MW01489356

The Alpha's Fated Encounter

Fated To Royalty: Book 1

Roxie Ray

© 2022

Disclaimer

All rights reserved. No part of this publication may be reproduced, distributed, or transmitted in any form or by any means, including photocopying, recording, or other electronic or mechanical methods, without the prior written permission of the publisher, except in the case of brief quotations embodied in critical reviews and certain other noncommercial uses permitted by copyright law.

This is a work of fiction. Names, places, characters, and events are all fictitious for the reader's pleasure. Any similarities to real people, places, events, living or dead are all coincidental.

This book contains sexually explicit content that is intended for ADULTS ONLY (+18).

Contents

Chapter 1 - Maddy

Abi was on the other side of the bar, pulling chairs down from table tops. It was Friday, so I was thankful for the help in getting the place ready for the evening rush. It would have taken me an hour if I had to do it on my own.

"Hey, Maddy? Do you want these tables moved farther apart?" Abi asked.

I stopped wiping the bar top and glanced over. "No, you can leave them where they are. It should be fine."

"Okay, cool." She flipped the last chair over, set it on its legs, and then slid it under the table. I'd moved behind the bar to start polishing the wine glasses when she came over and slapped her hands on the bar. "Holy shit, did I tell you I got my results back?" she asked.

I stopped mid-polish and looked at her with a raised eyebrow. "Results? What kind? STD? Pregnancy? SAT? What?"

She rolled her eyes. "Don't be an asshole. No, the DNA ancestry thing I sent off a few weeks ago. Remember?"

I did remember. The main thing I remembered was her hyperventilating before swabbing her cheek. We'd done it at her house, and I thought she was actually going to pass out when she saw the blood.

"I do. What did it say?"

"Well, I know you'll be shocked, but I'm seventy percent Irish."

I glanced up at the bright red hair braided down her back and the bright green eyes twinkling with excitement and shrugged. "No way. I was sure you'd be Argentinian or maybe Japanese."

"Very funny. Though, I did get a fun little surprise. I'm one percent West African."

"Ugh." I rolled my eyes toward the ceiling. "I really hope that doesn't mean you had some shitty slave-owning ancestor who liked to take advantage of the people he'd enslaved."

Abi's face fell and she tilted her head. "Well, damn. I hadn't thought of that. I kinda hoped my great-great-great grandma fell in love with some handsome mysterious man while on a sailing trip or something."

"Let's go with that. Much less depressing."

"You should do it, too," Abi said.

"What? Sail around the world and fall in love with a mysterious man? Deal."

"No, dummy, the ancestry thing. We can order a kit today. It'll be here in no time. It doesn't just tell you about your lineage, it also tells you if there are any diseases you're susceptible to. It's pretty interesting. I'm apparently twenty percent more likely to develop rheumatoid arthritis than the average person. Yay, me. Plus, I found three cousins I didn't know I had. I already friended one on social media."

The idea gave me a little flutter of anxiety. Finding out about genetic things did intrigue me. Being adopted, it would be nice to know if I had a higher risk of diabetes or heart disease, and would give me a head start on preventing things like that. But finding out about my birth family? That was more nerve-wracking.

When my parents had finally told me I was adopted, I'd gone through a full-on identity crisis. Who was I? Was my entire life a lie? Why did my biological parents give me away? All the things a young teenager would flip out about. It took about a year for me to come to terms with it. My mom and dad were the people who'd raised me from birth, and that was all I needed to know. I'd given up thinking about my birth parents a long time ago. The thought of stirring all that up again was mildly disturbing.

"I honestly don't care much about my heritage," I said.

"Okay, sure, but what about knowing if…I don't know…if whatever kids you someday have might have cystic fibrosis or if you're more likely to get breast cancer? Doesn't that interest you?"

It did, I had to admit that. I thought about it for several seconds as I finished polishing the last wine glass and started on the beer steins. I already had chronic anemia, for which I had to take supplements. What else could be lurking in my DNA? I didn't plan on having kids anytime soon, but knowing they might have some genetic anomaly before I ever got pregnant was always better than finding out last minute.

"Okay, if I did do this thing," I said, "how would I get a kit?"

Abi clapped her hands. "Yes! I'm so excited. Oh, what if we find out *we're* cousins or something?"

"The kit, Abi? How do I get one?" I asked, ignoring her comment.

"Hang on." She pulled her cell phone out. "I'll send you the link."

My phone pinged a few seconds later, but I left the text unopened. There was too much to do to get ready for the night. We finished prepping the bar before the first customers started to roll in—mostly regulars who'd just gotten off work. The night was way busier than I'd anticipated, but it was all good. People had made fun of me for getting a business degree only to turn right around and open a bar instead of going into corporate America, but I was pretty sure I made more than a lot of people my age. Twenty-eight and making over six figures a year? I'd take the busy and late nights. It was a pretty damned good trade-off.

Last call was at two in the morning, and by 3:30, I had everything cleaned up and the place locked. By four, I'd crashed at home and sleeping like the dead.

The next day, I rolled over in bed and grabbed my phone, the time on the screen showing it was noon. I saw Abi's message with the link to the ancestry site and stared at it for a few seconds, debating. I was still nervous about what I might discover. Whatever diseases I might be at risk for was not as scary as finding out about the people I had come from. I'd never been able to find any information about my birth parents. Would I find out they were serial killers? I chewed at my lip, thinking.

"Screw it," I said, and clicked the link.

Less than five minutes later, I'd purchased a kit. The company was based in Florida, and only a two-hour drive from where I lived here in Clearidge. It said I was eligible for free one-day shipping. I'd have it the next day. I put it out of my mind and went about my business the rest of that day and night.

Abi was at my place having lunch the next afternoon when the package arrived. I brought it in from the mailbox, and when she saw it, her eyes lit up. "It came. Nice. Let's do this," she said, putting her sandwich down.

"Do we really need to get a wad of spit out of me while we're eating?" I asked.

"Oh, come on, we were done anyway. Whip it out."

"Isn't that what you always tell your boyfriends?"

"Very funny. You know what I mean."

I cut open the box and pulled out all the items. It was pretty cut and dry. I poked my finger, put a drop of blood on a little cardboard sample card, and packed it back up. "Is that all?"

Abi nodded. "That's it. Just put that baby back in your mailbox and raise the little red flag. Are you excited?"

I shrugged, trying to hide my anxiety. "I don't know, maybe."

"What are you going to do if you have any DNA matches?"

That was the very thing freaking me out. Instead of directly answering her question, I told her I'd be right back and took the box out to the mailbox. Once I got back inside, it was easy to change the subject. The truth was, I wasn't totally sure what I would do if there were matches. I had no idea why I'd been given up for adoption. My adoptive parents had told me the adoption agency had no information about me. All they knew was that a guy claiming to be a social worker had brought me in as a baby. He told them he knew my parents and they didn't want to be involved in the adoption process or have their names put down. The problem, my dad had told me, was once the agency looked into the social worker, they couldn't find any trace or record of him.

That story had always haunted me. Had I been kidnapped? Or had they truly wanted to get rid of me? My parents didn't even have my original birth certificate. They'd found the hospital I'd been born at, but my birth mother's name had been registered simply as Jane Doe. All of it had pointed toward my birth parents being less than trustworthy. Why in the world would you not put your real name down when having a baby? The only thing I had from my birth parents was my name. The mysterious social worker had told the adoption agency my name was Maddison.

Thoughts of the test came and went over the next few weeks as I waited on the results. The website said it could take up to a month to receive them. A few weeks later, Abi asked again if I'd received the results.

"No, again, for the five hundredth time," I said with a groan. I was starting to get more irritated each time she asked.

"Sorry, sorry. I just like stuff like this. I get excited. Oh, you never answered when I asked what you'd do with any matches. Are you gonna stalk them on the internet? Friend-request them?"

The thought that my very existence could spell disaster for someone had started to rear its head. What if my birth parents had only been kids and given me up so they could go on with their lives? What if they had their own families now? Would shoving my nose into everything upend their entire lives?

I didn't blurt out what I was thinking. Instead, I took the safe route. "I don't know. I'll wait to see what the test says and go from there."

Fate didn't force me to wait long. My phone chirped a few hours later with a text that let me know the results were ready. I didn't open the email, though. My fear and anxiety spiked as soon as I saw the message.

I called Abi to let her know and see if she could come over. She was, of course, beyond excited about it and was at my place in less than twenty minutes.

I had my laptop open, the email link to the test ready. Abi walked in and pointed to the screen. "All right, sister, let's see it."

I took a breath and opened the link. The first couple of pages explained what the company had done and also assured me that my DNA wouldn't be shared or sold to outside companies. Finally, I pulled up the page with possible genetic markers for disease. Thankfully, there were none, except a negligible chance of developing irritable bowel syndrome at some point. Ugh, pleasant reading.

The next page brought up possible DNA matches. It was the one I was most excited and nervous to see. But the results were less than enlightening.

"Seriously?" Abi said, sounding dejected.

The only match was for some guy who'd lived nearly three hundred years ago. I didn't even know how they had any DNA from the guy to match me, but there it was. I leaned back, sighing in both relief and disappointment.

"I had like thirty different people matched to me," Abi said. "Most were distant, though. I can't believe you only have one. That's crazy."

"Yeah. Oh, well. We can't all have slave-owning rapists in our family tree," I said, nudging her.

"Hey, don't be an asshole. You can't choose your ancestors."

"Right. Let's go, we need to get the bar ready."

It was another Friday night, and my mind rested a little easier than it had the last few weeks. It was a relief to know I didn't have to make some big life-altering decision to contact a stranger and let them know I was their daughter. For the first time in weeks, I was able to enjoy my job without that weighing on me.

It was another busy night, and I was helping tend the bar because our normal two bartenders were having trouble keeping up. It was good for me, though. It kept me knowledgeable about cocktails and wine. It was difficult owning a bar without being in the know.

I was handing a couple of college kids some beers when Abi nudged me and nodded toward the door. "We got a crew of shifters coming in."

I glanced up and saw the guys she was talking about. You could always tell the shifters from the humans. There was...something about them. I couldn't even describe it, but it was obvious. I wasn't a bigot like some people. I'd never had any trouble from shifters and they were welcome at my place. All they wanted was some good bar food and good booze—both of which I could provide.

I nodded. "Yep, I see them," I said.

The guys, about a half dozen of them, made their way across the bar to an open table near the jukebox. One of them glanced in my direction and made eye contact. I forced myself not to roll my eyes. His face changed when he saw me, and then he changed course to come to the bar. I couldn't even count the number of times I'd been hit on in the years I'd owned the place. I was well-acquainted with the look he was giving me.

He bellied up and nodded to me. "Hey. Can I get a beer?"

At least he hadn't led with a pick-up line. I nodded. "Sure, what kind?"

He shrugged and gave an easy smile. "Whatever you recommend. You're the professional."

"Fair enough," I said, turning back to the line of beer taps. I'd made sure to have a cool and eclectic selection of beers when I opened the bar. I had almost two dozen options. I went right for my favorite: a micro-brew made by a couple friends of mine a few towns over. It had hints of orange and wasn't too hoppy. I slid the glass across the bar to him but held it back just out of reach. "I'll need to have your ID."

He grinned. "Yeah, sorry." He pulled it out and slid the license toward me. I checked the birth date, even though the guy was obviously over twenty-one, and slid the ID back. I pushed the beer the last foot over to him.

He caught it and took a sip. He furrowed his brows and looked at the glass. "That's really good. Nice choice."

I had a hard time not succumbing to his charm. He was cute and had a great smile, but I knew how these things usually went. I only nodded and took a couple of orders from some people beside him. Once I was free again, he waved me back over.

"Another round?" I asked.

He shook his head. "How long have you lived here?"

"Sorry, big guy, no personal info. I can do alcohol and maybe some hot wings from the kitchen if you want to ask for some of that."

He looked back across the room to his friends, who were all watching us. Most had their eyes on me. I wondered if he'd made a bet with his buddies on whether he'd be able to get my number. Turning back, he nodded at his glass. "Okay, house rules. I get it. I'll take another."

I filled another glass for him, and he went back to the table with his friends. I glanced over and they all seemed to be in deep discussion. Some of them looked pissed. I figured they were having a guys' quarrel. As long as it didn't escalate into shouting and fists, they were free to do as they pleased.

The same guy came back a few more times throughout the night. Each time was pure business. A pitcher of beers for his guys, then a big order of fried chicken sliders from the kitchen. Normal stuff, except that he only wanted to deal with me. He'd wait an extra ten minutes if I was busy. He completely ignored Abi, who tried to get his order and was being pretty obvious that she'd like to do more than just pour him a beer.

Toward the end of the night, he came up to settle his tab. I took his card, and while I was ringing him up, the question I'd been waiting for all night finally came up. "Okay, I'll finally stop bugging you if you just give me your name." He held up a finger. "And before you say it, a name isn't personal information. It's not private or secret. You can at least give me your name."

I chuckled and rolled my eyes. "Okay, fine." I put my hand out to shake. "Maddison Sutton. My friends call me Maddy."

He shook my hand and smiled that gorgeous smile again. "Good to know."

He turned without another word and started walking toward his friends, who were gathering at the door.

"Hey, don't I get your name?" I shouted after him.

He looked over his shoulder as he headed out the door. "Next time."

I watched the group go, thinking it was the strangest interaction I'd ever had. Usually, when you brushed off a guy, one of two things happened. One, they got butt-hurt about it and turned into pouty little incel shits. Two, they didn't take no for an answer and kept pushing until I had to be a bitch about it.

This was a refreshing change of pace. Maybe, just maybe, if he came back again, I'd entertain the idea of giving him my number. If he asked for it.

The bar slowly started to empty, and I didn't even have to make the last call. The final patrons were out before two. The bartenders got most of the place clean, and they and the kitchen guys were out by three, which left just Abi and me. I needed to mop the bathrooms and restock the paper towels, soap, and toilet paper—a twenty-minute job at best.

"Hey, Abi? Go on home. I've got this."

Abi yawned and rubbed her eyes. "You sure? I'm good to stay and help."

"It's all good. I'll see you tomorrow."

"Oh my God, thanks. I'm so damned tired. I'll call you in the afternoon for breakfast."

"You mean lunch?"

Abi shrugged a shoulder as she walked out. "Call it what you want. Whatever I eat after I roll out of bed is breakfast. Even if it's two in the afternoon."

I laughed and waved as she left. The rest of the closing stuff went by pretty quickly. It was kind of nice to have the place to myself and allow myself to zone out and decompress. All that was left to do was empty the under-bar beer glass cleaner. I'd worry about polishing the water spots off the next day.

While I was bent over taking the glasses out, I heard the front door of the bar open. Shit, I hadn't locked it after Abi left.

"We're closed!" I called out, still pulling glasses out.

I could hear a multitude of boots thumping across the wood floor of the bar. I hissed a frustrated breath out through my teeth. Standing, I shouted, "I said we're…"

I trailed off when I saw who'd come in. It was the guy from earlier in the night. The shifter. And he'd brought all his friends back. A knot of fear cinched tightly in my gut when I saw their faces. All of them, including the guy who I'd thought had been flirting with me, looked pissed. Like, ready-to-kill pissed. The worst part was the fact that they were all looking at me. Like I'd made them mad.

Trying not to let my fear show, I cleared my throat. "Sorry, guys. We closed over an hour ago. If you want service, you'll have to come back tomorrow night."

Ignoring me, the guy I'd been talking to stepped up to the bar and slammed his palms down on it. The impact reverberated through the bar like a gunshot. "You shouldn't even exist."

I took an involuntary step back, shocked by the disgust in his voice. He was looking at me like I was a smear of dog shit he'd found on his shoe. What the hell had happened in the last two hours? The jovial, charming grin was gone. All I saw now was the curled lip of loathing.

He looked back at his boys. "Smell that? Was I lying?"

The rest of his friends shook their heads, one of them sniffing at the air and making a deep, throaty growl. Cold sweat slid down my back, my eyes darting around at all the other men. None of their faces showed the slightest hint of compassion. Some had even moved to the ends of the bar, cutting off any escape I might have had. My breath started to hiss in and out my nose in panicked bursts. What was about to happen to me? Robbery? Murder? Gang rape followed by robbery and murder? A thousand nightmare scenarios flashed through my mind.

The shifter leaned forward, getting as close as the bar would allow. "Your bloodline should have been completely wiped out. The whole lineage was supposed to be dead. It looks like some of that tainted blood slipped through the cracks."

I bumped into the shelf of liquor behind me. A bottle of tequila and a pint of whisky fell off the shelf, shattering onto the floor. The pungent aroma of alcohol burned my nose. What the hell was he talking about?

"I don't know what you mean," I said, my voice uncharacteristically low and quiet.

He shook his head and spat on the ground. "Doesn't matter. You'll be dead soon enough. Go."

At the word, his men leaped to action. They moved so damned fast, I could barely register what was happening. Blurs of motion, screams and growls, the shimmering, angry flash of their red eyes. The last thing I remembered was a searing pain in my sides, followed by an explosion of pain at the back of my head. After that, everything went dark.

Chapter 2 - Nico

"Bro, I'm not going out," I said, leaning back into my couch.

"Come on," Sebastian moaned. "You've got to. It won't be the same without you."

I laid my head back, already exhausted. I didn't go out often. It wasn't really my scene. I'd been trying to beg off this little excursion for days. Sebastian had gotten more persistent all day, though. He was wearing me down, and he knew it. There was blood in the water and he was circling, ready to snap me up and drag me out for an evening of debauchery that probably wouldn't end until the sun came up.

"You don't need me to have a good time."

Sebastian flopped down on the couch beside me. "Nico, you're my best friend. How the hell am I going to have a good time if you aren't there?"

"I really wanted to turn in early tonight." The argument was as limp as it sounded. I almost never went to bed early.

Sebastian glared at me with a pretty hilarious look on his face. It was the closest he could ever get to looking pissed at me. "You've forced my hand." He put on a faux regal look and stood, pointing down at me. "Nicolas Lorenzo, I command you to come out, get drunk, have fun, and maybe if we're lucky, bring a hot chick home to bang. I command this as my birthday present."

"Are you being serious right now? Commanding me? Who the hell are you? Queen Elizabeth?"

"Did you get me a birthday present?" Sebastian asked.

I laughed and rolled my eyes. "What? I didn't realize you were turning seven. I haven't gotten you a present since we were in fucking middle school."

"Ha!" Sebastian pumped a fist. "There it is. Since you've neglected to give me a present for, like, two decades, you coming out will be the gift. I'll call it a wash."

"One night out is the same as twenty birthday gifts?" I asked, already knowing the argument was over.

"Well…you've got to buy me at least six beers tonight, but yeah."

I huffed out a sigh. "Fuck it, fine. Let me get dressed."

"Hell, yeah," Sebastian said, pulling his phone out. "I'll call the guys."

The rest of the guys showed up and we piled into Sebastian's massive suburban, then went out for dinner first. He wanted to go to this tapas place downtown because he'd "heard you can pull tons of tail out of that place." The food was freaking amazing, and he hadn't been wrong about the ladies. The place had a little salsa dance club attached to it, and there were tons of ladies out having a fun Friday night.

We were in the middle of a platter of roasted octopus, prawns, and Spanish sausages when a whole crew of chicks rolled up to our table. They were hot, yeah, but a little young for my taste. Barely legal college students, if I had to guess. They were literally all over my guys.

"Hey there, sexy," said a brunette with her tits almost falling out of her top, pulling a seat up next to me. She slid a finger down my chest and grinned. "Shifters are hot."

I grabbed another shrimp and popped it into my mouth. "Yeah, thanks…uh, same to you."

Sebastian leaned in and whispered into my ear. "Bro, what are you doing? She's hot, and she's throwing herself at you."

I glanced back and gave him a look that told him I wanted him to shut up. The brunette was joined by a redhead with smaller boobs but an ass that made even me look twice. She sat with her friend. "Meg? Who's the hot guy?"

I forced myself not to roll my eyes. Definitely college girls. They were both already three sheets to the wind and trolling for guys. I'd seen it a hundred times. Once the alcohol flowed, all inhibitions went out the door. If I were a different kind of person, I'd most definitely take advantage.

"Nico," I said, introducing myself.

Redhead furrowed her brow and grinned. "Oh my gosh, even his name's hot. Meg, let's go get this guy a beer. Be right back, babe," she said to me as she took her friend by the arm and hauled her toward the bar.

Sebastian grabbed my arm and shook it in excitement. "Holy shit, man. I swear, if you get a three-way on my birthday and I don't, I'm gonna be majorly pissed. Can I at least video it?"

"Dude? Seriously?" I winced in disgust. "I'm almost old enough to be their father."

"You're thirty-five, not sixty-five, no matter how much you try to be an old fart."

The girls returned with a beer, which I took with a nod of thanks. I downed it in four heavy gulps. Shifters didn't get drunk the way humans did. It wasn't that we couldn't, but our bodies ran hot. We burned the alcohol off two or three times faster than humans. I'd have to chug at least three times as much as a human to get drunk. I almost never did. I usually only drank because I liked to.

Redhead glanced at her friend Meg and bit her lower lip. They exchanged some unspoken conversation with their eyes. Meg turned away, face flaming, laughing and nodding. Redhead put a hand on my thigh as our server dropped the check for our food off.

"So..." Redhead said, leaning in close. "My friend and I think you're, like, really fucking hot. Have you ever been with two ladies at the same time?" She glanced over at her friend, then back to me. "We've never shared a guy before, so maybe it'll be a first time for everyone?"

I sighed and glanced around the table. All the other guys were doing their best to keep the shit-eating grins off their faces. I had a regular hookup I could call anytime I was in the mood. Taking home some random women didn't appeal to me.

I reached down and took her hand gently. "You and your friend are gorgeous. I'm just not looking for that kind of fun tonight, ladies."

I let them down easy, but they still looked dejected and left without another word. It could have been worse— they could have made a scene, called me an asshole, or thrown a drink in my face. As it was, I kinda felt bad; it looked like they'd spent quite a while working up the courage for that little proposition. Too bad they hadn't approached Sebastian instead. If they had, I'm sure the night would have been over. He'd have demanded a ride home to carnally annihilate himself. I might have even gotten into bed before midnight.

Sebastian shook his head and looked at me like I was a madman. "Dude? You just turned down a night of sexual glory most men would give their left nut for."

"Yeah, yeah, I get it. Boobs good, no boobs bad. Are we done here?"

With the ticket paid, Sebastian declared the next stop to be a strip club. After several minutes of arguing, we indeed ended up at a strip club. Thankfully, we were out of there in less than an hour and Sebastian didn't go bankrupt on lap dances. We bounced around to three more bars before Sebastian pulled us all aside.

"Dudes, I'm freaking starving," he said, holding his stomach.

"Christ, man," our friend Luis said. "We just had dinner."

"Man, that was hours ago. I know a great place down the road. Really good bar food. Fried pickles to die for, and some of these spicy chicken sliders that'll make you lose your mind. Let's go."

I glanced at my watch. "Sebastian, it's past three in the morning. They probably aren't open anymore."

"Nah, man. Gotta be open. It's Friday. Plus, it's my birthday."

"So you think they stayed open late just for you?" Felipe said, crossing his arms.

"Let's check?" Sebastian asked, wincing as though his hunger pangs were going to kill him.

I sighed. "Fine, but if this place is closed, that's it. Night's over. Got it? Some of us would like to sleep at least a little before sunrise."

"Ugh, you guys are lame. Okay, fine." Sebastian handed me the keys to his SUV.

Even with our increased metabolism, several of the guys were pretty buzzed. I was still basically stone-cold sober. Not only was I out late when I didn't want to be, but I'd become the de facto designated driver. I got into the driver's seat and started the car. I wanted to be pissed about the situation, but if I were honest, the night had been sort of fun. But I'd never tell Sebastian that. I'd never hear the end of "I told you so."

I knew which bar he was talking about, so I took a right out of the parking lot and got back on the highway. I was a hundred percent sure the place would be closed, so no matter what, I'd be back in my bed in an hour at the latest.

That thought vanished when I pulled us into the parking lot five minutes later. There was only one car there, but the front door was standing ajar and light shone out of the bar onto the pavement outside. It looked like all the lights were still on.

"See!" Sebastian shouted. "Told you they'd be open. Drunk food, here we come."

I frowned, but got out of the SUV with everyone else. Sebastian's chipper mood evaporated as soon as we were outside. The smell. All of us sniffed at the air. Luis and Felipe growled.

"Oh shit," Sebastian said. "Do you guys smell that?"

I did. Blood. Not only that, but I smelled humans and shifters. Not the lingering scents of those who'd been gone a while—all three scents were fresh. All three scents were coming from inside the bar. The blood was the prevailing smell, though. Strong, coppery, and thick. I wrinkled my nose at it.

"Should we call the cops?" Luis asked.

"Someone's hurt in there. Let's go." I didn't tell him that the blood was calling to me. That I couldn't ignore the pull of it. I had to see where it was coming from. There would be no waiting.

The guys followed me, their buzz drying up as adrenaline sobered them all. I was three steps away from the door when I heard what sounded like a stampede of boots inside. Not hesitating, I broke into a sprint, bursting into the bar. Usually, I had much more self-control. I liked to think I was cautious to a fault. Running headlong into an unknown place? A place that had the smell of blood? It was grade-A horror movie 101. But that scent? It was driving me, almost consuming me.

We plowed through the door and saw…blood. Lots of blood, and what looked like a woman covered in it, unconscious on the floor. I could still hear the sounds of feet sprinting out the back door. I could smell them too. Males. Shifters.

"Go get the fuckers!" I shouted. Sebastian and Felipe bolted for the kitchen door, trying to chase down the guys.

I knelt by the woman, Luis by my side. "Oh damn, Nico. What the hell did they do to her?"

I checked her over. Her breathing was shallow and ragged, and she was covered in blood. From what I could see, she had injuries to her sides and her head. Most of the blood seemed to have come from her head wound. I slid my hands gingerly into the hair and the back of her head. There was a massive lump and a large gash, but it wasn't soft or squishy like a crushed skull. It could have been cracked, but there was still a chance she might be okay.

I pulled my hand away and wiped sweat from my forehead with the back of my hand. The blood on my fingers passed by my face. The smell of it made me dizzy.

Like…like it was drugging me. I'd never smelled anything like it. It was so damned intoxicating.

I gritted my teeth as my wolf tried to rip free of my skin. I wanted to shift so bad, my whole body ached. What the hell was going on?

Luis was already pulling out his phone. I blinked and shook off the strange feeling. I grabbed his arm before he could dial. "Call the pack doctor."

Luis frowned at me. "Not the cops? Or an ambulance?"

I couldn't explain it, but I didn't want her away from me. The regular authorities would take her to a hospital, and every instinct I had wanted to stay near her. Plus, the pack doc *was* a real doctor. He'd be as good as an EMT anyway.

"No," I said. "Call the doc."

Luis looked down at the bloodied woman and shrugged. "Whatever you say, Nico."

He was on the phone, relaying what we'd found to the doc when Sebastian and Felipe came running back in from the kitchen. Sebastian stopped mid-stride and looked down, then back at me, his eyebrow raised in a question. Unsure what he was trying to convey, I glanced down. Unconsciously, I'd taken the woman's hand in mine and was holding it. When the fuck had I done that? Why was I doing that?

"We couldn't catch them," Felipe said, breathing heavily. "They had a car out back. They all jumped in and took off. We tried to chase them down on foot, but…" he shrugged. Shifters were fast, but not as fast as a speeding car.

"I only got a good look at one of them. I think he looked familiar. I'm pretty sure those guys were from Javi's pack," Sebastian said.

That made even less sense. "What fucking reason would Javi's guys have for wanting to hurt a human? A woman, no less?" I asked.

The others shook their heads, confused as I was. Luis hung up his phone and turned back to us. "Doc's coming. He only lives ten minutes away. This late? He'll probably haul ass and be here in five."

Luis was accurate in that prediction. We heard the squeal of tires in the parking lot a few minutes later. Doc came jogging into the bar and gasped when he saw the woman. "Holy shit. Is she alive?" he asked.

"For now," I muttered as I moved out of the way so he could work.

Doc checked her over. Blood pressure, broken bones, pupil dilation. I stood back with the others and watched him go through the process. Though, I stood a lot closer than they did. I couldn't seem to help it.

Doc pulled his rubber gloves off and sighed. "Well, the good news is she's not going to die tonight."

A breath of relief burst out of my mouth. Doc stood to go outside. "We'll need to get her to the clinic. She's gonna need quite a few stitches, and she's had a good bit of blood loss. I've got some O-negative blood at the clinic. Should be plenty to help her out." He nodded at Luis. "Come help me. I don't have a gurney, but there's a backboard in my van. We can use that to carry her."

He and Luis came back in with a seven-foot long board with handholds all along the sides. I'd seen similar things on TV. Doc also had an inflatable neck brace. I sat and helped him put the brace on her neck before we got her onto the board. He said he didn't think she had any spinal injuries but didn't want to rule it out before he had a chance to check her thoroughly at the clinic.

I rode in the back of the van with her, letting the guys follow in the SUV. I looked at her face, so covered in blood it was almost impossible to tell what she looked like. I caught myself praying that she'd be okay. Praying wasn't something I typically did. Why would I be so concerned about her? It was weird, to say the least. When Doc pulled into the clinic, I let out a pent-up breath.

I stayed by her side the entire time. We got her inside and into the exam room. Doc put a bag of blood onto an IV and slid the needle into her arm. While the blood worked its way into her, he started the stitching process. The guys were still there, but I'd almost completely ignored them.

Felipe nudged my arm. "What's going on with you, man?"

"Huh?"

Sebastian nodded at the girl. "You've been hovering like the damned angel of death, dude."

Thinking back, I knew I'd been acting weird from the moment I smelled the blood. It was like a switch had been flipped in my head. "I can't explain it. I feel strange, so does my wolf. I just need to make sure she's all right."

"Dude," Sebastian said, frowning deeply. "You're talking like you found your fated mate or something."

I looked down and saw that I'd taken her hand again. Even Doc was glancing over at me suspiciously. What Sebastian said couldn't be true. The woman was human. It wasn't possible for a shifter to be fated to a human.

I smelled the air again, and there was something else in her blood. Something that *wasn't* entirely human. A hint of something else.

Fear and curiosity filled me. I didn't say anything else. Instead I watched Doc work, and wondered who and what this strange woman was.

Chapter 3 – Maddy

The first thing I saw when I opened my eyes was a massive whitish blur. Blinking, my vision slowly cleared and I realized it was the ceiling. My whole body felt heavy, like a thick wet blanket was holding me down. My head felt groggier than usual. I was typically a morning person, but it was like my brain was trying to swim out of a deep pool of water.

Still, it was nice to be awake. The dream I'd had was not something I wanted to experience anymore. All those weird shifters beating the shit out of me. Why had I dreamed something so fucked up?

My thoughts stopped on a dime. The ceiling didn't look right. It was smooth, cream-colored drywall. My house had awful, bright-white popcorn ceilings. I'd been thinking of scraping it all off for more than a year, but hadn't gotten around to it. My heart rate spiked the second I realized I wasn't home. Where the fuck was I?

Trying to lift my arms, I found they weren't held down by a blanket like I thought, but were still super heavy. My mind cleared a bit, and I remembered my dream hadn't been a dream. That it had all really happened. Those guys *had* come back into the bar. They *had* attacked me. Was I…had they taken me back to their place? Was that where I was? Alarm set it—a thick, unflinching panic.

A tiny moan escaped my lips, but I wasn't able to form words. My head was starting to throb, too.

Before I could do anything else, a man in a white doctor's coat leaned over the bed. He glanced down at me and lifted one of my eyelids with a thumb, opening the eye much further than I wanted. He flashed a penlight into the eye twice. It felt like someone had shoved an icepick into my brain. He was a shifter. I could feel the strange electric buzz on my skin where he touched me. It was one of the reactions I always had when I was near one. I'd never known anyone else who reacted that way, but it was the way I knew for sure. There was also that strange sense of *otherness* they had that I couldn't put a finger on.

The realization made me even more scared. He was a shifter, which meant the fuckers who had tried to kill me really *had* kidnapped me. I must be in one of their complexes. A lot of shifter packs had their own doctors. Those who didn't had shifter doctors who worked in regions and made house calls. At least, that's what I'd heard.

My hammering heart was like a bass drum beating away in my chest. I moved my jaw and thought I could finally manage to speak.

"Whhh." The first sound I made was like a whisper of air, nothing else. He was checking my other eye with the flashlight. I swallowed and tried again. "What's…happening? Who are you?"

He clicked off the penlight and straightened. "My name is Doctor Carter. I'm the doctor for the Lorenzo wolf pack. You're in my clinic."

I coughed and my vision went blurry for a second. I was worried I would pass out, but I got myself under control. "So, you guys are the ones who attacked me?"

He frowned in surprise. "What? No, no, no. You misunderstand. You were attacked by a group of unknown shifters, yes, but that wasn't the Lorenzo pack. The Lorenzo alpha and his friends interrupted the attack and chased off the perpetrators. They probably saved your life."

With each moment that went by, my head cleared a little more and I was able to think. One thing he said made no sense. "If I was that bad off, why didn't you take me to a real hospital?"

Doctor Carter shrugged. "I had all the equipment here to fix you up. Some stitches and a pint of blood? Another IV for fluid and a heavy dose of pain meds? All here. Now, as for why they chose to call me first and not 911? That's something you'll have to ask Nico."

"Who's Nico?"

"Sorry, I didn't mention his name before. Nicolas Lorenzo, the alpha of the Lorenzo pack. He's the one who helped rescue you."

I struggled to slide my arms underneath me, trying to lift myself off the bed. I needed to get out of here. Abi was probably worried sick about me. Had they locked up the bar? Jesus, all the money in the register could be sitting there for anyone. I sat up, and the whole room seemed to tilt sideways. Overcome with nausea, I lay back down, gingerly resting my head back on the pillows.

"Easy there," Carter said. "You aren't going anywhere. The stab wounds on your sides were fairly deep. Nothing major, but it took a few stitches to fix. You've got a pretty good concussion, too. You'll be out of commission for a couple of days at least. I need to keep an eye on you until I'm sure everything is okay up there," he said, nodding toward my head.

"But my business—"

"Nico has quite a bit of pull around here. I'm sure if he took the time to bring you to me, he'd have someone make sure the bar they found you in is fine. Don't worry about that."

I sighed, exhaustion rolling across my body. I was in no condition to go anywhere, but it was hard to admit. I looked at the doctor and slowly shook my head. "Why did those guys attack me? I never did anything to them."

The penlight disappeared into his chest pocket. "That, I'm afraid, is the million-dollar question we've all been asking." He paused. "How do you feel? Pain-wise?"

I was honest. "Pretty bad. My sides hurt."

"Okay. I'll have my nurse get you another Vicodin, but a smaller dose than last time. I don't want you getting dependent."

I nodded, and he left the room. I didn't feel like I was in danger. There was no way to know for sure if he was telling the truth, but it felt like he was being honest.

A nurse came in a few minutes later with a small plastic cup. I took the small pill from the cup. As soon as I swallowed, I realized that it might not have been the smartest idea, but it was too late. Plus, the pain in my sides was getting worse by the second. The nurse left without a word, and I lay there. Ten minutes later, the drug kicked in. It was like someone was pouring warm honey all over my body. My eyes fluttered shut, and I drifted into sleep.

"Your bloodline should have been completely wiped out," the shifter said. His eyes were a glowing, bloody red, his teeth like steak knives ripping out of his gums in crimson spikes.

"I don't know what you mean!" I screamed.

"You'll be dead soon enough." His face had completely changed, a full wolf's head, but a wolf from the bowels of hell.

The others had shifted, too. The howls were loud enough to crack the walls. Crevices formed in the ceiling and floor, blood erupted from each fissure. It spurted up until it was inches deep on the floor.

The wolves were on me. Their paws tearing my clothes, shredding my skin. Me, screaming as their jaws clamped onto my body. The flesh ripping from my breasts, my cheeks, my stomach. The leader tearing at my insides while I screamed. Raising his maw to the sky, blood flying from his teeth, and howling—

I screamed and sat up, waking from the nightmare. The quick movement sent a fresh barb of pain into my brain. I clasped my hands to my head and lay back on the bed. I shivered and realized I was covered in a cold sweat.

The nurse came in a moment later, her eyes worried. "Are you all right, miss?"

I nodded. "I—sorry, it was a nightmare."

She shook her head. "No apologies needed. Here, I brought you dinner."

Dinner? I glanced outside and saw the window had a faint purple glow. The sun was almost down. There'd been bright Florida sunlight blasting through the glass before I fell asleep. It hadn't felt like that long of a dream, but I'd been out for hours. My stomach grumbled, though. I was starving. I sat back up, slowly and carefully this time.

She set the tray on a rolling table that she positioned over my bed. It didn't look like standard hospital food—a still-hot burger and fries with a pudding cup and container of diced fruit. There was a bottle of water beside it.

"I'm going to change some of your gauze while you eat, if that's okay?" the nurse asked, twisting off the water bottle cap for me.

"That's fine," I said, my words muffled by the burger I'd already started to stuff into my mouth.

She started pulling the old bandages off, and I didn't get the same buzzing sensation I got from the doctor. The nurse was human, which surprised me a little. I'd assumed the whole operation was run by and for shifters. I hissed while she pulled off the last strip of gauze. It was painful, but nowhere near as bad as it could have been.

I finished the fries and was chewing the last of the burger by the time she was done. Other than the one painful moment, she'd done a great job changing the bandages without causing me discomfort. She was pulling her gloves off when I decided to ask the question that had been percolating in my head since I'd talked to the doctor that morning.

"Is…uh…Nicolas around? Nico?" I asked, not sure which name he went by. "The doctor said he's the guy who saved me."

The nurse tossed her soiled gloves in the trash and started washing her hands. She spoke to me over her shoulder as she worked. "Alpha Nico isn't here right now, miss." She turned the water off and pulled some paper towels from a dispenser. "He'll be back soon, though. He said so. Don't worry." She gave me a weird look, then left the room.

I pulled the top off the pudding cup and ate dessert. Just what the hell was going on? What had that look been about? I finished the pudding and ate half the fruit before my stomach told me it was full. More than full, actually. It had been over twenty-four hours since I'd eaten anything, but I didn't want to make myself sick.

The nurse returned ten minutes later to take the tray. She put it aside and straightened my sheets, then checked my pulse and blood pressure again. "I know you asked about Nico earlier," she said. "It's kind of strange how he's been acting. Do you want another blanket?"

"Uh, sure, that would be nice. Nico's been acting strange?" I asked, not sure where the conversation was going.

She grabbed another blanket from a drawer and draped it across my legs, then nodded. "Very strange. Really protective of you. He spent most of the day with you, sitting right there"— she pointed at a stool that was beside my bed—"and making sure you had whatever you needed. Pretty strange for him. Do you...um...know him?" she asked, trying to shrug nonchalantly.

"No. I've never met him before. If he walked in right now, I'd have no idea it was him."

"That's what the doc and I thought, too. That's what makes his reactions so strange."

"Reactions? What do you—"

The door opened and Dr. Carter walked in. "How are we after a nap and some food?"

"Better. Thanks," I said, wishing he'd waited another minute or two before coming in. I'd wanted to know what the nurse was talking about.

Dr. Carter nodded to the nurse. "Thank you, Cleo, I think she'll be fine now."

The nurse mumbled a few words to him before leaving the room. The doctor stepped over and slid his fingers into my hair, probing gently at the base of my skull where I'd been hit. I winced in pain, and he pulled his hand away, making sure not to get his fingers tangled in my hair.

"Swelling is going down, but you'll have one hell of a knot on the back of your head for a couple of days. It'll probably be tender for at least a week."

"Do you think I'll be able to go home tomorrow? Has anyone talked to my friends?" I was still worried about

Abi. I'd even glanced around the room from my bed while I ate, trying to find my phone. I was pretty sure it was still lying on the bar, though. That's the last time I remembered seeing it.

"I don't know about your friends, but I know Nico will be here soon. He wanted to check in on you once you woke up. He's been…very worried about you."

"Okay, but what about my first question? When can I go home?"

Carter's eyes swept away from mine, breaking contact. His right hand fidgeted with a pen and the left slipped in and out of his coat pocket. Every bit of his body language screamed *I'm hiding something*.

It didn't sit well with me. I was about to press the subject when a throat cleared in the doorway.

Dr. Carter glanced over his shoulder. "Ah, Nico. I just told her you'd be here soon."

The doctor moved out of the way, and Nico stepped into the room.

My eyes widened, nostrils flared, and my heart rate went through the roof. I was glad I wasn't on the monitor, which would give away what I was feeling. I could imagine my embarrassment as my heartbeat went beeping all over the room as he walked in.

I sighed a breath out of my lungs, even as breath escaped me when he took another step into the room. Things had somehow moved into slow motion. Something inside me sparked to life. Something I didn't even know lived within me. I couldn't explain it. Was it an ache? A pang?

I watched the muscles in Nico's arms flex, and my eyes moved across his body and back up to his face. A burning need swept through my body, desire like nothing I'd ever experienced in my life. He was the most beautiful man I'd ever laid eyes on in my life. A voice in my head started murmuring a single word. As he drew closer, the voice rose in volume, first a whisper, then a shout, then an earth-shattering scream, all inside my skull.

Mine.

Chapter 4 - Nico

The wolf within me erupted with need. It was more possessive than I'd ever known it to be in my life. It was all I could do to keep myself calm as I walked into the room. I could practically feel my pupils dilate as I looked at her. It was the first time I'd seen her awake. Her own eyes had widened in what I assumed was surprise. I gritted my teeth as the wolf tried to release a growl of desire.

Doc stepped over and put a hand on my arm, stopping me. "Take it easy, Nico. She's been through a lot. She doesn't need an alpha scaring her," he said with a grin.

I knew he was trying to sound calm, but I could see something in his eyes. I must have had a strange look on my face. The look on his face told me I must have been radiating an aura of menace or anger. The problem was, that wasn't what I felt. I truly had no idea what had come over me since I first saw the woman.

I swallowed and took a breath as I nodded. I wasn't trying to scare her.

I gave my wolf a mental scolding, then patted Doc on the shoulder. "All good, Doc. I just want to make sure the patient is okay."

The woman, who was sitting up in bed, watched me as I crossed the room. Her eyes were taking in my every movement. Part of me thought she kind of looked like a prey animal, scared of the big bad wolf coming toward her. On second look? She was no prey animal. Her look was so intense that I had the feeling she was trying to dissect me with her eyes.

"Who are you? What the hell is going on here?" she asked.

I grinned and bobbed my eyebrows up. "I was hoping you'd help me with that. By the way, my name is Nicolas Lorenzo. Call me Nico."

"What do you mean, you hoped I could help? I was attacked by shifters. You're a shifter. Shouldn't you know more about all this than me?"

Her distrust towards me was coming off in waves. There was something else there as well, though. A look I couldn't quite put my finger on. My throat felt dry, and even though I was putting on a brave front, she was making me feel strange. I needed to figure out what the hell was going on, but that was going to be tough. Just being in the same room as her, and smelling that scent? It was almost too much. It was worse now that she was looking at me with those eyes.

"You still haven't answered me," she said. I realized I'd been standing there for several beats, not saying anything.

"Did you know the shifters who attacked you?" I asked.

She let out a heavy sigh and shook her head. "No. We get them in pretty frequently. Not those exact guys, but shifters. That night was the first time I'd ever seen any of those guys."

"Okay. Were they…I don't know…rowdy? Causing trouble? Did they threaten you during the night before coming back after closing?"

"No. Honestly, the guy in charge was"—she rolled her eyes—"kinda hitting on me most of the night. Or at least I thought he was."

"Do you think that's why they jumped you? Pissed off they got shot down?"

The look she gave me could have peeled paint off a wall. "I don't think six dudes would try to murder me just because I didn't want to bang one of them."

I held my hands up in an attempt to ward off her fury. "I get it. Okay. Can you describe them?"

"Probably. Yeah. At least a little bit."

"All right, hang on a second." I turned and pulled the door open. "Luis, I need you to hear this."

Luis appeared around the corner and made his way down the hallway. When he came into the room, I could see the suspicion in the woman's eyes darkening. I left the door open to make things seem a little less closed in. The last thing I wanted was for her to think we were ganging up on her with no escape. That was the exact thing that had happened to her the night before.

"This is my friend, Luis Ruiz. He's cool. One of my best friends and my second-in-command in the pack. I'm the alpha, he's the beta. Are we good?" I asked with a raised eyebrow.

She chewed at the inside of her lip, glancing between me, Luis, and the open door. After a few seconds, she nodded. "Yeah, sure. It's fine."

"Okay, can you describe what these dudes looked like? We're trying to figure out if we know them."

She thought for a second before starting. "The main guy was…younger? Maybe early to mid-twenties. Dark hair." She absently tugged at her earlobe. "He had an earring. Like a gold stud. He also had a tattoo—I think it was a crow—across his forearm."

She described the other guys in less detail, but she didn't need to. I glanced over at Luis as she spoke. He caught my eye and nodded almost imperceptibly. His shoulders tensed as the realization hit him. My own body was probably reacting the same way. The description matched some of Javi's guys.

"Does that help?" she asked when she finished. "Do you know those guys?"

I nodded. "I think we do know the wolves who attacked you."

Her eyes brightened. Not in excitement, but in relief. "Then what the hell is going on? Is it some kind of, I don't know, shifter gang war? Something like that?"

I winced. "It doesn't really work that way. Well, at least not usually. What else did they say when they came back?"

"That's the weirdest part. It made no sense. Maybe you guys know what it's supposed to mean. It could be some sort of shifter thing. He told me—and he was freaking pissed when he said this—he said I shouldn't exist. That my bloodline was supposed to have been wiped out. Whatever that means."

After she was done, she shivered. Her mind was obviously dragging the memory back up. My instinct was to step forward, sit on the bed, and wrap her in my arms. I wanted to protect her. My wolf was actually egging me on, trying to get me to do exactly that. I had to clamp my hands into fists to stop myself. I'd only met her five minutes ago, and she'd been attacked by shifters less than a day ago. That type of close contact wouldn't go over well.

"So, you have no idea what they meant?" I asked. "Do you have any other girls who work for you who are shifters? Could they have you confused with someone else? A case of mistaken identity?"

She shook her head. "No. They for sure wanted me. They even, like, sniffed the air, like I smelled funny or something. They definitely wanted me for some reason."

The hairs on my arms stood on end, and I could see Luis taking a slight step back. She did have a smell unlike anything I'd ever encountered. Shifter noses were just as good as the animals we shifted into. I smelled millions of different pheromones, odors, and chemicals each day. As soon as I caught a whiff of something new, my brain stored it away for later.

And she was something totally new. Not just a new person, but something I'd never encountered before in my entire life, which was pretty difficult to find.

Luis caught my eye and his brows knitted together, his eyes flickering with unspoken question. I wasn't sure what he was trying to get across. I'd have to ask him when we got back into the waiting room.

"Listen…shit, I don't even know your name." The realization made me feel like an asshole.

"Maddy Sutton. Maddison, but I go by Maddy," she said.

"Okay. Listen, Maddy. We're certain these guys belong to a different pack. It's run by a guy named Javi. He's…" I looked at Luis, who gave me a lopsided, humorless grin. "He's not a very good dude, let's put it that way. If his guys attacked you and didn't finish the job, then there's a pretty good chance they'll come back to…try and finish."

She stared at me for several seconds, her face impassive and emotionless. Then her eyes grew moist and her lower lip started to tremble. Her whole body began to shake, and she pulled the blanket tighter around her. "Why is this happening?"

She wasn't asking me, just whispering the question to herself as she cried, but I stepped closer to the bed, wanting to console her. "It'll be okay. I'm not sure why it's happening, but I promise I'll help you figure this thing out."

Her teary eyes flicked up to me warily. "Why? Why do you even care?"

That was a good question. One I couldn't answer. Whatever I said in response had to sound logical. No matter what, I didn't want to scare Maddy off. I had to figure out what was going on with this weird attraction I felt to her, and I couldn't do that if she was on the run. "Javi and I are rivals of a sort, if that makes sense. Now that I've involved myself, he'll be gunning for me. I'm sure his guys saw my pack. He'll know I stopped the attack. We're connected now. In a sense," I added quickly. "So I'm offering you the protection of the Lorenzo pack."

"So, you have no idea why? This is a mystery to you, too?" She looked equally confused and irritated.

I shrugged a shoulder. "No clue. But like I said, Javi's pack is after you for some reason. Whatever plan he has, he'll want to see it through. I fucked those plans up, so now there's going to be trouble for me. He'll assume I'm involved somehow. It's a long story, but we've got a bit of history. I need you safe until I can figure out what Javi's planning, and I can put a stop to it."

Her eyes went cold, and I could almost feel the chill in the room. Luis seemed to notice it as well and took a second step back, his eyes growing wary of Maddy.

"So, you're just going to use me? Furthering your own agenda? Am I bait or something?"

"It might seem that way, depending on how you look at it," I said. "Though, are you really going to refuse help when it's clear that Javi's crew is trying to kill you? Don't you want to know why you've been targeted? You could call the cops, sure, but what are they really going to do? Maybe get the few guys who attacked you, if they're really lucky. Then Javi sends more guys after you. Not a great plan, from where I'm sitting."

Her lips pinched together, and I was certain she was making the same connections in her mind. She slumped back against the pillows, huffing out a pissed-off sigh. "Fine," she said to the ceiling, then tilted her eyes toward me. "What does *protection* imply?"

Luis cleared his throat, holding up a hand to get her attention. "Two options, really. The first is that you'll come stay with the pack. I'm head of Nico's security, and we have a plot of land on the outskirts of the city. We've turned it into our own little gated community. If you choose that option, you'll always have someone around to keep an eye on you and protect you. We've got incredible security there, and there's almost no way anything will happen to you there.

"Option two is we have an around the clock guard tail you. Sounds less intrusive, but for it to be real protection, the guy would have to live with you. Crash on your couch or whatever."

"Okay, no," Maddy said. "I'm definitely not sharing my house with some stranger. Christ, how do I know he won't piss on the bathroom floor or something? Hard pass." She frowned and sat back up. "I'm not super fond of the first option, either. I have a life. I already have a place to live."

"You're totally free to reject both offers and try to protect yourself," Luis said. "The problem is, I know Javi, and I have to question how long you'll stay alive once he knows you're unprotected. I'm going to go wait for Nico out front. Think about it."

Luis turned to leave, and Maddy watched him go, her eyes narrowed into slits. "He's a real dick," she murmured under her breath.

I laughed, unable to help myself. Luis was honest to a fault and never sugarcoated things. I could see why he could look like an asshole to someone who didn't know him. It was still funny to hear her say it, though.

"This is all for your well-being. I hope you can trust me when I say that. But Luis is right—you can reject both options. You'll be all on your own, though." My wolf didn't like the sound of that. The beast was actually snarling at me. I thanked God only I could hear him. "Get some rest. I'll stop back by later tonight. You can tell me what you've decided then."

Maddy nodded absently, seeming lost in thought when I exited the room. My wolf whined, wanting to go back in there. To just see her. I fought the urge and forced myself to walk out the front doors of the clinic.

Luis was leaned up against my truck, puffing away on a cigarette. He flicked the butt off into the shrubs. "What the fuck is going on, Nico?"

All I could do was shake my head. "I don't know, man."

Luis pointed back toward the clinic. "Something is off about that chick. I can't put my finger on it, but…there's something weird going on here. Every time I get around her…I don't know. When she talked about Javi's boys sniffing her and saying all that shit? I can smell it, but I have no fucking clue what she is."

I knew exactly what he meant. "She's human, Luis. A human who needs our help. That's all we need to know."

Human, yes, but there was something else there. Something that was niggling at my mind right beneath the surface, if I could only see what it was. I was determined to figure it out, and so was my wolf.

For now, all I could hope for was that Maddy was smart enough to accept my protection. I didn't want to think about what would happen to her if she refused. I hadn't lied when I said Javi would be back to finish what he started.

Chapter 5 - Maddy

"What the hell, Maddy?" Abi said as she barged into my room in the clinic.

She'd been in a full-tilt panic when I'd called her that evening after another short nap. She'd opened the bar by herself, but had been freaking out when I didn't answer my phone or show up on time. After leaving the bartenders and the doorman to run things while she was gone, she must have hauled ass to get to me. Our place was a good fifteen minutes across town, and that was when the traffic wasn't backed up. She burst into my room less than ten minutes after I hung up the phone with her.

"I can explain," I said.

"Explain? I'd sure hope so. What the fuck are you doing in a shifter's clinic? And why do you look like you got the shit beat out of you?"

I sighed and lay back on my pillows. "Did you guys not see the blood on the floor when you came in to open the bar?"

Abi frowned. "Uh…no. Wait…blood? There was blood on the floor? What the fuck happened last night?"

I looked out the window, which was a dark square in the white wall of the clinic. No blood? I'd seen my pile of clothes in the corner of the room. They'd been covered in blood. There was no way I hadn't bled all over the place. Had Nico sent guys to clean the place up after he got me to the clinic? Locked it up all nice and neat, like nothing had happened?

Abi stepped over and put a hand gingerly on the scratches and cuts on my arm. "Maddy, are you in trouble? Who did this to you?"

I quickly told her about what had happened the night before, and how the group of shifters had jumped me after we'd closed. I even told her about Nico and his friends saving me and getting me to the clinic, and about the offer of protection. I added the last bit to see what she thought about their offer.

Abi had pulled up the doctor's stool to sit on as she listened to the story, her face growing more horrified as I went on. When I was done, she shook her head in wonder. "What the hell is going on here? Maddy, you're crazy if you turn down this Nico guy's offer to help."

"I know, but I don't know these people."

"No, but they saved your ass. They must be decent guys. You know, there are asshats in this town who'd find a bloody and beaten girl and wouldn't think twice about sliding the old zipper down and having a little fun while she's knocked out. These guys saved your life *and* offered to protect you from these other psychos? I haven't met them, but they pass the vibe test."

"But living in their, like, compound? Or worse, having some strange dude share my toilet and kitchen for however long? Does that sound like fun to you?" I wasn't sure why I was arguing against it so hard. There was something about Nico I inherently trusted, but I hated the idea of my life being upended. Although, the thought of being beaten to death was much less appealing.

"I don't care what you have to do to stay safe. I just don't want those crazy wolves to finish the job."

She had a point—the same point Nico and Luis had made. It made the most sense, but it still galled me to have my choice taken away. Something this important should have been a much more difficult decision.

"Okay. He's going to come by later to get my answer. I'll think about it. I'll be fine. You can head back to the bar. It's a Saturday, they'll be getting killed." I winced at the metaphor even as it came out of my mouth.

Abi rolled her eyes and wrapped me in a gentle hug, trying not to hurt my bruised and bandaged body. She looked me in the eyes as she pulled away. "You call me the moment you need me. Got it?"

"Yes, mom."

"Bitch."

"Whore."

"Love you," Abi said with a laugh as she headed toward the door.

"Love you, too, lady," I called after her.

I spent an hour going over the pros and cons of the decision I had to make. Lose some personal privacy, and not die. Have someone watching me 24/7, and not die. Uproot my life and move to a strange place, and not die. I huffed out an irritated sigh. The mental math was playing out 100-to-1 on the side of taking Nico up on his offer.

Less than thirty minutes after Abi left, Nico returned. He swept into the room, and I had to admit, I'd never seen a man look as smooth as he did. Somehow, he made even mundane things look graceful, like opening and closing a door. He nodded at me and pulled up the stool, taking a seat in front of my bed.

He glanced over at the hospital phone beside my bed. "I heard you made a call. Had a visitor."

"I had to let my friends know what was wrong. Did you guys clean up my bar? After you brought me here?" I asked, changing the subject.

Nico gave me a half grin. "I thought it would be for the best."

"You couldn't have grabbed my phone while you were there? I had to dial my friend Abi from memory."

"Uh...sorry. To be honest, I didn't even think of it to be honest." That had caught him off guard. Good. I was glad to see someone else as out of sorts as I had been the last twenty-four hours.

"It's fine. I'm just in a bad mood."

"Are you in that mood because you've made a choice you don't like?"

"That's a smooth way of asking whether I've made a decision," I said.

He shrugged. "I try."

"Okay, let's talk. First off, having a complete stranger living in my house is totally off the table. Not gonna happen."

Nico nodded once. "Understood."

"So, hypothetically speaking, *if* I did choose to stay with the pack, what would that look like?"

He raised an eyebrow and cocked his head. "As in?"

"Do I get to come and go as I please? Will I have my own place? Where would I live?"

"Oh." Nico looked relieved, as if it was an easy question. "You'll live with me. At my place."

That information sent a wave of tingles through my entire body, my heart rate kicking up a few notches. For some reason, the idea of being in close proximity to Nico, living under the same roof, made my body react in a way I wasn't ready for.

I couldn't deny that Nico was attractive. Jesus, he was gorgeous. I still had to remind myself that nothing romantic was going to happen between us. This wasn't him coming on to me or trying to seduce me. He was trying to protect me from certain death.

"You'll have your own room with an attached bathroom," Nico added. "Locks on all the doors, the whole nine yards. You'll have all the privacy you want, if that's what you're worried about."

"Okay. What about freedom of movement? Coming and going?" That was the big sticking point. I didn't want to feel like a prisoner.

He nodded. "Whenever you want. Just let me or Luis know and we'll make sure you have a tail. Someone following to watch out for you."

"Free meals?" I asked, only half joking.

He smiled, and the tingling in my body increased. "Whatever you want. I grill a mean steak, and I can make a killer pasta sauce. Grandma's recipe."

"Not exactly what I meant, but okay."

If someone had told me three days ago that I'd be getting ready to move into a shifter compound, I'd have called them crazy. But all I kept picturing was that other shifter's face. Him snarling at me that I shouldn't exist. The way they'd attacked me kept flashing through my mind, like a horror movie where the worst scene is on repeat. I'd come close to dying. Another two or three minutes without Nico and his friends, and I *would* have been dead. I owed Nico my life. The least I could do was trust him to protect me a little while longer.

"Fine," I said. "It seems it's in my best interest to take you up on the offer. When will I be moving in?" Once the words were out, I had the feeling that I'd crossed some proverbial Rubicon—the point of no return. Butterflies filled my stomach, but I couldn't figure out whether it was from worry or excitement.

Nico grinned. "I'll have everything set up and ready before you're discharged tomorrow. I'll be the main security point of contact. Doc said you'll need to come in a few times so he can assess your wounds and healing. Those stab wounds were pretty bad—not life-threatening, but Doc wants to monitor them anyway. I'll bring you to those appointments."

"Oh my God. It's like I'm gonna have a babysitter. Are you going to take me to play dates, too?"

"Having a babysitter is better than being dead, right? And I'll let you change your own diapers if it makes you feel any better."

"Very funny." It wasn't funny, but the situation was too dire to play totally straight. I appreciated Nico's attempt to soften the blow of all that was going on with a little humor. "One question. Why would this Javi guy leave me alone because you're watching out for me? Why wouldn't he say 'screw it' and still come for me?"

Nico crossed his arms and furrowed his brow, seemingly thinking how best to answer. Finally, he said, "Because I'm stronger than he is. He's a strong alpha, don't get me wrong, but I'm stronger. My pack is bigger and more powerful. He's probably still thinking of ways to get to you, but he'll think twice, and probably a third time, before going up against me. Knowing you're under my protection will make him nervous and worried. He doesn't want a war with me, so he won't make a move. That will give us some time to figure out why he's after you in the first place."

"If you say so." I stared at Nico in the eyes, hoping to get the importance of what I was about to say across. "I'm trusting you. With my life."

He gave me a grave nod. "I understand. You rest now. My pack will watch out for you—you have my promise. I'll be back in the morning to pick you up and swing you by your place to grab whatever you need. Whatever you want to bring is fine. I've got a good-sized SUV, so we'll pack it full if need be. Here." He pulled a scrap of paper from his pocket and handed it to me. "This is my number. Doc has it, but in case you need me during the night."

I took it, my fingers brushing his as the paper passed from his hand to mine. The warmth and smoothness of his skin sent another shockwave through me. What was it about this guy? I'd never felt like this before. "Thanks," I murmured. "See you tomorrow."

Nico nodded one last time, then latched the door behind him as he left. I used a button on the bed to turn the lights off in the room, scooting down and settling my head on the pillow as my eyelids grew heavy. Even after all the sleep I'd had, I was still exhausted. I closed my eyes and was asleep in seconds.

The next thing I remember was waking up. The room was still dark, but the first few rays of sunlight were starting to filter through the blinds. My head was turned toward the window, but I had the strange feeling that something wasn't right. A feeling of impending doom that I couldn't explain. I noticed movement to my left, in the direction of the door.

I turned my head, slowly, not entirely sure if I was in the middle of another nightmare. Surprisingly, there was a nurse with her back turned toward me. She held a small vial of liquid and was inserting a syringe into it. I watched her fill the syringe full, then slip the vial into her pocket. When she turned around, I saw it was the same nurse from the first time I'd woken up. Cleo? I think that was her name.

She still hadn't noticed I was awake. She took my IV and moved the needle toward the bag. There was a look on her face that sent a wave of fear through me. Something wasn't right. She looked nervous and worried. She even looked anxiously over each of her shoulders before moving the needle closer to the IV bag.

"What are you doing?" I asked, surprising myself.

She dropped the syringe, and gasped in surprise. The nurse locked eyes with me, and I saw terror in them. Abject, horrified terror flooded her gaze. My heart nearly exploded as I yanked the phone off the table beside my bed. I found Nico's number and punched it in even as the nurse sprinted from the room. I heard her stumble and fall as she was going. Then Dr. Carter was yelling at her, asking why she was in so early.

Even as early as it was, Nico's phone only rang once before he answered. "What's wrong?" His voice was calm, but there was worry in it.

"The…I don't know. I think the nurse here was going to do something. Can you send someone?"

"The nurse? Fuck. I'll be right there." He ended the call without another word.

An instant later, Dr. Carter burst into the room, looking harried and confused. He glanced at me and the phone, his expression asking a hundred questions. He walked over to me and rested a hand on my arm. "What's going on here? What happened?"

I took several deep breaths, trying to get the image out of my head. The look on the nurse's face had been one of the most horrifying things I'd ever seen. She looked like a woman intent on doing harm, even though she didn't really want to. I looked at the doctor. "Are you sure your nurse is trustworthy?"

"Trustworthy? What—"

"Maddy?" Both the doctor and I jumped in surprise as Nico's voice boomed from the front of the clinic. How could he already be here? It had barely been a minute since he'd ended the call.

He came running into the room and looked from the doctor to me and back again. "What the fuck, Doc?"

Carter shrugged and looked bewildered. "I...Nico...I don't know what's going on. I only got in five minutes ago. Cleo was already here. She wasn't even the nurse on duty."

I pointed at the syringe on the ground. "She was going to put that into my IV. I caught her. She was trying to do it while I slept," I said, surprised by the calmness in my voice.

Carter stooped and picked up the syringe. Nico stepped over to examine the syringe with the doctor. Carter grabbed a piece of gauze and squirted the liquid on it, then sniffed the liquid. Carter wrinkled his nose, then looked horrified. "Morphine?" His face went pale when he realized how full the syringe was. "This much would have stopped your heart in less than ten minutes once it was put in this IV. I don't...what's happening?"

My heart lurched into my throat. She'd been trying to kill me? I'd been seconds away from death. Had I not woken up, I'd probably already be dead. Twice in less than forty-eight hours someone had tried to kill me. I was living in a nightmare.

"Nooooooo!" a woman's voice screeching in fear and anguish came from the lobby. All three of us jumped at the sound.

A few seconds later, Luis burst into the room. He had the nurse pressed to his body, his left arm around her throat, the right had her arm bent painfully behind her. Tears coursed down her cheeks, and a bright red welt on her cheek was shaped like a handprint likely matching Luis's hand.

"Caught her," Luis grunted. "Wrecked her car less than a block away trying to get out. Ran her down like a fucking rabbit."

Nico stepped toward her, putting his face less than an inch from hers. "Who sent you? What were you doing here?"

Cleo winced away from him, her crying intensifying. Luis twisted her arm harder and she squealed in pain. "Alright!" she shouted. "A man told me to."

"What man?" Dr. Carter asked, his bewilderment fading into anger.

"A man came to me last night. I got home and my husband wasn't there. He showed me a picture of Jonathan. He was tied to a chair and his eye was swollen shut, and he...he...looked awful." She broke down into sobs for a minute before continuing. "The guy handed me a vial of morphine and told me what to do. He said I had to kill this girl or they'd kill my Jonathan." She dissolved into the most heart-wrenching cries I'd ever heard in my life. Her legs gave out and Luis let her body slide to the floor.

Luis looked down at her with his lips curled in disgust, then glanced at Nico. "I'll get her out of here."

Luis scooped the distraught nurse up and dragged her from the room. Dr. Carter followed them out. My entire body was shuddering, but I didn't even realize it was happening until I felt Nico's hand on my shoulder. My head snapped around to see him staring at me.

"Do you see now?" he asked. "The kind of trouble you're in? The attack the other night wasn't a one-and-done. Javi is going to keep coming after you. I need to protect you."

I was already nodding before he'd even finished talking. I'd never been so afraid in my life. Tears were leaking from my eyes, sliding across my cheeks to drip into my lap. "Why is this happening? I just want to know why."

Nico put a hand to my face, cupping my cheek. His voice went quiet and soft. "We'll figure that out together. I promise."

Chapter 6 - Nico

Doc gave Maddy another sedative so she could get some rest before he discharged. She hadn't been happy about having to take more drugs, but Carter assured her it was to calm her down and let her rest a little more before leaving. I stayed by her side until she was asleep, then slipped out to call Luis.

"Where did you go?" I asked as soon as he answered.

"Took the nurse lady to a secure location. She is…Bro, she's not in a good place right now. Never seen someone so fucking torn up. You'd think the husband was already dead. How's the girl?"

"Asleep. Doc knocked her out so she could rest before we moved her out. He might keep her one more day just in case, but he won't know for sure until later after he checks her wounds."

Luis paused, letting the silence draw out uncomfortably, before he spoke again. "So, what the hell is going on with Javi?"

I snorted a humorless laugh. "Not sure. This is weird. It had to have been him who approached the nurse, right?"

"Had to be. Probably not him directly but one of his boys. I don't get why he's got such a hard-on for this chick. She's hot, yeah, but other than that, I don't see anything special. I can't find any connection to Javi. I've been looking into it and asking around. She doesn't come from money. The bar looks legit, no sign of money laundering or anything like that. I just don't get it."

"Yeah." I grunted, not knowing what else to say. It was strange. Usually, when Javi made a move of some sort, there was always something obvious to be gained. Respect, money, territory, power, something. It would have made at least a *little* sense that he wanted Maddy for himself, but the whole attempted-murder thing seemed to rule that possibility out.

"What's our next play?" Luis asked.

He wouldn't like what I had to say next, but it was something that had to be done. "I need you to set up a meeting with Javi."

The pause on the other end of the phone was longer this time. "Are you serious right now?" he finally asked.

"I am. This might all be a misunderstanding. I don't want to go to war or get this girl killed all because it could have been sorted out in a five-minute conversation. Right?"

"I guess. But Javi is a stubborn piece of shit, you know that. He's not going to be happy you got in the way of his plans. Not once, but twice now."

"I get that. I've got to approach this like an alpha, Luis. I've got a responsibility to resolve things in the best way possible. I can't just drag the whole pack into something without exhausting every avenue. I've involved myself in this, and I've got to do my best to figure out an endgame."

"That's something else," Luis said, sounding confused and irritated. "Why the hell *are* you involved? Since the moment we pulled into that bar parking lot, it's like you've been a different person."

That was a question I still couldn't answer. It was part of the reason I wanted, *needed,* Maddy to stay with the pack. If I kept her close, maybe I could figure out what this feeling was.

I stayed silent, trying to figure out the best way to explain it. Trying to find a good reason to drag all my friends and family into something this dangerous. Instead, all I said was, "I don't know."

"You know what you're acting like, right? It's what Sebastian said. Like she's your fated mate."

I winced at the suggestion. "Luis, she's human. You know that isn't possible."

"I know that. Do you?"

"Yes. Fated mates don't apply to humans. All I can tell you is that every instinct in my body is telling me I need to protect her. I can't ignore that."

Luis sighed. "This is so fucking weird. I trust you, though. With my life, Nico. I'll stand by you on this. Whatever call you make on how to proceed, I'll have your back."

I was thankful for my friend. There was nothing like having someone who supported you. As an alpha, having someone like Luis as your beta made life easier and more manageable. "What's the plan for the nurse?" I asked.

"We're gonna keep her under lock and key. I'm going to check into the kidnapped husband. I'll keep you updated."

"Okay, sounds good. I'm gonna see if Sebastian can come watch Maddy. I need to get back to the house and get that spare room ready for her to move into."

I called Sebastian, who agreed to come over. I gave him the rundown on all that had happened and made sure he understood how serious it was.

"Shit," he said, eyes wide with confusion. "This is some heavy shit, bro."

"I know. I'll be back in a bit, just make sure she's okay. I trust the doc, but at this point, no one else gets in to see her. Got it?"

Sebastian nodded. "Yeah, yeah, we're good."

On the drive home, I went over the multiple ways the conversation with Javi could go. The scenarios in my head ran the gamut from intelligent adult negotiation that ended with a resolution we could all deal with to disaster that ended with shouts, screams, blood, and everything in between.

When I pulled into my house and saw the car sitting in the driveway, I sighed. It was not what I wanted to see. I loved my mother, but I wasn't really in the mood to have the conversation I knew was coming.

I found her in the kitchen.

"Nico? What is going on? Everyone is running around like chickens with their heads cut off. All over the pack compound. Is something wrong?"

With everything that had happened, I hadn't had time to let my family know about the situation. I rubbed my face and let out an exhausted sigh. "Mom, call Dad and everyone else. Have them come over. I'd rather explain it once instead of four or five times. I need to go clean up the spare room. I'm going to have a house guest."

My mother's eyes glittered with worry, but she did as I asked. I heard her on the phone with my brothers and dad while I was in the back room. The bedroom had mostly been used as my own personal storage area. It was full of boxes, bags of clothes, and books. I spent twenty minutes hauling items into the attic and garage before the room looked suitable for a guest. I grabbed some spare sheets and blankets from the linen closet in my bathroom and had just finished making the bed when I heard the rumble of conversation coming from the kitchen and living room. The Lorenzos had all arrived.

When I walked out, I saw my entire family sprawled through my house. Diego and Mateo were sitting on the hearth of my fireplace in quiet discussion. Rafael was with my parents at the kitchen island, it seemed like they were arguing, which was usual for them. My baby brother, Gabriel—the youngest of us all—was on the couch, scrolling through his phone, looking the least concerned out of everyone.

Dad glanced up and saw me standing in the hallway. "Nico?" Everyone else stopped what they were doing and turned to look at me. "What's going on here? I can't get any of your guys to give me a straight answer. I've called everyone. Why has the guard around the neighborhood been increased?"

I held my hand up. "Hang on, Dad, I'll get to that. Can everyone give me a second to explain?" I took their silence as agreement and launched into my story. I explained about finding Maddy half-dead and being attacked by shifters, recognizing them as members of

Javi's pack, the second attempt on her life, the nurse-and-husband issue, and my offer of security. I left out the strange feelings I'd been having toward Maddy since I first scented her blood. That seemed like information that would muddy the waters, and I had no time for that.

Unsurprisingly, Mom was the first to speak once I was done. "Nico, why are you involving yourself in this? It seems like this should be between this girl and the police. You're putting yourself and the entire pack in danger."

Dad chopped his hand down through the air like a knife. "Julia, you know what it means to be an alpha. Nico is a true alpha, and any alpha worth his salt helps those in need. He can't turn his back on this girl. This Maddy girl needs help, regardless of the pack. It's the right thing to do."

Diego cleared his throat, and we all turned to look at him. "And this could be a way to weaken Javi. Right, Dad?"

Dad nodded. He looked at me, and I noticed the calculating look in his eyes. "True, this could be the chance we've been waiting on to finally bring Javi down. Especially if we have something he wants. We can use that."

Mom's eyes blazed in fury as she turned on Dad. "Carlos, you're talking about war! Is that what you want?" She turned her gaze back to me. "Nico, you're being reckless. You can't put the entire pack in danger for one single human. You need to think this through. You'll understand that you can't—"

"Do you trust me as alpha, Mother?" I asked, my irritation turning to anger.

The room went deathly quiet. Gabriel turned back to his phone, averting his eyes from the uncomfortable situation. Mateo put a hand to his eyes, and Diego and Rafael looked on in greedy anticipation, ready to watch the fireworks of a fight between Mom and me. Dad looked like he was waiting to see how I'd handle the situation before chiming in.

The question seemed to be a slap in the face to Mom. I knew it would and didn't feel bad about it. She needed to understand. After staring into my eyes for several seconds, Mom finally lowered her gaze, face going red.

She nodded. "I trust you, Nico. Implicitly. You are the pack alpha," she murmured, sounding adequately chastised.

I sighed. "Then trust me on this. Can you do that, Mom? Dad does." I swept a hand across the room. "All my brothers do. Can you?"

Mom nodded again, managing to meet my eyes. "Yes. I trust you. I'm sorry. I...I'm just worried."

"I understand, Mom. So am I," I said.

Dad stepped over and patted me on the shoulder. "You're doing something here, Nico. I'm proud of you for this. Few would sacrifice so much for an innocent. The pack will follow you. I guarantee it. Come on, Julia, let's let Nico get the house ready for his guest."

Mom followed him out the door after giving me a hug goodbye. My brothers all seemed content to hang out where they were. The front door closed, and all four of them shared a glance with each other. I frowned as they all shared some unspoken conversation I wasn't privy to.

Diego stood and crossed his arms. "So, what's really going on? You're hiding something."

I groaned and hung my head. I hated how easily my brothers could read me. I'd really thought I'd done a good job keeping things hidden during my explanation. I gritted my teeth and kept my mouth shut.

Mateo chuckled. "You might as well spill it. We aren't going to let up. Unless you want us to tell Mom you've got a secret."

My eyes snapped up to his face. "You wouldn't fucking dare."

Mateo grinned and shrugged. "Maybe, maybe not. Do you want to risk that shit storm?"

I glanced at each of my brothers in turn, and they shared a look. There was no talking my way out of this. They wouldn't stop until I told them. It would be less headache to go ahead and get it over with now, rather than try to drag things out.

"Fine," I hissed, taking a seat on the stool at the kitchen island. "The girl I was telling you about? Maddy?"

"Yeah," Diego and Mateo said almost in unison.

"When I found her, she was covered in blood. Her blood. Once my wolf caught a whiff of that…it was like I couldn't stop myself. I was desperate to protect her. I was by her side for hours. I'm…drawn to her. I can't explain it."

Rafael frowned in confusion. "What you're describing is a wolf's protective instinct to its mate."

I pointed at him. "Raf, that's exactly what I thought, but that can't be it. Maddy is human. You know that's not possible. Humans and shifters date, sure, but being a fated mate? That's not a thing."

Diego grabbed a bottle of water from my fridge and opened it. "You've got to be careful. Something about this woman doesn't track. The fact that she's got this kind of power over you is something we need to watch out for."

The others nodded in agreement. Gabriel added, "We trust your judgment, don't get us wrong, but we have to make sure we're looking out for you."

"I get that," I said. "I've thought the same thing the last couple of days. I'll need all of your help keeping her safe. Can I count on you?"

"You've given her your word. We're here for you, and her, no matter what," Mateo said.

The rest of them nodded. Their expressions told me all I needed to know. They were taking this as seriously as I was.

A few minutes later, they all started moving toward the door. Raf put a hand on my shoulder. "Do you need anything else today?"

I shook my head. "No. I'm going to finish up here, then head to the clinic to pick up Maddy."

"Okay. Call if that changes. We're here."

Without another word, my brothers left, and I closed the door behind them.

I grabbed a set of towels and put those in the bathroom Maddy would use. I'd put a couple of blankets on her bed when my phone rang. It was Luis.

"What's up?"

"Doc's going to let Maddy out. Said he'd discharge her in about thirty minutes. Thought you'd want to be here. Felipe got here a minute ago. Full protection detail." Luis said.

I left almost as soon as I hung up the phone. My mind drifted as I drove. I tried to think of the best way to contact Javi for our face-to-face meeting. It needed to happen soon. The longer it went, the worse things were bound to get.

I pulled into the parking lot and found that wouldn't be a problem. As I stepped out of my SUV, I saw a figure standing at the far end of the parking lot, leaning against a bright blue 1968 Chevelle. The car alone told me who it was, even if I hadn't recognized him. Javi.

The distance was almost a hundred yards, but my supernatural sight and hearing made it seem like we were standing nose to nose. Javi seemed wholly unconcerned with my appearance. His hair was pulled back in a ponytail, his arms and legs thick with muscle. His knuckles were heavy, scarred, and made for fighting. Javi tilted his head up in a sort of nod. "Don't get involved, my man."

"Not an option. I'm already involved. Why are you after Maddy? What has she done to you?"

Javi winced. "Wow, first-name basis already. This isn't going to end well for you."

"You haven't answered me."

"This is bigger than you. It really would be best for you if you stepped aside before things get too hot. You're gonna make things a lot worse if you aren't careful. All you're doing is painting a target on your back, and you can bet that's not something you want."

I snarled, my wolf's rage seeping into my body. "That sounds like a threat."

Javi nodded. "Good. It was."

"Do we need to settle this right now, then?" My voice was rising in anger, my fists clenched.

All Javi did was laugh. "Not here, kid. I'll warn you one last time—you really have no idea what you're getting yourself into. When the shit hits the fan? Remember, I tried to warn you."

I stared at him as he opened his driver's side door and slid into the seat. The muscle car's engine roared to life, and Javi peeled out as he left the clinic, leaving a cloud of smoke and rubber in his wake. I stared at his car until it disappeared around a curve in the road.

Inside, I found Doc sitting at the front desk. "Is everyone in the back?" I asked.

Doc nodded. "Last I saw, they were at the end of the hall outside Maddy's room."

I hurried down the hall and found them all exactly where Doc had said. Before any of them could say anything, I relayed the exchange I'd had with Javi outside. Luis looked pissed and glared past my shoulder toward the parking lot where Javi no longer was. Felipe and Sebastian both looked worried. Things were getting heavy, and it was happening fast.

"I've got a bad feeling about this, Nico," Luis said.

"Yeah, man, what the hell is happening?" Felipe asked.

"I don't know," I said, shaking my head. "But we're involved now. It's too late to back out. We have to be prepared for whatever is ahead of us."

Chapter 7 - Maddy

"Hey, you ready?" Nico said as he walked into my room.

The minute I saw him and heard his voice, I knew something was wrong. The easy-going, charismatic Nico was gone. This version of Nico was tense and had a worried look on his face.

I didn't say anything about it. Instead, I simply nodded and started gathering my few belongings. Nico stood by the door with his friends.

He leaned toward his buddy who'd caught the nurse that morning. Luis? "Head out ahead of us. I'll call you with the address."

"Got it." He was gone an instant later.

Nico stepped over to me, his face a little less pensive than a moment before. "Can I take your arm? Lead you out?"

I was a little surprised that he'd asked permission. I'd actually been preparing myself for the full macho-man act—a hand around my waist, dragging me out the door "for my own protection" and not a hint of apology. This was a nice change of pace. It told me Nico really might be a good guy. I could tell he was, anyway, otherwise I'd never have taken him up on his offer. This helped me feel better about the situation, though.

"Yeah, that would be nice," I said. "I'm still a little wobbly from being in bed so long and all the pain meds."

That was the truth. I'd actually gotten dizzy getting dressed five minutes before he'd arrived. That was probably from my head wound, but I was sure all the other things that had happened in the last two days hadn't been great for my equilibrium either.

Nico put a hand around my arm and guided me down the hallway. He had two more friends standing at the front, both standing outside the door and scanning the area. If things weren't so dire, I'd have thought it was kind of cool. All these bodyguards should have made me feel like I was some movie star or something. But in reality, it scared me. Terrified me, really. People were trying to kill me. Literally. My life was at risk and people wanted me dead. I had no idea why, and these shifters were the only thing standing between me and a plastic body bag.

Nico walked me over to his SUV and settled me in the passenger seat. He went around the driver's side door and got inside. Once the doors were locked, he waited for his two friends to get into a car and pull up behind us in the parking lot. It looked like they were going to tail us to my place.

"Okay, what's the address? I'll have Luis get there ahead of us."

I told him the address. Nico pulled out his cell and relayed the info to his friend, then started the massive SUV and pulled out of the parking lot. I glanced back at the little clinic and wondered how such a nondescript building could have been the place where my entire life changed. Three days ago, my biggest worry was whether my shipment of red wine would come in on time, or if I'd have enough limes for the evening rush. I'd had a simple, pleasant, happy life. Now, I'd somehow found myself in a life-or-death struggle, and it had all started in a building that looked like it was home to an accountant's office. It really felt like it should look more sinister or dark. Instead, it looked like the least ominous place I'd ever seen.

After turning out of the parking lot, the building disappeared, and I found myself fully alone with Nico for the first time. Even the first time he'd questioned me, Dr. Carter had been right down the hallway. So this was different, and it felt a bit awkward.

"So…um." I had no idea what to start a conversation about. "I hope it wasn't too much trouble getting my room ready." Oh my God, what a moron. I did my best not to roll my eyes at myself.

Nico glanced over, then back to the road. "Nah. All good. I needed to clean out that room anyway. Only took me like half an hour."

"That's good. I'm a little worried about being bothered. I know you probably had your own life to deal with, and this is not really what you had planned. Unless you're constantly harboring women from danger, that is."

"First time, actually. I did save a vampire from some hunters once. That guy owes me one, big time."

I froze and blinked. "Wait…vampires are real?" The implication sent a new shiver of fear up my spine.

Nico barked a laugh. "Sorry, sorry, I thought you could tell I was being sarcastic. No, they aren't real…well, I assume they aren't." He chuckled to himself the rest of the drive, and my cheeks went red in embarrassment.

We pulled up to my house five minutes later, where Luis stood outside. He waved as we pulled in. His two other friends pulled their car in behind us. Luis was scanning the surrounding area as I got out of the car.

"Hang on," Nico said. "No going in until we clear the house."

I stopped mid-step and looked at my place. I didn't even contemplate that someone might be waiting inside for me. The thought was enough to turn my guts to water. It was my home, a place that should always feel safe. In one sentence, Nico had changed all that. Now every shadow, every angle, every nook looked like it could be hiding someone. A nightmare fantasy flashed through my mind— some dark figure crawling out of my linen closet, a knife clamped between his teeth, murder in his dark eyes. I shivered and crossed my arms across my chest, feeling cold even in the humid Florida heat.

I handed Nico the keys and waited with Sebastian and Felipe while Nico and Luis went inside. We stood in silence; both men kept looking up and down the road. I couldn't take my eyes off the house. When Nico came out three minutes later, waving the all-clear, I released a deep breath, relief swelling in my chest. I knew I was safe, being surrounded by four shifters, but still, the thought of an intruder being found in my place had been more stressful than I'd even imagined.

I stepped onto the porch and Nico nodded inside. "Take all the time you need. I'll be at the front door. Luis will go to the rear exit. We'll stay outside to give you some space."

"Thanks," I muttered.

The first thing I did was go to the fridge and throw out anything that wouldn't survive a week or two and put the trash bag by the door. In my bedroom, I pulled out my big suitcase and the carry-on bag I used whenever I traveled. I stuffed my carry-on full of my toiletries, phone charger, and other little things. I grabbed random clothes, shoes, and underwear, then dropped them into the larger bag. I was on my knees organizing the bag when I let my hands rest on my thighs. All I could do was stare at the things in the suitcase and wonder if it was enough. I would only be twenty or thirty minutes from my place. I could always have someone bring me back to grab whatever I'd forgotten.

Why was this happening? How long would I have to live like this? Bodyguards, safe houses, chaperones to and from the store and work? It was all too much to bear. I felt the fear inside me, but also a growing rage at the injustice of it all. I'd been a good person. I'd done all the right things and tried my best to help people who needed it. So why the hell had *my* life turned to shit?

I hadn't even realized I was trembling until Nico's hand brushed my shoulder. I spun around and leveled my eyes at him. He pulled his hand back and glanced at the suitcase. "I said your name a few times, and you didn't answer. I came to check on you. I was worried."

My mind must have totally zoned out to not have heard him. "Sorry, I must have spaced," I said, casting my eyes down.

"It's okay," Nico said. "It's a lot. I understand it's probably difficult to deal with it all."

I stared at him for several seconds. What was he trying to do? Was he only placating me? Trying to keep me calm by being nicer than he needed to be? All these questions and more bubbled in my head as I looked at him.

"Why are you doing that?"

"Doing what?" Nico asked, looking confused.

"Being so nice to me."

"Uh," Nico's brows furrowed. "Would you prefer I not be nice?"

I huffed out a sigh. "I know you're only using me to get what you want. To get this Javi guy or whatever. You don't have to pretend to be nice to me. That's all I'm saying."

Nico's eyes went hard, and his face was stony. "Us having a similar endgame has nothing to do with my personality or the way I treat people." His voice was icy, and I already regretted what I'd said. "I'm really sorry you haven't had good experiences with shifters. Truly, I am, but we aren't all the same. If that's what you think, then that's a pretty bigoted thought process."

"I didn't mean—"

"Yes," he interrupted, "I do need to figure out what Javi is up to. That's true. That doesn't mean I need to *pretend* to be a decent damned person to do it. I'll be outside."

He spun on his heel and stomped out. I closed my eyes and winced inwardly. Why the fuck had I done that? Shame and regret warred within me. Each emotion did its best to beat my ego to death. That had been a shitty, cold-hearted thing to say, and I couldn't think of a single reason to have said it other than that I was pissed at the situation and wanted to take my frustration out on someone.

"Dammit," I hissed and pounded my fist into my thigh. I was being a bitch to the one person trying to keep me alive.

Luis carried my big bag to the SUV while Sebastian took the bag of trash to my can and rolled it to the curb for me. Without looking at me, Nico took my carry-on from me. He put it in the back and climbed into the driver seat. "Is that everything?" he asked through the passenger window, still not looking at me.

"Yeah," I said as I opened the door.

We pulled away, and I didn't even get a chance for one last look at my place. All I could do was stare at the muscles in Nico's jaw clenching and unclenching in anger. He was still pissed, and I knew exactly why.

I let him drive for several minutes, watching the scenery change as we neared his pack lands, before I spoke again. "Look, Nico, I didn't mean to be so—"

"You'll be looked after the entire time you're in my care," he said, cutting me off before I could apologize. Yep, definitely still pissed at me. "Along with my friends you've already met, I've got four brothers. So, at least one of us will be around at any point. Usually more than one. We'll take you to and from work, and whoever is with you will stay there—one inside near the bar, and one outside checking the perimeter.

"I'm really not trying to uproot your whole life. I hope you understand that. I only want you to stay safe. Once we figure out what Javi is up to and stop him, you can go back to your life. You'll never have to worry about me bothering you again."

I pursed my lips, staring at my hands in my lap. I cursed myself again for being an asshole earlier. I'd much preferred Nico's kind tone over the harsh, cold one. Had I taken something that was already going to be a little weird, awkward, and scary, and made it even worse? It was looking that way. *Great job, Maddy, a really good idea.*

A few minutes later, we got to what I could only assume were the gated Lorenzo pack lands. Nico leaned out of the window and punched in a code, and the gate slid open. Once we pulled through and started driving by houses, my eyes almost bulged out of my head. Every house was really nice. I didn't know what I'd expected, but it wasn't these three- and four-thousand square foot monsters. Several had swimming pools and every lawn was immaculate. Another wave of shame cascaded across my mind as I realized I'd been anticipating shabby mobile homes or some big communal bunkhouse. I hadn't realized I'd been so judgmental. I guess all it took for the real me to come out was for my life to be in danger. The day was getting more depressing by the second.

The homes stayed pretty much the same the whole way down the road. I tried to forget my festering embarrassment by ogling the houses. Nico's pack must have had quite a bit of money to afford the luxury. The houses weren't mansions or anything, but they were definitely on the more expensive end of upper middle class.

We pulled into a cul-de-sac at the end of the neighborhood, and Nico pulled the SUV into the driveway. He clicked a button to open the garage door. The house was just as big and nice as the others.

Once the garage door was closed behind us, I climbed out of the car and glanced around the garage. It was sparser than most I'd seen, with just a few cardboard boxes and a shelving unit that looked like it held a bunch of tools, tire pumps, and flashlights. Typical DIY supplies. Nico already had the back hatch opened and my two bags pulled out. He rolled them to the entry door.

As he stepped through, Nico called over his shoulder, "Follow me."

I did as asked, still trying to think of the best way to apologize. When I stepped into the kitchen, my jaw dropped. Solid marble countertops, high-end tile floors, stainless steel appliances? The home was gorgeous. It definitely didn't look like a bachelor pad. I wondered if he paid for a maid or something.

Nico led me down a hallway, and I saw he'd decorated his house with various paintings. *Actual* paintings. Not prints or the lame pictures with paint splattered on them to give the impression of a painting, but honest-to-God paintings. One was a watercolor done in a way that could be confused with an abstract, but a second look showed that it was actually a howling wolf's head. It was really cool, and I was so mesmerized by it that I almost lost Nico.

At the end of the hallway, we came to a stairway. He hauled my bags up, opened a door at the top, and rolled my luggage in. "This is your place."

I stepped in and blinked in surprise. The bedroom and bathroom together were easily the same size as the tiny one-bedroom house I leased. I couldn't believe how much room I had. The bed was king-sized as well. I wouldn't know what to do with myself after spending the last five years sleeping on a full-sized bed.

"Anyway," Nico said. "Go ahead and get comfortable. Relax or whatever. We don't want your stitches opening before we go back to Doc's clinic. Once you're settled, come on down so I can show you how to use the security system."

Without another word, he strode toward the door to leave. I closed my eyes and sighed. "Nico?"

When I opened my eyes again, he'd stopped, half out the door. He didn't say anything; he just stood there. He didn't even turn to look at me.

"I'm really happy you're helping me," I said, hoping he could hear the sincerity in my voice. "I also wanted to say I was sorry about earlier." I swallowed my pride and went on. "When I was a bitch, I mean. I didn't mean to question you or your motives. That's all. I'm...I'm sorry. And thank you."

Nico finally turned to look at me, and the irritation and anger that had been there a few moments ago had cooled. The lines softened and the handsome face underneath it re-emerged. My heart did a stutter-step in my chest, and that voice started whispering to me again—the voice I'd heard the moment I'd first seen him. It was telling me the same thing it said yesterday. That this man was mine.

I shook the thought away because it made no sense. Probably nothing more than my hormones screaming at me since it had been almost a year since I'd gotten laid.

After a few seconds of staring intently at me, Nico smiled. "You're welcome. I'll see you downstairs."

I didn't breathe easy until he'd closed the door and I heard him descending the steps. I put a hand to my racing heart and tried to figure out what was going on with my head. I had enough going on with everything that was happening. I didn't need my body to take on a mind of its own and drool over a guy. Still...there was something intriguing about the thought.

Chapter 8 - Nico

The wolf inside me was going crazy with every stair I walked down. All it wanted was for me to go back upstairs. It was gnashing its teeth, slavering and whining, desperate to go back to Maddy. I'd never experienced anything like it before. Until I'd scented Maddy's blood the other night, my wolf and I had been on the same page. Two wholly different beings, locked inside the same body, living the same life, working like the perfect intertwined team. This wasn't something I'd ever encountered—or even heard of.

I stopped at the bottom of the stairs and looked up at the door to the guest room. I let myself entertain the thought for one second. Going back up the stairs, opening the door, taking Maddy in my arms. Flinching, I shook the thought from my head, and forced myself to go to the kitchen. I opened the fridge and pulled out a beer, my wolf still battering at my mind. Usually, I didn't need any help understanding what it was thinking, but this was one of the few times in my life it would have been really nice if it could talk. All I could get from it were these weird anxious and possessive emotions.

Popping the top off the beer, I pulled up one of the stools and sat at the kitchen island. She'd find me down here soon. While I waited, I fired off a text to the guys to let them know Maddy was getting settled, and I asked them to get together to figure out their work schedules so they could coordinate who would be with Maddy and when.

Almost immediately, the guys started texting back and forth. The conversation wasn't what I needed to see, so I silenced my notifications. I sipped at the beer and stared off into space, thinking about this strange situation and trying to rein my wolf in.

"Hey," Maddy's voice said behind me.

I spun and saw her standing in the doorway. "Hi. Everything all tucked away?"

"Eh, I'm not a very good unpacker. I tend to live out of my suitcase whenever I go somewhere. It's fine."

I grinned at that and walked to the fridge. "Do you want a drink or anything?"

Maddy raised her eyebrows. "What do you have?"

"I've got beer. I have some wine. Bottled water, soda, orange juice?"

"Beer works."

"Good answer," I said, pulling a can from the shelf and handing it over.

After taking a drink, she nodded toward the front door. "You were going to show me the security system?"

"Right." I walked to the door and pointed at the panel. "This monitors all the doors and windows. Once they're all closed, you hit the Home button and punch in the code. Five-seven-one-nine-five. You'll have to use the code manually at first. I'll get you a fob that you can use to lock and unlock it, though that might take a day or two. Then, it'll work just like a car. Simple but effective. If anyone tries to break in, the alarm is loud as hell, you won't be able to miss it."

Maddy looked at the panel for several seconds, her brow furrowed. Finally, she swept a hand toward the front door. "Can you tell me what makes this whole place so safe? I mean, the security system is great and all, but couldn't someone just sneak into the neighborhood?"

I couldn't help but smile. I liked that she was asking questions and looking for holes in our logic. It meant she wouldn't just go along with something because I said so. She was a thinker and wanted to know exactly what was going on.

"Good question. You saw the gate we came in through, right?"

"Yeah."

"What you didn't see was the guy hidden away, watching the gate."

Her eyes widened in surprise. "I didn't see anyone."

"Exactly the point. We have a rotating guard at the gate. We also have a fence that runs around the entire perimeter of the compound. We've got cameras at every entrance and randomly around the property. Someone's tasked with checking the footage all the time, looking for anything out of place. Now that Javi has proven how serious he is, we've got volunteers doing sweeps around the neighborhood and along the fence line."

"Okay." Grinning, she held up a hand. "I get it. Lots of security. Sounds safe. So, what comes next? What's the plan?"

"We need to figure out why Javi is after you. That's what we need to start working on."

I walked over to the back door and opened it, inviting her to sit on the deck with me. We settled into the chairs and drank our beers in silence for a few minutes before I broached the subject again. "First things first, let's talk about your connections."

"To what?" she asked.

"Shifters. Do you have any background with anyone? Ex-boyfriends? Business partners? Roommates? Anything?"

"None. I didn't, like, actively try to stay away from shifters. I just never had the chance to get to know any."

She looked a little embarrassed about the information, which I could understand. Lots of people hated shifters and wanted nothing to do with us. Ending the segregation of shifters had taken a long time, and some people still wished the old laws had never been revoked. Maddy didn't want me to think she was on the side of the racists.

"It's okay, I get it. I don't have many humans I deal with, if I'm honest," I said. "What about your parents? Could they have gotten into trouble? Maybe your father owes money or something like that? Maybe you're leverage for Javi to get what he wants from one of your parents?"

Maddy's eyes almost popped out of her face and a hand went to her forehead. "Oh shit. I haven't even called my mom and dad. Oh God."

That was probably something she needed to do. "Go ahead and give them a call. I'd keep what happened close to the vest, though."

"But shouldn't I tell my parents I was attacked? Nico, I almost died."

I nodded, raising my hands to keep her calm. "I know what you're saying. Still, if your parents aren't involved, the less they know the better. If you give them a bunch of info, they may become collateral damage. I don't want Javi going after them because they found out something they didn't need to know. Plus, if I'm honest, they'd probably demand you go stay with them. Can your parents protect you the way I can?"

Maddy chewed at her lower lip and glanced around the house, then gave a sad shake of her head.

"Good. When you do talk to them, try to get some information out of them. Be subtle with the questions. That way, we can try to rule them out early. I sent a guy to your bar. He's going to get your cell phone and bring it here. Until then, you can use mine," I said, pulling the phone out of my pocket.

She took it and immediately dialed her parents' number from memory. It was impressive, actually. I couldn't remember my own mom and dad's number. All I ever did was hit the button that said *Mom* or *Dad*.

I leaned back to listen to the call. My hearing was ten times better than that of a normal human, and this would give me the opportunity to hear if either of her parents sounded like they were hiding anything.

"Mom?" Maddy said, when the phone stopped ringing.

"Sweetie? Hi. I was starting to get worried. We haven't heard from you in a couple days. What phone are you calling from? It says unknown number."

"Yeah, sorry. Things got…uh…busy, I guess. I'm, uh…well I dropped my phone in the toilet. I'm using one of my employee's phones for now until I get a new one."

"Ew, that's terrible. But you said busy. Does that mean there's a boy?" her mother asked hopefully.

Maddy rolled her eyes. "Jeez, Mom, no. Listen, has everything been okay with you and Dad?"

"What do you mean?"

"Any problems or issues? I only wanted to check in. I have to make sure you guys are all right."

"I don't know why we wouldn't be all right. Your father got a new set of golf clubs and had one of the worst scores ever this weekend. He's been a little down about that, otherwise we're fine."

"Okay, so…" Maddy looked at me, then turned away again, "I didn't tell you guys this, but I did one of those ancestry tracker things. The ones where you send in a swab of spit and they give you a whole list of things about your DNA? Do you remember anything more about my birth parents?"

My eyebrows shot up in surprise. I hadn't realized Maddy was adopted. We hadn't checked on things like that when we looked into her. Could her birth parents be into something? That didn't make a lot of sense, though. You couldn't use someone as leverage if you'd never met them. It would be pointless for Javi to try and kill her if he had a feud or something with her birth parents. They didn't know her. It would be almost the same as killing a stranger.

As if she could hear my thoughts, Maddy looked at me and flashed a bashful smile.

Her mom sighed sadly. "We told you everything when we broke the news when you were fourteen, honey. There isn't a lot to tell. By the way, sweetie, are you taking your medicine?"

"I'm fine, Mom, seriously. Anyway, like I was saying. It was just weird. Abi did it and she had like three dozen matches. I did it and only got some random guy from, like, three hundred years ago."

I frowned. That was weird. But I'd never done one of the tests, so maybe it was more typical than she thought.

They went back and forth about the test and how much it cost and how long it took. I could already tell by her mother's tone of voice and verbiage that she wasn't involved. No one was that good of an actor. Her dad wasn't on the call, but it was unlikely it was him, either. Even if he'd lied or tried to keep things from his wife, anything serious enough to cause the death of his daughter would have been impossible to hide.

"I wish I knew more, Maddy, but we don't," Maddy's mother said. "I'm sorry. I'm sure that test stirred up a bunch of stuff. Are you okay?"

Maddy nodded and ran a hand through her hair. "I'm good, Mom. It's really not that big a deal, seriously. I was just intrigued. That's all."

"Are you sure? You know I'm here to talk anytime."

"Yes, Mom." Maddy smiled despite herself. "I'm good. I need to get going anyway."

"All right, sweetie. I'll tell your dad you called. Don't forget your medicine, either."

"Oh my God, yes, I won't forget. Thanks. Love you, bye."

"Love you."

Maddy hung up the call and handed the phone back to me. "Satisfied?"

I nodded and tucked my cell back into my pocket. "Yeah, I could hear the whole thing. She doesn't sound like someone hiding anything."

"Does that mean we're back at square one?" she asked.

"Well, we've been at square one for a couple days. There's no going *back* when we haven't been able to *leave* square one." I rubbed at the stubble on my cheek and decided to ask the question that had been percolating in my head from the moment I heard her mention it. "So, you really have no information on your parents? Your birth parents, I mean."

She shook her head. "Never met them, never heard from them. They gave me up when I was a baby, so I don't even have a connection from before."

"All right, we can probably rule them out then. There has to be a different reason," I said, then finished my beer. "What about other relationships? Ex-boyfriends? Friends you've cut ties with? Uh…current boyfriend? You know, stuff like that." I hoped she hadn't noticed the awkward way I tried to add that last bit.

"Nothing I can think of. I don't have a lot of friends. Abi is my closest friend, but she seemed totally shocked about what happened to me. I haven't had a boyfriend in almost a year. I honestly can't think of anything else." She slung her hair over her back. "Nico, I can't get it out of my head. What that guy said before he stabbed me."

Her face changed, and she clenched her hands together. Her eyes went dark, and she started trembling. I thought she was going to make herself bleed, she was biting her lower lip so hard.

Moving over, I put my hand over hers. "It's okay. You're safe. Can you remember exactly what he said? You told me before, but I'd like to hear it again."

A wavering breath breezed out between her lips, and she nodded. "He said I shouldn't exist and that my bloodline was supposed to be dead."

"See," I said, starting to get frustrated, "that still makes me think it has something to do with your family. Those phrases sound exactly like someone talking about family. Bloodlines? What else would that be about? It has to be something massive, too, if it's worth your life."

I leaned back in the lounge chair and thought about it for a few minutes. Maddy was beside me, nursing her beer, staring off into the lawn and scrub pines beyond. I went over a hundred other questions and leads I could try with her, but each one seemed more tenuous than the last.

Once I was totally out of ideas, I tapped her on the thigh to get her attention. "You said you had a match on that DNA test? Who was it?"

She put the empty beer can down on a side table and grinned at me. "You think they're trying to kill me because some ancient ancestor of mine pissed off one of their ancestors? That's a hellacious grudge to hold."

"Right, but if it helps figure this out, I'll even start checking into your old pets. Maybe you had a dog that got Javi's dog pregnant and he's looking for child support. Come on, what was the guy's name?"

Maddy looked up at the sky, her lips pursed. Finally, she shook her head in frustration. "I can barely remember it. Hang on, let me log in."

I handed her my phone and watched as she typed away at the screen for a few minutes. I knew something was wrong when she frowned. "I don't understand. It's gone."

I sat forward and tilted the phone screen so I could see. The DNA match window showed zero matches. Like there'd never been anything there to begin with.

"That's bullshit," Maddy said. "Abi was there, she saw it, she can vouch for it. There was one name there. Now it's gone? What the hell?"

That didn't make any sense. Not one single person in the world was linked to her? How was that even possible? A sudden sadness filled me. Maddy had to feel pretty alone. She had her adoptive parents, but not having any idea where you came from had to be a little depressing. "Do you remember any part of the name?" I prompted.

Maddy let out a frustrated sigh. "It was a weird name. I remember that. I can't be a hundred percent sure but…Udimus? Aidmos…Edemas?" Her eyes brightened. "I think that's it. Edemas."

A thousand phantom spiders seemed to be crawling up my spine. That name. What was that name, and why did it send shudders of fear through me as soon as she said it? Something from the past. My mind flitted through all the pack history I'd learned as a kid— thousands of years of lore and legends.

I remembered that name. It was unique. Connections started snapping together in my mind. Fog lifted and memory became certainty. The name had been unique, and the man it belonged to had been a madman.

Oh shit. No way. It couldn't be. That was…impossible.

"Maddy?" My voice betrayed my fear and wonder. "This Edemas? Was his full name Edemas Hollander?"

The look Maddy gave me sent another bolt of fear into my gut. She looked pleased and relieved. I'd just scratched an itch that had been tickling her mind, and it meant something awful.

She nodded. "That's it!" The pleasant surprise faded and she frowned at me. "How the hell could you know that?"

My blood ran cold, sending a dark chill up my arms. The puzzle was sliding together, revealing the picture. Her distinct scent? My wolf's reaction to her? It all made sense now. She didn't smell quite human because…she wasn't fully human. She was a descendant of a line of wolves.

Javi's guys were right. She *shouldn't* exist. All the stories said the bloodline had been fully wiped out down to the roots. Maddy was of the line of Edemas. The Hollander Clan. Sweet Christ.

I put a hand to my head, fighting back dizziness. Royal wolves. A line that was so hated and reviled that all written history of them had been erased and destroyed. I looked at Maddy, and true fear enveloped me. How the fuck could I protect her now?

Chapter 9 - Maddy

Something was wrong. I could tell by the way Nico was acting. Ever since I'd told him the name of my long-lost ancestor, he'd been behaving strangely. I'd finally gotten my phone back that night, and for the next two days, all I'd done was scoured the internet for info on this Edemas guy. It was, however, pointless. I kept getting medical links for pulmonary edema, articles about some nu-metal band from the late nineties, a few dozen people on social media with the last name Edam, but nothing else. Not a single thing that explained Nico's reaction. No birthdate or even birth country.

I'd pressed him for information as soon as I saw the expression on his face, but that had been pointless. He'd brushed it off as being tired and worried, so I'd tried to keep my distance from him for the last few days. For one, I didn't want to poke the wolf since he was obviously in a bad mood. Second, I was a guest in his house, and I didn't want to wear out my welcome by always being underfoot.

I'd managed to forget about Edemas *and* Nico by that afternoon, though. It was Thursday. I was going back to work, and I was nervous. Luis had already let me know that he'd be the one escorting me to the bar that evening. It took the better part of the day for me to work up the courage to go.

Luis arrived early. As we walked to the door, Nico appeared from his room where he'd spent most of his time the last couple days. "Are you sure you're okay to go?" he asked.

"Yeah, totally," I said, lying through my teeth.

Nico nodded and glanced at Luis, then back to me. "Make sure you call me if you have any issues. Luis will be able to handle anything, though."

"Thanks, I'm sure I'll be fine." Without another word, Luis and I left.

The ride to the bar should have been liberating. I'd been stuck in Nico's house for days. I was getting out and seeing a place I knew would usually be refreshing. Instead, the drive was filled with flashes of memories. A snarling face. Screams. The flash of a knife. By the time we actually got to the bar, I was almost shaking.

"Here we go," Luis said, turning his truck off. "I'll get you inside, then do a few circuits of the outside, make sure it's all clear. Once that's good, I'll be inside the rest of the night."

"Yeah. Sounds good," I muttered, fumbling with the door handle.

"Hey?"

I turned and looked at him, clenching my fists to keep my hands from shaking.

"Are you sure you're all right? You know, you don't have to go in there tonight if you don't want to. You…well, you don't look very good."

"Thanks. Same to you, buddy."

Luis blinked, then barked out a laugh. It was the first time I'd heard him laugh or even seen him smile for that matter. "Got it. I'll stay in my lane," he said, getting out.

The walk from the parking lot to the front door felt fraught with danger. Even with Luis right behind me, I kept glancing around. I wasn't sure what I thought would jump out at me, but I couldn't get the idea out of my head. Every shadow looked like a place someone could hide. The only thing that kept me going was the sound of Luis's boots thumping into the pavement. I'd be damned if I'd break down and lose my shit in front of him.

I stepped inside, the cool blast of the air conditioning refreshing against the late afternoon heat, but it also chilled me to the bone. My eyes locked onto the spot on the floor where the shifters had attacked me, and more memories flashed through my head—things I hadn't been able to recall while I recovered at Nico's. The shifters attacking. Me climbing over the bar, scrambling to try and get to the door. Then the *chink* sound of a thick beer glass being pulled from the shelf. I could almost hear it banging into the base of my skull. I could even recall the flash of metal in the last moment of consciousness. All of it came roaring back as I stared at the floor.

"Holy shit. Maddy!" Abi ran from the kitchen and threw her arms around me.

Luis nudged my side. "I'm going to check outside. Be back in a minute."

"Thanks. I'm good here," I said, walking back to the bar with Abi.

The rest of the staff was there, setting up. They all knew something had happened to me, but none of them had heard the truth. Only Abi knew, and I wanted to keep it that way. There was no reason for them to think it was unsafe working here. Shifters weren't trying to kill them. Only me.

"What do you want to do tonight?" Abi asked. "Kitchen? Stay away from everyone in there?"

I shook my head. "I'll help bartend. Staying behind the bar will feel safe, but I can still feel like I'm *here*."

As the night got started, it became obvious that I'd made a mistake. The first time a customer called to get my attention, I jumped and dropped a full bottle of beer on the floor. Then I heard a bunch of guys having a good-natured argument about whether the Dolphins or Buccaneers had a better chance at the Super Bowl that coming fall. Their happy, boisterous voices had seemed like rage-filled shouts for an instant. That was all it took to send me back to the kitchen, almost hyperventilating. It was all I could do to keep the staff from seeing me like that.

When I came back out, Luis raised an eyebrow at me in question. I waved him off and went back to work. Later in the night, I got another wave of near panic and went to the kitchen again to calm my nerves. I stood at the back door getting some fresh air, surprised to see Nico's other friend Felipe sitting on the tailgate of a truck watching the rear entrance. He spotted me and nodded. I forced a smile and waved back. I bit into the side of my cheek and went back out into the main room.

Abi nudged up against me. "Are you sure you're okay? The look in your eye is—"

"First night back jitters. Nothing to worry about," I lied. "All good."

Abi looked at me suspiciously, but didn't force the issue. Luis strolled up and tapped the bar with a knuckle. "Can I get a drink?" he asked with a smile.

I stepped over and started polishing a glass. "Is that really wise? Aren't you, like, on duty or whatever?"

He shrugged. "Shifters don't get drunk like humans do. Takes a lot. Mostly, I enjoy a well-mixed cocktail for the taste. Plus, I'm getting weird looks standing around a bar not drinking. What do you—"

Luis froze, then tilted his head to the sky, sniffing the air. I looked over his shoulder, and dropped another glass on the floor. The sound of shattering glass filled the bar, and almost all the customers cheered at the sound. I barely heard them. Instead, it seemed like the entire building went dead silent. A group of shifters had walked in the front door.

Abi saw them and moved to my side. "Hey, Maddy? It's okay."

I nodded and said nothing. My eyes flitted across every face as the group found a booth to sit at. None of them were familiar, none were part of the group who had attacked me. The memory of that voice returned, unbidden. *You shouldn't even exist.*

Luis was already in motion, striding over to the group of shifters. My body felt completely worn out. It was like I'd run a marathon and then come in to work a twelve-hour shift. I'd made a mistake, and I knew that. The way my hand shook as I watched Luis talk to the other shifters told me all I needed to know.

"Babe, go home. We can handle this," Abi said.

I nodded shakily. "You're right. I need to rest or something."

Luis finished his discussion with the shifters and returned to the bar. "All good. They're from a pack about four hours' north from here. It's a boy's road trip to a concert in Miami. They're cool." Luis looked at my face and frowned. "Hey, are you okay?"

"No," Abi answered for me. "She needs to go home."

All I could do was nod while staring at the men in the corner. Even though Luis had told me what was going on, I couldn't stop thinking that they were about to leap to their feet and rush me, knives and teeth flashing in the light from the bar.

Luis came around the side of the bar and took my arm. I glanced at Abi once before letting him lead me away. The bar's entire atmosphere felt strange as he escorted me out. It was no longer welcoming, warm, and pleasant. Now, it seemed every face had a hidden motive, every hand a concealed weapon, every word spoken a warning. I even glanced back at the table of shifters. Not a single one of them was looking at me as I left.

The ride back home was silent, for which I was grateful. The last thing I needed was some kind of lecture from Luis. I didn't even know what he'd say, but I imagined a ton of obnoxious and annoying things. The fact that he was the kind of guy who was fine with awkward silences was a blessing in disguise.

When we got back to the house, Nico wasn't there. Luis checked the house, making sure he wasn't in one of the other massive rooms. He took a seat at the kitchen island. "I'll hang out until Nico gets back."

"Sure, that's fine." I glanced around the house again, and had to ask a question that had been eating at me. "Luis, do you know where Nico's been going? He's either locked up in his room or he's away for hours at a time. Where the heck does he go? I've barely seen him since the first night, and when I do see him, he seems tense, distant. Is that normal for him?"

One corner of his mouth turned up in a humorless smile. "You'll know everything soon enough."

I didn't like the sound of that. It seemed overly ominous. "What do you mean? I'll know what?"

Luis shook his head dismissively. "Not my place to tell. Nico will explain it all in due time. That's all I can say."

I huffed out a sigh, but knew I wouldn't get any more out of Luis. He was like a living, breathing brick wall. No reason to keep beating my head against that wall.

I went upstairs and turned my shower on. While I waited for the water to heat, my stomach rumbled. I hadn't eaten anything for hours. I'd been too nervous before going to work, and I hadn't had any appetite at work. I jumped in the shower and cleaned myself quickly. Wrapping myself in a bathrobe, I headed downstairs to dig through the massive pantry and fridge for something to make for dinner.

Instead of finding Luis downstairs, Nico was sitting on the sofa. His face was hard and stony as he glanced up at me. The look in his eyes was not pleasant. He didn't look angry, but I'd never seen him so serious.

"Want to have a seat?" he said, gesturing to the other side of the couch.

"Uh…sure. I'm gonna grab a beer. I think I may need it based on your face."

He cocked his head. "Unfortunately, you're not wrong there. Grab me one too, please?"

I pulled the cans from the fridge and handed him the other as I sat down. Nico popped the can open and took a drink, then glanced across at me. "What do you know of shifter history?"

This was a strange subject, I thought, but shrugged and played along. "Um, only what you learn in school. Basic dates and big events. The Shifter's Rights Movement in the forties and fifties, the Shifter Purge in Russia back in the early 1800s, stuff like that. Why? What does this have to do with me?"

Nico downed his beer in three quick swallows and suppressed a burp. "Okay. Let me tell you this story. Wait until I'm done to ask questions. I'm sure you'll have a lot."

I was both scared and intrigued. Nico was one hell of a storyteller if this was how he was starting. I nodded at him to go on.

"There was once a royal line of wolves. Shifters who were part of the longest standing pack in history. The pack dated back hundreds of years and was the largest ever known—over a thousand members, if the legends are to be believed. My pack is considered massive and we've only got around sixty members, if that tells you anything. It takes an impressive and powerful will for an alpha to keep that many members in line and on the same page.

"They were all descended from a powerful wolf shifter who'd married a human woman. A human princess. He married into an actual royal family. One of his final descendants continued that tradition and married a widowed queen. Their children, like those before, were born as hybrids. Half-human and half-shifter. Something that was unheard of in other situations. Only this royal family bloodline had this ability.

"The alpha of this clan was legendary. Not because he was a royal or had hybrid heirs. He was strong, but what truly made him and his ancestors legendary were their distinct abilities. Shifters always go through a full change. We totally and completely become the animal we share the body with. These alphas? They could change different parts of their body at will. A human body but the head of a wolf? Upper torso of a wolf, and lower body of a man? A single hand changed to a paw? Changing their teeth to fangs? They could do all that. It was where the original stories of werewolves came from. They were also much stronger and faster than regular shifters." Nico paused and brushed a hand over his face.

"This final werewolf king was named Edemas Hollander. His pack weas feared not only by humans but other shifters. They were able to harness the power of the moon—again, like the old werewolf legends. It made them stronger than any other living being. On the day and night of the full moon, they were basically unstoppable and at their most powerful. It was this power that helped them reign over all shifters." Nico sighed and looked at me. "Is this making sense?"

I stared at him, my mouth hanging partially open. I had so many questions, but I needed to hear what he was telling me. We could sort it out afterward. At the moment, I was enthralled by the outlandish story he was weaving. I nodded for him to go on.

"Okay, good. So Edemas had children and they could shift, but this started to fade with each passing year. Especially within the royal line, the shifters chose to mate with humans. Every generation, the werewolf bloodline grew weaker. Even some of Edemas's own children couldn't shift. Edemas didn't like that the lineage was getting diluted, so he took a concubine—a shifter woman—and started mating with her to produce more pureblooded heirs. This caused issues Edemas didn't foresee. The family of the concubine considered themselves the pureblood line, and Edemas's legal wife and her children the half-breed line. There was tension, to say the least.

"While this ongoing issue was brewing within the royal family, the other packs feared how rapidly Edemas's family was growing. The fact that the strength of the bloodline was dissipating had given them some hope that eventually the Hollander pack would vanish from the earth. The new concubine and the full-blood children swept away that hope, and now they knew that Edemas's line would reign longer than anyone had anticipated. Maybe forever.

"The second issue was that there had been several females born to the concubine who had been born as alphas—something unheard of to this day. Those women were stronger than most male shifters. Edemas saw this happening, and started taking more concubines. It started to get out of hand. Some legends say he had upwards of three dozen children between his wife and concubines. He was trying to have as many children as possible, but that was frowned upon in the royal family. Usually you had children until you had a boy, then a second male child. After that, typically, the king would stop purposely trying to have children. I know it sounds weird, but it's how things were done back then. Anyway, a contingent of royals informed the alpha that he was not allowed to have any more children—official heirs or concubine bastards.

"This…this is where things get bad. The stories say Edemas flew into a rage. He slaughtered the contingent of family members, some of them his own nieces and nephews. His wife, the queen, was also a victim of his rage. He found her in the castle, and knowing she was the one who had orchestrated the proclamation, tore her throat out with his own wolf teeth. The news was like a nuclear bomb going off. Every human and shifter leader within hundreds of miles heard of the butchery, and they knew neither Edemas nor his lineage could be allowed to live. For more than three years, a resistance faction formed in the shadows, a combining of strength between all the shifter clans who were disloyal to Edemas as alpha and humans who knew they would be subjugated if the Hollander line was allowed to flourish. Also, some of Edemas's distant family joined the resistance. These were cousins and far-removed relations. None of them were werewolves, but they craved the power and fortune of Edemas. They felt slighted by their lack of station in his court. They were the main leaders of this resistance. A *new* royal family, basically."

Nico laced his fingers together and gripped his hands so hard, his knuckles went white. "On the night of the new moon, when Edemas and his children were at their weakest, the resistance attacked. It was bloody and brutal. Not a single descendant were to be left alive. The main party attacked Edemas in his stronghold, but hundreds of others tracked down his family. There…" Nico paused and made a pained face. "There are stories of pregnant concubines having their stomachs cut open, the fetuses inside killed. Children struck down in their beds, babies…" Nico put a hand to his face. I could see the horror in his eyes as he told the story. "Babies were killed in their cribs. The bloodline fully severed. Ended, wholly and completely." He finally raised his eyes and locked them on mine. "At least, that's what most shifters thought until this week."

I looked at him for several long seconds before laughing uncomfortably. "Yeah, but that's all just a story, right? You have to be joking."

Nico shook his head. "I wish I was joking."

"No." I jumped up and started to pace around the living room. "What are you saying? That story? That's...like, massive. That type of thing would be in the history books. Everyone would know that story. It sounds like something out of the French Revolution. Come on, Nico."

"History is written by the winners. Most of the shifters were ashamed of the atrocities they committed that day. It needed to be hidden. Not only because Edemas had been a madman, a fascist, and probably psychotic, but because the only way to stop him was to commit crimes no one wanted remembered."

I ran my hands through my hair. "How does this connect to me, though?"

Nico's eyebrows furrowed. "Your DNA test. The only match was for Edemas."

"But that has to be an error. If his entire bloodline was killed, I can't possibly be related to him. I can't." I was starting to get very scared. What did this all mean?

"Yes, it's confusing, but it's what we have to go on. The only thing that makes any sense at all is that someone got away. That a member of his family was able to escape and go into hiding. From there? You follow the family tree branches until they get to you."

"I still don't get how a guy who died three-hundred years ago has his DNA on this website. How is that even possible?"

Nico chewed at the inside of his cheek. "I thought about that. I think someone—a shifter family—kept a sample of Edemas's blood. It had to have been held for centuries. Once these DNA tests became standard, they probably sent it off. If I had to guess? They may be monitoring the sites, waiting for matches."

"Why, though? That's what you haven't answered."

"I don't know," Nico said, his voice barely below a shout. I realized he was as confused as I was. "There's more to the story."

"Oh great," I said, crossing my arms. "What more do I have to look forward to?"

"Edemas was pretty paranoid toward the end. He had a massive fortune. Gold, silver, jewels, everything. Millions and millions of today's dollars. He had it all hidden, and as far as I know, it was never found. If it was found, it was taken and hoarded by the new royal family. Basically any surviving heir"—he looked at me with a deeper seriousness—"would be entitled to that fortune if it was discovered."

"So, is this all Javi? Is he some history buff or something? Found out who I was and attacked me?" I asked, not even letting myself think of the mountain of Scrooge McDuck gold he'd mentioned.

"No, I don't think so. My best guess? For decades, there's been rumors that the members of the royal family, the ones distantly related to Edemas by marriage, are still alive. I think they're the ones who kept the blood sample and are trying to find any last descendants and kill them. If I had to guess, they're in control of Edemas's profile on that and other DNA test sites."

Realization started to dawn on me then. If he was right... "I've got shifter blood in me?

Nico didn't answer at first. Instead, he got up and walked across the room and leaned against the wall. He looked deep in thought. "I think so. It would explain your scent. You smell like a cross between a shifter and a human. It's faint, but there. Something I've never experienced before. It's the only thing that makes any sense whatsoever. It's very diluted, and I doubt you can shift. At least, I'm ninety-nine percent sure you can't." Nico's head dropped again, severing the eye contact he'd held. "It...uh...also explains my wolf's reaction to you."

"What?" I asked dumbly.

"My wolf. From the moment I first saw you, it's been acting strange."

"Strange how?"

He sighed and ran a hand across his face. "It's acting like you're my fated mate."

"You're kidding," I said. I knew what that meant. Everyone knew shifters had fated mates. It was a magical connection to whatever mate they were supposed to be with forever.

"I'm not, Maddy. I'm really not. As soon as my wolf scented your blood, all I wanted to do was be near you. To take care of you. There's no denying the feeling. Even my friends noticed it.

"The thing is, if you have even a drop of shifter blood in you? You're still a shifter. If you take a shifter mate and accept his bite, it will probably strengthen your blood. It could even make it to where you can shift. The mating bond makes both parties stronger. I hate to say it, but I'm a strong shifter. One of the strongest alphas around. I think my bite really could bring out your abilities. If that's the case, then the royals are going to want you dead. For him to be so hell-bent on taking you down means Javi's family must have descended from one of the families that revolted and helped kill Edemas and his family."

"So, he's trying to kill me because of something that happened hundreds of years ago?" I asked.

"If his family swore a blood oath or something to the royal family? Then yeah. He'd be honor-bound to do their bidding. That's the only thing that explains why Javi would involve himself. If I know one thing about Javi? He's a fucking man of his word."

The whole planet felt like it was spinning off its axis. I walked across the room, not knowing where I was going, only to turn around and walk back. I felt like a cow in a slaughterhouse, waiting for the final blow. There was too much to process. Too much to think about. I hadn't even started thinking about the fact that Nico had said we were fated mates, destined to be together. How the hell could I think about that when it sounded like everyone wanted me dead? It was hard to think about the future when every second, it could be ripped away from you.

Everything he'd told me sounded completely impossible. Yet, it all kind of made sense, crazy as it was. Was I really a shifter? It was nothing I'd ever even entertained. Had my parents known? Is that why they'd gotten rid of me? To protect me? Or to be rid of a death sentence?

"Can you find my birth parents with this information?" The words popped out of my mouth before I even knew I was going to say it.

"I'm not sure," Nico said. "If they're still alive, I'll do everything I can to help find them. If nothing else, it would help us get answers. And answers are what we need right now. More than anything."

The whole crazy story started to crash into me. I was a royal shifter. I was being hunted. I was supposed to inherit a fortune in gold and jewels...maybe. Not only all that, but Nico was my mate? The voice in my head that had been telling me he was mine was making more noise. A definite *I-told-you-so* vibe was coming from it. As all that spun through my head, I didn't even realize I was starting to hyperventilate.

I giggled and turned to look at Nico. "I don't want to alarm you, but I think I'm gonna—" Everything went dark as I fainted.

Chapter 10 - Nico

"Shit," I yelped as I jumped forward to catch her, halting her fall right before her injured head could smack into the tile floor.

After stopping her collapse, I lifted her and carried her up the stairs to her room. I managed to get the covers pulled back and laid her down without waking her up. I hoped she'd sleep all the way until the morning. She needed it after everything I'd dumped on her. It made me feel bad about forcing so much into her life so fast. In a week, everything she'd known had been turned completely upside down. I wondered how I would react if something similar happened to me.

Before I turned to leave, I looked down at her one last time. Her eyes were closed, and the long dark lashes twitched as if she was dreaming. Maddy's face was calm and serene. And beautiful. An ache formed in my chest and grew stronger the longer I looked at her. I leaned down and brushed a strand of hair from her face, letting my thumb trace the curve of her cheek as I straightened.

My mind circled back to all the feelings I'd had for her since that first night. The drive to protect and take care of her. The need to be around her. The...other desires. Maybe she truly was my mate. There was a flash of anger from my wolf. Apparently the word *maybe* wasn't good enough for it. That was the last thing I needed to focus on at the moment, though. If Maddy truly was a descendant of Edemas, then things were going to get very interesting. And dangerous. Javi had been right when he'd said I didn't know what I was getting myself into.

I tugged my phone out of my jeans as I closed her door to let her sleep. I called Luis and told him to grab the others and get to my house. I headed downstairs and sat at the kitchen table as I waited for them. I tried searching the internet for more information on Maddy, clicking away on my computer, searching for news stories and items of interest from the days and weeks when she'd been put up for adoption. Mostly, what I looked for were stories about murdered couples. Her parents were either in hiding or dead. It was the only thread we had to follow at the moment.

Ten minutes into my search, I heard the guys coming in the front door.

"Nico?" Luis called from the foyer.

"Kitchen," I called, slapping my laptop closed.

Luis, Sebastian, and Felipe rounded the corner and walked into the kitchen. They'd all been grinning and smiling, but something about the look I had on my face sent those expressions fleeing and morphing into serious concern.

"What's up, brother?" Felipe asked.

"Take a seat."

Sebastian snorted. "Well, that's not ominous as shit."

Once they were all seated on the couches, I took a seat on an ottoman and faced them, trying to figure out how to say what I needed to say. Would they even believe it?

"So, about Maddy…have you guys noticed she's a little different?"

At first there was no response, then slowly, all three of them started nodding. "Yeah," Sebastian said. "She, uh, smells funny. She's also hot as hell, but I don't think that's what you're talking about."

I gritted my teeth, my friend's typical humor setting my wolf on edge. Even hearing him joke about how gorgeous she was sent my beast into a jealous rage. But I choked back a pissy response and nodded in agreement. "Anything else?"

Luis leaned back and crossed his arms. "Can we stop beating around the bush, my man? Get to the damned point. You'll tell us whether we play fifty questions or not."

I sighed and pinched the bridge of my nose, feeling a headache starting to come on. "Do you guys remember the stories about Edemas? When we were kids?"

They shared a look and Felipe leaned forward. "The last werewolf king? Yeah. Why?"

"I think Maddy is his last descendant."

"Fuck off," Sebastian said, his mouth dropping open.

"What?" Luis asked. "How? His entire family was killed. All his children, all his grandchildren, all of them. Plus, it's been three hundred years since he died. Wouldn't we have some stories about heirs appearing over the last couple centuries?"

I went on to tell them about Maddy's DNA match. The name Edemas being her sole connection, and the fact that his name vanished from the website a few days after she was attacked. I even told them about Javi stopping by the clinic and threatening me before Maddy was discharged.

"Her blood is part shifter, that's not in dispute. Once you hear the story, the scent makes more sense. This is happening, guys. I think the hidden royal family is real as well. I think they're the ones pulling Javi's strings and going after Maddy," I finished.

My three friends sat, shock and awe on their faces. I knew how they felt. It was like someone finding out the story of the Pied Piper had been real or that Hansel and Gretel had really happened. It was almost too much to take in.

Luis held his hands up. "Hang on. I know what you're saying, but if that's true, what the hell are we supposed to do? Javi will be the least of our concerns if this is all actually happening."

I nodded and pulled my phone out again. Luis and the others looked even more confused until they heard me talking to my dad. I closed the phone and glanced up at them. "He'll be here in a minute," I said.

"What the hell is your dad gonna do?" Sebastian asked.

"He's the one who told me the stories when I was a kid. If anyone might know more, it's him. Plus, I know I can trust him with my life, with Maddy's life. Once this info is out, it can't go back. You can't put the toothpaste back in the tube, right?"

They had no argument for that, and we waited while my dad made his way over. His house was only three houses down. It was a blessing and a curse to have my family so close. In this situation, it was a blessing.

The knock came less than five minutes after I called him. He came walking in with a confused look on his face.

"Nico? I'm here. What was the big rush?"

I sighed, and for the third time in less than two hours, I relayed all my theories about Maddy and everything we'd learned about her. By the time I was done, my throat was sore from talking so much.

Dad took a seat and held his chin in his hand. It was the typical *Dad's thinking* look I'd seen from him all throughout my life.

"I was worried this might happen one day," Dad finally said.

All of us froze, unsure what he was saying. Had he known all along? Was this something shifters had been preparing for? If so, why didn't I know about it? I was the alpha, after all.

Sebastian raised his hand like he was still in school. "Hi, yeah, Carlos…er…Mister Lorenzo, Nico's dad, sir? I think I speak for all of us when I so eloquently ask…what the fuck?"

Dad snorted a humorless laugh. "There have been rumors for as long as I can remember that Edemas had been warned of the coming attack. In one of his very few moments of clarity, he understood that there was no way he'd survive. He found two of his children, babies who had both been born alphas, and sent them with a servant into hiding. This story is less known simply because it is so damned dangerous. Even mentioning this story to the wrong shifter could get you killed. In many circles, there is almost a religious fear of the Edemas lineage. We all know what religious fanatics are capable of."

That was true. Everyone knew of the Christian and Muslim attacks and the wars on shifters in the early centuries. To this day, there were certain villages in Asia where shifters were killed on sight due to the belief that they were demons. Religion was great when it helped the poor and needy. Once religious zealots started having opinions on things, it tended to get hairy pretty quickly.

"Anyway," Dad continued, "the children were small, only a couple months old. A boy and a girl, both pure-bred from Edemas and his shifter concubine. If this story is true, it could explain how Maddy came to be."

"There's something else I need to tell you, Dad. All of you." They all turned to look at me, waiting to hear what other bombshell I was about to drop. "I think Maddy is my fated mate."

"Called it!" Sebastian shouted, standing up and pointing at me, a massive grin on his face. "I knew it."

Dad ignored Sebastian and came over to stand in front of me. He put his hands on my shoulders. "This explains everything. It's why you've been so protective of her. This settles it. The Lorenzo clan is in full agreement. She is under our protection, regardless of who her ancestor was."

"Thanks, Dad. I appreciate the support. I've got a bad feeling that this is gonna get messy."

Luis cleared his throat. "Count us in, too. That was probably implied, but I wanted it on the record."

Felipe and Sebastian nodded. I'd always assumed my friends and family had my back through thick and thin. Seeing it actually happening was like a weight being lifted off my shoulders.

"We need more information," Luis said. "What about her birth family? Does Maddy have anything to go on? Some way of finding them?"

I shook my head. "No. Her whole adoption seems sketchy as hell. Some social worker dropped her off, but there's no trace of this guy before or after that day. Her adoptive parents were desperate for a baby, so they didn't look a gift horse in the mouth."

Dad cleared his throat to get my attention. "If Maddy is who we think she is, her parents may have known of their ancestry. Perhaps they gave her up to protect her. They hoped dumping her into the system with no connection to them would ensure she survived. I would have done the same for my children. Never knowing them would be better than seeing them killed in front of my eyes. It's a God-awful choice to make, but I would have made it."

"We are forgetting something pretty important here," Felipe said. "Javi. What the hell is his involvement? Why is he going for Maddy?"

"I think Javi and his clan are working for the royals," I said. "This extended family of Edemas who have been hiding throughout the centuries and searching for any offspring. If what my father is saying is true, they surely heard the stories of the two escaped Edemas babies. They want that line dead."

"But all this stuff happened back in, like, Europe or whatever. How does that get to America?" Felipe asked.

"Javi and his clan didn't always live in Florida," Dad said, grabbing our attention again. "He and his father got here back when I was a kid. I was maybe seven or eight. Javi was a few years older. I specifically remember that they had strange accents when they first got here. Those slowly disappeared over a couple years as they grew their pack and tried to fit in more. Now? You can't even tell Javi isn't a native. I think they came from the old countries. That could be how they're connected."

"Christ. We need to keep tabs on Javi," I said, looking at Luis.

"On it. We'll see what we can find. We'll have someone watching his movements. I was already going to do that, but now it's gonna need to be more intense."

"Thanks for coming over so late, guys. Go on home, get some sleep," I said, my own exhaustion starting to seep in.

The guys trickled out, eventually leaving me and Dad alone in the foyer. He wrapped me in a hug and pounded me on the back, then pulled away and looked at me. "If Maddy is your mate, I'm glad you're the one who found her. No one would have taken care of her the way you have." Dad winced and shook his head. "Your mother, though? Oof, she's going to lose her shit."

I groaned, knowing he was telling the truth. "Can you hold off on telling her? I know she'll try to pressure us into something Maddy's not ready for."

"My lips are sealed."

"We've got to make sure she's safe before any talk of claiming happens."

"Son, you don't have to persuade me. I wholeheartedly agree. Some things need to come first. I understand that. Your mother, however?" He made a face that told me all I needed to know.

"Good night, Dad. I love you."

"Love you, son," he said as he walked down the porch steps. "Get some sleep. You may not get much for the next few weeks."

I did get some sleep, which surprised me a little. I made my way down to the kitchen the next morning and started a pot of coffee. Before it was done brewing, Maddy's door opened and closed at the top of the stairs. She came walking down, still in her bathrobe from the night before. She didn't meet my eyes as she walked over and took a seat at the island, probably still trying to process everything that had happened the night before. I couldn't blame her.

I poured her a cup and slid the mug across the counter top to her. She took it. "Thanks," she mumbled. "Cream and sugar?"

I pulled a container of heavy cream from the fridge and a small jar of sugar out of the pantry, putting them beside her cup. "I need to go to work for a while."

Maddy finally glanced up. "How come?"

"Stuff still needs to get done. I own a car shop in town. I've had the team taking care of most of the day-today stuff while I've been doing research and other things. I need to get in there and touch base. Sebastian will be stopping by. He'll watch you most of the day. When I get back, I'd like to talk more about your adoption."

When she looked into my eyes, it was like she was diving right into my soul. It was all I could do not to look away. "Have you found something?" she asked, her coffee forgotten.

"My dad and I think your birth parents may have known about their bloodline. It's our opinion that they gave you up to protect you."

"I guess that makes sense. If things were as dangerous for them as they seem to be for me, it might have been their only option."

"Right. We may have a way to find the social worker, but I won't know for sure until I talk to Luis. I'm going to have him drive out to Tampa this morning, do some digging."

"Tampa? That's where the orphanage was where I was found."

"Exactly. Again, I don't want to get too deep into it, but we'll see where this goes."

"Sebastian should be here soon. I don't think you've been properly introduced, but you'll recognize him when you see him," I said. I knew what Maddy had been going through the last week. If anyone could lift her spirits, Sebastian was up to the task. "Even though he's here, don't hesitate to call me if you need me."

She nodded, lowering her gaze to stare into her coffee cup and the steam rising off the cup. I couldn't help myself. I moved around the counter and put a hand to her cheek, encouraging her to look at me again. She finally did, and I could see the fear in her eyes.

"I promise I won't pressure you into anything. I'm sorry if…if me telling you about my feelings was too much. I apologize. It's a lot, and I swear I won't make you do anything you don't want to."

We looked into each other's eyes for several seconds. The desire and need to kiss her was almost enough to break my will. My wolf was salivating and growling in lust and wanting. I fought off everything raging in my head, desperate to keep my word.

"Thank you," Maddy whispered after a moment.

I slid my thumb across her cheek like I had the night before. This time, she was awake, and I could see the color rise in her cheeks at the action. Thankfully, the doorbell rang before anything else could happen.

"Hey, yo? Nico? I'm here," Sebastian shouted from the entryway.

"I'll see you later today?" I said to Maddy as I walked toward the door.

"Yeah, I'll"—she shrugged and gestured to the house—"be around."

Sebastian walked in and waved at Maddy. "Hey, I'm Sebastian. Nico's most handsome friend. I'm like a solid eight. My humor probably gets me to a nine, so you'll need to control yourself around me."

I rolled my eyes and waved to them. Sebastian would either lift her mood or she'd kill him. I wasn't sure which scenario was more likely. I guess I'd find out when I got back.

Chapter 11 - Maddy

My first impression of Sebastian was that he was a moron. After a few hours alone with him, though, I realized he just had larger-than-life personality and liked to make people laugh. I'd decided to try and go to work again tonight, and he was cool with me doing that. I was happy that Nico hadn't ordered his men to put me under house arrest or something. That would have been too much. Cabin fever would have set in fast. Sebastian was a lot less serious than Luis, so I hoped he'd be able to keep my mind off the things that had freaked me out the night before.

"My car or yours?" Sebastian asked.

The guys had picked up my Jeep from my place after I moved into Nico's. I loved that car, and even took the doors off during the summer. I grinned. "My car, definitely. What do you drive anyway?"

"Miata."

I raised an eyebrow. "A Miata?"

"Yeah. Don't knock it till you try it. The thing corners like a dream. I also have a truck, but damn gas prices and stuff. I get, like, thirty miles to the gallon in that little guy. Makes way more financial sense."

"Okay, well, we're taking my car. No offense, but I don't want to try and cram myself into that little sports car."

"Suit yourself." Sebastian shrugged. "But your car, you drive. I'll ride shotgun."

"Fine by me," I said, grabbing my keys and heading for the door.

The whole ride to the bar, he tried to get me to give him an opinion on whether the Rays were going to make the World Series. I'd done my best to skirt the issue, but finally, I had to tell him I knew nothing about baseball and had never seen a game. It had been like I'd killed his puppy right in front of him. It was the quietest he'd been since he'd walked through the door. It made the last two miles to the bar eerily quiet.

Once we parked, he nodded to himself and looked at me. "That's it."

"What's it?" I asked, confused.

"I've found my life's work."

"Which is?"

"Making you a baseball fan."

I chuckled and opened the door. "Good luck with that. I can barely make it through a football or basketball game without falling asleep."

Sebastian's jaw fell open and he clutched a hand to his chest. "Blasphemer!"

"Oh my God. Come on." I got out and started walking toward the bar, hearing his footsteps behind me.

I walked in and was happy that the same anxiety I'd had the day before didn't rear its head again. I walked in and waved to the crew behind the bar. Abi came out of the kitchen and saw me, her face slipping into a scowl. She set the tray of clean beer mugs down and stomped toward me.

"Why the hell are you here tonight?" she demanded, thrusting her fists onto her hips.

"I need to work. I'd go crazy if I stayed locked up all day."

"And after last night? That didn't give you a clue that you should take things a little slower?"

"Abi, it's fine. I'm a lot better today. I think it was first-night jitters or whatever. Besides, my friend Sebastian here is gonna be watching out for me like Luis did last night."

"I could give a shit about this Sebas…" Abi's voice trailed off as she glanced around me and saw him.

Sebastian waved. "Hey, nice to meet you. Great place you guys have here. I stopped by months ago, and I've been wanting to try your chicken sliders again. Those things slap."

Abi's cheeks were reddening, and I could see the way she was looking at Sebastian. He seemed totally oblivious as he looked around the bar. Abi glanced at me while his back was turned, her eyes wide and surprised. She mouthed the words *He's so hot* to me, and I had to bite my tongue to keep from laughing. All I did was nod and head over to the bar to start getting ready.

Abi joined me, and we went through the opening checklist with the rest of my team. Sebastian checked all the entrances and even the windows in the bathrooms. As goofy as he could be, it looked like he took his responsibilities seriously. I kept catching Abi stealing glances at him. Maybe I could play matchmaker. I didn't think Sebastian was dating anyone, but I'd only known him for less than two weeks.

That thought made me pause. I frowned and did some mental math. Had it really only been that long? It felt like this new part of my life had been going on for months. Time was a strange thing.

The evening went by seamlessly. It wasn't as busy as it had been the night before, which was nice. Less stress meant less to worry about. Sebastian entertained the staff and several patrons with stories and jokes most of the night. By the end of the night, I was grateful he was there. I could also see that Abi was definitely on the way to being smitten. All in all, it was a great night. It eased a lot of my fears. I loved working, and I would have been devastated if I couldn't.

Sebastian even jumped in to help us close at the end of the night. It was the first time I'd been at the bar that late since the attack. Abi and several of the kitchen guys were helping out as well, but I still felt strangely alone as I wiped down the tables and put up the chairs.

Sebastian must have noticed. He walked over to me and nodded toward the door. "Expecting someone?"

"What?" I asked, straightening up from the table I was wiping.

"You've looked over at the front door like every minute since we closed. Again, expecting someone?"

I hadn't even realized I'd been doing that. In my head, I was still waiting for Javi's crew to show up again. Roll through the door, tell me I was an abomination and shouldn't exist. I thought I'd been hiding my thoughts pretty well. Apparently not. I hung my head in embarrassment, not wanting to meet his eyes.

Sebastian came around the table and put an arm around my shoulders. "Maddy, you're safe. If there is one thing I can promise, it's that."

"Thanks, I appreciate it. Seriously. You guys don't have to do this for me, and you are. Thank you."

"You're basically family now, so of course I'd do this. I mean, Nico is paying me like five hundred bucks a day in hazard pay to do it, but yeah, no problem."

I punched him in the arm and laughed as I went back to my task. Sebastian grabbed a broom and started sweeping the floor. Basically family? What did that mean? It hadn't registered when he first said it, but now I wondered why he'd said that.

I looked up to ask him to explain, but the front door opened. A familiar face walked in. Thankfully, it wasn't the face I'd been afraid would show up.

Nico came striding through the door like he owned the place instead of me.

My heart fluttered at the sight of him. My mind had drifted to him multiple times throughout the day, and seeing him now brought confusing feelings to the surface. He'd said I was his mate, and that was information I had a hard time processing. I hadn't really given myself much time to even think about it and what it meant. So much had happened. How could anyone get their minds around it? But I couldn't ignore the ache in my chest when I watched him move through the room. Nor could I ignore that voice deep inside my head, the one that had been begging me to stake a claim on this man from the moment I saw him.

I glanced at my watch and saw it was just after two in the morning. I looked at Nico and tapped my wrist. "Awful late for a drink, sir. Sorry, we're closed."

Nico gave me a smirk. "Couldn't sleep. I figured I'd relieve Sebastian and let him go home to bed."

"My liege? My lord?" Sebastian said in an atrocious British accent. "Thou art too kind to your humble servant." He threw the broom to the floor and bowed dramatically.

Nico shook his head. "Would you stop?"

"Okay, fine." Sebastian stood and waved to me as he headed for the door. "See you Wednesday, Maddy. I think Felipe will be with you tomorrow."

I waved and went back to work. Abi walked over and smacked me on the butt.

"Ow, shit. What was that for?" I said, rubbing my ass.

"Get out of here. Go on. We can finish up. Besides, your ride's here," Abi said, nodding toward Nico.

"Are you sure?"

"Get. Go on." Abi shooed me away with a bar rag as she walked back to the bar.

I looked at Nico. "Well, I guess I'm done."

He grinned at me and pointed a thumb toward the door. "Are you hungry?"

"I'm starving. I'd planned on making a grilled cheese before bed when I got home."

"Eff that. Let's go. There's a diner down the road. It's open 24/7. Great burgers, and a really good Greek omelet if you like olives."

I wrinkled my nose. "Olives? In an omelet? I'll stick with the burgers."

"Suit yourself. Come on."

He wasn't lying. The diner was only five minutes down the road. I recognized it. It was a place called Gena's. I'd driven by it at least a hundred times over the years, but had never actually set foot inside.

I realized the error of my ways as soon as I walked in. The building had that baked in coffee-bacon-grease-sugar smell of a really good, old-school restaurant.

The menu was classic diner fare, with a hundred different items. I always wondered how places like this were able to store so many types of food in such small spaces. We had a pretty limited bar-food menu at my place and still had trouble with space. Their menu had everything from chili dogs to chicken pot pie and Caesar salads. I shrugged and flipped the pages over to the breakfast section, deciding on a bacon-egg-and-cheese burger with hashbrowns.

"Damn," Nico said after the server left.

"What?"

"I like that. A real woman who orders what she wants. I like that."

I snorted and rolled my eyes. "I'm not the type to order a salad on a date to make the guy think I'm not a glutton or something."

Nico raised an eyebrow. "Is this a date?"

My cheeks went red. "Uh...not...that's not what I meant."

We sat in silence for several seconds. The awkwardness elevated with each moment that passed. Finally, we both burst out laughing.

"This is weird, right?" Nico asked, still laughing.

"So weird," I agreed.

"Look, this isn't how I pictured my life going, either, but like I said, I'm not going to push you into anything."

"I know. It's a lot to work through."

"My first priority is to keep you safe. Find answers and try to get your life back to normal. Well, as normal as it can be. Maybe it's all just a really big misunderstanding. I don't think it is, but I'm going to do everything I can to figure this out. I want you to be able to sleep easy at night."

His words dripped through my mind, gentle and kind. It made me all warm and fuzzy inside. It wasn't helping with the thoughts I was having about him. I stared at my fingers for a few seconds, trying to think of what to say. At last, I found the courage to look up to speak, but the words died on my lips.

Nico's brows were knit into a deep frown, and his body had gone stiff. He glanced around the diner. I could tell there was something wrong by the way he was holding himself.

"What's wrong?" I whispered.

"We're being watched."

An icy finger of fear stabbed into my chest. "What? How can you tell?"

"Instinct. Something feels…off. I can sense eyes on us. Like we're being watched."

Nico pulled his cell phone out and put it on the table. He flipped through the numbers until he got to Sebastian's name. He called him, all the while glancing around the diner.

"Bro, I'm not even home yet. What do you need?" Sebastian answered.

"There's eyes on us. I think someone followed me and Maddy to Gena's Diner."

"What? Are you sure?"

"Almost a hundred percent. Get down here. Luis is in Tampa. Call Felipe and tell him to get here. Move it."

"Okay, okay, I'm on it. Be right there."

"What are we gonna do?" I asked, my voice quavering. Memories of the attack flashed through my mind.

Nico reached across the table and laid a hand on my wrist. "Maddy, it's gonna be okay. We—"

He clamped his hand around my wrist like a steel vise. Before I could wince or tell him it hurt, he yanked on my arm, pulling me down at the same instant that the window beside us shattered. The world around us exploded into movement. The few patrons who'd been in the diner with us started screaming. The waitress and cooks were yelling at each other to call 911. More gunshots rang out in the early morning darkness. I lay on the floor of the restaurant and watched a coffee mug burst into a thousand pieces, then the cash register shattered as three bullets slammed into it.

Nico was on top of me, shielding my body from falling glass and porcelain. Once there was a break in the gunfire, he took my hand and we ran to the kitchen, staying as low as we could, basically running at a crouch. I heard a cook screaming into a cell phone as we made our way toward the back door. Nico opened the door and leaned out, checking the parking lot. I could hear squealing tires from the front of the diner, followed by the screaming roar of an engine.

"I think they're gone, but let's be careful," Nico said, helping me down the back steps.

By the time we got to the asphalt of the parking lot, my Jeep came tearing down the road at a solid hundred miles an hour. Sebastian had taken it home since I was riding with Nico. Any other time I'd have been pissed to see him driving it like that, but the moment, I'd never been happier to see it.

The tires screeched as it slowed and pulled into the lot. Sebastian threw it into park and jumped out of the cab. The jovial, happy-go-lucky guy was gone now. Sebastian had turned into a monster, angry and ready to kill. He ran to us, a scowl on his face.

"What the fuck happened?" he asked through clenched teeth.

"We were being watched," Nico said.

I heard sirens wailing in the distance.

"I passed a car driving like a bat out of hell on the way here. It must have been them. Big black SUV," Sebastian said.

"Probably," Nicol said. "I don't know where they were hiding. Once I saw the red laser dot on Maddy's temple, I yanked her ass to the ground."

What? My hand went to my mouth as I realized why he'd almost pulled my arm out of its socket. A laser sight? On my head? I remembered the bursting window and realized I'd been less than a second from dying. Again. I imagined my brains splattered all over the diner, and I started to shiver uncontrollably.

Nico led me to the Jeep and got me into the passenger seat. He cupped my cheeks in his palms and forced me to look into his eyes. "Hey, it's okay. You're safe now. I promised I'd keep you safe, and I will. I need to go hunt these assholes down, or try to. Sebastian will take you home and stay with you."

I nodded in response, unable to talk. My body was quivering so much that I couldn't even control it. If this kept up, I was certain I would shake apart. Nico pressed his forehead to mine, and almost instantly, I could feel a calming energy seep out of his skin and into mine. My heart rate slowed, and I was finally able to control my body better.

"How are your wounds?" Nico asked.

My sides were sore, but not painful. "Fine. I didn't rip out the stitches or anything."

"Good," he whispered and kissed my forehead. "I'll be home as soon as I can."

As he finished saying that, a truck came flying into the parking lot. I glanced up and saw Felipe behind the steering wheel. He leaned out the window. "What's the word?"

"We need to track down the guys who tried to kill us," Nico called over his shoulder.

Felipe's face went dark. "Son of a bitch," he hissed and pounded a fist into his truck's door.

Nico turned to join him, and I stretched out a hand. "Nico?" I called.

He slid to a stop and turned back to me. "Yeah?"

"Be careful."

He grinned. "Always."

Without another word, he jumped into Felipe's truck and they took off into the night. They headed down the highway, going the direction Sebastian had come from.

I leaned back in the Jeep's seat, my skin feeling hot and clammy. Sebastian came around to my side. "Maddy? Are you good? You don't—"

He jumped out of the way as I leaned out of the Jeep and retched. The fear and panic of the last few minutes had caught up to me. I gagged and vomited all over the pavement. Finally, when what little was in my stomach had been expelled, I relaxed back into my seat. The night felt ominous and full of horror.

Relief washed over me as Sebastian drove away from the diner. I fell into an exhausted sleep before we made it home.

Chapter 12 - Nico

Rage unlike anything I'd ever experienced surged through me. I sat in the passenger seat of Felipe's car, my fists clenched and shaking on my thighs. My wolf was snapping its jaws and howling, ready to break through. It was all I could do to keep the beast in check. I did not need it to come tearing out and forcing me to shift right here in the car.

I hissed out a frustrated breath through gritted teeth. They tried to kill her again. Not only that, but this time it was in public. Witnesses saw it happen, heard it. Someone probably saw the car as it ran. "Javi's getting sloppy," I muttered.

Felipe nodded and turned up the car stereo. He had his cell connected and had a police scanner app running on it. We could both hear the chatter of the cops, EMTs, and fire department. Apparently, the shooting had turned into an all-hands-on-deck situation.

"I don't know if it's sloppy," Felipe said. "Or desperate."

"No reason it can't be both."

We cruised through town, looking for the car Sebastian had seen fleeing the shooting. Felipe took every back road and alley through town, then got back on the highway. They'd probably hit the interstate and were long gone, but we had to be sure. He'd said it was a black SUV, which was pretty generic, but all I wanted was to get my hands on them. Choke them until they gave me Javi's location. Anything to get rid of some of this anger. So we had to try.

Felipe pointed through the windshield. "What is that?"

I leaned forward and stared off into the darkness. In the distance, and getting closer, was a boxy SUV on the side of the highway, the passenger and driver doors hanging wide open. As we got closer, the headlights illuminated more of it. The car was black, like Sebastian had said.

"That's got to be it. What are the odds? Almost four in the morning? Who stops to take a piss and leaves their doors open at this hour?" I said, glancing around as Felipe pulled up behind the car.

Once we were parked, I cautiously got out of the car, sniffing the air and straining my ears. These assholes had guns—no reason to be careless. Felipe did the same, getting out of the truck and crouching as we walked around. I smelled hibiscus, dandelion, and old piss from a dog that had marked its territory at least three days before. I could hear the flitting of bat wings above us and an owl hooting a half mile away. Nothing else. Whoever had left the car was long gone. Why did they leave it right here? There was no way we wouldn't find it. Even if they'd pulled it off the road five or six feet, we probably would have missed it.

"Wanna take a look?" Felipe asked as he stood to full height.

I nodded, walking toward the car. Even though no one was around, something felt wrong. Another scent tickled at my nose. It was faint. A human, but...distant...or fading? Had a human been in the car with them? Was I smelling the residual scent? Pheromones that had been left behind?

"Do you smell that?" I asked.

Felipe glanced at me as he was getting ready to peek in the driver's side door. "Human?"

"Yeah. So it's not just me?"

"Nope, it's there. Fainter than the smell of shifter. Maybe they stole the car from a human. Could that be it?"

I didn't like that explanation; it didn't alleviate the feeling of wrongness to the situation. The closer I got to the car, the stronger the smell got. Felipe checked the front seats, and I looked at the bench seats in the back. The car was totally clean. I caught the pungent sour smell of gunpowder, but nothing else.

"Back hatch?" Felipe asked.

"Sure."

Felipe hit a button on the hatch door and it rose automatically. In the darkness, I never would have seen it, but the dome light illuminated what was there. Felipe leaped back. I stood stock still, gritting my teeth and growling. A body had been stuffed into the trunk. A man, his eyes dead and sightless, stared back at me. His mouth hung open in a look of shocked pain. Thick black bruises circled his throat where I could see he'd probably been choked to death.

Now I knew where the smell was coming from. The smell of a dead human. A human who'd not been dead long enough to start stinking. I'd scented the fading remnants of life.

I looked back at Felipe, who was already on the phone. I frowned. "Who are you calling?"

"The cops, bro."

I hated talking to the cops. It never seemed to go well. There was an undercurrent of anti-shifter racism in the police force. I figured it was based in fear. We were stronger, faster, and more powerful than any human. It made us very difficult to deal with from a police perspective.

But I looked back at the body and knew Felipe had made the right call. I turned away from the awful sight of the dead man. This felt like a setup. Had Javi's guys dumped the body here on purpose, knowing we'd come across it? As crazy as it sounded, it had the *feel* of truth.

Felipe hung up the phone and shoved it into his pocket. "They have a cruiser nearby. Probably one of the ones who responded to the shooting." He glanced back at the corpse and winced before turning away. "Christ, man. What is this?"

"An attempted frame job from the looks of it," I said.

"Wait...seriously?"

I nodded. "It's not for us to take the fall. The cops aren't that dumb, but it will get us on the police radar. Make life difficult. That's my theory, anyway." I could hear a siren in the distance getting closer.

Felipe ran a hand through his hair. "Well, should we run? Get out of here?"

I shook my head. "No. We did nothing wrong. Besides, they're already here." I gestured back up the road. Red-and-blue flashing lights exploded the night sky as a police cruiser crested the hill and came toward us.

The car pulled up and two guys got out. Felipe and I knew how things like this could go, so we both raised our hands to show we weren't a danger to them. The cop from the passenger seat had a hand on the butt of his pistol as he came forward. It was all I could do not to roll my eyes.

The cop who'd driven the car looked much more at ease and nodded to us. "I'm Officer Duggan, this is my partner, Officer Keck. Are you the gentlemen who called the emergency line?"

"Yeah. We were driving and saw this SUV. Doors were hanging open, so we stopped to see if they needed help and found the body," I said.

Officer Keck raised an eyebrow and looked behind me toward the SUV. "And just what the hell were you two boys doing out so late? Couple of shifters like you? Shouldn't you be in bed?"

"No sir, just out late," I said.

"You boys been drinking?" Keck asked, stepping closer.

"Bryce?" Duggan said with a snap of irritation in his voice. "We've got a dead body to worry about. I think that's the most important thing. Call the station, tell them to send a crime-scene unit out here."

Keck eyed me for another second before turning to go back to the car. Duggan gave me an apologetic smile. "Sorry. Anyway, can I get your names? Then we'll try to go through a timeline."

We gave our names and told him the same thing I'd already said, sticking to the story that we'd randomly stumbled across the car on the way home. The asshole cop returned and continued to interrupt with questions about why we were out so late. It was starting to get me pissed. I wanted this over with so I could go home to check on Maddy.

"Just so I'm getting this straight," Keck said. "You just happened to be out on the highway in the middle of the night, and just so happened to find a dead body? You still haven't given me a good reason why you were out so late."

"Officer," Felipe said. "Is it against the law to be out late? I'm confused as to why *you're* confused."

"Watch your mouth," Keck snapped. "We're asking the questions here. Now, were you out late for some…I don't know…shifter thing? Need some time with the moon or something?"

Duggan grabbed Keck's arm and tugged him away. He whispered to his partner, low so he thought I wouldn't hear it, but they must not have known how sensitive our hearing truly was.

"Bryce, for fuck's sake, quit it," Duggan hissed.

"Doug, I'm telling you, these guys are hiding something."

"I know you're still pissed about Shawna, but this—"

"This isn't about that, goddammit. If she wants to end our marriage for some shifter cock, then good riddance. This is about the job."

"Enough, Bryce. Enough. These guys are shooting straight. Let's do the job, okay?"

"Whatever."

They came back over to us, Duggan looking embarrassed and irritated, Keck looking like he wanted to bite through steel. Duggan nodded toward the car. "We're gonna search it real quick. If you guys can stand by your car?"

"Sure thing," I said, leaning back against the hood next to Felipe.

The two cops went through the car even more thoroughly than we had. It took a while for them to get to the rear and check over the body. They never touched it or the surrounding areas—at least they knew how to do this part of their job.

After staring at the body for a few seconds, Keck turned around and looked at us. "Okay, son, last chance. Do you want to tell us why you killed him?"

"Excuse the fuck out of me?" Felipe barked.

Keck's hand went back to his gun. "Watch your mouth! You heard what I asked."

This time I did roll my eyes, and I made sure he could see it. "Officer, how stupid do you think we'd have to be to kill a guy and then immediately call the cops? That sounds like the dumbest thing I've ever heard."

"Nobody ever said shifters were smart. You—"

"Okay," Duggan broke in. "That will be enough of that. Mr. Lorenzo, you and your friend are free to go. Don't leave town in case we have more questions."

Keck turned and looked at Duggan like he was out of his mind. "Doug, are you serious? You can't do this. These guys had something to do with this. We can't let suspects go."

Duggan gave his partner a look that finally shut the other guy up. He glanced at us again. "You're free to go. Thanks for your time."

Felipe and I got into the truck and pulled away. I glanced through the window and saw the two cops arguing, close to a shouting match. Felipe shook his head. "Fucking bigot."

I nodded in agreement. "Can you turn your scanner back on? I want to see if we can find anything else out."

Felipe brought his app back up and I put his phone in the cradle. Before we got home, we heard the call come in that the crime-scene team had found the dead guy's wallet. The name was Johnathan McGuire.

Felipe and I looked at each other. That was the name of the nurse's husband. The one who'd been kidnapped. Javi had killed the guy.

"Fuck," Felipe muttered.

I pulled my phone out and called Luis. He needed to know.

The phone rang six times before he answered. "Huh, hello?" He sounded groggy, and I remembered it was almost four in the morning.

"Luis, it's Nico."

"What's wrong? What happened?" He was instantly awake and alert.

I gave him a quick rundown of the events until we were back in my driveway. We sat in the truck until we'd relayed all the information.

"And the dead guy?" I said. "It's the nurse lady's husband."

"Shit. I was afraid this might happen. Once she didn't complete the murder, Javi's crew would have had to kill him. No way you can let something like that slide. If you don't instill fear, you can't force anyone to do anything."

"I don't think I'm going to tell Maddy about this. There's only so much she can handle. She's already so shaken up, I can't put something else on her plate."

"Makes sense," Felipe said. "What's our next move?"

"I'm sending Javi a message," I said.

"What message?" Luis asked.

"I'm going to make sure Javi knows that Maddy is mine. He needs to know that any direct threats toward her or her life means he's declaring war on the pack. He may be doing the bidding of some shadow organization, but the Lorenzo pack is right here, not a thousand miles across the ocean."

"I guess we'll see if that gets him off our back," Luis said.

"I'm gonna try and get some sleep, guys." With that, I got out of the car.

"Good night…er…good morning, I guess," Felipe said.

"Talk to you tomorrow," Luis said.

I hung up and walked up the steps to the front door. Sebastian was sitting on the armchair, reading a book by a lamp. The rest of the lights were off and Maddy was curled up asleep on the couch with a blanket draped over her. Sebastian glanced up and put his book aside.

"How was she?" I asked.

He let out a sigh. "Not great. As soon as you left, I think it all hit her. She puked her guts out, then passed out. She didn't faint, I think it was mental exhaustion or something. I had to carry her in from the car."

"Thanks for taking care of her. Go on home and get some rest."

Sebastian left, and I scooped Maddy up in my arms and carried her up to her bedroom. Her eyes fluttered open and she woke up enough to give me an incoherent mumbled greeting. She was still wearing her work clothes. There was no way that attire would be comfortable to sleep in.

"Do you want to change?" I whispered.

Maddy nodded. "Mmhmm."

I got her in her bedroom and set her on the bed. I found a set of pajamas and handed the clothing to her. Her eyes still only half-open, she took them from me.

"Can you get my shoes and pants?" she mumbled.

"Sure."

I pulled her sneakers off and averted my eyes as I slid her pants down. At least, I tried to avert my eyes. Even in the dim light from the hallway ceiling fixture, I could see the muscular curve of her legs. Maddy was still half asleep and murmuring words I couldn't make out. She peeled her shirt off, the movement causing my gaze to slip across her body and up beyond her flat stomach to the mounds of her breasts. Maddy unclasped her bra and tossed it away. My breath caught in my throat, and I swung my head back toward her feet, but not before I'd gotten a glimpse of the dark brown nipples atop her perfect breasts.

I felt like a pervert, and she was still barely coherent and had no idea what I'd seen. She slipped the shirt I'd given her over her head and lay down, falling back asleep almost immediately. My heart was thudding in my chest. I quickly covered her with a blanket and left the room.

After latching her door, I leaned against it. My dick was throbbing in my pants, straining at the material.

Pushing the thoughts aside, I went to my own room, stripped off my clothes, and pulled on a pair of pajama pants. I brushed my teeth and set the alarm on my phone, hoping to get three or four hours of sleep.

Right as I was pulling my own covers back, Maddy called out to me. "Nico?"

Without hesitation, I was out my door and into her room again. She was sitting up, clutching her covers to her chest. I glanced around the room seeing if anything was wrong, then looked back at her. "What happened? Are you okay?"

Her head bounced in a sleep-drunk nod. "Nightmare. Could…can you stay with me?"

Without waiting for a second, I walked to the opposite side of the bed. Maddy watched me as I slid under the sheets. Once I was settled, she said, "I'm scared, Nico."

Her voice quivered. I didn't even ask what the dream was about. A thousand different things played through my head. I took her hand in mine and looked her in the eyes. "I'd be a little worried if you weren't scared."

Her face crumpled and tears started falling from her eyes. "I never asked for any of this."

Seeing her cry like that sent my wolf into a rage. It made me want to jump out of bed, get in my car, and drive straight to Javi's territory and beat the ever-loving shit out of him. Instead, I took a steadying breath and pulled Maddy close, pressing my forehead to hers. The connection sent a wave of calming energy through me. It must have done the same for Maddy because we both let out deep sighs at almost the same instant. It was one more sign that she was my mate. That she was as important to me as I felt she was.

"Maddy, I promise, I'll do everything in my power to end this. I'm going to bring this to a stop. No one is going to hurt you again. Ever."

She surprised me by not answering. Instead, she leaned forward and pressed a gentle kiss to my lips. I was speechless when she pulled away. She gave me a small, embarrassed smile before speaking. "Something in my gut is telling me to trust you, and since I don't have any other options, I have to believe you will keep me safe."

Without thinking, I slid my hands into her dark curls and pulled her to me. I kissed her—a passionate, possessive kiss that showed her all I felt for her. I pulled away, but only an inch, our lips only a breath apart. "You're mine, I swear I'll protect you. Anyone who wants to try will have to go through me and my pack first."

Maddy nodded and slipped deeper into the covers, curling into my body. I settled myself and draped an arm over her. In a few seconds, her breathing took on a deep steady rhythm that told me she'd fallen back asleep, the exhaustion of the day pulling her into unconsciousness.

I was tired. Bone-weary. But I stayed awake a long time after Maddy fell asleep.

Chapter 13 - Maddy

The morning after the shooting, I called Abi and the rest of the staff to tell them that I'd be shutting the bar down for a week. Nico had brought the idea up while we sat at the kitchen table eating toast and eggs.

"I think it's best if you try to stay out of public for a while. Plus, if the bar is closed, your staff won't be in danger. Javi's guys may keep stopping by to try and find you. If there was some altercation, someone might get hurt."

I'd jammed a corner of my toast into the yolk of my egg. I'd been irritated at the idea at first, but it honestly made sense. "Okay. I'll make the calls."

It was hard to argue with his reasoning, but it still pissed me off. Why should I be afraid to go to work? To operate the business I'd built from nothing? Except I was. I was terrified. After everything that had happened, all I really wanted to do was stay in Nico's house. I had promised everyone a full week's paycheck. I told them all to think of it as a paid vacation, which had excited everyone—everyone except Abi. She'd known something had to be very wrong for me to close the bar for a week.

"Maddy, are you okay?" she'd asked.

I'd told her about the shooting when I called, but had tried to change the subject to the closure of the bar. Abi hadn't bit on that, instead circling back to the main issue.

"Yes," I said, "I'm fine."

"For fuck's sake, Maddy, someone tried to kill you. *Again*. There is no way you're okay. Why don't you let me run the place for a few weeks. You'll take a big hit on business if you close for more than a day."

She was right, and I knew it, but Nico's warning about my friends' safety helped me stay strong in my decision. "I promise I'll be okay. If I lose a few customers, it'll be fine, truly. Abi, enjoy the time off."

She'd sighed in frustration. "Fine. I don't like it, but I'll trust you. You better not be lying to me that you're fine, though."

"Nico's taking care of me, so I'm good. Scared? Yes. Pissed off? Double yes. But I'm surviving."

"You better. Love you, chick."

"Love you, too. Talk to you later."

There was a knock at the front door, and Nico went to answer it. Sebastian had come rolling in for his day of watching over me, looking like he'd only gotten an hour of sleep. The dark circles under his eyes reminded me that he'd been out as late as the rest of us.

"Morning," Nico said. "I'm going to shower."

"Cool," Sebastian said, stifling a yawn.

"I'll be back down in a few," Nico said as he walked toward the steps.

Sebastian nodded to me. "How are you feeling?" he asked as he walked to the living room.

I rolled my eyes. "Like I've been run over by a truck."

He waved a hand at me. "Is that all? I feel like a pile of shit that was run over by a rusty tractor and then pissed on by a passing dog."

"Gross."

He grinned. "I win."

"You okay if I watch TV? It's really all I have the energy for right now."

Sebastian nodded. "Go ahead. I'm gonna use the bathroom. Just no reality TV, that shit gives me a headache."

"Deal."

I flipped the TV on as he walked down the hall to the bathroom. It was early and there wasn't much to watch, so I switched to the local news. The first thing I saw almost had the remote dropping from my hand. A scrolling banner at the bottom of the screen read: *Clearidge Man Found Murdered.*

I turned the volume up.

"...currently have no leads on the death. The body was found very early this morning inside an abandoned SUV by passing motorists. The county coroner has yet to complete an autopsy, but sources within the police department, speaking under anonymity, tell Channel Nine News that it appears the victim was strangled to death."

I couldn't remember the last time I'd heard of a murder in Clearidge. Strangled? Good lord. They flashed a picture of the man on the screen. I didn't recognize him, which I was thankful for. I wondered what he could have done to get killed in such a way—killed and left on the side of the road.

The next thing that flashed on the screen did make me drop the remote. My blood ran cold, and the hair on the back of my neck stood on end when Nurse Cleo appeared on screen, her eyes bloodshot and her cheeks red from crying. I left the remote on the floor and shuffled closer to the television, hoping I was imagining what I was seeing.

"I...I...my Johnathan is gone. I don't know what to do now," Cleo said, wiping fresh tears from her face. It looked like she was in front of a hospital.

"Mrs. McGuire, do you have any idea why someone would do this to your husband?" the reporter asked.

A feverish, terrified look crossed her eyes before she answered. "No. No idea at all." She looked directly into the camera, like she was trying to talk to Javi through the lens. "I don't know. I know nothing. I just miss my Johnathan. I need to go." Without another word, Cleo pushed the microphone away and walked off-camera.

"Stay tuned to Channel Nine—"

The TV flicked off, and I jumped, startled by the black screen and sudden silence. I looked over and saw that Sebastian had picked up the remote from where I'd dropped it. He grimaced and shrugged. "You weren't supposed to see that. Not yet, anyway. Nico and Felipe found that guy's body last night. Nico wanted to tell you."

As though he heard his name, the sounds of footsteps coming down the stairs pulled mine and

Sebastian's eyes away from each other. Nico stopped on the stairs. He looked startled that we were both looking at him.

"What? What happened?" he asked.

Sebastian gestured at the TV. "Maddy saw a news report. The nurse's husband?"

"Shit," Nico said as he descended the rest of the steps. "I really didn't want you to find out yet. I thought it might be too much, after everything else that happened last night."

I honestly couldn't disagree with him. It was a lot. I felt awful for the nurse. Yes, she'd tried to kill me, but only because the man she loved was in danger. If I'd been put in the same situation, what would I have done? If someone had my parents? It was terrible, but I knew that the decision wouldn't have been an easy one. Now Cleo's husband was dead.

"This is awful."

"You can't blame yourself," Nico said. "I know it's easy to go down that path, but that's not fair to you."

"No, yeah, I get that. I'm not being a martyr or anything. Javi is why that man is dead. I just feel…empathy. It's not my fault, but I can't help but think about how awful all this is for them."

Nico nodded and kissed me lightly on the forehead. "Good. I'm glad you see it that way."

"How is all this being handled, though? Sebastian said you and Felipe found the body. Did you tell the cops about Javi?"

Nico and Sebastian shared a look, then Nico shook his head slightly. "It's complicated. Shifters are held to the same level of law as everyone else, but there's a bias. All of us know it, so we have to be more careful. Felipe and I think the body was dumped where it was on purpose. They knew we'd be hot on their tail and would probably find it first. If someone else found it? Oh well. If we found it? Then we're on the police radar. If they can prove in any way that I had something to do with that death, it's a one-way ticket to prison. We have to be even more careful now."

"We don't need to worry about the nurse talking," Sebastian said. "She looked scared to death on the news a minute ago. When Luis set her free, he said she wouldn't be a problem. After seeing her on the news, I think he's right. I think Javi got to her again and made sure she knew she'd be next if she said anything."

The doorbell rang, and Nico groaned. Before he even had the chance to answer it, the door swung open and an older man and woman walked in. I could see instantly that the man was Nico's father. He was the spitting image of him, but about twenty-five years older. The woman, who I could only assume was his mother, looked harried and walked straight toward Nico.

"Do you know anything about this murder? The shooting at the restaurant and this body that was found?"

"Mom, calm down."

"Don't tell me to calm down. Tell me the truth. Does this have something to do with Javi?"

Nico sighed, glancing first at Sebastian before his gaze rested on me. "Fine. Sit down. Let me tell you what happened."

I sat where I was, feeling incredibly uncomfortable. I hadn't even met his parents yet, and now I was sitting here listening to what sounded like the beginning of an argument. Sebastian caught my eye, and I could see he also wanted to be anywhere else but in this room.

Nico went over everything that happened the night before. The shooting, the body, everything.

"Maddy's fine, though," Nico said, nodding toward the living room where I was sitting on the couch.

Nico's mother stood and hurried to my side, taking my hand in hers. "Are you okay, sweetie? Can we do anything for you? I can't imagine how awful this must be for you."

I was a little surprised by her reaction, but also happy. I'd been a little worried Nico's parents would hate the woman who had upended their son's life and put him in danger. I nodded. "I'm doing okay. Thank you. Nico's been great."

"That sounds like my boy. My name is Julia, this is Carlos. Do your parents live in town?"

"No, they…well, they live pretty far away. I moved here years ago to start my business. I got a good deal on an old bar. Plus, I always wanted to live in Florida. It always seemed sort of like California but less pretentious."

Julia laughed. "That's a good description." She patted my thigh. "That's fine. Since your parents aren't here, you can call me Mama Julia. All of Nico's friends do."

"We do?" Sebastian asked, frowning deeply.

"Shut up, Sebastian," Julia said over her shoulder. She got up and headed toward the kitchen. "I'm going to go ahead and make lunch."

Nico and I had had breakfast less than an hour ago, but my watch said it was past noon. We'd slept much later than I'd expected. No one protested, and within minutes, I could hear pots and pans being banged around in the kitchen.

I hadn't realized what an event *lunch* would turn into. Apparently the reason no one objected to having such an early lunch was because Julia was preparing a massive feast of six or seven dishes. She sent Carlos to the store to buy steaks, deciding to turn lunch into a cookout. Suddenly, Nico's house was being inundated by family and friends. It turned into a huge party. Nico introduced me to all his brothers and the friends I hadn't met yet. It seemed like everyone was here except Luis, who was still in Tampa, researching. It was all I could do to keep the names and faces straight.

Nico stayed close to me the whole day and into the evening. The food smelled amazing as it cooked, but I didn't have time to get hungry. I was involved in so many conversations that I could barely think about food. I also kept noticing the way Nico's mom continued to check on us. Her eyes followed us around the house. It made me a little nervous, so I partook of the makeshift bar Felipe had set up by the back deck. I'd always felt like I could hold my own, but the shifters were all pounding drinks and kept offering me more. It wasn't long after we ate that I realized I was the only person in the house who was getting drunk.

My bladder was screaming, so I excused myself from the picnic table and headed inside to relieve myself. I held the wall as I went, feeling more than a little tipsy and chuckling to myself as I locked the door. I groaned in relief as I peed for what felt like an hour.

After I washed my hands, I unlocked and opened the door, nearly yelping when I found Nico standing just outside. He looked at me in a way that sent rivers of heat across my body. Jesus, that look made me feel...I didn't even know.

"Are you good?" he asked.

The alcohol took over. Loosening my tongue and erasing any inhibitions I may have had a few hours ago. "It's not fair that you're so hot," I mumbled almost to myself, but he was grinning at me. I put a hand on his chest, feeling the thick hard muscle under his shirt. "You make my heart race, and this voice in my head...it's been talking to me since I first saw you. It says you're mine. Like, it's screaming in my head. Even now it says..."

"What does it say?" he asked, his voice a husky whisper.

I looked into his eyes and felt the tremble of butterflies in my stomach. My head was still dizzy from the liquor. "It says it wants you."

There was a flash in Nico's eyes, an explosion of hunger, and he pulled me to him. My body was pressed against his, and I could feel the hardness of his cock between my legs. It made my knees weak. Nico put his lips close to mine, almost touching them. "What do you feel now? *Am* I yours?"

"I..." I swallowed, my mouth going dry. "I don't know you that well, but everything tells me that you are."

Nico pressed his lips to mine. I sighed and opened my mouth, allowing his tongue to slide into my mouth. The alcohol gave me courage and made me bolder than I typically would have been. I slipped my hand down his chest and across his belt, until it came to rest on the throbbing bulge between his legs. Nico grunted and moaned into my mouth. His hands roamed my body, making sure to be gentle near my wounds. One hand caressed my breast, squeezing hungrily.

Nico brought his other hand to my belt and undid it. I was so horny, I didn't even give a shit that the door to the bathroom was open. All that mattered was him and me and this moment. I wanted it, needed it. Our lips were still intertwined as he slid his hand under the waistband of my pants and panties. I sucked in a breath as his fingers slid across my throbbing clit. Jesus, it had been so long, and it felt so good. I lay my head on his shoulder and thrust my hips as his finger slipped in and out of me. My breath was a ragged, nearly panicked rasp as the orgasm built. First a warmth deep inside my pelvis, then a rising sensation, like my body was being lifted off the ground.

With one last thrust of his fingers, everything came crashing down. I shuddered, my hips jerking and spasming against him until the last of the climax faded.

I sucked in a breath and chuckled against his neck. "Holy shit," I whispered.

Nico kissed the side of my neck and heard a throat clear. Nico and I both snapped our heads around.

Julia stood in the hallway looking at us. She looked as embarrassed as I felt. We pulled away from each other quickly. There was a mortifying moment when his hand got stuck in my pants before he could get it free. Thank God, my tits weren't out at least. I buttoned my pants, then ran from the room as quickly as I could. I raced up the stairs and closed the door behind me. Collapsing on the bed, I finally allowed myself a chance to breathe.

"Well, that was a good first impression, Maddy," I said to myself. I groaned and covered my eyes with my arm.

Chapter 14 - Nico

Maddy ran down the hall, turned the corner, and sprinted up the stairs. The thudding of her feet only stopped when the bedroom door slammed.

I closed my eyes and took two deep breaths, trying to release the anger I felt toward my mother for interrupting us. To say I was disappointed was an understatement. Once I finally opened my eyes, my mother stood in front of me, her arms crossed, an eyebrow raised.

She stepped closer, glancing over her shoulder to be sure everyone was still outside. "What are you doing, Nico?"

I huffed out an exasperated laugh. "I think that stopped being your business when I turned eighteen, Mom."

"Oh, stop it. You know exactly what I mean. All this?" She gestured to the bathroom, where I'd only moments before been engaged in one of the most erotic moments of my life. It made my skin crawl thinking about my mom seeing any of it. "You need to be careful. This is dangerous. I'm in agreement that the girl needs to be protected, but that's only so we can get to Javi. You need to remember that. You shouldn't get too attached to this woman."

I sighed and gritted my teeth. "Well, maybe things have changed."

Mom frowned and looked at me suspiciously. "What is that supposed to mean, Nico? What's changed? You can't possibly be thinking about mating with a human. If you want to sow your wild oats or whatever, you're an adult, and I can't stop that. Anything more? That's just crazy."

I glared at her. I'd never been so angry with my mother. "What if that's exactly what I do want? It's my choice who I mate with."

Mom gasped and again checked to make sure no one was around to hear. "Nico," she hissed. "That's taboo. It's not done."

I groaned and waved a hand at her. "Christ, Mom. You sound like those bigots who say interracial marriage is sacrilege, or that same-sex marriage is a one-way ticket to hell. Are we really having this conversation?"

I knew where this was coming from. Edemas. All the legends and stories shifters had been told for hundreds of years about the dangers of a hybrid human-shifter child. The very idea had turned into an almost religious terror, especially for the older generations. Mom had been raised on that ideology.

"We absolutely *are* having this conversation. If my son is about to do something this stupid, then I—"

"Enough, Mom. I'm not mating with a human. I just didn't like your insinuation."

Mom put a hand to her chest and let out a relieved breath. "Thank God. Maddy is a nice girl, really. Beautiful, but she isn't right for you. You deserve better."

I didn't like that. Not one bit. The anger spiked again, making me clamp my jaws together. All I'd wanted was for her to calm down and drop it, then she had to say something like that. My wolf was even more angry and a low growl escaped my throat. Mom's eyes went wide, and she took a step back.

"Mom, this is your one warning," I said through gritted teeth. "You will not speak about Maddy like that in my presence. In fact, you won't speak about her like that in *anyone's* presence. Is that understood?"

"Nico? What's gotten into you? Why—"

"I am the alpha of the Lorenzo pack," I said, barely managing to keep my voice below a shout. "Do you understand me?"

Mom nodded ever so faintly, a movement so slight, it was almost invisible. "What is going on here?"

"I'll tell you everything once you stop behaving like a superstitious child," I said as I pushed past her and headed toward the back door.

I burst out into the humid night air, everyone falling silent. My friends and brothers could all see I was in a pissy mood and left me alone as I stalked toward the scrub-pine forest behind my house. I needed to shift, needed it badly. It might be the only thing that would get rid of the tension inside me. My mind slipped back to those few moments with Maddy in the bathroom. There *was* something else that would help my tension, but that wouldn't happen now, thanks to my mother.

Dad was standing by the firepit with a beer in his hand. I walked over to him and nodded back at the house. "Can you keep an ear out for Maddy? She might need something while I'm gone."

He chewed at his lip and leaned in close. "Your mother?"

"I don't want to talk about it," I said as I stride toward the forest.

Behind me, he cursed under his breath and tossed his beer into the fire. I kicked off my shoes and stripped my shirt, tossing it to the side, shifting as I jogged into the woods. As soon as I changed, the anger and tension inside me dissipated. The freedom of shifting released all the pent-up frustrations and irritation. I heard crackling twigs and leaves behind me. A glance over my shaggy shoulder showed me that the guys had joined me, the three of them in their wolf forms running after me into the woods.

We ran for what felt like hours. The rush of the wind across my fur, the sounds of the night, the feel of the earth beneath my paws always calmed me. Shifting always brought out the true feeling of life. We crested a hill and sat in a circle, howling at the moon for several minutes. We weren't drawn to it, but we got a hilarious kick out of it.

I felt a thousand times better when I got back home. We must not have been gone as long as I thought because most of the crowd was still there. My father walked up to me as we stepped out of the woods and shifted back to our human forms. "Maddy?" I asked.

"Seems fine. Hasn't come out of her room, from what I can tell. Your mother went home. She told me what happened."

"Shit. I thought she would."

Dad put a hand on my shoulder. "It'll be okay. She'll come around when she hears the whole truth. I know she will."

"That's fine, but I don't want her treating Maddy poorly until then. I won't have it, Dad, you know I won't."

"I know that, but do you really think your mother would be disrespectful to Maddy? That she's that kind of person?"

He was right. Mom would push the issue with me, and in private. She was too kind to ever say or do anything that would make Maddy feel less than. She might not think Maddy was the right person for me, but she'd never say something like that to Maddy. I nodded. "Yeah, I know."

"Good. Let me help you clean up a bit, I think everyone is starting to leave."

He was right. The party was winding down, and people were beginning to make their way to the door. Dad, my brothers, and my friends all cleaned up the backyard and the living and dining rooms. By the time everyone but me had left, the house was pretty much back in shape.

I made my way up to my room and turned on the shower. Once I'd piled my clothes into the hamper, I stepped into the steaming heat of the shower spray. I sighed in relief as the water ran over my body.

As I washed myself, the last of the tension left my body. My mind drifted back to the furtive moments with Maddy in the downstairs bathroom. My cock stiffened, so I shut the water off and got out of the shower, not wanting to get wound up. After drying off and brushing my teeth, I wrapped a towel around my waist and went out into the bedroom. I yelped when I saw Maddy standing in my doorway.

She smiled shyly. "Sorry. I just came to see if I got you in trouble with your mom."

I tightened my grip on the towel and chuckled. "I'm a grown man."

Maddy rolled her eyes and took a couple steps over toward my bed. "Yeah. I'm a grown-ass woman, and I *still* get told off by my mom sometimes."

She sat down on the foot of the bed and fidgeted with her hands, looking nervous. I stepped over and closed my bedroom door. No one else was in the house, and the doors were all locked, but it felt right to close the bedroom. There was tension in the air, so thick and tight that I could barely breathe. I could feel Maddy's eyes on me as I walked back from the door.

Anticipation and nervousness flooded through me. My cock was hard again. Her eyes were almost like hands fluttering across my body. Licking my lips, I gazed at her. "Um…can I get dressed?"

Her gaze slid up my form, then her eyes locked onto mine. "Yeah. That's fine."

I took a breath and decided to do something aggressive. Instead of retreating to the bathroom to change, I grabbed a pair of pajama pants out of my dresser, and dropped my towel. An almost imperceptible gasp left Maddy's lips. I knew the entire right side of my body was visible to her, including my rapidly thickening cock. I'd never done anything this forward in my life, but when I was around her, I couldn't seem to help myself. I slipped the pants up and glanced over, seeing her gaze flicking between my legs until my cock was obscured beneath the waistband.

I took a breath to calm myself before walking over to the bed. Maddy leaned across it and looked at me in a way no one had ever looked at me before. All thoughts and ideas of staying calm jumped out the window. I gestured toward the bed. "Are you comfortable?" I asked, my voice gruff and heavy with desire.

Maddy nodded, her eyes filled with a deep-seated hunger—hungrier than I'd ever seen. I could read her body, could hear her breaths coming in small pants, and I could smell the nervous sweat on her skin. She wanted me. She wanted me as much as I wanted her.

"I promised I wouldn't force anything. I'm sorry about earlier. I shouldn't have—"

"Shut up, Nico. I wanted that. I wanted that…I wanted more. I've always been super-guarded with men, but with you? It's like I don't need to be that way. Or that I don't want to be that way. I have no idea what's happening with us, but I don't want to fight it. It feels too good to fight. I'm not ready to be claimed yet, but I know I want you."

I knelt on the bed and hovered over her, looking down into her eyes, my body almost vibrating in anticipation. "Is that the truth? Or is it just the booze talking?"

Maddy grinned and shook her head. "I sobered up pretty fast after I was caught humping your leg and hand."

I chuckled and leaned in, kissing her deeply. Our tongues twined and flicked against each other. I pulled away after a few seconds. "Are you sure this is what you want?"

Her only answer was to slide her hand down under my waistband and wrap her hand around my cock. I let out a sigh as Maddy smiled at me, sliding her hand up and down the length of my shaft. I dug my fingers under her shirt and slid it up until her breasts were free. I looked at the enticing flesh, and my heart started hammering in my chest. I leaned forward and took her left breast in my mouth, licking and sucking at the nipple. Maddy's back arched, and she sucked in a deep breath. Her hand moved more insistently between my legs.

I tugged my pants off, tossing them across the room. Grabbing the waistband of her shorts, I tugged them off her in one swift movement. Maddy giggled and sat up slightly, wrapping her hand around my cock before slipping her lips over the head and taking my length into her mouth.

"Oh God," I whispered, looking down to see her bobbing her head up and down on me. The heat of her tongue on me was ecstasy. Nothing had ever felt so good, nothing had ever made me feel like this.

I leaned forward and slid my hand over her hips, staying away from her bandages. My finger trailed across her thighs, then between her legs, my finger slipping into the moist cleft of her pussy. Maddy moaned, my cock still in her mouth, and the vibration of her mouth almost made my eyes roll back in my head.

I rubbed a finger across her clit. The faster I moved, the quicker she bounced her head on my cock. I had to have her, I was desperate for her, but I wanted to take things as slow as she wanted. We teased each other for what felt like an eternity, until finally she pulled her mouth free and looked up at me while still stroking me. "Fuck me, Nico. Now."

I took two quick breaths and watched her hand working at my shaft. "Are you sure?"

She reached down with her free hand and clutched my hand, pushing my fingers deeper into her pussy. "Now."

The wolf growled, and I rolled her onto her back. I leaned over her and kissed her breasts gently, letting my lips drift across her nipples. Maddy reached between my legs and guided me inside her. We locked eyes as I entered her. The warmth, the slick wetness of her sent shivers of pleasure through me. Inch by inch, I slipped inside her. Maddy's mouth dropped open as I filled her. Finally buried inside her, I started thrusting, losing myself in the feel of her.

Maddy groaned and pressed her face into the hollow of my shoulder. Everything about her pushed me closer to the edge. Her smell, the sound of her moans, the feel of her pussy as it clenched around my cock...I was drifting closer to the point of no return. Slipping a hand between us, I started rubbing her clit in time with my thrusts.

Maddy threw her head back. "God...I'm gonna come." Her breathing became erratic as she dug her nails into my back.

My own orgasm started to build, a heavy pressure at the base of my cock. I moved quicker, slamming into her. Maddy whimpered with each thrust. She tensed, clutching at my shoulders, veins bulging at her neck, her face going red as her orgasm tore through her. I came an instant later, my body shaking and shivering as I pounded my hips into her, releasing everything I had, feeling more pleasure than I'd ever experienced in my life. It was the single greatest orgasm I'd ever had. My wolf howled in my head, a sound of triumph and happiness. We collapsed together, wrapped in each other's arms.

Chapter 15 - Maddy

I was in the kitchen, wiping down the counters. I was going stir-crazy not working and decided to help clean up Nico's place, though it was surprisingly clean for a bachelor. Sitting at home for days on end was grating on my nerves, so I had to do something to keep myself occupied. I'd already binge-watched everything I'd ever wanted to see and had read six books that had been on my to-be-read list. I was starting to see how the guy from *The Shining* had gone bonkers.

While I rinsed the rag I'd used to wipe the counters, my phone rang. It was Nico. He was at work, so it must have been important.

"Hello?" I answered.

"Hey, I just heard from Luis. He's almost back home."

A tremor of excitement went through my chest. Luis had been in Tampa for a week. I'd been anxious to hear what he'd learned, and now it seemed like I was finally going to find out. "What did he say?"

"He wants to tell us in person. He's on the interstate right now and said he'd be at my house in about two hours. I'm going to finish up what I need to here, then I'll be there. Are you good with that?"

I'd have preferred if he came home now because the waiting would be torture, but he still had a business to run. I'd have to busy myself and try to keep my mind off whatever Luis was going to say. I nodded to myself. "Yeah, it's fine. I'll be okay. Felipe is here, so it's not like I'm alone."

Felipe raised his can of Coke. He was sitting on the couch watching a baseball game. He was much quieter than Sebastian, but still a nice guy. I liked all of Nico's friends, which was good.

"Okay, cool," Nico said. "I'll try to finish as soon as I can. Call me if you need me."

"I will. See you soon."

"See you."

I set my phone on the counter and stared at it. In a couple hours, I might have some information. The thing I've hungered for my entire life. Since the moment my parents had told me I was adopted, all I'd wanted was to know where I'd come from, but then I'd come to terms with being adopted. The DNA test had stirred that hunger for knowledge again, and now...could today be the day?

It took a second to realize I was chewing my nails. Pulling my hand from my face, I started wiping again, cleaning the same things I'd already gone over.

Felipe turned and peered over the couch. "Was that Nico?"

I nodded, unable to make my mouth work.

"What did he say?"

Pulling in a steadying breath, I tried to compose myself. "Luis is on the way. He has information."

"Oh wow. Okay. Uh...are you all right?"

I nodded. "I'll be fine. It's just that this place is filthy and needs a good cleaning."

Felipe raised an eyebrow. "You realize you're cleaning the kitchen island for, like, the third time today. And that's only the times I've seen."

Flicking my arm, I sent the rag flying into the sink. "You're right. I'm going to try to take a nap. That will kill some time."

"Naps are good. Naps are really good," Felipe said, turning back to his ball game.

But all I could do was stare at the ceiling. My hands twitched and twined together, and I couldn't stop fidgeting. I lay there for a solid thirty minutes. My mind kept spinning, and I envisioned a thousand different ways this could play out. After what felt like years, my eyes finally drifted closed. I didn't wake up until I heard the front door open over an hour later.

My eyes snapped open, and I was out the bedroom door before I'd even fully awoken. Making my way downstairs, I could hear Nico and Luis talking to Felipe. By the time I made it to the landing, Felipe was heading out the front door. Luis looked over and saw me, nudging Nico.

"Maddy, hey. Felipe said you went to sleep. Feel better?" Nico asked.

"I'll feel better when I hear what Luis has to say."

"Fair enough," Luis said. He had a file folder and a laptop under his arm.

I sat on the couch and Nico sat beside me, taking my hand in his. He squeezed my hand reassuringly. Luis sat opposite us and shifted his things onto his lap. "Okay. We'll start simple first. Once I arrived in Tampa, I did some initial digging. I stopped by a couple group homes, adoption centers, few churches. I asked about social workers who dealt with babies, specifically men, since that was the only lead I had from what your mom told us," Luis said, nodding toward me.

I nodded back. "Yeah, she said all they knew was a guy had dropped me off at the adoption agency."

"Right. That little tidbit helped a lot actually. Apparently less than fifteen percent of all social workers in the country are male. That means a guy should probably stick out and be memorable, right? Well, he was. The story gets a little sticky, though."

"Sticky how?" Nico asked.

"Well, there are social workers who specialize in shifter babies. Not every shifter clan is as well off as we are. Lots of them are poor. For richer packs, there are always mated couples who can't seem to conceive. There's an undercurrent of—for want of a better word— *sold* children."

"What?" I was horrified.

Luis made an apologetic face and shrugged. "It's difficult. The parents have no money and no way of providing for their child. They sell the kid to a family who they know will give the child everything they can't, and they get a nice chunk of change to try and better themselves. I see both sides of it."

"Does this happen with humans?" I asked.

"Not usually. Shifter communities are way more insular. We have our own doctors, our own internal laws and ways of policing ourselves. It's much easier for a shifter child to change hands than a human child simply because there's more red tape in the human world. Anyway, as I was saying, I think I found the guy your mom was talking about."

Nico and I both leaned forward, drawn into the story. It was interesting on multiple levels. One, because it dealt directly with me. Two, hearing about all this was like learning a big secret about the world. As awful as some of it was, it was exciting to learn.

"There was apparently a social worker in the Tampa area named Kenneth Reid. He was the go-to guy for handling shifter babies. He had lots of contacts with local shifter clans and was pretty well-liked in his agency, so no one ever looked into his shady dealings. I found these…" He pulled two documents out of his file folder and handed them over. "In that one, there are some descriptions of an unborn baby girl. No name, just a due date and the address of a shifter clinic. The due date is about nine days before your birthday, Maddy."

I stared at the paper. It was basically an email with almost no information on it. "What is this supposed to be?"

"I found it in an ancient filing cabinet in the bowels of the agency Reid worked for. There were two dozen more for different babies. I think this was a simple description that he could use to find takers for the babies when they came. The other paper is the one that's even more interesting."

I glanced at the other document. It looked like a contract. I read it twice to be sure I understood what it was saying. It more or less promised the unborn baby girl to Kenneth Reid.

Luis pointed at the paper. "That is the very last thing I found from Kenneth Reid. No other papers, no other documents. His employment record ended not long afterward. Once *this* transaction was completed, he vanished. I think this contract is about you, Maddy. If you are who we believe you are, it must have been incredibly dangerous for this guy to do what he did." He pulled a third sheet of paper out and handed it over. "This is your birth certificate."

I pulled the paper from his hand greedily, desperate to see it. At the top was my name, Maddison, but the last name was different. It said Samuels. Maddison Samuels? That was my real name? On the line with the mother's name were two words. My breath caught in my throat as I read the name. My birth mother. The woman who had carried me for nine months and birthed me. Gabriella Karson.

Luis pointed to the top of the paper. "This is a shifter clinic, which is weird, because your birth mother wasn't a shifter." He pulled yet another sheet of paper out. "This is your biological mother's birth certificate. Human. And this clinic? It shut down and all staff members disappeared less than a week after you were born."

A chill ran up my spine. It was like something out of a movie. This couldn't be real life, could it? I turned the birth certificate around. "I don't see a father on this."

Luis nodded. "I think she knew you were going to be targeted, so she didn't put anything on the certificate. It looks like she had good reason to be afraid." He opened his laptop. "I used her name and the area to find out where she went to high school, which led me to finding these."

He turned the computer around and clicked to expand an image. It was the smiling face of a beautiful girl. It looked like a senior picture from a yearbook. I looked into her face and felt a twinge in my chest. My birth mother. I had her eyes.

"This is her. I got the school to let me in and scanned some images from the library where I found the yearbooks. It gets more interesting." He started clicking through more images. They showed the woman and another boy. My jaw fell open, and Nico whispered a curse.

The guy looked just like me. The resemblance was uncanny. There was no way he wasn't my birth father. One of the images was of the two of them embracing and laughing. Above the picture were block letters that read *Cutest Couple*. Luis pointed at him. "This is David Samuels. Four months before you were born, this happened."

He clicked open a link that brought up an old newspaper story about a high-school graduate who had been found murdered in an alley only a mile from the school. There were lots of quotes from friends and family. Beside the headline was a close-up of David Samuels with a huge smile on his face. Again, I had that strange sense of dissociation. I had a father, the one who raised me and loved me, but this was the man who'd helped *make* me. I shared his DNA. I had his facial features and dark hair. This man was my father, too. It was so strange to finally see him, and bittersweet to know that I'd never get to meet him. Knowing he was dead didn't hit me the same as it would have if my dad had died, but I still felt a deep, weary sadness. It was especially tragic looking at how happy he'd seemed to be in life.

"This is the heir of the Edemas family bloodline. I think someone figured it out and killed him because of it," Luis said. "He was nineteen when he died, and your bio mom had just turned eighteen when she gave birth to you. She was young and terrified. The love of her life had just been killed, and the baby she carried was likely to be a target. I don't know if David Samuels knew his lineage, but from what Gabriella did to hide you, I think he did and told her about it. She gave you up to save you. It was done out of love," he finished, his voice gentle and quiet.

I nodded. "I think you're right." I shook my head, confused and overwhelmed. "How the hell did you figure all this out?"

Luis cleared his throat and glanced at Nico before answering. "It's kind of my gig. I'm a private investigator. I've got contacts and experience doing stuff like this. As good as I am, though, this was still pretty hard to dig up.

I'm still looking into your birth father, but I'm positive he was killed because of the Hollander lineage. It was the royal family who found him and had him killed. I don't think they ever found out about the girlfriend and baby, otherwise they'd have hunted you down before you ever even learned to walk."

"What about Gabriella? Where is she now? Can...could I try to meet her?" I asked. The idea suddenly started building in intensity in my mind.

Luis glanced away, his face falling. "I don't think that'll happen. The last thing I found for her was her name on an organ donor list. She needed a transplant, and everything I could find seemed to point toward her not getting it. I'm pretty sure she's gone. I'm still checking on her, though. There could be a chance some records weren't updated...I'm not holding out hope, but I'm still looking."

I sank back into the couch. Suddenly, a deep and exhausting weariness washed over me. I'd napped, but I still felt like I'd been going for days. There was so much to think about. I'd found my birth parents, seen their faces, and found out their names. All that should have been exciting, but instead, it only filled me with sadness. They were both dead. David had died because some weird royal shifters had decided he was dangerous. Gabriella had to give up her child to keep her safe. I wondered if she'd actually died of a broken heart. I couldn't imagine giving away a child, never knowing what happened to her. To never see her smile, hear her cry. No first steps, no twinkling eyes on Christmas morning. It had to have weighed on her.

"Anyway, that's all I've got for now," Luis said, standing.

Nico stood and gave him a quick hug. "Thanks, bro."

"I'm gonna head out unless you need anything else."

"We're good. See you tomorrow?"

Luis nodded and headed for the door. Nico showed

him out and locked the door behind him. He came back over and plopped down on the couch next to me. He rubbed my thigh and let me sit in silence for a few minutes before speaking. "How are you? After all that?"

I sighed and gave a one-shouldered shrug. "It's a lot to process." I leaned forward and grabbed the file folder Luis had left. It had printouts of all the yearbook photos of my parents. I flipped through and couldn't help but laugh at some of them. They looked so young and in love. So much promise and happiness ripped away for something so crazy.

Nico pointed to a picture. "I still can't believe how much you look like your dad."

"Yeah. It's crazy. I never knew them. Never even saw their faces until today, but I already miss them. Is that stupid?"

Nico shook his head. "No. Especially now that you've learned they didn't give you away for no reason. Your mom tried to save you. I think if your dad hadn't died, your life would have been really different."

"I would have never had my current parents. That's...God, there's no way any of this could have played out without some kind of tragedy."

"Well, now we've at least got some answers. We have a place to start. Luis will try to find this Kenneth guy. The fact that they never found him dead means he probably went into hiding. If we find him, we get even closer to the truth."

"Yeah, you're right. It's all going to play out the way it's supposed to. All I can do is go along for the ride."

Nico leaned over and kissed me. A soft, lingering kiss on the lips that almost completely pulled the stress from my body. He pulled away after a few seconds and looked me in the eyes. "We'll figure out all of it. I promise you that. Until then, I'm going to protect you. I promised to keep you safe, and I keep my promises. I'm not afraid of a royal family that hasn't mattered in hundreds of years. They won't take you from me. I'll do everything I can to make sure we get to have our happily ever after."

Chapter 16 - Nico

The day before, a guy had brought in a 1960 Porsche 911 Coupe, and all my guys knew I'd want to work on it. I jumped at the chance, since we didn't often get rare, mint-condition cars in the shop. Most of what we did were newer custom cars. This one probably cost over a hundred thousand dollars. I called Gabriel to come over and hang with Maddy before giving her a quick kiss and heading to the shop.

The thing was amazing. As soon as I walked in and saw it, I was in love. Bright candy-apple red, fully restored, custom rims—it was a thing of beauty. The guy who'd brought it in said the engine kept misfiring. It sounded like a pretty simple fix—spark plugs and ignition coil being the top two candidates. I rolled up my sleeves, put the car on the lift, and got to work. It was a good way to distract myself while I waited for Felipe's call.

He'd been working back channels to get a meeting set up with me and Javi. I needed to talk to him face to face. To let him know, in no uncertain terms, that he needed to back the fuck off. It was probably pointless, but he needed to understand my position and the danger he was in. If he tried to touch Maddy, I wouldn't hesitate to rip his throat out.

The spark plugs looked fine, as did the distributor cap. I followed the chain to the carburetor, and then the coil. I was right about the coil being bad.

I was elbow-deep in the replacement when Felipe called. I nearly dropped my wrench when his number popped up. I knew what it meant, and the anxiety was already building inside me.

I put my tools down and answered. "Talk to me."

"Hey, Nico. I finally got a hold of one of Javi's nephews. I sweet-talked him into giving me his cell number. Javi actually took my call."

"And?"

"Meeting is set for today. One hour in the parking lot of the grocery store downtown. Public, but not *too* public. Far end of the lot, away from most of the parking and the entrance. I already called the other guys. We'll be nearby, hidden away in case things go sideways."

My heart was beating heavily in my chest. "Alright. I'll finish up here and head that way. Try to get there early."

"Good deal. If things go well, you won't see us, but we'll be there," Felipe said.

"Later."

Shoving the phone back in my pocket, I went back to work. The grocery store was only a ten-minute walk from my shop. My concentration went to shit, and it took fifteen minutes longer than it should have to finish the repair.

Once I was done, I headed out to my car and drove to the grocery store. The ten-minute walk was only a two-minute drive. A text came through from Felipe as I pulled in, letting me know he had eyes on me. Javi was nowhere in sight, so I got out, leaned against the SUV, and waited.

The waiting went on for longer than it should have. The time for the meet arrived, and Javi had yet to show up. I gritted my teeth. It was obvious what he was doing, and it pissed me off. There was no doubt he was coming. He wouldn't have agreed on the phone and then not show up. Javi would have just told Felipe to go fuck himself. No, he was making me wait on purpose in a roundabout way to assert his dominance. A true alpha didn't wait for anyone. That was the message he was sending. It was loud, clear, and irritating.

Ten minutes after the scheduled time, Javi's muscle car came roaring into the parking lot. It took everything I had not to sneer in disgust as he parked and got out of his car. I needed this to be diplomatic. I had to push my anger below the surface.

Javi's salt-and-pepper hair was pulled back into a ponytail, and he wore his usual leather jacket. I never knew how he survived the Florida heat and humidity with that damned jacket on. It was almost fall and still over ninety degrees.

He nodded to me. "Nico."

"Javi."

"Well, I'm here. I don't have a lot of time. What are we discussing?"

I sighed. "You know exactly what we're talking about."

Javi raised an eyebrow and ran a hand through his gray goatee. "Elaborate, please."

"Stay away from Maddy," I said, forgoing any more preamble. Javi's eyes narrowed at the mention of her name, but he didn't respond. "Maddy is mine. I'm going to claim her, and that makes her part of the Lorenzo pack. Now and forever, she'll have our protection."

"Claim her?!" Javi shouted. The change on his face was so pronounced that it startled me. "You're going to try and claim that *thing*? You goddamned fool. You have no clue what she's capable of."

"Watch your mouth when you talk about her," I hissed, pointing a finger at him.

"You idiot!" Javi raged. "Do you have any idea what she is? Or are you just trying to get some hot little piece of ass?"

I didn't justify that with an answer. Instead, I relaxed back against my car, crossing my arms. We glared at each other for several seconds, Javi's anger growing hotter by the moment.

"Okay," Javi said, raising his hands. "Let's lay it all out. Maybe you really are that dense. She's a monster, Nico. An abomination that can destroy us all. The blood that flows through her veins is tainted." He pointed in the general direction of the Lorenzo compound. "That *woman* you and your family are harboring? She is a beast unlike anything you've ever seen. If you're stupid enough to awaken the monster inside her, then you deserve the shitstorm that'll follow."

"All I hear is an old man who's scared of a woman. Is that what this is, Javi? Is that what your clan is scared of?"

Javi clenched his hands into fist. "Goddammit! Listen to me. Her great-grandfather was a carrier of the blood of Edemas. You know what that means? I know your father told you the stories. Everyone does."

This was information Luis hadn't uncovered yet. I wanted to hear everything he knew, so I nodded for him to go on.

"The grandmother was a half-breed. The bloodline is there, but her father was born with human genes and her mother was fully human. That means the Edemas line is diluted."

"I'm gonna stop you there," I said. "If the bloodline is so diluted, why is Maddy such a threat to you?"

"That's what I'm trying to tell you, goddammit. It's the reason she can't be allowed to survive. If she were to mate with a shifter, there is a chance the dormant beast inside her will react to her mate. It will awaken the latent genes. She could become a shifter."

I'd assumed as much, but still didn't think it was reason enough to kill an innocent person. The legends about the cruelty of Edemas probably had some truth to them, but that didn't mean every single descendant was some psychotic monster that had to be wiped out.

Javi jabbed a finger toward me. "We can't allow her to become a wolf. She needs to be destroyed. If there was even a one-percent chance she could go on to have a child that was an alpha, then the werewolves could return. You can't let that happen…unless you want to risk the lives of your entire clan."

Rage swept across my body. I took two heavy steps toward Javi. "Is that a threat?"

"No. You're confused. That's not what I mean. I'm not the threat, that woman is. If the Hollander bloodline was to be restrengthened and the werewolves come back, she'll be the main reason we are destroyed and subjugated. It will be a bloodbath."

My mind went to Maddy. Nothing about her seemed like the type of person who would go mad with power. She was kind and gentle. Everything Javi believed was urban legend, paranoia, and bullshit. "Listen, I know exactly what Maddy is capable of. She's none of the things you're talking about. The blood is so diluted, even you're sitting here talking about 'maybe' and 'possibly.' You have no idea what you're talking about. You even said her father was a half-breed and her mother was a human. What could you possibly fear from someone like that?"

Veins stood out on Javi's neck and he slammed his palms into his thighs in frustration. "She's not what you think she is. Blood doesn't lie. You're blind."

"Blind or not, Maddy is mine. Tell your puppet masters they need to stop pulling your strings. If this *royal family* or whatever keeps going after her, they'll be in for a fight they'll regret."

Javi's eyes widened in surprise and he took a step back. Apparently, he hadn't thought we'd know about the people commanding him. He'd thought it was a secret only he knew. He yanked his car door open. "Fine. Have it your way. Don't say I didn't warn you, Nico."

He sped away, not sparing me another look. I watched him go, my mind processing the information. I didn't need any more proof for who and what Maddy was. But I couldn't help but wonder if Javi's story was true. Had it really been centuries since any of Edemas's descendants could shift? It seemed crazy that none of them had mated with a full shifter. Shifters made up a full third of the earth's population. The odds that it had never happened over the course of three centuries seemed outlandish.

I nodded to myself. Javi was full of shit. Maddy wasn't dangerous, and I'd prove it. I pulled out my cell and called Luis.

"I'm here. Are you good? We just watched Javi drive away like a bat out of hell."

"I'm fine. He's still on his bullshit. Listen, we need to dig into Maddy's paternal family history. We need to figure out everything we can about David and his ancestors. Every resource we have, spare no expense. Buy what you need, bribe people if you need access to records, whatever it takes."

There was a slight pause before Luis responded. "Are we okay here?"

"Yes. I need to prove that Javi is full of crap. Get to work on it, and let me know if you find anything or need help."

"On it, brother."

By the time I got down the street to where the guys had been holed up watching the meet-up, Luis had already gone off to start his research. Felipe got out of Sebastian's car and got into mine.

Sebastian leaned out his window. "What did that jackass have to say?"

I shook my head. "Not much other than he thought Maddy was some kind of monster that needed to be put down. He was talking about her like she was a rabid dog."

Sebastian lip curled in disgust. "What a dick."

"Yeah," Felipe muttered. "Before all this, I had a pretty good idea he was a piece of shit. This situation with Maddy has removed all doubt."

"Speaking of," I said. "I want to get back home to her. Let's go."

We walked in the house, and the first thing we noticed was the cackling laughter coming from the living room. Felipe glanced at me and gave me a questioning frown.

"I told you!" Gabriel shouted, still laughing, "It's one of the best comedies of the nineties, I told you."

Felipe and I walked down the hallway and found Maddy on the love seat, her face red with laughter. Gabriel sat on the couch opposite her, seeming to revel in her enjoyment. On the TV was some kind of slapstick comedy with some guys who used to be on *Saturday Night Live* back twenty-five years ago.

"Having fun?" I asked.

Gabe and Maddy both turned to see us and burst out laughing again, Maddy covering her face. I couldn't help but smile back. She was beautiful when she laughed. My heart skipped a beat. There wasn't a cruel or malicious bone in her body. Regardless of what blood ran in her veins, this was not someone who would end the world.

"Well, if it's that funny, can we join you?" I said.

Maddy patted the seat next to her. I took a seat, putting my arm around her. Felipe sat next to Gabe and put an arm around him. My brother shrugged him off. "What the fuck, bro?"

Felipe grinned, nodding toward us. "I was just trying to fit in."

Gabe sneered at him. "If that's what you want, you need to pony up the big dough. I don't put out on the first date unless it's for a sugar daddy."

We all laughed again and settled in to watch the rest of the movie. After five minutes, Maddy leaned in close to my ear. "Is everything okay?"

As an answer, I kissed the top of her head and nodded. "Everything's fine."

It might not have been the full truth. We were in danger. The world was balanced on a knife's edge. But at that moment, everything was perfect. I'd do everything I could to keep it that way.

Chapter 17 - Maddy

Nico was at work again, and he'd said he would be late. His auto shop had gotten a new contract for servicing the county post office vehicles. All twenty vehicles had to have their oil changed, tires rotated, and general tune-ups done by the next day. He'd said he probably wouldn't be home until after nine.

Sebastian was here, but he'd brought his new motorcycle and was in the garage working on that. The mudroom door was open, so if I needed him, I only had to shout, but I was starting to feel lonely.

It had been over a week since I'd seen Abi, so I texted her to see if she wanted to come over. Her response had been enthusiastic, and she told me she'd be there in thirty minutes. I grinned and put my phone away, then went to let Sebastian know.

"Hey," I said, knocking on the doorframe.

Sebastian was on his knees, trying to remove some type of chain from the engine of the motorcycle. He glanced up when I called him. "Yeah?"

"I've got a friend coming over. Abi, from the bar. I wanted to let you know so you wouldn't freak out when she got here."

"Oh." Sebastian smiled. "That's cool. No problem."

I went back to the living room and read my book until I heard the knock at the door. Abi came in holding a massive bottle of red wine. "Refreshments," she called as she held the bottle over her head.

"Oh, thank God. I could use a drink."

"Well, get the glasses, sister," Abi said as she peeled the foil off the top of the bottle.

A few minutes later, we were on the back porch, sipping wine and watching the sun go down. Abi glanced around at the house for about the tenth time. "So, how is it living in a mansion?"

I scoffed and took another sip of wine. "It's not a mansion. It's just a big house."

"How many square feet is this thing?"

"I don't know, I think Nico said it was like six thousand-ish."

Abi raised an eyebrow. "Mansion."

"Whatever. It doesn't even have a pool."

"No, but they have a neighborhood pool. I saw it as I came through the security gate."

I waved a hand at her. Who cared how big the house was? I'd lived in a place less than a quarter this size for years. My parents' house had been half this size. It didn't matter how big a place was. It was more about who you shared it with. That's what made a house a home.

"You're thinking," Abi said. She raised an eyebrow. "Are you imagining Nico naked?"

I almost spat my wine out. "What?"

"You heard me. Girl, you are literally dating a *Chippendale* dancer. Gorgeous face, like zero-percent body fat, big sexy muscles. Not only that he seems like an actual good and sweet guy. You're like…super lucky."

I blushed. "It's nice. I have to admit that. He's pretty awesome."

"Okay, the big question," Abi said, leaning in. "How big?"

"What?"

Abi rolled her eyes. "Don't play coy. How big? Seriously."

"You mean—"

"His wang, crotch sausage, pleasure tube, muscle snake, whatever you wanna call it. How big?"

I blushed furiously, giggling. "Do you really want to know?"

"Maddy, I haven't been laid in six months. If I can't live vicariously through my best friend, my lady bits might shrivel up and float away."

"Well," I said, glancing over at her. I raised my eyebrows and gave a massive, toothy smile.

Abi's jaw dropped. "For real? He's got a big ol' porn star dick, doesn't he?"

"That's all I'm giving you. I'll simply say that it's satisfying."

Abi sat back in her chair and took several more sips of her wine. I could tell she was contemplating something. I wondered whether she'd asked me what he was like in bed, but what she did ask surprised me.

"Maddy, why did these guys come to your rescue?"

I chewed at my lower lip and stared down at my wine glass. "What do you mean?"

"I know you got attacked by shifters, but...bringing you here to live? Twenty-four hour bodyguards? It's a little weird for a robbery gone wrong."

It was a lot. Most people wouldn't believe the story, but Abi was my best friend. If I couldn't tell her what was going on, there was no one I could tell.

I sighed and put my wine glass down. "Are you still sober enough for this?"

Abi sat her own glass down and leaned forward, eager and excited. "Spill it."

I took a deep breath. Where to begin? My family? Did I go chronologically? Or did I start with the night of the attack? I decided it would be easier for her to understand if I started from the night the shifters walked into the bar. Tell her everything in the order I learned them. I began, and though I wasn't a great storyteller, I did a pretty good job. Abi gasped and cursed at all the parts I thought I would have if I'd heard the story myself. I finished with the story we learned about my birth parents. By the time I was done, my mouth was so dry from talking so much that I grabbed my glass of wine and drained it.

Abi sat in stunned silence, trying to take in everything she'd heard. Finally, she shook her head and looked at me. "So...you're like...long-lost royalty? Literally a missing princess or queen or whatever?"

"I don't know that I'd go that far."

Abi gasped. "Holy shit. You're like the shifter Anastasia."

I snorted a laugh. "Nothing that dramatic."

Later I got Abi a cup of coffee to help her sober up before she drove home. Nico got back about ten minutes after she left, and Sebastian took off on his newly repaired motorcycle.

"You got home early," I said. It was only seven.

Nico shrugged. "Surprisingly, the postal trucks weren't a complete disaster. I'd assumed the worst. I'm starving. Do you want to get something to eat?"

"Sure," I said. Any chance to get out of the house was a welcome change of pace, but it didn't ease my worries. "Are you sure it's okay? I mean…with Javi and his clan being out there?"

Nico nodded. "I made sure Javi understood. He got the message loud and clear. Go on. Get changed. Don't let him worry you. I'll be right by your side the whole time."

Nico took me to an Italian place downtown. I'd been there before and loved it. I was a little on edge the whole night, though. Nico had given me his word that Javi would stay away, at least for a while, but it still made me nervous. After the shooting at the diner, nowhere but here felt safe. To Nico's credit, he helped take my mind off things.

It was like a normal date. We talked about the mundane things new couples always talked about. He told me about his childhood, being the heir alpha and all that entailed. I told him about growing up with my own family. How it had been simple. Camping trips, Disney trips, beach trips—all the normal family stuff. Then the revelation that I was adopted when I'd just started high school. It had thrown me for a loop and made life difficult for a year or two.

After dinner, Nico took me for a walk through downtown, and we talked some more. It was one of the most romantic evenings of my life. I couldn't even explain why. A small part of my mind told me it was the bond we shared. We both knew we were fated mates. That had to have played into the bliss of being with him, but I didn't care. All I wanted was to keep walking down the sidewalk, holding his hand, and talking.

It was almost eleven by the time we got home, and I had a huge smile on my face. The night couldn't have gone better. I was still a little buzzed from the cocktails we'd had at a classy little bar downtown. My whole body had a warm fuzzy feel to it as we strolled in the door from the garage. Nico caught my arm and spun me around. I was startled, but when he kissed me, the surprise melted away.

His hands slid down to my hips and he pulled away. "I wanted to say I really love having you around."

"I love being around," I murmured.

My skin was hot and the voice in my head was chattering away. I'd come to the conclusion that it was my wolf—dormant, but still very much alive. It wanted Nico. Desired him in a way I couldn't even understand. It wanted to claim him, to mark him as mine. The alcohol was lowering my inhibitions just enough for the creature living inside me to start taking over. Carnal thoughts exploded through my mind, thoughts of what I could do to Nico, thoughts of what he could do to me. Warmth radiated from between my legs, and I was dripping wet already. The quick and powerful reaction was a little startling.

"Are you okay?" Nico asked.

I hesitated for an instant before speaking. "I...there's a voice in my head telling me to...take you. It wants you. It's scary because I don't know if it's me that's thinking that or some *other* thing."

Nico's eyes grew intense as I spoke. "Don't ever turn from your instincts. The voice you hear is dormant, but the feelings are natural." He leaned close, his lips almost touching mine. "You're mine. I'm yours. Don't hold back." His hand slipped lower, cupping my ass. "Don't ever hold back."

The words seemed to tip a scale in my head. One moment, I was scared to give up control to the thing in my mind. The next, every barrier in my mind was torn down. All the hesitation, fear, worry, and shame drained away. It left me standing there, wanting to take him. To take control like I never had before. I wanted to have him in every way imaginable.

I pressed my lips to his, sliding my tongue into his mouth. I pressed against him, pushing him out toward the kitchen, then toward the couch. I shoved him down onto it, and the look of surprise in his eyes somehow made me even wetter.

I tore my shirt over my head and stripped my bra off. Nico saw what I was doing and started pulling his own clothes off. Excitement flooded my body, like hot lava searing through every vein. The crotch of my panties were soaked through when I peeled them off and tossed them to the side. Nico was naked by the time I collapsed to my knees and grabbed his thick, twitching cock. I locked my eyes on his and slid the full length of him into my mouth.

"Shit," Nico whispered, laying his head back onto the couch.

The hot, thick flesh in my mouth sent my wolf into a frenzy. It was the closest I'd ever felt to her. The being who shared my mind told me to take this man. Take him, make his eyes roll up in his head. To give him something so amazing, he'd never look at another woman, never even think of another woman.

I tightened my lips around the head of his cock and sucked at him, slipping my tongue back and forth across his flesh. One hand caressed his balls, the other stroked his shaft. He was vibrating beneath me. Small whimpers and whispers of pleasure fell from Nico's lips. My pussy felt hot, my clit was engorged and aching. I sucked at him for several more seconds before I couldn't take it anymore.

I stood, turning around, then lowered myself onto his cock. Nico gasped as I moved against him, my body feeling completely full and whole. His thickness nearly split me in two, but the voice in my head urged me on. I leaned back into him, feeling the heat of his chest and stomach on my back. Nico's hands rose and caressed my breasts. I looked down, watching him gently pinch my nipples, rolling the dark brown flesh between his fingers. It sent electric tingles down to my crotch. Nico slid a hand down my stomach and stopped at my clit. His fingers rubbed and slipped across the wet flesh, a sigh of ecstasy hissed out of my lips.

Nico's hips thrust up, slamming the full length of himself into me. Every movement was like a shot of adrenaline. Every motion he made was somehow both too much *and* not enough. I growled and stood, pulling him free. Turning, I straddled him, reaching between my legs to slide him into me again. I looked into his eyes. "Fuck me, Nico."

He growled, grabbing my hips and ramming into me. My head hung down, pleasure rocking through me as he moved. I kissed and sucked at his throat, leaving hickeys across his neck, collarbone, and chest. My breasts bounced and swayed as he had his way with me. I ground my hips onto his cock in time with his rhythm, bringing us each closer to orgasm. Sweat sheened our skin, both of us desperate for what was about to happen.

Nico wound a hand into my hair and tugged gently, pulling my face up so he could look into my eyes. "Look at me when you come. Look into my eyes," he whispered between grunts of exertion.

As though he could read my mind or sense the changes in my body, I could feel the building pressure, the aching rise of pleasure deep in my pelvis, tendrils starting to arch out into my limbs. I trembled, my breathing now only fast gasps. My nails dug into his arms, like I was afraid I was going to fly off his body at any second. I looked deep into his eyes as the final cresting wave crashed over me. Explosive, deep, and earth-shattering, the euphoria erupted across me. I clenched my jaw as it burst through me.

Nico hadn't finished, though. Even in my state of bliss, the wolf still urged me on to finish him.

I shoved his shoulders back into the couch and slammed myself down on him. The look on his face was one of abject happiness, pleasure, and surprise. Over and over, I fucked him, until his mouth dropped open into the *oh* of a silent scream. His face went red, and with a grunt, he came. His cock twitched and spasmed within me. I rode him until he was fully spent and gasping for breath.

I collapsed against his chest. Nico wrapped his arms around me and we sat, stroking each other as we silently enjoyed the afterglow of our lovemaking.

Chapter 18 - Nico

The next morning, I woke up and found my neck and chest covered in hickeys. I looked like a high schooler after a horny night out with his girl. I wasn't ashamed of them; I saw them as badges of pride. They were physical symbols of how much Maddy had wanted me.

Maddy was already up, doing some of her laundry when I got downstairs. "Hey, sexy," I said as I walked up behind her.

"Morning. Are you all rested?"

I grinned at her. "Barely. I'm heading down the street to Luis's place to see the guys. I'll be back in a little while. I texted Mateo, and he'll be outside mowing the yard. He'll watch the place while I'm gone."

"Okay. See you in a little bit."

I kissed her and left. As soon as the door was closed, my wolf wanted me to go back to her. After the night before, I'd expected Maddy to be more chipper, but she'd seemed a little down. My wolf wanted me to go check on her, but that would have seemed overbearing. At least, that's what I thought it would seem like.

I walked down to Luis's house. Everyone else was already there. It was a little weird, especially for Sebastian, who didn't enjoy getting out of bed before ten every morning. As I walked in, the first thing I heard was Sebastian himself.

"Oh shit! Did you get into a fight with a vacuum cleaner?" He ran up to me and pulled my collar down, revealing more of the marks Maddy had left on me.

I slapped his hand away and straightened my shirt. "Get the hell off me."

"Good lord, man. What did she do to you?" Felipe asked.

I grinned at them. "You boys wouldn't understand. Gotta get hair on your balls first. Once that happens for you, come on over and talk. Daddy Nico will explain the birds and the bees then."

"Ha," Luis said dryly. "Can we get started?"

"Yeah, sure."

We sat and discussed the security measures for our neighborhood. Things seemed pretty buttoned-up, and I didn't think there was anything more we could do. Luis updated me with the info he was researching, but he didn't have a lot.

"I have a call out to a buddy of mine. He's a retired cop from Tampa. He lives in New Smyrna now, but he still has contacts. He's trying to look into Maddy's grandfather and stuff. Won't know anything for a few days."

I sighed. "Okay. We can only do so much, I guess."

"Speaking of doing," Sebastian said, nodding at my neck again. "Seems like Maddy's starting to connect with her wolf, maybe? Looks like she's getting…aggressive. Even if she can't shift, maybe she's, like, becoming one with that part of herself."

"I've actually thought about that," I said.

"And what did you think?" Felipe asked.

I tapped my finger on my knee. "I think maybe it's because she's been around us so much."

"Huh?" Sebastian looked confused.

"Dude, wolves are pack creatures. There's a reason shifters live in communes and neighborhoods like ours. We thrive on being around others of our kind. She's been living with us for almost a month. That, plus the fact that we're fated mates, could mean the wolf is trying to break free."

"So does that mean she might actually become a shifter if you guys complete the mating bond?"

My mind drifted back to the night before. I'd never had sex like that before. We'd both been so free and aggressive. Open. Wanting. We could have done anything to each other and we would have loved it. I remembered her riding me, her back against my chest. I'd been in the midst of losing my mind in lust, and I'd contemplated giving her my bite right then and there. I'd even picked out the spot. An area right between her shoulder blades. Her skin had been sweaty and the muscles flexing. I could almost taste her. I'd tamped down that instinct.

I wanted to claim her, but we couldn't jump to that stage yet. It was something that needed to be discussed. A decision that big couldn't be made at the drop of a hat. Plus, even though I didn't think Javi was right, I didn't want to put Maddy or others into even more danger. As hellbent as Javi and his crew were to kill her, if her dormant wolf actually did wake up…I didn't want to think what they'd do to go after her.

I shook my head and shrugged. "I don't know, honestly. All I know is that anything might happen. Maybe nothing will, maybe she does become a shifter. I'm not ready to cross that bridge yet."

The conversation shifted to more banal things. Sports, cars, food, all the stuff we usually talked about when we were together. With nothing important left to talk about, I said my goodbyes and headed back home.

I walked and breathed in the humid Florida air. It was a beautiful day, and even after everything that had happened with Javi, I couldn't help but think things would work out okay. I waved to Mateo as I walked up the path. He wiped sweat from his forehead and waved back. "Hey, brother."

"Hey. Is Maddy all good?"

Mateo nodded and grinned. "She's fine. I checked on her once. Have fun in there."

I frowned. "What's that supposed to mean?"

He shook his head and started loading the mower back into my garage. "Not what you think."

Without another word, I unlocked the door and went inside. As soon as I stepped into the kitchen, I understood what he'd meant. It wasn't some dirty joke, it was a cryptic warning. It was just like one of my brothers to leave me hanging, then stand back and watch the fun. Instead of finding Maddy, my mother was waiting for me in the kitchen.

"Uh…hey."

"Hello, Nico," Mom said as she thumbed through a magazine.

"Where's Maddy?" I glanced around and didn't see her.

Mom nodded toward the stairs. "Said she had a headache. Went for a nap."

Turning on my heel, I headed straight toward the stairs to go check on her. I only made it three steps before Mom called to me. "Nico, I need to speak with you."

I closed my eyes and took a deep breath before turning around. "About what, Mother?"

"Don't '*mother*' me. Come sit down."

This was not going to be good. I knew how these talks went. I'd had them my entire life. When I was a kid, it was about school, rules, and picking on my brothers. Now that I was older, it was always general life things. My shop, the pack, when I was going to settle down with a mate. It was never fun, and I had the feeling this might be the least fun talk yet.

Not wanting to fight, I walked over and sat on the stool across from her.

Mom closed her magazine and folded her hands on the table. "I don't want to sound rude, but something seems to be off about Maddy."

I gritted my teeth but stayed calm. "What do you mean? Off how?"

She lifted her hands an inch and flopped them back down. "I'm not totally sure. It seems like she's struggling with something internally. Not her injuries or things like that, something up here," she said, and tapped her temple. "She was whispering to herself. She seemed frustrated and exhausted. Finally, she excused herself with that excuse of having a headache." Mom twisted a ring on her finger, a tic she'd had as long as I'd been alive. It meant she was worried. "Nico." She glanced around, as though someone might hear. "Have you ever smelled Maddy?"

I stiffened at the mention of it. It was something that was so slight, even the other guys hadn't really noticed it until I pointed it out to them. Mom had always had an incredible sense of smell, though. Stronger than almost anyone else I'd ever known. I should have realized she would have noticed it. I stayed silent, letting her go on.

"Something just seems...off. That's the only thing I can say about it."

It made me feel bad that out of our entire family and all my friends, my mother was one of the only ones out of the loop. That being the case, I still didn't need her pressuring me or Maddy, or trying to pry into our lives.

"Mom, everything is fine."

"Nico, I don't think it is."

"I said, everything is fine." My voice got louder, and I was one step away from being angry.

She seemed to get the hint. She grabbed her magazine and stood. "Okay. I had to tell you what I thought. I can't do more than that." She walked to the door and opened it, then she turned to look back at me. "Be careful, Nico."

Without another word, she walked out, closing the door behind her. I let out a heavy sigh and rubbed my face. That had been more stressful than it needed to be.

Maddy was still upstairs sleeping, so I went to check on her. I found her on her bed, not asleep, a hand to her forehead. I stepped over and sat on the bed, putting a hand on her thigh. "Are you okay?" I asked.

Maddy shook her head. "The voice."

"Huh?"

"The voice in my head. It's getting louder."

She'd mentioned it before, but I wanted to make sure it was what I thought it was. It was probably like the link I had to my wolf. We shared and passed emotions and feelings back and forth to each other, not words, really. If it was something else I wanted to help her. "Can you describe it to me?"

Maddy shook her head. "It's like this tickling at the back of my mind. A whispery voice that isn't mine." She huffed in irritation. "I keep calling it a voice, but it's strong emotions that sort of push me in directions and mess up my head. It's hard to concentrate." She put a hand on either side of her head. "It's like there's pressure building in my head."

That wasn't anything I'd ever experienced before. Maybe it was her dormant wolf recognizing its mate. Wolves became very emotional and insistent when they found their fated mate. It might be acting out because it can't be claimed like it wanted to be. They could even turn feral if the mating bond wasn't enacted in a timely manner. Could a dormant wolf become feral? It made me more desperate to find out about Edemas's descendants. I needed answers to help Maddy.

I slid in close to her and pulled her body into my arms. "We'll figure all this out," I whispered.

Maddy dug her fingers into my arm. "I'm scared, Nico."

I tightened my embrace. "Don't be afraid. I'm here and I've got you."

We sat together for almost thirty minutes, enjoying the silence and darkness. Finally, I heard her breathing grow deep and heavy. I eased her off my lap and nestled her head onto a pillow. She was so exhausted that she didn't even stir as I moved her. Leaving her to rest, I went to my home office and called Luis.

"I'm on the road, what do you need?"

"On the road?" I asked.

"Yeah, got a lead I need to run down."

"Anything you need to tell me?"

"Not yet. Trying to figure all this stuff out about Maddy, too soon to say anything."

"Speaking of, she's not doing well. Her wolf is being...I don't even know how to describe it. It's like it's trying to break through or something. It's making her miserable. Headaches and voices. Honestly, if someone didn't know what was happening, they'd think she had schizophrenia or something. I'm worried as hell about her."

"Don't worry. I'll find you some answers. I'm not going to let you down."

After getting off the phone with Luis, I called my dad. I needed all the advice I could get.

"Hey, boy. Your mom came home a little irritated after visiting."

I rolled my eyes. "Dad, I feel bad about that, but I've got bigger things going on."

He seemed to hear the worry in my voice and dropped it. "What's wrong?"

It took a few minutes, but I explained what was going on with Maddy. By the time I was done, I was more worried than before I started talking.

Dad took a deep breath and sighed. "I have to be honest, I've never witnessed or even heard of a dormant wolf. You and I both know that half-breeds are pretty taboo, but they still happen quite a bit. Even they can shift, though. Her shifter blood is pretty diluted, but the bloodline she comes from may be part of the cause. Edemas and his entire line before him were the strongest and most powerful shifters to ever live. It would make sense that an…uh…anomaly like the Hollander line would maybe cause some weird things down the genetic trail."

"Does that mean things will get better or worse?"

"I can't even begin to guess. Edemas was the strongest of all his family, all the way back to the beginning. He was drunk with power, crazy with it. Son, I don't want to scare you, but that blood *is* in Maddy. Even if it is diluted, her wolf will be incredibly strong. Now that it's been recognized by its mate, it's probably fighting for dominance. It's like a caged animal gnashing its teeth to be free. A caged dog will tear its mouth to bloody shreds trying to rip its way out of a prison. Who the hell knows what will happen whenever that creature is finally set loose."

Dad's words echoed across my mind. The warning from Javi was still crystal-clear. He'd warned me things would get out of hand. That I had no idea what I was getting into.

I wondered if there was some truth to what he'd said.

Chapter 19 - Maddy

When I woke up the next morning, I felt more rested than I had in days. The wolf was still there, a murmur beneath the surface. Almost like being in a room where a TV was on but the volume was so low, you couldn't make out what it was saying. It was still weird, but it made me much more functional. I was probably pushing things, but before lunch, I'd started to get the itch. I wanted to go back to work. I'd always been a workaholic, especially once I'd built up my own business. The bar had been closed for a week, and I was dying to get back there.

Nico had come home for lunch and was making us both sandwiches. I decided it was a good time to bring it up. He was opening a bag of chips when I walked in and leaned on the counter.

He glanced over at me and grinned at me. "You look like you want to ask a question."

"How did you know?"

"No clue, but I can tell. What's up?"

I tapped my fingers on the counter, watching as he put a pile of potato chips on each plate. "What would you think about me opening the bar back up? Going back to work?"

Nico didn't even hesitate. "I think it's a great idea. I know you love that place. I'll still make sure you have a guard, though."

I blinked in surprise. I'd really thought it would take a lot more to get him to say yes. "Uh…wow, okay. Yeah, that's fine. I probably wouldn't be comfortable without someone there to watch out for me."

Suddenly, I was giddy. Other than Abi, I hadn't seen any of my team since that last night at the bar. I missed them. It was weird since I was technically their boss, but it was true.

Nico handed me my plate and a bottle of water. "As long as you are comfortable, I'm cool with it. When did you want to open back up? Next weekend?"

"Umm...well, I kinda wanted to do it tonight."

Nico froze, the sandwich halfway to his mouth. "Tonight?" He looked surprised.

I nodded and took my first bite. Through a mouth full of food, I said, "I was gonna text Abi and see if she could check with everyone."

"Crap, okay. Felipe is free. I'll see if he can take you over tonight."

"Sweet." I put my sandwich down and pulled out my phone. My thumbs flew over the screen as I texted Abi, who responded almost immediately.

Me: *Hey! How do you feel about getting back to work tonight? I want to open the bar.*

Abi: *uuuuuuuuhhhhhhh what?*

Me: *You read that right. Do you think everyone else might be free?*

Abi: *I think so, actually. I can start calling them. Are you serious about this? Are you sure you are up to it?*

Me: *Totally. I'll put the announcement on my social media and the media pages for the bar. Do you think you and everyone else can do the same?*

Abi: *On it. I'll start getting a hold of the guys and gals. We'll need to go in early. I bet that place is dusty as shit after being closed a week.*

I closed my messaging app and immediately started posting about the reopening. With each passing second, I felt happier. It took fifteen minutes before I even tried to start eating my lunch again. I usually wasn't this impulsive. Most of the time, I tried to think things through and plan them out a little better. I was sure the wolf had something to do with it, but I didn't care.

Nico walked back over and put his dish in the sink. "Felipe said he was down for tonight."

"Awesome. Can he come over in..." I glanced at the clock on the microwave. It was just past twelve-thirty. "Like thirty minutes?"

Nico's eyes bulged in surprise. "You're going to go in that early?"

"I know, but the place will be a disaster. We'll have to rewash and polish all the glasses, dust the counters and floors. If we want to open at five like usual, it'll take a little extra work."

Nico chuckled and shook his head. "Let me call him back."

Felipe was free, and we got there just after one. Abi and two of the bartenders arrived twenty minutes later. The staff actually seemed excited to be back at work. I hoped they would want to, but I'd been worried they might be a little pissed that I'd closed the place to begin with. Thankfully, none of them seemed the least bit put out by the closure. It made things feel like old times, and before I even realized it, we were open.

The night went like it usually would have. It was busier than I thought it would be, and that helped a lot—the wolf was quieter when I was busy. I bounced all over the place: helping make drinks, running food out, cashing out tabs, and cleaning up. The clientele was typical: folks getting off work and wanting to wind down, groups of friends wanting to relax over a drink together, and the people who always came to places like this looking to get laid.

One of that last type came in around nine. He looked like he was a little younger than me, probably mid-twenties. He was cute, but I could tell just by the way he carried himself that he was out on the prowl, which made him a little more unattractive. I was happy to serve people like him, but there was usually an air of desperation to them that always made me wonder how they ever got lucky.

He came up to me an hour after he got there to get a drink. "Hey there, lady. How are you doing?"

"Doing great. Can I get you a drink?" I asked, barely taking my eyes off the table I was clearing.

"Yeah. Maybe you can give me your number along with it?"

I grinned, honestly thinking it was funny. He definitely couldn't read body language. "Sorry, it's against the rules. I can grab you that drink, though. Beer? Cocktail?"

He grinned drunkenly and leaned in. "*Cock*-tail? Mmmm, you talk dirty for a girl who doesn't want to give up her number."

My good nature was rapidly dwindling. Usually, I was great at dealing with these situations. I was self-aware enough to know that I was attractive. I kept my body in good shape and I was traditionally pretty. I wasn't blind to that when looking in the mirror, so I was used to this. Men were always hitting on me. Most of the time, I was able to pivot away and get things back on track to customer and owner. Easy distinction, easy way to get rid of someone without hurting feelings or losing a customer for good. For some reason, this time, anger built rapidly in me. All I wanted was for this guy to go away.

"Listen, pal, I've got a dick at home to play with. I guarantee it's nicer than yours. So order a drink or leave me alone."

Internally, I was shocked I said something like that. I was never vulgar toward customers. Part of me was mortified that I'd lowered myself to his level. Another part of me was grinning in pride and...growling? The wolf was doing this, I could feel it.

The guy's eyes narrowed, and his grin became less flirty and meaner. "You got a smart mouth on you. Maybe I need to shove something in it," he said, grabbing my arm roughly.

Rage. When I glanced down and saw his hands on me, that was all I could feel. Rage. Red-hot and boiling. Lava-hot and razor-sharp. I looked up at him and his face changed. The look on my face must have been terrifying. My lips peeled back from my teeth. I visualized grabbing the beer stein on the table, slamming it against the wall until I held a jagged glass handle, then shoving it into his throat. The image of him gagging and stumbling back, blood spurting from his mouth and throat, should have horrified me. Instead, it made me excited.

Thankfully, before I could do anything that crazy, a heavy hand slapped down on the guy's shoulder. Felipe stood behind him. He yanked the guy back, and I was released as the creep stumbled away. Felipe twisted his hand into the dude's shirt and grabbed his free arm, yanking it up behind him until the asshole yelped in pain.

"What?" Felipe asked. "You mean you don't like being touched when you don't want to be? Ain't that some hypocritical shit?"

Felipe dragged the guy through the bar and shoved him out the front door. As the door swung closed slowly, I saw the guy stumble to his knees in the parking lot. The bar fell silent, then suddenly the crowd erupted in applause. Felipe grinned and gave everyone a pageant wave as he came back over to me, his expression serious as he got close.

"Are you good? Did that piece of shit hurt you?"

I shook my head, still wondering at how I got so angry. I'd never been so pissed in my life. And that bloody fantasy that had flashed through my mind? What the fuck was that? Never in my life had I visualized killing someone. Not even the guys who'd tried to kill me. Those weren't my thoughts, I realized. The wolf had been the one thinking those things. It scared me more than I could explain, even to myself.

The next hour went by much slower. I did my best to put on a brave face, but I knew I couldn't hang at the bar much longer. I put on my best fake smile and found Abi.

"Whew, busy night, right?" I asked.

"Yeah. Sorry about that guy. I should have found you and warned you. He was hitting on me earlier. I figured turning him down would have shut him up. I guess that was too much to ask for."

"Mm hmm," I said, doing my best to act normal. "Listen, I'm exhausted. Are you good if I head home a little early?"

Abi waved me off. "No problem. It's not too busy now, we should be fine closing up. You need the rest anyway. How are your sides, by the way? Did you get the stitches out yet?"

"Yeah, yeah, all good. I'll find Felipe and let him know. Let the team know they can have a round on the house once you guys close up."

"Sweet," Abi said, smiling, then her eyes narrowed. "Maddy, are you sure you're okay? That douchebag didn't mess you up, did he?"

"I'm fine, seriously."

That wasn't true, of course. I was anything but fine.

Felipe got me home, and I collapsed on the couch. It wasn't even nine yet, and since I was working at the bar, Nico had gone in to do some paperwork and parts ordering. I was still on the couch when he got home. It only took one look at me for him to come running over.

"What's wrong? What happened?" he asked as he sat down beside me.

I explained everything that happened, making sure he understood that it wasn't the guy but my reaction to him that had me so freaked out. My body was actually shaking in fear as I told him. I kept seeing that mental fantasy of me slamming that piece of glass into the guy's neck. I told him about that.

"Do...do you think I really would have done that? Could the wolf make me kill someone?"

Nico rubbed my back and sighed. "It's okay, Maddy. Don't think like that."

"No, Nico!" I shouted, sitting up. "What if I am a monster? What if Javi is right? Maybe I do need to be put down like a rabid dog."

"No. You are not a rabid dog. Stop talking like that. You have to understand something. Being a shifter is like being two separate beings at once. The wolf is a reflection of you. They feed on your emotions. If you're happy, they're happy. If you're angry, they're angry. If they're host is an asshole like Javi? Then the wolf is an asshole.

"Your wolf is different. It's been dormant your entire life. It has no idea how to connect with you. You can't shift, so it's probably confused and frustrated that it can't do what it wants. Plus, it is a wolf. Wolves hunt and kill. Nothing about that is unnatural, it's just that it doesn't know how to control that yet. It hasn't had your influence on it long enough. You. Are. Not. A. Monster. I don't ever want you to say that again."

Everything he said made sense. It also calmed me down and made me feel better. It was good to know I wasn't some uncontrollable beast. The thought that I could lash out and murder someone was a horrifying thought. I was glad Nico was here to explain it all to me.

I slid closer to him and curled into his lap. Even the wolf inside me seemed calmer. It was like we both understood each other better after hearing the explanation.

"I know I can't shift yet, or maybe ever, but I'll try to do better connecting to my wolf. Do you have any tips about how to do that? Walking around talking to myself is a one-way ticket to the nut house."

"Come on." He shifted me and stood up, grabbing my hand. "Maybe this will help.

We walked out the back door and toward the woods behind his house. Nico held my hand as we walked, stopping once we got to the edge of the forest. "Okay," he said. "Shifters usually connect with their wolves for the first time at ten or eleven. In rare cases, it might take until twelve or thirteen. More or less when you hit puberty."

"Oh shit. Human puberty is bad enough," I murmured, remembering how awkward and weird that time of my life was. I could only imagine how much worse it would be to suddenly have another being inside you to go along with the hormones, acne, and extra hair.

"It's not that bad, really. It kinda makes it easier, to be honest. Anyway, once you make a strong connection to your wolf, subsequent shifts get easier. You trust it, and it trusts you. You have to call on it, *knowing* that it will answer the call and come forward."

Without another word, Nico took a step back and shifted. My jaw dropped as I watched. It wasn't like seeing shifters on TV or hearing about it. This was…different. Everything transformed and morphed so seamlessly that it was like someone had hit a switch. I stood, frozen in surprise and delight, watching him transform.

Nico padded forward and rubbed at my legs. His fur was so soft and thick. I knelt and ran my hands through it, then laughed and buried my face in the coat. The wolf in my head was sad, almost nearing despair at not being able to come out and interact with her mate. I could imagine if the tables were turned, and I wasn't able to be with Nico in his human form, how depressed I'd be.

I closed my eyes and concentrated on the wolf within me, doing my best to send my thoughts to her. I promised her that if Nico and I had enough time, she'd be able to be with her mate. I had to learn to shift and make our connection stronger, but I let her know that it would be soon. Finally, I asked her to trust us.

Almost immediately, the pressure in my head vanished. I sighed with relief. I hadn't realized how exhausting the insistent presence had been until it was gone. I almost shouted in victory.

After letting me pet him for a few minutes, Nico shifted back. He took my hand and helped me back to my feet. "Maddy, I really can't wait for the day when we'll get to experience this together. There really is nothing like it. Running through the woods as a wolf is one of the most freeing and exciting things you can do. Doing it with your mate…I can't even imagine how amazing it will be."

I felt the exact same way. I wanted that freedom, that wide-open release, to have that connection with Nico as we ran through the woods. I truly couldn't wait for it. I grinned to myself and let him pull me into a hug, resting my head on his chest.

Chapter 20 - Nico

My shop was open seven days a week, but I'd decided to take a few days off, including the weekend. After the way Maddy had reacted to her wolf trying to assert its dominance, I knew she needed something special. For the past month, she'd just spent her time in my house and had only gone to work a few times. She had to be going crazy with boredom.

Plus, from the moment I met her, chaos had been the name of the game. Nothing had been normal, nothing had been simple. In a different world, I'd have wooed Maddy. True *dating* stuff. We hadn't really had the time to do any of that. I decided the time was right to get away for a bit.

The Lorenzo pack had done well for itself, and about fifteen years ago, my parents had invested in real estate—mostly rental properties around Florida, but we'd also purchased some cabins up in Tennessee. They were vacation rentals near the national park, tucked away in the mountains, quiet and beautiful. They brought in a hefty sum each year. I'd checked with the company who managed the rental program and found one of them were open for the weekend. I booked it and decided to let Maddy know we were going on a weekend getaway.

"Tennessee? Like...banjos and stuff?" Maddy had said when I told her about it on Wednesday.

"It's not like that. Well, some of it probably is, but so is Florida. Have you ever been?"

"Not that I remember, but if you say it's nice, then I'm game. When do we leave?"

"I thought we'd head out tomorrow, if you think you can get away."

Maddy only had to think about it for a second before agreeing. "Why not. Let's do it."

We both packed a single bag and hopped in the car the next morning. Maddy had left Abi in charge of the bar in her absence, and I'd told Luis and the guys where I was going. Javi and his crew hadn't made any more attempts on Maddy's life, but I knew it was only a matter of time before they made another move. I'd even contracted a security company to keep tabs on Maddy's parents. They wouldn't know they were there, but knowing they were being protected made me feel better. I didn't mention that to Maddy, though. She had enough to think about without worrying about her parents.

For the first time since we'd met, we were away from danger. The drive was pleasant. We went up through Georgia and talked the entire time. Now that we were away from the day-to-day danger and anxiety, we were able to fully open up to each other. We had some of the most regular discussions I could remember us having. Our favorite James Bond actor? Mine was Sean Connery, hers was Daniel Craig, to which I explained her grievous error. Favorite books? Hers was *A Tale of Two Cities* by Dickens, mine was *Blood Meridian* by McCarthy. Her favorite movie was, surprisingly, *Fight Club*.

"I don't think I've ever met a woman who really liked that movie," I said as we passed through Atlanta.

She shrugged. "There's a lot of nuance to it. People think it's just toxically masculine men punching each other, but that's just the surface. It's like the movie is wearing a mask, and once it's off, the real movie comes through. What's yours?"

"*Gladiator.*"

Maddy raised an eyebrow and gave me a disappointed look. "Seriously?"

"What?"

"What's the phrase? 'Basic bro?' Is that what you are?"

"Hey! You just said your favorite movie is freaking *Fight Club*."

"Right, but I'm a woman, which makes my choice interesting and unexpected. For a guy to say his favorite movie is *Gladiator*? Like, were you choosing that between *Gone in 60 Seconds* and *Terminator 2*?"

I burst out laughing, mostly because I *did* like both of those movies. "Okay, fine, whatever, I still like that movie. And it won best picture."

A few hours later, we started climbing into the mountains. Maddy rolled the windows down and watched the scenery. I hadn't been up here since I came with my parents to pick out which cabins they wanted to purchase. I'd been nineteen or twenty at that point. I'd forgotten how nice it was. In Florida, it still felt like summer, but it was October and there was no place as beautiful as eastern Tennessee in the fall—at least, none that I'd seen.

The cabin was located outside a touristy area. The town was called Gatlinburg, and it was more or less a family-friendly Las Vegas tucked up in the mountains. Thankfully, the cabins were far enough away from the chaos that it felt like we were in the middle of nowhere. As we pulled up in the driveway, Maddy let out a deep, relaxed sigh.

"I feel like we're a million miles from home. It's so beautiful," she said as she got out of the car.

I stepped around and took her hand. "This is one of best units. I wanted us to really disconnect, so I talked the lady who runs the rental company into stocking the fridge and pantry with food and stuff. We don't have to leave at all. There's a hiking trail system that's only about a hundred yards up the hill; a creek runs through the property, too. Oh, and there's a hot tub on the back porch."

Maddy raised her eyebrows. "Oh, a hot tub?"

I chuckled and led her toward the door. "Let's start relaxing."

That first night, we talked even more about ourselves. Learning and finding out things we didn't know previously. Maddy let me know about her time in college and majoring in business. She then asked me how I got into fixing cars, and it occurred to me that I'd never really told her the extent of my own business.

"We actually do more than just fix up cars," I said. The weather outside was much cooler than in Florida, and we'd put on hooded sweatshirts while I cooked steaks on the grill on the back porch.

"I'm confused. Didn't you just get that big contract with the post office?"

I nodded. "Yeah, but that was more like a favor. It was a pretty big contract, but the last company that took care of their fleet was going out of business, so the guy asked me to take it over. Not a big deal. Our real money is in custom stuff. Building and repairing custom and one-of-a kind cars. We had a gorgeous Porsche a few weeks ago. That was some basic repair stuff.. We do everything you could imagine, and people pay a ton of money for what we do."

Maddy sipped at her glass of wine. "So, when you say you build cars…"

"From the ground up. We have machines that create custom tire rims; we can build motors and transmissions all the way from a plain block of metal into a roaring beast of an engine. I've even got a portion of the shop set up for custom paint jobs and stuff like that."

"So, are you making those import-tuner cars? Like back in the old *Fast and the Furious* movies?"

I groaned. "I mean…we've done those, yeah. There's an actor in Hollywood who loves that shit, even though it's at least a decade out of style. About once a year, he puts in an order for a Mitsubishi Eclipse or an Acura Integra, or something. He always wants it with eight hundred horsepower and some ridiculous fiberglass spoiler. I swear if I have to put one more giant robot decal on the side of one of his cars again, I may throw up."

Maddy laughed. "A famous actor? Like a movie star? Seriously?"

"Yeah. But the stuff I really like doing is more interesting stuff. Modifying things in ways people have never thought about. Had a guy who bought his wife an '89 Lamborghini. Thing was mint condition. Only had like four thousand miles on it. But his wife didn't know how to drive a manual. Me and the guys spent six weeks designing and installing a custom automatic transmission. Stuff like that. Or people will just ask for other modifications. It's a really cool job."

"Sounds like you love it," Maddy said, setting her empty glass aside.

I took the steaks off the grill and put them on a plate. I nodded. "I do. I'm good at it. So, that's nice."

The next day, we went for a hike. We headed out early in the crisp air. It never got that way in Florida except maybe in the dead of winter, and even then, it still had a humid quality that never let you think it was actually cold. It was invigorating, and as we hiked, I told myself we should try to come up here at least once a year. I was kicking myself for waiting this long to visit in the first place.

When we cleared the top of a ridge that looked out over the Smoky Mountains, the entire mountain range looked like it was on fire. Clouds hung so low on the ridges and valleys, they looked like massive patches of smoke. That explained how the mountains got the name.

"This is amazing," Maddy breathed as we stood there.

"It is," I agreed.

She slipped her hand into mine, her fingers pleasantly cool. "Thank you for bringing me here."

"No problem. It's my pleasure."

"I get so caught up in work, I sometimes forget to do stuff like this. I have enough money to go on a vacation every year, but I never make the time for myself."

I laughed. "Same here."

"Too bad it took almost getting killed for me to take an actual vacation."

We spent our last day making the pilgrimage down to Gatlinburg. It was an adventure to say the least, but still kind of fun. Maddy enjoyed the kitschy stores and gift shops. She even bought a gawdy airbrushed T-shirt as an ironic souvenir. We had lunch at a surprisingly good deli downtown where I had one of the best Reuben sandwiches I'd ever tasted.

That afternoon, we spent over an hour sitting in the hot tub. It was the most relaxing hour of my life. We spent the whole time in a natural, comfortable silence, watching the breeze billowing through the red, orange, and yellow leaves. Back home, everything was still completely green.

"Are you getting hungry?" Maddy asked.

"I am. But I'd prefer to stay here the rest of the night," I said.

"Well, you'll shrivel up like a prune. And there's certain parts of you I don't want shriveling up."

"Oh, well then. Let's get out of here."

Maddy found ingredients to make spaghetti and meatballs in the kitchen, including salad and a loaf of Italian bread. After dinner, when the sun had almost set, I lit the big fireplace in the living room of the cabin. Within minutes, I had it crackling and roaring. We sat on the couch and snuggled together, watching the flames. The last few days had been pretty amazing. I could already tell we were closer than we'd been before we left. I needed to let her know how I felt. It was a need I couldn't ignore.

"Does it feel like two months?" I asked.

"What? Uh." Maddy laughed. "Has it really been that long? In some ways, it feels like it's been shorter. In others, it feels *much* longer."

"True. I just wanted you to know that I feel like this has been the best couple months of my life. I know that night was probably the worst of yours, but I wanted you to know that I'm happy I was the one who found you. The one who saved you. I don't really want to think what my life might be like without you. I guess what I want to say is thank you for letting me take care of you."

Maddy looked at me and smiled, then raised a hand to my cheek. "Nico, I'm so happy fate brought us together. Even if it was bad, I think things worked out for the best. I can honestly say you're one of the best things that ever happened to me."

She leaned forward and kissed me. As soon as our lips touched, the hunger sparked inside me. Desire and need. Absolute *want*. I pulled her closer, letting my tongue slip into her mouth. Maddy sighed and slid her hands across my chest. Her breasts pressed against me, and I could feel their warmth through our shirts. A happy and excited growl escaped my throat.

Maddy pulled away and looked into my eyes. The same hunger I felt was mirrored in her eyes. Without asking, I began to undo the button and zipper on her pants. As I worked, she pulled her shirt off and stripped her bra away. I groaned at the sight of her breasts, her nipples hard and inches from my face.

With her pants finally undone, she stood to take them off. I worked on my own clothes, tearing them off in urgent need. Maddy stood in front of me, illuminated by the flickering fire behind her, her skin colored a glowing orange. I looked up at her, in awe of her beauty. I touched her thigh, the fingers sliding across the smooth skin of her body. My thumb slipped through the short tuft of hair between her legs, and she smiled faintly and closed her eyes. My other hand slipped across the flesh of her stomach and both hands moved up until her breasts filled my palms. I drew circles around her nipples with my thumbs, and I leaned forward to kiss her stomach, her chest, gently tracing shapes over her breasts and trailing my fingers across her nipples. Maddy was breathing heavier, eyes still closed.

Finally, she opened her eyes and took my hands in hers, interlacing our fingers as she stepped forward and knelt on the couch with me. My cock was rock-hard and she deftly positioned her hips above me and slid down onto me. I gasped, letting the warm wetness of her envelop me. Inch by inch, she slid down my length. Her eyes never left mine. Once she was seated, my full length inside her, she leaned toward me and kissed me again. This kiss was more primal, carnal, a statement instead of a question.

Maddy began rocking her hips back and forth. I grunted as she picked up speed. The room was draped in shadows, brightened only by the spastic flames in the fireplace. It felt like the entire world had disappeared. We were the only things in the universe, our pleasure the only thing that mattered.

She moved faster, almost bouncing on me. Her swinging breasts drew my attention. I took them in my hands and squeezed gently but desperately. Our lips touched in light, feathery kisses, brought together only by the movement of her body. She moved her hands into my hair, pulling my face to her chest as she began to move faster still. I released her breasts and wrapped my arms around her, hugging our bodies together.

"Take me, Nico," she breathed into my ear.

I slammed my hips into her, lifting her up off the couch as I did. The pressure was already building within me. I fucked her harder, every second making me hungrier. I needed her, wanted to come inside her more than I'd ever wanted anything in my life. I could hear her murmuring in my ear, but her words were too low to understand, too quiet to overcome the sound of my breathing and the sounds of our flesh striking together.

Finally, I felt her pussy clench around my cock, tight beyond belief, and Maddy released a long groan of pleasure as she shuddered in my arms. The feel of her clamping around me sent me over the edge, my own orgasm bursting forth. I sucked in a breath, then released myself inside her. Totally spent, we rocked together, holding each other, our bodies sheened in sweat and our breaths slowing. The rest of the world still seemed insignificant with her in my arms.

Chapter 21 - Maddy

As soon as we were out of the mountains, I missed them. It had been such a beautiful and tranquil respite from the world, from all the awful things that had happened, and might still happen. All I wanted was for him to turn around, go back to the cabin, and escape everything. I mentioned that to Nico, and he reached over and put a hand on my thigh as he drove.

"We'll come back. I was actually thinking how silly it was that my family owned these places and I never used them. Maybe we can make it a yearly trip."

The feelings I already had for Nico were surprising. I cared for him. Deeply. I wasn't used to that. It had been such a long time since I'd done any kind of dating. I liked it. It made things even more special. I really and truly did like him. It wasn't just that he'd saved me, or that he was gorgeous, or fucking amazing in bed, or even that our wolves were fated mates. It was that he was exactly the kind of person I'd always wanted in my life. As we made our way home, a voice in my head—this time, not my wolf—started to think I might be on the way to more than just liking him.

The trip back was bittersweet, but we made it fun anyway. We stopped at a gas station halfway through Georgia and bought enough snacks, candy, and soda to put an entire kindergarten class into a food coma. We listened to each other's favorite songs and listened to most of the first *Harry Potter* audiobook. It was like an amazing dream I didn't want to wake up from.

We got back home safe and sound. The real world couldn't wait anymore. The day after we returned, it was back to work. I went into the bar that afternoon with Sebastian. Everything was exactly as it should be. Everything except Abi. The entire time we prepped to open, she seemed off. Kinda pissy and easily irritated. Not at all like herself.

"Hey," I said, nudging her halfway through the night. "What's up with you?"

"Nothing."

The one word answer without the hint of a smile told me that *something* was wrong. Later, while I was cleaning up spilled beer, I saw Sebastian chatting up a young woman at the other side of the bar. Even though he was flirting with her, I kept seeing him scan the room, like he was looking for someone else. Abi was near me, staring daggers at the two of them.

"Piece of shit," Abi muttered.

I did a double take and made sure she actually *was* looking at Sebastian. She'd always seemed sort of smitten with him. "Abi, what the hell is going on here?" I asked, gesturing to her and then over to Sebastian.

Abi sighed and threw her bar rag onto the floor and came over. "So…Sebastian and I…might have hooked up over the weekend."

Remembering that shifters had enhanced hearing, I glanced over at him, knowing he could hear the conversation. We locked eyes, and I gave him a look that basically said, *shut your fucking ears and stop eavesdropping.* Sebastian looked like a whipped puppy and looked away.

Abi leaned against the bar and crossed her arms. "You know, I realized it was going to be a casual thing. Something fun that we could enjoy. Still…" Abi gave a dejected shrug and let her arms flop down to her sides. "I really kinda thought Sebastian might actually like me. Now I'm pissed at myself for getting my hopes up."

My heart hurt for her, and I also wanted to kick Sebastian in the nuts. I put a hand on her arm and lowered my head to look into her downcast eyes. "Don't beat yourself up over this. Did you have fun?"

Abi rolled her eyes. "Yeah. It was pretty great. A couple of pretty great times actually."

"Well, that's something. You had fun and nothing came from it. That sucks, but at least you have some good memories to think back on."

"Ugh." Abi grunted and threw her head back dramatically. "You're right. I guess two adults should be able to handle a little fling."

"Right. Now, can we get back to work? It'll get your mind off it?"

Abi nodded and picked her towel up off the ground and went to help the bartender. Throughout the night, I kept catching her glare at Sebastian. It was a little exhausting and I wasn't even involved. I'd probably have to talk to him about not having sex with my employees. It was nice that he was here watching out for me, but I didn't need him causing drama. That was not okay. I didn't fully blame him, though. I'd seen how Abi had been eyeing him up like a juicy steak. I was sure they both played a part in whatever had happened.

The rest of the evening passed by pretty uneventfully. No fights, no shifters, nothing that would cause any problems. At least until an hour before closing, when the old guy walked in. I noticed him as soon as he set foot in the door. My place sort of catered to a younger crowd. We rarely got anyone over fifty trying to come in. Part of that was my marketing—I wanted my place to be hip and cool. The other part was I'd only been open a few years, and most of the older clientele already had watering holes they'd been frequenting for decades. Once someone was loyal to a bar, tavern, or pub, they tended to stay there.

The guy who'd walked in was in his early to mid-sixties, if I had to guess. I'd never seen him before, but he walked in like he owned the place. He pushed through the doors and walked straight toward the bar. People were generally suspicious and cautious creatures. The typical habit for humans was to get the lay of the land and check out the area before getting comfortable. This guy just stepped right in like he came here every day.

He pulled up a stool and started eyeballing the rack of liquor behind the bar.

One of my bartenders turned to see what he wanted to order, but I held him off, putting a hand on his arm. "I'll get it, Kyle. You take care of those sorority girls at the end of the bar. They think you're cute."

I turned to the man. "What can I get for you, friend?"

He seemed to be looking at our gin selection. I thought he was ignoring me at first, but finally he pointed a finger to a bottle on the top shelf. "I'll have a Tom Collins, if you please."

I nodded. "Coming up."

The bottle in hand, I poured it, the simple syrup, and the juice of a lemon into a shaker. While I prepped the drink, the older guy turned and scanned the crowd. Was he meeting someone here? Maybe an online date? No reason it couldn't happen even if he was older. But there was something about him that was…off. I couldn't put a finger on it, but it was very pronounced. I poured the shaken ingredients over ice in a chilled Collins glass. I grabbed the soda gun and filled it the rest of the way with soda water. Putting a lemon wedge on the edge of the glass, I set it in front of him.

"That'll be fourteen dollars. Do you want to pay now or start a tab?"

The man squeezed the lemon into the drink, then took a long sip from the straw and smacked his lips together. He spoke without looking at me. "You know, you don't look like some kind of evil beast. I guess looks can be deceiving."

The world seemed to collapse in on itself, everything in the periphery vanished, and tunnel vision set in. All I could see was this man. The one who'd called me a beast. He wasn't a shifter, so how did he know about me? Who was he? Was he here to kill me? Maybe Javi had hired a hitman or something. My heart slammed as I glanced around his body, looking for the bulge of a gun or something.

Before I could force myself to speak, Sebastian was there. He'd obviously used his enhanced hearing to make out what the man had said. He slapped a hand on the old guy's shoulder. "Is there a problem here?" he asked.

The stranger raised an eyebrow and glanced at Sebastian's hand. As though he were totally unconcerned, he turned back and took a second sip of his drink. Sebastian gave his shoulder a slight shake. "Hey, old man, I'm talking to you."

The stranger nodded. "Oh, I know."

The whole situation was becoming surreal. Next to Sebastian's thick muscular body, the old man looked incapable of hurting anyone, but he must have had some sort of death wish. Sebastian was getting furious, I could tell by his face. He could literally break this guy in half if he wanted to.

Sebastian made a funny face and seemed to sniff the air. The anger on his face turned to confusion.

"What do you want?" I mumbled.

The old man shrugged. "Hey, you guys are the ones who were looking for me."

I frowned and looked up at Sebastian. He had an equally puzzled look on his face. He took his hand off the guy's shoulder and moved to his side so he could look him in the face. "What are you talking about, buddy?"

After another sip of his drink, he finally turned and made eye contact with Sebastian. "I said, you guys were looking for me. I decided it would be better to come on in and see what you wanted." He turned his eyes to mine. "Figured I needed to show my face before your PI friend found me and blew my cover." He nodded toward me. "You know, you look a lot different from the little bundle I dropped off at that adoption agency all those years ago."

I sucked in a breath, my eyes widening in surprise and shock. Kenneth? Was this the social worker? The man who'd brought me to my parents and disappeared? "Sebastian," I whispered. "Call Nico."

Kenneth grinned. "Ah, the boyfriend. Yeah. He needs to hear the whole story."

Sebastian was gaping at the man, but pulled his cell out and dialed. "Nico? Get your ass to the bar. We have a lead…no, bro, Maddy is fine…yeah, yeah, just get the fuck down here."

Kenneth took another sip and smacked his lips together. "Hot damn, that's a good drink."

Chapter 22 - Nico

My SUV almost rocked over onto its side as I slammed on the brakes in the parking lot. Most of the cars had already cleared out, due to the late hour. Sebastian had been cryptic as hell on the phone. He'd said Maddy was safe, but I had no idea what was going on.

I jogged across the pavement and into the bar. There were still a half-dozen customers milling around, finishing their last drinks, but no sign of Sebastian or Maddy. I was on the verge of a panic attack when I saw Abi.

She waved to me and nodded toward the rear of the building. "Back office. They told me to tell you when you got here."

I sighed in relief. "Okay, thanks."

I jogged through the kitchen and past the dishwashing area. Bursting through the door to Maddy's office, I found her and Sebastian sitting at her desk, and an older guy sitting to the side. "What's going on?" I didn't like how panicked my voice sounded.

"Well," Sebastian said. "Nico, meet Kenneth. Kenneth, meet Nico."

Kenneth? The name erupted up from my memory. The name of the social worker who'd dropped Maddy off as a baby. He was here? "No shit?"

"I shit you not indeed," Kenneth said, giving me a humorless grin.

Sebastian pushed a chair toward me, and I gratefully took it, collapsing onto it. "Okay…what's, uh…have we found anything out?"

Kenneth sat forward, resting his elbows on his knees. "We were waiting for you to get started. Now that you're here, I can tell you everything I know."

"Please," Maddy said.

Kenneth nodded. "Okay then. Your friend Luis is pretty good at his job. I have little ears everywhere." He fluttered his hand around the room. "Word got back to me that a shifter was looking for me. Asking about my last-known whereabouts or known associates. He was starting to get close. I couldn't have him blowing my cover, so I decided to come to you. Get this little conversation out of the way. Then I can go back into hiding."

"Wait, why are you hiding in the first place?" Maddy asked.

Kenneth smiled at her. "Because, just like you, I shouldn't exist."

"Huh?" Sebastian asked dumbly.

Kenneth pointed at Maddy. "You, my dear lady, are my niece. Your father and I were half-brothers. I carry the blood of Edemas as well."

My jaw dropped. What? I shot a glance at Maddy, and she looked equally shocked. Sebastian had a hand to his forehead and said, "I knew you smelled weird."

Kenneth nodded at Sebastian. "Yes. You probably scented the partial shifter blood within me."

"My father had a half-brother?"

"Yes. Our father had...appetites, I guess you could say. I was a love child he had with a co-worker. I was never acknowledged as a true member of the family; however, my father did tell me about my lineage. He told me how powerful the blood in my veins was and that there were people who would love nothing more than to see me dead.

"I met your father when we were...I don't know, I guess I was thirteen and your dad was maybe eleven. My dad paid off my mom every month to keep her from spilling the beans to his wife. Your father and I still became friends. We were both only children, and finding out we had a sibling—even a secret one—was pretty exciting. I have no idea how Dad got David to keep quiet about me to his mom, but as far as I know, she never found out who I really was."

I held my hands up, still reeling from the new information. "So…you know what happened to Maddy's parents?"

Kenneth's face grew somber and he nodded. "Yeah. Dad got cancer, and on his deathbed, he told me and David that we needed to go into hiding if we were ever discovered. That we had to protect ourselves and run. He was very adamant about that. The royals would do anything they could to kill us if they found out about us. After Dad died, David met Gabriella. They fell in love and one thing led to another. Things happened," he said with a shrug.

"How did David die?" Maddy looked like she was both desperate to know and terrified to find out.

Kenneth rubbed at the gray stubble on his cheeks. "I don't know how the royals found out about your father and me. Things happened so fast. We didn't really have the time to figure that part out. People started asking around about us—strangers, shifter strangers. We knew exactly what was happening. We had been forewarned, after all. All David could think about was Gabriella and the baby in her womb." He looked at Maddy and gave her a sad smile. "He was young, but he was fucking brave. You guys were his only concern. One day, there was a frantic knock on my door, and I found your dad and Gabby on my front door step. David was…Jesus, he was so panicked. He said some shifters had located them and were chasing them. Gabby was crying and holding him. He pushed her to me and told me to save her. Three cars came roaring into the parking lot of my apartment complex. I didn't even think about it, just took Gabby with me and ran." Kenneth's eyes welled with tears. "We could…uh…hear the fight. Then the gunshots. It was over fast."

Maddy put a hand to her mouth and looked like she wanted to cry. I stood and walked to her side, putting my hands on her shoulders. I didn't know how to comfort her. Maybe I couldn't.

"Anyway," Kenneth went on, wiping at his eyes. "I helped your mom hide. She was due to give birth any day.

She was terrified, and rightfully so. She talked about getting the baby somewhere safe. David and Gabby knew I helped get unwanted shifter babies to different homes. The rumor was I *sold* the babies, but that was always bullshit. All I did was help people who didn't like going through the traditional channels, either because of legal reasons or safety issues. She begged me, absolutely begged me, to get her baby to a family where she would be safe. A well-off family who would give her a good life. Where she would be loved." He looked at Maddy again. "You need to know that this was not an easy decision. She cried for days once she'd decided.

"I found a couple who wanted a baby girl. Made contact with them, posing as a social worker, and let them know I'd meet them at an adoption agency in downtown Tampa. Your mother and I were holed up in a motel on the outskirts of town when she went into labor. I got her to a hospital and she gave birth to you. She held you, Maddy, she did. She held you so long and cried so hard that I truly believed she was going to change her mind. I could tell how much she loved you the second she looked at you. You need to know that. Your parents loved you more than life itself. Your father died to protect you and your mother. And your mom gave up every ounce of her own happiness to make sure you were protected. If you learn nothing else, I need you to know that."

Maddy nodded. Tears were streaming down her cheeks, and I knew she probably didn't trust herself to speak.

"After about an hour and a half, Gabby kissed you on the head one more time and handed you to me. I took you to your new parents, posing as a social worker, and vanished before the adoption agency could get any more info on me. Your mother died about nine months later. She had heart issues and needed a transplant, but there was no match. I don't know if I believe that. I think she died of a broken heart, not a sick one."

After a few moments of silence, Sebastian spoke up. "Alright, the bloodline of Edemas? Is it true what the legends say? Is that really why the royals are trying to kill Maddy?"

Kenneth nodded. "The bloodline is real. Maddy and I are true descendants of Edemas."

A question that had been nagging at me for weeks resurfaced. Now was the time to ask it. "There were obviously people who survived the slaughter of his family. In all these years, have there been any dormant shifters who mated with a shifter? Brought the bloodline back to prominence?"

"The royals are very thorough. Anytime there's even a mention of a living descendant, they *take care of it*. There have been dozens of people throughout history who were probably killed because they were only thought to be descendants. They'll kill a hundred innocents if it means getting one descendant of Edemas. Most of the lineage were killed before they ever got to their adult years. They never even had a chance to mate. Of those few who did get to that age, I've never heard of anyone reactivating the dormant blood. That's why Maddy is in so much danger. If she really is fated to an alpha, then the odds of her reactivating Edemas's bloodline are greater. The blood has been so diluted over the years, no one really believes she'll become a werewolf like Edemas. A shifter? Probably. The royals are too scared, and they want that treasure Edemas left behind. I think that's what all this is about."

"Wait," I said. "What could be valuable enough to kill kids and babies? It sounds like these royals are powerful enough as it is. Why do they need more money?"

Kenneth shook his head. "It's not that kind of treasure. Legend has it Edemas left behind a vial of his own blood. That he hid it in a vault a few days before the revolt that killed him and his family. It can only be opened by one of his descendants. One drop of that blood could reawaken even the most dormant of genes. It would create a whole new line of werewolves. It can give them a one-way ticket back to power, and the throne."

"Holy shit," Sebastian muttered.

"Do you think the story is real?" Maddy asked.

"The vial of blood?" Kenneth shrugged. "The royals think it's true. That's all that matters. It's why you and I are in so much danger. Speaking of, I've told you all I know. It's time for me to go back into the shadows."

"Can't you stay with us?" Maddy looked hopeful, but I knew it would be a bad idea.

Kenneth seemed to know that as well. "Can't stay in any one place too long. I'll meet up with you all again. I'll get you a time and place. We can discuss more at that point."

At any other time, I'd have thought he was being paranoid. After hearing that story, I knew his paranoia was based on legitimate fears. He'd survived this long by doing things his way. We needed to let him do his thing.

He got up to leave and Maddy gave him a hug. Kenneth looked awkward at first, then he seemed to relax and patted her on the back before departing.

I took Maddy out the back door. I didn't think she'd be in the mood to talk to anyone, even Abi, after that story. She seemed a little shell-shocked, so I let her sit in silence as we drove. I was worried about her. I couldn't imagine how I'd feel if I'd heard that story about my family. She sat in the passenger seat, staring down at her hands. Maddy had never been this silent before. By the time we got home, I wondered whether she was in shock or something. It would have been better if she was sobbing or expressing her sorrow in some way. The stoic, blank stare was starting to freak me out.

We finally got inside and I sat on the couch with her. I held her for a long time, wondering if I should call Doc to come take a look at her. Then she finally spoke.

"It's so sad," she whispered.

I nodded. "I know." I didn't know what else to say.

"David died for me. Gabriella had to give me away. I can't imagine how sad she must have been, or how scared David was. I...it's..." Maddy started crying. Deep, broken sobs rocked her entire body.

I put my arms around her tighter as she cried into my chest, the tears soaking into my shirt. "It's gonna be okay."

She cried for several minutes before getting herself under control again. I grabbed tissues so she could wipe her face and blow her nose. I ran my fingers through her hair and looked into her eyes. "Well, one good thing came from this. We know why the royals are after you. That gives us an advantage. I promise you, with all I have inside me, I won't let your parents' sacrifices go to waste. Come on, let me put you to bed."

I guided her to our room and got her tucked away. She was asleep before I was even able to get the covers over her. I looked down at her for several seconds before stepping over to the window. I looked out into the dark night and wondered what it would be like to die for the people you loved the way her father did. To give away the most precious and beautiful thing you would ever have the way her mother did.

I knew they were dead, but it didn't stop me from speaking to her parents at that moment. "I'll keep her safe," I whispered. Hoping that somewhere, somehow, her parents heard and believed me. I would keep her safe, and if I could, I'd stop the royals' hunt on the bloodline forever.

Chapter 23 - Maddy

The next afternoon, Luis returned home. Once Kenneth had revealed himself to us, there was no reason for him to stay out on the road. He was a little pissed when he got back.

"That sneaky asshole," Luis had hissed. "I was right on his tail. I would have had him in another two or three days."

"Well, I think that's why he came to us, right?" Sebastian asked.

Luis sighed. "Yeah, I know. It's just…if I was out hunting a bear or something, and I spent hours and hours tracking him down, searching until I found his cave and everything, then while I'm in the woods he strolls up to the porch of my buddy's house…it's disheartening. That's all."

I giggled at him. He was so dejected that his quarry had sensed him on his tail and one-upped him. It didn't make things any better that Luis was always so serious. Nico went over all the information Kenneth had given us, including the secret vault where the vial of blood was supposedly hidden.

"Well, there's my next job. Figuring out where that blood is. Once we find it, we will have major fucking leverage against the royals," Luis said once Nico finished talking.

The idea of finding the blood had me stiffening. Nico had his arm around me and felt my reaction. He leaned over and whispered, "What's wrong?"

"Do we really want to find it?" I asked.

"Why wouldn't we?" Felipe asked.

"It's too dangerous. If it can really do what they think it can, wouldn't it be dangerous? Creating a whole new line of these god-like werewolves?"

Nico shook his head. "No, that's not what we want. We need to find it so we can destroy it. Once that blood is found, we can get rid of it. If there's no chance of Edemas's bloodline returning to power, the royals won't have any reason to go after Maddy or any other descendants."

It was a good plan, but I wasn't sure it would be that simple. This royal family had guarded the secret for hundreds of years for good reason. If one drop could reawaken a dormant wolf, what would happen if someone drank the entire thing? It would be like Edemas himself was reborn.

I mentioned my fears and Nico nodded. "True, it will be hard to convince the royals we have no intention of using the blood as a weapon, but I don't know what else we can do."

My hatred toward the royals seemed to build each day. After hearing Kenneth's story, the rage inside me slowly built until it was basically boiling within me. Knowing that they'd sent agents out to murder innocent children, all because they might one day find some hidden blood somewhere on earth, was too much to even fathom.

One night, while working a slow evening at the bar, I was staring into space, and for a moment my thoughts turned dark. I started to imagine taking the blood, just a single drop. I could almost taste the mineral, coppery taste. Once I did that, they'd be sorry. I'd lay waste to the entire royal line. How would they like it if I did to them what they'd done to me and mine? I would take the blood, then spill every drop of theirs.

The dark fantasy broke at the sound of a wine glass shattering. I jumped in surprise and saw a customer had dropped her glass. Abi was running over with a towel and a fresh glass for the woman. I didn't help because I was too shaken up about the thoughts that had been circulating inside my head. Had I really been contemplating taking Edemas's blood? The thought made me shudder.

Mateo had been my guard that night, and he came over. I must have looked like I'd seen a ghost. "Are you okay?"

"I'm fine. The glass breaking startled me. No big deal."

He'd gone away, buying the story.

Nico hadn't been as easy to fool. The next day, his whole family was getting ready to come over, and he pulled me aside while we were cooking. "Something's wrong, Maddy. I can tell. What's up?"

"Nervous is all. No big deal."

"Nervous? About what?"

"Everything, I guess," I said, hiding my dark thoughts away inside my own mind.

Nico had looked at me skeptically before reluctantly going back to cutting lettuce for salad. The family started trickling in a little while later. First Nico's brothers, then an aunt and uncle and a few cousins. His parents arrived last. I forced myself to mingle and chat, but my heart wasn't in it. In fact, it was painful. Trying to keep a fake smile on my face and laugh at jokes and tell stories was worse than anything. I wasn't a fake person by nature. I was usually a social butterfly, hence why I'd opened a bar. But this was all too much.

After dinner was over and everyone had gone outside to enjoy the Florida fall evening, I made my way downstairs into Nico's man cave. There was a pool table, dart board, a videogame cabinet that seemed to play half the old arcade games from the eighties, and a massive TV with theater-style seating in front of it. The room was blessedly quiet, and I sat in one of the thick leather chairs in front of the TV. The silence was like cool water on a wound, and it was exactly what I needed.

The respite didn't last long. After five minutes, I heard the *shush* sound of feet on the carpeted stairs. A glance over my shoulder showed me it was Julia. I gritted my teeth, wishing for just a few more minutes of peace. I quickly plastered the false smile on my face and stood.

"Hey, Julia. Did you need something?"

She waved at me. "Sit back down, dear. No need to get up on my account."

I sat and Julia walked over to join me. She took the seat next to me and chuckled. "You could almost drown in these things. They're so big."

"Yep," I said, hoping she'd get the point from one-word answers.

She didn't. Instead, she put her hands on her lap and seemed to be thinking of something to say. Finally, she sat forward, put a hand on my knee, and said, "Can I ask you a question?"

I sighed in exhaustion, failing to hide my weariness. "Sure." His mother was nice, but she could be pushy. No need to try to get out of the inevitable. If she was going to ask me a question, she was going to ask it. Whether I wanted her to or not.

"What are your intentions with my Nico?"

"I don't think I understand what you mean," I said, truly *not* understanding.

Julia sighed and looked uncomfortable. "What I mean is…well, here's the thing. Nico is an alpha. You understand?"

"Right. I knew that already. What does that have to do with anything?"

Julia twisted her fingers together, obviously flustered. "He's *the* alpha of the Lorenzo pack. He took over for Carlos several years ago. He's done fantastic job leading us, and I don't—"

"Julia," I interrupted, rubbing at my temples and becoming more irritated by the second. "Can we get to the point here?"

"Well, as the alpha, he'll need to settle down and have children at some point. He needs an heir. Someone who can take over as alpha the way he took over for his father. I really don't mean to sound like a bigot here, but the future alpha can't be a half-breed."

The words slammed into me. It was like I'd been slapped. My teeth tore into the side of my cheek so hard, I tasted blood. It was all I could do to keep my face composed and not lean forward and scream in this woman's face. The dark part of my mind wanted to ask her what she'd think if I was a werewolf—the full embodiment of Edemas. Would she think I wasn't good enough for her precious boy then? Was that what I needed to be to be accepted?

How dare she? Who the fuck did she thing she was? I opened my mouth to tell her exactly what I thought of her. Instead, I said, "Thanks, Mrs. Lorenzo. I'll take that into consideration. I appreciate that you feel comfortable enough to approach me with your concerns."

Julia smiled and patted my knee again. "I'm sure you all enjoy each other. A young fling is fine. You just have to know that nothing more can come of it. Come back up and rejoin the party when you want, sweetie."

Without another word, Julia stood and headed back up the stairs. I watched her go, and as she disappeared at the top of the landing, my vision went red and my hands clenched into fists. Leaping to my feet, I could actually feel my wolf wanting to jump out of my skin. It was the closest I'd ever been to her. I was vibrating with rage, and tears were leaking out of my eyes. They weren't tears of sadness or shame, but tears of anger and outrage.

I wasn't sure how long I stood like that. Time seemed to slow down. It could have been five minutes or five hours. I heard more footsteps coming down the stairs. I turned to look. If it had been Julia again, I really thought I might have jumped onto her and torn her hair out. I wasn't myself at all. Thankfully, it was Nico.

"Maddy? Are you down here? Oh, there you...Jesus Christ! Maddy? Holy shit, what happened?"

He ran to me and took my fists into his hands. I finally glanced down and saw bright red blood dripping from my shaking hands. Blood had oozed out on both hands and made bright red lines between each finger and dripped onto the hardwood floor. Nico gently pried my fingers open, and we both saw what had happened. I'd clenched my fists so tight, my nails had torn holes into my palms. There were four crescent-shaped wounds on both palms.

"What the fuck, babe?" Nico asked, breathless. "What the hell?"

"Nothing," I muttered. "Nothing happened."

Nico pulled me toward the bathroom and turned the sink on. He took a towel, wet it, then dabbed it on my hands. "That's bullshit. You wouldn't do this if something hadn't happened. Maddy, I've been worried about you. Ever since we talked to Kenneth, you haven't been the same. Please. Tell me what's going on in that head of yours."

I stared down at my bloody palms and shook my head, not trusting myself to talk. The wolf was receding, leaving me alone with my anger and fear. Nico put a hand under my chin and lifted my face to his. "Tell me. If you can't be honest with me, then who can you be honest with? You're my mate, and I will always put you first."

My lower lip trembled, and this time the tears were from sadness. The words started to pour out of me. I spilled my guts. I told him about the dark thoughts I'd been having, about secretly wanting to take the blood, and how I thought it made me evil. I told him about how sad I was about what happened with my parents. Then I told him what his mother had said and how it set me off, and that I didn't think I'd ever truly belong in his family. When I finally looked back up into his face, he looked pissed—angrier than I'd ever seen him other than when Javi had tried to kill me again.

"It's okay. Those thoughts are normal, Maddy. Everyone would want revenge. That doesn't make you a bad person or a monster. What you're going through is rough. There's no other way to put it. I would be surprised if you *didn't* have some dark moments. That's normal for anyone in your position." He put a hand on my chest and then his own. "You and me? We are a team. Please don't hide stuff from me. The longer you keep it bottled up, the worse you'll feel. I'm here for the good times and the bad, the tears and the laughter, the fear and the happiness. Whatever it is, always know you can come to me."

Those words took a load off me. My entire being felt lighter. I could tell by the look in his eyes that he really did mean it. I'd never been with anyone who cared for me so much. I felt stupid for not opening up sooner, but now I realized that I really could.

Nico kissed me. I could taste my tears as he pressed his mouth to mine. When he pulled away, he looked into my eyes. "We'll make it through this."

I was suddenly exhausted, like I'd run a marathon with a weighted vest on. Even my eyelids started drooping. "I need a nap or something," I mumbled.

"You do look tired. Here, come this way."

He led me across the game room to a door at the back. Inside was a small guest room with a twin bed. It looked like the most comfortable thing I'd ever seen. Nico pointed to it. "You can nap here if you want. I thought you might not want to go upstairs with everyone still around."

I nodded. This did seem to be the better option. I didn't think I could face his mother again, at least not right now. The little room would be the perfect place to rest. "Thanks. It's great," I said, already kicking off my shoes.

Nico helped me get under the covers and tucked me in before kissing me on the forehead. He sat on the floor beside the bed, holding my hand. "I'll stay with you until you're asleep."

I nodded and yawned. I closed my eyes and let my exhaustion sweep over me. In moments, I could feel sleep taking me. I drifted down into unconsciousness.

I dreamed then. About the full moon.

Chapter 24 - Nico

I clenched my jaw so hard as I went back upstairs that I was afraid my teeth might crack. I'd never been so pissed off in my life. I stomped through the kitchen and out into the backyard. There were still about twenty people here, drinking, eating, laughing. I had no patience for any of that at the moment.

"Okay!" I shouted, getting everyone's attention. "Out. Everybody out."

The crowd silenced, my brothers all looked confused. No one moved, which only made me angrier. "I said out!" My voice boomed out like a grenade. "Everyone but Mom and Dad. Get the fuck out."

The crowd started moving, everyone quickly putting their glasses and plates down and heading toward the door. Dad was with Mom, whispering questions to her. I was happy to see that Mom looked abashed. She knew what I was mad about and looked worried.

My brother Diego walked up to me before leaving. "What the hell, Nico?"

I glared at him. "Not now, Diego. Not. Fucking. Now." I hissed the words through gritted teeth.

Diego lifted his hands in surrender. "Got it. Got it. Point taken."

My eyes locked on Mom while the last few people trickled out. Once the back door was closed, I was free to express my rage. "What is wrong with you?" I asked her.

Her jaw dropped. "Nico? What's going on here?"

My voice rose an octave. "I said, what is *wrong* with you?"

She crossed her arms and shook her head. "I was looking out for my boy. That's all."

Dad sighed and rubbed at his face. "Julia, what did you do?"

Mom swept a hand toward the house. "Carlos, that girl in there is a human. Nico can't be allowed to mate with a human. There won't ever be an alpha to take over the pack. You know that. Everyone does. I was the only one who seemed willing to say anything."

"I can be with whomever I want, Mother. I'm a grown man. I'm the alpha. I am in charge of my own life."

Mom shook her head. "No, Nico. It feels that way, I know. You are still my and your father's son. You have a duty to the pack. I only told Maddy the truth. I couldn't let her get her hopes up that there could be more with you. There can't be. Don't you see that? She can't—"

"She's my fated mate!" I bellowed in rage. "Stop talking about her like that."

Mom's face went pale, and Dad stepped over and put a hand on my shoulder to calm me down. "Son, easy. Take a breath," he murmured in my ear.

Mom took two steps toward me and pointed a finger at my chest. "No. I won't have you lying to us to keep shacking up with some girl. Humans and shifters can't be fated. You know that. Stop lying. You're being a child, Nico."

Dad, finally letting his anger show, turned to her and held up his hand. "Julia, would you stop? Jesus, just stop for a second."

"You can't actually be on his side? Carlos, you know what's at stake here! The future of the Lorenzo pack."

Dad sighed and looked at me. "I think it's time you tell your mother everything."

"Everything what? Oh my God, is she pregnant? Is that what's happened?"

"Julia," Dad hissed, "I love you with all my heart, but will you please—and I say this from a place of utmost love—please shut up for one second?"

Mom gasped and put a hand to her mouth, but she stopped talking.

Dad patted me on the back. "She'll understand once she hears."

I took a breath and nodded. Calming myself, I unfurled my fists. "Mom? Do you remember all the old stories about Edemas?"

Her brow furrowed in confusion. "The Werewolf King? Yes, why?"

"The stories said that when he and his family were slaughtered by the other side of the royal family and his subjects, the entire bloodline was wiped out, correct?"

"Nico, these are scary stories we tell little shifters at Halloween. What does this have to do with that girl in there?"

"A secondary legend tells that he was able to spirit away two of his descendants. Two babies who were full werewolves like he was. They were alphas, too. Two strong blood links to the Hollander line."

Mom sighed and shook her head. "I'd heard that once or twice, you still aren't—"

"The stories are all true, Mom. Edemas did get two children out before the assassinations. They passed their genes down through the years. The new royal family has been searching for and killing any child that came from those descendants. That is who Maddy is," I said, pointing back toward the house.

Mom froze, glancing from me to Dad and back again. "What are you saying?"

Dad took a step toward her, putting his hands out in a pleading gesture. "What he's saying is true, Julia. Maddy is a descendant of Edemas. She *is* a shifter, but the blood became so diluted over the centuries that her wolf is dormant. It's locked inside her, unable to come out."

"What about Javi? How does he factor into this?" she asked, still looking like she didn't completely believe us.

"Javi's family came to America when Dad was a kid. They came from Europe. We think Javi and his entire pack are under the royals' direct control. They are here, in this country, to hunt down and kill anyone who might be a descendant of Edemas.

"Javi's crew was seconds from killing her. Her father died saving her mother, and then her mom had to give her away the day she was born to try and keep her safe. She died not long afterward. There's a bullseye painted on Maddy's forehead, and she has enough to deal with without the mother of the man she loves talking to her like she's a piece of shit." I was breathing heavily by the time I finished talking.

My mother looked at my father. "Is this all true?"

Dad nodded. "It is. If you're honest with yourself, you'll know it too. You've surely caught some of her scent. She's not human, not completely. The stories are true, and that means the danger is as well."

Mom put a hand to her mouth and looked at the house, tears welling in her eyes. "Nico, I didn't know. I thought—"

"You thought I was thinking with my crotch and not my head?" I was still pissed at her and wasn't ready to be forgiving just yet.

"No, it's just...I'm sorry."

"Nope. Don't apologize to me. You'll need to apologize to Maddy. And it better be some real groveling-type shit. Kiss her toes, do her laundry, whatever the hell she needs."

"Yes, yes, I promise. I'm sorry, I have to ask, how do we plan on keeping her safe? You can intimidate Javi all you want, but if this royal family is real and they are after her, nothing will stop them. Even if Javi ends up dead, they won't stop."

"We know," I said. "Maddy's uncle is still alive, and he told us about another legend. Apparently, Edemas left behind a vial of his blood. If Maddy or any descendant was to drink that blood, the werewolf line would return. That's what terrifies the royals—the kings of old would be back. He's going to help us find this secret vault. Once that vial of blood is destroyed, we think the royals will back off. Kenneth is going to contact us again within the month."

Mom's look of shame and humiliation had given way to worry. "I don't feel good about you all going on some manhunt for some vial that may or may not actually exist. Especially when you don't know where it is. How are you even going to go about finding it?"

Dad raised an eyebrow. "She has a point, Nico. Do you have any leads on this blood?"

I nodded. "Kenneth has been researching it for decades. Basically ever since his dad, Maddy's grandpa, died. He and Luis have been in contact through secure emails and texts on burner phones. He's got some info. We aren't certain, but all the old legends say Edemas had his seat of power somewhere in Norway. The odds of the vault and the blood being in that country are pretty high. Luis is making connections. He and Kenneth are both trying to make inroads over there. We won't make any type of move until we're at least ninety percent certain."

Mom nodded and glanced back up at the house, then laughed humorlessly. "Nico, I'm sorry. I don't...I never should have been that way with Maddy. Whether she was a shifter or not, human or not, that's not the way I want to be. I don't know what came over me."

"Well, you're not wrong," I said. "You can make it up to her later."

If she'd been hoping I'd say, 'I forgive you,' she was mistaken with how this would go. She had a long way to go with Maddy first before I'd be able to say those words.

She must have realized it and nodded sadly. She and Dad left, leaving me standing in the backyard alone. I was itching to go for a run, but I couldn't leave Maddy alone. Besides, she might wake up at any time. I spent the next thirty minutes picking up all the paper plates, beer cans, plastic cups, and trash my guests had left behind. I would normally have been irritated, but I hadn't really given anyone the chance to dispose of their trash. I chastised myself for how I'd reacted. I'd need to apologize to everyone at some point.

Once the yard was cleaned up, I headed inside to check on Maddy. When I opened the door to the guest bedroom, she was already awake. She was lying on her back, reading on her phone. She glanced over at me. "Hey. Is everyone still upstairs?"

I shook my head. "All gone."

"Ugh." She flopped her arms down on the bed. "All your friends and family are gonna think I'm some stuck-up bitch. I'm always shutting myself away whenever there's a get-together."

I sat with her and pulled her upper body onto my lap. "They understand. You've gone through a ton of stuff. No reason to worry about what other people think anyway. You've got enough to deal with."

"I guess you're right. It still feels kinda antisocial."

"How did you sleep?"

"It was weird," Maddy said. "I had the strangest dream."

"Oh yeah? What about?"

"The moon. It was like I was connected to it. The whole dream was me walking through a forest or something, and I was looking up at the full moon. I could feel the light of it on my skin and it made my entire body tingle. There was a link between me and it. It wasn't like anything I'd ever felt before. For a little while, it didn't even seem like a dream. It was like I was lucid." She shook her head. "I can't figure out what it means. Maybe it doesn't mean anything at all."

Hearing her talk about her dream brought back memories of the stories my father had told us as kids. How Edemas and his ancestors had become more powerful as the moon grew full. When the full moon was out, they were basically living gods, nearly unbeatable in battle. It made me wonder how strong Maddy could be if she became a full werewolf like her forefathers. I needed to get my mind off that subject.

"So…Mom knows."

Maddy turned and looked at me. "She knows what?"

I nodded. "All of it. I chewed her ass pretty good. I'd be expecting an apology at any time."

"Oh, jeez. I hate that you had to do that."

"Don't be sorry. She's the one who should be sorry, and she is."

Maddy curled into me. "Well, I'm glad she knows. It still doesn't make me happy that she thought so little of me for being human."

I sighed, understanding exactly what she meant. "Mom's a traditionalist. Not always cool, but hopefully, we can show her a better way. I don't want my mom to think that just because someone's human, they can't be in her family. Like, what if one of my younger brothers falls for a human?"

"I'm still more human than wolf, though."

I leaned down and kissed her neck, moving my lips higher until I was close to her earlobe. I could feel her body reacting to me. "I could put a little more wolf in you," I joked, my voice barely above a whisper.

Maddy burst out laughing. "Oh really? Could you?" Her laughter turned to moans as I took her earlobe in my mouth and sucked gently.

She slid her hand onto my lap and kneaded the fabric of my pants, making my cock hard in an instant. My own hands drifted across her body, sliding across the mounds of her breasts, across her stomach, and sliding over her ass. Maddy started tugging at my belt, and in less than a minute, we were naked on the bed, our lips and tongues exploring each other's bodies.

I lifted her hips and slid under her. With her legs straddling my head, I slipped my tongue into her wet pussy. Maddy groaned and arched her back while I flicked the tip of my tongue across her clit. Lowering her head, Maddy took my cock into her mouth, the warm, slick wetness of her tongue sliding and wiggling across the head and shaft. I sucked in a breath, laying my head back as she worked me.

Her head slid up and down as she fucked my cock with her mouth. She sucked the head. It was like she was devouring me in the most amazing way. I came to my senses and put my lips around her clit and sucked while sliding a finger inside her. She sighed, my throbbing flesh still in her mouth, and nothing had ever sounded so erotic in my life. I clutched her ass with my free hand, pulling her closer and sucking on her clit, engorging it with blood. I could hear her breathing getting heavier as she ground her pussy into my face.

She pulled my cock out of her mouth. "Make me come, Nico. Make me come."

Not wanting to disappoint her, I slid my tongue into her pussy, fucking her with it as I rubbed her clit with my thumb. I moved faster. She started to tremble, and I could feel her getting close. As she neared her climax, her mouth worked even harder and faster on me. There was a building pleasure deep in my pelvis, just beneath my balls. I couldn't help myself, thrusting my hips in time with her mouth.

I slammed my tongue into her one final time, and she jerked and spasmed against me. Maddy moaned in pleasure, even as she continued to suck me off. I laid my head back, enjoying the next few moments. She added her hand and sucked the tip while her fingers stroked the length of me. A few seconds later, my eyes bulged, and I gritted my teeth. My fingers dug into the sheets as I erupted. The orgasm was exploded through me. Maddy continued stroking me as I shivered in pleasure beneath her.

Chapter 25 - Maddy

Something was wrong. I could feel it, but didn't know how to verbalize it. For days, I'd been moody and easily pissed off. The night before, I'd blown up at Travis, one of my bartenders—something I never did. He'd been carrying a jar of olives out of the back and had slipped on a wet patch on the floor. He'd caught himself but had dropped the whole jar. It shattered, throwing olives, brine, and glass everywhere. I saw it happen, and instead of asking if he was okay, I'd flown into a fit of rage.

"What the fuck, Travis? Do you know how much that jar costs?"

The rest of the staff had turned and looked at me in shock. They'd never heard that type of anger in my voice.

Travis looked confused. "What? Are you serious, Maddy?"

"Yes I'm serious. If it happens again, it's coming out of your next paycheck. Clean that shit up."

Travis had gritted his teeth and shook his head, starting to pick up the olives, gingerly watching out for broken glass. He muttered under his breath. "This is bullshit. It was just an accident."

"I'm sorry?" I shouted across the room. "Is there something you want to say?"

"Nope!" he shouted back, his face flaming with anger.

It wasn't like me at all. It was like I was watching myself do and say these things, but couldn't stop myself. I chalked it up to PMS, but it was some next-level monster PMS. I mentioned it to Nico after another situation where I'd cussed a guy out for bumping into me at the post office. Felipe had been with me as my guard and had to pull me out the door because I was ready to fight the guy. He was a solid hundred pounds heavier, and all I could think of was busting his face in.

Nico frowned. "I mean, you've been under a lot of stress lately. Maybe that could be it?"

"I don't know, Nico. I don't like being like this. Could it be my wolf? Can they cause mood swings and stuff?"

He sighed and leaned against the counter, crossing his arms. "Usually not. There's some anxiety and things like that. I've never heard of anyone getting that mad, or out of control. Maybe you should take a day or two off to relax?"

I didn't think he was right. It wasn't his fault. I was an anomaly. None of the other shifters had ever seen or dealt with a dormant wolf trying to push free. She was stirring inside me, and I could feel it. Almost *physically* feel it. Like her body was right at the surface, beneath my skin. It was disconcerting, to say the least.

That night, Sebastian took me to work, and I went directly to my office. I didn't want to be around any of the staff in case I had another blow-up. I felt bad enough walking through the building and seeing the look Travis gave me. I'd always prided myself on having a family work atmosphere. I was rapidly ruining that with my behavior, and I didn't know how to stop it. Fifteen minutes after I sat down, a knock came at the door, and Abi leaned in.

She quirked an eyebrow. "Can I talk to you?"

"Sure. Why not," I said, closing my laptop.

Abi closed the door and sat in the chair across from me. She clasped her hands in her lap and took a deep breath before speaking. "So, why have you been such a bitch lately?"

There it was. The first person to call me out on it. I groaned and put my head down on my desk. "I'm sorry," I moaned.

"Seriously, Maddy. What the fuck? I had to talk Travis out of quitting. You treated him like a dog last night. What's gotten into you? Do you need a break?"

It was the same thing Nico had said. I didn't like that idea. Ever since the attack, I'd only been working two or three days a week at most. I'd always prided myself on being independent and able to handle anything. Most weeks, I would put in five or six days easy. Sometimes, if someone needed a day off, I'd do seven full days. It was all okay because it was *my* place, the thing I'd built from nothing. I wanted to be here, wanted to lead my staff. I'd become so codependent on Nico that I was having a hard time differentiating the two of us. Always having one of his friends or brothers guarding me, not being able to do anything by myself…it was starting to become unsettling. I knew I needed the protection. I wasn't stupid, but I was starting to feel suffocated. That, along with whatever the wolf was doing to my head, was making it tough to think straight.

"You may be right, but I *need* this, Abi. I can't drop everything and leave you guys alone."

Abi rolled her eyes. "Sorry to break it to you, boss, but we can run a pretty tight ship without you. I know how to run this place, and the team knows what to do each night."

"Ugh, I know. I didn't mean to say you couldn't handle it." Nothing seemed to be coming out right.

"I know, I know. I'm just busting your balls. What I'm saying is that it's okay if you want to take some time. Since the attack, you've not spent more than a week away. Most people would have taken a whole month off. I think it's starting to get to you."

"Maybe. I'll think about it. For now, I'm going to try and let you guys do what you do. I'll try to stay off the main floor. I'll work in my office or help the kitchen team if they need help. That's a little less stressful than being out in front of customers."

Abi grinned and stood. "Good call. I promise we won't call you out front unless it's something major. Okay?"

"Deal."

Luis was due to leave the country the next day. He and Kenneth had narrowed down the search area to something they could probably go through in a week or two. He wanted to come by and confer with Nico in person before flying out.

He got to the house at lunchtime. Nico had ordered pizza to feed him before his big trip. Felipe and Sebastian came over as well, wanting to hear what the plan was.

We sat around the coffee table in the living room, eating while Luis explained what was going to happen. Everyone seemed pretty on edge about the whole thing.

"Kenneth is already over there," Luis said. "Some of the contacts he's made have really helped. There's apparently a pretty significant undercurrent of distrust for the royals in the old countries. It was surprisingly easy to get information—relatively speaking, that is. There's a lot of fear, too. Everyone, it seems, is scared of them. It took a while for him to gain their trust, but once he did, we got a lot of good intel."

"Like what?" Nico asked, grabbing another slice of pizza.

"Well, he's found the location of the original castle that Edemas ruled from. The human textbooks list it as the stronghold of a feudal lord, but in reality, it was Edemas. Kenneth has high hopes that it's the location of the vault or safe or whatever the hell the vial is stored in. I sort of doubt it."

"Right?" Sebastian said. "Wouldn't, like, the first place they'd look be in the castle he lived in?"

Luis shrugged. "It's what I think. Kenneth thinks there may be some hidden areas the royals couldn't find. We'll see. It's a good place to start anyway."

While they talked, I sat there, pizza growing cold in my hand, remembering my dream from a few nights before. The moon. My wolf was stirring. It was almost as if she was trying to communicate something to me. The images of the dream kept replaying in my mind, niggling at my subconscious. Was there something there? In the dream? The trees, the night sky, the light of the full moon. Over and over again, it flashed through my mind. Along with the images, there was a sense of wanting something.

"Hey," Felipe said, nodding toward me. "You okay, Maddy?"

Nico turned to me and put a hand on my thigh. "Are you all right?"

I nodded. "It's listening to Luis talk about Norway. There's something inside my head that wants to be *there*. I don't know where *there* is, though. It's frustrating."

Nico wrapped an arm around me. "It's okay."

A flash of anger surged through me, and I shrugged his arm off me. "Stop coddling me, dammit. I'm not some damned damsel in distress who needs to be saved. I have things to offer."

Nico's face fell, and he looked surprised by my reaction. I wanted to apologize, but the wolf had me, and there was no way she'd let me back down now. He held his hand up in surrender. "I didn't mean anything by it. I'm sorry. Are you sure everything is okay?"

I glared at him for several seconds, feeling the awkwardness in the room build as his three friends sat there, mid-chew, as I blew up at Nico. Finally, as the wolf's anger subsided, I sighed, and my body relaxed. I put a hand to my face. "I'm sorry," I said and leaned into Nico. "I told you something is wrong with me. I can't explain it."

"It's almost like she's going through puberty," Luis said.

"What?" Nico and I said in unison.

"Well, it usually isn't so…aggressive, but it's like the mood swings we had right before our first shift." Luis put his pizza down and leaned on his thighs. "Sometimes, if someone is a late bloomer, then the wolf can get angrier. Instead of fight or flight it's more like fight or…fuck," he said, smiling awkwardly. "You're *way* beyond just a late bloomer. This isn't like a kid who is fifteen and finally connecting to his wolf. Yours has been pent-up inside you for almost thirty years. If you're this easily keyed up, it sounds like you're nearing your first shift."

I shook my head. "I can't shift, though. It's impossible."

Luis bobbed his head back and forth. "Maybe. But maybe your wolf knows something you don't."

Luis left not long after for the airport. His words sat with me the rest of that night and into the coming days. It was confusing and scary. I couldn't shift. The blood was too diluted, but now that I was with Nico, my wolf knew its mate was *right there*. What would happen as this kept progressing? Would I finally snap and kill someone for doing something dumb? Would I claw out some old lady's eyes for stepping on my foot at the grocery store? Run someone off the road for cutting me off?

The other thing that scared me was if Luis was right. What if my wolf wanted to shift? Needed to shift, but couldn't? What would happen? Would I literally explode? It was all too confusing, too terrifying. I wanted it over with.

The next day, I was sitting on the back porch and staring up at the full moon. I felt calm and at ease for the first time all week. The way the light of the moon fell on me it was almost like cool water washing over me. My body had felt hot and on the verge of igniting for so many days, it was a welcome respite.

Nico found me out there and sat beside me, taking my hand in his. He didn't say anything. Instead, he leaned back and gazed up at the sky with me. I could tell he was waiting for me to say something. He was giving me the time I needed to put things into words.

"Nico?"

"Yep?"

"What does it mean if I…feel something moving inside me?"

He sat forward and turned his head toward me, looking concerned. "Describe the feeling? How long have you felt it?"

"It's been going on for a little while. Kinda since I started feeling…weird. It's almost like there's movement deep inside me. A tingle under my skin. An…almost butterfly feeling in my stomach. Every now and then, I can almost sense something just beneath my skin, sliding across the inside. It's weird. I don't know how else to explain it."

Nico stared at me for a long time. The look on his face was a combination of shock and confusion. "That shouldn't be possible. What you're describing is what kids experience before their first shift. But..." he shook his head and looked at the moon for a minute before turning back to me. "Maybe you have more shifter blood in you than we thought. That, or your wolf is so strong, it's trying to break free of the bonds holding her inside you."

That didn't sound good. "Is that a thing that happens? I thought the human part was still mostly in control."

"It is," Nico admitted. "I honestly don't know. Until a couple months ago, your entire existence was a mystery. I have no idea how strong the Edemas wolves were. Maybe it can fight through the dormancy?"

He must have seen the worried look on my face. He took both my hands into his. "Hey, don't worry about this. No matter what happens, you aren't alone."

"But what if—"

"If your wolf manages to break free, I will be here. I promised you I would make sure nothing happened to you. That doesn't just mean Javi and the royals; it means whatever is happening inside you, too. I'll be there to walk you through it every step of the way. You have my word on that."

I relaxed, knowing he was right. I could put my faith and trust in him. After everything, he'd proven that time and again. I leaned against him. "Thanks. It's so scary. Sometimes I don't even know how to act."

He wrapped an arm around me. "I'm here. Don't forget that. When things seem too crazy or weird, always remember, you are not alone."

We sat there for a long time. The silence wasn't awkward or strange. We were simply two people who cared for each other, enjoying the night. I stared into the milky whiteness of the moon and let its calming effect pour through my body. It called to me, pulled at me.

Deep in my mind, my wolf growled hungrily.

Chapter 26 - Nico

Maddy's confession had freaked me out. There was no way I'd let her see how concerned I was about her, though. Something was very wrong. She should not be able to shift. If her blood was as diluted as it was supposed to be, it should have been impossible. Her wolf was so strong. There should have been no way she could actually feel the mental movement of the wolf within her.

I remembered how it felt as a child. The awakening of the wolf, the way it was hungry for release. It really had felt like something was crawling beneath my skin. It was the exact description Maddy had given me. I was worried for her, worried what it all might mean.

I pulled my phone out to text Luis. I needed advice, and he was with the one person who might be able to give me the answers I needed.

Me: *I need to talk to Kenneth.*

Luis: *What's wrong?*

Me: *Something's going on with Maddy. I think she might be on the verge of shifting.*

Luis: *What???*

Me: *That's what it sounds like. What she's experiencing sounds just like the lead-up to the first shift.*

Luis: *That shouldn't be possible.*

Me: *Exactly why I need to talk to Kenneth.*

Luis: *He's out in a village on the outskirts of Oslo. Had a lead about a descendant of a human who'd worked as a servant for Edemas.*

Me: *Tell him to call me as soon as he gets back. Got it?*

Luis: *Will do.*

The next several hours went by excruciatingly slowly. Maddy was out grocery shopping with Felipe. I really hoped Kenneth would call while she was out. I didn't want to hide away. That would have been strange and hard to explain. Thankfully, I got a call not long after she'd left.

I answered the phone, almost dropping it in my haste. "Hello? Kenneth?"

"Yeah, it's me. Luis said you had an issue?"

I sighed, took a breath, and explained everything that was happening with Maddy. Her dreams, the sensations, and feelings. I went into detail about her mood swings, and how she felt like something was inside her. I laid it all out, and once I was done, I waited for Kenneth to tell me what he thought.

"Well, I'd hoped this wouldn't happen, but I guess we don't always get what we hoped for."

I blinked and shook my head. "Wait…what? You expected this?"

"Based on my research, I knew it was a possibility."

My blood ran hot, and I gripped the phone hard enough for my knuckles to crack. "You knew this might happen, and you didn't think I might need that fucking info? That *Maddy* might need the info?"

I could hear him sigh on the other end of the phone. "I didn't want to stoke fears based on a hunch. There was no reason to freak you all out if there was no proof or if there really was no reason to be worried."

"Well, what the hell is going on? Maddy shouldn't be able to shift. So what the hell is going on with her?"

"My research goes all through the genetic lines back to when Edemas was assassinated. I've gone back hundreds of years. Of course, I can't say I've found every single descendant, but from what I've discovered, Maddy is the first instance of a first-born female being born to the bloodline since the fall of Edemas."

I didn't understand what that had to do with anything. My frustration was boiling to the surface. "Why does that matter?"

"There have obviously been other females born, but in three hundred years, none have been first-born. Ask yourself this, Nico. What bloodline, out of all the different bloodlines, ever produced female alphas?"

I knew what he was saying. Female alphas were practically unheard of. The only time you ever heard about them was in legends. Stories about... "Oh shit," I whispered.

"Exactly. If the stories are true—and at this point we have no reason to assume they aren't—what does that tell you?"

The dots started to connect inside my mind. Puzzle pieces clicking together, revealing a picture I didn't like. "Maddy's an alpha?"

"That's what it looks like," Kenneth said. "I'd wondered about it. Worried is a better word probably. So, I kept tabs on her. I went so far as to hire a private investigator to stake out her house and watch her as she neared puberty. Nothing. Not a whisper of an imminent shift. I kept watching her until she was almost twenty years old. Still nothing. I'd decided we were in the clear. I didn't anticipate her finding a fated mate, or that it was even possible. I think now that she's found her mate, the alpha wolf is trying to break free. To take over."

"Will it hurt her?" It was the only thing I could think to ask. My concern for Maddy was growing by the second.

"No, I don't think so. She still shouldn't actually be able to shift. She'll just feel all the emotions and feelings of her wolf. It will be intense. You need to be there for her. Treat it just like a teenage shifter getting ready for their first shift. But you need to remember that she's an alpha. She's gonna have some bite to her."

That was true. It was a known fact that alpha wolves were much more aggressive during the initial change. After that first change, the shifter was able to bring it under control and begin the symbiotic relationship that would define their lives.

If you'd never shifted, though? Jesus, how long would it take to control it?

"Okay. Thanks. I need to talk to my dad. See if he has any suggestions."

"Glad I could help. Call if you have any more questions. I don't know if I can answer them, but I'll try."

I sat for a minute, letting the information ruminate in my mind. The hope I'd had before his call had evaporated. Now, I had more to think and worry about.

Before Maddy got home, I headed out the door and walked down to Dad's house. I'd never needed his advice more than I did now.

"Nico?" Dad looked surprised by my unannounced visit.

"Can I come in, Dad? We need to talk."

He raised an eyebrow. "Your mother didn't do something again, did she?"

I waved him off as I stepped in. "No, nothing like that. I need advice. You have experience with this."

"With what?"

"Raising a teenage alpha shifter."

Dad squinted at me. "Uh...do you have some love child I never knew about?"

As stressed as I was, a laugh managed to escape my lips. "I don't. It's Maddy." I went on to explain everything that had been going on with her. Then I told him about my conversation with Kenneth, and the fact that it looked like Maddy was a female alpha.

Dad listened patiently. Once I was done, he whistled and tilted his head back to stare at the ceiling. "That's a lot to deal with, son."

"Kinda what I thought," I said with a nod. "I can't even begin to understand how Maddy must be feeling. Like going through puberty all over again, but this time with a wolf breathing down your neck manipulating your emotions. Christ, Dad, it was bad enough when I was eleven, and I knew what to expect."

"So, we still don't think she can actually shift, right?" Dad asked.

"No. Kenneth and I both don't think her blood is strong enough to allow that."

Dad nodded and leaned forward. "There's only one thing you can do, and that is to have patience. I remember when you hit puberty. We already knew you were an alpha, so we had a bit of warning." Dad grinned ruefully. "You?

Oh man, you were a handful, though. Pissy attitude, angry outbursts. It was all your mother and I could do to handle you. I'll tell you, that first night when you finally shifted, I'd never been so relieved in my life. It was exhausting, but we loved you. We supported you through it. That's what you'll have to do with Maddy. That's the only advice I can give you. Until she's comfortable and the wolf settles into the fact that it will never shift, you'll have to be understanding."

I walked back home and saw Felipe sitting outside. He was on the steps of the porch. When he saw me he sighed and stood. "Thank God, bro. I don't know how much longer I could handle her," Felipe said as he stood.

"What's wrong?"

Felipe rolled his eyes and nodded toward the house. "Maddy just about killed a lady." My eyes bulged, and Felipe patted the air in front of me, motioning me to calm down. "Not literally. Some chick in the grocery store pissed her off. To be fair, the lady was an entitled bitch. Just yanked a pack of hamburger out of Maddy's hands. Like, big as shit, ballsy as hell. Took it out of her hand. Even my jaw dropped at the audacity of it. Maddy gets in the bitch's face and more or less tells her to back up and get out before she beats the shit out of her. I've never seen a person look so scared. Lady beat feet and got the hell out of there. Left her cart and didn't look back.

"So, then the whole rest of the time we were shopping, Maddy was raging about the chick. I couldn't calm her down. Then the whole drive home?" Felipe shook his head in exhaustion. "I'm tired, bro. I'm gonna go home and take a nap."

"Great," I said and walked inside.

I found Maddy pacing in the kitchen. She kept going back and forth, not even noticing me until almost a full minute had gone by. She jolted to a stop and looked at me. "My period started," she grumbled.

Oh good, I thought. Late-onset wolf puberty *and* PMS. Secretly, I wondered who I'd pissed off in a past life to deserve so much stress in this life.

I stepped over, and before I got close, Maddy released a growl. I stopped dead in my tracks. The sound had been exactly like a shifter growl.

"Something's wrong, Nico," she hissed. "It's not just stress. Something is wrong *inside* me."

"I know," I said, taking a seat on a stool. "I think I know why."

The anger on Maddy's face gave way to surprise. "What? What's wrong with me? Tell me." She sounded so desperate that it made my heart ache.

"I called Kenneth. I wanted to get his opinion on how you've been acting. He is almost a hundred percent sure that you're a female alpha. The first one in almost three hundred years. It means your wolf is stronger, more powerful than usual. It's why things have been so rough for you."

Maddy put a hand to her chest. It took her a few seconds to respond, and I could almost see the questions forming inside her head. She took a seat beside me, and she already looked more relaxed. "So, you guys are sure?" she asked.

I nodded. "It's really the only explanation for what you've been feeling. I can't say it's a hundred percent because no one has dealt with this before. You're kind of like a unicorn. We're learning as we go."

Maddy groaned and flopped her arms onto the kitchen island. "Why is my life so fucked?" She gave me a sideways glance. "So, I'm basically going through puberty a second time?"

I shrugged. "Kinda."

"Well, the first time wasn't very fun. I remember screaming at my parents for stupid stuff. I'd break down, crying for literally no reason. And, oh God, so much masturbation. Like...so much."

I couldn't help but laugh. A grin spread on Maddy's face, and it delighted me to see it. At least she was a little more relaxed. Sometimes the most stressful thing in the world was to not know. Once a name had been given to something, it became less scary and easier to deal with.

She turned to me and wrapped her arms around me. "Thanks for not hating me. I'm sorry for being such a moody bitch lately."

"Hey, at least you didn't threaten to kill me like that lady at the store."

"Fuck." She put a hand to her face, covering her eyes. "Felipe told you?"

"He did. Pretty cool story."

She sank into me. "How long does shifter puberty last anyway?"

I grimaced. "It, uh, it could be months."

"God almighty," she muttered and put her face into my shoulder.

I rubbed her back. "It'll be okay. We'll get through it. I survived, and so will you. We'll just take it one day at a time."

"Can you promise me that you won't hate me? Like, if it gets worse? I don't want you to get so frustrated with me that you start to despise me."

"That's impossible," I said, lifting her chin to meet her gaze. "How could I hate you when I love you so much?"

Maddy's face went pale and her mouth dropped open. "What did you just say?"

It took me a second for her words to sink in. A light clicked in my head. It was the first time I'd ever said it to her. I meant it.

"I love you."

"Do you mean that?"

I grinned. "I wouldn't say it if I didn't mean it."

She kissed me, hard and long, sliding her hands through my hair. When she was done, she pulled away and studied my face for a long time. Then a grin spread across her face. "I love you, too."

Chapter 27 - Maddy

After talking to Nico, it felt like I had a better handle on things. It wasn't perfect, but I seemed to be holding it together better than I had.

I'd even come back to work. I was still a little snippy, but I was usually able to rein myself in before I blew up at someone. Although, Sebastian had been on the receiving end of one of my pissy episodes. I'd finally told him he needed to stay away from the bar due to the way Abi reacted when he was there.

"Maddy, come on. Seriously?" he'd whined.

"Yes. Don't I look serious?" I asked while we sat in the living room.

"It was a one-time thing. I didn't think it would be that big of a deal."

"I'm going to stop you right there. I've known Abi for years. She's my best friend. I've known you for a couple months. You're great, but who do you think I'm going to side with here?"

My tone must have been getting angry because Nico had come around the corner and given me a raised eyebrow. "Are we good in here?"

Sebastian had turned to Nico to plead his case. "Nico, can you talk some sense into her?"

Nico puffed his cheeks. "Oh, see, now you've messed up, bro."

Sebastian had turned back around and flinched at the look I gave him. I stepped forward and started poking him in the chest, asking questions. "What do you think Nico is going to do? Am I not the owner of the bar? Is it not my decision who does and does not get to be there?" My voice rose with every question. "Do you think Nico has any say in *my* business? You're the one who fucked one of my employees. You're—"

"Okay, okay, okay," Sebastian had said, holding his hands up, warding me off. "Shit, all right. I get it. I'm sorry."

I froze at the fear in his eyes. The man who was a solid six inches taller and seventy pounds heavier than me looked like he was terrified of me. It took a physical effort to calm my face, but I did my best. I crossed my arms and took a step back to give him some room.

"I really am sorry. I didn't mean to make things awkward," Sebastian said.

"It's fine. I shouldn't have blown up like that. Felipe can take me to work tonight. I already texted him," I said, then took a deep breath to continue calming myself down.

It hadn't gone perfect, but I was happy I had been able to tone down my tirade before it had gotten out of hand. Maybe things were getting better. Felipe arrived thirty minutes later to pick me up for work.

Nico pulled me aside before I left. "You're sure you'll be fine? Are you still working in the back or are you gonna be out on the floor?"

"I'll be in the bar tonight. We have a couple people on vacation. I'll be fine. It's a Wednesday. It won't be too busy."

Nico didn't look happy, but I could tell he was walking on eggshells to keep me from exploding. "Alright. I'll be texting Felipe through the night to see how things are going. Fair warning, if I hear of something I don't like, I'll be there in a flash. Okay?"

"Yes, Dad," I said, rolling my eyes at him.

"I'm serious." I could see the emotion in his face and felt like shit for belittling his concern.

I put a hand to his cheek. "I know. I'm sorry. Yes, if you need to swoop in like a knight in shining armor, I'll be excited to see you. Okay?"

He nodded and kissed me goodbye. Felipe and I rode in silence to the bar. He was a pretty quiet guy, and if I had to guess, he was a little worried about pissing me off. It was fine. I needed the quiet to get my head right. I desperately didn't want to have an angry outburst that night. Especially not toward any of my staff.

Thankfully, the night went by pretty seamlessly. It wasn't crazy busy, but there were enough people to keep any of us from getting bored.

The issues started around midnight. When a guy started hitting on Abi. I'd seen him chatting her up over the course of the night, but hadn't thought anything of it. At least not until I saw her face. I could see she was getting frustrated that the dude wouldn't leave her alone. For her part, Abi was handling things as professionally as she could. I could hear some of the things he was saying, and I was starting to get pissed.

Finally, Abi had had enough. I heard her even over the din of the bar. "Listen, dude. Not interested. Take a hint and get lost."

"Hey," the guy said, looking upset. "You don't get to talk to me like that. The customer is always right, remember? Besides, let's not be like that. You don't know how good I can make you feel."

I slowly made my way across the bar, hoping Abi would diffuse the situation before I got there. Abi had shaken her head. "Dude, if I wanted to fuck a tiny dick, I'd go buy a bag of baby carrots and have a full on gang bang. Even then, they'd probably be bigger than whatever you're packing."

Well, shit. I moved faster, gently trying to move people aside. I looked up and saw that Felipe was watching the interaction from the far end of the bar. At least I'd have back-up if necessary.

The drunk guy was getting belligerent. "Fuckin' whore. Who do you think you are? Maybe I'll make you suck my dick. Show you how a good girl should act."

He reached a hand out to grab Abi, but I got there just before his fingers could close around her arm.

I tugged at his shirt, hard, and he spun around to look at me. His eyes were burning pits of rage. He stared down at me. "Oh, you want some, too? That's fine. I've got enough cock to go around. Maybe I'll ram her pussy"—he nodded toward Abi—"then I'll fuck your little booty hole. How'd that be, sweetie?"

I gritted my teeth. "Sir, I'm going to have to ask you to leave."

He leaned down and got within an inch of my face. Out of the corner of my eye, I saw Felipe starting to move across the room. I could smell the beer on his breath as he talked. "Fuck...you...bitch."

"Listen, you piece of shit. Get out or I'm calling the cops," I said. My vision was going red. I was so angry. Beyond pissed off. My entire body was shaking. I could hear growling deep in my mind. The growling of a wolf.

"You know what?" the guy said. "This is what uppity cunts like you need."

Without another word, he reared back, cocking a fist and slamming it straight toward my face. The entire world seemed to slow down. I waited for Felipe to jump between the guy and me. To stop his fist from crushing my nose and breaking my teeth. He'd slam the guy to the ground and call Nico to come whisk me away.

That's what I thought would happen. It was not what everyone witnessed.

The fist, like a rocket, shot straight toward me, so fast that it was a blur. Behind those knuckles was two-hundred pounds of muscle. As fast and strong as he was, one punch would probably send me to the hospital. Abi was screaming, the bartenders were yelling. Felipe was shouting and shoving through the crowd. And then my own hand shot up and snatched his fist out of the air.

The entire bar seemed to freeze. Everyone, even Felipe, stopped and stared as I caught the guy's fist in mid-air. It was like he'd punched a wall. I looked at my own hand in surprise. It vibrated as the guy tried to push through me to slam his knuckles into my face.

"What the fuck are you?" he grunted as he tried to pull his hand out of mine.

I remembered the names he'd called me, the way he'd treated Abi and me. Then I remembered that less than ten seconds ago, he'd been trying to turn my face into jelly. A wolfish growl escaped my lips, and I gripped his hand and twisted. He yelped in pain and spun as I twisted his arm, desperate for his arm not to break. I grabbed the back of his jacket, and using his own body weight, slammed his face into the brass tube that ran the length of the bar. Blood burst out of his nose and the cracking sound of his nose echoed through the room.

The entire crowd jumped back. He slid to the floor, clutching his face and crying. I let go of him and stepped back.

I looked down at my hands in shock. What had I just done? Felipe was there, hauling the guy up to his feet. "Buddy, we're gonna call this a wash. You tried to assault a woman, she defended herself. Now, I'm gonna toss your ass out and you're not ever coming back. Got it? No need for the cops."

The guy's voice was thick after having his nose broken. "Is she a fucking shifter? What the fuck just happened?"

Felipe dragged the guy toward the door, but not before shooting me a wide-eyed glance. I bolted, running through the kitchen and into my office. I locked the door behind me and sat at my desk. I couldn't even understand what had just happened. I'd taken some basic self-defense classes back in college, but what I'd just done? That had been more instinct than skill. I'd felt so strong. So powerful. Like my arm wasn't even my own. A satisfied little growl echoed up through my brain, and I knew my wolf must have had a part to play in the display out there.

I sat in my office, stewing over what had happened. Twenty minutes later, there was a knock on my door, and Nico let himself in with the key I'd given him. He didn't say anything. He came in, closed the door behind him, and watched me closely.

I glared at him. "Would you stop fucking looking at me like that?!"

Nico raised an eyebrow, and I winced. "I'm sorry. I didn't mean to talk to you like that."

He walked around my desk and sat on the edge, looking down at me. He didn't seem upset at my tone of voice. Instead, he looked totally unperturbed. I could sense myself spiraling. It was like I was weightless, and the wind was blowing me along, and I had no say in where. Everything was so scary. I groaned and tugged at his shirt, pulling Nico to me. He came and wrapped me in a hug.

"Felipe told me what happened," Nico finally said as he stroked my hair.

Tears slipped across my face, but my voice was steady. "Nico, I didn't even know what I was doing. It happened so fast. I've never moved that fast in my life."

"Wolves have fast reflexes," Nico explained. "I think your supernatural senses will start to develop soon. Everything is awakening since you're going through puberty. I have no idea how strong you'll be, but from what I've seen, I think you'll be as strong as a fully shifted adult wolf, especially since you're an alpha. It's gonna be part of the process. We'll have to take it as it comes. It'll get weird, but like I've said, I'll be here for you."

He was right about that. Things got very weird over the next week. On Friday, I'd been sitting in the living room reading a book when a disgusting smell wafted into my nose. The sour sweet smell of rotting plants. I'd gone all over the house searching for the smell, even going outside to see if some plant in the landscaping had died. Finally, I'd found an old bag of salad in a drawer of the fridge. It was still sealed, but I'd been able to smell it. Through the plastic, the door, and across the room. I threw it out in disgust.

Saturday night, a car a block from the bar had been T-boned. The horn had blared for over ten minutes until the cops and EMTs got it disabled. For everyone else it had been a dull hum in the background, totally ignored. For me? I'd had to go into my office and wrap my ears in dish towels. It seemed so fucking loud, it gave me a migraine. By the end of that night, I was totally exhausted. My body was going through so much that even with full nights of sleep, I didn't feel completely rested.

Felipe walked me out to the car. It was nearly three in the morning, and all I wanted was to go home, put some damned earplugs in, and pass out. Felipe took a few steps in front of me to open my door. My senses were completely overloaded and raw, like an exposed nerve.

I heard the creaking sound and tilted my head. My senses told me what it was even though I'd never heard it before—the sound of a ligament twitching, flexing. My eyes widened in surprise when I heard the next sound. A click, the sound of a trigger being slowly pulled back.

I grabbed Felipe and yanked his body to the right just as a bullet smashed through the window, where he'd been standing a moment before. The sound of the shot burst across the parking lot as we tumbled to the ground.

"Shit!" Felipe pushed me to the other side of the car as bullets started punching into the tires and metal of the car. A hunk of pavement burst up out of the ground as a bullet slammed into the asphalt.

"Call Nico!" Felipe shouted as he pulled out his own gun and returned fire.

I did exactly as he asked, hitting the speed dial. Nico answered groggily. "What's happening?"

"They're shooting at us!" I screamed, trying to be heard over the gunshots.

"I'm coming," Nico sounded fully awake now. I took heart in knowing he'd be there soon. But would it be soon enough?

Felipe fired back at the shooter. We'd been the last people to leave the bar. I'd sent everyone else home, and Felipe and I had finished mopping and locking up. We were alone.

Fear tugged at my gut, making goose flesh rise up on my arms. Felipe got up on his knees and glanced over the top of the car, scanning the woods on the other side of the highway. A bullet pinged off the hood six inches from his face. He dropped and cursed.

"Well, I've got five shots left. Probably would have been a good idea to bring more bullets. Oh well," Felipe said, sounding astonishingly calm given the situation.

"What are you gonna do?" I asked.

"My best."

Without another word, he took his shirt off and flung it to the right. The flash of white must have drawn the shooter's eye. There were two quick shots toward the front of the car, where the shirt had now fluttered to the ground. During the two shots, Felipe stood and braced his gun on the hood of the car. As soon as the second shot rang out from the highway, Felipe fired three quick rounds toward the muzzle flash we could both see.

When his third shot was out, Felipe dropped down again. We waited in silence for a few seconds, then we heard it. Screams of pain. Felipe grinned and looked at me. He stood quickly and dropped back down twice, trying to draw more gunfire. Nothing came. He inched around the front of the car and snatched up his shirt, he waved it over his head, and there was still no shot. He pulled the shirt back on and waved for me to follow him.

We stayed low and continued to run and hide for cover as we made our way to the highway. The screams of pain were getting increasingly louder. Once we were sure there was only one shooter and we were safe, we stood and jogged the rest of the way to the road.

Headlights appeared over the hill, and I could hear the screaming engine of Nico's SUV. He pulled up next to us, tires squealing. He leaped from the truck and scooped me into his arms, checking me for injuries.

"Are you okay?" he demanded, looking more terrified than I'd ever seen him.

"I'm fine. I think Felipe got the guy who was shooting at us."

Nico growled and looked at Felipe. "Where?"

Felipe gestured toward the woods. Nico went with him, and I followed closely behind, not wanting to be left alone. The underbrush gave way to a small clearing. Even in the dark, I could see the man's set-up perfectly. My night vision was already getting better. He had a big fallen log that had been fitted with a tripod for a rifle. The gun had fallen over the side of the log. The man was thrashing on the ground, screaming and clutching his leg. I almost gagged seeing it. Felipe's shot had gone right through the man's knee. It looked like the bullet had torn straight through his knee cap. The leg hung down like there were no bones connecting the lower portion of the leg to the upper. He was in so much pain that he didn't even try to go for his weapon when he saw us enter the clearing, just continued to clutch his ruined leg and scream.

Felipe jumped forward and yanked the man's sidearm out of the pistol holster at his waist. Nico quickly patted the stranger's pockets and searched him for more weapons, finding a wicked-looking six-inch curved knife from a holster at his back. Nico looked at Felipe. "Grab his fucking arms."

I had no idea what Nico had planned, but Felipe didn't hesitate. He put his own pistol into his waistband and put his hands under the would-be assassin's armpits. Nico stepped down to the guy's feet and looked the man dead in the eyes. "You'll probably want to be asleep for this." Nico kicked the man's ruined knee. The shriek that burst from the man's throat sounded like death. It was high, keening, and full of pain. He stopped screaming long enough to vomit on the ground, then passed out from agony.

"Holy shit," I whispered.

Nico grabbed the guy's legs and lifted. "It's what he deserves for trying to kill my mate," he snarled as he and Felipe hauled him through the forest.

Once we got to the highway, we checked to see if anyone was around before hustling the body to the back of the SUV and tossing him inside. Felipe took the driver's seat, and Nico huddled in the backseat, holding me close and stroking my hair. Felipe pulled away. "Where to?"

"My shop. We'll try to get some answers there. It's far enough from anyone that they won't hear if he tries screaming for help."

Felipe nodded and drove straight to Nico's shop. Once we were there, Felipe and Nico carried the stranger inside and strapped him to an office chair, then tied a rope around his waist and his good leg to hold him down. Once he was secure, Nico and Felipe stepped back and looked at the man.

Felipe pointed at the guy's face. "Doesn't look like he's from around here, does he?"

I could see what he meant. The assassin's face had a distinctive Eastern European look to it, but that didn't necessarily mean anything. After all, this was America—the melting pot.

Nico took a step toward the man and slapped him across the face. He jerked awake, his eyes rolling in their sockets, making him look like a panicked horse. He started screaming again and looking down at his ruined leg.

Felipe grabbed a massive wrench on a work table and positioned it over the knee. "Yeah, it fucking hurts, but if you don't shut the hell up right now, I pound the whole thing to jelly. Got it?"

The man's eyes jerked up to Felipe and then the wrench, and he made a Herculean effort to bring himself under control. The screaming stopped, but he continued to stare at his dangling leg. He started to gibber in a language I didn't understand.

Nico glanced at Felipe. "What the hell is he saying?"

Felipe shook his head. "Don't know. Sounds Slavic? Maybe Polish or Czech? No fucking idea." He slapped the man's face. "English, motherfucker, English!"

The guy licked his lips and glared at us, then turned his eyes toward me. "She-beast. Is alive. Woman must be…uh…eradicated."

Nico stepped forward and towered over the man. "Say that again."

The assassin cowered in fear. "Please. No hurt. Please." He had a thick accent that made understanding the words difficult.

"Who sent you?" Nico asked. We, of course, already knew, but Nico probably wanted to hear it anyway.

"Orders were…kill female. Kill she-beast. Werewolf cannot resurface."

I stepped forward, taking strength in Nico and Felipe being right there. "What do you mean? My wolf can't surface. I'd need Edemas's blood for that."

He glared at me and spat on the floor. "Stupid bitch. You know nothing?"

Nico brought a palm across his face, the sound of the slap echoing through the garage. Blood dribbled out of the man's mouth. "Call her a bitch again and see what happens."

The man coughed and spat a wad of phlegm mixed with blood on the floor, nodding that he understood. "Fine, yes. No bitch."

Nico pulled the gun they'd taken from the man's holster and pressed the barrel against the man's good knee. "Start talking. Otherwise you'll need to get fitted for a wheelchair. First off, what's your fucking name?"

The man stared at the gun in horror and fear before swallowing. "Uh...my name Bogdan."

"Okay, Bogdan. Tell us what you know."

"What is known of the..." He stopped himself from saying what he wanted, remembering Nico's warning. "Of woman's father?"

Nico lowered the gun. "We know he was killed by the royals because he had some distant relation to Edemas. The last werewolf king. You all are killing all the descendants until the bloodline is totally gone. That's all we know about you sick fucks. You kill kids."

Bogdan gaped at Nico, then glanced at Felipe before his gaze finally rested on me. After a few seconds, he barked a laugh. "You know nothing. Father was not killed because he was a distant relative. Father was killed because he was a full-blooded Hollander wolf. The first in three centuries."

Chapter 28 - Niko

"What do you mean he was a full-blooded wolf?" Nico asked.

"Uff, for Americans, you not good at the hearing. I say what I say. David Samuels was a full-blooded wolf."

"How is that possible?" I asked, my voice barely above a whisper.

Bogdan took a deep breath and winced at his leg again, trying to find a more comfortable position. "You know the story of Edemas, yes? That he sent away two children? A boy and a girl?" We all nodded. We remembered the story. Bogdan nodded. "Good, yes. He split the babies up. Both were pureblood. Both alpha. The boy he sent to a pack of wolves that worship Edemas. They were almost like a cult. Fanatics. They ensured the boy only had children with other wolf shifters. None"—he paused for emphasis—"of his offspring were alpha. Not one ever. None of his line carried the werewolf gene. Edemas wanted his progeny to survive, but mostly because he wanted an uprising. A resurgence of the werewolf to rise up and cast down the new royals and avenge him. No alpha? No uprising. Simple."

"What about the girl?" I asked.

Bogdan shrugged. "Girl is girl. Much harder to track lineage. Last name changes. Women, especially in the past, were sent away for marriage more often. Hard to trace. The boy? We killed all of his line." He looked pleased with himself after mentioning the last part.

"You think it's something to be proud of that you all butchered babies and children?" I growled, my voice icy and cold.

Bogdan looked confused. "But is abomination. All must be wiped out. No descendants, no werewolves. You must see." He nodded toward me. "It is why she cannot be allowed to live."

Felipe tapped the man's bad knee with the barrel of his pistol, eliciting a scream of pain. While he screamed, Felipe shouted to be heard. "You'll want to stay on the story, big guy. Any more talk about Maddy, and I'll personally put a bullet into your crotch."

Bogdan got himself under control again, nodding and wiping sweat from his forehead. "Yes. The royals got too comfortable. We all assumed that the girl had died or that her line had run its course. We were wrong. She had created a family with a human man. Their children created their own families." He made a spreading motion with his fingers. "You see? But the blood was diluted with each generation. No longer a threat. Or so the royals believe. A great-great-granddaughter of Edemas's child found a man. They fall in love, they mate. The man? He is wolf shifter. The boy that was born? He is not an alpha, but he has the strongest blood link to Edemas. Rumors come that a boy is showing signs of resurgence of the Edemas werewolf line. The couple go into hiding, knowing the royals will come for them." Bogdan raised an eyebrow. "What better hiding place than a whole new world." He raised his arms and gestured around us.

I nodded. "They came to America to hide." It made sense. Run as far as you can.

"Yes. They hide, and for a time are successful. The boy that was born began his own bloodline. His son grew to a man and met a shifter woman." Bogdan, despite his injury, grinned. "This is where story gets good. We only discovered this after blood tests. The pair were actually related. Very distant cousins. Both carried the blood of Edemas in their veins. The odds are millions to one that this should happen. They had a son, a single child. He was not an alpha, either, but never before, in three hundred years, had the blood been so pure again. He was unable to shift, of course, but he still had power in his blood." He looked at me and waggled his eyebrows. "Have you figured out who that boy was yet?"

Maddy nodded. "David Samuels?"

Bogdan grinned at her. It wasn't a nice grin. It was dark and filled with malice. I didn't like it.

"Your father. We came for him. He had to be killed. He was not alpha, but there was a chance he could have a child of his own. That child could be alpha. A fear…that was true." He continued staring at Maddy. "I can smell it on you. You are alpha?"

None of us gave him the answer, deciding it was better to keep him in the dark. Maddy was an alpha. She could open the vault, and she could become a werewolf if she drank Edemas's blood. Not just a shifter like we'd thought, but a full werewolf. A being so powerful that they had ruled over all the shifters of Europe. A being so powerful, thousands of people had spent centuries trying to ensure it never came to pass again.

The prospect terrified me. I could only imagine what was going through Maddy's head.

"My mission has failed," Bogdan said, grimacing in pain. "I am a failure. Know this, she-beast. We will never stop. You must not be allowed to rise."

His arms were unbound because we hadn't considered him a threat. His leg was destroyed so he was in too much pain to shift. He had no weapons near him, but he still made one final move. He flicked his wrist, and a tiny blade that Felipe hadn't found snapped out from beneath his sleeve. It was too small to have done any damage to us, but he didn't plan on attacking us with it. Instead, he drew the blade across his own throat. I screamed as the fan of dark red blood burst out of his neck.

"Oh, holy fuck!" Felipe screamed and jumped back away from the arterial spray.

I grabbed Maddy and turned her from the sight. I was too late, though. She'd seen. I watched the way Bogdan's eyes had bulged as the blade split his skin open. The man convulsed a few times and gurgled one last wet death rattle before going still.

It was something I'd never forget for the rest of my life. It hurt me to know that Maddy had seen it and would think about it for as long as she lived.

I sat her in my office while Felipe and I hauled the body deep into the woods out back and buried it. Maddy didn't speak. She seemed stunned or in shock. I couldn't even think what to say to bring her out of it.

Just before dawn, I came back in with Felipe, sweaty and tired. We walked over to the office, and while Felipe cleaned the blood, I called Luis. It would be almost lunch time in Norway. I was exhausted, and instead of holding the phone to my ear, I placed it on the table on speaker.

"Luis?" I asked.

"Yeah, what's going on?"

"Is Kenneth there?"

"Hang on."

There was a rustling sound and Kenneth's voice came on the line. "This is Ken."

Sighing, I glanced between Maddy and Felipe before going on. "Kenneth, did you know that David was a full-blooded wolf?"

"I don't know what you mean."

"What I mean is that not only was your father a shifter, but David Samuels' mother was one as well."

"No, that's not true. David's mother was a human." Kenneth didn't sound as sure of himself as he had before.

"Nope. We've just had a...let's call it a conversation with an assassin the royals sent to kill Maddy. David's birth mother was a shifter. Not only that, she was also a descendant of Edemas."

"What? That...that can't be. Dad would have told us."

"Looks like your old man had a lot more secrets than you realized," Nico said, chuckling humorlessly.

"Why, though?" Kenneth asked. "Why not tell his own children the truth?"

"I think your father was protecting David. Maybe he thought he might be the one to finally bring about Edemas's revenge."

"Jesus," Kenneth hissed. "You might be right. Dad was always talking about Edemas in more of a happy light than most people do." He paused. "We need to meet soon. How long until you and Maddy can get to Europe? Until you can, you need to get Maddy into hiding. Immediately."

"We already have her in hiding at my place."

"No. That isn't safe anymore. Hide her some place they'll never think to look for her," Kenneth said.

"Why? What's different now?"

"Look. If what you're saying is true, then Maddy should have been a shifter since she was a kid. I have no idea why her wolf has been dormant for so many years, but once the royals know their assassin wasn't successful, they'll increase the pressure. You have to be more careful. Something bad is coming."

"Shit, Maddy, what's wrong?" Felipe asked.

I spun in my seat. Maddy looked terrible. Her face was pale, and her eyes were unfocused.

She shook her head. "I… don't…" She never finished the sentence. She slumped over. I barely managed to catch her before she hit the floor.

"Jesus, she's so pale," Felipe said behind me. "What happened?"

It was all I could do to stay focused. I needed to help her. My anxiety was almost too much. I'd made a promise to take care of her, and now was the time. "Felipe, call Doc. Tell him we're on our way."

The next hour went by in a haze. Maddy never quite lost consciousness, but she spoke like she was in a gauze-covered dream. Nothing seemed real to her. I couldn't tell if she was hallucinating or maybe talking while in a semi-sleep state.

Doc worked on her and hooked up an IV, and I held her hand the entire time, Felipe paced back and forth at the other end of the room. It all reminded me of that night when I'd found her half-dead on the floor of her bar. I'd been right in that same room, holding her hand. The déjà vu wasn't pleasant.

Sometime later, I felt a poke at my chest. I'd fallen asleep beside her bed. My head jerked up, and my eyes sprang open. Maddy was there, smiling at me. She looked so much better that I almost cried out in joy. I rubbed my eyes, reaching out to take her hand in mine.

"What happened?" she asked.

"Not sure yet. Doc took some blood to run some tests. You kind of fainted. I'll be honest, you were a bit of a drama queen."

She could see the sarcastic grin on my face and chuckled. "You know me. Anything for attention." The smile slid away from her face as the memory of everything that had happened must have come back. "Nico, I've got a bad feeling things are gonna get worse."

I tightened my grip on her hand. "Probably. But I'll be here for it."

Before we could say anymore, Doc walked back in. The look on his face told me that he'd found something he didn't like. Doc pulled up a seat next to me and looked at us. "Your bloodwork came back, Maddy."

She struggled to sit up straighter. "Okay?"

"So," Doc began. "When you came in the first time a few months ago, after the attack, I took blood samples. You were unconscious and I needed to check for any diseases that might be in your system so I could treat you properly. The blood I took from you then and the blood I took today are almost completely different."

Maddy and I stared at him in confusion. I shook my head. "What do you mean?"

He handed us a report. "This is a little hard to read, but look at the third column. It shows the red and white blood cell counts as well as platelet levels. The top line shows Maddy's numbers from today. White blood cell counts are extremely high, like a shifter. That's why we almost never get sick. The platelets are off the charts, which is the healing factor we have. Makes total sense, right? Since Maddy has shifter blood." We both nodded, but Doc shook his head. "That's the problem. The blood from earlier shows that she's completely human. Cell and platelet counts are right on par with an average human. Somehow, over the last few months, the blood has totally changed."

I furrowed my brow, not understanding. "Well, could it be that her wolf is awakening?"

"That's the entire issue, Nico. Why the hell was her wolf dormant to begin with? You told me this morning her father was a full-blooded wolf. Even if her mother wasn't, Maddy would have had strong enough blood to be a shifter. None of this makes any sense."

As we talked back and forth, Maddy remained silent. All she did was stare down at her hands.

Glancing over at her, I saw she had a strange expression on her face. Some combination of guilt, embarrassment, and shame.

I cut off my conversation with Doc and turned toward her. "What's wrong?"

Chapter 29 - Maddy

Feeling like an idiot for not mentioning it before, I took a deep breath and sagged back into the pillows of my bed. "I have a blood condition. I take medicine for it."

Doc frowned. "What type of condition?"

"Chronic anemia. I've taken meds for it since I was a kid. I ran out weeks ago and forgot to get my prescription refilled."

Nico looked at Doc. "Could that be it?"

Doc looked even more confused. "Maddy, what medicine do you take for this...um, condition?"

My face went red in embarrassment. "I don't actually know. My mom always calls it in for me."

"Maddy, you're almost thirty years old and your mom still calls in your meds?" Doc asked.

My embarrassment grew with every word. "Not all of them, no. Just this one. She gets a discount or something on them. She gets it cheaper than I could if I ordered it."

"Maddy, I hate to break it to you, but that makes no sense," Doc said.

My embarrassment faded a bit and was replaced with anger. "What do you mean? It makes perfect sense."

"It doesn't," Doc said, taking the blood report from Nico. "This blood test doesn't say you are anemic."

"What?" I must have heard him wrong. That couldn't be possible.

"Maddy, this test *and* the test from a couple months ago have perfectly adequate amounts of iron in your blood. You aren't anemic now, and you weren't then, either."

I sat back up and tore the paper from his hands. "That can't be right. I've had chronic anemia since I was eleven. It started after my first period. It had been a heavy flow. I—" my voice stopped as old memories resurfaced. Panic and fear fluttered in my chest.

"What is it, Maddy?" Nico asked.

I swallowed hard. "Um, I was acting out. Lashing out at my parents and kids at school. I can remember being frustrated and like there was something inside me trying to get out." As I said the words, the meaning began to crash down over me.

"Oh, holy shit," Nico whispered.

I shook my head, trying to push the thoughts away. "No, it was just normal puberty. Everyone gets pissy and emotional for a few years."

"Maddy? Have you ever heard of suppressants?" Doc asked.

"Are you shitting me?" Nico practically shouted.

Doc held a hand up to calm him and looked at me again. "Have you?"

"Uh, not really," I said.

"Not surprising," Doc said. "They're a bit frowned upon. It's a type of drug used to suppress shifter activity. It's mostly used in countries where being a shifter is *very* frowned upon. It's also been used by humans who have adopted shifter babies. It's very hard to get, very illegal, and hard to hide. Most kids start to question why they are taking meds at a certain age—"

"No!" I cried out, jumping off the bed. "My parents wouldn't drug me. They wouldn't."

Doc held his hands up. "Sorry. I didn't mean to imply something. If it's a normal medicine, why don't you call your mother and find out the name. Then we can rule that out."

The suggestion should have been an innocent enough request, but I had a panicky, dissociated feeling rising up inside me. What if they had lied to me? Had I been taking drugs to suppress the shifter inside me? The thought of calling her and getting that answer was terrifying. Except, I knew I had to. The only way to be sure was to ask my parents.

I nodded. "Fine. We'll call and settle this right now." I walked to my purse to get my phone.

Stepping over to me, Nico sighed and took my hand. "Maddy, if the answer isn't what you want it to be, you have to remember that they are still your parents."

"I know that, Nico," I snapped as I pulled out my phone. I regretted it as soon as the words were out of my mouth.

It was past three in the morning, but I didn't care. The phone rang seven times before Mom answered, her voice groggy. "Hello?"

"Mom? It's Maddy."

"Maddy?" She was almost immediately awake and sounded worried. "It's late. What's wrong? What happened?"

"Easy, Mom. I just have a question."

"A question at three in the morning?"

"Who's on the phone?" I heard my dad ask.

"It's Maddy, dear, I'm talking to her. Maddy, what do you need?"

"Mom." I took a deep breath. I knew the quickest way to ask was to come right out and see what happened. "Mom, I've run out of my medicine. Can you tell me what the brand name is, so I can have my doctor order more?"

There was a long pause, and I could hear my mother's breathing get heavier. "Your...meds? You're almost out, or you *are* out?"

"I'm out. I forgot to tell you. I ran out a few weeks ago and things have been crazy so—"

"Maddy! Dear God, you have to take your meds right away. Oh my God."

"Mom, Mom, calm down. I'm not going to die from anemia, right?" I asked the question, but there was a dark pit opening inside me. The way she was acting was almost a dead giveaway.

"No, you *have* to take it. I think I have some here at the house. I'll drive down tonight."

"Jesus, Mom. It's a six-hour drive. Are you being serious? I'm at a doctor's office right now. Tell me what it is and he'll call it in."

"No, no, no. You know I have to call my doctor. I get the discount for it. I—"

"Enough!" I shouted into the phone. Everything went still. Doc and Nico froze where they were; the look on Nico's face was resigned regret. Mom went silent, and I could hear Dad murmuring to her, asking questions. "The truth, Mom. Right fucking now."

"Maddy, baby, you have to understand—"

"All I have to understand is what the hell is going on. What medicine am I on? Tell me. Right now…or…or I'll never speak to you again." In that moment, a part of me meant it. How could I trust my parents if they couldn't tell me what was happening even when I came right out and asked.

When Mom spoke again, I could hear the tears in her voice. "You don't have anemia, Maddy. When that strange man called us and said he had a baby we could adopt, your father and I were so happy. He told us you were a shifter, though. Or at least a half-shifter. He said we'd need to give you suppressants once your beast, or whatever, started to emerge. He said if anyone found out you were a shifter, your life might be in danger. That's all he told us. We found a doctor who could get the suppressants into the country.

"We really didn't think we'd need them, but when you got close to puberty, you started acting out. Almost to the point that we were afraid of you. You lashed out, you were aggressive, and totally out of control. We got scared and started giving you the pills. They keep the shifter transformation from happening. The doctor said it makes the creature go dormant."

I was sure Nico could hear everything on the phone. He'd taken my free hand in his and his head hung down. I'd never been so angry and sad at the same time. It was like my whole life had been pulled out from under me. The people who were supposed to take care of me and be honest with me had lied to me my entire life. I could hear Mom crying on the phone.

"We only wanted you to have a normal life, Maddy. We wanted you to be safe and normal. You seemed so much happier once the pills took effect."

My wolf growled, and the sadness was fading. All I felt now was rage. An anger so deep that I wanted to get in the car and drive to their house to scream at them. To shout, to throw things, to show them the wolf they'd tried to suppress for almost twenty years.

"Maddy?" Nico whispered. I ignored him until he hissed in pain. I glanced down and saw that the hand he was holding wasn't my hand anymore. At least it wasn't like the hand I'd always known. My fingernails had transformed into claws, digging into his flesh. I gasped and released his hand, dropping the phone. I stumbled backward, clutching my warped hand.

The phone clattered to the floor, and I could hear Mom screaming my name on the speaker. Nico scooped the phone up and started talking, but I tuned it out. I slumped into a seat, already starting to hyperventilate. Doc slid next to me and was trying to talk to me, but all I heard was the dull roar of my blood coursing through my body and the growl of my wolf. I could feel her rage at finding out she'd been suppressed for our entire lives. I could still feel the claws on my hands. I kept them hidden under my armpits, then bent over, staring at the floor.

I tried to tell my wolf that I was sorry, doing my best to make sure she could feel my sorrow. So many years of lies and secrets. I apologized, and almost instantly, my wolf's anger subsided. It was like she knew how sorry I was, that I'd had nothing to do with the deception. It was the first time I *truly* felt like a whole new being was inside me. I started to sob, and my wolf seemed to wrap some sort of emotional blanket around me. I could hear her whining, hurt by my own pain. I continued to repeat that I was sorry in my head. Over and over again, I apologized, not stopping until I managed to gain some semblance of control. Finally risking to open my eyes, I saw that my hands had gone back to normal. I released a sobbing sigh and smiled.

Doc helped me stand and walked me toward the bed. "I want you to stay here tonight. I need to keep you under observation. I've never known anyone to be on suppressants for so long, so I have no idea what the side effects or withdrawal symptoms might be. I'll get you a Xanax, so you can sleep."

"That sounds great. I could really go for being stoned," I said as I climbed into one of the clinic beds, déjà vu hitting me from the night I was attacked the first time.

Nico walked over to me and took my hand again. I could see the angry red puncture wounds on the back of his hand. I frowned when I saw them. "I'm sorry about your hand."

He shook his head. "No big deal. Seriously. I'm sorry. Not because I did anything, but for"—he gestured toward the phone on the table—"for all that. For having to go through it all. I can't imagine how you're feeling, but we'll get through it. I promise."

"Yeah, I know," I murmured.

Nico pulled the sheets back and kicked off his shoes before climbing under the covers with me. The bed was made for one person, but was still wide enough that he could pull me into his arms as Doc left. I laid my head on his chest and let him comfort me. As I drifted off to sleep, I still couldn't believe what my life had become.

Chapter 30 - Nico

My phone was ringing again. Maddy didn't want to talk to her parents. Even bringing it up would set her off. After the fifth or sixth call, I finally gave her mother my personal cell number. I felt terrible, but I couldn't fully cut off contact. Maddy was angry, but they were still her parents. I was the go-between for them. Still, three or four calls a day was starting to wear on me.

I answered the phone. "Hello again, Mrs. Sutton."

"Oh, hello, Nico. How are you?"

I chuckled. "The same as I was three hours ago the last time you called."

She sighed and laughed. "I'm being a pain, I know."

"No, it's fine. I get it. I spoke with your husband about an hour ago."

"Oh lord. I didn't know he'd called."

"What can I do for you?' I wanted to get this over with. There wasn't anything I could pass along that I hadn't already.

"I just…I was thinking and…I don't want her to think I'm ashamed of her. Of what she is. We've always loved her. We're so, so guilty about all this. We miss our girl. We want her to know that. And we're happy that she's with such a nice young man as yourself."

Maddy hadn't told her parents about us. That fact didn't make me mad. She'd had a ton of things going on. When I mentioned our relationship in one of our first phone calls, her mother had been surprised. Over the course of the last few days, we'd kind of gotten to know each other a bit. She was a nice woman. Her father was pretty cool, too. Both of them had made some pretty shitty decisions when it came to lying to her, but I could tell they did love her.

"Well, Mrs. Sutton, I appreciate that."

"Nico, all we want is to fix things with Maddy. It's all either of us can think about."

"I know. Just give her time. She's angry. Not only that, but she's also dealing with her wolf trying to emerge. It's a lot. I know you don't understand that part of it, but all I can say is that it's not a great time."

"Can you let her know that her father and I love her?"

I sighed. This was depressing. "I can tell her. Don't worry. A few more days, and she'll calm down. Then you can tell her that yourself."

"Thank you, Nico. I'll try not to bother you too much."

"Totally fine, Mrs. Sutton. Have a great day."

The one good thing was that it seemed like Maddy was getting control of herself and her wolf. Ever since she'd found out about the fake medicine, she'd been in a much better mood. No more snapping at people or losing her cool. I hadn't seen her so calm and at ease in weeks. When I came home that afternoon for lunch, I found her reading a book. Over the last little while, it had been all she could do to sit still for five minutes, much less sit and read for an extended period.

"Okay, what's going on?" I asked as I sat beside her.

"What do you mean?"

"You're totally chill. Have you made peace with your wolf? I'm not complaining," I added quickly. "But it seems crazy how fast things changed."

Maddy marked her page and sat the book aside. "I'll be honest, it was what happened at the clinic."

Over the last few days, I'd refrained from talking about her hands turning into claws. It happened sometimes when shifters went through puberty. It was very rare, but I'd heard of it before. It was almost like the way the werewolves of legend could change certain parts of their bodies. I doubted that was what she meant when she was talking about what had happened at the clinic. I sat silently and waited for her to go on.

"I'm angry, and frustrated, but I feel like I'm finally making contact with what's inside me. It's sort of like meeting up with a long-lost relative. Plus, my wolf understands that I didn't knowingly take the pills. I think that was the main issue. Our connection was so slight and distant that she couldn't understand what I was doing or why. I think the wolf knew I was taking something that was holding her back, but the rest was sort of a blur. The anger was mostly because she thought I was doing it on purpose. As soon as she knew what was happening?" Maddy shook her head in wonder. "It was like a light switching on. Everything became a little less intense, a little more cohesive, I guess. That's the only way I can explain it. It's been nice not to have some kind of war going on inside my head."

"I'll bet. I'm happy that things are going better. Um…your parents said to tell you they love you."

Maddy let out the most dramatic sigh I'd ever heard. "I guess I need to talk to them at some point."

I shrugged. "That, or you're gonna have to buy me a new phone, because they'll wear mine out if it keeps going on like this."

"Okay, fine. I'll do that once all this is figured out. Speaking of, have you heard when we're meeting Kenneth?"

"I'd wanted to wait until I was sure you had everything under control. Having a wolf in puberty on an airplane is not a good idea, trust me on that. I called him this morning. He says he's positive the royals are going to up the pressure. The fact that their assassin was ineffective has probably pissed them off. Luis actually dug into the guy and found out he was in a shifter division of the Polish Special Troops Command. It's basically Poland's version of the special forces. He was a big piece to play, and we blocked it. They have to be pissed and nervous. That's a dangerous combination."

Maddy nodded. "Well, no worries about the plane. The wolf and I have an understanding. We can go whenever. The longer this stretches out, the worse it is."

"Right. I'll start making plans. I need to tell my folks. I guess there's no time like the present. I'll walk down the street now, if you're cool with that."

Maddy nodded. "Sure. Is it okay if I don't tag along?"

Maddy still had a weird relationship with my mother after the whole blow-up they'd had. Mom had apologized. She'd actually been about a half-step from groveling at one point. Maddy said she forgave her, but it didn't seem like she was completely ready to be buddy-buddy with Mom yet.

"Yeah, it's fine," I said. "Keep reading your book." I headed out the door to my parents' house.

"What the hell are you talking about?" Mom shouted.

I rolled my eyes. "I said Maddy and I are going to Europe. Kenneth and Luis think they have some leads on how to end all this." The conversation wasn't going how I'd planned.

Mom ran her hands through her hair. "Carlos, what do you think of this?"

Dad had his arms crossed over his chest as he stared at me from across the room. "Well, Julia, can you think of a better way to keep Maddy safe? The royals think she's here in Florida. The best way to hide might be to get out of the country."

Mom groaned. "You're probably right. I just hate the idea of Nico going *toward* the royals. They live in Europe. It's where their seat of power is."

"True," I said. "But like Dad said, they won't be expecting it. It may give us the breathing room to find this vault before they figure out what we've done."

Mom glared at me, but then her face relaxed. "Fine. You're probably right. It doesn't mean I have to like it."

Dad stood and walked over to us. "I'll watch over the pack while you're gone. We'll get things buttoned-down just in case they decide to turn the volume up and bring the fight to us."

It was one of my biggest fears. I had a duty to the pack, and I worried about what might happen if I wasn't here. Knowing Dad was good to step up and take over while I was gone was a huge load off my shoulders. I could go on this quest with Maddy and have one less thing to worry about.

"Also, Dad, do you know anyone with a private jet?" I asked.

"Seriously?" he asked with a raised eyebrow.

"Safer than flying commercial, right?"

"Good lord. Let me make some calls. I think I actually do have a contact."

Dad made good on his promise. Within six hours, he put me in touch with a guy who had a Learjet available for charter. After we had that, it was a waiting game.

We waited four days until Kenneth made contact with us. He called on Monday morning. Thankfully, I was home and able to take the call with Maddy.

"Are you guys ready?" Kenneth asked.

"Ready as we're gonna be. Where are we meeting you?" I asked. I had the phone on speaker on the kitchen island.

"Sweden."

Maddy and I exchanged a look before I spoke again. "Why Sweden?"

"I've got a safe house there. It's where I've spent most of the last twenty-five years. The royals have never found me. It'll be a safe spot to make our home base. It's as safe as we can get. We can plan our next moves there."

I took a breath, the reality of what we were about to do finally setting in. "Okay, Kenneth. I'd like to do this as soon as possible."

"Hell. Can you all fly out tomorrow?"

Maddy was chewing nervously at her nails when I glanced up at her. She caught my eye and shrugged. "Why not?"

"Okay," I said. "We'll make the preparations."

That night was one of the most stressful of my life. Things felt like they were coming to a head. The atmosphere was tense and nerve-wracking as Maddy and I packed. Even though we were going on a private jet, we decided to just do one carry-on bag each and a couple of backpacks. The last thing I wanted was to be lugging around a ton of luggage on what was supposed to be a secret recon trip.

That night, neither of us slept for shit, and the next day seemed to crawl by. We'd decided to fly out at night, hoping anyone watching might lose us in the darkness. I had a feeling that there were still eyes on us, and I had no plan to reveal our plans in the light of day.

Felipe and Sebastian came over right after dusk to see us off. Felipe put our bags in the back of my car and hugged Maddy and me in turn. "Be safe, guys. I'll be really fucking pissed if you get killed over there."

"Nice pep talk, Felipe," I said, hugging him back.

Sebastian was uncharacteristically quiet and also hugged us both. If I didn't know better, it seemed like he might have been on the verge of crying. I put a hand on his shoulder and looked into his eyes. "We'll be back soon, bro."

Sebastian nodded, flashing a feeble smile. "Yeah, yeah. See you guys soon."

He hugged Maddy, then we got into the car and drove away. There was a strange finality to it, as well as a nagging feeling that now that we were on our way, things would never be the same again.

I hoped I was just being paranoid, but the feeling wouldn't leave. Maddy must have felt something similar because she sat beside me, not uttering a single word. She seemed lost in thought.

We'd barely gotten over the county line when things started to feel weird. I slowed the car, knowing something was off. I couldn't even describe it, but it felt like someone was standing right behind me. I could almost feel the breath on my neck.

"What's wrong?" Maddy asked, noticing I'd slowed down.

I'd chosen to take some back country roads to the airport, hoping it would throw off any tails we might have. As we crested the hill, I saw that my plan had been for shit. There were three cars parked across the road, blocking us from going any further.

"Oh no," Maddy whispered.

"Grab my phone. Text the guys that we've got an issue," I said, bringing the car to a stop.

I glanced in the rearview mirror, hoping to back up and make a quick U-turn. Instead of an open road, a massive SUV with its lights off pulled out of the woods to block our escape. Son of a bitch. I'd never even seen the car as we came through.

This was bad. I did my best to look calm for Maddy, but I was freaking out inside. I put the car in park and stared through the windshield. My fingers gripped the steering wheel so hard, my knuckles were white.

Javi stepped out of the shadows. He raised his hands, gesturing that he was unarmed, and nodded at me to get out of the car.

Maddy curled her fingers around my thigh. "You can't. Nico, you can't go out there."

I sighed. "There's not much else we can do. I'm sorry. I guess I didn't plan this as well as I thought. At least out there I'll have a shot. If it goes bad, I can shift and try to fight them. Give you time to run."

Maddy's eyes were full of tears as she shook her head, flinging her hair back and forth. "No. They'll kill you."

I put my hand on her cheek. "Let me see what Javi has to say. If you see me start to shift, that's your signal to run. Got it?" The remarkable calm in my voice surprised me.

Maddy didn't agree. All she did was loosen her grip on my leg. I took that as acquiescence. I opened the door and stepped out slowly, holding my own empty hands above my head, then stepped towards the front of my car.

"Hey, Nico."

"Hey, Javi. Can I help you with something?"

A rustle of noise came from the right and left. I glanced around and saw more of Javi's pack coming out of the woods. We were fully surrounded. He had at least a dozen guys out here.

I had no chance. I was an alpha, but even then, there was only so much one shifter could do. My wolf was snarling and snapping inside my head, itching for a fight. My human mind calmed him and tried to think of a way out. I wasn't successful.

Javi put his hands down. For the first time, I noticed he didn't look well. His typical cockiness was missing. Instead, he looked worn-down and exhausted. There was fear in his eyes. I could see it, but I had no idea where it was coming from. He had me dead to rights. The guys were at least thirty minutes out, if they even got the message. Felipe and Sebastian would never get here in time. What did he have to be afraid of?

"Well?" I asked, trying to fill my voice with as much courage as I could muster.

Javi glanced down at his boots before answering. "Nico, I'm not here to fight. I'm not here to capture you, and I'm not here for Maddy, either."

I looked at him for a long moment and cocked my head. I wasn't sure I'd heard him correctly. "Then what are we doing here?" I asked.

"I need your help."

The words hit me, and it was all I could do to keep my jaw from dropping. Doing my best to keep the surprise off my face and out of my voice, I asked, "What the hell do you need my help for?"

Javi motioned for his guys to move into the glare of the headlights. "Come on, guys, enough intimidation, get the fuck over here." Once all his people were in front of me, Javi shook his head. "The royals want my head. And they want my pack dead."

Frowning, I shook my head. "Why? You're their attack dogs, aren't you? Do all their bidding? Try to kill innocent women?"

Javi nodded but looked pained, like the admission hurt him. "My family swore a blood oath to the royals centuries ago. I'm the alpha now, and my father told me years ago that the time would come that we would be called upon. We've always been loyal. They finally called on me months ago. They found an heir to Hollander. Some type of online DNA test. Once they found her, they ordered us to kill Maddy." Javi winced and gritted his teeth. "I really thought I was protecting the world when I sent my guys there. Then, two weeks ago, they told us we had another mission. A shifter orphanage down in El Salvador. Allegedly there was a group of triplets that had connections to the Edemas line."

As I listened to him talk, I was having a hard time understanding where the story was going. I glanced back and saw Maddy had the phone to her ear. Probably talking to Felipe or Sebastian. Maybe even one of my brothers if she couldn't get a hold of my friends.

"We went," Javi said. "The orders were to take out the kids and any witnesses." Javi shook his head and wiped a hand across his face. "Nico...I'm not going to kill kids, man. The triplets were only like eighteen months old. Christ, they didn't even smell like wolves. The blood had to be so diluted, it was pointless. I refused. The moment we got in there and saw what we were dealing with, I said fuck it, and ordered us to pull back. I gave the nuns running the place a heads-up to get those three kids out of there as soon as possible.

"The royals found out, and now there's a target on my back. My back, and the backs of every member of my pack. We have the same enemies now. I want an alliance with you. We have a common goal. Take down the royals."

I blinked several times before answering, trying to get my thoughts in order. "Javi, you're men still tried to beat Maddy to death. How can I trust your men? There's no way."

Javi chewed at his lip and nodded to one of his guys, who went to the back of one of the trucks and opened the back hatch. In the light of the headlights, I saw a man's body. Even at that distance and with all the bruises and blood. I could see it was the guy who Maddy had described as the leader of the gang who attacked her. His eyes were open and lifeless. "What the fuck?"

Javi nodded. "Yeah. Some of us were more committed to the royals than others. The guys I sent after Maddy were…zealots, to say the least. It's the main reason I sent that specific group of guys. When I ordered us to turn back at the orphanage, they revolted and demanded we kill the kids. So, we killed them instead. Simple as that. I brought this one back to prove my pack's trustworthiness."

I stared at the dead body for several moments. He'd killed his own pack members. That was unheard of. It should have been unforgivable, but the reason he'd killed them had been honorable.

Plus, we needed all the help we could get. I had to ask for assistance anywhere I could get it. After making my decision, I nodded. "Okay, Javi. I'll give you a shot. But you still killed an innocent man. I can't fully trust you, but I need the help. My pack can't do this alone. You turn on me…" I pointed at him. "And I'll skin you alive. Got it?"

Javi held his hands up and nodded. "Got it."

Chapter 31 - Maddy

Seeing the dead body in the back of the SUV had been one of the most shocking things I'd ever seen. His dead eyes had stared out and seemed to be staring right at me. The sight should have been horrifying, but my wolf took pleasure in it.

I recognized him immediately—his face had haunted my dreams for months. Knowing he and all the others who'd attacked me were dead filled me with a strange combination of happiness, relief, and sadness.

I'd heard Nico agree to work with Javi, and I agreed. It made sense to have more help. I didn't get out of the car, though. Making a deal with the devil didn't mean I needed to cozy up to him.

Nico called Felipe and Sebastian, who'd been pushing their car to the limit to get here in time. He explained what was happening, and once they arrived, he put them with Javi to start making plans. Nico even called his dad and gave him a heads-up. When we finally pulled away, Felipe had Nico's father on speaker phone and all four men were deep in discussion on how to protect both packs.

"Do you think we made the right choice?" I asked once we were a few miles away.

Nico shrugged. "I hope so. We need as much help as we can get. Plus, Javi has women and children in his pack just like we do. Even if Javi is a dick, those people deserve help. We'll have to wait and see. The guys and Dad will make sure things go smoothly."

I couldn't imagine how difficult it was to be a pack alpha. There were so many decisions and things to worry about. I was glad Nico was in charge. At least he'd make the best choices to keep everyone safe.

The rest of the drive to the airport was spent in silence. I could tell that Nico was thinking about something.

I could almost sense his anger. When we got to the private airstrip and got our bags loaded, I finally asked him what was wrong.

"I can't stop thinking about that story. About Javi's pack going down south to that orphanage."

When I'd heard the royals had ordered the murder of three babies, my own blood had boiled. The shock, disbelief, and anger had been almost more than I could stand. I nodded. "I feel the same way. I mean, I know it's incredibly distant, but those kids are my relatives. They've been targeted simply for existing. They're just babies. How could anyone think they were a threat?" My tone kicked up a notch with each word I said.

Nico put a hand on my shoulder as we walked up the stairs to the plane. "Stay calm, Maddy. Remember what I said about the plane. Not a good place to have a stressed-out wolf."

He was right. As the plane took off, it was like my skin was too tight. My wolf and I had come to an agreement, a happy truce. Even then, the flight was rough. My anxiety was high and my senses were at an all-time high. It was an exhausting flight. Thankfully, I finally fell asleep after three hours of dealing with it.

I didn't wake up until we landed in Sweden. The thump of the landing gear hitting the pavement jolted me awake. I rubbed my eyes and glanced outside, chuckling softly. I was actually in Sweden. It wouldn't to be a fun trip, but it was still a pretty cool moment.

"What's so funny?" Nico asked.

"I've never been to Europe. It's kinda neat. Even though we're on a life-or-death mission."

A car waited for us on the tarmac. Nico had arranged it beforehand. The keys were hidden on one of the tires. After we loaded the car up and got in, Nico punched in the coordinates that Kenneth had given him, then the next leg of our trip began. It was midafternoon there, and already the jet-lag was dragging at me. It didn't, however, stop me from checking out all the sights as we went.

The safe house was a four-hour drive from the airport, and for the first hour or so, things were fine. But the deeper we got into the countryside, the more anxious I became. It was different from what I'd experienced on the plane. This was more intense, a bone-deep worry. My wolf was pacing and whining inside my head, pushing my anxiety even further.

Nico must have noticed. Two hours into the drive, he finally said something. "Maddy, are you all right? You seem...I don't know."

I nodded, continuing to stare out the passenger window. "I'm fine. Don't worry about me," I said, hiding the anxiousness. I tried to calm myself and my wolf down, but it wasn't working.

After stopping for a snack, we continued to follow Kenneth's directions and turned onto a smaller country road that took us deeper into the mountains. I closed my eyes and pretended to nap, but in reality, I was just trying to hide my building anxiety. It felt like an eternity before Nico finally pointed out the window at a cabin up the road.

I sat up to look and saw that the thing was like something out of a storybook. It was flanked by a distant waterfall and completely surrounded by old growth trees. The sky was barely visible through the canopy, giving the place an early evening look. It was so shrouded in shadows that I had a hard time making out just how big it was.

The trees seemed familiar. I frowned and looked around as Nico pulled the car up and put it in park. The entire area seemed familiar. I'd never been here before, so why would this piece of property jog something in my memory?

My eyes snapped wide open. I knew where I'd seen all this before—in my dream about the moon. This looked just like the forest I'd walked through in that dream. Instead of calming me down, the realization made me even more nervous.

Kenneth stepped out onto the porch and waved us in. We grabbed our luggage and walked up the steps.

"Glad you all made it," Kenneth said, taking one of the bags from me.

He hurried us inside, closed the door, then quickly locked it and set what appeared to be an alarm panel. I gaped at it. "How the hell did you get that installed way out in the middle of nowhere? I didn't even see any power lines running to this place."

Kenneth grinned. "You learn a lot of things over the years when you're trying to stay hidden."

He surprised me by dropping the bag and enveloping me in a massive hug. I stared over his shoulder at Nico. His eyes were wide, and he had a shocked grin on his face. "Uh...nice to see you, too," I mumbled as he set me back down on the ground. But before he released me, I returned the hug. He was my uncle, after all.

"Sorry. You start to miss human interaction when you live alone like this. Plus, I miss your father, and you remind me of him."

"It's okay," I said.

"I was just getting some food ready for an early dinner. Hope you like Swedish food. Smoked fish, roasted potatoes, and of course meatballs. I made a bit of everything, I wasn't sure how hungry you'd be."

Other than some dill-flavored potato chips and a Swedish chocolate bar, we hadn't eaten anything since leaving America. Nico and I both dived in, devouring everything Kenneth had put together.

After eating Kenneth's entire spread, the three of us sat and relaxed by the fireplace. Nico and I on the couch, Kenneth on a recliner.

"Well, we have news about Javi," Nico said as he sipped a cup of hot chocolate Kenneth had made for us.

"Is he dead?" Kenneth asked hopefully.

Nico shook his head. "Even crazier. He's allied himself with us. He turned his back on the royals after they ordered him and his pack to kill three eighteen-month-old babies in El Salvador."

"Eighteen months old?" Kenneth said in horror. "Because they have some shred of the old blood in them?"

I nodded. "Yeah. Javi had to…eliminate some of his own guys who wanted to go along with the plan."

Kenneth slapped his thigh in anger. "Those baby-killing sons of bitches," he hissed. "Those kids are…well, hell, they're our family, right?"

"That's what I told Nico," I said.

"They're sick. This has to stop somehow. Maybe you're the one to do it," he said, pointing at me.

"Why me?" I asked, taking Nico's hand for comfort.

"Because," Kenneth explained, "your dad was a full-blooded shifter. I'm not sure that he ever brought his wolf out—the blood had diluted so much over the centuries, he'd probably need to meet his fated mate or drink Edemas's blood to do it—but he was a full wolf by blood. You are an alpha, Maddy. You might be able to take the throne. The true throne. Not this…whatever the royals have been playing at for three centuries." Kenneth sat back and sighed. "Well, I guess the term *royals* is just a name they use now. They don't run a country, they don't have a real throne. They just use the fortune they've amassed to fund an army of child butcherers. They have power because they have money. There are God knows how many politicians, authorities, and journalists in their pockets. It's part of the reason why they've manage to stay hidden so long." Kenneth pointed at me. "That fortune is one you have rights to."

"I don't want money, Kenneth. I want them to stop murdering people. Killing kids? Having this awful shadow government? It's all got to come to an end. Until they're stopped, no one with even a passing relation to Edemas will be safe."

"That's why we need to find that vault. Get the vial of blood. Force their hands," Kenneth said. "It's the one thing that will give us leverage. Make the royals back off."

"Right," Nico agreed. "Once we get that, we might have a shot."

They both sounded so confident, but I had doubts. It couldn't be that simple. Finding one simple thing wouldn't be enough to make them throw up their hands and say,

"You got us. All done. Enjoy your life." If they'd held power for so many years, even having that secret weapon wouldn't be enough to stop them.

I opened my mouth to mention my worries, but I froze. The words were already forming on my lips, but I couldn't speak. My entire body was racked with sharp, shooting pains. I almost gagged because the pain was so bad. I wrapped my arms around my stomach and bent over, letting out a hiss of pain.

"Maddy?" Nico said, his voice laced with concern.

His hand was on my back, but I barely registered the touch. All I felt was pain. Finally, I managed to suck in a breath. Instead of telling them I was all right, a scream erupted from my throat. A scream of agony and torment. It was like my skin was trying to split apart, like I'd swallowed glass, like every cell in my body was trying to explode. I sank to my knees as a cold sweat broke out all over my body, dripping off my nose onto the floor.

"What's happening?" Nico shouted.

"Christ, I don't know!" Kenneth yelled.

I gritted my teeth and felt my wolf rising up inside me. She was right there. I could almost feel her breath on my neck. She was so close. As close as she was, it still felt like she was a thousand miles away. She was in pain—I could feel it. Her pain and mine were melding, making it even more agonizing. Something was pulling at us both. A magnetic tug that was trying to rip us in two.

"God," Kenneth whispered. "Look. That's got to be it. I didn't even think about it."

I managed to lift my eyes to see what he was talking about. Anything to figure out how to stop this pain.

Kenneth was gesturing toward a window. It looked out on the waterfall in the distance. It was the only opening in the entire forest canopy. The sky was already dark.

Sitting there in the sky, casting its glow down on us, was a milky white full moon.

Chapter 32 - Nico

I held her for hours. The pain she felt must have been intense. She alternated shivering and burning up. Screaming, then hissing breaths through gritted teeth. I carried her to the bathroom so she could vomit. I was starting to worry that we'd need to go to a hospital. I'd never seen anything like this.

I traced a finger gently over her cheek. "Maddy?"

"Ugh...ugh." It was all she could say. Ligaments stood tautly on her neck as she clenched her jaws in pain.

I had an inkling of what was happening. I wanted to see if she felt it, too. "Are you trying to shift?"

Maddy jerked her head in a spastic nod. I sighed. This was not how this was supposed to go. The first shift was always a little uncomfortable, but it tended to happen so fast that whatever pain or discomfort there was vanished in a second or two.

But this had been going on forever. Her wolf wouldn't come through for some reason.

"Maddy?" I asked again. "Is your wolf having trouble coming out? Is that the problem?

She looked at me, her eyes filled with desperation, sweat dribbling across her forehead and down her cheeks. "Stuck. I...feel...stuck."

Finally, out of sheer exhaustion, Maddy fell into a fitful sleep. I settled her on the bed and put a cold, wet cloth on her head. Kenneth came in to check on her. He looked as worried as I felt.

"How is she?" he asked.

"Asleep. Sort of," I said. She was unconscious, but she continued to twitch and convulse as wave after wave went through her body.

"I heard what you asked her," Kenneth said. "Is this really what a first shift looks like?"

I shook my head. "No. This is awful. The moon is having an effect on her. It's her first full moon since she got all that medicine completely out of her system. I wish I could make it better."

Maddy let out a low groan, and I watched in horror as her body began to ripple. Patches went from skin to fur and back again. It happened all across her body in waves.

I knelt on the bed and took her in my arms again. She shivered as her body continued to try to shift. Her claws emerged, then receded, her teeth morphed into fangs. Instead of the magical change that usually happened, the wolf teeth seemed to tear through the gums before sliding, leaving blood around her lips.

"Kenneth, get me...fuck, I don't know. Get some water or something!" I cried out. Panic was rising in my gut. I was afraid. More afraid than I'd ever been in my life.

Kenneth arrived a few seconds later with a bottle of water. I tried trickling some into her mouth to keep her hydrated, but she spat it back out and gagged. It continued like that for hours, until the moon finally set and the glimmer of sunrise began in the east.

As if a switch had been flipped, Maddy collapsed, motionless, into my arms. She was so still that, for a heart-stopping second, I thought she'd died. Then I saw the steady rise and fall of her chest, and I let out a sigh that was close to a sob.

I stripped her clothes off. They were completely soaked through with sweat. Once I got her under the covers and her head on the pillow, I left the room, closing the door behind me so she could sleep off what had just happened.

I flopped into a kitchen chair and covered my face with my hands. I was more tired than I'd ever been in my life. I could only imagine what Maddy felt like. Kenneth set a cup of coffee in front of me, and I greedily took it, sipping the scalding liquid.

"How are you doing?" he asked.

I shrugged. "Tired. Freaked out. Worried. All of the above."

"It's the moon. She has the power of the werewolf in her blood. It made the pull of the moon stronger than it would be if she'd been a normal shifter."

I nodded. "That's the only thing that makes any sense. I've never seen something like that. I've heard rumors of suppressants being used on shifters. There's always a bit of a withdrawal stage, but they never have anything like that happen when they start to shift again."

Kenneth nodded, then sipped at his coffee. "Last night, the werewolf inside her was reacting to the pull of the moon. The legends say the night of the full moon is when they were at their strongest."

"I don't know how to help her get over the hill," I said. "How do I get the wolf to come out?"

Kenneth tapped a finger against his mug and eyed me over the bridge of his nose. "Have you and Maddy discussed claiming?"

I stared at my cup. "After last night. this is going to sound stupid."

"Try me."

"Well, I've been holding off on discussing it with her. I wanted to wait"—I gestured toward the bedroom—"until the *danger* was over," I said ironically. "Looks like a different kind of danger was waiting in the wings, though."

Kenneth stared back at me, not saying a word. I stared back, getting more frustrated by the second.

Then it clicked into place. My shoulders drooped and my hands slid off the table. Christ, I was an idiot.

Kenneth pointed at me. "If you become mated, you'll share each other's strengths. It could be the last little kick in the butt her wolf needs to figure out how to come out. Once you claim her, her wolf might become strong enough to come forward for the shift."

It made sense. Every claimed set of mates I'd met had always had an intense connection. It was the only thing I had to go on. I'd discuss it with her once she woke up, but that ended up taking quite a while. She slept the entire day. I took a three-hour nap, and when I woke up, Kenneth said she'd barely stirred.

Finally, hours later, just before dusk, her eyes fluttered open.

I sat on my knees beside her, taking her hand. "Hey. Damn, you gave us a scare."

"I feel like I was hit by a bus," she hissed as she ran a hand down her side.

"Do you want anything to eat?" Kenneth asked from the door.

Maddy glanced toward him and nodded. "I'm starving."

Kenneth nodded. "I've got a can of soup. I'll make you a grilled cheese to go with it while it heats up."

I'd never seen someone so hungry. Maddy devoured the sandwich and the soup before it even had time to cool. Kenneth found a can of pineapple and a couple granola bars, which she also polished off quickly. Once she was finally satisfied, she seemed much stronger and ready to talk.

"So," I said, "this is our theory."

"On?" Maddy asked.

"On how to fix what happened last night. To keep it from happening ever again."

"How?"

"Claiming."

Maddie's eyes went wide, and a line formed between her eyebrows. "How would that help?"

"Once the mates are entwined by the act of claiming, their strengths mingle, making each other stronger. We think that if I claim you, it'll give your wolf the strength she needs to complete the first shift." I interlaced my fingers and leaned forward. "I promise you I won't force this. I don't want you to do something you don't want to do. I swore from the beginning that I'd do anything to protect you, and it's pretty painful for me to watch you go through that kind of agony. I can't do it, Maddy. I can't see you like that again—"

She stopped my rambling by putting a hand on either side of my face. "It's okay, Nico. I think this is where it's supposed to happen. I know it."

I shook my head slightly and frowned. "How do you know that?"

"The trees and the moon. They're the exact same from my dream. It's meant to be. I think my wolf somehow knew this was the place I'd end up. I don't have any idea how it could know that. I don't even have the energy to question it. I choose you, Nico," she said, looking deep into my eyes. "I already did—weeks ago. I just never felt like there was enough time to discuss it. So much was going on, I didn't want to push."

I pulled her toward me and kissed her. I pulled back and looked into her eyes. "I love you, Maddy. No rush, but I really don't want to see you in that kind of pain ever again."

"Before the next full moon? How about that? We'll be back home by then, probably. Once we have time?"

"Perfect. We've got a lot to do, but it'll be soon."

The sound of a clearing throat echoed across the room. We turned and saw Kenneth sitting by the door. We'd both forgotten he was sitting right there. "So, do you guys need some alone time?"

Chapter 33 - Maddy

I'd never been so sore in my entire life. My muscles felt like they were being pulled apart every time I moved, my bones ached, even my hair seemed to be throbbing. The only good thing was that my wolf seemed calmer now that the full moon had passed. It took a few days of recovery for me to understand that my building anxiety when we arrived had been the wolf knowing that the full moon was approaching. She'd known what was coming and had been freaking out. She was trapped inside me.

The first day I spent in bed, then each passing day, things got better. By the third day, I was pretty much back to normal. Sore but normal.

I found Nico in the kitchen that morning. He was just putting his phone down.

"Who were you calling?" I asked as I poured myself a cup of coffee.

He glanced at me and shrugged. "Your parents."

I gritted my teeth. I was still angry at them. So many lies. So much that had been hidden. I didn't know how long it would take for me to forgive them. I loved them, yes, but I also hated them for keeping me in the dark. I hadn't talked to them since that last phone call at the clinic.

"Have you been talking to them a lot?"

"Uh…I'm gonna tell your mom she's paying my cell phone bill next month," Nico said. "They call all the time. I mean, it's like two in the morning back home, and they're calling."

I sighed and sat down. "Are they worried?"

"What? Worried that their daughter is in a different country and there's a secret society of psychopaths after her? Why would they be worried?"

I gaped at him. "You told my parents everything?"

He waved me off with a smile. "No, of course not. They do know you're in a different country. I didn't say where, in case the royals have their phone tapped or something. They know you're in trouble, but that's all I've said. They know you're with me and safe. That was all they were really concerned about."

I slowly turned my cup in my palms, warming my hands. I'd need to speak with them as soon as all this was over. I couldn't keep them out of my life forever. I didn't want to, either. I just needed to get my head around it. "I just need time to come to grips with…well, my entire life, I guess."

Nico nodded. "They get that. Trust me, they do."

We ate a breakfast of toast and jam. Nico said he had some more calls to make to the guys back home, so I went outside for a stroll. I'd been in the cabin for three straight days and was desperate for some fresh air. I put on a light jacket and took the path by the house that led up to the waterfall. The air was brisk, much colder than back home. It honestly felt good. The icy air against my skin helped to focus my mind. Helped me think about everything.

The waterfall had seemed fairly close to the cabin, but it must have been an optical illusion because it took almost ten minutes to get to it. There was an ancient-looking stone bench beside the little river that was fed by the waterfall. I took a seat and stared at the water, losing myself in the roar. The spray churning up out of it turned into mist in the air, the early morning sunlight making it burst into rainbow colors. It was the most at ease I'd been in weeks.

It was nice. I must have completely zoned out because I never heard Kenneth make the climb up. I jumped, startled when he sat next me.

"Sorry, didn't mean to scare you," he said, giving me an apologetic smile.

"Oh, it's fine. I was out of it."

"You look like you were doing some intense thinking. How are you holding up?"

I wanted to give him a simple answer—"I'm fine" or "I'm dealing with it." Instead, it was like a dam broke inside me, and words vomited out everywhere. I spilled my guts to him.

"It sucks. Everything sucks. My whole life has been turned upside down. People are trying to kill me. I'm apparently a shifter. Not only that, but I might also be able to become a werewolf or some shit. I've been treating my friends like crap for weeks. Nico's mother hates me. The only good thing to come out of all this is Nico. God…if it wasn't for him I'd have probably lost my mind by now."

I gasped for breath after unleashing the volley of words, and Kenneth grinned back at me, chuckling. "I guess things are going well then?"

I stared at him for several seconds, then burst out laughing. It wasn't that funny, but it seemed like the only thing to do at that moment. Kenneth smiled and shook his head. "You know, you remind me of your father."

My laughter gradually died at the sadness in Kenneth's eyes. I put my hand on his, not knowing what else to do. Sorrow, almost like a living thing, grew and took over his face and body. His shoulders slumped and a line formed between his eyebrows. I wondered what memory he was thinking about to cause the change. Was it happy? Sad? I had no way of knowing, and I wasn't comfortable asking. All I could do was hold his hand.

"You know," he finally said. "I promised I'd keep you safe. I really thought I'd done enough." He shook his head in frustration. "I…I just can't believe I never thought to look into David's mother. I just took my dad's word for it. I never really knew her. She died not long after I met him. If only I'd looked into it, maybe I could have put two and two together. If I'd known you were what you were, I might have been able to help. You might never have been attacked in the first place."

I could see he was racked with guilt. He stared at the ground, unable to even meet my eyes. I didn't blame him. His father had done the same things my parents had done. They'd hidden things they thought would protect their kids.

I patted his thigh. "Kenneth. It's okay. I don't blame you. You never could have known."

He nodded, wiping at his eyes. "Well, regardless, I promise I won't drop the ball again. I'll do what I need to do."

We sat like that for a few more minutes, enjoying the silence, before heading back to the cabin. We found Nico pacing the porch, looking distraught, gripping his phone.

A small voice came from the speaker. I hurried to get to him, and only when I got close could I tell that the voice on the other end was Luis.

"Are you okay?" Nico asked.

"Yeah," Luis replied. "They jumped me, but I got away. I'm in Norway. I'll tell you, it was close. I just barely made it out." Nico seemed to visibly relax once Luis told him that he wasn't hurt.

"Where in Norway were you?" Nico asked.

"I went to the castle ruins. The one Kenneth found. It's where Edemas lived during the last part of his reign. I think we're getting too close for the royals' comfort."

"Did you find the vault?" I asked.

"No. I didn't see any evidence of a vault or crypt or anything. The whole palace has been dismantled over the years. It's just a generic historical monument now. Besides, it wasn't the castle I was interested in. Once I saw there was nothing to be found in the ruins, I started to leave. That's when I saw the graveyard in the distance. There were a bunch of tombs and headstones. I had a hunch that maybe the vault was hidden in plain sight. If this thing was supposed to be so well-hidden, the best place to hide it was the most unlikely place—the tomb where Edemas was buried."

My blood buzzed and excitement burst with in, though I had no idea why. It was like my wolf knew something, but couldn't get the thought across to me.

"That...that would be a strange place for it," Kenneth admitted. "As far as I know, no one has ever looked there."

"Right," Luis said. "I decided to return at night. I went as carefully as I could. I know for a fact no one was tailing me. No one knew I was going to go back. I even snuck out a back window of the inn I was staying at so anybody watching the front door would think I was still inside. But the royals had a team at the graveyard."

"They were already there waiting for you?" Nico asked.

"Yeah. I got out, but it gave me a theory. I think they've known where this vial of blood was the entire time. It's not some hidden thing. I don't think they're even killing descendants to keep them from opening it. Kenneth already said the legends made it clear that someone with Edemas's blood would be the only one who could open the vault. What if that's what they want?"

The words hung in the air. Nico glanced back and forth between me and Kenneth. They *wanted* it open? Why? I thought the entire thing was that they never wanted the blood to get out again.

"They've been killing people and trying to use their blood to open the vault for centuries. I think this is one big con. They aren't some all-powerful group trying to *save the world* from the werewolves. They're hoping to become a new ruling family themselves by using the strength of Edemas's blood."

"If that's true," I said, "wouldn't my birth father's blood have been strong enough to open it?"

Kenneth shook his head. "Your father was pureblood, but he didn't have the ability to shift. It's why I always assumed my dad's story that David's mom was human like mine was true. He also wasn't an alpha; he was just a step away from being strong enough. They probably tried it, but it didn't work."

I had a mental flash of David, lying dead after giving Gabriella and Kenneth time to get away. Someone stabbing his body with a needle to pull his blood out. My heart ached at the brutality of it. He never got the chance to live his life. To meet me. All because an already powerful family wanted to be even more powerful. It made me irate and heartbroken all at the same time.

Kenneth nodded toward me. "This is why they're really after Maddy. They want to kill her, yes—it just isn't for the reason we always thought. They want her blood. They *need* her blood. It's the only way to open the vault."

Nico sighed and shook his head. "If Luis is right, this makes things even more difficult. They already know where the vault is. They saw Luis, so they know we're in the country now. They'll freak out. Pull all their pawns and soldiers in close. We've got a much tougher fight on our hands."

"What do you want me to do?" Luis asked.

"Lay low. I'll be in touch when we have some sort of plan," Nico said, then ended the call.

I chewed at my lower lip. Everything seemed to be speeding up. We were on a rollercoaster, headed for a massive drop. The fear was returning. Would I ever feel safe again? Would we get out of this alive? I had no clue. All we could do was try.

Chapter 34 - Nico

"One thing I just can't get my head around," I said. We were sitting around the fireplace after getting off the phone with Luis.

"What is it?" Kenneth asked.

"Maddy's blood. Why are they still after it?"

"What do you mean?" Maddy looked as confused as I did.

"Well, during the first attack there was…well, there was a ton of blood. Why didn't they just take it then? They had plenty of opportunity. Why isn't this all over? I mean, either her blood works or it doesn't. Or am I not thinking this through?"

"I think you're on the right track, but you're forgetting something," Kenneth said.

Maddy sat up straight and put a hand to her lips. "The suppressants. Remember what Doc said? He said my blood now looks totally different from my blood the night of the attack. They did take my blood; it just didn't work. But now that the drug is completely out of my system, it probably will. That has to be it. My wolf was dormant, now it isn't."

I frowned and ran a hand across the stubble on my cheeks. "It *doesn't* make sense, that's what I'm saying. Yes, I get that your blood is different now. But how the fuck do the royals know that?"

Maddy and Kenneth's eyes both went distant as the implication sank in on them. They understood where I was going with my train of thought. If they had taken her blood, and it hadn't opened the vault, why were they still pursuing her? Did they really want all the descendants dead? Maybe, but their real mission was finding the blood that would open the vault. Unless someone had told them about the suppressants.

I glanced at Kenneth, but brushed away the possibility that it was him. He wouldn't do something like this to his only family, would he? Especially since the royals killed his brother. What about Doc? Could they have something on him like they did his nurse? How many people knew? Just my inner circle. Could one of my best friends be working with the royals behind my back? The thought made me sick to my stomach.

"I need to go to the bathroom," I said and excused myself.

As soon as I was locked away, I pulled my phone out and texted Luis.

Me: *I think we have a mole. Someone is informing the royals.*

Luis: *I was thinking the same thing.*

Me: *It's not you or Felipe or Sebastian. I'd bet my life on it.*

Luis: *Wow, I love you too, bro. Who does that leave?*

Me: *It leaves Kenneth or Doc. They're the only other ones who know.*

Luis: *You need to watch your ass around Kenneth. Doc is a ten-hour flight away. If it's him, he'll have limited info to give them.*

Me: *Okay. Stay safe. I'll keep my eye on Kenneth. I'll let you know if anything gets weird.*

Luis: *Got it.*

The next couple days were pretty stressful. I was living in a house with a guy who might be helping the people who were trying to kill me. That was not a comfortable place to be. It was even worse because it seemed like Maddy and Kenneth were growing closer each day. That relationship and the way he acted with her made me doubt his involvement even more.

The original plan had been to stay at Kenneth's cabin until the vial was found. Now that we knew that the royals were guarding it, our timeline had changed. Plus, I was nervous about staying there. The thought that we were being set up for a trap wouldn't stop nagging at my mind. Luis and I had been texting back and forth, trying to come up with a plan to get into the tombs undetected. We went through what felt like a hundred scenarios before coming to one we thought would work.

Luis had the idea to orchestrate a massive diversion that would get the guards out of the graveyard long enough for him to get in. It sounded like it might work, but there was always the possibility it wouldn't. We couldn't wait any longer. My wolf felt like it was getting boxed in. Every sense I had was cranked up to DEFCON one. We had to make a move, and this was the best we had.

I gave Luis the go-ahead to do some up-close recon and see how many guards were actually there, if there was some type of security system—anything that could give us the information we'd need. If he felt good about it, Maddy and I would join him in Norway and make our attempt. Now, I had to sit and wait for Luis to tell me what he found.

Unfortunately, I got more than I bargained for. The day after I told Luis to move in for his recon, he called me. I was sitting at the kitchen table, finishing dinner with Kenneth and Maddy, when the call came in.

"This is Nico."

"Bro, are you alone?" It was Luis, and he sounded like he was out of breath.

"Hang on, let me get somewhere." I covered the speaker and looked across the table. "I'll be right back."

"Is everything okay?" Maddy asked.

"Yeah, all good."

I went to the back porch and closed the door behind me. "Luis? I'm here."

"Nico, you and Maddy have to get out of the cabin. As soon as possible."

"What did you find?" Dread seeped into my bones. Dread and fear.

"I got into the cemetery without anyone noticing me. I snuck behind one of the tombs and a few of the guys guarding it had grouped up on the other side. They were on a phone call. I heard him, bro. It was Kenneth. He was telling them they needed to come for Maddy. He said her blood was viable now. It's Kenneth! He's fucked us. He's the mole, dude. Get the fuck out now."

Breath hissed in and out of my nose, and I gripped phone hard enough to make the glass and plastic creak. My rage was almost too much to hold in. I turned and looked back over my shoulder through the window. Maddy and Kenneth were talking. Maddy was laughing. Kenneth was also laughing, but I caught him sending a nervous glance up to the window. Our eyes met through the glass and the smile on his face slipped away. That fucking motherfucker.

"I'm on it," I said to Luis. "I'll call you when we're safely out."

I shoved the phone back into my pocket and slammed the door open as I stepped back inside. "Maddy, grab your stuff. We're leaving."

She jumped, startled by the anger in my voice. "What's going on?"

"Just got off the phone with Luis. We're making our move. Gotta hit the road. Come on." It was easier than trying to explain in front of Kenneth. I'd break the news to her once we were driving away from this place.

Kenneth held his hands up and gave me a brittle smile. "Hey, now. I think it might be safer to wait until morning, right? Go in fully rested?"

I glared at him. I didn't say a word, but the look in my eyes broadcasted everything that needed to be said. Kenneth swallowed hard and clamped his lips together. Maddy glanced back and forth between the two of us. Her brow furrowed, and I could see horror dawning on her face. She was starting to put it together.

I pointed at the bedroom. "Maddy, grab your stuff. Come on."

Before she could even make a move for the bedroom, Kenneth jumped out of his chair and backed up against the front door. He pulled a gun from inside his jacket and aimed it at us. "You can't go," he said. The barrel of the gun wobbled in the air as he pointed it.

Maddy let out a sigh that was closer to a sob. "Kenneth? You?"

"Hush, Maddy, just hush. Okay? I can't let you go. Not until the royals get here."

"Why?" Maddy cried out. The word was both a question and an accusation.

He winced like he was in pain and grunted in anger. "You don't know what it was like. I was the older brother, but I was always second in my father's eyes. I was the offspring of some drunken fuck-fest. Something to be ashamed of. David was the golden boy. I was less than a half-breed in my father's eyes. Neither of us could shift, but at least he knew David was a full-blooded shifter. That was all that mattered to him—a secret that I was never privy to. Even all those years ago, my father couldn't be bothered to give the poor bastard son all the information.

"I've been searching for the vault for my entire life. All I want is to open it and take a drop of that blood. Then I can finally be what I was always supposed to be." Anger laced every word as his voice rose in volume. The gun weaved dangerously in the air as he lost himself in a fury that had been building up inside him over the last few decades.

Maddy took a step toward him, heedless of the weapon. "Did you get David killed?" Her lip curled in disgust as she asked the question.

"That's not the point—"

"The hell it's not!" Maddy shouted. "Did you get him killed?"

Kenneth sucked on his teeth for a moment, then gave a humorless chuckle. "I hated my brother. It's true. I loved your mother, Maddy. I loved her from the moment David introduced us. I loved her in a way a man shouldn't love his brother's fiancée. I didn't call the royals. I can swear that to you. They found him on their own. I took the chance to save your mother. I got her out, and I made sure I got her baby to a safe place."

My disgust with the man grew with each passing second. I couldn't help but think that there might have been a moment all those years ago that he could have helped Maddy's father get away. He said he didn't call the royals, but did he *truly* do everything he could to save his brother? I had a sneaking suspicion that he hadn't.

"If you loved her and wanted her baby safe, why are you betraying me now?" Maddy asked, tears streaming down her face.

"I only helped them once I found out what you were. Once I knew that David had been a full-blooded wolf, I knew how valuable you would be to them. I want the power that is owed to me. I'm the firstborn son. I should be what I was meant to be."

"You son of a bitch! You've killed me! I'm going to die and it's all because of you," Maddy wailed.

I growled and stepped beside her, putting an arm around her. She was vibrating with fury. I couldn't imagine the betrayal she felt. This man, who had slowly become a member of her family, a connection to her past, a man who she thought was growing to love her, had slammed a knife into her back for his own greed.

"No!" Kenneth said, shaking his head. "I don't want you dead, Maddy. I lied to the royals. I gave them false information. They won't be here for at least another day. I just need your blood. Now that Luis found the vault, I can use your blood to get in and take the vial of Edemas's blood. I can finally become a shifter. My blood isn't pure enough to become a werewolf, but that's not what I care about. I just need to be what I was born to be. You and Nico will be able to get away safely. I'd never break my promise to your mother. I loved her too much to help them kill her child."

"You're a traitor," I said, stabbing a finger in his direction. "How can you expect us to believe you? You're only telling us what we want to hear."

Kenneth shook his head vehemently. He tossed his gun across the room where it bounced safely on the sofa. He held his hands up and shrugged. "I promise, I don't want you dead. You just can't leave until I have her blood." Tears dripped from his eyes. "Please, Maddy. I loved your mother. I love you because you are your mother's daughter. Please believe me."

"He's telling the truth," Maddy said. She sounded confused, dejected, and sad. "I can feel it."

I turned to look at her, unable to believe what I was hearing. "What?"

"I can't explain it. We can talk about it later." She turned back to Kenneth. "I'll make you a promise, *Uncle*. Cut off all contact with the royals. Put your trust in me and Nico. If you do that and stay out of our way, I'll make sure you finally meet your dormant wolf. Do we have a deal?"

Kenneth stared at her for several seconds, then I witnessed a grown man breaking down. His face crumpled, and he slowly sagged down to his knees. He was sobbing like a baby. "Thank you. I'm so sorry. I never meant for things to get so out of hand. I'll go back into hiding. I have another safe house. I promise you, the royals will never hear from me again." He glanced over at me, and even though I still wanted to rip his head off, I let him speak. "Nico? I'm sorry. I never wanted Maddy hurt."

I shook my head. "Kenneth, it—"

I never got to finish that sentence. A burst of air slammed through the cabin—the sizzling, buzzing sound of a bullet. It crashed through the back window, crossed the room, and slammed into Kenneth's forehead. A neat little black hole appeared like magic between his eyes. A spray of red-and-gray gore splattered on the wall behind him. Kenneth's eyes rolled to the back of his head and his body fell forward. His head bounced lifelessly on the floor.

Maddy's scream ripped through the air.

Chapter 35 - Maddy

My scream was still reverberating through the cabin. My eyes were locked on Kenneth's body. All I could see was the massive pool of blood spreading from his head. He was gone. In an instant. One second, he was alive and talking to me. The next, he was just gone.

I was shaking violently, like I was freezing to death. My mind was starting to dissociate. I was dangerously close to going into shock, and I was fully aware of it. There was So. Much. Blood.

"Move!" Nico hauled me through the front door, almost tearing my shirt off with the grip he had on me.

I hadn't even noticed the other gunshots. Bullets were knocking out windows and snapping through the wooden doors. Nico and I stumbled down the steps and sprinted into the woods. He tugged me along, his breath remaining steady. Nico was running so fast that a normal human would never have been able to keep up. I was just barely able to stay with him because he was pulling me along. My foot snagged on a tree root, and I crashed into the ground. The forest floor was thick with pine needles, so I thankfully didn't hurt myself.

Nico slid to a stop and crouched down with me. "Are you okay? I'm sorry, I didn't realize I was going so fast."

"Are they still shooting?" I whispered.

Nico looked back the way we'd come and shook his head. "Not right now. I don't hear them following, either. It doesn't mean we're safe. We really need to keep moving."

I nodded and wiped dirt off my hands and knees. "Okay, just not so fast."

Nico took my hand and led me deeper into the forest. He stopped every two or three hundred yards to find a break in the trees and check the position of the moon. It felt like he was leading us somewhere, but I had no clue where. Nico had never been here before. He had to have some sort of plan, but whatever it was didn't make sense to me. All I could do was follow. I didn't even want to risk whispering. Shifter senses were strong, and the people who'd killed Kenneth could still be on our tail. I didn't want to give anything away.

After nearly forty-five minutes, we emerged into a small clearing with a narrow gravel road that led east and a big lump of something that was covered by a camouflage tarp.

"Thank God. I wasn't sure I'd remember how to get here," Nico said, relief coating his every word.

"What the hell is this?" I asked.

Nico led me toward the tarp, then took hold of one corner. With a jerk of his arm, the plastic sheeting slid away, revealing a small Swedish SUV. I looked at Nico like he was some sort of magician. How the hell had he managed to get a car to this clearing?

He must have seen the look on my face. "I didn't put it here—Kenneth did. There's three or four gallons of water and some shelf-stable foods in there. And a pistol in the glove box."

"Kenneth? How did you know he had this here?" My mind was still reeling from everything that had happened in the last hour. This was the last straw.

"After the night of the full moon. You were out of it. You slept the entire day. He told me he had an escape plan if things went bad, then brought me out here and showed the car to me. I snuck out a couple nights ago after both of you were asleep to make sure it was still here. I had a terrible feeling that Kenneth was involved in all this crap. Turns out I was right to make sure. It was the only thing I could think of when the bullets started flying. Thank fuck the guys with guns came from the back of the house. If they hadn't circled, there's no way we could have gotten here."

"Kenneth? So he basically just saved our lives? Even though he was selling us out to the royals?" I still had a hard time believing he'd done that. He was dead now, so I could never get all the answers I wanted.

Nico nodded. "I think he originally had good intentions. He got all twisted up in his own jealousy and greed. Some shame as well. It doesn't forgive what he did, but it explains it a little. At least he did this for us," he said, gesturing at the car.

I released a weary sigh and did my best not to think of the way Kenneth's body been splayed out on the cabin floor. "Let's get out of here."

Nico helped me into the car and we took off, spraying gravel off the access road as we went. I sat in the passenger seat, my lips clamped tightly shut. The images of the last few hours kept flashing through my head like a nightmare that wouldn't quit. Remembering the blood and look of surprise on Kenneth's face made me want to vomit.

Nico took my hand, his other hand gripping the steering while tightly. "It's gonna be okay."

I felt really fucking far from okay, but I nodded and smiled at him. Once we were back in cell range, Nico's phone started ringing. He handed it to me. "It's Luis. Answer it. I need to keep both hands on the wheel in case something happens."

I answered, immediately putting the phone on speaker. "Luis? It's Maddy."

"Where's Nico?" He sounded more panicked than I'd ever heard him before. "Is he all right?"

"I'm here, man," Nico said.

"Oh, shit. Thank God. I've been calling you for like two hours. What the hell happened?"

"The royals showed up. At least, we assume it was them, I never got a look at them. You were right, Kenneth was the mole," Nico said. "They took him out. He's dead. We've got to abort the plan. God only knows what's going to happen now. We need to drop back and reset." Nico pounded a fist on the steering wheel. "They were already at the cabin, Luis. Kenneth said he'd given them bad info, but they were already there. Fucker lied right up to the last second."

"No," I said. "He wasn't lying. I know it. I'm not sure if it was because we were family or because my senses are overloaded, but when he told us that, I could…" What I was about to say sounded crazy, but it needed to be said. "I could hear his heartbeat. It never sped up or did anything weird. He was telling the truth. The royals double-crossed him."

"Either way," Nico said, calming down a little. "We need to get out of here. Luis, get your ass out of Norway. However you can, get back home. We're on the way to the airport. I already messaged Dad to have his pilot buddy send the plane to us. He was in Britain, so he should be there when we get to the airport."

"Got it," Luis said. "I've got a plan. Found a shifter commune in Finland. A distant cousin moved there years ago, and I contacted him. They've got their own little airfield. I think I can get out there, or at least get someplace a little friendlier, then I'll make my way home from there."

"Okay. I'll let you know when we get to the airport."

"Talk to you later."

The call disconnected, and the silence that fell over us allowed me to slip back into my sadness and mourning. It was crazy to mourn someone who'd betrayed me, but I guess I was the type to see the best in everyone, even when they didn't see it themselves.

I pitied Kenneth. He'd never been able to make contact with the wolf buried so deep in his DNA. I couldn't imagine life without mine now. He'd spent his whole life desperate to feel whole. He did betray me, but it didn't stop me from crying for him as we continued driving. I turned my face away so Nico wouldn't see my tears.

A few hours later, we arrived at the airport, and sure enough, the jet was waiting for us. Nico didn't rush toward it, though. We spent nearly an hour watching and checking the surrounding areas for any sign of the royals. Once Nico was as sure as he could be, we finally drove up and onto the tarmac, then boarded the plane as quickly as we could.

The flight was scheduled to be almost ten hours. I was absolutely exhausted and fell asleep in one of the fold-down beds. I slept the entire flight. When I woke up, it wasn't because I'd had enough sleep. I woke up because my wolf was frantic and pawing at my chest, desperate for me to wake up.

I sat up in bed and rubbed my eyes. "Is something wrong?" I asked. It was then that I realized the plane wasn't moving. We'd landed.

Nico was staring out the window. "I'm not sure. Come on. Stay behind me."

I walked over to him. A glance out the window showed me what he was so worried about. A woman stood on the runway, staring at our plane. She stood there with her arms crossed, hair pulled back into a severe ponytail. She wore a designer suit and dark black sunglasses even though it was dark outside.

The pilot looked at us in confusion. "Uh…do either of you know this woman?"

Nico grunted and shook his head. "Thanks for the flights. Can you open the door?"

I tugged Nico's arm and pulled his ear close. "Is that smart? Should we go out there?"

Nico sighed, and I'd never seen him look so exhausted. "Babe, we're out of options. The jet's out of fuel, and we can't just keep hopping around the globe. We've got to hope this isn't the end. That's all we can do. If it goes bad again, I'll make sure to give you as much of a head start as I can."

I swallowed and slipped my hand into his as the pilot opened the door and lowered the steps. The moment I stepped outside, I caught a whiff of the woman, and my wolf started growling and snarling inside my head. As we stepped off the stairs, the woman took a few steps toward us, then pulled her sunglasses off.

She smirked at us. "Good evening. My name is Viola Monroe."

Her accent was thick. European. Similar to the Bogdan guy who'd tried to kill me, but not exactly the same. She turned her gaze on to me and I could see the hunger in her eyes. Nico growled and stepped in front of me, blocking me from her sight. Her smirk turned to a smile as she turned her gaze to Nico.

"I am the head of the royal family." She chuckled. "Well, I guess that's somewhat trite. We don't have castles or armies anymore. We do have mansions and assassins, though. We don't make laws, but we have the money to keep those who do make the laws in our pockets. Our titles died out centuries ago, but our power still makes us royal."

"Listen, chick, are you done spouting off about how fucking special you think you are?" Nico growled.

Viola curled a lip in disgust and sent Nico a withering look of disdain. "Dogs should not speak unless they are spoken to. You'd do well to remember that, Mr. Lorenzo." She looked back at me again. "Miss Sutton? Or should I say Miss Samuels?"

"My name is Maddison Sutton. I *would* have been Miss Samuels if you hadn't murdered my father and forced my mother to put me up for adoption."

Viola gave a slight nod of agreement. "True words. Well, Miss Sutton, your existence has put what we've built over centuries at risk. You are a disruption."

I shook my head and laughed. "You mean what you've built with Edemas's money? Is that what you mean? The fortune you tore from the bloody hands of his dead children and grandchildren? The fortune"—I glared at her—"that belongs to someone else?"

Rage flashed in Viola's eyes, and it took her a moment to pull her features back into a cool and calm smirk. "Young lady, we will tear you to pieces if you think you're owed even a penny of that money. Simply because you have the blood of a monster in your veins doesn't mean you understand what a monster really is. We've had decades and centuries to learn how to be monsters. Do not talk so flippantly with me, little girl." She crossed her arms again. "Besides, if your full beast awakens, you'll find yourself in the same position Edemas was all those many years ago—lying on your back with a sword slamming down into your throat. Honestly, we're probably doing you a favor by taking your life sooner. Probably best for everyone that way."

Nico took a heavy step toward Viola. "If you touch one hair on her head, I'll bring death and destruction to your doorstep. I'll make what Edemas did look like child's play."

There was a moment's flash of fear in Viola's eyes, but she recovered quickly. "I'll make the two of you a deal," she said with the fakest smile I'd ever seen. "We've spent centuries ridding the world of the sin of Edemas. Cleansing the earth of all his seed. In that time? We've learned some of his tricks." She raised a hand and snapped her fingers. A man emerged from the car behind her. He carried a manila envelope.

Nico took an instinctive step back, raising an arm to guard me from whatever the man was planning. The man didn't even glance at us, though. Instead, he walked right up to us and dropped the envelope on the ground in front of us, then turned on his heel and strode back to the car. Nico glanced at me over his shoulder and raised a questioning eyebrow. I nodded at him.

Keeping his eyes on Viola, Nico bent and picked up the envelope. Viola nodded toward the package in Nico's hand. "I think the contents of that envelope will help you make your decision. Give us what we want. The blood of Edemas, or see what happens. I'll be taking my leave now." She turned and strode toward the car. Once she was there, the man opened the back door for her, but Viola turned back to us. "One last thing. It's not a drop of blood we need from you, Miss Sutton. We need you on the brink of death. We need enough blood that would kill a normal human. Hopefully, your mate claims you soon. That may be all that saves your life."

"Who the fuck said we were giving you what you want?" Nico barked.

Viola smirked. "Look in the envelope, Mr. Lorenzo, and tell me you'll say no."

Without another word, Viola slid gracefully into the back seat. We stood there, waiting until the car pulled off the tarmac and disappeared down the road. Nico held the envelope so hard his fingertips turned white.

"We have to open it." I said, fear screaming through my mind. I had no idea what was in there, but I knew I wasn't going to like it.

Nico nodded. "Yeah. I guess we do." He ripped the envelope open with a finger.

Chapter 36 - Nico

Two days. It had been two days, but it felt like so much longer. The moment I'd opened that envelope, everything changed. All my plans had gone out the window. I'd thought we were ready for everything. I was so completely wrong. In fact, I'd never been this wrong in my entire life. Now we were paying for my missteps.

Maddy was upstairs in her room. She'd locked herself in there as soon as we got back. Nothing I said could get her out. She refused to speak to anyone. All we could do was leave food outside her door.

Thankfully, Dad came over. I needed his advice. The house felt too quiet without anyone to talk to.

We were sitting in my office, the contents of the envelope scattered across my desk. Dad was leaning forward, staring down at the pictures. One set showed Abi, bound and gagged, tied to a chair. The picture caught her mid-scream, tears streaming down her face. The second set of pictures were of Maddy's parents. They were also tied up, but looked worse than Abi. Her father's left eye was swollen almost completely shut, there was blood running from his nostrils, and a thick purple bruise on his right cheek. Her mother's hair was filled with leaves and dirt, and she had a blood-swollen lip and a gash on her forehead. The royals had discovered Maddy's weakness.

As soon as the pictures slid out into my hand on the tarmac, Maddy lost it. She screamed and ran after Viola's car, even though it was already out of sight. I had to grab her and keep her from sprinting off the runway and onto the highway. The scariest thing was that she wasn't screaming at Viola in rage. No, she was calling for Viola to come and take her. It only took Maddy an instant to make the decision to sacrifice herself to save the people she loved.

Would I have made the same decision? Probably. Would I have been able to make it that fast? I don't know. I'd had to fight her to get her into the car. She screamed at me to call the royals, to have them come and take her.

"We have to save them," she sobbed into my face as I tried to buckle her in.

"I can't let them take you. They'll kill you, Maddy."

She lashed out and slapped me across the face. "You don't get to tell me what I get to do with my life."

"Yes, I do!" I yelled at her. "I love you, and you love me. That means we *do* have a say when one of us wants to do something stupid." I took her face in my hands before starting the truck. "I promise you, I will do everything I can to get them back safe."

Tears streamed down her face, and I watched her face crumple. "You can't promise that. You don't know that you can. You've made a lot of promises you couldn't keep." She'd turned her face from me, pressed her forehead to the window and cried silently.

Those words had been like a punch in the face. I couldn't even be mad about it. Because she was right. She was devastated and had no way of getting her frustrations and heartache out, so she sat in her room in silence.

I looked across the table at Dad. "Well?"

Dad shook his head and ran a hand through his beard. "I'm sorry, son. I never even thought about her friend Abi. That's on me. I should have had someone on her friend. This is my fault."

In the corner, Sebastian sat with Felipe and Luis, who'd finally gotten back home the night before. Since finding out about Abi, he'd been fuming. He slapped his thigh and put his face in his hands. "I should have thought about it. I was too busy being a dickhead. Fuck," he hissed and slammed a fist into the armrest of his chair.

"Did you find out what happened with Maddy's parents?" Dad asked.

I gritted my teeth and nodded. "Yeah. The guys I hired to watch them were found floating in a lake about a mile from their house. Throats were slit. They were professionals. Whoever they sent after Maddy's parents knew exactly what they were doing."

"Did you read the file I sent you about this Viola chick?" Felipe asked.

"Yeah, she's a real sweetheart," I said.

Viola Monroe was well-known in certain circles. Pretty famous actually, but not in the way celebrities were famous. The general public would have no idea who she was, but she was famous in rich and powerful circles. If billionaires had their own celebrities, she'd be right at the top. Everything Felipe had dug up showed that she and her family gave millions of dollars every year to causes for the needy and downtrodden. They even funded orphanages all over the world. That last little tidbit pissed me off. The only reason they funded those was to find the descendants of Edemas and then kill them in their fucking beds. They were like saints. We couldn't find any dirt on them, not even a whiff of scandal. I was sure there had been something over the years, but the type of money they had could buy away their troubles.

"We've got the fight of our lives on our hands," Dad said.

His words hung in the room like an omen. He was right. Our pack was strong, but against this? Against a centuries-old family with more money than God, and decades of practice at killing and covering it up? It sent shivers of anxiety through me just thinking about it. I looked around the room and wondered if any of the people here were going to get out of this alive.

"We're running out of time," Luis said.

That was also true. Inside the envelope, along with the pictures, had been a note saying we had until the next full moon to hand Maddy over. There was an address and nothing else. We all assumed the royals had already opened the tomb and brought whatever vessel the vial of blood was in. They'd get Maddy there and bleed her dry trying to open it. I'd be damned if I let that happen.

I nodded at Luis. "Yeah. Less than four weeks. One thing I still don't get…why are they so desperate to get into this vault or whatever? They're already more powerful than almost anyone on earth. Is this vial of blood really that big of a deal?"

"I think there has to be something else inside there. Other than Edemas's blood," Luis said.

"Maybe," I said.

Dad held up his hands. "We need to take a step back here. We're getting caught up with all the extraneous stuff, but we need to focus on Maddy. She still hasn't shifted yet. We need her at full strength, whatever that is. She can't do that without you," he said, nodding toward me. "You've got to focus on her. We can plan afterward."

As though fate heard my father's words, I found Maddy in the kitchen a couple hours later. I'd come down from my room for a snack, and she was standing at the counter, making herself a sandwich. I froze and stared at her. It was the first time I'd seen her in almost a full day. My wolf whined at the sight of her. It was desperate to go to her, to hold her. I hesitated to act on those desires. I didn't know how she'd react to me. The last words she'd spoken to me weren't the loving kind. I didn't blame her for that, but it terrified me that something between us had been broken.

Maddy noticed my presence and turned from the plate she was working. I stood in place, unsure what to do. She surprised me by dropping her butter knife and crossing the room. She swung her arms around me and pressed her face into my chest, hugging me tightly. I almost sobbed in relief and put my own arms around her, pulling her close. Nothing had ever felt so good as having her body pressed into mine.

"I'm sorry," Maddy whispered.

"For what?"

"For what I said to you. I'm sorry. I was panicking and freaked out and scared. I didn't mean to say what I said to you. You have kept your promises. I wasn't thinking clearly. All I could do was picture my family and Abi in those pictures. I just want to save them, Nico."

I gently pulled her away from me and looked into her eyes. "We're going to figure this out." I didn't make another promise. No matter what she said, I knew I hadn't done a very good job at making good on my promises. "I love you. Losing you is not an option. I'm not going to hand you over to them so they can do God knows what to you."

"I think I have a plan to help."

I raised an eyebrow. "You do? Let's hear it."

"I want you to claim me. I think I'll be able to shift after you do. If the royals are afraid I can become some big powerful beast, then maybe I can. Once I'm a full shifter, I can train and get stronger. Put the fear of God into them. If I can control the power inside me, then maybe we can use it."

I frowned and thought for a second before answering. "Maddy, I plan on claiming you. I want you forever, but becoming a shifter won't make you all-powerful. The guys and I are scared that we won't be enough as it is. One more shifter won't make that much of a difference."

Maddy pulled her lower lip into her mouth and nibbled at it. I could see she was trying to think of what to say. Then she looked me dead in the eye and said something I wasn't prepared for. "I don't think my wolf is normal. I think she's...much more."

"Huh?"

"You guys talk about feeling sensations and emotions from your wolves, but my connection isn't anything like what you guys describe. Her *voice* is so strong, almost like it's another person standing beside me, whispering in my ear. I noticed it the night of the full moon. She's powerful, Nico. Very powerful. If we can finally break her free, she might be the secret weapon we need. It's only a hunch, but I think I'm right."

"Maddy, I don't want to claim you on the basis of a hunch."

"Are you serious?" Maddy asked.

"Uh...I...what?" I stumbled over my words, trying to come up with an answer. I wasn't entirely sure what she meant by that. Serious about not claiming her, or that it was more than a hunch? I didn't know what to say.

"I want you to claim me anyway, you big idiot. I already promised myself to you. I love you. That's not going to change. I want you, and I want you completely and totally. If you still want to wait, then that's up to you. I'll wait, but just know that I'm ready to be yours. Completely yours."

I thought my wolf was literally going to jump out of my chest. Hearing her lay it all out like that had sent him into a frenzy. It almost felt like he was going feral. The desperation I felt in him was like nothing I'd ever experienced before. It was all I could do to hold him off. I wanted to take her more than anything. I wanted to pick her up and slam her onto the kitchen island. Rip her clothes off and fuck her brains out, then sink my teeth into her, claim her, and make her mine forever.

I blinked the thoughts away, I still didn't want this to be some spontaneous thing. I wanted it to be special. To mean something.

I cupped her cheek. "A few more days, I promise. Not much longer. We'll talk about how to get you through your first shift. Soon."

Maddy leaned forward and kissed me. "I can wait. If that's what's best."

"We're going to make it through this, Maddy."

She nodded. "I know. Fate didn't bring us this far for us to fail."

Chapter 37 - Maddy

We'd been back home for a week, but a part of me still felt like I was stuck in Sweden, stuck in some purgatory where I had to relive everything. Kenneth's death, the pictures of my parents, of Abi, the running and the fear. I didn't know what the symptoms of PTSD were, but I had a sneaking suspicion that I was close to going down that route.

I'd been on edge since returning home. It was all I could do to keep from having a full-blown meltdown. It was so hard to have faith, to trust that the royals were being honest. That they wouldn't hurt them yet. That they were still alive. That we'd get the chance to rescue them. I had no idea if my faith was misplaced or not, but it was the only shred of hope I had, so I clung to it with a mental death grip.

Nico and I had been spending a lot of time out in the forest behind his house. We'd walk through the trees, and he had me hold my hands out, touching the leaves and branches as we went. He told me connecting with nature would help me connect with my wolf. He was mentally preparing me for my first shift. The next full moon was the expiration date. Either Nico would claim me, or I'd go through another agonizing night as the moon tugged my body towards it.

Nico was still not ready to claim me. We hadn't even had sex since we'd gotten home. Part of me wondered if the things I'd said to him the night we got back had ruined what we'd had between us. I'd apologized, but it hadn't seemed to make a difference. He was still sleeping in his own room, leaving me in mine. I'd cried myself to sleep the night before, thinking I'd messed things up so bad that he would never want to be with me like that again. No claiming, no love-making, no nothing. He said he loved me, but I missed the closeness of our bodies. So, not only did I have guilt about my family getting kidnapped, but now I had guilt about what I'd said to the man I loved.

There was no way I could keep working at the bar. Not with Abi being held in some godforsaken basement or dungeon or something. I messaged the entire staff and said we were closing temporarily. Like before, I'd keep cutting them a check each week. They were understanding, but I knew some of them would start looking for another job. Why wouldn't they? They could double their money by taking my check *and* working somewhere else. Then when it was time to finally reopen, most would never come back.

The thought filled me with a depressing ache. The bar had been my life. My baby. Now I was on the way there with Luis and Sebastian to pack up the money in the safe and discard anything that would expire before we reopened.

Once we were inside, I took a second to walk around, my fingers trailing across the bar's wood counter. I really did hope I'd get to reopen. After I had my moment, I went about helping Luis and Sebastian close the place down. We disconnected the CO_2 tanks to the soda machines and threw any refrigerated stuff into the dumpster or packed it up to take back home. I let Sebastian have the recipe for our chicken sliders, which made him happier than I'd seen him since he'd heard the news of Abi being taken.

As we worked on removing the trash and doing one final clean, my thoughts went to Nico. I wish he'd been there with us. I was a little disappointed when he said he wasn't coming. This was difficult for me, and I would have liked to have had him here for it. He'd given me a pretty lame excuse about needing to be home for a video call. Like he couldn't take that on his cell at the bar. It made me think I'd done some irreparable damage to our relationship.

His absence from shutting down the bar made more sense when Luis pulled up to Nico's house to drop me off. There were rose petals and candles on the walkway leading up to the front door. I glanced over at Luis and gave him a quizzical look.

He shrugged. "Don't ask me."

I got out of the truck and walked up the path to the door and opened it. Inside, there were even more candles and rose petals strewn along the floor. I rounded the corner and found Nico standing in the living room. He held an open bottle of champagne and two flutes. He was dressed in a tuxedo. The thing must have cost a couple thousand dollars. I'd never seen a suit that fit someone as well as fit him. He looked like he'd walked right out of some old 1920s twenties cocktail party. He looked amazing. Probably the most gorgeous I'd ever seen him, and that was saying something.

I took a few steps toward him. My face must have betrayed my confusion. He put the bottle and glasses down, then took a step toward me and grabbed my hands. "Maddy, I have a proposal for you."

"Oh really?" I said, wincing inwardly at how dumb my response sounded.

He grinned. "I love you. Forever and always. I promise I'll protect you and keep you as safe as possible. I want you to be my partner for life. Shifters don't typically do this the way humans do, but…well, here it goes," he said and got down on a knee, still holding my hands and looking up at me. "Will you take me as your mate? Can I claim you and make you mine forever?"

I put a hand to my face as tears blurred my vision. I'd never been so happy in my life to hear something. I'd gone days thinking I'd messed things up. Instead, Nico had been planning this. He'd been getting ready to propose to me. My head was already bobbing up and down before I could speak. "Yes. Yes, Nico, yes, I will."

He grinned and stood, pulling me into his arms and hugging me. He kissed me, and I tasted my own tears on our tongues. He pulled away and licked his lips. "Mmm, salty."

I burst out laughing, and Nico poured us each a glass of champagne. We walked up the stairs, sipping at the champagne as we went. Once we got into his bedroom, I started undressing, looking into his eyes as I did. He stared back at me as he pulled his own clothes off. My wolf was growing impatient and pushing me toward Nico. She wanted to be claimed as much as I did. She was desperate to have what she'd wanted for so long—a mate, and to be able to come out into the world.

I slid my panties down my legs and unhooked my bra. The cool air in the room kissed my skin, and my nipples hardened. I stared across the room as Nico removed the rest of his clothing. His thick cock was already getting hard. His muscles, much like that you'd see on a marble statue in Rome, rippled. Urged on by my wolf, I made the first move, walking over to him. I looked into his eyes, wrapped my hand around his cock, and kissed him. He groaned, the rumble echoing into my mouth.

I stroked him as we kissed, our tongues dancing as my fingers slid up and down his shaft until he was rock-hard and fully erect. Nico slid his hands up my hips, then up to my ribs until he filled his hands with my breasts. I sucked in a breath as his thumbs circled my nipples. I dropped to my knees and took him into my mouth. Feeling him fill me like that sent a cascade of warmth to my pussy, I was already dripping wet, desperate for him. His back arched as I sucked his cock. A pleasant happiness filled me, knowing I was making him feel so good. I moved faster, then slipped a hand to his balls, caressing them as I sucked him off.

After a few moments of that, Nico tugged me up off the floor and laid me on the bed. When I was on my back, he knelt beside the bed, lifted my legs and slipped his tongue into me. I clutched the sheets and gave a quiet sigh as he went to work. He slipped his tongue from inside my pussy up to flick across my clit, then down to circle my anus. Nothing in life had ever felt so good as the way his mouth did. I moaned and panted for breath, letting him do what he wanted to me. A finger slid into me as his tongue probed my ass, then a thumb rubbed at my clit—all three sensations damn near making my eyes cross with pleasure.

I finally patted his arm. "Make love to me, Nico. Please," I whispered.

He looked up from between my legs and grinned. "Yes, ma'am."

He crawled up onto the bed, licking my left nipple as he moved up, eliciting another gasp from me. I slid my hands along the thick ropes of muscle that made up his body, in awe of this man who was mine. All mine. My wolf licked her chops and growled. The sound erupted from my own mouth.

Nico smiled and raised an eyebrow. "Are you ready?"

I nodded, not trusting myself to speak. Nico moved his hips until I felt the head of his cock right against my pussy. He pressed until it had just barely started to slide into me. He leaned down and kissed me while he slipped the rest of his length into my body. Each inch filled me until I could feel his balls pressed tight against my ass. He was so thick, and I shuddered, my orgasm cresting just from having him inside me.

When he started thrusting, the entire world seemed to disappear. Everything vanished. It was like we were making love in the darkness of space, surrounded by nothing and everything all at once. I dug my fingers into his shoulders, urging him to fuck me harder. His full length slammed into me over and over again. I was almost dizzy with lust. The building orgasm felt like a wave cresting, but this was a tidal wave, massive and almost terrifying in its mass.

My breath burst in and out of my lungs as my hips rose to meet his. His cock crashed into me, and the first flash of heat and pressure exploded inside my pussy. I called his name as wave after wave of pleasure rocked my body. My legs were vibrating, and I couldn't catch my breath, but Nico was still moving, going faster with each thrust.

I was whispering into his ear, begging him to claim me. To make me his forever and all eternity. Finally, I felt his shoulders tense and a deep satisfied groan erupted from him. His cock pulsed within me. Still moving his hips, he sank his teeth into the fleshy hollow between my neck and shoulder. I felt the icy hot flash of pain, and my eyes bulged as the blood seeped out of my skin. The pain somehow melded with the pleasure of the sex, and a second and even more powerful orgasm rocked me. I wrapped my legs around him, locking my ankles together to hold him.

Nico rocked against me, slowly grinding into me as I continued to shake involuntarily. The wolf was there. I could feel her. Stronger than I thought. I only thought I'd felt her before. She was so powerful, like a storm inside my mind. I felt encompassed by her, our two souls twisting together. I could see her in my mind, teeth bared and strength growing with each passing second.

There was no doubt about what she was. Everything about her screamed alpha.

The Alpha's Fated Encounter

Fated To Royalty: Book 1 Part 2

Roxie Ray

© 2022

Disclaimer

All rights reserved. No part of this publication may be reproduced, distributed, or transmitted in any form or by any means, including photocopying, recording, or other electronic or mechanical methods, without the prior written permission of the publisher, except in the case of brief quotations embodied in critical reviews and certain other noncommercial uses permitted by copyright law.

This is a work of fiction. Names, places, characters, and events are all fictitious for the reader's pleasure. Any similarities to real people, places, events, living or dead are all coincidental.

This book contains sexually explicit content that is intended for ADULTS ONLY (+18).

Chapter 1 - Maddy

"Right there," Nico hissed, pointing at the screen. "Zoom in."

Felipe clicked the image and expanded the area Nico had pointed to. Felipe and Sebastian had brought over the pictures Viola had sent us of my parents and Abi. They were trying to find the location of where they were being kept. Nico was sure they could use the metadata of the images to figure it out. I sat to the side, watching as they converged in front of the screen. We were working on the photo of Mom and Dad, but I couldn't even tell what he was pointing to. To me, it looked like a red-and-black blob.

"Is that what you're talking about?" Felipe said.

"Yeah," Nico said, nodding. "Is that a billboard? Out the back window?"

Sebastian leaned forward, squinting. "It says...Resorito's. I think it's a restaurant billboard."

Nico jabbed a finger at Sebastian. "Search the name."

I twisted my hands together as Sebastian searched on his phone. A few seconds later, his face broke into a massive smile. "Resorito's Restaurant. Only one in the whole country from the looks of it."

"Where?" I asked, my voice trembling with nerves and excitement.

"Looks like right outside Chicago." Sebastian's voice was almost vibrating with happiness. I had to admit; I felt a similar wave of satisfaction. It was a tiny win, but it was still a win.

Nico nodded. "Okay. Let's see if we can do some research and find out how many of those billboards they have and where they are. We should be able to narrow down the location pretty quickly."

Within fifteen minutes, they'd found a street-view picture of the billboard. It had the same pine tree in it that was in the photo. There was only one house at the correct angle for it to be visible through the basement window. We'd found them! I sighed in relief.

Nico gave my thigh a reassuring squeeze. A glance over at Sebastian made the smile on my face fade a bit. He wasn't looking at me. In fact, he seemed to be actively trying to ignore me, and it had been going on ever since we found out Abi had been taken. I knew he felt guilty about it, but the way he'd completely cut me off irritated me. We'd been becoming friends, now I had to feel the loss of a new friend along with the loss of my family and the woman who was the closest thing I had to a sibling. As much as I didn't want to, I could feel my heart begin to harden toward him.

The guys went through the same process with Abi's picture, and within the hour, we'd pinpointed her location as well. Hers had been more difficult. Instead of a window, there was a mirror behind her that reflected a window. Outside was a set of street signs. The image was incredibly blurry, but Felipe was able to enhance it enough for us to find the intersection. Again, only one house had a window that faced those signs. Even though it had all been done on the computer, we all looked exhausted by the end. Felipe and Sebastian had left not long after to help Luis recon the houses. Felipe gave me a quick hug goodbye, and Sebastian mumbled a departing word before ducking out the door without even making eye contact.

I got up and went to the kitchen sink, sighing heavily. Everything hurt—literally my entire body. As I leaned over the kitchen sink, Nico stepped over and started rubbing knots out of my shoulders. My groans and moans could have been misconstrued as sounds of pleasure. Instead, they were the grunts of a woman who felt like her whole body had been run through a meat grinder and then glued back together.

"Oh shit, right there," I hissed.

Nico dug his thumb into a spot below my shoulder blade. "It's your body getting used to the change. It'll take some time for you to get used to it."

"Christ, does it go away? Or do I learn to live with the pain?"

"It goes away. The first week or so is the worst. Honestly, the pain will probably go away faster once you shift."

It had been two days since Nico had claimed me. Even though my wolf was incredibly strong, I still hadn't shifted yet. She was right there under the surface, but for some reason, the wolf wouldn't come out. I wasn't sure what else I needed to do to bring her out. We'd all thought that when Nico claimed me, it would be pretty immediate. Now, I could do nothing but sit and wait. It was frustrating.

"When do you think that will be?" I asked.

Nico sighed. "Well, I'm not sure. I think you may need a little more time. The wolf probably needs to adjust to the change the same way you are."

That wasn't the answer I'd been hoping for. I couldn't worry about it too much, though. It would happen when it happened. Nothing else we did would speed it up. The other thing that had my attention was the change that had come over Nico. Ever since he'd claimed me, things had been different with him. It wasn't anything bad, but there was something about the way he carried himself, his natural aura, and his confidence. All of it was... more intense. I'd discussed it with his friends, and they'd noticed it too.

It started the morning after my claiming. He didn't actually *act* any differently, it was just that even his presence was more demanding. I found myself fighting the desire to submit to him. I wasn't a submissive person by nature, so the feeling I was fighting whenever I was around Nico was strange. I'd learned enough about how powerful an alpha could be and knew that when they finally paired up with a fated mate, they became even stronger. A chosen mate could increase strength, but a fated mate? It was beyond anything I'd anticipated. I'd even watched Luis and Sebastian when they were around him. They bowed their heads in respect, but it seemed to be subconsciously like a physical force was emanating out of Nico and forcing us into submission.

The weirdest part was that it was kind of pleasurable. My body seemed to crave to submit to an alpha. There was probably some ingrained part of our DNA that desired a strong alpha to lead us, to take care of us, and to intimidate our enemies. If that was what he was going for, then he was doing a damn good job of it.

Nico sighed. "Okay, my fingers are going numb. Is that any better?" he asked.

"Much better. Thanks," I said.

As much as I wanted to be excited about the developments of the day, I couldn't muster that emotion within me. Instead, the all-too-familiar anger started to boil up inside me again. The rage reared its ugly head anytime I thought about the royals. My imagination always took over, and I couldn't stop myself from thinking about the awful things they were doing to my parents and Abi. My wolf bared her teeth; she was as pissed off as I was. A growl erupted from my throat.

Nico raised an eyebrow at me, and my cheeks flamed. I slapped my hands down on the island. "I'm sorry. It makes me so mad, though."

Nico wrapped me in a hug from behind. "I know. I'd be acting the exact same way if this were happening to my family. There's nothing wrong with being angry."

"Those assholes. If they were here right now..." I growled again and clenched my eyes shut.

Nico kissed the side of my head. "It's okay. But, Maddy..."

"Huh?"

"You're gonna ruin the marble if you aren't careful."

I glanced down. My nails had turned to claws and were digging furrows in the stone of the counter. "Shit, sorry." I took a few deep breaths and watched as my claws morphed back into nails.

"You're really getting those partial shifts figured out," Nico said with approval.

"Thanks." I rolled my eyes. "Now, if I could only figure out how to shift completely."

Nico took his seat beside me again. "Look, I think you'll go through the same adolescent stages most shifters have to experience. Your wolf was dormant for so long that it's no surprise that it's weird. The pills your parents gave you probably messed up your hormones or something. That's probably why you're having trouble shifting. Like I said before, be patient and give it time."

It still made me angry that they'd done that to me. The fact that my parents had hidden so much from me wasn't something I could easily forget or forgive. The only thing that worked as consolation was the fact that I truly did believe they gave me the pills because they thought it was for my own good. Besides, Kenneth had told them I needed the pills to stay alive. It also weighed on me that the last time I spoke to my parents, I'd yelled at them. My rage at being lied to had spilled out of my mouth in furious words. I tried not to imagine that being the last thing I'd ever say to them. The thought was too much to bear.

"I think it's time to start your training," Nico said.

"What training?"

"For when you have full control of your wolf. You can't shift yet, but that doesn't mean we can't get you ready for when it does happen. You need to be around other wolves, to understand how we fight when we've shifted, to learn what our movements are like. I don't know whether we'll ever be in a full-on brawl with the royals, but we have to train for that possibility."

That actually sounded fun. I grinned at him. "When do we start?"

"Tonight, when Javi and his pack come over. We need to make sure we're all on the same page."

"Javi?" Even the sound of his name filled me with apprehension. The guys who'd attacked me weren't in his pack anymore, but he'd still been the one to send them after me. He'd also killed Nurse Cleo's husband—a totally innocent man.

Nico sighed and nodded. "I know. I get it, but we've got a bit of a truce going on right now. We need the backup. We've got a common enemy."

"Can you really trust him?" I asked.

"I have to believe so. Javi's conscience wouldn't let him kill innocent babies. That put a target on his back. He's in just as much danger as we are. His family swore a blood oath to the royals centuries ago. They won't take kindly to the fact that one of their purebred attack dogs has now turned and bitten them on the hand."

I sighed, still not convinced we could trust Javi or anyone in his family. "If you think it's necessary, I'll go along with it."

"I do, Maddy. I think we'll really need the manpower. I've got a bad feeling that when we go to rescue your family, it's gonna get ugly. We'll need everything we have to pull off the mission."

I couldn't argue with that. I had the same feelings.

Chapter 2 - Nico

I dug my fingers into my biceps and clamped down and squeezed, trying to massage away the strange sensation I'd felt for a couple of days. It wasn't helping. Since I'd claimed Maddy, it had been as though I was going to rip right out of my skin. All I could do was try to keep it together so no one else noticed or worried about me. My attempts to do that had been fairly successful but not perfect.

Luis sat on the other side of the table. "What the hell's going on?"

I glanced up and saw Luis looking at me, one eyebrow raised in question. His eyes were glued to my hand, massaging my other arm. If there was anyone I'd never be able to fool, it was Luis. He was a professional investigator, for God's sake. He was too damned observant for his own good. I pulled my hand away so quickly that it probably looked like I'd been burned.

I shook my head. "Nothing's wrong. Why?"

Luis crossed his arms and tilted his head. "You say that, but your body language says different. Spill it."

We stared at each other for several long moments. I was hoping he'd get the message and drop it, but he was obviously not going to. My irritation slowly gave way to acceptance, even though it pissed me off to no end that he'd beaten me.

"Fine," I hissed. "It's this new power I've got."

"New power?"

"Yeah. Ever since I claimed Maddy. It's like… I don't know. Imagine how strong you are now, then take all that power and strength and plunge it right into the body of a thirteen-year-old kid or something. That's what it's like—almost too much to handle. Good lord, I can almost feel it seeping out of my pores."

Luis nodded. "I can go ahead and confirm that's true. Even sitting this close, I can feel it coming off you. It gives me these weird instinctual feelings. Sort of like I want to get on my knees and swear fealty to you like you're some ancient king or something. The others also feel it. It's weird. I'll admit that. Sort of difficult to be around, honestly."

I lowered my head into my hands. "I'm sorry. I can't control it yet."

"Don't worry about it." Luis waved me off. "It's not a *bad* thing. We aren't scared of you or anything. Besides, I think it'll get better once you learn to harness this new power. You know, control it. It's new. Just like what Maddy's going through."

"Right, but shouldn't I be dealing with this better? I was born a shifter. Changes should come easier to me," I said. Maybe he didn't understand what I meant, but it made sense in my head. I was the one who'd been changing since I was eleven years old. I was well-equipped to handle this, but I still felt like my skin was about to explode from my body.

"Correct," Luis said. "But the issue is the power you're sharing. We know Maddy's lineage. That's some powerful shit. We know you aren't trying to *force* us all into submission or anything. We're here, bro. You'll be fine in a few days. I'd almost guarantee it."

"I can only hope some of your positivity rubs off on me." I shook my head and sighed. "You know, I really thought claiming Maddy would be all about me helping her through the changes. I didn't think I'd have to worry about myself."

Luis left a while later, and I was stewing in my own thoughts. Maddy was grocery shopping with Felipe, and the house felt simultaneously too big and too small. If I could describe how I felt, it was probably closer to going through puberty than anything else. It ticked all the boxes: strange emotions, weird things happening to my body, new strength.

I took a little while to sit on my bed and do some breathing exercises. Perhaps meditation would help me focus on my new power. I listened to music and took slow, deep breaths, letting the new sensations wash over me. At first, I felt weird, like some new-age guru trying to "find his center", but after a few minutes, I really thought it was helping. Luis was probably right—it would probably take a few days to really get a handle on it. There was just so much power. It was a testament to Maddy's family tree. Being fated mates likely increased the power even more. I couldn't even imagine what was going on inside Maddy's body.

In the afternoon, Javi and his packmates showed up. Although the meeting was scheduled, it didn't alleviate the tension. There were lots of glares and whispered words from my pack as Javi and his crew pulled in. The cars came in a big convoy, almost like a parade, and parked at the edge of the forest at the far end of the Lorenzo property. We were using a large open field, which was usually only used for flag football games on Thanksgiving. It was the best place for the training I had in mind.

My pack stood in a clump behind me, and everyone looked nervous about our long-time rivals being so far into our lands. Dad, Maddy, and my brothers stood with me. Luis, Felipe, and Sebastian were in a small semi-circle between my family and the rest of the pack. Javi got out of his muscle car and gave me a nod, which I returned. His crew piled out of their cars and slowly approached us. Several members of my pack growled behind, and I heard my three friends quieting the dissent. I was thankful for them because the last thing I needed was to appear weak and unable to control my own people.

"Hey, Nico. How goes it?" Javi said as he got within a few yards of me.

"It goes fine. How are you and yours?"

Javi sighed and kicked a clump of dirt to the side. "Pretty sure the royals are shopping out my neighborhood. Nothing concrete, but there've been some sightings. This little"—he gestured around at all of us and his pack—"get-together seems like a really good idea. The longer this goes on, the more danger we're all in."

I nodded and raised my hands, turning so everyone in both packs saw me. The murmurs of conversation faded, and I tried to project my voice so everyone could hear me. "The two packs that have come together here have been rivals for as long as I can remember. As of today, we are one team brought together by a mutual enemy. An enemy who wishes us harm. An enemy who would kill each and every one of us, our friends, and our families, to further their gains. On this day, we stand and begin a partnership that will benefit and protect both packs. Tonight, we learn to fight together. This is the day we spit into the eye of the royals.

"It won't be easy, but I know we will make this work. For the next month, we are allies. I expect every member of my pack to abide by my word. If anyone has a problem with that, they are free to leave right now. Otherwise, we learn to fight alongside each other, not *with* each other. Are we good?"

A resounding bellow of agreement erupted from my pack. I turned and stared at Javi. He nodded and glanced back at his people, asking a silent question with a simple raise of an eyebrow. His pack all nodded in agreement. He looked back at me and shrugged. "We're good if you're good."

"Okay," I said. "We shift, then we separate into groups, a mixture of your people and mine working together. I'd like the first session to have our strongest people acting as the royals. That will show us what we're truly working with when it comes to our younger and more inexperienced people. We can organize once we've shifted. Good?"

Javi nodded. "Sounds like a plan."

"Maddy, head off to the side. I don't want you getting trampled by a hundred wolves." She nodded grudgingly and trudged away from the two main groups.

There was a ripple of movement as dozens of men and women started shifting. I realized in the instant before I shifted that I hadn't done this since Maddy and I mated. I had about a half second to think about what changes might be in store for me as I morphed into a wolf.

Almost instantly, I felt a well of power brimming within me and cascading out of my body. It felt like a physical wire connected Maddy and me. I looked around, surprised at the reaction the others were showing. Every shifter had bowed down, kneeling on their front paws, heads lowered, several of them whining in submission. Most surprising was the fact that all of Javi's pack, including Javi himself, were doing the same. They looked uncomfortable and twitchy, but it was like they couldn't help falling prostrate in front of me.

The feeling was overwhelming. The power I had over my friends, family, and allies was more than I could handle. The aura emanating from me was like a weapon, and I was too scared to use it. I shifted back as quickly as I could.

Panting for breath, I held up my hands in surrender. "I'm sorry. I'm sorry," I shouted, hoping everyone could hear me as they started to raise their heads.

Dad shifted back to human and hurried over to me. "It's all right, Nico, don't apologize. This is what being an alpha is. A true alpha, with your mate beside you. This is the power you are meant to have. You will be the strongest alpha in hundreds of years. Harness this power, trust it, and use it to lead us. Lead, Nico. It's what you were born for." Dad gave me a broad smile that emanated his pride.

I glanced over at Maddy and, for the first time, I felt her power emanating from her. As she watched us, I could tell she didn't even realize she was doing it. Her aura was pushing out dominating energy almost equal to mine. It reminded me that she was also an alpha. Two alphas as mates? What would that do for the pack? I'd never heard of that occurring. After a moment's thought, I decided it could only make us stronger.

I grinned at her, and she gave me a hesitant smile. I shifted back to my wolf form and did my best to reel in the power. It seemed to work. Everyone acted like they weren't as intimidated by me. I went to Javi and nudged him. The two of us organized the packs into two groups, and then we went through a dozen different scenarios. It was exhausting and difficult, but nothing degenerated between the two packs. I was pleasantly surprised at how both groups worked together. By the end of the first night, my sliver of hope had blossomed into something a little more substantial.

When we were done, Javi and I stood, slicked with sweat and panting for breath. I put out my hand to him. "Thanks for coming out. Let's shoot for another session tomorrow?"

Javi stared at my hand for several seconds before reaching forward and taking it. He looked into my eyes. "Nico, thanks for trusting me. Me and my pack. I know I haven't done much to warrant your faith, so this means a lot."

I shook his hand. "Stay the course, and do right by us. If you can do that, then we will do right by you."

Javi inclined his head and grinned. "Fair enough."

That evening, Maddy and I didn't get home until well after the sun set. She'd been quiet since the session with Javi's pack started. It was obvious that she was thinking about something, but I wasn't going to pry. I went about making a quick dinner for us, letting her work it out in her head.

I was unwrapping a frozen pizza when she spoke. "I could feel everyone's energy."

"What?"

"It was like I could read the energy of everyone there." She looked at me. "You're so strong."

"Much stronger now since we've mated," I said, nodding.

Maddy gave me a look that told me she knew I was being deliberately obtuse. "No, Nico. I mean you're *really* strong. Plus, I could tell you were holding back out there. You… I think you'd have beaten any shifter out there if they'd attacked you. Even if they worked together."

Hearing her say that filled me with a bit of childish pride. Maddy had seen how strong I was, and it had impressed her. I shrugged and slid the pizza into the oven. "I held back, yeah. I didn't want to hurt anyone. I'm still getting used to this new energy I've got—sort of like you are. You aren't worried about me, are you?"

Maddy studied me, worry creasing her forehead. "I worry about what that power can do to someone. Something like that can go to your head. Remember what all that power did to Edemas? I'm scared that the same thing could happen to either of us. It's so new and intense. What if it changes us before we really understand it?"

I circled the kitchen island and wrapped my arms around her in a tight embrace. She threw her arms around me and pulled me just as close. I put my lips to her ear. "We are not Edemas—no matter what. Plus, we have each other. Neither of us will let the other turn into some soulless, power-hungry monster."

Maddy pressed her hands into my back and tried to pull me even closer. I could sense the terror vibrating within her body. She was terrified that we'd lose ourselves to this newfound strength. If either of us succumbed to the power, it would be the downfall of the entire pack. I wondered if, maybe, she was right to worry.

Chapter 3 - Maddy

Nico was out at his auto shop, checking on things. For the first time since we'd met, I was wholly alone at home. His friends were all working on researching the safe houses where my family was hidden. Nico had been uncomfortable leaving me by myself and had mentioned getting one of his brothers or his father to come to watch out for me.

"Nico, you won't be gone that long. It'll be fine. I'm safe here. Nothing is going to happen. I promise," I'd said.

The expression on his face told me he was obviously uncomfortable leaving me alone at home. Finally, he nodded. "Okay. I won't be gone for more than an hour-and-a-half. Okay?"

"Sounds great," I said, and within ten minutes, I was sitting in the blessed quiet.

Having protection was great, but God, it was exhausting having people around all the time. Sometimes being alone was all a person needed to recharge. I found a comfy spot on the couch and decided to catch up on some reading.

I was three chapters into a new book when my phone rang. I glanced at the screen and frowned. It was the Clearidge police department. A thousand different thoughts ran through my head before I finally answered.

"Hello?"

"This is Officer Turner. Is this Madison Sutton?" The female voice was clipped and professional.

"Yes, what's this about?"

She sighed and said, "Are you the resident of twelve twenty-three Cypress Lane?"

I hadn't spent the night in my own house in weeks. After the attack at the bar, the only time I'd been there was when we went to pick up my things to move in with Nico. A week or so later, Nico had Felipe fetch the rest of my clothes. I'd been meaning to have all my other items brought over by movers and get rid of the house. It was pointless to keep paying for it when I wasn't living there anymore.

"That's my address, yes," I said, a small sliver of panic sliding into my chest.

"Well, I hate to be the one to tell you this, but thirty minutes ago, a fire was reported at this address. The fire department was dispatched, and they are currently working on the blaze."

My jaw dropped open. My house was on fire? I thought about all my keepsakes and pictures. Confusion swirled in my head. How had this happened?

"Ma'am? Are you there?" Officer Turner asked.

I blinked, realizing I'd been silent for several long seconds. "Umm, yes. How...how did it catch fire?"

"Unsure, Ma'am. That will be for the fire marshal to determine. Your number was given to us by one of your neighbors. The fire department is doing its best to bring it under control, but your neighbors thought you might want to come by. Some items might be salvageable once the fire is tamed."

"Right," I said. "I'll be right there."

I ended the call without saying goodbye. Fear and alarm warred within me. I couldn't even think straight as I grabbed my car keys from the kitchen counter and ran out the door. I wasn't completely out of it, though. Nico would lose his mind if he found out I'd left the shifter compound without an escort, but I needed to get to my house. I tried calling him, but the call went to voicemail. Instead of leaving a voicemail, I sent him a quick text, telling him what happened before I got in my car and drove as fast as I could toward my old neighborhood.

As I passed the guard shack, I waved to Nico's Uncle Miguel. The look of confusion on his face as I sped by made me feel even more uncomfortable going out alone. I'd become used to having a full-time guard. Even when I went to the grocery store to buy tomatoes, someone went with me. But, I'd told Nico where I was going, and the police and fire department would be there. It wasn't like I'd be all by myself.

The drive to my neighborhood was strange. It almost felt like someone else was driving my car. The closer I got, the more surreal the trip became. I kept glancing through the windshield, trying to see the streaks of black smoke that would be my home burning.

It wasn't until I turned onto my street that I realized something was wrong. Terribly wrong. I pulled my foot off the gas when I saw my house. It sat quiet and calm—completely fine. Not a trace or hint of fire. My wolf snarled in the back of my mind. *Trap.* I glanced around frantically, looking for any sign of the royals' agents but saw nothing. How could it be them, though? The police department's number had been on the caller ID.

My phone rang again. I didn't even look at who was calling. It had to be Nico. "Nico? I screwed up. You need to come—"

"Young Miss Sutton, this is not your dog." Viola's voice was sickly sweet and disturbingly close through the speaker.

"Who...how?" I couldn't seem to form a coherent sentence.

"No worries. We are cleverer than you seem to understand. I know I said you had until the full moon but...oh." She sighed and chuckled. "I find that I am used to getting what I want when I want it. When my team proposed this plan, I never thought you'd be so gullible. It truly is delightful."

I heard the screaming of an engine and had just enough time to glance in my rearview mirror. A massive black truck was careening down the street. I never got the chance to scream. As the truck slammed into the back of my car, the world turned into flipping and spinning chaos. Somehow through the sound of crunching metal and shattering glass, I could still hear Viola laughing through the tiny phone speaker.

Chapter 4 - Nico

The crew had done a good job in my absence to keep everything running smoothly, but I needed to stop by more often. No matter how good the crew was, they needed to see me. I didn't want the guys to think I didn't give a shit about them.

My head mechanic Blake was working on doing a custom suspension for a nineteen-sixty-four Ford GT40. It was going well, but changing out the double wishbone suspension for MacPherson struts was proving to be a bitch.

"Blake, do we need to reroute the exhaust here to get this to fit?" I asked, pointing to the undercarriage. The car was on a lift, so I could stand up straight beneath it.

Blake walked over, wiping grease from his hand, and glanced at the area I was pointing at. It looked like the exhaust manifold might bump the new suspension upgrade if the car went over a bumpy stretch of road. Blake sighed. "Shit. I think you're right. This isn't a daily driver, but if this guy wants to take it on a road trip to a car show or something, he will dent the shit out of it if he goes over a speed bump."

"Okay, let's get Davy and Josh on this as soon as we can."

Blake nodded. "You got it, boss."

"Thanks."

I stepped away and slid a hand into my pocket to grab my phone, but it wasn't there. Checking my pockets, I found them empty. Where the hell was it? After glancing around the shop, I remembered I'd put it on my desk as soon as I got there. I wanted to check in on Maddy.

As soon as I stepped into my office and grabbed my phone, I knew something was wrong. I had a missed call and a text from Maddy. My heart was hammering in my chest as I opened the message.

My house is on fire. Going now. Meet you there???

Her house was on fire? How the hell did that happen? A glance at the time the message was sent showed it had come in about ten minutes after I got to the garage—fifteen minutes after I'd left home. I looked out my office window. Terrifying thoughts buzzed through my head, and I snatched up my truck keys and bolted. Without even glancing at the team, I sprinted through the shop and out the massive open garage doors to my truck. The tires squealed and left a strip of rubber on the ground as I headed toward Maddy's old neighborhood.

I pushed the truck well past the speed limit, not even bothering to look for cops who might be out and about.

I just wanted to get to her. Something didn't feel right, and my entire being was on edge. Even my wolf was freaked out. Whatever this was, it was not good. When a house fire was the best-case scenario, something was seriously wrong.

When I turned the corner onto her street, every fear I had was realized. The scene before me played across my vision and my mind in seconds. The house was unharmed, and Maddy's car was flipped over on its roof. A giant black SUV was parked behind her wrecked car. Two men were at Maddy's door, trying to pull it open and drag her out. I snarled as I slammed my truck into park and leaped out, sprinting toward the men.

Maddy was halfway out of the driver's side window, kicking and screaming at them, then she saw me.

"Nico!"

I leaped into the air, shifting as I did. The first assailant spun on his heel in time to see my massive bulk and snapping teeth arching through the air. I slammed my paws into his chest, sending him stumbling backward, and his masked head bounced off the pavement, instantly dazing him. The second man released Maddy and tried to pull a pistol from a holster at his waist, but I lunged toward him, my teeth clamped around his wrist, yanking his hand away from the gun.

Maddy scrambled to her feet and rushed the kidnapper. She slammed her hands into his back, tipping him forward. His shins hit my side, and I released his hand and thrust my back into his legs, forcing him to fall forward. The man fell to the ground face first. Blood and teeth burst out of his mouth on impact.

The first man I'd attacked managed to get to his feet and ran over to start to pull his partner to his feet. He had his hand to his face to keep the blood and teeth from spilling from his mouth. The less-injured assailant glared at me, his hand drifting toward his own gun. I took two steps toward him and growled deep in my throat.

The man froze before moving his hand away from his weapon. "Fuck it," he said with a snarl and quickly helped his friend into his SUV.

The vehicle had a heavy brush guard on the front, so it had almost no damage, unlike Maddy's small car. Within seconds, they were driving away, tires squealing and the engine screaming as they went. I stood there, making sure they were gone before I shifted back to human and turned to Maddy.

"What were you thinking?" I said, pulling her to me.

"I–I don't know. The caller ID said it was the police. Like the actual cops. If it had been a weird number, there's no way I would have come here." She was shaking with fear and shock.

I thought about that for a moment. Had they cloned the local police telephone number? Or did the royals' influence and reach go as deep as the Clearidge police department? Both were possibilities. If the royals had agents in the police department that were helping them, it was one more reason to stay off their radar.

"I'm gonna get the guys from the shop out here to tow your car," I said, pulling my phone out of my pocket.

Maddy looked like she was going to protest, but the same thoughts I had must have run through her mind because she closed her mouth before she said a word. While I was on the phone, one of Maddy's neighbors came out to see the accident.

"Maddy? What the heck happened?" a little old lady said as she tottered down her short driveway. "I heard a big bang, and by the time I got out of the bathroom, I saw that black car speeding away. Did you get hit? Oh my god, look at your car." She put a hand to her cheek and gaped at the upside-down car.

I quickly told the guys the address and told them to haul ass. I wanted the car gone before anyone called the cops.

Maddy swept a hand toward her car and spoke to the old woman. "The guy came out of nowhere.

Flipped my whole car." She did a good job selling it. Maddy was tough and already seemed to be recovering from this new attack.

"Oh my god, sweetie, have you called the police?"

Maddy turned to me, a questioning look in her eyes. I waved at the neighbor and gave her a vague answer. "Tow truck's on the way."

Within five minutes, my guys showed up with the truck and started righting the car and getting it on the bed. Maddy thanked the neighbor for her concern and followed me to the truck. I continued to glance up and down the street, waiting for the cops to show up. The more I thought about it, the more I was sure the royals must have someone in the department who was helping them. "Anyone else on the street who might call nine-one-one?" I asked as we buckled up.

Maddy shook her head. "No. Everyone else works during the day. Mrs. Doogan is the only one who's home most days. There's a stay-at-home mom down the street, but her house is probably too far away to have heard anything."

"Okay, good. Let's get you home," I said, relief finally settling in as we pulled away.

I reached out and put a hand on Maddy's thigh, squeezing gently. She put her hand on mine. The feel of her skin reminded me of what I'd almost lost. We spent the drive home in silence, both knowing how close we'd come to losing each other. We'd have to be more careful.

Chapter 5 - Maddy

The moon's strength tugged at me, filling me with power and seducing me with its glow. My body ached to shift. The hissing sound of my feet stepping through the grass and the moss followed me as I walked, naked, through the forest. Cool, moist air kissed my body, quenching the heat surging over my skin. Finding a spot where the tree canopy opened, I turned my face up to the moon. Its light swept over my body like a lover's hand. My flesh tingled, and my nipples grew hard. Upon opening my eyes, I saw the moon's massive white face hovering in the sky and shining down upon me.

An almost orgasmic sense of power surged through my body. In an instant, I started to shift—my flesh turning to fur, my bones reshaping themselves, my jaw elongating to that of a wolf. In less than three seconds, I stood, fully changed. I was a wolf, like Nico, but different. Glancing down, I saw that I walked on two powerful and thickly muscled legs. My hands weren't the stubby, clawed feet of a wolf. Instead, they were a hybrid of hand and paw, tipped in wickedly sharp claws.

Instead of being frightened, the sight of my new body filled me with bloodlust. The desire to hunt, chase, and kill overpowered my senses. I surged forward into the forest. My new body was lightning fast, and I crashed through the trees and undergrowth faster than I'd ever moved in my life. I howled up at the moon, relishing this newfound power.

My sprint came to an abrupt stop when a smell caught my attention. The scent of a wolf. My chest heaving from exertion, I stopped and searched for the source. After a second, a young gray wolf came padding out from around a tree. It froze at the sight of me. Its yellow eyes locked onto mine as it trembled, and a fearful stream of steaming urine spurted from between its legs. I snarled, enjoying the fear coming off this creature—a beast so below me that it barely registered as a cousin to me. A new desire filled me. I needed to dominate, to subjugate, to annihilate.

I took a heavy step toward the wolf, a mere child in my eyes. The beast was shaking as though it was having a seizure before it finally collapsed to the ground, bowing down to me. It understood I was the alpha. Not just of this creature but of all his kind—his kind and the shifters. I wanted this thing to succumb to my power. That wasn't enough, though. This was only the beginning. I'd make the world bow to me. My jaw would close on the throats of my enemies, and their blood would burst into my mouth and course down my throat. The mere thought sent an almost sexual buzz through me. I raised my maw toward the moon and released an earth-shaking howl.

I jolted up in bed, gasping for breath and drenched in an icy cold sweat. I would have screamed as I woke, but my throat was tight with fear. I swallowed and wiped my brow. The dream was fading even as Nico stirred beside me. The images may have been rapidly vanishing from my mind, but the emotions and feelings were still overwhelming. Maybe even more vivid than when I'd been asleep.

"Maddy? Are you okay?" Nico mumbled as he rolled over.

I jumped from the bed without answering and sprinted for the bathroom. The memory of my werewolf body running through the forest seemed to come back, making me feel like I was in some strange alternate reality or experiencing déjà vu. My knees slid on the tile as I hit the base of the toilet and heaved into the bowl. Vomit burst up and cascaded out of my mouth in a hot, burning spray. Nico came in behind me and swept my hair back out of my face, holding it away as I gagged and puked three more times. The memory of the dream made me more nauseous the longer I sat there. Finally, with nothing left in the confines of my stomach, I collapsed to the side and leaned against the tub, sweat trickling down the side of my face.

"What happened?" Nico asked.

I took a deep breath and grabbed a wad of toilet paper to wipe my mouth before answering. "Bad dream. Really bad dream."

"Come on," Nico said as he bent over and scooped me into his arms.

I didn't even try to decline. I let him lift me, resting my head on his chest as he carried me downstairs. It was nice to be carried. There was something nostalgic and comforting about the act. Almost like I must have felt when my daddy had carried me when I was little. In the living room, Nico set me on the couch and covered me with a blanket before moving to the kitchen.

"I'm going to make you some tea," he said.

"Thanks."

"Do you want to go outside to drink it?"

I glanced out into the forest beyond Nico's house through the glass door. The memory of the dream and how powerful I felt in the woods made my stomach do another little flip-flop. I shook my head. "Inside's fine."

A few minutes later, he walked over to me with a steaming cup. He handed it to me and sat down next to me. "Okay, let's hear it."

"I don't think you want to." I shivered and took a sip of my tea, my hand trembling as I raised the cup to my lips.

"I think I do. I've never had a nightmare bad enough to send me into convulsions of vomiting."

I sighed and held the mug in my lap, wrapping my hands around the ceramic. The heat of the tea bled through to the exterior of the cup—nearly hot enough to burn my fingers. But I didn't move my fingers. I welcomed the pain because it reminded me that I was still awake—that I was still me.

"You're sure?" I asked.

"Wouldn't have asked if I wasn't."

I took one more sip, then relayed the entire dream to him—all the parts I could remember anyway. Through my retelling, I made sure he understood exactly how I'd felt, how drunk with power I'd been. When I was done, I sank back onto the couch.

"Am I turning into a monster? Some soulless beast?" I asked. "Like Viola said I was?"

The fear that I'd become some psychotic maniac like Edemas had been toward the end of his reign weighed on me. That madman's blood was in me. I could see myself getting seduced by the power. Would I be strong enough to control it? Would anyone?

Nico shook his head. "You aren't going to be a monster." He scooted closer and took me into his arms, setting my mug aside. "Blood or not, I know what kind of person you are. You know it, too. We promised to keep each other focused. If you feel like you're losing yourself to this power, tell me. I'll be right there to reel you back in, okay?"

I nodded, grateful that he was here. I couldn't even imagine what kind of freaked-out mess I'd be if I'd woken up alone. "Thanks. That means a lot, Nico."

"No problem. Are you ready to go back to bed?"

I glanced at the clock over the stove. I'd assumed it was getting close to daylight, but it read three forty-five in the morning. "Ugh, yeah, I guess so."

Nico led me back upstairs and helped me get back into bed. I lay back on my pillow and assumed I'd lie there staring at the ceiling for the next four hours. Thankfully, I was asleep before Nico even got in bed. Better yet, my sleep was dreamless.

Later, I woke up, and Nico was already up. I rolled over and saw it was almost eight in the morning. The house was quiet, but I could hear noise coming from outside. I lay in bed, trying to figure out what it was, but the sound was too distant for me to make it out.

I got up and dressed quickly. While I was brushing my teeth, I glanced out the window toward the big field at the back of the Lorenzo property and saw what I'd been hearing. There were a few dozen shifters running around. They looked like they were moving in some predetermined formations and attack patterns. Nico must have rounded everyone up for another training session.

Once I was ready, I headed out to the field to watch them train. The closer I got, the clearer the noise became. It was a combination of human yells and screams, wolf howls and chuffs, the scraping sound of boots and paws on dirt and grass, and above it all, Nico's voice calling out orders. I stopped about a hundred yards from the group and watched.

While I stared at the men and women running around, shifting and shifting back at will, I sensed my own wolf deep within me. She wasn't happy as she paced in irritation in the back of my mind. Her mood probably stemmed from the fact that she still hadn't figured out a way to come forward yet. Every day I communicated with her, trying to let her know I was here for her, that it was safe to come out. So far, none of the techniques I'd used had worked.

I'd asked around, and most shifters had told me the behavior was pretty normal for a newly awakened wolf, but that didn't make things any better or less uncomfortable. At this point, not being able to shift was like having a pebble perpetually stuck in my shoe. Not pleasant at all. The wolf was more irritable than usual today, and it quickly became obvious why.

Across the field, Nico had shifted, and he was amazing. His wolf was something to behold, larger and more forceful than any of the other wolves. Ever since we mated, he'd been a different person. Pheromones pulsed off him like crazy and were sometimes too strong. My wolf had to be reacting to that, too. She must have been desperate to meet him—I would have been because I reacted in a similar way when he was in his human form.

"It's okay," I whispered. "Whenever you're ready, I'm here."

She must have heard me because she calmed down almost immediately. The feeling I got from her was relaxed and kind. I smiled as I sat to watch Nico and the other shifters. My smile didn't fade even when my mind drifted back to the nightmare I'd had. My wolf wasn't like that awful thing I'd become in my dream. I had to believe that.

Nico and the rest practiced and trained the entire day. At noon, I put in a massive pizza order for delivery, and after everyone had refueled, they were back at it. It was impressive to watch. Their stamina, strength, and speed were incredible. By late afternoon, everyone was exhausted—and rightfully so. I felt a little guilty watching them all walk off the field and toward their cars and houses because I'd spent the day catching up on my reading while they'd busted their asses in training.

I headed back home to see about dinner but found Nico's mother in the kitchen, cooking what looked like a feast for an army. It smelled like she'd already been cooking for hours. My mouth watered, but I hesitated to step further into the kitchen. I still remembered that she'd basically told me I wasn't good enough for her son.

Before I could turn and disappear, she glanced up from stirring a pot and locked eyes with me. Instead of any venom or vitriol, I only saw surprise mixed with a little shame and anxiety in her eyes. I'd be lying if I said I didn't relish the abashed look. She'd made a few attempts to make up over the last week or two, but the road wasn't fully smoothed over.

"Oh, Maddy. Sweetie, do you want to help me cook dinner? I could really use the help."

I chewed at my lip in contemplation, then decided to be the bigger person. "Yeah, sure. What can I do?"

Julia smiled and tapped the cutting board. "If you could dice some tomatoes and cucumbers for the salad, it would help so much."

I stepped over and started chopping. From the corner of my eye, I watched Nico's mother hesitate. She was standing over a bowl that held what looked like dough for some type of bread. She had a pained look on her face, and I could almost guess what was going through her head.

"Maddy?" she said, "I'm… so very sorry."

"For what?" I asked, knowing full well what she was talking about. A small part of me was ashamed of my pettiness, but it was a *very* small part.

Julia put a hand to her forehead. "I was—to use a vulgar term—a bit of a bitch to you."

I almost dropped the knife. I stopped chopping and glanced across the kitchen island at her. I didn't respond. Instead, I just looked at her and waited for her to continue.

Julia sighed and wiped her hands absently on a dishtowel. "I should know better than to have such bigoted thoughts. I'm sorry I said those things to you. My kind has been through awful things over the centuries, and I think I still have some ingrained things in my head about family and what an alpha and his mate should be. The thing is"—she finally looked into my eyes again—"you make my boy so happy. That's the only thing a mother should worry about. Is her boy happy? Does he love the woman he's with? Is she good for him? You, my dear, check all those boxes. From the moment Nico was born, I told myself I would do anything for him to be happy. And then," she said, sounding exasperated, "he finds the one person who makes him happy, and I treat her… well, I treat her like shit. Your whole life has been turned upside down. Your friend and parents were kidnapped. It feels like I'm the absolute worst person on Earth when I think about what I said to you. I'm so sorry. Is there any way we can start over?"

I stood there, dumbstruck and on the verge of tears. Finally, I nodded slowly. "I think that would be nice. To start over, I mean."

Julia's face burst into a smile that was both happy and relieved. She'd probably thought there was a fifty-fifty chance between me forgiving her and me waving the chopping knife in her face until she ran screaming. She stepped forward and put a hand on mine. "Thank you for giving me a chance. The... the chance I didn't give you. I'm here for you. I'd love for you to look at me like a mother one day."

A single tear spilled over and onto my cheek, and I wiped it away quickly as I smiled and nodded. "Yeah. I think that would be great."

Dinner was amazing. All of Nico's friends and brothers came over along with his dad, and even after all the guys stuffed themselves, there was a ton of food left over to send home with everyone. Julia pulled me into a hug before she left, and I almost broke down sobbing as I hugged her back. Once everyone left, I went out to the back porch to be alone.

Nico found me there once he'd finished cleaning up the kitchen. He wrapped his arms around me, and I rested my head on his chest. "What are you thinking about?" he whispered in my ear.

I was honest with him. "My family. Being around yours is wonderful, but it makes me think about my parents being tied to those chairs."

Nico squeezed me tight. "It'll be okay."

I chuckled humorlessly. "That's what I keep telling myself. It's all I can do to stay sane."

"We won't let them hurt your parents."

"What if they're playing us, Nico? What if they're lying, and they're all already dead?"

"Don't think like that. We have something they want. Viola is a businesswoman. The first rule of business is if you have leverage, you use it—you don't get rid of it. They are alive. Never think differently."

I fed off his confidence. He sounded like he truly did believe it. I hugged his arm, clinging to him and his hope, praying it would rub off on me. All I could do was hope that what he was saying was true. I also had to wish things would go the way we wanted. One thing I would never tell Nico was that if it came down to me or my parents and Abi, I'd sacrifice myself every time.

Chapter 6 - Nico

Maddy had another bad night. Her bad dreams had woken her up three times. She was taking a nap upstairs, completely exhausted from lack of sleep after so much disruption. It seemed like the nightmares were getting worse every day as we got closer to the full moon. I'm sure the kidnapping attempt hadn't helped, either. I was worried about how things would be in the days before the full moon. Hopefully, she and her wolf could figure things out so she could shift before they both became too distraught and exhausted to do anything, much less fight, run, and whatever else we would need to do.

Dad and the guys were coming over for a meeting that morning, and Luis was going to give us an update on the reconnaissance of the locations we thought Maddy's family was being held. They were in different locations, in completely different states. I didn't have high hopes that things would be simple. We'd managed to score a win when we'd identified the locations. I had no doubt the royals wouldn't be that lax on anything else.

"Do you want the bad news?" Luis asked as we all settled in.

"Not even going to pretend there's some good news?" Dad asked.

Luis shrugged. "I'm a pragmatist."

"Okay," I said. "Let's have it."

Luis opened a tablet and swiped until he found what he was looking for. He turned it around and showed us a picture of an abandoned house.

"We're pretty sure this is where Maddy's parents are being held."

Sebastian squinted at the screen. "It doesn't look bad. What's the big deal here? Can't we just do a smash and grab? Go in the dead of night and pull a Seal Team Six sort of thing?"

Luis shook his head. "We thought about that. I checked some street cameras around the area. Found some nasty stuff." He started pointing at different areas of the picture as he spoke. "Multiple people inside the house. I paid a local investigator to take some pics. From the images he sent, it's safe to assume they're all armed. There are cameras all around the location, so they'd see us coming. We wouldn't have the element of surprise. Good news is they look like a closed circuit, so only the guys inside can access the feed. My guy is also pretty sure the apartment building next door has two different guys on elevated floors. If those guys have scoped rifles, we're dead before we even get to the door."

"Well, shit," Felipe muttered.

"Exactly." Luis swiped the screen again and showed another building. "It's pretty much the same thing. You want me to be honest?" he asked, looking me dead in the eye.

I nodded. "I wouldn't have you here if I didn't want you to be."

"There's no way we get them out without several of us getting injured or killed."

Dad raised an eyebrow. "Pragmatist?"

Luis grinned back and nodded. "Yup. Look, I think that's why they separated them. The royals were worried we'd go for a rescue operation. By separating them, we'd either need to choose one to go after or split our people into two teams. In the first option, they have a heads up and can move Abi or the parents. The second option is that our teams are too small or weak to actually get them, and it's a bloodbath."

I sank back into the couch and put my face in my hands. Both safe houses seemed to be in residential areas, which meant that not only were the royals there, but if something big happened, the neighbors who lived nearby would call the cops. Then we'd have to deal with that, along with not getting our brains blown out by a sniper or guard. It was a chess game, and they'd set up the board perfectly.

"Fuck," I hissed. "Those sons of bitches are smart."

I'd been hoping to come up with some sort of leg up on them, some way to outsmart them, but that was looking like childish wishful thinking. It shouldn't have been surprising. They'd been planning, scheming, and murdering for centuries. They had more experience at this than anyone. I should have known better.

A decision needed to be made, and I was the one who had to make it. We'd need to wait. Maybe something else would happen to give us the advantage we needed. "All right, no one makes a move on any of these houses. Not without my express order. Understood?"

They all nodded, but Sebastian was slower to respond than the others. I could see him chewing at the inside of his cheek, his brow furrowed in concentration. He hadn't been the same since Abi had been taken. It seemed like he almost blamed himself. Maddy had filled me in on their fling, and I wondered if he thought the kidnapping could have been prevented if he'd actually pursued Abi instead of having a weekend of debauchery and then going about his life. Sebastian had never been the type to stew in guilt. Usually, he let things slide off his back. Abi being taken had really messed him up. It made me wonder if there wasn't some part of him that actually *did* want something more with her.

"Sebastian? Are we good here?" I asked. I didn't need him going off half-cocked and trying to be a one-man rescue team. It would only get him killed.

He stared at me, then nodded again. "I got you."

"Okay," I said. "I guess we're done here for now. Anyone hears, sees, or finds out anything, let me know as soon as you do."

Sebastian hung around when everyone had left. I thought he knew I needed some company. I used to enjoy my alone time, but since mating with Maddy, I'd become uncomfortable being by myself. It was almost like my pack instinct was heightened. Clearly, Sebastian also didn't want to be alone. I wasn't sure if it was because he felt bad about Abi or if he was simply lonely. That had never been something I'd considered. Sebastian was always so outgoing and fun-loving, but that didn't mean he didn't have issues. If we did get Abi back, I wondered what might happen between the two of them.

I was making breakfast burritos when Maddy came down the stairs. She wiped at her eyes, smiling when she saw Sebastian. The problem was, I knew it was not a true smile. I could see it. She was trying, but it didn't look genuine. There was still some anger toward him lurking under the surface.

Apparently, Sebastian could sense it too, because he headed to the front door. "Hey, guys, I need to get going. See you later."

He strode out the door, and Maddy came into the kitchen to brew herself a cup of coffee. I really wanted to build that bridge between them. Having one of my best friends and the woman I loved at odds with each other was exhausting. Something needed to be said. I finished wrapping the burritos and plated them, then slid one over to Maddy.

We ate in silence for a few minutes before I decided to broach the subject. "So, you and Sebastian?"

Maddy swallowed and glanced warily at me. "What about us?"

I sighed and put my food down. "It seems like things are... I don't know... strained between you two."

Maddy shrugged. "It is what it is."

"Well, that's a little vague. What do you mean?"

Maddy huffed out an irritated breath. "Look, he screwed my friend and left her out to dry. I understand two grown adults can get horny and want a little release, I'm not a prude, but he just straight-up ghosted her. That's pretty shitty. I figured it was not a massive deal, not cool, but whatever. After Abi got kidnapped? I don't know. I guess I'm more than irritated. Like, maybe if he hadn't done it, she wouldn't have gotten taken."

I forced myself not to roll my eyes, instead clearing my throat and angling my body toward hers. "You know that's not accurate. We don't even know where she got snatched. It could have been in the parking lot of a grocery store or something. Are you saying that if Sebastian had pursued her, she'd be safe now?" It was the same silly line of thinking I believed was plaguing Sebastian, and I didn't want Maddy going down the same rabbit hole.

Anger flashed in Maddy's eyes. "Maybe. How the hell do you know she wouldn't?"

I held my hands up to keep the peace. "Hey, whoa, hold on. There's no reason to get angry. I'm trying to figure this out and smooth things over between you two."

Maddy stood, dumped the rest of her food in the trash, and tossed the plate into the sink. I winced, thinking the plate would shatter. Instead, it bounced around loudly in the basin. She whirled on me—her face a mask of fury. "Did anyone ask you to do that? Smooth things over?"

There was a challenge in the air. Like she was pushing me, trying to assert her dominance. My wolf did not like that. I walked over to her, doing my best to exude every bit of my alpha energy. "Maddy, you need to calm down."

Her eyes flashed. "I am fucking calm. You need to not talk about things you don't understand."

"I do understand. Sebastian fucked up. He feels like shit, and he doesn't need you or anyone else making him feel worse about it."

Maddy was enraged, her wolf exerting her influence. Was this what it would be like to have two alphas in the same house—both of us fighting the other for supremacy? I couldn't even contemplate it. I was too busy trying to restrain my own wolf; he was desperate for Maddy to back down, desperate to assert his own authority.

"I'll make him feel like shit if I want to," Maddy snarled. "It's my prerogative. You don't get to tell me what I can and can't do."

Things were starting to slide off course, and I felt the undercurrent of something else— something familiar but strange. I'd never had this feeling when I was angry before. My brain was scrambled, and I was horny as hell. This argument was stirring something deep inside me, almost like my wolf had wanted this fight. My cock throbbed inside my pants.

"Maddy, I'm telling you, stop. Okay? We... we need to think about this."

She pressed herself against me, her breasts pushing against my chest. "Why? Maybe it's best if we get it all out now."

I couldn't concentrate. I was so angry, but also... I didn't know. I felt dizzy. "Maddy, I'm the alpha. I'm in charge. I'm telling you, fighting about this isn't the way to go about it."

Maddy leaned forward even closer. I could see the anger in her eyes, flashing like lightning. But there was hunger there too—a hunger similar to mine. She bared her teeth at me, and a growl erupted from her throat. "Are you gonna fuck me or not?"

There was a moment of silence as her question hung in the air. Our eyes locked on each other, our angry, heaving breaths the only sound in the room. My rage suddenly morphed into something else. I pressed my lips to hers, kissing her hard, harder than I'd ever kissed anyone before. She returned the kiss almost violently, her fingers gripping my hair. She was already grinding her hips against me, rubbing herself on my stiff cock, straining my pants. We were both growling, the anger and lust mixing into an intoxicating madness.

I slid my fingers up her body to the neck of my old T-shirt she was wearing. I yanked at the fabric, tearing the shirt in two. Her nipples were already hard, and Maddy gasped when I pinched them. Our lips still were crushed against each other's, our tongues waging a war. She slid her hand down and tugged at my zipper, sliding it open and digging into my pants with fervor. It was like we were still fighting, but I'd never had a fight that felt this good.

My cock swung free, and a groan rumbled up from my chest as she stroked me. I thrust my hips in time with her hand. Maddy pulled her lips away and slid her cheek along mine until her lips were tickling my ear. "I said, are you gonna fuck me or not?"

My vision became hyper-focused, a singular mission now before me. I would do as I was asked. I pulled away from her and spun her toward the kitchen island, then tugged her pajama shorts down and pushed her over so she was face down on the counter. I spread her ass apart with my hands and slid my tongue into her.

"Oh, fuck." Maddy groaned, and I worked my tongue deeper into her, rubbing her clit with my thumb as I did.

My cock was throbbing, desperate to be inside her. I stood, clutched her hips, and slammed into her. Maddy cried out in ecstasy as I buried myself to my balls. She was wet, hot, and tight. I gritted my teeth, all my frustration vanishing as I moved within her.

Maddy held on to the edge of the island and turned, looking at me over her shoulder. "I want it hard. Do it. Fuck me hard, Nico."

Excitement filled me at her words. The *want,* the absolute *need,* was almost too much. I looked into her eyes and began slamming into her. Her eyes almost rolled to the back of her head, and she laid her face on the cool granite as I worked on giving us what we both wanted so desperately.

The sound of our skin slapping together mixed with our groans and grunts of pleasure. My balls were clapping against her clit with each thrust. Suddenly, Maddy took a deep, gasping breath and started to tremble. She murmured curses under her breath, stiffening as she came. I didn't slow my movements. My wolf was too hungry, the man part of me too horny. I slammed into her again and again. Her ass shook with shock waves each time my hips crashed into her. The pressure of release was starting to build deep in my balls.

"God, oh god, oh god..." Maddy murmured as I continued fucking her.

A second and then a third orgasm rippled through her body, her pussy clenching around my cock each time. Her legs were shaking uncontrollably, and sweat dotted her forehead. It was the sexiest thing I'd ever seen. The look of abject ecstasy on her face sent me over the edge. An explosive, earth-shattering orgasm welled within me and burst forth. I came so hard that I had to swallow back a scream. I continued moving, slower with each thrust, until I pulled free of her pussy and rested my head on her back as we gasped for air.

After we cleaned up, we lay on the couch and cuddled. I had never experienced anything like what we'd just done. I'd loved it, but I hadn't liked the anger and rage we'd both had during the fight that led up to the sex.

"I'm sorry. I shouldn't have pushed," I said.

Maddy shook her head. "I don't know what happened. It was like I couldn't let it go. My wolf was inside me, almost goading me. I'm the one who should be sorry. Sebastian didn't do anything to get Abi kidnapped."

I nodded. "It's our wolves reacting to each other. They're both alphas, so they both want obedience from their pack. They're butting heads."

"Is it always like this?" Maddy asked.

I shrugged. "I've dealt with a few alphas before, but no. Not that intense. There's always some tension. Guy stuff. Whose dick is bigger— metaphorically, that is."

Maddy giggled.

I frowned at her. "What's so funny?"

"Nothing. I just suddenly got a mental image of a bunch of big bad shifter dudes whipping their cocks out and passing around a ruler."

I snorted. "Okay, bad analogy, but you get the idea—basic male-dominance stuff. I think it's different with us because we're mates. It's weird because when we were fighting, my wolf hated that you weren't backing down, but it seemed to like it at the same time. It was a weird feeling. We've never met a female alpha, so I don't know if this is always the reaction, but I'm not complaining."

Maddy nodded. "Maybe we should work on being able to have a normal disagreement. I don't want every fight to devolve into teeth and claws coming out, followed by us fucking all over the house."

I laughed. "Well, I guess there are worse ways to argue." My smile faded, and I became more serious. "This is going to take some adjustment, though. Having two alphas in the same house is going to be tough, but we'll get through it."

That night, Maddy fell asleep quickly, and I hoped she'd have a nightmare-free night. Unfortunately, I didn't fall asleep as easily. I lay there with her for almost thirty minutes, staring at the ceiling, before I got up and went downstairs. The only light was a small night light on a lower outlet in the kitchen. I didn't turn any more lights on as I headed for the back door and went out on the porch.

Warm air drifted over me as a breeze moved in from the west. I took a deep breath and looked up at the sky. The same breeze that cooled my skin was also pushing clouds to the east, revealing the moon. I stared at the bright white orb. It had moved to another phase and was getting ever closer to the full moon—to our deadline. As I gazed up at it, I felt a strange tug. It was almost like soft, stretchy threads were attached to the moon and were tied to my eyes, heart, and even my balls. Every tender and important part of me felt like it was connected to the moon, being pulled forward, tugged in a direction I didn't understand.

I'd never had the sensation before. It wasn't unpleasant, but it *was* weird. I wondered if it was because I was mated to Maddy. Could she be, somehow, sharing her connection to the moon with me? It made me wonder what else might come about from our mating. What other surprises lay in store for us?

Chapter 7 - Maddy

My eyes snapped open to a dark room. I was drenched with sweat. Gasping in air, I pressed a hand to my chest. My sternum ached like it was about to break in two. In fact, my entire body ached like I had the worst flu in the world. Nico awoke almost instantly and rolled over to check on me.

"What's wrong? Maddy? What's happening?" He fumbled with the light switch on the nightstand and turned on the lamp.

My body felt like it was on fire. My skin was so sensitive that when Nico touched me, I hissed in pain and waved him off, unable to speak. The sound of snarling reverberated through the room, and it took a moment for me to realize it was coming from my own mouth. I couldn't even attempt to form human words.

Nico straddled me and leaned in. I could hear him talking, but I was too freaked out to comprehend his words. I thrashed around, gasping for air, and then fur started to sprout on my skin. I looked at it and felt more terror at the sight of it. My breathing became more erratic, and I was on the verge of hyperventilating. The panic that flooded through my body pushed the fur away. My skin was all that remained, clammy and sweaty as it was.

I was finally able to tell what Nico was saying. He wasn't even talking to me. He was talking to my wolf. Trying to calm it down and easing its frustrations. It must have worked because I finally started to feel more normal. It took nearly twenty minutes for the episode to wind down, and I lay there exhausted and panting.

My wolf's irritation and anger at not being able to come out was rising. I wished she'd find a better way to express herself. This was starting to get ridiculous. Easing myself up onto my pillows, I wiped a hand across my forehead and gave Nico a wan smile.

He sighed and shook his head before pulling me into a hug. "Maddy, you have to stop fighting your wolf."

"I didn't think I was." I didn't like the whiny sound that crept into my voice.

"I'm not sure if you're consciously doing it, but it's pretty evident that you are."

I sighed and fought back tears. "I didn't know what was happening. I was scared."

He nodded and brushed my hair back from my cheek. "I know. You haven't shifted yet, and the longer you go without shifting, the harder it's going to be. I think that's the problem. You're scared. That fear is holding her back. You can't fear her. She's a part of you now. I can see why it would be scary."

"But—"

"I know what else you're scared about. I swear I won't let you turn into Edemas. I promise."

He'd known what my argument was going to be. It was true. The dreams I kept having made me feel like becoming a power-hungry beast was right on the horizon. Like there was no way to avoid it. Why else would I be having nightmares?

"I'll go make you some chamomile tea. I'll be right back," Nico said, standing and heading toward the door.

As I waited for him, I tried my best to talk to my wolf. Her anger and resentment were like a wet blanket on my mind, suffocating everything else. Nico returned a few minutes later with a mug of tea.

"I'm going to go downstairs and drink it," I said.

"Babe, you need some rest. Are you sure you don't want to try and get some more sleep?"

I stood and put a robe on. "It's fine. I need some time to think anyway."

"Okay, I'll come and sit with you," Nico said.

"No." I put a hand on his chest and kissed his cheek. "It's fine, really. You go back to sleep. I'll see you in the morning."

He didn't protest. Once he was in bed, I took my tea and went downstairs. As I walked down, I tried again to communicate with my wolf.

"You can't try to come out in the middle of the night," I whispered. "It freaked me out."

That was a bit of a lie. Yes, it had freaked me out, but would it have been any different in the daytime? I didn't think it would have been. I really was terrified of shifting the first time. Panic would have set in no matter where my wolf had tried to come out. I had no idea how to get beyond the fear of shifting. My wolf didn't like that line of thought.

After sitting on the couch for a few hours, I finally managed to sleep for a few hours, curled up on the cushions. I woke to Nico heading out the door. I'm sure he hadn't wanted to wake me. He'd done his best to close the front door quietly, but my new senses were much more sensitive. I rubbed my eyes and felt the strange, heavy exhaustion that came from sleeping but not sleeping enough. Like your body *knew* it had been screwed out of something and was gonna make you pay for it the moment you started moving.

I got dressed and grabbed a book. Nico had scheduled Javi's guys to come over again for another training session. I didn't know if this one would be an all-day affair like the last one, but I wanted to be prepared. My wolf stirred as I headed to the field. She was pissed at me. I couldn't blame her. If the tables were turned, and I was stuck inside her and couldn't get out, I was pretty sure I'd be angry as hell.

I continued my internal monologue with her as we walked, but I wasn't sure it was getting through. I found my usual spot beneath a tree and read a few chapters before glancing up to watch the training.

It looked like Nico was working on defensive maneuvers. They were broken up into multiple smaller groups. Nico had one person trying to defend themselves against everyone else in the small groups. It was scary watching one lone shifter try to fend off three or four others. None of them were doing well and kept getting overrun. Was this how it would be when the fight with the royals finally happened? Would we be swarmed and destroyed?

Nico must have seen the same thing I did. He called for a pause and gathered everyone into a circle. "Okay," he called. "Let's get a better understanding. Javi, come here." Nico waved to the leader of the other shifters, and he strolled into the circle. "I'm going to have Javi come for me. Most shifters think like a wolf when we go into battle. We go for the throat, the inner thighs, the balls. All the soft spots. That's what you have to defend. Watch." He motioned toward Javi. "Come at me."

Javi shifted and circled Nico before lunging toward him. He snapped at Nico's throat, but he was able to lunge to the side and made a motion with his hand toward Javi's stomach. He straightened and pointed. "See? Be ready for the attack, know where they are going to go, and be prepared to counterattack. If I'd had a knife in my hand, I could have laid Javi's guts open. We'll do it a few more times so you can see what I mean."

I watched as Javi and Nico sparred, going back and forth, shifting to wolf form and then back again. It was all pretend, nothing but a training session, but anger welled up inside me. The sight of someone attacking my mate made my wolf go crazy. She was gnashing her teeth and pacing inside my mind. I tried to ignore her and watch what was going on.

Javi circled Nico and managed to get inside his defenses, striking against Nico's ribs. It was only at half-strength, and Nico didn't even flinch. It was harmless, but my wolf couldn't stand it. I blinked, and there was a blur, like looking out a window of a speeding car. There was rage too, a red, seething bubble of anger and indignation. It all happened so fast that I couldn't process what was happening.

When my vision coalesced again, I was standing in the circle. There were screams and shouts of alarm and surprise all around me. I kept blinking, glancing around, and seeing all the looks of confusion and fear in everyone's eyes. I looked over at Nico. "What... what happened?"

Nico held a hand up and looked wary. "Maddy? Can you put your... your hand, er, claw down?"

"What?" I turned to look at my hand. I froze. My entire right hand had morphed into the clawed hand of a werewolf. The longest claw was pressed right against Javi's throat. A single drop of blood slid down toward his collarbone from where the skin had barely been pierced. "Oh shit," I hissed.

"Yeah. That's… well, that's not good," Javi said but didn't sound terribly worried. "If I'm honest, I'd rather it be my neck than my nuts."

"I'm sorry. I don't… I didn't realize—" I couldn't figure out how I'd even gotten into this situation.

"Cool, cool, cool. Could you maybe put that thing away?" Javi asked.

I realized my claw was still at his throat. Pulling it away, the flesh immediately returned to human skin. My nails were mine again, no longer wickedly long. "I'm so sorry," I said to Javi.

Javi raised his hands. "No big." He smiled. "You did know we were only practicing, right?"

I slunk off in mortified embarrassment. Nico called my name, then ordered Luis to take over the training session. I tried to walk faster when I heard his footsteps behind me but gave up once we were back at the tree. I turned to face him; the skin of my cheeks must have been blood red. Heat was radiating off my face.

"I'm sorry, Nico."

"Hey, it's fine. Javi's cool. No harm, no foul."

I rolled my eyes. "I almost killed him, for God's sake."

"It's all good. Everyone was a little… surprised, I guess."

"You don't understand," I said, anger lacing every word. "I couldn't control it. It came out of nowhere, and I didn't even realize I was doing it until it was too late. It's all my wolf. She got pissed that he was attacking you and took over."

Nico put his hands on my shoulders. "Big deep breath. Calm down, Maddy."

I tried slinging his hands away but only managed to flop my own arms around ineffectually. Tears started pouring across my cheeks. "I feel like

I'm losing control. My wolf doesn't understand my fear and hesitation. I'm having to deal with my own shit *and* all this crap going on in my head with this wolf. I'm worried I'm going to go crazy before I can get it under control."

I was out of breath by the time I was done venting. Nico stood there, letting me finish my freak out. My body was exhausted, and I knew that each day would only get worse. Everything that had happened since I bought that damned DNA test had been a living hell—everything except Nico. It still made me wish I'd never bought the stupid fucking thing.

"Come with me," Nico said.

"Where? The freaking psych ward?"

"Stop that. Come on."

He took my hand and led me to the back edge of the field. I averted my eyes from the crowd as we passed. I didn't want to see the stares I was probably getting. Nico continued walking even as we entered the forest. Holding his hand, I let him lead the way, no idea where he was taking me. After about four hundred yards, the sounds of training vanished, muffled by the leaves and undergrowth of the forest. We finally felt truly alone, and some of my anxiety started to fade.

We rounded a small copse of trees and found a seven-foot-wide creek running through the woods. The water burbled and swirled among rocks. It was the most calming thing I'd ever seen. Nico walked toward it and dipped a hand in up to the wrist. "I used to come here when I was younger."

"Why?" I asked dumbly.

"Well, as you can see, it's a pretty quiet place. A good spot to get your mind right."

"So… do I drown myself or something?" I asked, but the joke fell flat.

"Sit with me. I'll try to show you a way to control the feelings you're having," Nico said, patting the mossy ground beside him.

I sat cross-legged next to him, and he put a hand on my thigh. He looked me in the eye and took a deep breath. He didn't say anything, just gave me a look that told me he wanted me to follow along. I obliged and matched his breathing. Three seconds in, three seconds out. After a few minutes, I was much more at ease. Most of my anxiety was gone.

"My dad taught me some of this when I was getting ready for my first shift," Nico said. "Close your eyes and think about running along this stream."

I did as he asked, closing my eyes and visualizing running beside the gurgling water. Even in my imagination, I was clumsy and tripped over a rock.

"Now, imagine you aren't human anymore. Imagine you have four legs. Try to see yourself sprinting along, the wind in your fur, the ground beneath your paws."

I did that, and almost immediately, my wolf calmed, like she was getting to experience the actual sensation of running through the forest. My heart rate slowed so much that I only felt it beat every few seconds. When I finally opened my eyes, I felt more rested than I had in days.

Nico grinned at me. "How's that feel?"

I nodded. "Better. A lot better, actually."

"Good. I think I know part of the problem. Your wolf is an alpha. There's a territorial aspect to things that humans don't ever feel. Not in the way we do, that is."

"Territory? What do you mean?"

"As an alpha, your wolf is trying to figure out

where she fits in. She probably doesn't know where she belongs."

"Doesn't she belong with you?"

"Yes. But she's never experienced the world until she was awoken within you. It's all new. Imagine being born and waking up, but you're in an adult's body. You've got the mind of a child but none of the history or background to know how to react to the world around you. All you've got is an innate instinct. That's what your wolf is dealing with. She wants to belong. We are pack animals first and foremost. If you still view the world from the eyes of a human, you won't ever be at home with the pack. If you aren't at home here, then she never will be. If you can truly open yourself to being one with the pack, then I think things will get better."

He was right. I hadn't thought about that. I wasn't human anymore. I was a shifter. My wolf settled even more as realization dawned on me. My life was different. It was different in a good way. We were home. This was where we belonged.

Chapter 8 - Nico

My last visit to the auto shop had been cut short by the kidnapping attempt on Maddy, but I knew I couldn't keep neglecting the shop. I got Felipe to come and watch over Maddy while I headed out to finish what chores I had left there. The team was good and, thankfully, didn't ask too many questions about my abrupt departure the other day. After a few hours there, I decided to head back home. There was too much uncertainty. As much as I enjoyed working at the shop, I had other responsibilities. I walked out to the parking garage, swiping through my phone to see if I had any messages. I did have a few texts, mostly from Maddy, some from the guys, but nothing crazy or important.

I put my phone away and walked slower. Something didn't feel right. I glanced around with every step I took. Sniffing the air, I noticed an unfamiliar scent. The hair on my arms rose, making me nervous. I even thought about calling for backup, but the smell was faint. Whoever had been here had left hours ago. I had the sense that I was safe for now.

I walked around my car, even looking underneath it. When I was about to unlock it, I saw something that made no logical sense. There was a jeweled case with either a CD or DVD in it lying on my driver's seat. I glanced around one more time and tried my door handle. It was still locked. What the fuck? Memories of old gangster movies with car bombs filled my head, but that wasn't what was happening here. The royals wanted Maddy to give herself up. Killing her mate was a one-way ticket to making sure that *didn't* happen. Though they had been brazen enough to try to take her, I didn't think they were desperate enough to do something so rash.

I unlocked my door and got into the truck, picking up the case as I did. Flipping it over, I found a piece of paper taped to the back.

A friendly reminder that the full moon is approaching. In case you forgot how serious we are.

I gritted my teeth and started the car, then sped home. Maddy was downstairs in the living room when I came in. I tucked the jewel case into the waistband of my jeans. I needed to watch it before I showed it to her. That way, I could help prepare her for whatever blow awaited.

Felipe nodded. "Hey, man, are you good if I go now that you're back? I need to run some errands."

"Yeah. Fine." I grunted the words as I headed toward the stairs, desperate to get to my office and my laptop.

"You good, Nico?" Felipe asked.

"Yeah. All good."

"Are you gonna even say hi?" Maddy called from the kitchen. I winced, realizing I'd totally ignored her.

I turned around and plastered a fake smile on my lips. I prayed it looked more genuine than it felt. "Sorry. I need to order some parts for the shop. It's something I should have done a week ago, so I want to get it out of the way."

I gave Maddy a quick kiss. Felipe called a goodbye, and we both heard the front door close. Maddy stared into my eyes, and I realized I was totally fucked.

"What's wrong?" she asked.

"Huh? Nothing."

"You're lying, Nico. I can tell. I can hear your damned heart beating a mile a minute. Something happened. What was it?"

My shoulders slumped as I came to grips with the fact that whatever was on that disc would be out in the open soon. I wouldn't get the chance to watch or listen to it first. I just hoped whatever was on the disc wouldn't devastate her. Slowly pulling the case out of my waistband, I held it up between us.

Maddy's eyes narrowed. "What the hell is that?"

"The royals left it. They somehow managed to break into my truck. It was on the driver's seat with a note. I have no idea what it is. I wanted to check it first before I showed it to you. If it was… something bad, I wanted to be able to prepare you for it."

"Well, it's here now. Let's see what those assholes sent," Maddy murmured. She looked less confident than she sounded.

I got my laptop from my office and set it up on the kitchen island, sliding the disc into the drive. It only took a few seconds for the media player to pop up. It was a video file. A knot twisted into my guts, like snakes fighting each other. Video would be worse. There was no way it wouldn't be.

"Push play," Maddy whispered.

I hit the button, and within seconds, it felt like the floor had dropped out from under us. Maddy's mother was on the screen. She was still tied to a chair, her hair matted and greasy. Sweat and dirt coated her skin, but otherwise, she looked healthy and unharmed. She was staring to the left of the camera and nodding. Someone must have been giving her instructions.

Finally, Maddy's mom looked at the camera. "Maddy, baby. We… need you to do what the… the royals say. It won't be that bad. They've… uh… they gave me, and your father guarantees that nothing will happen." Maddy's mom glanced to the left again, possibly listening to more coaching, then she focused on the camera again. "They only need some blood. They—" Maddy's mother gritted her teeth and snarled at the camera. "Don't do it, Maddy! Do not do it. Your father and I will die for you. It's our job. We're your parents. I forbid you from trying to save us or doing—"

Her screams were cut off. She began to convulse in the seat. Her eyes rolled up into her head as she jerked and jolted in her restraints. It was then that I saw the collar around her neck. There was a buzzing, clicking sound on the video. They had her in a goddamned shock collar. The bones of my fingers cracked as I clenched my fists.

Foam oozed out of her mother's mouth, and she slumped, passed out, and exhausted, her chest heaving. From the edge of the camera, a familiar form appeared. Viola was dressed in another designer suit. This time her hair was slicked back away from her face. She stood directly in front of Maddy's mother.

"Bitch," Maddy hissed, vibrating with rage. I'd never seen her look so angry.

Viola turned to the camera. "Well, this was unfortunate. We only typically use shock therapy on the ones who don't fall in line. As evidenced by this"— she curled her lip in disgust—"display, your mother has been a tough one to break."

Maddy snarled at the screen, and I put a hand on her lower back to steady her. The fact that Viola could torture someone like this and act like it was no different than swatting a fly made it clear she wasn't sane. "I'm going to kill her," Maddy hissed.

I believed her. A chill ran down my spine.

"Maddy," Viola said. "You can end all this. Your parents and your little friend can all be set free. All you need do is join us at the disclosed location in a few weeks. Very simple really. I hope to see you soon. Your family hopes I do as well."

The video clicked off. There was a moment of complete silence, then Maddy went berserk. I stumbled back as she started swinging her arms around the room. She pulled books off the bookshelves. She slammed her hands into the wall, punching holes in the drywall. Her hands flashed between claws and fingers so fast that it was almost like watching a strobe light.

"Maddy, calm down!"

She rounded on me. Her eyes were filled with a fury I couldn't begin to understand. Her eyes were blood red, then they were back to normal, then red again. Her lips were peeled back in a snarling growl, and I watched as she and her wolf were both fighting for dominance, fighting to see who was the angriest.

I held my hands up, patting the air in a calming gesture. "It's okay. I'm here. Maddy, take a breath. Remember what I told you at the stream? Focus."

Maddy's body twitched as though she wanted to lash out more, but she ended up taking a single steadying breath, then visibly relaxed. I sighed and realized I'd been scared. Hell, I was still scared. I'd never seen anything like it.

Maddy opened her eyes, and though they were calmer, they didn't have the look I'd expected. She wasn't crying. She didn't even look sad. There was only a deep and vicious fire in her eyes. That scared me almost as much as her destructive outburst.

"I know what you're thinking, and you need to get that out of your head," I said. "I'm not letting you sacrifice yourself."

Maddy gave a single shake of her head. "You don't know what I'm thinking."

I frowned. What was wrong with her voice? It didn't sound like her at all. It was deeper. Throatier. What the fuck was happening?

Maddy clenched her hands into fists and shook them in front of her. "I don't want to sacrifice myself. I don't want to die. I want the royals to die. I want to force them to sacrifice themselves." Her words grew in volume. The more she spoke, the more alien her voice sounded. "I want Viola's sightless, unblinking eyes to stare up at me from where I have her head on a platter. All these years of lies and deceit, so much time spent scheming. I know what they are. Years and years, I've dealt with them. I want them to scream for mercy. They've done this for so long, they don't even see how evil they are. I want to gut them and see their faces as they watch their insides slide from their bodies—"

I ran forward and clutched the sides of her face, putting my eyes right in front of hers. "Maddy! Snap out of it."

As though a switch had been flipped, she blinked, and then she was Maddy again. Only her. She took a deep gasping breath and put a hand to her chest. "That wasn't me, Nico. That was my wolf speaking through me."

I blinked at her. "What? That..." I frowned. "That isn't possible. She can influence what you say. Give you impressions and emotions, but they can't talk through you."

Maddy shook her head, worrying her bottom lip between her teeth. "None of those words were mine. I didn't say any of that."

"But you were talking about knowing the royals. Having memories of them. That can't be your wolf. How would your wolf have any memory of them? It was only *born* when we mated."

"I don't know, Nico." Maddy dragged her hands through her hair. "That's what I've been telling you. I don't think this is the typical way a shifter's wolf is born. I keep telling you this is weird."

My mind spun with the possibilities. How could her wolf have memories of the royals? How strong was it that it could actually take over her body and *speak* through her? Why hadn't it come out yet if it was so strong? I needed someone with more experience.

"Are you cool if I call my father over?"

Maddy nodded and paced around the room like a caged tiger. I grabbed my phone and called Dad. He was at our house in less than five minutes. We met him downstairs and sat down to explain what had happened. He listened carefully as we explained what we'd seen on the video, Maddy's reaction, her outburst of anger, and then the way the wolf seemed to speak through her.

He held up a hand. "Wait, wait, you're saying the wolf itself spoke?"

"Yes," Maddy said, desperation seeping into her voice.

"Right," I added. "She says none of the words were hers."

Dad sat back and rubbed at his beard. I remembered the look from my childhood. It was what he always looked like when he was contemplating something very important. Finally, he shook his head. "I've never heard of anything like this."

I sighed in frustration. I hadn't held out much hope, but I had hoped he could help us make sense of this.

"Theoretically, it is possible," Dad said. "We share bodies with the wolf. We even give over our bodies when we shift. Our minds are melded in a sort of symbiosis. We are one being of two halves. If the wolf can completely change our bodies and use our other senses, there's no reason it couldn't use our voice. I mean, they sort of do already when we growl or snarl. I've just never heard of a wolf strong enough to do that."

"What about the things it said?" I asked. "The memories and stuff?"

Dad looked at Maddy. "Is this anything the wolf could have gleaned from your memories? The dealings you've already had with the royals?"

Maddy shook her head. "I don't think so. She was talking like she already knew them, not like she knew *of* them."

Dad shook his head again. "None of this makes any sense."

Chapter 9 - Maddy

Things weren't going well. Seeing the video of my mother being tortured had done something to me. Not only to me but to my wolf. My temper was shorter than usual, and I kept having to catch myself. Multiple times I wanted to lash out at Nico or Felipe and Luis, and especially Sebastian. It was so bad that I tended to stay away from everyone when they came over.

A delivery driver had dropped off a package the day before. It was a package I had ordered, but he put it on the first step of the porch instead of the welcome mat by the door. It was such a small thing, but I'd nearly lost my mind. I'd gone stomping down the walkway toward his truck, yelling at him. Thankfully, Nico had been there to haul me back inside. I'd really been ready to chew the poor guy out for something so trivial and stupid.

Deep down, I knew most of what I was feeling wasn't anger—it was fear. Fear of what would happen to my family. Fear of what the royals were planning. Fear of what the hell was going on with my wolf. I wasn't a violent person by nature. I didn't have any concerns that I would actually hurt someone, which was nice and one less thing to worry about. Still, as much as I was sure I wouldn't hurt anyone, the memory of how I'd reacted to the video haunted me. Never in my life had I felt such an overwhelming and blood-boiling anger. The weirdest part is that the anger stemmed, not from my mother's torture, but from the sight of Viola herself. My human anger had been terrible, but the wolf's anger had been apoplectic. She'd been infuriated beyond belief.

A few days after we'd watched the video, Nico found me sitting in the dark in his office, my back to the door as I stared out the window. I was trying to do some of those calming meditations he'd shown me and was having varying degrees of success.

"Maddy?" he asked hesitantly.

I spun in his office chair to face him. "Yeah?"

"Do… do you want to go out and get a coffee or something?"

My spirits lifted almost immediately at the thought. I liked coffee, yes, but that wasn't the main reason I was excited. Ever since we'd returned from Europe, I'd spent nearly all my time in Nico's house or around the shifter neighborhood. With the bar closed and the royals doing God knew what, it hadn't felt safe to be out in town. But, Christ, I was getting cabin fever, which was probably exacerbating the irritation and anger I'd been experiencing. There were only so many rooms to go to, only so much yard to stroll through before you started to hate what you were looking at.

I stood up. "Hell yes!"

Nico and I hopped into his truck and made our way to the downtown area of Clearidge. I rolled my window down and let the wind blow across my face. Nico's house was a step or two away from being a full-fledged mansion, but it had started to feel like a prison. Getting out was freeing in a way it had never been before. Nico, for his part, let us drive in silence. It was a companionable silence, though, not awkward or strained. I think he knew I needed this more than even I did.

We pulled up outside a small mom-and-pop coffee and pastry shop that looked out over the Clearidge park and pond. I'd always thought the shop looked cute but had never managed to get in there over the years. When we walked in, the earthy smell of freshly roasted coffee and the sweet smell of baked goods lifted my mood in an instant.

I ordered a vanilla iced coffee and a chocolate croissant. Nico got a cappuccino and a piece of strawberry pound cake, then we found seats that overlooked the park. I glanced over at Nico as he took the first sip of his drink. "Thanks. I was getting a little stir-crazy."

He nodded and dabbed at his mouth with his napkin. "I could tell," he said with a knowing grin.

I sighed and rolled my eyes. "I'm sorry for how I've been acting."

"It's not your fault. I think we've established that."

I nodded. "Yeah. Still." I shrugged.

"You know, the last few days, I've been wishing we could still talk to Kenneth," he said wistfully.

The mention of my dead uncle filled me with multiple emotions. I was sad because he'd been the one connection to my birth family I had, and I'd grown to really like him over the days we spent with him. I was also filled with anger—anger at him for betraying us, but also at the royals for killing him. They were the reason he was so tortured in the first place. If not for them, my birth father would be alive. Maybe he and Kenneth could have figured things out over time. He could have been a different person without them.

I took a drink of my coffee before answering. "It would be nice to talk to someone with some insight, that's for sure."

"What if we tried to find more of your family?" Nico asked.

I frowned. "What family? Everyone is dead. At least anyone I can think of to try and find. The royals have made it their mission to kill anyone associated with the Edemas bloodline. Kenneth was probably the only person worth talking to."

Nico jerked his chin toward me. "Obviously, the royals aren't as good at finding the descendants as they thought they were. You're a perfect example. Maybe there are others they've missed. Also..." He gave me a weird look. "What if Kenneth was keeping secrets up until he died?"

"What other secrets?"

"I've been wondering lately... What if your birth mother was still alive?"

I nearly choked on my coffee. I wiped my lips with a napkin and gaped at Nico. "What? Where are you going with this?"

He held up a hand. "Hear me out. Right at the end, he told us that he'd been in love with her. Once your birth father was dead, he may have hidden her away to keep her safe. If he loved her as much as he said he did, he might have orchestrated her death to get the royals to stop trying to find her."

I sighed and shook my head. "Nico, I feel like you're grasping at straws here."

"Sure, it's a long shot. Except, the more I think about it, the more it makes sense. You were there. You saw what Kenneth was like when he talked about her. He didn't seem heartbroken or grieving—it was more like there was a longing in his tone when he talked about her. As though she wasn't *gone*, just out of reach. It feels like it could be right."

"Okay," I said. "Let's say we do believe she's alive. What's the move? If Kenneth hid her so well that the entire world thinks she's dead, how do we find her?"

"We've got her picture and her name from the yearbook. The royals think she's dead, which means they wouldn't have been looking for her. After all these years, she may have become less wary of being found. I bet Luis would have a good chance at locating her if we really went all in on this."

From his enthusiastic tone, it sounded like Nico had been thinking about this for a few days. I had to admit the idea made me nervous and eager at the same time. I didn't want to get my hopes up, but we had nothing else to go on.

"I really think that she may have some answers about your wolf and why she's acting the way she is. If your dad had some knowledge, he probably shared it with her. He was closer to your birth mother than anyone, even Kenneth."

It did seem like a last-ditch effort, but I didn't know what else we could do. We'd exhausted every other option. I shrugged. "Okay. Let's see what we can find."

We finished our drinks and snacks before heading back home. After getting our computers, we searched using the name we had. We turned up over a dozen different Gabriella Karsons, but every time we were able to pull up a picture, it looked nothing like the beautiful young woman from the yearbook photo. Then we decided to try different combinations of her name and my birth father's name. The variations went on and on. Gabriella Davids,

Gabby Samuelson, Karson Samuels. We even tried crazy things like Davidina Gabriella. No luck.

Hours later, I flopped down on the couch, a headache forming behind my eyes. "This is a waste of time, Nico. She's dead. We have to admit that."

"No, I don't think so. Maybe we aren't thinking about it the right way."

"If she was alive and Kenneth loved her as much as he said, I doubt he'd have stayed away from her for long stretches..." I trailed off, an idea forming.

"What are you thinking?" Nico asked, obviously seeing the look on my face.

"Kenneth had that safe house in Europe, but where did he stay when he was in America? If she's alive, he'd have wanted to be close to her."

Nico grabbed his phone. "Let me call Luis. He had the most contact with him while they were searching for the vault."

I walked over, listening to the phone ring.

Luis finally answered. "This is Luis. What's up?"

"Hey, I'm here with Maddy, and we have a question," Nico said.

"Okay, what've you got?"

"When you were working with Kenneth, did you get any info on where he lived while he was in the states?"

"Well, if you recall, I was searching for him before he came strolling into the bar of his own accord. I'd found some traces of him in Tampa. That's where I'd been looking."

"Did you ever pinpoint his location?" I asked.

"Nope. Once he revealed himself, I gave up. No reason to keep looking when he was right there. I don't know if he lived right *inside* Tampa, but he had to be close. The fact that he'd heard we were looking for him means he couldn't have been too far removed from my search area. Are you guys working on something?"

Nico chewed his lower lip and looked at me questioningly. I gave him a nod to go on. "We think, maybe, Maddy's birth mother might still be alive. I've got a theory that Kenneth hid her away and faked her death to keep her safe."

"Oh shit. Seriously?" Luis asked.

"Like I said, it's only a theory, but we want to run it down. One way or another, we need to know for sure," Nico said.

"Okay. I'm more than happy to keep running down leads. If she's alive, I'm pretty confident I can find her. I don't want to toot my own horn, but I'm pretty damned good at what I do."

"I think he's right," I said, nudging Nico. "We've got too much to deal with to add this investigation to it."

Nico nodded. "All right. Luis, you get on this. We'll focus on training the packs and trying to get Maddy through her first shift. I really think she's close."

"Okay. I'll dig up my info from before and head out to Tampa tomorrow morning sometime. Send me whatever you have on Maddy's birth mom. I'll go from there."

After we got off the phone, we sent Luis the few pictures of her that we had. There weren't many, but it would probably help. We also let him know the name and address of the high school she'd attended. I looked at her smiling picture on the screen after we sent it and felt a pang of sadness for Kenneth. I couldn't imagine loving someone and not having them reciprocate. I glanced at Nico as he worked on his computer and wondered how I'd feel if that happened between us. Me pining away for a man I knew didn't want me that way. Ugh, it sounded depressing as hell.

When we were in bed that night, I had another semi-anxiety attack. My wolf was acting up again. Sweat broke out on my body, and I had a tremor in my hands. My breathing elevated, and my pulse started to ratchet higher with each passing moment. The wolf was trying to assert herself again. Nico held me close and whispered that things would be all right. It wasn't a bad attack, but I was still consumed with guilt and shame once I'd regained my composure. Nico must have noticed.

"Are you okay? Do you need anything?"

I shook my head. "I feel like I'm putting you through so much more than I need to. Like I'm this heavy burden you have to bear."

He stroked a hand through my hair. "That's what I'm here for."

"Thank you for being so patient with me. I don't know what I would do if you weren't so understanding all the time."

"Well, I'd be a pretty shitty mate if I couldn't help you through this—a shitty mate and an even shittier alpha. I protect my pack. That means everyone in it. My mate most of all." He pulled me closer. "You can rest easy. I've always got your back."

For once, I did rest easy, falling asleep in seconds. The entire night went by in blissful, dreamless sleep.

Chapter 10 - Nico

I woke before dawn, still running through the possibilities of Maddy's birth mother being alive. Even when I'd been asleep, it felt like all I did was dream of the information she might be able to give us—of the closure Maddy might be able to get by meeting her. My head was spinning so much that I felt like I hadn't gotten any sleep at all.

Maddy was still sleeping, her breathing deep and calm. If nothing else, I was happy she'd gotten a good night's sleep. A glance at the bedside clock showed that it was a little before six-thirty in the morning. I decided to head downstairs and make some coffee. I'd need massive amounts of caffeine to get through the day.

I turned on the kitchen light just as my phone rang. I looked down at the pocket of my pajama pants. The phone rang two more times before I pulled it out, bewildered by the timing of the call. The screen showed me that it was Luis.

"Hello?"

"Saw the light come on. Let me in," Luis said.

My head still had one foot in dreamland, and I wasn't completely sure what he'd said. "You're outside?" I asked dumbly.

"Yeah, bro. I'm at the door. I waited until I saw the light come on before I called. I didn't want to wake you."

"What if I'd slept in? How long have you been waiting out there?"

"Dude, you told me what's been going on with Maddy. Honestly, I thought when I got here, you guys would already be awake. Can I come in or what?"

"Christ. Hang on."

Realizing the day would be even more exhausting than I'd initially thought, I went ahead and started the pot of coffee brewing before going to the door to unlock it and let him in. Luis looked bright-eyed for so early, and it made me wonder exactly how long he'd been up. He stepped in and glanced around the living room, kitchen, and dining room. "Is Maddy still asleep?"

Yawning, I nodded. "Yeah. First night in over a week that she slept through the night."

"Okay. I wanted to stop by before I head to Tampa. Straight talk. Do you really think this Gabriella chick is alive?"

Knowing how Luis was, I wasn't surprised by the question. If he was going to put in the leg work on something, he'd want to be exactly sure of what he was looking for. Did he need to focus his search on an actual person or a gravesite?

"I'm not a hundred percent sure, no. All I can say is I have a feeling about it. Everything is so strange. Kenneth said she died not long after having Maddy. Cancer. The thing is, in all our searching yesterday, we never found any type of death announcement or obituary. Could she have died while in hiding? Maybe, but that seems weird. The whole thing feels like a cover-up."

Luis nodded. "Right, it is a little too perfect. Not that death is perfect, but it usually isn't tied up nice and neat with a little bow like this seems to be. Disappear, have a forbidden baby, die quickly afterward? Life doesn't *usually* work like that. Not that it couldn't happen, but it seems a little convenient."

I nodded, glancing at the stairs to make sure Maddy wasn't in sight. "Right. If I had to guess, Kenneth was still protecting this woman all these years later."

"It would make sense. You guys said he was hung up on her romantically?"

"That's what he alluded to when... well, a few seconds before he died. He was in love with her. Unrequited love from the way it seems."

Luis sighed and gave a little half-shrug. "I'll do the best I can. If she's out there, I'll find her."

"Thanks. Do you want some coffee for the trip?"

Luis shook his head. "Nah, got an energy drink with three hundred milligrams of caffeine in the car. I'll be cracked out of my mind in a little bit. I'll call you when I have some info."

"All right. Be careful. The royals think she's dead. Don't be the reason we lead them back to her door if she's not."

"I got you," Luis said as he headed out the door.

I sat on the back porch and drank two cups of coffee before pulling my phone out and texting all the guys, my brothers, Dad, and Javi. Training was off for the day. Maddy was getting closer to her first shift, and I wanted to spend the day working with her. Her stress levels increased with every passing day. Nothing about sitting and watching us all shift and run around was going to help her. If anything, watching us was probably making her wolf even more anxious and frustrated.

Maddy finally woke up an hour later, looking more rested than I'd seen her look in days. I waited until she'd eaten breakfast and woken up properly before telling her what I had planned for the day.

"Do you want to come back to the creek with me?" I asked.

She looked at me and raised an eyebrow. "What for?"

"Well, it seemed to help the other day. Maybe if we go out there more often, it will get you relaxed and calm enough for the shift to happen."

Maddy put her cup down. "Whatever helps. I'll get dressed."

Twenty minutes later, we got to the stream and settled in. I wasn't some yoga guru or anything, but I'd read enough about breathing techniques and meditation that I thought I could help her.

"Okay, just like last time. Close your eyes. Deep breath, three seconds in and out."

Maddy did as I asked. I knelt behind her and gently kneaded her shoulders, trying my best to relax her entire body. I could feel the tension start to release from her as she continued her breathing exercise.

I lowered my lips to her ear and whispered, "You are strong, Maddy. It isn't just your wolf. You are as strong as she is. Remember, you are in this together."

I continued giving her prompts and encouraging words. We worked on it for almost an hour before we finished. Maddy opened her eyes and smiled. "I feel a lot better actually. My wolf also seems calmer."

I breathed a sigh of relief, happy that it helped. "Maybe we can do this more often."

"Yeah."

I nudged her with my elbow. "You still don't sound totally good. What's on your mind?"

Maddy tugged a handful of weeds from the ground and tossed them into the water. The green sprigs fluttered in the wind before hitting the water and floating away. She was silent for so long that I started to think she wasn't going to answer. When she finally spoke, it was so sudden that I almost jumped in surprise.

"I still regret ever doing that DNA test. None of this would have ever happened if I hadn't done that. My guilt is so overwhelming. Everything that's happening with my parents and Abi is my fault, or at least I feel that way. It would have been better for everybody if I hadn't been so curious."

Her words hit me hard. Not only because she shouldn't feel guilty, but because of the unknown that went along with them. If that DNA test hadn't happened, would we have found each other? We were fated mates, but that didn't mean we were guaranteed to locate one another.

As though she could read the thoughts bouncing through my head, she glanced over at me. "I don't regret you. Nico. You're the one good thing that's come from all this. I only wish we could have met under different circumstances."

That was something I could definitely get behind. Life would have been so much simpler if I'd just strolled into her bar on a random Friday night. Flirted a bit, exchanged numbers, and then *boom*, a normal relationship. What was done was done, though. There was no way to go back, and there was no reason for anyone to feel guilty about anything. Sometimes fate was a brilliant and wonderful lady— other times, she was a sadistic bitch.

Maddy tossed another handful of grass into the stream. "I need to get over it. I know that. Wallowing in the mistakes of the past won't change a damn thing." She turned to look at me. "I want to try and shift again."

"Right now?" I asked, surprised by the sharp left turn the conversation had taken.

Maddy stood and brushed her pants off. "Yeah. Let's give it a try."

The next couple of hours were spent trying to talk her through what I did when I shifted. It was honestly sort of difficult to explain. For me, it was so innate and simple that it felt like I was trying to explain exactly how to blink or how to flex every muscle and fire every nerve it took to take a breath. Instead of trying to focus on the biological mechanics, I tried to get her to open her mind and body up to the wolf.

Maddy tried to give me cues as we worked on it, letting me know how her wolf was feeling at certain points. We tried running, lying on the forest floor, even taking our shoes off and wading into the stream to get her more connected to nature. A lot of shifters were more at home in the wilderness, but that didn't seem to help either.

"What if I shift?" I asked. "Do you think that might bring her out? My pheromones are really strong, especially now that we've mated."

Maddy seemed nervous. "Sure. Let's give it a shot."

"Don't fight your wolf's reaction to me," I said. "Stay calm, and remember the relaxation techniques. It'll only take a second for her to take over and shift."

Maddy nodded, and without hesitation, I shifted, falling to the ground and landing on four paws. Maddy's breath hissed through her nose as she chuckled. "Uh… she's… I don't even know how to explain it, but she knows you're here."

I moved to Maddy's side and slid myself along her legs, rubbing my scent on her. Maddy clenched and unclenched her fists and fidgeted on her feet. I looked up and saw the expression on her face—she looked both confused and anxious. She was whimpering and talking to herself, but it was so low and quiet that I couldn't make out what she was saying. I took a few steps back when she started to snarl and growl.

I could feel Maddy's wolf. Her presence was right there, so close I could practically smell her. I'd never felt that before. She was close. So damned close.

Maddy shook her head and looked bewildered. "She's not ready."

I shifted back and took Maddy's hand. "What do you mean? Do you mean you aren't ready?"

"No, she isn't."

"How can you tell?"

"She told me so."

The idea of my wolf actually speaking to me was beyond my comprehension. Every time Maddy said something like that, it confused me even more. Was it a werewolf trait? Some more powerful connection they had to their wolf? Jesus, could they talk when they were in their werewolf form? That was a pretty scary thought and added to the pile of questions we already had.

"Did she say why she didn't come out?" I asked.

"She said as much as she'd love to come out, it wasn't the right time." Maddy took my hand and smiled one of the first genuine smiles I'd seen on her face in a while. "I don't know what changed with my wolf, but I think things are going to be okay. We just have to be patient."

She kissed me then. I had no idea what had changed, but she seemed more at ease than ever before. I kissed her back, wrapping my arms around her. After several seconds, I pulled away to look into her eyes. "I trust you. I don't really know what or who your wolf is, but I trust you."

I said that, but it was still strange to me to think of a wolf having its own thoughts. The thought of my own wolf having its own motives and being able to dictate to me when and where he was going to reveal himself was bizarre. But her wolf *was* part of Maddy. It had become rapidly clear over the last couple of months that she was unlike any of us. We had so much to figure out. I'd do whatever it took to help her understand.

Chapter 11 - Maddy

Now that I'd learned some ways to stay calm and collected, things seemed to be a little bit better. My wolf and I had grown closer. I couldn't put a finger on what had caused it, but I was grateful. It was probably the reason I was able to look past my own anxiety about shifting and could feel hers. She was just as anxious as I was, if not more.

My wolf wanted to be with her mate, but she said it wasn't time. The waves of emotion I felt from her were sometimes overwhelming, and I still found that difficult to understand. Nico told me it was normal. In fact, he said it was more normal than the words I heard from her. Nico's wolf shared its feelings, emotions, fears, and desires with him. Every shifter had that symbiotic relationship with their wolf. Although mine was on a wholly different level, and no one could understand it.

Yet, it made sense to me. A living and thinking being shared my body, so why wouldn't she speak to me? Apparently, that was unheard of. It wasn't a constant hum of words buzzing through my mind all day. It was sporadic and usually in simple two, sometimes three-word bursts. Enough for me to know she was there, but not enough to drive me mad.

Regardless, I felt better than I had in days. It was a relief to sleep well for a few nights in a row. As a side benefit, Nico was also more relaxed. He and I were connected through mating, so I was sure my issues had weighed on him physically. When I sat down to watch the next training session a day or two later, I felt almost totally normal.

It was a little while after lunch when I sensed someone walking up behind me. I glanced over my shoulder to see Nico's mom, Julia. "Oh, hi. Did you want to have a seat?" I asked, patting the grass beside me.

Julia and I had made up, and things were much less strained between us. It was still a little awkward because we were trying to get to know each other, but it was a pleasant awkwardness.

Julia shook her head. "Do you have a minute?"

I nodded. "Sure, what's up?"

She took a seat next to me, folding her hands into her lap as she looked out over the field and watched her husband, sons, and the rest of her pack running, leaping, and fighting. "I know you're going through a lot. I wanted to see if you wanted to talk about it or if you needed anything?"

I raised my eyebrows in surprise. "Thanks, I don't think so. I can only talk about it so much. After a while, it starts to feel redundant."

Julia put her hand on my arm. "Your family is in danger. Your friend. There is nothing redundant about talking about that. Sometimes that's the only way to make sense of a situation."

My heart warmed, knowing I wasn't being annoying and that everyone around me really did want me to feel better. "I know. If I need to vent or something, I know who to come to."

Julia smiled. "I hope you do. I'd be happy to be the person you come to if Nico isn't available. You have the support of everyone in the whole family. The whole pack, really."

My talk with Julia lifted my spirits doubly, and I found myself talking to my wolf even more than usual. I couldn't force her into coming out, but I could make sure she was calm and at ease. The breathing and meditation helped. It kept my mind off what was possibly happening to Mom, Dad, and Abi.

Each day brought the full moon and our deadline closer. If we couldn't figure out a way to rescue them, we'd have to make a decision. Nico didn't think there was a decision to make, but there were several options on the table. One of them was sacrificing myself. He'd never go for that. Not in a million years. Not even in a billion. But they weren't his family, his friends. They were mine, which meant the final decision was mine. I hoped we wouldn't get to that point.

That evening after the training session ended, Nico came running inside while I was working on dinner. He looked out of breath and waved his phone in the air. "Luis. He's calling."

I turned the stove to simmer and joined Nico in the living room. He answered the phone right before it went to voicemail. "We're here," Nico said.

"Hey. Just checking in," Luis said.

I sat forward, eager to hear any news he might have. "Have you found anything yet?"

Luis chuckled. "Unfortunately, investigations like this aren't easy or quick. When someone wants to pretend they're dead, they tend to do a good job of hiding."

"So nothing yet, it sounds like?" Nico asked.

"No. I'll call again in a day or two for another update. I've got a couple of leads I'm working on. There're only a few hospitals in town, so I'm trying to track down the people who would have been head of oncology around the time Maddy's birth mother supposedly died. Probably pointless, though. If it was faked, then they'll have no memory of her. Like I said, I'll let you know."

"Okay. We'll talk to you later. Stay safe out there," Nico said.

After dinner, Nico and I sat on the porch. The weather had gotten cooler over the last few weeks—cooler for Florida, anyway. He had his arm around me when he leaned over to speak. "What do you think you'll do if she is alive?"

"What?" I asked, pulled out of my post-dinner haze.

"Your biological mother? If she really is alive, how do you think you'll react?"

That question had been nagging at me ever since Nico brought up the possibility. I still thought it was a long shot, but I had to admit I had no clue what I'd think or do if it turned out to be true.

"I'll be honest. I have no idea how it'll affect me until I'm face to face with it. The parents who raised me, my *real* parents, are great. Amazing even. I love them so much—it's why I'm so torn up about them being kidnapped." I swallowed hard, trying to fight back the tears. "Am I still mad that they suppressed my wolf with drugs all those years? Sure, but they had their reasons. Kenneth basically told them I'd die if they didn't. I think they should have told me once I was older and let me make my decision myself, but that's behind me. I've had a great life, and it's sort of scary to think that I might never have had that.

"It makes me really sad to think about a life without Mom and Dad in it. Even if Gabriella and David were truly fantastic people, they aren't my parents, not really. They gave me the DNA that made me, but my adoptive parents raised and loved me. Nature versus nurture, you know?"

Nico looked pained and patted my arm. "I'm sorry. I shouldn't have brought it up."

I sat forward and put a hand on his shoulder. "No, don't be like that. It's not bad. I don't feel bad. I miss them, yeah, but that just means I really love them."

"Okay. I felt like I was rubbing salt in the wound for a second there."

I shrugged. "I get it." I looked down at the floor, thinking. I remembered all the vacations with my parents. The way they saved to send me to college. Even the awkward silence when I told them I was using my business degree to open a bar, followed by more love and support. My lower lip started to tremble, and tears filled my eyes. "Nico, we have to save them. Even if my birth mother is alive, she didn't hold me when I scraped my knees. Dad did. She didn't sit and hold me for an hour when my first boyfriend broke my heart in high school. Mom did."

Nico pulled me close, and I took comfort in the warmth and strength of his body. His lips were by my ear. "I'll do everything I can to fix this. I'll go until I'm damned bloody and beaten before I stop trying to get them back for you. We won't let the royals win."

His words stirred something deep inside me. My wolf reacted to the words, and anger and rage radiated off her. I tried talking to her in my mind, using calming and placating words. None of those words meant anything because even I knew they were lip service. I felt the same emotions she did. The wolf's fury coalesced in my stomach and chest like a stone. I could almost see her stoic furry face, the pissed-off fire in her eyes. It didn't feel like an animal—it felt like something more than that.

I pulled away from Nico and shook my head, bewildered by the sensation. "I know I keep saying this, but my wolf is… strange."

"What happened?" Nico asked, looking worried.

"The same as all the times before. It's like she knows more and feels more than other wolves. At least from the way you describe it."

Nico nodded, but he didn't say anything else. He already knew what I meant. It was part of the reason he was probably desperate to find my biological mother. We needed answers. More mysteries and questions were not welcome. Answers. Please, God, just some answers.

Chapter 12 - Nico

Two weeks. That was what we had left. The full moon would be here in half a month. Each day that passed seemed to go faster than the one before it. Luis hadn't made any headway yet, and it was taking all my mental energy to keep Maddy from getting too worried. She was so scared for her parents, and I knew I needed to be strong for her, to give her something to lean on. The problem was, I was equally worried. I couldn't show that, though, and it exhausted me.

Felipe and Sebastian came over that afternoon to talk about the safe houses where Maddy's parents and Abi were being held. Luis had left behind pictures and even blueprints he'd managed to get from the city planning offices. As we talked, the same problem kept surfacing.

"We all die," Sebastian said, flopping back onto the couch.

"Not necessarily," I said.

Sebastian pointed at the pictures. "Okay, fine. We don't all die. Only, like, eighty percent of us die. Then they put a bullet into the hostages and vanish. Great. Then the twenty percent of us who survive can live the rest of our lives with the guilt."

Felipe spun the pictures back and forth. I couldn't tell what he was doing. I nodded at him. "Do you see something there?"

He frowned at one of the blueprints for a few seconds before looking up at us. "So... we've basically come to the conclusion we can't do this, right?"

"Yes," Sebastian said.

"No," I said at the same moment, shooting Sebastian a glare.

Felipe held his hands up to calm us. "Okay, no need to come to blows here. What if we get help?"

I sighed and gestured to the outside world with my right hand. "We already have that. Even with Javi's guys assisting, it'll be a bloodbath."

Felipe closed his eyes for a minute, and I had the distinct feeling that he felt like he was talking to an idiot. I crushed my lips together to keep from calling him out for it.

When he opened them, he looked calm and clear-headed. "I realize Javi has aligned himself with us. Wolves are great. I'm talking outside the box. What about other shifters?"

Sebastian and I both froze. The thought hadn't occurred to us at all. Honestly, I didn't think any other shifter clans would want to help us. The royals had been werewolves. From the stories, they'd been pretty one-sided when it came to who they associated with. Would any other shifter breeds give a damn?

Sebastian raised an eyebrow. "Who do you have in mind? Who else are we trying to get killed?"

"You guys are still thinking brute force," Felipe said. "What if we went the stealth route? I know some reptilian shifters in Alabama. They can shift into snakes and lizards and stuff. They aren't powerful, not like wolves or bears or dragons or anything. They don't shift often because of how vulnerable they are when they do. Imagine going from a full-sized man to a three-foot-long snake. Not a safe place to be, right?"

"Get to the point, Felipe," I said.

"The *point* is that they can get really small and sneak into these safe houses. Once they're inside, they shift back and *boom*." He slammed a fist into his palm. "We immediately have guys on the inside. We split their defenses, startle them, and throw them off balance. Then, and only then, we go in—full-bore special-forces takedown. Kick in the doors, the whole nine yards."

Hearing him describe it sent chills up my arms—in a good way. The idea had merit. More than that, it was the best any of us had come up with after days of planning. Could it actually work?

"These friends you've got? What would it take for them to help us?" I asked.

"Leave the negotiations to me," Felipe said. "If you think we can use them, I'll hit the road this afternoon and head up that way."

I thought it over, then nodded. "Do it. Any help is better than no help. The plan has value. Whatever they want—within reason. Make the deal, and see how soon they can get some people down here to us."

"Sweet." Felipe stood up. "I'm going to head home and pack a bag."

I walked Felipe out and returned to the living room to find Sebastian sitting on the couch, arms crossed, staring into space like he wanted to beat the shit out of the air itself. I walked over and looked down at him. "What's up with you?"

Sebastian gave an angry shrug. "I wish I was doing more."

"There's no more you can do, man."

He gestured toward the front door. "I didn't have any snake shifter friends. The best I can say is I got laid by a chick who claimed to be a deer shifter once. Christ, I'm such a fuck up."

I'd never heard Sebastian sound so dejected and self-deprecating. I knew what was causing it. His guilt about Abi was growing. Every day she was still in the hands of the royals, he seemed to be falling deeper into a despair that was similar to Maddy's. The falling out the two had after Abi disappeared hadn't helped either of them. I was getting tired of them avoiding each other. I was exhausted enough with what was going on without having to navigate this too.

"You need to talk to Maddy," I said.

Sebastian shook his head. "She won't want to hear anything I have to say."

I sat on the couch beside him. "You are holding a shit ton of guilt, bro. That's not healthy. You aren't doing yourself any favors by beating yourself up." Sebastian didn't answer. I sighed, my frustration increasing. "You and Maddy were becoming friends before all this happened. I know you avoiding her is probably hurting both of you."

Something I said must have broken through. The hard angles of his face softened, and his shoulders slumped. "Do you really think so?"

"Yes, I do."

"Okay, okay. I'll talk to her. I promise. Soon."

"I've heard that before."

"Ugh, I got it. For real this time."

I gave him a decisive nod. "Cool. I'd have you do it right now, but she's out shopping with Dad and Mateo." I jabbed my finger into his arm. "Next time, though."

Sebastian gave a rueful shake of his head and grinned at me. "Yes, Father."

I smiled back at him, knowing we were okay. "All right, get the hell out of here. I'm tired of babysitting you."

"Yeah, yeah. I need to get some work done on my yard anyway." Sebastian gave me a quick hug before leaving.

Not long after, Luis called with another update. I didn't have huge hopes, but as soon as I answered the phone, I could hear the excitement in his voice.

"Nico? Is Maddy there, too?" he asked.

"No, she's out with Dad and Mateo. She told me she was going stir-crazy and needed to get out. Thought it was safer for her to go with two of them. What's going on?"

"I think I've found something. Well... I guess I've found the *lack* of something. I can't find any record of Gabriella Karson's death."

"What?" Chills ran up and down my arms. "No record at all?"

"No. I sent requests for records to every coroner and funeral home in and around Tampa. Took three days alone. Nothing. I got a hold of a guy I know of who ran a nationwide search. All I found were two matches. There's a Gabriella Karson in Kansas who was ninety-seven and died of a stroke. Another was an infant in south Texas who died three days after she was born due to severe birth defects. One hundred percent not Maddy's birth mother."

"Holy shit," I whispered, starting to believe that my theory might actually be right.

"It gets better," Luis said. "I can't find her name in any registries anywhere. The last place her name pops up is on an application for The University of South Florida Morsani College of Medicine. She never registered or attended. She vanishes without a trace at about the exact same time as the David Samuels murder."

"Did you try name changes? Those are recorded."

"Right, but if she changed her name, she didn't do it the legal way. No records there. I even took the time to do what you guys did and searched every name combination I could come up with. Nothing came up that was the right age or race. I even went so far as to use facial recognition software on that yearbook photo. Nothing. It's like she dropped right off the planet. I've never seen anything like it. If Kenneth really did help her disappear, the guy was fucking good. He was hidden well, but I was still able to find traces of him. This is a whole different level."

You'd do anything for the person you loved. I thought about what I'd do to keep Maddy safe. How many hoops I'd jump through, the bribes I'd pay, the people I'd blackmail. I'd have done anything for her to be safe. I was certain Kenneth would have done the same if he'd loved Gabriella the same way. "What's your next play?" I asked.

Luis sighed. "I'm still digging. If there is anything to find, I'll get it. Anyway, I need you guys to think about something."

My brow furrowed. "Us? What do you need?"

"Well, I was thinking last night that the one lead we never really pursued is still sitting right in front of us—Maddy's adoptive parents."

"Luis, they're captured. How can they help us?"

"They *are* held hostage, but their house isn't. Those two people are the only ones who had contact with Kenneth, and I'm betting they may have had contact with Gabriella too. They lied to Maddy about a lot of stuff. I think you guys should go to their house and see what you can find. Old records, letters, anything that might give us some more information."

It seemed silly that we hadn't thought of checking there already. With all the chaos, it never crossed my mind. Maddy's either, for that matter. I wasn't sure it was going to lead to anything, but I decided we had to do our due diligence. Even a small clue might lead to bigger things. "Okay. When Maddy gets home, I'll talk to her about it. If she's cool with it, we'll head out in the morning."

"All right. I'll let you know if I find anything else important."

Maddy got home a few minutes after I hung up. Dad and Mateo hung around for a few minutes to help pack away the groceries before they left, but once we were alone, I pulled Maddy over to sit on the couch, and she turned her worried gaze on me. "Is everything okay?"

"Yeah. I got off the phone with Luis a little while ago."

The worry on her face morphed into excitement and eagerness. "What did he find?"

"There's absolutely no record of your birth mother's death. At all. No death certificate anywhere in the country. He's doing some more digging, but he suggested we go to your parents' house."

"Mom and Dad's?"

"Yes. He thinks they may have some clues hidden away there. Did your mother or father have an office or anything? Keep records or documents?"

She shook her head and put a hand to her forehead. "I guess there's a couple of places that might be worth looking at, but I don't know how much help it'll be. My adoption records were sealed. I doubt there's anything worthwhile to find. Wouldn't it all be in the state records office?"

"Maybe. But your parents kept a lot of secrets. Maybe there are a few more we can uncover?"

Maddy's shoulders sagged. "That's true." Sighing, she said, "Okay. Let's do it."

We got up early the next morning and started driving. Maddy had been born in Tampa, but she'd grown up in Naples. It was over two and a half hours south of Clearidge. The drive was long but nice. It reminded me of our trip to Tennessee. We talked, joked, and debated over music and films. Maddy seemed more relaxed than she'd been in a while. For two hours on the interstate, things felt relatively normal. Once we got past Fort Myers and started seeing signs for Naples, she grew quieter, and her mood started dipping.

We were too close to turn back, but now I worried about what we'd walk in on when we got there. Would there be blood or something from the struggle? I cursed myself for not thinking of it before. I tried to keep things light-hearted for the rest of the trip, but Maddy only gave short, curt answers as she stared out the passenger-side window.

Maddy's old neighborhood was a nice subdivision. All the houses were in the classic Spanish style with clay roof tiles and white or cream stucco. Her parents definitely had some money, but it didn't seem like they were pretentiously rich. Their house was at the end of a cul-de-sac, and as we pulled into the driveway, Maddy stared at the front door with a mixture of horror and sadness.

As I got out, I saw an older lady walking a shih tzu toward us. Maddy groaned. "Ugh. Mrs. Garvey."

"Who?"

"My neighbor. I'll get rid of her. Hang on."

Maddy got out of the car, plastered the biggest fake smile I'd ever seen on her face, and walked toward the woman. "Mrs. Garvey?" Maddy's voice was tinged with surprise and excitement, which was not at all what she'd sounded like a second ago. She was a damned good actress.

"Maddy? Oh goodness. I haven't seen you since last Christmas. How are you?"

"I'm great. And how is little Princess?" Maddy knelt and petted the dog. I had a hard time not rolling my eyes.

"She's chugging right along like the good girl she is. Maddy, where have your parents been? I haven't seen them in a couple of weeks."

"Well," Maddy said, standing back up. "Cool story. Mom won an all-expenses paid trip to Italy and Greece."

Miss Garvey put a hand to her chest. "No! Seriously? That's exciting. When did that happen?"

"About a month ago. It was one of those online sweepstakes. Mom signed up for it since it was free, and she won. It was only a ten-day trip, but they decided to go to Spain and France as well. They'd always wanted to go. So, it was almost like two vacations for the price of one. I'm a little jealous that I didn't get to go. They called me and let me know they forgot to put a hold on their mail, so I came to get that and check on the house."

"Well, I cannot wait to hear about their trip when they get home," Mrs. Garvey said.

"They should be back in a couple of weeks."

"Okay, then. I'll let you and that handsome young man go." She waved at me, and I nodded back.

Maddy walked back toward me, rolling her eyes. I nudged her as we walked up the path to the door. "She seems nice."

Maddy glared at me. "Ugh. She puts on a show, but she's just a nosy old bitch. She's also the president of the HOA if that tells you anything. I've never been a fan."

"Coulda fooled me."

Maddy didn't answer. Instead, she reached her hand out and tried the doorknob. It turned, and the door swung open. The lights were still on, and I put a hand on the small of her back and escorted her in, closing the door behind us. Maddy's gasp drew my attention to the living room.

The living room was a disaster. Couch cushions were haphazardly strewn across the floor; a lamp was turned over, the bulb busted and glass shards littered the carpet. There was a thick dent in the drywall by the hallway. I imagined Maddy's father being shoved into the wall hard enough to put a hole in it. Several pictures had been knocked off the wall. One was Maddy's college graduation photo. Her parents flanked her, looking happy and proud. A spiderweb crack ran across the photo, almost totally obscuring Maddy's face. The struggle must have been intense. There was no blood, thankfully, but that didn't make it any less awful to see.

Maddy stood, frozen in place, with a hand to her mouth. I walked through the scene, looking around at what had transpired, trying to form the picture in my head. At least three men. They'd come through the front door, most likely under the cover of night. In a nice neighborhood like this, Maddy's parents probably didn't lock the doors unless they were out or going to bed. It had been vicious and fast. Her parents had barely had time to react, much less fight.

Behind me, Maddy sniffled. I turned to see tears tracking down her cheeks. I went to her and took her in my arms. She pressed her face into my chest, and I could hear her trying to hold back the sobs. I rubbed her back. "It's okay. Let go," I whispered.

As though all she'd been waiting for was permission, her sobs escaped her mouth, quiet and tense at first but slowly growing until she lost herself in them. I had to wrap my arms tightly around her to keep her from collapsing. It was the cries of heartbreak, fear, and anger. I let her drain it all out. All I could do was be there for her as she released it all.

Chapter 13 - Maddy

Nico let me cry for ages. He walked me over and sat me down in the recliner by the fireplace. The tears simply wouldn't stop. Every time I thought I was done, another sobbing fit crashed through me. He just knelt there, holding my hand the whole time. Every few seconds, I'd look around the living room and see the disaster again. The room where I'd sat and unwrapped Christmas presents, the kitchen I'd helped Mom prepare Thanksgiving dinner, the table we sat around for Easter dinner. It was the same, but now it felt violated. I doubted I'd ever be able to look at it the same way.

Finally, I managed to get myself under control. I'd needed to vent the emotion out, but I couldn't afford to fall apart completely. I stood and wiped my eyes. "Come on. Let's clean this up before we look around."

Nico's eyes widened in surprise. "Are you sure? It's okay if you need some more time, Maddy."

I shook him off. "No. We need to get this done. Come on." I sniffed.

We spent the next fifteen minutes fixing the room, cleaning up the glass, and putting things back where they belonged. I'd thought it would keep my mind occupied, and it actually did help. Once the evidence of the abduction was gone, the house felt like a home again. It still seemed desecrated in some way, but at least it wasn't overt.

Nico and I went out, grabbed our bags, and brought them back in. Thankfully, none of the other neighbors were out and about. I didn't have the energy to fake another conversation. We stowed everything in my old room. Mom and Dad had converted it into a guest room, but they'd left a lot of my things as decorations. A shelf along one wall still held all my trophies—gymnastics from when I was little, basketball when I'd been in elementary school, and track from high school. All of them were still lovingly dusted and arranged. My heart hurt at the sight, but I needed to push through the sadness. Push through and figure out a way to get them back.

We went to the kitchen next, and I sighed when I walked in. It looked like they'd been taken while making dinner. There was a sour smell of spoiled meat, and we found a whole chicken in the sink—raw, greenish with slime, and covered in flies. There were potatoes sitting in a pot on the stove that Mom hadn't even started cooking. The top was covered in a fuzzy gray-black mold. A large salad sat in a bowl on the counter. The lettuce and vegetables were wilted and slowly turning into a black soup of putrefaction.

"Ugh," I groaned. "We should have started in here."

Nico rubbed my lower back. "It's fine. We'll get it cleaned up before it stinks up the rest of the house."

Thank God Mom had some rubber gloves under the sink to deal with the chicken. Nico took care of that because I didn't think my stomach could take it. He stripped the gloves off and started rinsing out the sink and washing his hands. "I should have thought about this too," he said. "I could have had a team come and clean things up before we got here."

After another fifteen minutes, the kitchen was back in better order, and the window over the sink had been opened to air out the stench. As bad as the kitchen had been, I had no desire to cook. I pulled my phone out and put in an online order for Chinese delivery.

"General Tso?" I asked Nico.

He wrinkled his nose at me. "Maybe we don't do meat. I'm gonna have PTSD from that rotten food for a while."

I glanced at the sink. "God. Right. How about vegetable fried rice?"

He gave me a relieved smile. "Much better idea."

While we waited for the food to arrive, I took him up to my dad's study. It was one of the best places I could think of where something important might be hidden. When I opened the door to reveal the room, Nico whistled appreciatively. It had two floor-to-ceiling bookcases on each side of the room, the carpeting was thick and dark red, almost brown, and Dad's desk was a massive mahogany antique he'd found at an estate sale when I was around seven or eight. There was a big globe beside his desk, along with a cocktail station with crystal bottles of whiskey, bourbon, and gin.

"Uh… was your dad like… *The Godfather* or something?" Nico asked as he stepped into the room.

"Close. He was a real-estate lawyer."

"Close?"

"A joke."

Nico chuckled. "Right." He gestured around the room. "This doesn't really match the aesthetic of the rest of the house."

I nodded and sat in the plush leather seat behind Dad's desk. "Dad told me once that when he'd been in law school, he'd always dreamed of having a big, over-the-top office like big-shot lawyers had on TV and in the movies. He became a partner at his firm when I was… I don't know, ten or eleven? After that, he had the generic office here that was remodeled to look like this. It's pretty cool, huh?"

"Cool is an understatement," Nico said as he perused the books on the bookshelves. "Does he still practice?"

I shook my head. "He retired about four years ago."

Nico moved over to an antique filing cabinet. "What's in here?"

"That's where he kept important documents and transcripts from some of his biggest cases. Lots of important things in there, probably the best place to start looking."

Nico and I pulled every manila folder, accordion file, envelope, and notebook out of the cabinet and spread them across the floor in front of the leather couch beside Dad's desk. We only got through a couple of files before the doorbell rang. Nico ran down to grab the food and some drinks from the fridge. We ate while we worked. We poured over so much stuff that it felt like we'd been doing it for days. My eyesight was getting blurry after reading so much legalese. I had no idea how anyone could make head or tail of some of what was written in these documents.

By midnight, we'd gone through everything Dad had in his filing cabinet. There was still another filing cabinet he kept in the garage, plus all the boxes and stuff in the attic, then there were their computers and Mom and Dad's personal stuff in their room. It was overwhelming.

Nico rubbed a hand over his face. "Let's give it a rest for tonight."

It had been a long day. A really, *really*, long day. "Yeah. I don't think I'll be worth a damn if I have to look through one more file tonight."

Nico and I made our way to my old room and got ready for bed. While I was brushing my teeth, he must have taken a closer look at my room. I came out, and he was holding a trophy, a look of bemused confusion on his face. I saw the one he was holding and rolled my eyes.

He held it up and grinned. "What the hell is Miss Teen Naples?"

I walked over and tried to yank it out of his hands. He took a step back, chuckling. He nodded toward the shelf. "And The Florida Teen Pageant?"

"Fuck off, Nico," I growled.

He laughed and finally let me have the trophy. I put it back on the shelf beside the other one. I flopped on the bed and gestured toward the awards. "So, my mom had always wanted a beauty queen. She did pageants when she was younger and loved them. Like *loved* them. I did a couple here and there, plus those two when I was in high school, but I hated it. Much to Mom's disappointment. I preferred sports."

Nico sat beside me and nudged me gently in the ribs. "I'm struggling to picture you as a pageant chick."

I sighed and shook my head. "It wasn't *that* bad, but I'd never want to do it again. Something gross about getting all made up and in a fancy dress, then having people decide if you were the prettiest and most bubbly and shit. It was all very fake. I don't like being fake."

"Fair enough. Looks like you were a pretty accomplished athlete in high school, though," he said, looking at the other trophies.

"Most of those are from team stuff. I was above average, but nothing special. Let's just say there were exactly *zero* athletic scholarships being sent my way. That's actually how I met Abi. On the track team."

"Seriously? You guys have been friends that long?" Nico asked.

"Yeah. We both did the hurdles. I did the one hundred meters, and she did the four hundred. I also did the long jump, but I was terrible at it. Abi and I tried out when we were freshmen and immediately bonded over our very average athleticism. Two peas in a pod from then on."

"That's pretty cool. Did you enjoy high school? I feel like there are two types of people, those who loved it and those who hated it. Which one were you?"

I shrugged. "I guess I'm an outlier. I was pretty apathetic to the whole thing. It never seemed like this life-defining time that the movies and television make it out to be. It was a place I went to learn. I didn't hate it, but I also didn't enjoy it enough to pine for *the good old days* all the time. It was sort of the Abi and Maddy show. We did our thing and didn't let anything get between us."

Nico grinned. "That sounds like you guys." He raised a questioning eyebrow. "Any crazy stories?"

Of course, there were. We *had* been kids after all. I chewed on the inside of my cheek as I thought of a good one, then almost burst out laughing. "Okay, here's one of the best. So, this guy, I think his name was Aaron, started rumors about Abi and me."

"Rumors?"

"Real douche stuff. He was on the football team and started telling everyone that he'd had a threesome with us. No one actually believed him, but it pissed us off. He had this giant red truck his daddy bought him when he turned sixteen. So, Abi and I decided to get back at him one night. We snuck into his parents' driveway with three cans of paint."

"Oh shit."

I chuckled again. "Yeah. By the morning, it was bright neon pink. It also had several dicks painted on it. I don't know if he ever actually figured out who did it, but the rumors stopped almost immediately."

"Damn," Nico said. "Couple of badasses over here."

I shook my head. "Nope. Just dumb kids. If we'd gotten caught, we would have been in a hell of a lot of trouble. I'm sure it was several thousand dollars in damage, but I will admit, it was pretty cathartic."

Nico stood and stretched his arms over his head, groaning. "Are you ready for bed?"

Just the thought of sliding under the sheets and passing out sounded amazing. "Very ready."

My head had barely touched the pillow before I was asleep and dreaming.

I was walking down a corridor. It was familiar somehow, but I'd never been there before. The walls were ancient, covered in lichen, dust, and caked-on soot from the dozens of candles in sconces along the wall. Even as I walked along the stone floors, I had the sensation that this was more than a dream. It had the hazy realism of an old, almost-forgotten memory. How was it possible?

Before I could think about it, my thoughts were pulled away by the murmur of voices ahead. I moved farther down the corridor, glancing at the tapestries and oil paintings along the stone walls. One of the paintings showed a man with a thick black beard hanging almost to his chest and wavy black hair that fell to his shoulders. The look on his face was one of pious conceit. I had a moment of recognition as well as love and devotion. Who was this man? Why did it feel like he was important to me?

"We must do something," the voice down the hall hissed. It pulled my attention away from the painting, and I continued down to the doorway.

I stopped outside and pressed myself against the wall, eavesdropping on the conversation. There were at least three distinct voices, maybe more, but I couldn't be certain.

"Our queen has sullied herself by laying with a beast and creating demon spawn. By God, her soul is probably already bound for hell."

"Hush! Raging against the queen in shadowed rooms won't help. Action. That is the way," a voice said.

"Yes," agreed another. "Perhaps an herbal concoction that would leave her barren? Then there would be no further abominations slithering out from between her legs."

A powerful and throaty voice spoke up. "These ideas are only the prattle of disgruntled royal cousins. You are all blind to the true problem. Edemas has created dozens of offspring. He's making bastards left and right. If he or the queen were to die, then the next in line would simply take over, subjugating us for another generation. We must not only cut the head off the snake but chop up the body and burn it to ash. We should start with the Crown Princess."

A flutter of fear jolted through my chest as the strange voice said the words. I didn't know why there would be so much terror inside me. Did I know this woman they were talking of killing?

"He's right. If the princess is allowed to live, then she may become a monster like the father. I'm told there are two newborns that Edemas has sired with a couple of his whores. The rumor from the wet nurses is that they, too, are alphas. This has to end. Starting with the princess would be best. It will put

Edemas on edge and also sow fear and distrust within his inner circle. It is a good plan."

"It must look like an accident. Overt murder will only turn his suspicions on us. If we are to be successful and wrest this crown from his head, we must be careful. The princess is kind and gentle, yes, but we all know what might happen soon—once she wears the crown. No, this is for the best."

A whimper of fear escaped my throat, and I clutched at my chest, wishing I could take the sound back.

"What was that?"

"Is someone at the door?"

Without waiting another moment, I turned and ran, my bare feet slapping on the stone floor as I went. Shouts erupted from behind me. The conspirators had spotted me and were in pursuit. Fear pushed me forward. I could see the staircase ahead of me. In the back of my head, I knew that if I made it there, I could try to take the stairs two or three at a time. Three floors down, I could find the captain of the guard—if I could only get there.

My left foot touched the top step just as rough hands splayed over my back. My head snapped back as I was pushed over the stone banister. I tipped over the edge, and the hard slate floor thirty feet below me rushed up at me. My breath exploded out of me as my fear gave way to shock and disbelief. I spun in the air, looking up at an unknown face as I fell. Stern eyes watched as I neared the ground with every second. Then—

I jolted up in bed, gasping for air and clutching at the sheets. My heart pounded so hard that I was worried I might have a heart attack. I hadn't screamed like I usually did when I had a nightmare, and Nico was still asleep beside me, breathing steadily. I put a shaking hand to my mouth and tried to calm my breathing.

My wolf was right at the surface of my consciousness. She was hurt and terribly sad. Were my dreams actually memories? Could wolves be reincarnated? Could my wolf have lived all those years ago and lived in that castle? If these were memories, who had my wolf been in that past life?

Chapter 14 - Nico

  I left Maddy to sleep the next morning and went downstairs to scrounge up some breakfast. Most of the stuff in the fridges had expired and rotted. I threw out the milk, eggs, and everything else that looked dangerous to consume. In the freezer, I found some frozen burritos. Shrugging, I went ahead and threw the burritos into the oven.

  I walked around the kitchen and took a closer look at the refrigerator doors. It was completely covered in photos and magnets commemorating a visit to Disney World, another for Disneyland, and there was a magnet with a beach scene from a trip to Jamaica. The photos were the best part, though. There was one of Maddy when she must have been twelve or thirteen years old with a mouth full of braces. Then there were several with her at various ages through middle and high school. The senior picture showed the beautiful girl I knew so well.

  I checked on our frat house breakfast and found they were almost done, so I headed upstairs to wake Maddy. To my surprise, she was already up. She was sitting in bed, staring out the window.

  "Hey, good morning," I said.

  "Morning." She didn't look at me, and it seemed like her mind was elsewhere.

  "Umm, breakfast is almost ready. I made beef and bean burritos. The sour cream is still good, and I found some jalapeños and salsa."

  "Sure. Be there in a minute." She didn't bat an eye at the strange breakfast. Over the last several weeks, I'd learned to let Maddy be. She was going through things I couldn't begin to understand.

"Okay, cool. Come down whenever you're ready."

She came into the kitchen wearing a robe just as I was putting the burritos on a plate. When I looked up at her, Maddy seemed a little more awake and not as distant. She took the plate and raised an eyebrow.

"How late did I sleep?" she asked.

I smiled at her. "It's only eight o'clock. It was the best I could do. There's cereal, but I had to throw out the milk."

Maddy nodded, and I slid the container of sour cream and a bottle of hot sauce toward her. "It's fine. I'll have to leave a bad review for this restaurant online, though."

I chuckled. "Damn. There goes my livelihood."

We ate in silence before getting dressed and tackling the office again. As we got going, I noticed her slipping back into the strange, contemplative mood she'd been in when she woke up. I didn't pry, giving her the space she needed to work through whatever was going on inside her head. While she did, I flipped through her dad's address book, checking every person by doing a search on my phone. Every name was benign—other lawyers, a plumber, family and friends who had no connections to anything more powerful than the accounting or marketing firms they worked for.

I put the book aside and nudged Maddy with my toe. "Hey? Space cadet? What's going on in there?" I said, gesturing to her head.

She jumped, startled out of her reverie, then gave me a guilty smile. "It's silly."

It made me a little sad that she'd think anything she said would seem silly to me. "Out with it. I won't think it's dumb, I promise."

Maddy let out a heavy sigh and took a minute to think before speaking. "Do you think reincarnation is real?"

That was definitely not where I thought this was going. She caught me off guard with the question, and I must have had a surprised look on my face. Maddy shook her head and blushed. "It's stupid, I told you. You know what? Forget I said anything."

I leaned forward and put a hand on her arm. "Wait. Sorry, but you sprung that on me with no warning. I wasn't ready for intense spiritual matters, so I apologize. Now, again, reincarnation?"

Maddy rolled her eyes. "Right. Well? Do you think it's real or not?"

"I'll be totally honest. I've never given it a lot of thought. I think it's possible. The very fact that shifters exist kind of puts everything on the table. Ghosts? Angels? Reincarnation? None of that sounds as crazy as people who can turn into animals on command, does it?"

Maddy laughed and bobbed her head back and forth. "Pretty good point."

"Why is this on your mind, anyway?"

"I had another dream last night."

"A nightmare?"

Maddy winced. "Sort of. Not like the others though. It was bad, but the entire time it felt like it was more of a memory. Like it really happened. You know how dreams always seem sort of fuzzy and strange while they're going on? Like anything could happen at any second, and it would make total sense? Like, 'oh my flashlight turned into a popsicle, or the car vanished, and now I'm floating along the highway two feet in the air'. No big deal, right?"

"Yeah."

"Well, this felt totally real, exactly like a memory, but it wasn't mine. I was in an old castle. There were men in a room having a secret meeting. They were talking about killing Edemas and his family. They were going to kill his oldest daughter, the princess, first. In my dream, I accidentally made a noise, and they chased me. One of them pushed me over the side of the banister, and I fell thirty feet. I... I died."

I shook my head. "Wait. They were going to kill Edemas? So this was like three hundred years ago?"

Maddy nodded. "When I woke up, my wolf was really unhappy—sad and betrayed, completely distraught. Could my wolf have been reincarnated into me? Is she showing me memories of her past life?"

I had no clue if what she was saying was possible or if reincarnation even existed. If this was real, it opened a lot of deep *deep* questions about reality itself. I couldn't take the time to dive into metaphysical philosophy. Maddy needed answers. Again I let myself wish that Kenneth were still alive. He might not know anything, but it would have been nice to ask the only true expert we'd known.

"It might be nothing," Maddy said. "But it was just too vivid and *real* to dismiss. That's why I wanted to talk it out with you."

"Right now, the only things we have to go on are the legends that were passed down in secret. We know Edemas had a ton of kids. The only ones the legends specifically mention are the two babies who were sent into hiding. Maybe there was another daughter? The eldest child who was the first to die before the massive coup? It's possible."

Yes, it was possible, but the idea of that princess's wolf being reincarnated into Maddy's body was fairly crazy to think about. It almost made me dizzy. It was only a theory, though. Could we confirm it? How the hell would we be able to do that?

I rubbed a hand across my face. "Okay, let's come back to this once we've finished working on this search. There are only so many things we can do at once. We find some information on your adoption, see if we can find your birth mother, then we think about the...the possibility of a reincarnated ghost wolf. Okay?"

Maddy nodded. "Yeah. Sounds good."

We'd turned the office completely upside down. There was not a single thing we hadn't looked through. Maddy had even flipped through every book on both massive bookshelves to see if anything had been tucked between the pages. All she found out was that her dad liked to use empty candy-bar wrappers as bookmarks. We moved on to her parents' bedroom.

While Maddy went through the dresser drawers, I checked in the closet. There was a big cardboard box on the shelf above the hanging garments. Deciding to start there, I pulled the box down and lifted the lid. The first thing I saw was a thick envelope on the top of several photo albums. The hair at the back of my neck stood on end. My instincts told me we'd found something.

"Maddy?" I said, walking out of the bedroom with the envelope in one hand and the box in the other. "I think I found something."

Maddy dropped what she was doing and hurried over to me. We dumped the contents of the envelope onto the bed and went through them. My initial excitement faded quickly. They *were* the adoption papers. Everything Maddy's parents had done to complete the process of becoming her parents. It told us nothing we didn't already know. Kenneth's name was listed as the social worker. Maddy's birth mother's name was there, but it was her given name, no alias we could use to try and find her. Every line was cut and dry. We even flipped through the photo albums, and other than a walk down memory lane, there was nothing useful.

"Damn it." I'd really thought there might have been some clue here.

Maddy gave her head a sad little shake. "I hate to say it, but I was pretty sure we'd never find anything here. We were grasping at straws."

I sat on the bed and stared at the floor for a second. I was pissed that this had all been for nothing, but there was nothing else to be done. I shrugged a shoulder. "I guess we can put this back where we found it."

"I'll do it," Maddy said, putting her hand on my thigh. It looked like I was more depressed about this than she was.

"I gotta show you where. Come on."

I led her to the closet and showed her the spot on the top shelf where I'd found the box. Maddy stepped on a plastic crate on the floor to reach the shelf. Her foot slipped, and the crate flipped onto its side. Maddy tripped but caught herself and the box she was holding.

"Shit. I almost broke my neck. What..." Maddy trailed off mid-sentence as she bent to right the crate.

"Maddy? What is it?" I leaned around her. The plastic crate had cracked under her weight and spilled its contents. There were dozens of envelopes, postcards, and letters. "What the hell is all that?" I asked.

Maddy shook her head. "I don't know, but they're all addressed to me."

"Grab it. Let's take it to the living room. There's more room there."

Maddy shoved everything back inside and picked up the broken crate, following me to the living room. I helped her spread the contents out on the couch and ottoman. She was right. All the letters were addressed to her. Some looked old. I grabbed what looked like the oldest letter and handed it to her. "It's your mail. Might as well open it."

Maddy took it from me with trembling hands. The letter had never been opened. Her parents had kept them but hadn't even opened them? Maybe it was supposed to be a sweet gift. They'd written her letters throughout her whole life, and they'd present them as some emotional gift the day she got married or had a baby or something. That idea was a nice one, but something told me that was not what this was.

Maddy pried a finger under the seam of the envelope and tore it. The shredding sound of the paper had a strange finality to it, like we were crossing over into something we were never meant to see.

I leaned over her shoulder as she pulled the piece of folded paper out and opened it. I read along with her.

Dear Madison,

I hope you are doing so well. I bet you're getting big. I wish I could be there for your first birthday, but things are weird right now. You wouldn't understand, but I wanted to let you know that I love you very much. I miss you every single day. I don't want you to ever think I gave you up because I didn't want you. It was something I had to do to keep you safe. Your new family will make sure you have the life I couldn't give you. I do wish I could see you. Sometimes I dream about you. I got to hold you for an entire day before my friend took you to your new mommy and daddy. I can still remember the way your sweet baby hair smelled and how soft those little cheeks and fingers were. Oh gosh, I'm crying now. I need to stop writing. Happy birthday, sweet girl. I miss you.

Love, Momma

Maddy stared at the letter in open-mouthed shock. I probably had the same look on my face. Maddy set the letter aside and grabbed a postcard at random. It had a picture of a penguin wearing a Santa hat.

Maddy! I hope you had a wonderful Christmas. I'm sure Santa brought you everything you wanted. I know you've probably been a very good girl all year. I love you, and I hope you're enjoying third grade!

Maddy was openly crying when she grabbed the third envelope, almost tearing it in half in her haste to see what was inside.

Dear Maddy,

I know I can never tell you where I am, but I wish I could. I'd love for you to be able to know something about me and where I live. Anyway, I was able to make a pretty nice Thanksgiving dinner. My friend came from Europe to spend it with me. He's always looking out for me and helping me. Do you have any friends at school? I'm sure you have tons. I love you, and I hope you had a good ninth birthday.

Love, Momma

"Why?" Maddy sobbed, covering her face with her hands. "Why did they hide these from me? She loved me and missed me. She wrote all these letters, and I never even knew."

I put an arm around her and pulled her close, letting her cry into my shoulder as I looked down at the dozens of items that had come out of the box. So many. It looked like Maddy's birth mother had sent a letter for every single birthday and holiday she'd missed, plus a lot more that must have been sent at random times. Moments when she missed the baby she'd given up and wanted to make contact. This confirmed my theory. Gabriella hadn't died a few months after Maddy had been born. These letters went on for years and years. She'd survived. She might still be out there.

Once Maddy had managed to pull herself under control, we organized the letters by date. I could tell she was trying not to read the words, but I kept seeing her pause every few minutes to glance at a line here or there, and her eyes would well up again. Once we were done, we could see that the last letter had been dated the day she turned eleven years old. That one was the longest of them all.

Madison,

I'm so sorry, but this will be the last letter I send you. I'm so sorry, but I have to cut off contact with you. It's not safe for you anymore. Part of why I'm sending this is to let you know exactly who you are. Maddy, you are descended from a long line of shifters. You know who they are. They're the men and women who can change into animals. You might start to notice changes in yourself, but maybe not. I know you're on medication that might keep that part hidden for a long time if we're lucky.

You are a very important person. I've always known that, but something in your blood makes you even more important. It will cause a lot of bad things if anyone finds out. You'll be different from other female wolf shifters. I need you to try to restrain yourself at all times. I know that's hard, but you have to in order to stay safe. There are bad people who will come for you if they find out how strong you are. I'm going to do my best to protect you, and I hope one day you'll forgive me.

All I can tell you is that you aren't alone in this. Someone will be there to help you through it all when you find out. I'm so sorry I can't say more. I have to disappear for your own safety. Hopefully, we can be together again one day. Watching you grow all these years has been one of the few joys I've had in life. Please, please, remember how much I love you.

Love, MS

Chapter 15 - Maddy

The last letter fluttered out of my hand and landed in the pile of the rest of them. A thousand emotions toiled inside me. There were so many thoughts and feelings swirling inside me that I couldn't even keep track of them as they crashed through my mind and heart. Anger and sadness were the two that seemed to be fighting for top billing.

So many more questions. It was like every time I thought I was going to get some answers, more questions sprang out of the darkness. Until a few months ago, I'd always thought my life was basic and boring. Now it seemed like all I could do was wait for the next mystery. This wasn't fucking fun. I wished I could go back to having a dull life.

Eleven years. I couldn't even comprehend it. Over a decade of letters, and every single letter tucked away safe and sound. It looked like Mom and Dad had planned on giving them to me at one point. When? I'd probably never know. The fact that they'd kept them safe took some of the sting away. If I'd found out they'd thrown them away, I wasn't sure how I'd ever forgive them. The woman who wrote these letters deserved to have them read. So much love and heartache had been put into the thousands and thousands of words she'd written. At least now they could be read. Maybe I'd read them all on the drive back home.

I picked the last letter back up and reread it, going over the same section several times. She told me to practice restraint, that bad people would find me, I was stronger than other females, and that she'd do her best to protect me. What had she meant by that? If she'd been trying to protect me for all the years since this last letter had been written, she'd done a good job staying hidden. What the hell did she mean?

"Maddy!" Nico's voice came echoing down the hallway, and I jumped, surprised that he was gone. I'd never noticed him leave.

"Yeah?" I called back.

Nico hurried down the hall, holding something. It looked like a bunch of slips of paper. He nodded toward the letter in my hand. "What was the signature on that letter?" He looked spooked.

"Uh." I glanced down. "It's not a name really, just initials. M and S."

"Holy shit," he hissed.

"What? You're freaking me out, Nico."

He handed me the stack of papers. Some were yellowed with age and had curled edges. I took them and frowned. "What are these? Where were they?"

Nico ran a hand through his hair. "I was giving you a minute alone. I thought you might want to go through the letters. I came back to your parents' room to do more searching. I found these in a plastic container under their bathroom sink. Look at it. The signature on those."

Glancing down, I saw what he was talking about. The papers were all old prescription receipts. Each one had a photocopy of the original prescription with it. At the bottom of each was a simple scrawled signature. MS. My jaw dropped. I could feel my heart beginning to race.

"Do you have any memory of who your pediatrician was when you were a kid? What did she look like?" Nico asked.

It had been years and years since I'd seen my pediatrician. My memory was fuzzy, but it definitely *had* been a woman. The problem was, even with all the time that had passed, I knew one thing for certain. I shook my head. "I know what you're thinking, but that doctor looked nothing, absolutely nothing, like the pictures in the yearbook."

Nico nodded and rubbed at the stubble on his cheeks. "What if she had plastic surgery to make her unrecognizable? If she was on the run from the royals, then maybe that was one more step she and Kenneth decided on to keep her safe. It makes sense."

I looked at the last letter again. Another sentence jumped out at me. *Watching you grow all these years has been one of the few joys I've had in life.* Watching me grow? The words hit me like a fist. Had my childhood doctor been my birth mother? I'd seen her at least once a year, usually three or four times a year. All those visits and I'd never known.

Nico and I went straight back to work, tearing through the office again. We moved from there to the garage, then the bedroom, grabbing every box or envelope we could find and digging through them. We searched for anything that might have the doctor's full name on it. School absence notes, vaccination records, anything that could give us a hint as to who she was.

Hours later, we'd still found nothing. All that was left was a small shoebox in the closet. I pulled it down, certain we'd run into another dead end. At first glance, it looked like the box was full of my parent's medical records. There were several cholesterol tests for Dad. OB/GYN paperwork for Mom. At the bottom, beneath all that, we hit pay dirt.

Nico swore. There were several records from doctor's visits when I was very little. From the dates on them, I'd been three years old. They were blood tests that showed my red blood cell count matched those typically found in shifters. I ignored all that—I already knew I was a shifter. What I wanted was what was at the bottom. Beside a messy scribble of a signature was the printed name of the person who those pen marks belonged to. Malia Stanford. That was most definitely not the name Gabriella Karson had gone by in high school. Could this woman be the person who gave birth to me?

Nico had his phone out and was already dialing before I'd completely come to grips with what we'd found. I knew he must have been calling Luis, and it didn't take long for him to answer.

"Luis? It's Nico. We found something… Yeah, at Maddy's parents' place… Better than that. I need you to search for a doctor. A pediatrician named Malia Stanford."

Nico spelled the name for Luis and gave him the address of the office out of which she'd practiced. The whole time they talked, I tried to conjure her face from my memories. I'd been so little that it was hard to pull up any specific moments I'd shared with her. I did remember that she'd been really nice. I wasn't sure if it was my own mind shading the memories or not, but I kind of thought I remembered her always having a huge smile on her face when I came in. Maybe she *was* my birth mother, or maybe she'd just been a really nice woman who liked children.

"I'm gonna put you on speaker," Nico said, then set the phone down on the table.

"Hey, Maddy," Luis said.

"Hi." It was all I could manage at the moment.

"I told Nico I'm going to do a quick search. With this being a doctor, they'll be much easier to find than most people. They have to be licensed and carry all kinds of additional liability and malpractice insurance. I should have something in a few minutes."

"Cool," I muttered. Nico moved closer to me and put an arm around my shoulders.

There were several moments of silence. All Nico or I could hear was Luis typing on his laptop. When he finally spoke again, he sounded pleased with himself. "Holy shit. I think I've found an address. It's the one from her employment paperwork. It's an insurance renewal form from about the same time Maddy turned eleven. It shows it as this Malia chick's home address. No way of knowing if it's where she still lives, but it's the best lead we've got so far."

The odds of her still living there almost twenty years later—while hiding from the royals—was pretty slim. Though, like Luis said, it was the best lead we had.

"We'll wait and try to head that way tomorrow. Text me the address," Nico said.

"I'll send it now. Are you guys good, or do you want me to head that way to assist?"

Nico looked at me questioningly, and I shook my head. "We're good," he told Luis. "Thanks for offering."

"Why don't we go now?" I asked when the call ended. To have answers so tantalizingly close and to wait another ten or twelve hours felt like a special kind of torture.

Concern flashed over Nico's face, but he schooled his features before he spoke. "Maddy... I guess we can if you really want to. I sort of thought you'd want to process everything before we go knock on this door."

Disappointment made my shoulders sag, but waiting made the most sense. A night's sleep might bring things into focus. The problem with all of this was that it felt like I was caught in an awful whirlwind, and I wasn't sure when it was going to stop. Maybe it wouldn't, and it would just get faster and faster before I hurtled into the abyss.

Chapter 16 - Nico

When dawn came, I began to wonder if we'd made a mistake in waiting to go to visit the address Luis had given us. I knew I'd barely slept the whole night, and judging by all the tossing and turning Maddy had done, she probably hadn't fared any better. Both of us seemed groggy and acted like zombies as we got up and started getting ready.

Maddy and I went about mundane things like brushing our teeth and trying to eat, though all we managed was a couple of handfuls of granola from the pantry. Maddy moved around the house at a manic pace. I could tell she was on the verge of a freakout. I tried to see things from her perspective but realized pretty quickly that there was no way I could. The situation was one I could never imagine. Anything I said would sound either trite or asinine.

Instead of dealing with it, I packed our bags and put them in the car. After I had it all secured, I went back inside. Maddy was sitting on the couch, bouncing her heels and fidgeting with her fingers, staring off into space.

I waved a hand in front of her eyes. "Are we good?"

Maddy blinked in surprise. "Huh? Yeah. All good."

Sighing, I sat next to her. "Seriously? Because it seems like that isn't exactly true. It's okay to be anxious."

"Shit." Maddy huffed the word out and stood, pacing the room. "It's... I don't know. What if we do find her? What should I say? What should I do?

Do I shake her hand or hug her or what? What if she wants to kiss me on the cheek or something? I have no idea what to do here, Nico."

I put my hands on her shoulders, stopping her pacing. "That's why I'm here. If it gets too much, I can take over and do all the talking. It'll be fine."

Maddy sagged under my hands. "I hope you're right."

We went through the house one more time, making sure all the lights were off. Maddy stopped in the doorway of her parents' room and looked in. She stood there for several seconds, gazing around the room. I let her be, knowing she was taking one last look. I assumed she was soaking it all in. If we were unsuccessful, then this would be the last time she was in that house when her parents were still alive. The next time we were here, it would either be a family get-together or to prepare for a funeral.

The thought was morbid, but I had to be mentally prepared. I had every intention of getting everyone back alive and in one piece, but fate sometimes had a way of fucking over even the best plans. I prayed I wouldn't have to see that happen. I wasn't sure how Maddy would handle it, but I could guarantee it would be heartbreaking to watch.

She turned away from the bedroom and looked at me. "Ready."

I nodded and led her to the front door, locking it behind us as we left. Once we were in the car and pulling away, she gave one last look at the house before settling in for the trip. I put a hand on her thigh. "It shouldn't take long."

Maddy nodded but didn't say anything. The address Luis had given us was for a place about twenty minutes from the house. We drove the entire distance in silence. It was just before ten in the morning when we reached the address. Maddy and I both stared at the place and wondered if Luis had given us the right address.

Most of the houses in the neighborhood were well kept and appeared to be actively lived in. The house we were looking at had the distinctive look of abandonment. The paint on the porch handrails were peeling, and the siding was faded and broken in a couple of places. On the roof, I could see at least four missing shingles, and the yard was overgrown. Weeds had run rampant through the beds, and the gutters were overflowing with old leaves and pine needles.

"Do you think she had to run?" Maddy asked. I couldn't tell if she sounded disappointed or dejected.

"Not sure," I said, shaking my head. "Only one way to be sure, I guess. Let's go."

We parked on the curb and walked up the footpath to the front door. I stopped to open the mailbox. Inside, there were several letters that had gotten wet and then dried into a thick papery clump before the post office finally realized the home wasn't occupied.

"It looks pretty rough compared to everything else around here," Maddy said. "You'd think someone would buy it or that the city would condemn it and have it torn down to build something new."

"It's not totally dilapidated," I said with a shrug. "But if someone doesn't do something soon, that's probably what's going to happen."

We were almost on the porch when Maddy stopped walking and gave a surprised little growl. I turned to look at her, immediately on guard. "What's wrong? What is it?"

Maddy gave me a confused look. "I smell Kenneth. It's one of the first times I've actually been able to recall a scent. It's strange."

"What? That can't be possible. We watched him die."

She shook her head and furrowed her brow. "It's super faint, but it's there. Like he'd been here at some point in the past."

I looked at the house and the footprints we'd left in the dust on the porch steps. The idea of scenting someone who'd been gone for that long was incomprehensible to me. Not even the most sensitive shifters had senses that strong. Even if Kenneth had been here right before going back to Europe, it was still nearly a month ago. Just how powerful was Maddy?

I raised a hand to knock. My knuckles sounded like a gunshot against the bone-dry wood of the door. We waited several seconds before knocking again. There was still no answer, so Maddy reached forward and tried the doorknob. It turned easily, and the door swung open. The inside looked as untouched as the outside. Dust caked every surface and heavy cobwebs hung in the corners. It was clear to see that it had been several years since anyone had been here.

Maddy took my hand as we walked across the threshold. There was a single moment where I winced, anticipating some sort of booby trap. Nightmare images of a hidden gun pointing at us, a trip wire leading to its trigger, filled my mind. Thankfully, she stepped into the living room with no repercussions. I let out a little sigh of relief.

"Are you okay?" Maddy asked.

I nodded and chuckled ruefully. "Yeah. I think I've seen one too many adventure movies."

Maddy smiled at me. "I had the same thought. Poison darts?"

I laughed out loud. "Tripwire and a gun. Your idea was way cooler."

The strain dissipated a bit with our little jokes. It made me less anxious, and I hoped it meant the same for Maddy. The house was strangely untouched. Nothing had been taken, and a few pictures still hung on the wall. Others had fallen, leaving behind faded squares where they'd once hung. The furniture was right where it should have been. It had the look of a place that had been abandoned quickly. Had the royals found this woman? Did she have to run in the middle of the night, leaving everything behind, not even bothering to lock the door behind her? Perhaps.

Maddy sniffed the air and gave a little shake of her head. "I was right. It does smell faintly of Kenneth. There's another smell, one that seems familiar, but I don't know why. I can't really place it. This way," Maddy said, motioning for me to follow her.

She led me up the stairs. We went slowly, still wary of anything that might jump out at us. The house seemed totally dead, though. Once we were at the top of the stairs, we followed the hallway to the end, where we found a small bedroom that seemed to have functioned as an office. Unlike the rest of the house, which looked untouched, this room had been ransacked. Whoever had been in here had been in a hurry. Papers were scattered across the floor, a couple of filing cabinets had been left hanging open, and several files were strewn in a pile beneath the open doors. A container of pens and pencils had been knocked over onto the floor. It was chaos.

The filing cabinet looked like the best place to look for clues, so I went straight for it. Maddy moved around the room slowly as I pulled file after file out and skimmed through them. They were coated in dust, but everything was still legible. There was no way for me to know what I was looking for, but that didn't stop me from looking through everything. After the first few, it was obvious they were old medical files of patients Maddy's birth mother must have had. Every chart had her alias signature at the bottom. Malia Stanford, MD.

I wondered if she'd *actually* gone to med school. Had Kenneth gotten her a new identity, plastic surgery, and all the false records needed to enroll? Or had he faked everything? Had this woman been practicing medicine for decades with a fake medical degree and license? I didn't want to think about that part.

Patterns started to jump out of the file. Every single file was for a shifter patient. All these people were shifters. They also all had birthdays that were within a month of Maddy's. Slowing my search, I tried to figure out precisely what she was looking for. Maddy was quiet. I should have checked to see if she'd found anything, but I was too consumed with my own search. Then I saw it. On the third page of every file, there was a DNA report. A single line had been highlighted on all of them: a genetic marker search. For some reason, Maddy's birth mother had been trying to match the markers to something—but to what?

I dug back into the filing cabinet and saw a file that made my breath catch in my throat. Madison Sutton. Maddy's name was tagged on the chart. I yanked it out and opened the file to the third page. Every other report had been circled in yellow highlighter. Maddy's was circled in bright red ink. Whoever had circled it had been so excited by what they'd seen that they'd put four or five circles around the results and put three check marks beside them. Whatever marker this woman had been searching for, it looked like Maddy was a match.

I turned to show Maddy what I'd found, only to find her standing motionless at the other side of the room, staring into a closet. I took a few tentative steps toward her, and before I could ask what was wrong, I saw what she was looking at. There was an entire wall of the closet that was devoted to her. There were literally dozens of pictures of Maddy. The oldest looked like they'd been taken when she was a toddler. Maddy's skin had a more olive complexion back then. She looked a lot more like her biological father in those photos. A photo of Maddy at around seven years old was pinned up next to a yearbook picture of David Samuels. The resemblance was uncanny.

The pictures showed her growing up. Many appeared to have been taken with a telephoto lens from a good distance. Maddy stepped into the closet, and I was able to see more. The entire room was some sort of memorial to her. Maddy didn't make a sound as she looked at all the pictures. The newest photos were of her at her graduation ceremony. Her birth mother had been there? Or had someone been there on her behalf? Kenneth? I had no doubt that if Gabriella had asked him, he'd have done this for her. Maybe he'd taken most of these photos for her. The entire thing was a strange combination of creepy, sweet, and sad. So many years this woman had spent wanting nothing more than to be with the daughter she'd given up. It hurt my heart to see it. I knew it had to be having the same effect on Maddy. The same effect but magnified a thousand times.

Chapter 17 - Maddy

When I'd opened the closet door, I'd expected to find piles of boxes, maybe some moldy clothes still hanging on hooks. I'd not been prepared for what I found. The pictures were almost too much to take in. I was so flooded with emotions that I couldn't pinpoint exactly what I was feeling. My entire life was plastered on the walls of the closet.

There were pictures of me running track, a newspaper clipping of me coming in second at a countywide science fair in sixth grade, along with the most random picture. It was Abi and me. We were dressed for prom, and we were standing in front of the massive old oak tree that stood in front of the high school. The picture was taken from a different angle, and from farther away, Mom and Dad's backs could be seen as they took the photos I remembered from that night.

I'd decided to try softball one season when I was twelve, and there was a picture of me swinging and missing a pitch. Beside it was a handwritten note.

You did such a good job at this game!

One of my pageant pictures was on the far side of the wall with another note pinned up next to it.

Maddy, you are so beautiful. I'm so proud of you. I wish I could tell you in person.

It went on and on like that. Photos and notes, notes and photos. This wasn't Kenneth's doing. It was too personal, and the notes had a feminine quality to them. He'd been here, though. His scent was all over the place. It was stronger in this room than anywhere else in the house.

"Hey," Nico said softly. I turned to him and saw he was holding a file in his hands. "I found something."

I took it from him with numb fingers and glanced at it. In my current state, all I could see were random words and numbers. Nothing made sense to me. I shook my head to try and clear it. "What am I looking at?"

Nico pointed out a line on one of the pages. "I found a ton of other files like this. It looks like she was running DNA tests looking for this specific marker." He pointed at a line someone had circled repeatedly with red ink.

"Is this her way of trying to trace the Edemas line or something?" I asked.

"That's all that makes sense. It *has* to have something to do with that. Why else would she be doing this? All these other files were tested for the exact same marker, and the kids are all pretty much the same age as you. That's weird."

"Show me." I wanted to see what he was talking about.

Nico showed me the filing cabinets, and I flipped through the files to see for myself. He was right. Almost every kid here had a birthday within a month of mine. It was like she was trying to match these other kids to me. Or see if they had the same marker I did? I scanned through every file, desperate to figure out what exactly she was looking for. I wasn't a geneticist, and neither was Nico. Without more information, there was no way we'd figure out what this marker was or what it meant.

Between the files and the closet, it was obvious Doctor Stanford had been keeping tabs on me my whole life. It was enough to take away almost all the doubt I had about her being my birth mother. Why would a random pediatrician do all this? Why would a pediatrician have pictures of me in her closet? Sure, there were unhinged people who created relationships in their heads. Stalkers. But this didn't feel like that. This wasn't sinister. Most stalkers tried to make contact with their target. She'd gone out of her way to keep things as distant as possible, only seeing me a few times a year at her office.

It should have given me some relief knowing, for sure, that she was my biological mother, but it didn't. Instead, it made me wonder.

"Where do you think she is?" I asked Nico.

"No idea. It's weird that she'd keep track of you for so long and then vanish off the face of the earth. What was the oldest picture in there?"

"Looked like there were a couple of pictures of my college graduation. Nothing later than that."

"So she pulled up stakes and vanished six years ago?"

I shook my head. "I guess." I didn't know how to feel about any of this. I felt drained. "What do we do now? This was our biggest lead."

"If she's half as careful as I think she was, I doubt we'll be able to find anything about her whereabouts. It looks like she's spent decades maintaining a very careful façade. As far as we know, the royals *still* don't know she's alive."

"I don't know about that," I said, gesturing around the room. "It looks like she left in a hurry. She didn't take any pictures or personal items. She ran, and she ran fast. I bet all she had time to do was get rid of anything that might lead them to her. Maybe they didn't know it was actually her—maybe they only thought this was one of Kenneth's safe houses. Either way, she got out of here in a hurry."

"True," Nico conceded.

I glanced back at the closet of pictures. I'm sure she had to run for her own safety, but she'd left behind all those pictures. The only things she had of her only child. It stung a little bit even though I knew she had to have cared. I'd read the letters she'd sent. No matter what I told myself, I was still feeling rejected and abandoned, as silly as that seemed.

Nico and I searched the rest of the closet and found nothing. It was disheartening. This had all felt like some sort of treasure hunt. We'd found and followed clues, traveled so far. Not having some sort of closure was almost unbearable. What had it all been for if this was a dead end?

We were putting everything back and doing as good a job as we could to clean up the little office. I nudged Nico. "Do you think it really did help?"

Nico stopped what he was doing. "What do you mean?"

"The very last letter she wrote to me alluded to the fact that she'd done her best to protect me. I think she's talking about the suppressants. Do you really think they helped? I mean, the royals found me anyway. I almost feel like it would have been better without them. At least then, my wolf could have come out. I'd be able to defend myself if I was a full shifter."

Nico put his arm around me. "I think she did what she thought was best. Keeping your lineage secret probably saved your life. Remember what Javi said? They found those three little kids in South America. If you'd been a shifter, the odds of them finding you were probably way higher."

He was probably right. The entire thing was crazy. My life over the last few months had gone from wholly mundane and blissfully quiet to a never-ending, drama-filled chaotic mess.

"Do you want to look around the rest of the house?" Nico asked.

I shrugged. "We can walk through it. I doubt we'll find anything, though."

We went through the two bedrooms and the bathroom upstairs, then glanced around the kitchen, giving the drawers a cursory open as we went. Nico made the inexplicably bad decision of opening the refrigerator. I'd thought my parents' place had been awful, but this was a million times worse. The inside was almost black with mold. Every item had spoiled, rotted, liquified, then dried into a black-and-gray paste that covered almost the entire interior.

Nico slammed the door. "Holy shit. That was awful."

Seeing the disgusted look on Nico's face sent me into giggles, then into a full belly laugh. Tears streamed down my face as I tried to catch my breath.

Nico nodded appreciatively. "Yeah, I know. Dumb move. You can stop laughing."

I only laughed harder. I doubled over, clutching my knees—until we heard the front door slam shut. My heart nearly leaped into my throat, and Nico was by my side in an instant, snarling. I caught a whiff of something in the air. The same familiar scent

I'd noticed when we'd walked in, only now it was stronger. Nico took me by the arm and led me toward the living room. As we rounded the corner of the hallway and came into the den, everything seemed undisturbed. No one was waiting to jump us, but one thing had changed, and both of us were staring at it. On the wall beside the coat closet, a picture had been taken off the wall. Where it had been, there was a wall safe sitting with the door wide open.

Someone had snuck in while we were in here and opened the safe? The thought made my skin crawl, knowing a stranger had been right here in the house and neither of us had noticed. The scent must have mixed with the faint smell of the home. I couldn't help but glance around the house, furtive and afraid. Were they still here?

Nico and I walked over and glanced into the safe. All that was inside was a thick eight-inch by twelve-inch sealed envelope with a piece of paper sitting on top of it. My fingers trembled as I reached inside. This was important. I could feel it in my bones. Every bit of laughter was now a distant memory. The safe was so well hidden that the odds of me finding it accidentally were astronomical. I felt Nico's presence beside me, but I couldn't look at him. My eyes were locked on the letter.

Maddy,

I know you have so many questions. All I can say is I'm sorry I can't answer them in person. I know that your wolf has awoken and that the royals have found you. I'm sorry that this is something you'll have to go through, but I know you're strong enough. My girl can handle anything. I know it.

You need to understand the truth about your lineage and your history. It's a lot, and I'm sorry, it won't be easy learning what it is that's sharing your body with you. It's all in the envelope. Read it, understand it, and be careful.

I love you.

My entire body was shaking by the time I was done reading the letter. Somehow, I managed to reach into the safe and pull the envelope out. It felt much heavier than it should have. The seam was almost calling out to me, demanding to be torn open. As much as I wanted to, another, stronger part of me was too afraid. All I'd wanted was answers, and now that they were here, in my hand, I was terrified to know.

"We should get out of here, Maddy. It doesn't feel safe anymore."

All I did was nod at him and tuck the envelope under my arm. Nico put his arm around me, leading me out. He was on edge, glancing all around, ready for anything. We hustled to the car as quickly as we could. Nico got me into the passenger seat and then walked quickly to his side of the car and got in. Before he could start it, a shadow moved toward the back of the house.

"What is that?" I asked, pointing through the windshield.

Nico leaned forward, squinting. "It looks like a person. They're running through the woods. I bet that's who was in the house with us."

He grabbed his door handle, probably to jump out and go after them, but he froze. I saw it at the same time he did. Black smoke was billowing from the back of the house. Within seconds, flames were licking up toward the shingles of the roof.

"Shit," Nico hissed. "They lit it up. We gotta go. If we're here when the cops and fire trucks arrive, they'll have a shit ton of questions we can't answer. Buckle up."

I did as he asked, and within seconds, we were racing down the road back toward the highway. I glanced back one more time before we turned. The roof was already fully engulfed. It was burning fast. There was a momentary pang of sadness. That had been the place my birth mother had called home. In a few minutes, it would be nothing but ashes. A question nagged at the back of my mind. Had she set the fire? The shadow disappearing into the forest—could that have been her?

Chapter 18 - Nico

It didn't take long before the house fire hit the news. We heard it on a radio traffic report as we drove back home. The drive was mostly in silence as we both tried to process what we'd seen and discovered at the house. I had to admit, I was fairly freaked out by the whole experience. The house had been creepy, and having the shadowy stranger appear and fuck with us at the end was enough to send goosebumps rising all over my skin.

I glanced over at Maddy. She was looking through the windshield, a look of worried concentration on her face. The envelope from the safe was lying flat on her thighs—her fingers curled tightly around it. She hadn't even attempted to open it. My own curiosity was screaming to know what was in there, but I knew Maddy was going through a lot, and she didn't need me pressuring her to open it. She would need to do it in her own time.

"Are you hungry?" I asked.

Maddy blinked and turned to me. "Not really, but we can stop if you are."

"No, it's fine. I do need gas, though, so I may grab a snack at the gas station."

"Okay."

I reached over and squeezed her thigh reassuringly, then took her hand in mine. Maddy sighed and relaxed a little bit. I needed to make sure she knew I was there for her. With everything she was going through, it was the least I could do. Honestly, it was pretty much the *only* thing I could do. If I'd gone through as much as she had and discovered so many earth-shattering revelations, I probably wouldn't have held up nearly as well as she was. Still, at some point, we would have to open the envelope.

By the time we finally got home, Maddy looked ready to pass out. It was still early afternoon, but I could tell by looking at her that she desperately needed a nap.

"Let's get you inside and into bed. You can sleep for a couple of hours."

Maddy opened her car door and nodded. "That sounds great."

I led her up to the bedroom and helped her get her shoes and pants off before tucking her in. I kissed her forehead once and then her lips. "Rest up. I love you."

"Love you too." As Maddy said it, her eyes flicked to the nightstand where the envelope sat.

I didn't say anything about it. Instead, I turned the light off and closed her door. As I headed back downstairs, I pulled out my phone and texted Luis, Sebastian, and Dad. I wanted them to all come over so I could tell them exactly what had gone down when we were in Naples. It was important for me to keep my inner circle in the loop. The whole situation was becoming overwhelming. There was no way to know if any of them would have any major insight, but if nothing else, it would feel good to share the burden of knowledge with them. I wished Felipe could be there, but he was still in Alabama. Hopefully, his trip wouldn't be for naught.

I headed outside and got our bags out of the car, and Dad was already walking up the street toward my house. It hadn't taken him long to get my text.

"Well, you look like a wrung-out dish towel, boy," Dad said as he stepped up and leaned on my car.

I laughed ruefully. "Good to know I look exactly like I feel."

"Bad?"

Right to the point—my father was good at cutting through the shit. I gave him a one-shouldered shrug. "We learned a lot, but now we have more questions. It seems like the way it always goes."

"Is Maddy okay?" Dad asked, glancing up at the house.

"She's taking a nap. It was an intense trip. She needs time to decompress. I'll tell you everything once the guys get here."

"Let me help with that." Dad grabbed the other suitcase and followed me inside.

Ten minutes later, we were sitting around the coffee table in my living room. My phone was on the table, and Luis was on speaker. He was still doing research in Tampa. Having them all there as backup made me feel better.

"Okay, give us the dirt," Sebastian said.

"Yeah, the build-up is killing me," Luis said, his voice electronically hollow coming from the phone. "What did you find at that house?"

"Maddy's parents' house?" Dad asked.

"No, the other one," Luis said. "The address I found for you."

"Hang on," I said. "We'll get to that. The trip was definitely worth it. We found a lot."

Dad sat forward. "Maddy's birth mother?"

I nodded. "We went to her adoptive parents' house first. The living room had been ransacked when her parents were taken. It was not a good scene—that's all I'll say about that.

"Maddy and I searched the place top to bottom and found some letters her birth mother had sent her. These letters went all the way up until she was eleven years old."

"So the whole 'your mother died right after she gave you up' was another fucking lie Kenneth told us?" Luis asked.

"Basically, yeah. Pretty sure he helped her disappear, and even at the end, he held that information close. He may not have been loyal to us, but he was goddamned loyal to Gabriella. Took her secret to the grave. Anyway, in the very last letter, she signed her initials. M and S. I found a bunch of old prescription scripts for the suppressant pills Maddy's adoptive parents had given her. Same exact initials."

"Hang on." Sebastian sat forward, looking beyond confused. "The doctor's initials, you mean?"

I nodded at him grimly. "Yup."

"Maybe I'm not following," Sebastian said, glancing between the two of us. "Did this doctor and the mother have the same initials?"

"They are one and the same. Right?" Dad asked.

"Exactly," I said. "Apparently, Kenneth helped Maddy's birth mother get a whole new identity: plastic surgery, new name, school records—the whole nine yards. She was Maddy's pediatrician from the time she was three or four years old, maybe earlier."

"What the fuck?" Sebastian flopped back onto the couch with both hands on his head. "She was right there the whole time?"

"Right," I went on. "So, she spent years watching her during check-ups and stuff and provided her parents with the drugs to keep her wolf suppressed. Once we had that, it was easy to find her alias. Malia Stanford, MD. Luis did a search and got us her address. We went straight there the next day—the place hasn't been lived in for years. Looked like she'd run last minute. There was a whole shrine to Maddy. Pictures that either she or Kenneth had taken through her whole life. Kindergarten, preschool, college, and everything in between."

"Creepy," Sebastian said.

"Not creepy," Dad said, giving Sebastian a withering look. "The woman gave away a baby she desperately wanted to keep. It had to be heartbreaking to give away your child to keep her safe. I couldn't imagine living my whole life without my boys. The heartache? The sadness? A few pictures here and there were probably all that kept her from a depression so deep it could have led to madness or even suicide. Never underappreciate the power of the love of a mother for her child."

"Sorry," Sebastian murmured, his cheeks going red.

"The house?" Luis said, nudging the conversation back to my story.

"Yeah, we went inside to find the pictures and a filing cabinet. It was full of children's medical charts. Maddy's birth mother had been testing all kinds of kids. DNA tests. From what we saw, she was trying to cross-reference a single genetic marker in Maddy's DNA with dozens of other kids. No idea why that marker is significant though. It has to have something to do with Edemas's bloodline. Nothing else in the house, but then someone snuck in while we were there, moved a painting off the wall, and opened a hidden wall safe."

"While you were inside the house?" Luis asked, amazed by the audacity.

"Yeah. When they left, they slammed the door. They *wanted* us to know they'd been there. This person wanted us to find the safe. There was a thick envelope and a letter written by Maddy's birth mother. We took it and got the hell out of there.

"Once we were in the car, we saw whoever it was running through the woods away from the house. I was going to go after them, but they'd set the fucking house on fire. We had to leave before God and everybody showed up asking us why we were there. Then we came back home."

"Well? What's in the damned envelope?" Sebastian asked once my story was over.

"No idea."

"What?" Luis asked, incredulous.

"We haven't opened it yet. It's not my property. It was left for Maddy. She needs to be the one to open it. We have to be patient. She's been through so much, and I don't want to force her into something else until she's had time to process what's already happened. Whatever is in that envelope might be another world-shaking revelation."

"Exactly," Sebastian said. "It might be important. She's only got like ten or twelve days until the next full moon. Shouldn't we... I don't know... not demand her to, but give her a little nudge toward opening it?"

I held my hand up to calm them all down. "I'm not an idiot. If it takes more than a day or two, I'll say something. Trust me."

"This person who burned the house down?" Dad asked. "Did you get a look at them?"

"Not very good. They were already pretty deep into the woods when Maddy spotted them," I said.

"I can try to see if there are any street cameras nearby. Maybe I could attempt to hack into their feed and get a better look," Luis said.

"I don't think that's necessary," I said. "I've got a pretty good hunch that it was her birth mother. Only she and Kenneth would have known about that safe, and Kenneth is dead. It had to be her. She's still keeping herself hidden for some reason."

My phone rang, and the screen said that it was Felipe. I stood, snatching the phone off the table. "Luis, I'll call you back. Felipe is calling. Maybe he has news."

"Okay, let me know," Luis said and disconnected.

"Felipe? It's Nico."

"Hey, man. How's it going?"

"Weird, which is pretty normal at this point. What do you have for me?" I asked, pacing back and forth across the room. Dad and Sebastian watched me as I did.

"Well, I got my guy Randal here. He's the alpha of these reptile shifters I was telling you about."

"Will they help us?" My voice was almost breathless. We needed help, and if these guys wouldn't throw down with us, I didn't know where we'd turn next.

"He wants to talk to you before he agrees to anything. I said you were one hell of a conversationalist."

"Okay, put him on."

There were some rustling sounds as the phone was passed between the two men, then a deep voice spoke through the phone. "This is Randal. Are you Nico?"

"Yes, sir. You got me."

"My friend Felipe here gave me the rundown. I'll tell you what, this doesn't sound like something I want to get my people into."

It felt like I'd been punched in the chest, but I kept my composure. "I know it's pretty dangerous."

"Dangerous? Boy, you're talking about the royals. A bunch of crazy-ass humans who think they're in control of what shifters can and can't do. The only good thing about them is that they usually only give a shit about wolf shifters. I'm not really trying to get them to look our way. We live a nice, quiet, peaceful life. I'd like to keep it that way."

I could feel the desperation building inside me. "Listen, Randal. This is the mother and father of my fated mate. This is her best friend. It's the only family she has, and I can't fail. I have to get them back. There's no way you could understand how bad this is. They've been tortured. I am the only one who can get them back, and I have to have help. I'll do anything for you. *Anything*. Money is no object. Give me a price, and I'll pay it. Gladly."

There was a long moment of silence on the other end of the line before Randal spoke again. "I don't want any money. You know, son? You sound like me in my younger days. I have a mate of my own and children. I would go to the ends of the earth for them. I can hear in your voice that you love her like I love mine.

"If I was in the same spot and asked for help, I'd sure as hell hope I'd get it. I know how hard it is to ask. An alpha is supposed to be the end-all-be-all of the pack. It isn't easy admitting that you need assistance. Here's my deal. I'll send my sons down to you. They're the best operational guys I have. They can get in and out of anywhere undetected. That's all I can do."

I let out a heavy sigh of relief. "Thank you, Randal. Thank you. I know you said you didn't want any payment, but I'll tell you right now, the Lorenzo Wolf pack now owes you an incredibly big debt. You give me a call the moment you ever need it."

"I do appreciate that. Don't worry. If it ever comes to that, you'll be my first call, Mr. Nico. Take care of my boys."

"I will, sir. Thank you again."

They swapped the phone again, and Felipe was back. "That went better than expected."

"Yeah, how soon can you guys get back?"

"Late tomorrow maybe. We'll leave here once they are ready."

"All right. I'll see you when you get here."

I turned around after hanging up and looked at Sebastian and Dad, pumping my fist in victory. Dad gave me a relieved nod while Sebastian grinned and relaxed his posture.

I texted Luis to say that the reptile shifters were on the way and to get his ass home. I didn't see any reason for him to keep looking for Maddy's birth mom. I needed to consolidate my forces, and having him gone didn't help. Besides, it looked like that woman was even better at hiding than Kenneth had been. I wasn't sure even Luis would have been successful.

Sebastian left not long afterward, but Dad lingered. I could tell he wanted to ask me something. I poured myself a scotch and Coke to help my nerves and gestured toward the bottles. "You want one?"

Dad shook his head. "Your mother would kill me; it's not even five in the afternoon. How's Maddy's state of mind? This is a lot to take in. How do you think she's holding up?"

I took a sip of my drink, letting the burn linger in my throat before answering. "I really don't know.

She's stressed out, for sure. I'm a little worried. It's like every single day something else gets piled onto her. I know she's worried about her family, plus she's found out her whole life was a lie. Then there're mundane things like her business being shut down. I'm afraid she's getting close to a breaking point."

"I think you're right."

"What do I do, Dad? I don't think a *vacation* is the right thing, not with so much going on right now. She's got too much going on to enjoy a weekend away."

"I'll be honest. The best thing you can do for her is to be present. Make sure she knows you're here for her while she works through all of this."

I nodded. "I'm trying my best, Dad. I really am. The problem is, I don't know if my best will be good enough."

After Dad left, I let Maddy sleep. I was sure she needed it, so I made dinner. I wanted something special for her when she got up. Maybe a bunch of her favorite things would help get her mind off everything for a few minutes.

Thirty minutes later, Maddy came down, and I saw her give me the first real smile I'd seen on her face since her laughing fit when I'd opened the fridge at Gabriella's place. She walked up to the table and saw everything I'd made.

"You made me spaghetti and meatballs? That's my favorite!"

I bobbed my head back and forth. "Well, when we were at your parent's house, I may have stumbled across your mom's recipe book and taken a picture of this one. She'd written *Maddy's fave* in the margins. So, I'd love to say I was good at guessing, but that would be a lie."

"Wait. This is my mom's actual recipe?"

"Yup."

"Oh my gosh. Get me a fork. Now."

I laughed. "Yes, ma'am."

Over dinner, Maddy opened up to me about how she was feeling. It was exactly what I'd thought. She was fully overwhelmed by everything.

"I feel like my entire life is balanced on a razor's edge. Nothing seems to relieve the stress. Even when I go to sleep, there's a pretty good chance I'll have some crazy dream or hellish nightmare, so there isn't even any respite there. That envelope sitting there in my room isn't helping. We'll have to open it, but I just mentally can't. Not today. God only knows what's inside that thing. Who knows, maybe it'll make things even worse."

"Whatever you decide, I've got your back," I said, putting a hand over hers.

Maddy put her fork down and gave me an appreciative smile. "Thank you."

She leaned over and kissed me. Her lips lingered on mine a moment longer than necessary. Hunger exploded inside me, and I slipped my tongue into her mouth, flicking across hers. Maddy moaned and deepened the kiss. Things became more passionate. One of my hands found her thigh and slid up until it was on her waist, then I was lifting her into my arms. We stood, dinner forgotten, and moved toward the stairs.

Our kiss finally broke as we started climbing the steps. I held her hand and led her to the bedroom. All I wanted to do was take her mind off everything. If I could take away her stress and worry for even ten minutes, I would.

I pulled her close, staring into her eyes as I began to undo her pants, letting them slide to her pants. I tugged her T-shirt over her head and slid my hands across the bare skin of her shoulders down her collarbones, then I slipped my fingertips onto the smooth flesh of her breasts. Her breath caught as I circled her nipples. Maddy bit her lower lip and unzipped my pants, sliding her hand inside and tugging my cock out. I let out a sigh as she stroked my shaft, her cool fingers as soft as velvet.

I pushed her onto the bed, and she bounced on the mattress. Maddy giggled as she pushed herself up to give me room. I tugged my pants and socks off, then threw my shirt across the room. I climbed onto the bed with her and rolled her onto her stomach. I began to massage the knots out of her shoulders, and Maddy gave a surprised and happy little groan. I prodded at the muscles and worked my way down to her lower back, digging into the tense muscles as I went. When I reached her ass, I rubbed at the muscles there, making her moan in pleasure. My cock was throbbing. I couldn't keep this up for much longer.

I spread her legs apart as gently as I could. Her breathing became heavier as my fingers slowly moved closer to her pussy. I massaged her inner thighs, moving higher and higher. My thumbs slipped across her lips, and she sucked in a breath as I slowly circled her clit, making her hips move against my hand.

Maddy pressed her face into the pillow and groaned as I slipped a finger inside her. My free hand continued rubbing her clit while my finger moved in and out of her.

"You're so wet. Do you want me to fuck you?" I asked, my voice barely above a whisper.

"Uh-huh. Fuck me, Nico. God, I want you in me."

Without another word, I raised myself onto my knees and put my hands under her hips, lifting her ass toward me. I lowered my face and slid my tongue across her pussy, then moved forward, sliding my cock into her, all the way to my balls. Her pussy was so warm and wet that I moaned and held her there for a moment, enjoying the feel of her.

"Holy shit," Maddy said in a breathy whisper. She slid her hand down and started rubbing her clit.

I pulled almost all the way out, then slid back in, slower this time, taking my time. My hands were on her hips, and I could feel her shaking ever so slightly, overcome by pleasure.

"Jesus, Nico. You've got to fuck me. Please."

I leaned down close to her ear, my cock completely inside her. "How do you want it? Slow? Hard?"

"Hard," she growled.

I gripped her hips and grinned. My thrusts came fast and rough, but not too rough. The sound of our breathing filled the room. I was gasping as I got closer to climaxing. Maddy was clutching the sheets in her hand and grunting in pleasure with each thrust of my dick, her free hand rubbing furiously between her legs.

"I'm gonna come. God, oh god..." Maddy started to shudder beneath me.

She stiffened beneath me and cried out as I continued to slam into her. Her pussy clenched tight around me, and I felt myself go over the edge, the explosion of sweet ecstasy erupting from within me. My body went warm, and I could feel tingles through my balls as I finished, grinding myself against her. We collapsed onto the bed. I wrapped an arm around her and gently cupped her breast. Maddy reached back behind her and ran a hand through my hair.

"I needed that," she said. I could hear the smile in her voice.

"Glad I could be of assistance."

Chapter 19 - Maddy

I stood in the shower, letting the warm water cascade down my body. I did not want to get out. There was something comforting about being there. The glass door was closed, steam filling the room, the steady static-like sound of the splashing water at my feet. It almost helped me zone out and forget about the envelope still sitting on my bedside table. Almost, but not quite.

Nico and I had been back for several days, and I still hadn't opened it. It wasn't just that I hadn't opened it—I hadn't touched it. Like it was radioactive or venomous. Every time I walked into the bedroom, I actively tried to avoid glancing in its direction. I was being stupid, and I knew it. That envelope most likely held all the answers I'd been so desperate for. Now that it was right there, literally at my fingertips, I couldn't bring myself to open it.

Dunking my head under the spray, I let the water drum onto my head, blocking out the sound of my own thoughts. It would have to be soon. I felt the pull of the moon more and more every day. Maybe today?

Setting my jaw, I cranked the knobs and turned the water off. Once I was dried off and had my robe on, I headed out to the bedroom and stood in front of the nightstand, staring down at the envelope. My determination faded as the brownish-yellow color of the package sapped all my resolve. Fear overrode any curiosity I might have had a moment before. Sighing, I turned away to get dressed. Maybe *not* today?

Once I was dressed, I glanced out the window and saw Nico leading a group down to the field to train. The pack had become much better at working as a cohesive unit since Nico started getting everyone to spend several hours each week working on fighting. Instead of simply relying on their natural strength and speed, they were able to work together seamlessly. I decided to go down with them and watch again. It would give me something to do to get my mind off that damned envelope.

Dressed and with a piece of toast in my belly, I headed down to where I could hear the training. The first thing I heard, though, made me frown in worry. Nico's voice was loud and broke through the din of the practice. He sounded irritated. By the time I got close enough to make out his words, I knew something was off.

"Mateo? What the fuck are you doing? You cut off Greg, for Christ's sake. If you did that during battle, you'd both trip over each other's feet. Jesus, this shouldn't be this difficult."

Mateo lowered his head and looked abashed, kicking at the grass in frustration. The group started again, going through some maneuver where half of them remained in human form, and the other half shifted, and the two parties worked together. Another group seemed to be pretending to be enemy soldiers.

"Stop! Stop, goddamn it!" Nico shouted as he picked up a rock and threw it in frustration. "Gabriel, can you please think about what you're doing for one second? You were supposed to be in the group that stayed in human form. Why the hell did you shift?"

For the second time in ten minutes, Nico had chewed out one of his brothers. This wasn't like him. He was usually very patient with the guys, especially his brothers. He was stalking around the field, looking like he wanted to break something. As I glanced around, I saw his behavior had everyone on edge. What the hell was up with him?

During the next forty-five minutes, I watched him snap at two other men for simple mistakes. Finally, Nico called for a break, and everyone moved on to grab some water, a snack, or go to the bathroom. Nico didn't look happy. I needed to talk to him and figure out what the hell was going on.

"Nico?"

At the sound of his name, he turned toward me and walked toward me. "Hey, what's up?"

"That's what I was going to ask you. What the hell is the matter with you?"

He frowned at me, looking surprised. "What are you talking about?"

I gestured toward the field. "All that. That's what I'm talking about."

Nico glanced around and seemed confused. "What?"

Sighing, I pointed toward his brothers, who stood in a clump, pulling bottled water out of a cooler. "You chewed Mateo's and Gabriel's asses out for some pretty simple mistakes. Then you made that kid over there feel like shit for just stepping wrong. Everyone out here is walking on eggshells around you today because you're snapping at them left and right. What's going on?"

As I spoke, I could see Nico's face go from a defensive scowl to an embarrassed frown. He sighed. "I'm sorry. It's the stress. It's almost too much to handle. I didn't even realize I was being like that."

"Do you want to talk about it?"

Nico shrugged. "It's a big day. Luis is supposed to call this afternoon."

Once Felipe had returned with the brothers from the reptile shifter clan, Luis had gone to work setting up the plans to infiltrate the safe houses. Today was the day they'd planned on attempting reconnaissance of one of the houses. I knew it was important, as well as dangerous, but that didn't make it any easier to see Nico like this.

"I really just want Luis to call and let me know if things went well," Nico said.

Luis and the brothers were going to fly into a nearby city and drive the rest of the way. It would have been quicker and more efficient to fly directly into the city they were being held in, but the royals were smart. They'd likely be watching incoming flights. Plus, with the kind of money and influence they had, they could just pass along a few bribes to get the passenger manifest to any flight they wanted. They'd know Nico or his friends were on the way before they ever landed. Luis was doing this the safe way. It simply made things take a lot longer.

Thankfully, both safe houses the royals had used were in the United States. The final meet at the end of the month would also be in the States. At least that's what we all thought. I knew it didn't really matter where that final meeting took place—it wouldn't end well.

"I think you need a break," I said. "Let one of your brothers or Felipe run the training session the rest of the day. What do you say?"

Nico looked pained and glanced back at the field. I knew he wanted to stay.

"Listen, you were pretty hard on everyone today. It might be best if they take a little break from you."

Nico sighed sadly and gave me a single nod. "Yeah. Probably for the best. Maybe I can do better tomorrow. Hopefully, I'll be in a better mood."

"I think that's a good idea," I said, relieved that he agreed with me.

"Felipe?" Nico called as we walked toward his friend.

"Yeah?" Felipe was in the middle of eating a granola bar.

"I need to blow off some steam. Can you take over for me?"

Felipe raised his eyebrows and glanced around to make sure he couldn't be heard. "So, Maddy told you to stop being a dickhead?"

"Shit," Nico hissed. "Basically, yeah. Can you make sure we run the op I was talking about? Out in the woods with limited visibility?"

Felipe waved him on. "Got it, got it. Go relax."

Nico took my hand, and I led him up to the house. I could tell he felt bad about how the day had gone. By the time we got to the back porch, he was in a pretty pathetic mood.

"I hate that I was so hard on everyone. I'm the alpha, but the Lorenzos have always led by being calm, kind, and levelheaded. Like my dad and my grandpa before him."

I stopped walking and put a hand on his chest. "Hey, it's okay. Everyone has a bad day. Even an alpha. I bet if you asked your dad, he could tell you some stories about times he was a really annoying asshole."

Nico laughed at that. Seeing his smile was better than the depressed frown he'd been wearing. It gave me a happy little flutter in my stomach, knowing I'd been the one to lighten his mood. I wanted to kiss him. The moment for that disappeared as his phone chirped in his pocket. He yanked it out, and his eyes went wide.

He glanced up at me. "It's Luis."

"Answer it," I said in a hushed whisper, as though I might ruin the mission if I spoke too loud even though they were hundreds of miles away.

We stepped inside the house as Nico answered the phone on speaker. "Luis? It's me. Maddy's with me."

"Hey. All right, we landed about two hours ago. We're going to get settled for a day or two, maybe do some exterior recon first. These guys can shift into pretty small lizards, so the plan is for them to infiltrate and do as much recon as they can. I'll be nearby. Hopefully, we can figure out whether it's Maddy's parents or Abi being held here. They say they'll do their best to get us what we need. Once I feel confident that we're safe to go in, I'll let you know it's time. At that point, we can go over what they saw."

There were lots of different kinds of shifters. It was one of those things you *knew* but never really paid attention to, like all the different languages in the world—you understood they were out there, but it wasn't something most humans really focused on. I'd never heard of reptile shifters until this, and I was completely fascinated. It made me wonder what other types of shifters there were out there. Sharks? Bats? I made a mental note to ask Nico about that someday.

"Sounds good," Nico said. "I want updates. Stay safe out there. I owe their father a massive favor, and I want to make sure his boys come home safely. Remember, they didn't *have* to help us."

"I know," Luis said. "I'll get back to you as soon as I can."

"Good luck," Nico said.

"Yeah, good luck," I added.

Nico was still tense. Hearing from Luis hadn't relieved the tension like I'd hoped it would. He stuffed his phone back in his pocket and walked to the kitchen, where he yanked open the fridge door and pulled out a bottle of water. Nico uncapped it and chugged it down in a few gulps.

He shook his head as he wiped his mouth. "I don't know how I'm going to relax until I know those guys are safe and we have the intel on the safe houses." He looked at me with almost manic desperation in his eyes. "I have to find out, for sure, where your family and Abi are being held. Once we know, we can come up with a plan to save them. Maybe then I'll be able to take a breath." He shook his head and looked forlorn. "I'm scared, Maddy."

That admission surprised me. Nico had been my rock throughout this entire ordeal. It had never occurred to me that he was afraid. He'd been steady and constant, always ready to act or come up with a plan.

"Nico, what are you afraid of?"

"I don't want to fail you. I *can't* fail you. If…" He trailed off and took a steadying breath before continuing. "If something happens to them, I don't know how I can ever look you in the eye again. I have to get them out. Otherwise, I don't know what we're going to do."

I couldn't let him keep taking all the pressure. We were in this together, and there was one last thing we could do to get them back. It was something only I could do—the one weapon I had in my arsenal that was the exact thing they wanted.

I put a hand on his cheek and gave him a sad smile. "Nico, if we don't get them out of our way, then we'll have to do it their way. I'll simply meet up with them and give them what they want."

Nico's eyes flashed in surprise and anger, and I could feel him almost flinch away from my hand. "No. Maddy, absolutely not."

"Yes, Nico. I have all the faith in the world that we'll be successful, but we have to understand that it might come down to that. I would die for Abi and my parents—"

"Well, you aren't going to," Nico growled. "I'm not going to let you give yourself over to them. They'll bleed you dry and more than likely kill you. I won't allow it. I can't."

I was patient with him because I understood his anger and could see it from his side. If the roles were reversed and it was his parents and one of his friends who had been taken, and he'd told me he was going to do what I'd suggested, my reaction would have been the same. It wasn't something I wanted to think about. It would have pissed me off. So, I understood his response.

"I'm not going to let my family be tortured and killed. I couldn't live with that."

Nico grabbed my hand and pulled it from his face, intertwining our fingers. "Maddy, even if this plan doesn't work, we'll think of something else. Something will work. I refuse to let you be some guinea pig for these people."

"It's the very last option, but it's on the table. It has to be."

He was getting frustrated. I could see it in his face. Then he asked the question I'd been thinking about moments before. "What if it were me, Maddy? If the royals wanted me to give myself over to be bled out, would you do it?"

Hearing the words out loud was more visceral than just thinking them in my head. A chill ran down my spine, and my wolf reacted by emitting a low, angry growl. Nico grinned knowingly. "See? Neither of us can stand the idea of losing the other."

There was nothing else to say. Nico pulled me close and wrapped me into a tight embrace. I put my arms around him, and we sat like that for a long time, enjoying the feeling of our bodies pressing against each other. I could feel his heartbeat through my own chest, and I knew he could also feel mine.

After a moment, I murmured, "We'll figure something out. I'll stop thinking of sacrificing myself. Okay?"

He relaxed beneath my hands when I said it. He pulled me even closer. "Thank you."

Nico made lasagna for dinner that night. It was his grandmother's recipe, apparently, and he was excited for me to try it. When I offered to help, he shooed me away. Instead, he poured me a glass of wine and sent me out to relax on the back porch. Not one to turn down wine and a quiet night, I took him up on it and left him to make dinner.

The sun had already set, and the moon hung heavy in the sky. I sipped my wine as the moon tugged at me. It was stronger tonight than it had ever been. The aching of my bones sent waves of warmth through my entire body. I couldn't take my eyes off the bright, milky white of it as it sat there in the sky—not full yet, but getting closer.

My wolf was right at the surface. I couldn't feel any emotion from her, just a heavy presence, like someone reading a book over my shoulder. To me, it was like she was there watching. Waiting. For what, I had no idea.

I recalled the dream from a few nights ago. The dream that was more a memory than a dream: the whispered voices, the fear, the running, and the rough hands shoving me over the railing to my death. It had all been so vivid. As if I'd actually been there, experiencing those things.

Glancing into the kitchen, I made sure Nico was still absorbed in cooking, then set my wine glass on the table. "Are you the daughter of Edemas?" I whispered, talking directly to my wolf.

There was no response. Not even a flicker of emotion. I frowned, wondering if she could even hear me. Was she too entranced by the moon? Or was she simply ignoring me? I decided on a different question. "Do you want revenge?" Still nothing. I sighed. "Okay. I can't understand what you went through in this past life—if that's what this is—but I'm here," I said. "I'm on your side no matter what. We share this body. We're in this together."

There was a sense of stirring in my mind. Months ago, the sensation would have been disturbing, but I'd gotten so used to it by now that it was second nature. I could feel her emotions coming forward. Relief. That was what was flooding my body now. Deep, grateful relief—and curiosity. Not mine, but the wolf's. I glanced up at the second floor, to the window of the bedroom. The envelope waited. It couldn't wait any longer. We needed to open it.

I looked over my shoulder at Nico chopping vegetables for a salad. He looked content. Happy. It could wait until tomorrow. We could have one more night before whatever revelations were in the envelope were brought out into the world.

Chapter 20 - Nico

The night before had been one of the most relaxing we'd had in a long time. Maddy had enjoyed my lasagna, which pleased me, and we spent most of the night on the couch, talking and watching silly TV shows. It was such a normal night that I could have almost forgotten what was going on in our lives.

We went to bed early, which was exactly what we both needed. I'd slept through the night, and I wasn't woken by Maddy having any nightmares. I hoped that meant she got to have a good night's sleep. When I awoke the next morning, I made my way downstairs, trying to be as quiet as possible to give Maddy more time to sleep.

I was brewing coffee and opening a package of bagels when Maddy came down the stairs with the envelope. A smile had been forming on my lips when I first saw her coming down, but once I saw what was in her hand, the grin died on my face.

"It's time?" It was a question, but my tone made it sound more like a statement.

Maddy nodded as she put the envelope on the counter. The little package of paper looked heavier than it should have. Like Maddy had laid the entire Library of Congress on the counter. I half-expected the kitchen island to crumble under its weight.

"Are you sure you're ready?" I asked. We needed to do it, but I didn't want Maddy to push herself to do something she wasn't completely sure of.

She nodded once, with finality. "I can't put it off anymore. I shouldn't have put it off this long. I should have opened it the second we found it."

"All right. Whenever you're ready."

As though she wanted to get it done before she could talk herself out of it, she tore the top off the envelope and pulled out a letter. A quick glance showed her birth mother had written it. I sat beside her and read it over her shoulder.

Maddy,

I'm so sorry for everything. If you're reading this, then I know you're alive, which is a blessing to me in so many ways. You must have so many questions. I can only answer what I know. I'll do my best.

First, I'm sure you're wondering why I would give away the greatest thing that ever happened to me. My baby girl. Your father, David, and I were so in love. I was an advanced student in high school. By the time I was a sophomore, I'd already completed enough credits to graduate early. Call me a silly, love-blind girl, but I didn't want to leave David yet. Instead, I stayed and took advanced-placement courses. When David was a freshman in college and I was a senior in high school, I'd already completed enough coursework to graduate with a degree in biology. Our plan was for me to join him and start studying for my medical degree. We would finally be able to get married. It was a wonderful dream, but one we would never see come to fruition.

Your father had always known the royals would come for him. His father had told him about his heritage and what his bloodline meant. I knew all this, but I loved him too much not to stand by his side. David had also kept an immense secret. Not even his father and his half-brother knew this. David could shift. He was a full shifter. When the royals came that night, he did everything he could to protect me. Maddy, your father was very powerful. When he shifted, it was like nothing I'd ever seen before. Still, as strong as he was, there was only so much he could do against all the men with guns. He sent me to find his brother and stayed behind to give us as much time as he could.

I gave you away because it was the only way I knew to give you the life you deserved. The thought of raising a child while on the run was too much. Kenneth helped me find a wonderful family for you, then he helped me fake my death. I had to make sure the royals thought I'd died. If there were even a chance I could be pregnant, they would have never stopped looking for either of us.

Maddy's hands shook as she looked at me. "My father *could* shift? It wasn't just in his blood—he was a full shifter. How did Kenneth not know?"

I nodded. "The fact that he was able to keep that hidden is amazing." The initial phases of becoming a shifter were very uncomfortable. It was what Maddy was going through right now. This David guy had to have had a will of iron even when he was eleven or twelve to keep something like that hidden so well that even his father and brother didn't know.

I slipped my hand into the envelope and pulled out a set of three photos. One was of a very tiny baby—obviously Maddy. The resemblance was clear even as young as she was. It looked like it had been taken less than an hour after she'd been born. The other two photos were of her with her mother. In the first, she was still covered in sweat, but she had a bright smile on her face as she held the baby to her breast. Maddy reached a hand forward and slid a finger across the photo, letting the tip of her finger linger on her mother's cheek. I glanced over and saw tears welling in Maddy's eyes.

The second was of the two of them again. This time she was in a newborn onesie, and her mother was dressed and looked recovered from the birth. She was cradling Maddy in her lap. The smile was gone now. Instead, she was looking at the small child, and I could see a soul-crushing sadness on her face. There were tears in her eyes as she looked down at the baby. This must have been the moment she gave Maddy to Kenneth to take to her new family.

"God," Maddy whispered. "I can't imagine how this must have felt."

"That's the truest love I've ever seen," I said, and I meant it. "Giving away the thing you love more than anything else in the world to keep them safe? It's the bravest thing I think I've ever heard of."

Without another word, she picked the letter back up to continue reading.

Once you'd been safely placed, Kenneth arranged for me to undergo plastic surgery. I have to say, it was bizarre to wake up with a totally different face. He helped me forge documents to show I'd completed my degree under my new name. I went to med school and focused on pediatrics, with a focus on shifter children. I was a fast learner and graduated early again. I did a one-year residency, then pulled strings to ensure I got a job at the practice where your parents took you for check-ups.

You were three-and-a-half years old the first time they brought you in. It was all I could do not to burst into tears when you came walking into that exam room. Kenneth made sure to contact your parents and let them know that they could safely get the suppressants from me. It was another one of our ideas to keep you hidden from the royals.

I used my position as a doctor to run tests on all my patients. I never told the parents, which I felt bad about. Still, I was doing it for their benefit. I had to make sure they weren't descendants of Edemas. Those children would be targeted, and it was my way of protecting them. I could hide their information.

At this point, I'm sure your wolf has awoken. I know you're angry about her being suppressed, but you have to understand why we did it. You have to know what is coming. If you haven't shifted already, then it'll happen soon. The suppressants weren't only to keep you hidden from the royals but from everyone around you too. When your father shifted, he wasn't cruel or evil, but there were times when the wolf took over. It became more pronounced and exerted more of its personality than typical shifters experience from their wolves.

During the full moon, it was worse. He could sometimes be scary, almost feral. He came home multiple times, covered in blood, needing to clean up before anyone saw. He'd have no memory of the night before. One of the things that weighed on him was that he had no way of knowing if the blood was animal or human. It was terrifying for us, and eventually, it broke your father. He decided he wasn't going to shift anymore. He was strong enough mentally to hold it back without drugs, but it was a struggle. It was physically painful for him to hold the wolf back. This is what I was afraid your wolf would be like. It's the other reason I decided to put you on the *suppressants. You need to be very careful. I've included some articles in this packet.*

I slid out several pieces of cardstock that had newspaper clippings pasted to them. The stories were of murders and deaths that had taken place in and around Tampa in the years leading up to Maddy's birth. The descriptions were of people who'd been torn open and eviscerated as though they'd been attacked by a wild animal.

"Oh, Jesus," Maddy said, putting a hand to her mouth.

I shook my head. "This doesn't make sense. When I shift, my wolf comes to the forefront, but I'm always still in charge. She's saying that your father sometimes completely lost himself in his wolf? That... that's a little terrifying to think about. A lot of the urges my wolf has are not socially acceptable. If I wasn't there to temper those desires..." I trailed off, shaking my head, unsure how I'd cope with something like that.

I think those deaths were caused by your father's werewolf. I used my connections to get blood samples for these victims and did a DNA check. Every one of these people had familial connections to the royals. I think when your father shifted, the wolf took over and hunted down royals where he could find them.

Your father told me the legend of Edemas. You may have heard them too, by now. The thing is, the standard legends are not correct. They are a warped version of the events, propaganda that was propagated by the royals.

The legends say Edemas wanted full-blooded shifter children, that he had a harem of shifter women to complete this desire, that his human wife, the queen, was not giving him sufficiently powerful offspring, and when she balked at his concubines, he had her killed, which is what started the revolt against him. This is not true.

The hidden part of this story is that Edemas's wife was murdered by her own family. They were greedy and jealous of Edemas's power. His wife was killed, as was his eldest daughter, the heir to the crown. His daughter was thrown from the staircase. That is what set Edemas off. The loss of his two most loved family members is what twisted his mind and drove him into madness. It brought about his murderous rampage. He'd always been hungry for power, and yes, he did have concubines, but he was never cruel until the murder of his wife and eldest daughter.

Your father believed he was the reincarnation of Edemas himself. He had it in his mind that he would be cursed to relive the same fate as his ancestor. David often had nightmares, visions, and memories of things from the past. Things he thought were real images from Edemas's life. He saw things he couldn't possibly have known. These memories were how he knew that the legends and stories were wrong. He lived the truth in his dreams.

Chapter 21 - Maddy

My whole body was shaking as I read the letter. Each word I read seemed to hit me deep in my soul. My birth mother's handwriting, the information she was giving me, the pictures? It was all too much. I put the letter down as my wolf began to stir. Was she reacting to my emotions? Or was it the story itself?

In my mind, I spoke to her again. *Are you the reincarnation of Edemas's daughter?*

Her hesitation was almost physical, something I could feel inside my brain. There was something she wanted to say, but she was afraid. Then, in the deepest part of my mind, in a voice so small I almost missed it, she answered. *Yes.*

I gasped, feeling the weight of that statement slam into my chest. Nico put an arm on my shoulders. "Hey? Are you okay?" he asked.

Shaking my head. "It's true. My wolf. She just told me that it's all true. She's the reincarnation of Edemas's daughter."

"Seriously?" Nico wouldn't have looked more surprised if I'd slapped him.

"Yeah."

"What else is in here?" Nico said, digging through the envelope. We hadn't finished the letter, but I was curious too.

He tugged out a small, folded stack of papers wrapped in a rubber band. The band was old, dry, and rotted, and snapped apart when he tried to pull it off. Once unfolded, it was obvious what they were. The masculine block letters were not my birth mother's handwriting. These were journal entries. They were from David Samuels. My birth father. I immediately set my mother's letter aside and took the stack from Nico, beginning to read them.

May 9th,

I had another dream last night. It was the same as two days ago. So damned real. I'm going to write them here so I can try and piece together what they mean.

I was in a strange building, like a castle or something. It felt really old, ancient. It was dark, but there were candles and torches along the passageways and rooms. I was angry about something. Not just angry, but heartbroken. There was a man leading me along the passage, he was trying to tell me something, but I couldn't hear him. We came around the corner, and there was a girl lying on the floor. She was young, maybe around my age. Nineteen or twenty? Not sure. When I saw her in that dream, I can't even describe how I felt. I was so sad, and I screamed. Not even a scream really, but a howl, like my wolf was sad as well. The girl was obviously dead, her eyes staring up lifeless, and a huge pool of blood spread out from her hair. That's when I woke up. What does it all mean?

May 19th

Another dream. Thankfully, this one was different. I really didn't want to see that dead girl again. Although, this dream was worse in some ways. I know I was in the same castle as before, but I was outside, walking along a parapet or something. I was yelling at a man beside me. The guy was wearing familiar colors and kept bowing to me as I spoke. He was some type of servant. I couldn't make out the words, but I knew I was not happy with something he was telling me. The dream was more emotional than the last one. Betrayal, paranoia, anger, sadness, and panic were all boiling inside me. When I woke up, I was covered in sweat and breathing heavily. I'm starting to think I know who these dreams are about. If that's the case, what does that mean?

June 11th

Am I ever going to have a good night's sleep again? This dream was strange in a lot of ways. I was fighting with a woman. She was beautiful and familiar, though I don't remember ever remember seeing her in my waking life. She was asking me to stop making children. She seemed to be angry about my harem. I was angry. Didn't she understand I had to have more children? The only shifter child we'd had was our daughter, who was now dead. The rest had been born with my blood but were not able to become werewolves. I had to have heirs, and they needed to be shifters.

Her anger was enough for me to start to fear her. Was she going to betray me? Could she do something like that? My dream flashed to a massive room that was full of gold, jewels, silver-adorned weapons, carved alabaster, jade statuettes—so much treasure that I couldn't even focus on any one thing. I knelt and placed a small chest of gold coins on the ground. I turned and stepped out, sliding the big stone door closed behind me. Next to me, an ancient witch stepped forward and placed a hand on the door, and began chanting, sealing it with magic.

June 23rd

      I dreamed that I was in a dungeon—maybe? The walls were rough and seemed to be made of rock instead of the stone of the castle I'd been dreaming of, but this still felt familiar. I thought I was deep in the bowels of the castle. There was the same twisted old crone of a woman standing beside a fire. I was afraid of being betrayed. Possibly even by my own wife. This was my last chance to make sure my bloodline would live on. The old witch took my hand and drew a blade across the back of my wrist. A flash of pain, then my blood ran in rivulets off my arm. The witch caught it in a glass vial, and capped it with a small cork stop, then dipped the top into thick, red, melted wax. I was wrapping my wound in a cloth as she murmured incantations over my blood. Hope swelled in my chest as she completed the spell, then sealed it away in the vault. If my fears proved to be true and I was cast down from the throne and all my family killed, this blood, strengthened by the spell, would bring my distant descendants back to full power. God willing, this small vial of blood would allow the werewolves to again walk the earth.

      I woke up this morning, after that dream, feeling good for once. There was an excitement inside me. A feeling that was matched in my wolf. This dream had not been as nightmarish as some. It actually filled me with hope.

July 2nd

      This was the worst one yet. I almost had to run to the bathroom and vomit when I woke up. I was standing in a different chamber, and my hands were covered in blood. I was screaming when the dream started—on my knees and screaming in rage and loss. Beneath me, on a massive bed, was a beautiful woman. Her eyes were closed, but her throat was open. It was a massive, red, gaping wound. Blood had gone everywhere. Somehow I knew that this woman was my wife. This was the queen, and someone had murdered her. Two family members dead. Both killed while inside my castle.

The more of these dreams I had, the more difficult it was to separate myself from this person in the dreams. It did feel like I'd lost my own wife. I didn't think I could feel more heartbroken than if I woke up and Gabriella was lying there dead. That sounds crazy to write down, but it's true. My wife and daughter. Seeing my queen like that, I knew my daughter's death wasn't an accident. I was being betrayed. There were rats in those walls. Just before I woke up, I felt my mind starting to crack apart. I was going to lay waste to my enemies. I'm sure now. It's Edemas. I am Edemas. The reincarnation of him.

July 30th

Nearly a month. I almost thought I was through with it. I was ready to put the nightmares behind me, but last night I experienced something I can barely describe. I was lying on the floor, staring off down a hallway. I could hear the sounds of screaming and crying. Children, women, and men. Then the awful wet sounds of swords and axes piercing into flesh. The screams tore at my heart, and my rage was like a boiling hot fire in my chest, but I was weak.

Above me, a man came into view. I knew him. He'd been the captain of my guard. I'd been betrayed one last time. Beside him were my *queen's brothers and cousins. They'd killed their own blood to take my crown. I tried to shift, but I was too weak. The men raised their swords, and before they did anything, I croaked out a warning, telling them I'd be back. I would return along with my daughter to avenge our family. The blades glinted in the candlelight as they slammed down toward me.*

The stories of Edemas are false. He wasn't a mad psychopath. He'd been driven to revenge by betrayal and the deaths of his wife and daughter. I would have done the same thing in his place. This changes so much. The only thing I can't understand is why my wolf is showing me these things when I sleep. What am I supposed to do with this information? I can hear my wolf whispering that it wants revenge, but I have no clue how to go about doing that. The royals are going to find me. I know they are. Now that Gabby's pregnant, what will they do if they know I have a child?

Seeing my birth father's thoughts and feelings written out on the pages should have been heartwarming because I had a chance to get a feel for how he thought. Instead, it was like getting kicked in the gut. He'd experienced the exact same type of dreams I had. Visions of the past were given to him by his wolf while he was asleep. The very fact that he knew he was the reincarnated soul of Edemas must have been terrifying. As scary as me knowing I was the reincarnated daughter of the old king. It made me feel like my head was going to explode, and my father had probably felt the same. With a sigh, I picked up my mother's letter to finish reading it.

Maddy, I believe that your father really was the reborn Edemas. You'll find some of his journal entries in this envelope. The visions he had were so vivid, and they caused him so much fear and pain. Before the royals came, he would often put his hand on my belly and tell me that he thought our baby was going to be the reincarnation of Edemas's daughter. If that's true, then I'm afraid of what you may become. Please don't ever lose yourself to the power of your wolf—ever.

You can't let the royals get their hands on the vial of blood. Your father told me, in the days before the royals came for him, that he didn't think they wanted to destroy the blood. He thought they wanted it for something worse, something more sinister. I believe him. After all my research and everything I've seen them do, I have no doubt that they want nothing more than to use it for something terrible. Don't let them get their hands on that, Maddy. There's a hidden treasure they are free to have. Let them have the hundreds of millions in gold and jewels as long as they never open that vial of blood.

Be careful, Maddy. Stay safe and protect yourself. Do whatever you have to in order to stop the royals from completing their plans. All I can tell you is how much I loved you. Your father too. He loved you so much. Giving you up is the biggest regret I have in life. Second is the fact that you never got to know him. That, even for a day, he didn't get to hold you. I love you, Maddy.

Love, Momma and Daddy

I felt emotionally exhausted. My mind was so overwhelmed that I was a little worried I was going to pass out or get dizzy. Nico must have seen the look on my face because he hugged me close.

His breath tickled my ear as he whispered, "It's all going to be okay."

All I could do was laugh hysterically. My chuckle turned into maniacal laughter. Once I got myself under control, I pulled away to look into his eyes. "How is that even possible? There's nothing okay about any of this. I have to somehow get that vial before the royals do, we have to save my parents and Abi, and now I have to figure out how to live with the soul of a reincarnated wolf inside me. How much more can be on my plate?" I didn't like the whiny sound in my voice, but I couldn't really help it.

"Maddy, you aren't obligated to do anything. Getting revenge for some murders hundreds of years ago and getting that vial are not your concerns. Getting your family back—that's what we are worried about. Don't worry about those things."

My wolf didn't like hearing that. I could feel her irritation welling up inside me. "Nico, if these people are capable of killing children and kidnapping Mom, Dad, and Abi, then there's no telling what they might do. We have to destroy that vial before they get it open. But that brings us back to the same place we were before. Finding the vault."

Nico bobbed his eyebrows up and sighed. "Well, when Luis was in Europe, he was pretty sure they had guards stationed at a graveyard near the old castle. He was fairly certain that was where it probably was. No other reason to have guards there."

"Well, how big was the cemetery?"

"It was old. Probably a few acres at least, with a ton of crypts and tombs," Nico admitted.

I shook my head. "We'll never find it before they stop us. We need more details."

"Hang on," Nico said, pulling his phone out.

"What are you doing?"

"Texting Luis."

Realization dawned on me, and I allowed myself a little grin. "Are you doing what I think you are?"

He nodded as he typed with his thumbs. "Yeah. We need the info on the safe houses, but now we need to see if we can hear any details on the vault's location. If it's that important, someone may talk about it, especially if they believe they're alone."

Nico sent the text and sat staring at his phone, waiting for a response. They would have gone forward with the mission at any time. We could only hope they got the message before they moved ahead.

Finally, Nico's phone chirped and opened the text. "Hell yes!" Nico pumped a fist. "He got it. They'd just pulled into an abandoned parking lot when I sent it. The brothers are going to listen for any info."

I released a breath I hadn't realized I'd been holding. "Great. Maybe we'll get lucky."

Nico didn't respond. Instead, he placed his phone on the table and looked at me. He had a weird look on his face. "Maddy?"

"Hmm?"

"The envelope? Your dad's journal entries?"

"What about them?" I could still remember the words. They were burned into my mind.

"Are your dreams like that? Almost like... I don't know... like you're living in a movie or something?"

I sat there for a minute, thinking about his question. "Kinda, yeah."

"Do you want to tell me about them?"

I did. I talked for a while, giving him detailed descriptions. Especially the one where I'd been walking through the woods and the memory of being murdered. Before I started talking, I thought it would be traumatic to relive it out loud. Instead, I actually felt like a weight had been lifted from my shoulders. When I was done, he looked shocked.

He chuckled mirthlessly. "I can't believe this is really happening. Like, it's all *real*. Does your wolf seem hostile or bloodthirsty? Kind of like what your birth mom said in the letter about your dad's?"

"No, not at all. She's angry with the royals, but that's it. Honestly, there's a lot of fear in her, which makes sense now after learning everything. I mean, they murdered her in a past life—she has every reason to fear these people. Of course, it's not the same people, but after hundreds of years of money and power, I doubt they've become any less awful. In our experience, they may actually be worse. I think my wolf isn't the same as Edemas's. I can't see her taking over my body to go hunt descendants of the royals like what happened to my father."

Finding out my dream was real gutted me because I could still remember the fear and horror she felt as she was pushed over the railing. The way the hard stone floor had rushed up toward her. I gritted my teeth. "I'm not entirely sure what she wants, but I know that I want vengeance for her."

"Don't forget what your mother said in that letter," Nico warned. "Control your emotions. Don't let yourself get carried away in those emotions. If she's like mine, hate, anger, and revenge will just feed her and make it hard for you or her to think straight."

I took a steadying breath. He was right. Knowing what we did about how Edemas and my father interacted when they were in the same body gave me pause. Could the wrong emotion at the wrong moment send me down that same path? Would I show up at home, covered in blood and gore after being gone for days with no memory of what I'd done? The thought made my blood ice over.

Chapter 22 - Nico

As I'd read along with the letters and diary entries, and after seeing all the pictures and news articles, I got the feeling things were going to get bad. If I had been the one seeing these memories in my dreams, it would have destroyed me. I'd seen Maddy shut down after experiencing things like this before, and now I understood why. That was what I was worried about. I was surprised by the change I saw in her. It was the complete opposite of what I'd expected.

"Teach me to fight," she said through gritted teeth.

My eyes widened in surprise. "What?" Maddy looked ready to go to battle right there and then.

"You heard me, Nico. I can keep my wolf's emotions in check, and I can control my own, but if it comes down to it, I need to be able to defend myself. I'm tired of sitting on the sidelines. I sit under that damned tree and watch Javi's pack and our pack training. I need to know how to fight."

I didn't want her to think like that. If she had to fight, then it meant I'd have failed in some way. Her protection would have been compromised. The royals or their agents would have gotten to her. It was too anxiety-inducing for me to even think about. I put my hands on her shoulders. "Maddy, there's no reason for that. I will never allow anyone to come near you. They'll never even get the chance to attack you directly—"

"For fuck's sake, Nico. Stop that," she said, shaking my hands off her arms. "Stop coddling me! I'm not some porcelain doll that's gonna break if the wrong person touches me. Anything can happen. You and I both know that. I can't shift yet, but hopefully, I will soon. If nothing else, I should be able to defend myself in human form as well as when I'm a wolf."

I tried to find an argument against her learning to fight, but it all sounded stupid. If we weren't in this situation and everything was normal, wouldn't I want her to be able to defend herself against a mugging or an attempted rape? Why was it different with the royals? Why was I so afraid for her to learn to fight? It was ridiculous. I had to admit that.

"Okay," I said, the tension leaving my shoulders as I came to terms with it. "You're right. I've been treating you like you're some fragile thing that shouldn't be anywhere near the fight. The fight is coming to you, though. We can start tomorrow. Does that sound good?"

Maddy visibly calmed and gave me a small smile. "That does sound good."

Maddy met me in the backyard the next morning. She was dressed in a T-shirt and shorts while I wore athletic pants and opted to go shirtless. Our pack hadn't had any true battles in years. My father and grandfather before him had always done a good job of keeping the peace. Other than Javi's crew, we'd had very little reason to have any disputes. Even with that in mind, the Lorenzos had always made sure the pack was properly defended. Everyone old enough to learn was taught how to fight, both as humans and as wolves. Dad had taught my brothers and me multiple techniques—Jiu Jitsu, Krav Maga, and Aikido. Even though we'd had no true reason to use it over the last several years, it was a matter of pride that our pack was able to defend ourselves against any attacker.

"So," Maddy said. "Where do we start?"

This wasn't supposed to be easy, so I decided to start things off the way my father had started with me. Without answering her, I stepped forward, grabbed her arm, spun, dug my hip into her belly, and twisted my upper body. Maddy yelped as she spun head over heels and landed on the grass on her back.

Groaning, she coughed. "Fuck. What the hell?"

I winced inwardly. I didn't want to hurt her. That move had been minor, but it still made me feel bad. I'd need to be a little more careful. I lifted my shoulder in a shrug. "This is how I learned."

Maddy rolled over and dusted the grass off her butt. "Well, damn. Okay, then."

Over the next hour, I showed the initial stages of fighting: footwork and placement, balance, guarding, and spacing. After that first hip check, I found myself holding back, being more careful with her. The lessons my father taught me seemed to totally disappear from my mind. It got so bad that Maddy actually managed to get a few hits in before lunch. Not because she was picking it up that fast or that she was inherently good. She was athletic and a quick learner, but if I was honest with myself, it was because I wasn't able to give it my all.

When I was a boy, Dad loved us. He loved us, but he still knocked the shit out of us when he was teaching us to fight. That was what Maddy needed, especially with such short notice. I couldn't do it. The realization was brutal. I could teach her a lot of things, but I couldn't be the only one. I needed someone who wouldn't hold back—someone who wouldn't hurt her but would be able to knock her around more than I was able to.

"Hey?" I said to Maddy when we took a break.

She finished chugging her water bottle and looked over at me. "Yeah?"

I took a moment to gather my thoughts before continuing. "I think we need someone else here."

Maddy raised an eyebrow. "Hey, buddy, I'm not into that three-way stuff."

I snorted a laugh. "No! Not like that. I'm not able to give it my all when I'm sparring with you. I need someone who's going to give you a true challenge. That's the only way you'll learn. I'm doing that thing you were talking about. Treating you like a glass doll."

"Oh." Maddy nodded. "Was it seeing me on my ass in the grass?"

I nodded. "Basically. Let's say I'm too much of a gentleman."

"Who do you want to do it? Felipe? Luis?"

I sighed and shook my head. "You'd be surprised, but they aren't the best fighters among my brothers and friends."

"Who then?"

"I'm gonna grab my phone. I'll see if Sebastian can be here soon."

"Sebastian?" Maddy looked like she'd just choked on her spit.

Less than thirty minutes later, Sebastian and Maddy stood face to face in my backyard. He looked as uncomfortable as I'd thought he would. I conned him into coming over by saying I needed him for some one-on-one sparring. Of course, I neglected to tell him exactly who he would be sparring with. As uncomfortable as he looked, Maddy looked equally as irritated. She stared back at Sebastian, her arms crossed over her chest.

I was starting to think this might not have been such a good idea. Although, the two of them needed to get a grip. When Abi had first been taken, Maddy hadn't seemed to hold any ill will towards Sebastian, but that had changed quickly. His own guilt had kept him from going anywhere near her. They'd been becoming friends, and that conscious separation had hurt Maddy more than I'd realized. Plus, I think she needed someone to blame. The royals were so far removed and impossible to strike out at that she focused her anger and hurt at the only person who was nearby. Sebastian. For his part, he'd done a shit job. He'd promised multiple times to talk it out with Maddy, and so far, he'd been too afraid to do it. This would be the chance for them to hash it all out—as long as they didn't accidentally kill each other in the process.

"Okay," I said. "Do we understand the assignment?"

Sebastian gave a hesitant nod. "I... uh... try to take her down, right?

"You can try," Maddy said with a roll of her eyes.

I grimaced inwardly. "Okay then, whenever you guys are ready."

Sebastian took a couple of tentative steps toward Maddy. After having some success against me, Maddy was probably more confident than she should have been. She took heavy steps toward Sebastian and tried to chop at his neck. Sebastian easily blocked it, slapping her hand away. The *crack* of skin on skin made me wince. Maddy clutched her hand to her chest, hissing in pain.

"Shit, sorry," Sebastian mumbled.

"It's fine," Maddy said, her teeth clenched.

They went at it again. This time Sebastian took a more active stance, bending his knees and moving in low. Sebastian knew more fighting techniques than me, Luis, and Felipe combined. While a lot of kids played baseball or football growing up, all Sebastian had enjoyed was martial arts. Once he became an expert in one specialty, he'd beg his parents to enroll him in a different one. He'd even gotten into boxing in college. The guy was an encyclopedia of fighting. I wasn't even sure what style he was using when Maddy tried to grapple with him again.

Sebastian shot a hand under her striking hand and grabbed a handful of clothing. He yanked it forward and braced his leg, forcing her to fall face-first onto the ground. From there, things got heated. I stayed back and let things play out. As much as I wanted to intervene, I knew they needed to get this out of their system.

They went back and forth, and to my surprise, Maddy *was* a quick learner. Once she saw Sebastian use a move, she made sure to watch out for it. Sebastian made sure to still give her verbal clues and explain why she'd been taken down each time, though I could tell he was getting irritated with her for not acknowledging the instruction.

Fifteen minutes later, they were both pouring sweat and grunting while they each tried to get the other into a joint lock. Sebastian was trying to get Maddy's left arm while she attempted to bend his wrist back. They were so close to each other as they struggled that their foreheads were almost touching. Their teeth were bared as they struggled.

While they tried to get the upper hand on each other, their feet got tangled. Yelping, they tumbled to the ground. They lay there, gasping and covered in sweat, looking sufficiently exhausted.

I stepped forward and crossed my arms as I looked down at them. "Now that you've both had a chance to get your frustrations out, are we ready to bury the hatchet? Do we feel better now?"

Sebastian nodded as he heaved in gasping breaths. Maddy gave me a nod as well as she winced and massaged her thigh where Sebastian had kicked her.

I nodded and looked at Sebastian. "Good. New plan. Along with saving Maddy's parents and Abi, we're going to try and get info on the blood of Edemas. We want to get to it and destroy it. Are you down?"

He nodded, rolled over, and got up to his knees. "Yeah. When do we plan on going in? I want to be there with the team that hits the safe house Abi is in. I want to be there. I owe it to Abi for being such a shit to her. I owe it to her... and Maddy."

Maddy sat on her butt and sent Sebastian a withering look. "You don't owe me anything other than to stop wallowing in guilt. I want everyone to get out of this safely, not just Abi or my parents. If you go in there to save Abi, then I want you to do everything you can to stay safe."

Sebastian blushed, and he kept his eyes downcast as he tugged blades of grass from the ground. "I'm sorry."

"About what?" Maddy asked. "About what you did with Abi or about basically blowing me off and barely talking to me for a month?"

When Sebastian glanced up, he looked abashed. "Sorry. I thought you hated me, so I stayed away."

"Sebastian, we're friends. Friends don't abandon each other when things get tough. Okay?"

He nodded, smiling shyly. "Okay. Deal."

"Good," Maddy said. "Now you can stop being an asshole."

He laughed. "You were a little asshole-ish yourself."

Maddy raised her eyebrows. "Can't argue with that."

I took a deep breath of relief as they laughed. It was one less thing to worry about. It had become exhausting having my best friend and mate at odds with each other. I needed everyone on the same page if we were going to be successful.

After dinner, Maddy sat on the couch and winced as she rubbed at her lower back. Concerned, I sat next to her. "Are you okay? Did we do too much today?" I was worried either Sebastian or I had hurt her.

Maddy shook her head. "No. It's the same body aches I've been having for days. They get worse at night when the moon comes up."

It was her body wanting to shift. It had been over two weeks since I'd claimed her, and we'd done everything we could think of to get her wolf to come out. It must have been taking an awful toll on her. I couldn't imagine how badly my body would hurt if I went this long without shifting, especially for my first shift.

Her wolf had to be desperate to get out, but for some reason, it just wouldn't. I wondered if she'd even be a full wolf when she shifted. Would she always be a werewolf? Or would it be something she could control?

"Come on. I'll run you a bath," I said.

Ten minutes later, I had the big jacuzzi tub in my bathroom full of water and Epsom salts. Maddy stood behind me in a robe, looking longingly at the hot water. "Is it ready?"

I nodded and dried my hand on a towel. "Good to go."

"Okay." Maddy shrugged off the robe and hung it on a hook.

My eyes locked onto her body as she moved toward the tub. Her breasts swayed with each step, and as she stepped into the tub, the muscles in her ass flexed, going taut. My cock was immediately hard, straining against my pants. I kept my composure but gave Maddy a grin and raised my eyebrow as she slipped into the water.

"Don't get any ideas, big guy," she said as she rested her head on the edge of the tub.

I pressed a button, and the massaging jets switched on, making the water roll with bubbles. "No ideas other than the ones I always have. What hurts the most?"

"My fucking shoulders. It's almost like the damned wolf is setting up camp right at the base of my neck."

Pulling up a small stool from the corner, I sat behind Maddy and started massaging her neck, digging my thumbs into the knotted flesh between her shoulder blade and neck. She groaned in response. My cock twitched again at the sound. After several minutes, I moved my hands up into her hair and started massaging her scalp.

"Oh, shit. That feels good," Maddy whispered.

"Glad you like it."

I wanted her to feel good and to release all the tension and frustration that had been building up in her all day. Looking down, I saw the rippling water lapping at her breasts, and I couldn't hold back any longer. My fingers caressed her shoulders once more and slowly moved to her collarbones, drifting across the delicate flesh there. Maddy's breath caught as I slipped my hands lower. I massaged the muscles of her chest, and her breaths began coming more rapidly. I could feel her heart beating faster.

I circled her nipples, rubbing gently around the areolas. Maddy closed her eyes and arched her back, pressing her breasts into my hands, her nipples erect and warm. I rolled them between my fingertips.

"God," Maddy breathed, and I saw her hand start to drift between her legs.

"Nope," I whispered. "That's my job."

Continuing to massage her chest with my left hand, I leaned forward and slipped my right hand down her body, across her belly button.

"Do you remember those ideas I told you not to get?" she whispered, her lips inches from my ear as I leaned over her.

"Yeah?"

"Forget what I said. Do whatever you want."

I grinned and slid my hand through her pubic hair, then slipped two fingers inside her. Maddy moaned and let out a deep satisfied sigh. I slid my fingers in and out of her, fucking her with my hand. With each thrust, my palm slapped softly on her clit. My own lust was growing with every second as I watched her body react to me. My cock had been tight in my pants before, but now it was ready to explode.

Maddy spun in the tub, surprising me. She pressed her lips to mine, her tongue fluttering across my teeth, lips, and tongue. Water splashed onto me as she reached her dripping wet hand down to tug at my belt. In seconds, I was undressed and sliding into the bathtub with her. The warm water and her slick, wet skin caressed me and welcomed me in as I slipped into her embrace.

Maddy wrapped her arms around my neck and moved her hips under the water until she slid down my length.

"Christ, you're so tight," I whispered between kisses.

"You're thick," she said with a coy smile, then nipped playfully at my lip.

I started slamming into her, heedless of the water that was splashing over the edge of the tub and onto the floor. Maddy twined her legs around me and pulled at me, forcing me to go faster.

Our foreheads were pressed together as we moved in sync. Maddy slid her hands down and clutched my ass, pulling me in deep. "I'm gonna come," she said, her voice shaking with lust and anticipation.

"Do it. I want to feel you come for me," I said, grunting as I increased my pace.

The orgasm washed over her. I could feel and see it. Veins popped out on her neck, her jaw dropped open, and her body convulsed. An inarticulate scream erupted from her throat as I finished inside her. My own climax rocked me and sent a powerful explosion through my body, erupting from my cock and spreading through my balls, up my back, and out through my limbs.

I hugged Maddy close, still inside her. "Are you relaxed now?"

She nodded, still trying to catch her breath. "I am. Are you ready?"

"Ready?"

She ground her hips against me again, and I laughed in surprise. "Seriously?"

"You started it."

Chapter 23 - Maddy

By the end of that first day of sparring with Nico and Sebastian, I felt pretty good about what I'd learned. I wasn't some badass heroine in an action movie, and I wasn't sure I'd be able to get any hits if it came down to a fight between me and someone else. Though, I was on the way there, or at least I felt like I was. More practice was necessary, but I didn't feel like a complete failure.

That night, after I coaxed Nico into a second round in the bathtub, we were lying in bed, happily exhausted, and I told him what I wanted.

"Can I join the training session tomorrow?"

Nico looked at me warily. "Are you sure? Maybe you should work with me and Sebastian a few more times."

"No. I need all the time we have. There's only so much you guys can teach me. I want to be in the chaos of a battle. Even if it's pretend. It'll give me more experience, and if I find myself in something similar, I might not freeze up or freak out."

My argument was sound, but Nico still made a show of thinking it over. After several long seconds, he nodded grudgingly. "Okay, we can see how it goes tomorrow. If it gets to be too much, let me know, and we'll pull you out. I'm planning on doing more forest work. Lots of cover and short lines of sight. Be prepared for it to get a little crazy."

"Awesome," I said as I laid my head on his chest. Within seconds, sleep overtook me.

The sun was barely up when we started. Javi's pack wasn't able to come today, which was nice. As awkward as it already was, I didn't need a bunch of people I barely knew watching me make a fool of myself.

Nico took half the pack and put them into a team by themselves, pretending to be the royals. Since they were all playing humans, he told them they weren't allowed to shift. He took the rest of us and broke us into groups of two. He told me he was going to have one group act as traitors and help the royals. He didn't tell anyone else his plan, which irritated me. I felt like he was only telling me because he was still coddling me, but I hoped he only wanted to let me in on his little scheme because he was excited and proud of the little twist.

I was with Sebastian, of course, and once things got going, I realized Nico hadn't been lying. It was crazy. We sprinted through the woods and could hear screaming and shouting. Then the exploding sounds of paintballs as they slammed into the trees. Apparently, Nico had other tricks up his sleeve to make things more chaotic. He'd given the "royals" team paintball guns to simulate the weapons they'd probably have when we went toe to toe with them.

"Shit," Sebastian hissed. "Nice of him to tell us."

"What if someone gets shot in the face or eye?" My heart was racing a rapid tattoo against my chest.

"Well… don't do that," Sebastian said as he led me into the woods.

He spent a good amount of time explaining strategy to me as we worked our way to the "royals." We even caught a couple of guys unaware, and Sebastian had me stay back and watch what he did to take them down. He was amazing. He took both of them out in seconds. They lay on their backs, groaning and holding body parts that would be bruising within minutes. After they submitted and sat on the ground, pretending to be dead, he took one of the paintball guns and gave it to me.

"I thought I was learning to fight hand to hand?"

"First rule of fighting, always find a way to get the upper hand. If you can't get the upper hand, then level the playing field. Until you can shift, taking an enemy's weapon is the next best thing."

It went on like that for over an hour as each side went through attrition. Eventually, Sebastian and I were both taken down by paintballs to the back, which hurt like a bitch. Before we were taken out, we took out almost a dozen enemies. The good guys did eventually win, but we lost a lot of people. Nico was happy with the result but not pleased by the casualties.

He sent everyone else out for lunch, but Sebastian stayed behind with me to work on disarming and incapacitation hits.

"Remember what I said in the woods about leveling the playing field?" he asked after everyone had gone off to eat.

I nodded. "Yeah."

"Good. In movies, they'll tell you that going for a guy's throat, eyes, or balls is dirty fighting. It's cowardly and not fair, right?"

I shrugged. "I guess so."

"Well, that's bull-fucking-shit. If you go into a fight and you're afraid for your life, there are no rules. You hit that fucker where and whenever you can."

He showed me the best way to attack a person's soft spots: striking the throat with the space between your thumb and forefinger; eye gouges; ways to position yourself for a solid crotch hit; the proper way to do a heel stomp on the bridge of a foot; and where the solar plexus was for a palm strike.

It was only the end of the second day, and I already thought I had quite a few tools at my disposal to get myself out of trouble and run. I was even more confident than I had been yesterday. Actually *knowing* you had a chance in a fight was a glorious feeling.

Nico came down later and brought us both some sandwiches, which we basically inhaled. I couldn't remember the last time I'd been so hungry. He nudged me with his elbow as I finished. "How was it?"

"Good," I said.

"Yeah," Sebastian added. "She's learning fast."

"Nico, do you think it would be okay if I headed out to that creek? I want to do a little decompressing."

"Sure. Do you want me to go with you?" I could tell he wanted to, but I really did need some alone time.

"No, I'll be fine. I just want to work on some of those relaxation exercises you showed me."

"Well, all right, but keep your phone on if you need me. You're on the Lorenzo pack lands, so I'm not worried about you being safe. I just want to be there if you need me. Do you remember how to get there?"

I stood and brushed my pants off before heading toward the woods. I nodded over my shoulder to him. "I do. I'll see you in a little while."

Nico and Sebastian raised their hands to wave. I smiled to myself as the trees enveloped me, and silence fell. I loved people and being around them. It's why I'd chosen to open a bar. However, as much as I liked people, sometimes you just needed to get away for a little bit. I'd also had very few chances to be truly alone since all the drama in my life started. It was almost a novelty having time all to myself.

After getting turned around once, I was able to find the creek fairly easily. I smelled the water long before I saw it, and once I was there, I sat right at the edge. After a few minutes of tossing some stones in the water, I closed my eyes and started the breathing and meditation exercises.

My wolf had been on edge and withdrawn since we'd read the contents of the envelope. She hadn't spoken to me since we read the letter. It almost seemed like she was hiding herself now that I knew who she was for sure. I wanted to try and help her feel at ease. Her worry and hesitation made me anxious. It honestly felt almost like I had a terrified little girl hiding inside my mind.

I took several deep breaths and relaxed my entire body, listening to the gurgle of the water as I did. After a few minutes, I felt my heart rate slow, and the muscles in my shoulders, back, and legs loosened. I began to reach out to my wolf once I could feel her relaxing.

I decided not to speak to her because it might be too much. Instead, I reached out toward her with my body, visualizing our forms becoming one. Shifting. Imagining my fingers turning into claws again like they'd done before. I could still remember the sharp claws that had dug into the countertop of the kitchen all those days ago. That was what I wanted to do again but not have the partial shift be fed by pure emotion. It should be a controlled and conscious change if I were to master it.

For the next fifteen minutes, I focused my mind on shifting my hand and continued to send positive thoughts toward my wolf, letting her know everything was okay and that it was safe. About the time I thought it might not work, I felt a tingle run down my arm to my hand, then there was a not-unpleasant pulling sensation.

Glancing down, I saw that my fingers had actually turned into claws. They were the long-fingered claws of a werewolf rather than the stubby paws and toes of a wolf. I grinned and let my wolf know she'd done a good job. I concentrated on trying to do it again. By the time we stopped, I was actually sweating with the mental exertion of it, but I could make my hands change at will. It was crazy and strange and exciting all at once. My mind and body were exhausted, so I lay back on the moss by the creek to rest.

"You're doing a great job," I whispered to my wolf.

There was a surge of relief and happiness from her that made me smile. My mind drifted back to the memories I'd dreamed about. My eyes sprang open when something in my mind clicked into place. I remembered the whispered voices of the conspirators from the dream. They'd talked about the princess, but there was something that stuck out at that moment that hadn't before. Those men had said the princess *may* become a monster like her father. That things *might* happen. They had talked in possibilities, not facts.

I reached out to my wolf again with my mind. *You never shifted before? In your past life?*

The first emotion that flooded into my mind from her was sadness. It started small, a tiny ache at the back of my mind, then grew until I could feel it in every inch of my body. Then a low, almost embarrassed growl whispered in my mind. *No.*

My heart ached for the girl. She must have been very young when those awful men killed her. Maybe only eleven or twelve? A child. Her hesitancy, confusion, and wariness all made much more sense now. We were both trying to figure out how to shift together. She'd never had the chance to come to her full power. She'd been killed because of what she *might* become. I really couldn't blame her for being afraid to come out into the world.

After resting for another while, I managed to get up to head back. I needed to tell Nico what I'd discovered and see if he had any ideas on how to proceed. Surely there was a way to help put my wolf at ease.

I found him in the field, watching as the pack continued a different drill. He wasn't participating. When he saw me emerge from the woods, he smiled and waved a hand toward me. Skirting the practicing group, I walked up to him and pulled him aside.

"How was it?" Nico asked once we were away from the noise.

"Great, actually, I made some real progress with my wolf. If I concentrate really hard, I can make my hands shift."

Nico's eyes widened in surprise. "Wow, seriously? Can I see?"

"Uh, it's a little exhausting. I'll try to show you later. I wanted to talk to you about something else. I think I know the real reason my wolf is having such a hard time coming out."

"Okay, let's hear it."

Once again, I went over the dream of her death and told him what the men had said. Then what my wolf had confided in me—that she'd been killed before ever having her first shift, that she was as inexperienced as I was. When I was done, I could see realization dawning on Nico's face.

"Damn," Nico said when I was done. "You're right. Shifter puberty is tough, but it's even tougher on girls." He nodded toward two women running across the field with the group. "Those two are my cousins Eliza and Francisca, and they had a really difficult time when they first shifted. I feel like I'm a good resource for you, but I was never a prepubescent female shifter. Maybe you could talk to them and see if they have any pointers for you. If you want to, that is."

"At this point, I'll do anything if it helps."

After the practice session was done for the day, Nico introduced me to his cousins. They were gorgeous, and I could tell they must have been twins. They weren't identical, but they looked alike enough to make it obvious that they were related.

"Eliza, Francisca, this is my mate, Maddy."

I nodded and gave a little wave. "Hey."

Eliza raised an eyebrow. "Oh, we know you. The woman who finally nailed Nico down. Impressive."

My cheeks flamed, and I grinned, shrugging awkwardly. "That's me, I guess."

Francisca hugged me. "Don't mind my sweat."

Returning the hug, I said, "You're fine. I'm probably pretty stinky from this morning too."

"You guys have heard the deal right?" Nico asked. "About Maddy being a shifter?"

Francisca and Eliza looked at each other and exchanged exaggerated eye rolls. Francisca crossed her arms and raised an eyebrow. "The entire pack knows, Nico. It's not really a secret."

"Right. Anyway, I thought you guys could hang out this afternoon. I've given her all the pointers I can about shifting, but you guys might have a better understanding of how it is to be a female and go through your first shift."

"We *might?*" Eliza said scathingly, glaring at Nico.

"Oh, hell. You know what I mean," Nico said, and the two women giggled.

Francisca took my arm and started walking away. "Come, Maddy. We must give you all the secrets we mysterious female shifters have. The men aren't to know our mystical ways."

Nico sighed. "You guys are assholes. You know that?"

Francisca and Eliza laughed as we walked across the field toward a house at the end of one of the three streets of the Lorenzo compound. Once we were inside, Eliza immediately opened the fridge and pulled out a bottle of white wine. "Who's down?" she asked, waving the bottle over her head.

"Me." Francisca raised a hand.

I nodded. "Absolutely."

The three of us took seats on the couch, wine glasses in hand, shoes kicked off. It was strange. I'd met the two of them less than fifteen minutes before, and we hadn't even started our conversation, but I already felt like I'd known them for years.

"Okay, Miss Maddy, what do you want to know?" Eliza asked before taking a large sip of her wine.

"Well, uh, I guess I wanted to know exactly what you guys went through when you did your first shift. What was it like? Any tips for getting over the hump, so to speak?"

"Oh shit," Francisca murmured. "We could go on for days on that."

"For real," Eliza added.

"Is it really that much different from men at that age? Like, isn't it basically the same?" I felt dumb for even asking the question, but I wanted to know.

Francisca chuckled and leaned forward. "Sweetheart. Think about what you're saying. When normal human men go through puberty, they grow some hair on their balls, their voices get deep, and then their dicks get bigger and start getting hard at the drop of a hat. Women? Jesus, the boobs, the hair, fucking cramps, blood leaking out of you, and so freaking many hormones. It's a whole ordeal. Now, imagine that, along with a fucking magical creature living inside you and wanting to come out and change your body. It's so much more difficult. Girls usually don't have their first shift until after most boys, simply because so much shit is happening with our bodies that it's hard to focus on shifting. Boys are usually nine or ten. Girls are ten or eleven, on average."

I drained my glass and sat it down so Eliza could refill it. "So, tell me what you do to get that first shift out of the way?"

The sisters gave me pointers that were sort of on the same line as Nico's meditations, but they also went deeper into what to say to the wolf. They had tidbits of wisdom and some funny stories about their own attempts to shift the first few times. We sat and talked for a couple of hours, finishing two bottles of wine. Nico's cousins were plowing through glass after glass, and I was doing my best to keep up as the conversation went on, but I was getting tipsy.

"Oh shit," Francisca said, glancing at her sister. "Look at Maddy's eyes."

Eliza leaned forward and looked at my face. I had a hard time not giggling at her. "Damn. We've literally been sitting here talking about how she hasn't shifted yet, and we let her get drunk."

At the back of my drunk and fuzzy mind, I remembered shifters metabolized alcohol ten times faster than humans. It looked like I hadn't received all the benefits of shifterdom yet. I was buzzed while they still looked fit to drive cross-country.

"Umm, I better get going," I said, rising unsteadily to my feet. I felt a dizzying rush swoop through my head. "Oh damn." I put a hand out and balanced myself on the couch.

"Welp, let's get you home," Francisca said, standing up and putting her glass on the table.

She walked me home, and as I moved, I realized I was plowed. This wasn't buzzed. This was way more drunk than I'd been in months. By the time we got to Nico's place, I wasn't stumbling over myself and hanging on Francisca, but I was still fairly hammered.

"Can you get the rest of the way in, or do you need me to get you inside to a chair or something?"

I patted her shoulder. "No thanks." I chuckled and leaned in to whisper conspiratorially. "I'm gonna go in here and try to get Nico's pants off. After that, I'll—"

"Gross, stop." She held her hands up and looked like she'd throw up. "Whatever you do, have fun, but I don't want to hear about my cousin knocking boots."

I made my way, carefully, up to the front door. I glanced over my shoulder as she left, waving at her before I went inside. I fumbled through, locking the door behind me, and walked in to find Nico standing in the kitchen, looking delicious as hell. I did my best sexy saunter toward him, though if I was honest, I probably looked more like a drunk sloth than Jessica Rabbit.

"Well, how did that go?" Nico asked.

Moving close, I ran a finger down his chest. "Good. But not as good as things are about to get." I blinked hard two times as the room started spinning slightly.

Nico glanced down at my finger as it slipped past his belly and down to slip across his crotch. He smiled. "Is this what I think it is?"

Confusion swirled in my head, and I looked down at my hand. "Uh… it… it is a penis, right?"

Nico burst out laughing and shook his head. "No."

"It's not a penis? What the hell am I touching then?" I was so confused, and I had a hard time focusing.

"No, I mean, are you trying to seduce me?"

I looked up into his face and grinned. "Yup."

"I think maybe you should sleep it off. Maybe try the whole seduction thing sober tomorrow morning if you want."

Raising an eyebrow, I said, "Oh really? Are you going to say no to this?"

Lifting my hands to my chest, I swear to God I thought I was trying to pull the buttons apart to reveal my bra. My wine-addled brain had forgotten that I was wearing a T-shirt and not a button-down. Instead, I grabbed the cotton fabric and yanked, doing nothing but stretching my shirt and hurting my fingertips. "Well, shit." I looked down and pouted. "I was trying to show you my tits."

"Okay, that's the cue to get you to bed." Nico put an arm around me and helped me up the stairs.

We lay in bed, getting ready to fall asleep, and I patted Nico on the chest. "I really like your family."

"We're mated now, Maddy. They aren't just my family. They're yours too."

That sent a warm, tingly feeling through my whole body, which had nothing to do with the alcohol. Having his family welcome me like they had was a nice way to soften the pain of having my own family taken from me. Feeling loved like that was exactly what I needed.

"Thank you so much, Nico. I don't think I can ever thank you enough."

"You don't need to thank me. You're my mate, and I love you. You *are* my family, and that means I put you first."

A new thought formed in my head as I ran my fingers over his chest. An idea I'd not allowed myself to contemplate until right then. Maybe the alcohol had opened some doorways I didn't know were waiting to be opened.

"What are your thoughts on family? I mean... a family for us?"

Nico shifted his position in bed. "I've always wanted kids. You've seen my brothers. I had a big family. It's definitely something I want. What about you?"

"Yeah. I do. One day anyway. Things are a little crazy right now to plan something that big, though."

Nico rubbed my back. "Right. How about this? One day, when all this craziness is over and behind us, we can revisit this conversation. When I know for sure, you and your family are safe."

A smile crept across my lips. "That would be fantastic. I'd like that."

Chapter 24 - Nico

Luis had sent me a text early the next morning, saying it was time to infiltrate the safe houses. My shoulders tensed as I read the message. I tightened my grip on the phone, then eased it off, worried the screen might crack.

Glancing over my shoulder at Maddy, I said. "It's Luis. Today."

Those three simple words carried a metric ton of meaning. Both of us knew how difficult and dangerous this was. In my mind, I felt like I was at war. I wanted Luis and the other shifters to be safe, but I also wanted as much information as possible about Maddy's family. If anything happened to Luis and his team, I'd be swamped with guilt. My own anxiety spiked as I texted Luis back.

Maddy looked equally nervous. Her face was pale. She wanted this to be over. She was desperate to get her mom and dad and Abi back, but she knew as well as I did that the next few days would be incredibly dangerous.

"I told him to hold off starting until I can get everyone together. I'm going to call everyone over," I said as I got up and dressed.

Nodding, Maddy stood and started dressing. "Umm, do you want me to, like, make breakfast for everyone?" I could tell how nervous she was. Maddy probably wanted to stay busy to keep her mind off what was about to happen today.

I gave a little half nod. "Sure. Let's... I guess let's try and keep the day as normal as possible. There's literally nothing we can do but wait."

I wasn't very hungry, but normality would keep things a little less stressful.

After Maddy headed downstairs, I called Dad, Felipe, and Sebastian and told them to come over as soon as possible. Once I was off the phone, I headed down to the kitchen. Maddy was sliding a big pan of frozen biscuits into the oven while bacon sizzled in a skillet and eggs cooked in another. Surprisingly, as the food cooked, my stomach growled. It seemed I had an appetite after all.

Dad arrived first, with Felipe and Sebastian right behind him. I helped Maddy finish up and put plates down for everyone. Everyone was pretty quiet as we ate, even Sebastian. We all felt the pressure and seriousness of the situation. As hungry as I'd felt a few minutes ago, I barely managed to eat anything. Instead of talking, I exchanged texts with Luis. Once he let me know he and the brothers were ready to go, I stood and put my half-eaten food in the sink.

"Okay," I said once they'd finished. "Luis said they're about to leave the motel. Let's go and sit in my office. There are enough chairs for everyone in there."

The five of us trudged up the stairs and found spots in the office, then waited for the call to come in. I was in my leather office chair, rocking back and forth, staring at my phone on the desk.

"Bro, you gotta chill," Felipe said. "Won't help if you're freaking out like you are."

Forcing myself to stop fidgeting, I nodded curtly at Felipe. I hadn't even realized I was doing that until he pointed it out. I really was stressed. Before I could think about it or really calm myself down, the phone rang. I hit the speaker button, and the Bluetooth speaker at the edge of my desk came to life with Luis's voice.

"We're here. I dropped them off two blocks away. They're gonna walk about one more block in human form, then make sure no one is looking and shift. We need to be fast, so I gave them forty-five minutes, max."

"What's the plan?" I asked.

"Full interior floor plan recon. While they do that, they'll try to see who they have held in there, the number of assholes with guns, and listen for any info on the vial of blood. That's all I could think of," Luis said.

Dad glanced over at me, and I saw the look in his eyes. We both knew there wasn't any more we could look for right now. We nodded at each other in agreement. "That's good," I said.

"Okay. I'll call again when they're out and safe."

"Cool. Talk to you soon," I said.

My chair creaked as I leaned back to wait. The waiting was complete torture. Sebastian got up and paced the room. Felipe and Dad tried to talk about soccer and baseball, but the conversation seemed forced, as though neither one wanted to talk but didn't want to sit in silence either. Maddy and I sat together, holding hands in silence. The whole time, I tried to keep my mind off what might be happening. So many things could go wrong. If something went wrong, I'd be responsible. Sometimes I hated being the alpha.

When the phone rang over thirty minutes later, all of us jumped in surprise. I answered the phone so quickly it almost slid out of my hand and off the desk. "Luis? Are you guys okay?"

"Yup." He sounded like he was walking fast. Not out of breath, but breathing heavier than if he was just strolling. "I ditched the car in a parking lot and met the guys on foot. We're heading back to the car, and then we'll get back to the motel. I just wanted to give you an update that they're out and safe. I'll call again in less than ten minutes."

The call disconnected before I could say anything else. Damn him. Couldn't he give me a little update? Something? I sat back in my chair and gritted my teeth. "Sebastian, can you get me a beer?"

"It's ten in the morning," Sebastian said, giving him a crooked smile.

I knew how early it was, for God's sake. I huffed out a sigh. "I don't care. I need to take the edge off."

"Grab me one, too," Felipe said.

Sebastian rolled his eyes and left, returning a few moments later with three beers. Felipe took his and nodded at the third beer in his hand. "I thought it was too early?"

Sebastian flopped into his chair. "Well, hell, if you guys are doing it, I might as well join you."

A few minutes later, Luis called again, and this time he sounded calmer. "Hey. We're back. I had to make sure we didn't have a tail."

"So no one saw you?" Dad asked. "You went undetected?"

"Looks like it. No way I would have missed someone following. We're good. Here, let me give you to the guys. They were inside and can give you the most details. This is Darren and Marcus. You talked to their dad about a week ago."

There was some rustling as the phone was passed over, then a new voice. "This is Marcus."

I sat forward. "Marcus. Good to speak to you. I'm Nico Lorenzo. I want to thank you for what you and your pack have done for us."

"Not a problem. Pop said you all were on the level and needed help. We're glad to do it."

"Thank you again. Can you tell us what you found?"

"Yeah, man. I can give you the whole layout."

Waving a hand to gesture toward Felipe, I said, "Felipe, grab that notepad. Draw what he tells us."

Marcus gave us a detailed layout of the building. As he talked, Felipe sketched the general floor plan. There was an attic that had nothing but some old boxes. The main floor was set up like any other house, bedrooms, bathrooms, kitchen, and living room. It only got interesting when he started to describe the basement.

"As soon as we got downstairs, we knew there was some crazy shit going on," Marcus said. "Looked like it had been gutted down to the stud walls, then a couple of shitty walls were put up half-assed to make prison cells or something. They did a crap job, but they're solid."

"Could you get a look inside those?" I asked.

"My brother Darren climbed up and got a look through a space they left at the top of the wall. One cell was empty, but the other had a girl in it."

"What did she look like?" Maddy's voice burst out. "Did she look hurt?"

"She was in her late twenties or early thirties, reddish-blonde hair, probably five-foot-five or six. She was a bit dirty and had some good bruising around her cheek and on her arms and legs, but otherwise seems healthy. She wasn't tied down or anything—she was sitting on a shitty cot they had for her to sleep on."

It was Abi. That was where she was being held. I breathed out a sigh of relief and leaned over to rub Maddy's back. She looked relieved but still worried.

"She did have what looked like a LoJack on her left ankle," Marcus said.

"A what?" Maddy asked.

Sebastian piped up. "A LoJack. It's an ankle monitor. Basically a GPS so you can find where someone is. They use them on guys who are on limited-release probation. So the cops know where they are at all times."

"Right," Marcus said. "They want to keep track of her if she does manage to escape. Hey, let me hand you off to Darren. He heard something you need to hear."

The phone changed hands. A different, slightly deeper voice took over. "Yeah, so I was scoping out the living room upstairs while Marcus was in the attic. I heard these guys saying something about the girl in the basement. They said they wanted to move her to 'the other house, so they'd all be in the same place for the *big night*.' I'm not sure what they mean by that, but it sounds like she's getting moved soon."

"Is there anything else you can tell us?" I asked, hoping for as much information as possible.

"We did see about six guys in that house. All of them were armed. Other than that, we told you everything," Darren said.

Six men to keep one girl prisoner. They were probably well-trained and armed. I chewed at my lip for a second, contemplating that scenario.

"Thank you. You guys lay low for now. I'll text Luis when we have a plan."

Once the phone was hung up, Sebastian was the first to speak. "We need to move. Now."

I held up a hand. "Hang on. We need to talk about this first."

"No way. You heard them. They're gonna move Abi somewhere else. They're probably moving her to where Maddy's parents are, and that will consolidate their forces. It'll be easier to break one person out. Why not move in right now?"

"Because," Felipe said, "all we have there is Luis and two reptile shifters versus six armed guards. You want Luis to go in with a couple of guys who can turn into fucking geckos or some shit?"

"He's right," I said. Sebastian needed to understand what was at stake here. "We can't get there, and I don't have any favors to call in where they are. I'm not going to get Luis and those two guys killed. Not when we still have some time to come up with a plan. Besides, they still need to check the second safe house."

Sebastian looked upset, but he slumped back in his chair and shook his head. I could see he was mad and that he really wanted to be able to try and save Abi. I was glad that he was fighting for her, but this was too precarious to go off half-cocked.

Grabbing my phone again, I started typing and said, "I'm going to tell Luis to head to the other safe house. They can get there in a day or two if they go now."

"We should fucking go in now," Sebastian hissed under his breath, staring out the window. He really was pissed. I couldn't believe he was pushing me so hard on this. Sebastian was usually the easiest going of all my friends.

Without looking up from my phone, I shook my head sadly. "I know, man. I totally understand, but we have to do this the right way." After my message was sent, I looked at Sebastian, locking eyes with him so he'd be sure to get my full meaning. "We need to know the layout of the other house. Once we get that, we can formulate a plan that can be put into place. Synchronize and go in at once. Do you want to get in there and save Abi, only to tip off the royals? If we get Abi, they might kill Maddy's parents."

Sebastian paled and looked like he was going to be sick. "I didn't think about that. Sorry, you're right."

I nodded at him, smiling sadly. "We'll save her. I promise, but we have to be smart about it."

Maddy hadn't said much. As I glanced over, I saw her left hand under the desk. Her fingers were changing from claws back to human fingers. I grinned. She was controlling it. If she could control that, then she really was getting close. Maddy caught my gaze, and the determination in her eyes almost startled me. It scared me. As much as I hated it, I knew there was nothing that would stop Maddy from getting her family back. She was hell-bent on not being a fragile princess or a damsel in distress. She wanted to fight. I had to make sure I was ready for that. I'd be damned sure.

Chapter 25 - Maddy

The next few days would only add to my anxiety. I was sure of it. Waiting the hour for Luis to give us an update had been bad enough. Now we had to wait for them to travel to the next safe house. Then we'd have to redo what had just happened. I was not looking forward to that. After everyone had left, and the house was empty, I decided I needed to get my mind off it by practicing my partial shift.

Nico came down from his office a few minutes after everyone was gone and found me sitting in the living room staring at my hand.

"What are you doing?" he asked as he plopped down on the couch.

My fingers turned to claws, then back to my fingers. I'd been able to do that consistently since first doing it out by the creek, but I wanted to go further. I shook my hand and glanced at Nico. "Working on shifting."

He gave me an appreciative smile. "You're doing really great. I saw you doing that in the office earlier. What do you want to try next?"

"Well, I want to do my whole hand."

"Give it a try?"

Taking a deep breath, I glanced down at my hand and concentrated. My mind reached out and tentatively touched my wolf's, and I told her it was okay. I visualized what I wanted and stayed calm and open to her. After what felt like an eternity, a buzzing tingle ran through my hand, and I opened my eyes.

My entire hand and halfway up my forearm was a wolf's paw. Fully covered in hair, bigger than a typical wolf, but otherwise, exactly what you'd see on an animal in the woods. "Holy shit," I said, on the verge of freaking out.

"Calm down," Nico said. "Just take a breath and relax. It's okay. This is part of who you are. It's something you're doing. It's not something that's being done to you against your will."

He was right. I needed to stay calm. Still, it was hard to explain how weird it was to see part of your body completely change and look unlike anything it had ever looked like before. Sucking in a heavy deep breath, I steadied myself. Nico leaned forward and gently took my paw in his hand and ran his fingers along the fur. The feeling was strangely soothing.

"It's a regular wolf's paw," Nico muttered to himself.

That was a weird thing to say. Was I supposed to have a horse's hoof or something? "Why do you say that?"

He looked at me, shaking his head. "I just wasn't sure if you'd shift into a wolf or a werewolf. When you only did your fingers, it looked like one, and this is the other."

He was right. I'd been wondering about that. Would my first true shift be simple, or would I be something that was strange even in the shifter world? My birth mother's letter made it sound like my father had only ever been able to shift into a werewolf, and it was part of why he'd tried to stop shifting altogether.

I pitied him. He must have been incredibly strong mentally. To have Edemas's reincarnated wolf inside your mind had to have been much more difficult than what I was going through. My wolf had been a young girl, a child really, when she died. That's what I had in my head. David Samuels had an angry, powerful, and enraged former king inside his mind. It had to have taken a toll on him. There's no way it hadn't.

Nico and I worked on it a bit more the rest of the day, but it was exhausting, and we finally took a break. Luis texted that they were en route to the other safe house, which didn't help my anxiety. I wanted this all over, but I also didn't really want to go through all that it entailed.

We had a little over a week until the next full moon. In some ways, it seemed to be taking forever to get here. In others, it seemed like it was coming in the blink of an eye. I was happy that we'd been able to locate Abi, but we still had to lay eyes on my parents, make a plan, and then implement it—all of that in less than two weeks? I wasn't sure we'd pull it off.

I couldn't stop picturing that video of my mother getting electrocuted with that shock collar. Abi was mostly unhurt, but who knows what would happen the closer we got to the full moon? My resentment and anger at the royals was getting more intense with each passing day.

"Do you think you're getting closer to shifting?" Nico asked as we picked at our lunch.

"A little. My wolf seems a little calmer and more at ease, but there's still a lot of nerves and anxiety."

Nico gave me a concerned look. "I just hope we get there soon. It would be nice if your wolf could stop fighting it. I'd love to know exactly what we're getting into."

"You and me both. You have no idea how stressful this is."

"Shit, I almost forgot," Nico said, grabbing a newspaper that was sitting off to the edge of the table. "I saw this a while ago. I think it explains why they chose the next full moon as the deadline."

He handed me the paper, which was open to the life and sciences section. There was a headline about the next full moon being a super moon. I glanced through the article. It explained that it was when there was a full moon that passed as close to Earth as it possibly could. I looked up after reading it and frowned at Nico. "Do you think this is part of their plan?"

"It has to be. If you don't shift before then, there's no way your wolf would be able to resist the pull of a super moon. It'll drag her out. I think the royals want that. That moon will have a shifter or werewolf at its strongest. Even I'll feel it. That strength will be in their blood. I think they want to take your blood that night so it gives them the highest chance possible to open that vault."

"I guess that makes sense," I said.

"Right. These people have spent centuries kidnapping shifters and using their blood, then discarding them when they aren't strong enough. They've murdered innocent children. There is nothing they won't do. It has to be for the treasure that's supposed to be hidden there."

"What about the vial of blood? Isn't that the main thing they want?"

"I'm sure they probably want to destroy it, yeah, but the treasure has to be the true endgame. It belongs to the actual descendants, but that doesn't matter to them, of course."

Sure, they wanted the treasure, but there had to be more to it than this. The royals were already incredibly rich and powerful. What was a little more money when you already had billions? No, they wanted the vial. My mother's suspicions had seeped into me. The things I'd read inside that envelope had filled me with a sense of impending doom. Something sinister was on the way. Something that involved that small container of blood. I needed to get my mind off all this for a little while.

"Can we go check on my bar?" I said.

"Now?" Nico asked in surprise.

"Yeah. I just want to make sure things are okay. I miss it, and I haven't been by since we shut it down."

"As long as I go with you, sure. I don't want you going anywhere alone in town right now."

"I wouldn't have it any other way. I wouldn't feel safe on my own anyway."

"Let me grab my stuff, and we can go."

As we drove to the bar, my thoughts drifted to my staff. I'd spent so much time worrying and fretting about Abi that I hadn't really had the chance to think about how they were doing. I'd continued to send them paychecks every week, so they were being taken care of. I was sure they were enjoying the paid vacation, and I knew this was all temporary. Still, I loved the bar and the people who worked there.

Unable to help myself, I glanced at everyone we passed, wondering whether they were agents of the royals. They probably thought they had a boot on our necks, so the chance of them actually trying something right now was low. They needed me, so I was physically safe, but there was no reason they wouldn't try to kidnap me again. Having Nico by my side made me feel much safer.

A wave of sadness hit me as we stopped in the parking lot. I got out of the car and looked at my place. It looked dead and lifeless. It hurt my heart, and I promised myself things would change one way or another.

"I'm gonna go in and check around for a second."

"Need me to come in?"

"No, I won't be long. Just stay by the door. If I need you, I'll text you."

Nico seemed anxious about letting me go, but he didn't argue. I walked up the steps and unlocked the door. As soon as I stepped in, I relaxed. It was almost like coming home. I was happy to be there, but it also filled me with sadness. Abi wasn't here. She always helped me open. We'd spent so many hours here. The smell of the wood floors, the sweet-sour smell of spilled alcohol, and the scent of cooking grease from the kitchen mixed together. I smiled as a strange nostalgia came over me.

The smile that formed on my lips died as a new scent came wafting in, canceling the rest. The smell was both new but strangely familiar, and it absolutely shouldn't have been here. I yanked my phone out and sent Nico a text. I would have called out, but if anyone were in here, they'd hear me shouting.

Within seconds of me sending the text, Nico burst through the door. His head swiveled as he tried to see whether every shadow was a threat. He came to me and put an arm around me protectively.

"So you smell it?" I asked.

Nico sniffed at the air, then nodded. "I do. I think it's coming from the back. It's stronger toward your office."

Nico eased me behind him as we walked to my office. He moved slowly, cautiously. Even though the scent was faint, there was no telling what was back there. Every step forward was like a step toward the unknown. My office had always been one of the places I felt safest. Now, the wooden door held a fear of the unknown. My wolf was pacing inside my mind. She was as anxious and nervous as I was.

Nico reached out, his fingers brushing the doorknob. I had the strangest urge to yank his hand back as though he was going to burn himself. Clenching my jaw, I stopped myself from doing that. He spun the knob and pushed the door open. Instead of a dangerous enemy, a monster, or poison gas, all we saw was my empty office. It was a bit anticlimactic. I frowned as I glanced around, sure something had to be hiding in there.

Nico stepped through the threshold and turned in a circle, checking every corner. He looked at me and gave a little frown. "You came in here before you texted me?"

"Huh? No. I only made it to the main room out front."

His frown grew deeper, and he looked around the room once more. "That doesn't make sense. When's the last time you were in here?"

What the hell was he talking about? I shook my head, trying to remember. "It's been weeks. The last time I was in my office was when we came to shut everything down. I haven't even been in the building since then."

"Then why does this room smell like you? Not just like you, but like you were just in here not long ago?"

Chapter 26 - Nico

Maddy stared back at me like I was insane. I could tell by the look on her face that she was being honest. Then it hit me. Maddy's mother. That's who had to have been in here. I sniffed the air again. The smell was very similar to Maddy, and if you weren't paying attention, it could be mistaken for Maddy. She'd been here. In this very room.

After coming to that conclusion, I looked at Maddy. In her eyes, I saw that the same thought had occurred to her. I could see it dawning on her.

"Gabriella," I said, stating what was becoming obvious.

Maddy took a few tentative steps into the room and put her hand on the desk. "She was here? Right here?"

"It's the only thing that makes any sense."

"Yeah," Maddy said, nodding, "I guess it is, but why? Why would she come here?"

"I think she was the one who set fire to the house in Naples. She was the one who snuck in and made sure we found that safe. I never thought she'd follow us here, though."

Maddy huffed and started moving around the room, checking drawers and shelves. She was looking for anything that may have been left behind. It made sense. The last time Gabriella had snuck up on us, she'd left a massive amount of information. I joined Maddy and started to move around the room. We spent nearly ten minutes turning the place upside down. We even took the time to get on our hands and knees and look under the furniture.

When it became obvious that nothing had been left, Maddy's irritation kicked up a notch. Instead of placing things back neatly after she'd checked them, she let the items fall to the floor. After checking the last drawer of her desk, Maddy growled and yanked the entire drawer out, slinging the contents across the room.

"Are you okay? Maddy?"

Maddy ran her hands through her hair and gritted her teeth. "She was here. Inside my fucking business and couldn't be bothered to tell us why?"

"I'm not sure. Maybe—"

"She gave me away all those years ago, and it looked like she actually cared. If she cared, why won't she show herself to me? Why, Nico?" Tears were running down her cheeks.

Knowing that her birth mother had been this close twice in one week and hadn't bothered to speak to her or even leave another note seemed to break Maddy. She was under so much stress already that this was almost too much to bear. I could see it in the way her shoulders slumped and in the deep sadness in her eyes.

"She abandoned me," Maddy went on. "She abandoned me, and she's been here the whole time. Hiding. Not telling me who she was. How can someone do that when they say they love you? How can someone possibly do that to someone else?" Her voice had risen almost to a shout. I didn't try to calm her down. She needed to vent. So, I would let her vent.

When she finally went quiet and flopped into her chair, I sat on the desk and put a hand on her shoulder. As angry as she was, I tried to think about all the things I'd do to keep my own child out of harm's way. I didn't even know this woman, but for some reason, I felt like I needed to explain her motives. "You know she probably did it to keep you safe, right? Not saying that it was the right thing, but it's probably the main reason."

Maddy had a hand on her forehead as she looked up at me. "I realize that. It doesn't make me any less angry or frustrated. If she wanted me to be safe, wouldn't it be a lot easier to just fucking talk to me? All this weird cryptic shit is getting on my nerves. Why is this better than face-to-face?"

That was something I couldn't answer. Maddy was right—an in-person meeting would have made things much easier to understand. On the other hand, when someone had spent decades on the run and hiding, it was probably difficult to put that mindset aside. I could see both sides, but I loved Maddy. I had to side with her on this. It would be simpler for her birth mother to just come out of the shadows and tell us all that she knew.

I squeezed Maddy's shoulder. "Let's lock up and go home."

Maddy sighed sadly. "Yeah. Okay. I'm sorry I blew up like that."

"That's okay. It's what I'm here for."

"You're here to listen to me have a hissy fit like a spoiled child?"

"I wouldn't call it that. We'll call it... therapy."

Maddy chuckled. "Okay. I'm sorry, regardless."

We went through the building, turning the lights off as we went and making sure the back door was locked. This made me wonder exactly how

Maddy's birth mother had gotten into the bar in the first place since we had to unlock the front door. Once everything was locked up tight, Maddy and I walked back to the car. I'd parked parallel to the building, my driver's side door facing the road and the passenger side door facing the front of the bar. I helped Maddy up into the truck, and as she buckled in, I walked around the side to my door.

A bright yellow sticky note was stuck to my door, my name written in bold block letters at the top. Below it was a scribble of something else. I didn't take the time to read it. Instead, I yanked it off the door and shoved it into my pocket.

"Something wrong?" Maddy asked as I opened the door. "You look like you saw a ghost or something."

I shook my head. "I thought I saw a scratch in the paint. It was just a scuff of dirt. No big deal."

We drove home, mostly in silence. The whole way, I tried to think of why I'd snatched that note off my door and not told Maddy about it. Was it the fact that she'd already been through enough? She'd just gotten done spouting off about how pissed she was about all the cloak-and-dagger bullshit. Or was it because it had my name on the top? Was this something meant only for me? That seemed like a selfish and childish reason. Though, what if it was something dangerous? If that was the case, then I definitely wanted it to fall to me and not Maddy.

I tried to act casual, but the note in my pocket seemed to take on more and more weight with each hour that passed. I forced myself not to take it out. Whatever was written there might make it more difficult to keep up my façade. By the time I tucked

Maddy away in bed, it felt like there was a red-hot coal in my pocket, burning and blistering my skin.

"Aren't you coming to bed?" Maddy asked as I headed toward the door.

"In a bit. I'll be up later."

"Okay. Goodnight. Love you."

"Love you too. Sweet dreams."

I went to sit in the kitchen. With my hands clasped together, I stared at the wall. I managed to wait ten minutes, then pulled out my phone. I called Sebastian and Felipe over, telling them not to knock or ring the bell. I didn't want them waking Maddy.

"Bro? What's going on?" Felipe asked.

"I'll explain when you get here. Hurry up."

While I waited for them to get there, I pulled the note from my pocket. Below my name was an address and a time. Three o'clock tonight. My fingers shook as I stared at the note. It was definitely a woman's handwriting. My instincts told me Maddy's birth mother had left this for me. Was there really going to be a meeting?

I searched for the address on my phone. The satellite image showed a house on the outskirts of town. It wasn't in a subdivision. The house sat by itself on about two acres of land. It was just secluded enough to be a good spot for an ambush. I shoved that thought away quickly. The best place for an ambush would have been the bar today. If this was a trap, it was a poorly executed one. No, this was something else. Why only me—why not Maddy? Well, I wouldn't know until I got there.

Felipe and Sebastian arrived a few minutes later. They came in quietly, just as I'd told them to, though Sebastian was over exaggerating it by tiptoeing across the foyer tile.

"What's the big secret?" Felipe asked.

I glanced toward the stairs first, making sure Maddy hadn't come out of our room for some reason. "Maddy and I went to check on her bar today. I think she was getting sort of stir-crazy, and she missed the place. Anyway, we got there, and everything was untouched. Exactly like when she left it."

"I'm assuming we're going to come to a problem at some point?" Sebastian said.

"Getting there," I said. "We both catch a scent. It's not anything we recognize from the bar. Then it hits us. It's Maddy's birth mother."

"No shit?" Felipe said.

I nodded. "Yeah. It was similar to Maddy's smell but different enough for us to realize what was going on."

"But she wasn't there?" Sebastian asked.

"Not in the building. Maddy kind of lost her shit, understandably. She was pissed about her mom sneaking around her bar but not coming out to meet her. When we left, I found this." I handed the sticky note over to Felipe. He and Sebastian looked at it.

Sebastian raised an eyebrow. "You aren't going here, right? This sounds sketchy as shit."

"I thought the same thing at first, but there's no reason she'd attack me. And if it was some trick by the royals, they could have tried to take us right there at Maddy's bar. No, this is a legit meeting. I'm not stupid. That's why I called you guys over. Sebastian, I want you to stay with Maddy. Felipe, you're coming with me."

"Three o'clock?" Felipe said. "The witching hour?"

I rolled my eyes. "Trust me, the symbolism wasn't lost on me. Werewolves, shifters, and secret societies? Why not throw in a nod to witches? Are you ready to go?"

"A little early, isn't it?"

"It's a bit of a drive to the outer edge of town, and it wouldn't hurt to get there early and check the perimeter. I don't think this is a trap, but there's no reason to go in totally blind."

An hour later, Felipe and I pulled up a half-mile from the address. We went the rest of the way on foot, walking in silence, not discussing anything, simply doing what needed to be done. I loved Sebastian like a brother, but he liked to talk when he was nervous, and this was *not* the time for that.

The house looked safe. We made two different circuits. Once at a five hundred yards out, and another at a hundred. Neither of us saw anything that looked like a trap. There were also no signs of the royals' soldiers. This place was clean. Felipe and I sat in the woods, and a quick glance at my watch told me it was time to move in.

"Ready?" I asked.

Felipe nodded but gave me a weird look. "I'm ready, but do you think anyone is in there?"

I glanced at the house again. Even from a hundred yards away, I could see what he was saying. The lights were on, but the house *felt* empty. There were no shadows passing by the windows, no lights turning off or back on, and there didn't seem to be a car in the driveway.

"Only one way to find out," I said.

The walk up to the house was strange. It felt like we were here to peddle something like traveling salesmen or religious missionaries. *Hello, do you have time to talk about our Lord and Savior Edemas?* I shook the thoughts away as we stepped inside the gated fence that cordoned off the front yard. Felipe nudged me and gestured toward the porch. The front door wasn't fully ajar, but it was definitely open a crack, a sliver of light clearly visible. I nodded to him, letting him know I'd seen.

At the top of the stairs, I took a tentative step up to the door. I gave the wood a single sharp knock. The front door swung in about three inches. Felipe nodded to me, so I pushed the door the rest of the way open. The brightness of the interior hurt our eyes after being in the dark for so long.

"Hello?" I called. There was no answer.

Felipe and I walked through the house, announcing our presence. There was no one here. Our instincts had been correct. I kicked a chair in the living room, releasing my frustrations.

"Nico? I found something," Felipe said from the kitchen.

I rushed to the kitchen, where Felipe stood at the kitchen table. I looked down at what he'd found and released an irritated sigh. On the table was another damned envelope. My name was written on it in black marker.

"What is this damned woman playing at? I don't like games," I hissed as I picked up the envelope and opened it.

Felipe gasped, and my eyes widened. Maddy's birth mother wasn't playing games. She was giving us more information. Stuff we'd never have gotten on our own.

"You've gotta call Luis," Felipe said as we dug through the contents.

I pulled out my phone and dialed. Miraculously, Luis answered on the second ring. "What the hell is wrong?" he asked, obviously barely awake.

"Call off the plan. Right now. We don't need it. We've got something better," I said, trying to keep my voice calm.

"What? Hang on." There was a rustling as Luis probably sat up in bed. "What are you talking about?"

"Maddy's birth mother. She just gave us the fucking mother load. We don't have to do a blind breach on these houses." I looked down at the pile of information. "I've got pictures of the safe houses, pictures of Maddy's parents and Abi. Shit, man, her father was moved to a different house. We didn't even fucking know that. There are three houses, for Christ's sake."

"Holy shit, are you serious? A third safe house? I… sonofabitch… what else is there?" Luis sounded fully awake and greedy for intel.

"There's schematics for each house, bypass codes for all the security systems at each house—"

"Fuck me, Nico," Felipe said, holding up a piece of paper. "Look at this shit. How the hell did she get this?"

The paper he handed me had a list of addresses. It was easy to see they were the three safe houses. Below each address was a list of names with times beside them. The times were for ten-hour increments. It took a second for me to realize what I was looking at. "Oh damn. Hot damn."

"What? What the hell is it?" Luis screeched.

"It's the security team's schedule. The times they're on duty, off duty, on break, and their fucking names!"

"You're shitting me," Luis said, sounding as stunned as I felt. "Do we think it's legit? Is this good intel?"

"Listen, I have no way of knowing how the hell she got this stuff, but there's no reason for her to lie. No reason she'd give us all this only to send us to our deaths. All this woman has done since the moment she got pregnant with Maddy was to keep her safe and out of the hands of the royals. We have to believe this is accurate, but we need to move soon. Who knows how long these schedules or security codes will stay up to date."

"Okay, okay. I'll let the guys know the original plan is off. Do you want me to head back home right away?"

"Yeah, get back here. I need to think about this before we start planning something new. Once you get back here, we'll make a plan."

We hung up, and Felipe had all the items stuffed back into the envelope. One more check around the house, and we were out the door. I was exhausted, both physically and mentally, as we started walking back to my car. When we got to the end of the driveway, we heard a voice call out of the darkness.

"Protect my daughter. Protect her because I can't anymore."

Felipe and I whirled in the direction of the sound. She'd called out from a pretty good way off, and the voice had been quieted by the surrounding trees and distance. If it hadn't been almost four in the morning, we probably never would have heard her. There was a moment where I thought about bolting, shifting, and trying to chase her down. Corner her and get real answers. At the back of my mind, though, I knew she'd have planned for that. She'd be gone before I ever got there.

Chapter 27 - Maddy

The sound of closing doors and voices woke me up. I lay in bed for several seconds, trying to figure out what was going on. It sounded like a dozen people were downstairs. Had something happened? No one was screaming or yelling, but the voices sounded urgent and perhaps excited.

I dressed as quickly as I could and made my way downstairs. My feet froze halfway down the steps. There really were about a dozen people all over the house. Nico's dad and brothers were running around, several of them on phones. Felipe and Sebastian were at the kitchen island, standing over a pile of what looked like papers and printouts. Nico and his friends looked terrible. All three of them had deep dark circles under their eyes. Had none of them gone to sleep last night?

A few other members of the pack were bringing in large takeout containers of food. None of this made any sense. My anxiety started to escalate. This much activity had to mean something had happened. Something big.

Mateo walked by with a phone to his ear. I only caught half of what he was saying. "You tell him to figure it out. I don't care..." His voice trailed off as he moved through the house.

Nico glanced up mid-sentence and saw me. He gestured me over. When I got there, he dug out a food container from one of the bags. "Here, I ordered breakfast for everyone. No time to cook, and we all need the energy."

He sat me down and opened the container. It held an omelet, bacon, and a few slices of toast. "Nico, what the hell is going on?" I asked, ignoring the food.

"I promise, I'll explain, but you do need to eat. All of us do."

Grudgingly, I set about eating breakfast. I wasn't actually hungry, but something about Nico's demeanor told me I should follow orders. Around me, the pack continued moving about. The entire house had the feeling of a stock-market trading floor. Everyone was moving at a speed of a million miles an hour. The food passed my lips and went down my throat, but I couldn't have told anyone what it tasted like if my life depended on it.

Once I was done, I stood and walked over to Nico. "Okay, what the fuck is going on? This is madness," I said, sweeping my hand across the room, gesturing to everyone.

"Okay." Nico pulled me aside into his massive pantry. "Yesterday at the bar? You remember when we left?"

My brow furrowed as I squinted at him. "Of course. What about it?"

"Your birth mother left me a note. It was stuck to my driver's side door. Right where only I could see it. It had an address and time. Last night at three in the morning."

I gaped at him. Was he being serious? She really had been right there?

"Seriously?"

"Yes. I didn't want to say anything to you until I had it figured out. The note also said only I was supposed to come. Not you. Felipe and I went late last night. She wasn't in the house when we got there. What we did find was another envelope."

I gritted my teeth in irritation. "More envelopes? What is this? Can't she come out and say it for once?"

Nico gave me a sad smile. "That's sort of what I said, but that doesn't matter right now. What was in that envelope was huge. Gabriella somehow managed to get a massive amount of security info on the royals' safe houses. Stuff we'd never have known without her. Maddy, your dad was moved to a different house. It's not just two safe houses now; it's three. She also got us the bypass codes for the security systems at each house. Biggest of all, she got us the names and schedules of all the guys working security at the houses. We've got a real chance here. She gave us everything we needed."

My jaw was open. I couldn't have been more shocked if the Easter Bunny had come hopping into the room. First, how had she managed to get that? Second, did this mean we'd be getting my family back safe? I'd prayed that we would be successful, but a small part of me still thought I'd be attending funerals in the near future. The excitement I saw in Nico's eyes gave me genuine hope for the first time since they were taken.

"You didn't see her at all?" I asked.

Nico shook his head. "No, I didn't see her. I did hear her, though."

"Hear her? What do you mean?"

"As Felipe and I were leaving, she yelled at us. She had to be at least a couple of hundred yards away. It was faint but audible. She told me I had to protect you because she couldn't anymore."

My eyes were locked onto Nico's. My body seized up tight like a bowstring. "What do you think that means?"

"I'm honestly not sure. It's probably the fact that she can't get us any more information. She's leaving your safety in my hands now that she's exhausted all her sources."

A deep, inexplicable sadness spread within me. It was almost heartbreak. Something about this whole thing felt so final. For my entire life, I'd never had any desire to meet my birth mother, but once all this started moving like an unstoppable freight train, my thoughts changed. I wanted to meet her now. It was like I'd been cheated out of something. Would I never get to talk to her? Each day that passed seemed like it was less and less likely.

Closing my eyes, I tried to push those thoughts away. Instead, I tried to focus on what was happening now. "Show me what she gave us."

Nico gestured to the kitchen island and showed me the stack of papers. I saw the pictures of Mom, Dad, and Abi. There were blueprints that had been blown up until they were almost the same size as the island itself. They showed each building perfectly.

Nico pointed at them. "She gave us the standard sizes. I called a guy in town who makes banners and signs and stuff. Paid out of the ass to get him up early to blow these up to size for us. It makes it easier to see what we're looking at."

Nico's father walked over, holding a notepad. "Nico?" he asked. "I think I've got a good plan started. Do you want to go over it with me?"

Before Nico could answer, the front door opened, and Luis barged in, looking harried and exhausted. "Made it!" he called as he stepped inside.

Nico glanced at his watch in confusion. "How the hell did you get here so fast? I called you barely four hours ago."

"Got lucky with flight times. Landed about forty-five minutes ago and hauled ass over here. Let's see what we've got."

We all sat around the living room going over the intel. Nico and his father went back and forth on how best to orchestrate the rescues. Luis gave them the information he and the lizard shifters were able to glean from their infiltration. The plan was coming together, but there was one bit of information we didn't have.

Nico looked at Luis. "Those guards said they were moving Abi soon? Right?"

Luis nodded grimly. "They did."

Nico's dad leaned back on the sofa and put his hands on his knees. "So, the real question is, are they moving them all to the mother's location, the father's location, or an entirely new fourth location that we don't know?"

"We have no way of knowing," Nico said. "That means we've got to move fast. This has to be done before they move them. My guess is it'll be a totally new location."

"What's the play?" Felipe asked.

"I don't think we'll need a ton of manpower," Nico said. "Not with the information we have. It'll still be complicated getting three different operations to happen at the exact same time. It'll be three teams, and we need to move in the next thirty-six to forty-eight hours. If we wait longer than that, we may find ourselves breaking into empty houses. Our one shot will have been pissed away."

"We can do this. I know we can," Nico's brother Rafael said. He looked driven and ready. I'd spent more time with Nico's friends than I had his brothers, but all of them sat around the room, and each one looked as ready to go into battle as Nico did. It filled me with happiness and comfort to know this entire pack was ready to fight for my family.

One part of the plan didn't sit right with me. Throughout all the discussion, there was no mention of me. It was easy to see that I would be left behind.

I pointed this out, and the room went silent. Multiple eyes went to Nico, but no one said anything. Finally, Nico cleared his throat. "I think it's best if you stay here, where you'll be safe."

It made rational sense, but it didn't mean I had to like it. "Can't I at least go with you, Nico? If I have to sit here waiting to get a phone call that someone I love is dead, it'll drive me crazy."

"You have to stay out of this. If you go out into the field, it'll give the royals the opportunity to snatch you. You have to remember that's what this is all about. They kidnapped your family and friends to force you to give yourself over to them. You'd be playing right into their hands if you went with us. If I had a guess, this will be chaos at best. All it would take is for you to be out of my sight for a second," he snapped his fingers for emphasis, "and they'd have you. I couldn't live with that."

I'd started unconsciously biting at my nails as he spoke. Everything he said was accurate. All of it. That didn't mean I had to like it. I pulled my hand away from my mouth. "I'm worried, Nico. I'm scared one of you won't make it back. You, your friends or family, my parents or Abi. I'm terrified that's going to happen, and I'm going to be sitting here on my ass, useless."

Nico's father leaned forward and put a hand on my thigh. The warmth of his fingers sent a wave of comfort through me. There was something about a father's touch, even when it wasn't my father, that could ease the fears of a scared child. He looked me in the eye and nodded. "Julia and I will be here with you, as well as the rest of the pack who won't be going on this mission. All of us. Don't worry about Nico. My boy is smart and strong. All my boys are."

I chewed at my lip and nodded at him. "I know. Thank you. What do we do when they retaliate though?" I asked. "If—no, *when*—we succeed, they'll be pissed. There's going to be retribution, isn't there?"

Nico glanced around the room and nodded hesitantly. "Yeah, probably. We can't worry about it. One crisis at a time. The number one priority is to get your family back to you. After that, we'll deal with the counter punch the royals throw. That's all we can do."

"Okay," I said. "I trust you. All of you," I added, looking around the room at the men who were getting ready to put their lives on the line to save my parents and best friend. Tears welled in my eyes. This was the type of thing that showed what humanity really was. There were those who would say these people weren't truly human, and maybe they weren't, but in many ways, they were even *more* human than people who weren't shifters. Bravery, sacrifice, courage, love, and force of will—those things were the best parts of the human race. After this, if I ever met a bigot who thought shifters were second-class citizens or beneath full-blooded humans, I'd probably have to be dragged off them.

The rest of the day slowly returned to normal. The three rescue teams were formed, and everyone dispersed to their own homes to pack bags and make final preparations. Plane tickets for the next morning were purchased. By the time the sun went down, only Nico and I were left in the house. We'd skipped lunch in all our planning and discussion. My appetite had disappeared, but Nico managed to get me to eat some chicken salad and crackers for dinner. Even that light meal seemed to sit in my stomach like a lead weight.

After I ate, I made my way outside to do my new favorite thing—stare at the ever-fattening moon. The milky whiteness was much brighter than usual tonight. The familiar pull was strong, tugging at my bones and muscles. The connection was so strong, I could even feel it in my hair. I imagined I could close my eyes and actually float into the air, held aloft by nothing more than the moon's gravity.

Nico came out to join me not long afterward. He sat beside me and put an arm around my shoulders. "How are you feeling? Be honest."

"That obvious?"

He nodded and grinned. "I could feel your worry all the way inside the house. Mates share a deep bond, remember? When you're happy, I'm happy. The same goes for bad feelings too."

I let out a slow breath, then said, "I'm worried about you. I'm worried about everyone. I'm scared the people I love are going to die. It's too much to handle."

Nico pulled me closer. "Nothing in this world is going to hold me back from returning to you. I would literally cut down mountains if they were between you and me. Nothing will stop me. That's one thing you don't have to worry about."

I leaned into him, grateful that he was trying to ease my fears. He'd probably never know how much it meant to me. His hand slowly drifted down my back to my tailbone, then slid back up. His fingers slipped along my back in a gentle motion, but I could hear his heart. The speed of the beating told me he was getting excited. Letting him continue to rub my back, I trailed my fingers across his knee, down his thigh, until I was right at his crotch. I could feel his bulging hard-on beneath his jeans.

Nico grunted and leaned into my ear. "Do you wanna go to bed?"

"Mmhmm," I said and got up off the seat.

He took my hand and led me inside and up the stairs. Both of us knew what the other wanted—needed. There was no need for preamble. I wanted him, and he wanted me. A part of my consciousness told me this might very well be the last night we would have together. If things went wrong, I would never get to hold him in my arms again. If that were true, I wanted this night to be a night I could always bring back up in my memory—one perfect night of passion and happiness.

Nico pulled his clothes off, and I took in every movement. The way his abs flexed as he took off his shirt, the contraction of the muscles of his arms and forearms as he slid his pants and shoes off. He moved with such fluid grace that I was already wet before he was halfway done. There was something about a man who was so confident in his motions that made me hot. He tugged his underwear off, and his cock sprang free. The thick, muscular appendage bounced twice before going fully rigid.

My own undressing went similarly. I stood at the far side of the room, stripping off layers, all while Nico drank in my body. It was almost like he was making love to me with his eyes as I got undressed. The cool air made goose flesh rise up all over my body once I was naked. Not waiting for him to make the first move, I stepped forward, crossing the room in three quick steps. Once I was close, I pressed my body to his. His hardness slipped up my belly. The warmth of his chest on my breasts sent another pulse of lust between my legs.

Nico kissed me, cupping the back of my head and pulling me close. The desperate desire in that kiss alone almost sent me over the edge. I'd never felt so wanted, so *needed*. I moaned into his lips as heat pooled between my legs. His free hand slid across my stomach until it found my breast. Sighing, I pulled my lips from his, looking down to watch him play with my nipple. A pleasant electrical tingle ran from my chest to my clit, and I could feel it engorge, pulsing in time to the beat of my heart.

Nico lowered himself to his knees, peppering kisses over my chest and stomach. He paused long enough to flick his tongue over my right nipple, eliciting a gasp from me as he moved lower. He turned me and pressed me against the wall before lifting my left leg over his shoulder. I was pinned against the wall as he pressed his face against my pussy.

I groaned with pleasure as his tongue slipped deep into me and threw my head back until I was staring at the ceiling, reveling in the feeling of him licking me. He slid in and out of me, fucking me with his tongue. His right thumb moved up to rub at my clit, the left pressing gently against my anus. My head spun as the orgasm built quickly. The rhythm of his thumb and his tongue had me arching my back, pressing my crotch into his face, desperate for more.

I dug my fingernails into the wall, trying to find purchase. My body was about to explode. Then it happened—the building wave, the growing mountain of pleasure. It seeped out from my pussy to my inner thighs, then sent waves of heat up my stomach and lower back. My world seemed to snap like a twig. I groaned through gritted teeth as I came, hard and unyielding, but Nico didn't pull away. If anything, the pace of his tongue and finger increased. My breath hissed in and out of my nose and mouth as wave after wave rose and crashed over me.

Trembling, I dragged myself away from his mouth. I wanted him inside me, more than anything I'd ever wanted. Tugging at his shoulders, I made him stand, then pushed him onto the bed. His cock stood straight, rock hard, and waiting for me. Without hesitation, I wrapped my lips around the head and then enveloped all of it. The hot, thick flesh slid across the roof of my mouth, and my tongue pressed and flicked the underside of his cock until I felt it at the back of my throat. When I raised my head, I glanced up and saw a look of ecstasy on Nico's face. I kept eye contact as my head bobbed up and down again and again. Every time I came back up, I sucked hard at the head and ran my tongue teasingly over it.

"Jesus, Maddy, I'm not going to last if you keep that up," Nico whispered, his voice husky with desire.

I let him slide out of my mouth and grinned at him. "Well, we don't want that."

His cock quivered as I stroked him three more times. I sat up and crawled onto him, positioning my hips right over him. Slowly, I lowered myself. As the lips of my pussy spread apart, allowing him to enter, I watched his face. The look of pure bliss I saw there brought a smile to my face, and I started to ride him.

I tilted my hips so my clit rubbed against him with each movement. Nico took hold of my breasts, massaging and clutching, as he grew ever closer to coming. I had my hands splayed on his chest to keep my balance. Through my fingers, I could almost feel his heart trying to break through his rib cage as his hips rose and fell in time with mine.

My nails dug into the flesh of his chest as another orgasm reached its crescendo. Nico grabbed my hips, slamming me down onto his cock. I gave myself over to him as I rode out the wave of my orgasm. This time it was a sharper, more focused orgasm, as though it was concentrated directly on my clit. I lay my head on his chest until I felt the throbbing pulse of him deep inside me. Nico let out a long, slow groan as his thrusting slowed until he finally stilled.

We lay together like that, catching our breath for a long time as the sweat cooled on our skin. While we recovered, I sent up another prayer, pleading with God to make sure everyone came home safe. I didn't know how I would survive losing anyone, especially not Nico.

Chapter 28 - Nico

My parents came over right before we all left for the airport. Dad told me he wanted them to be there to support Maddy while we were gone. I appreciated that my mother was also there. She and Maddy had made up, but action meant more than words. It looked like they really were in a good place.

"Nico, honey. My boy, you be safe. Understand?" Mom said as I picked up my bags.

"I will, Mom. I need to get out of here. The van will be here in a minute," I said.

Maddy came out of the living room and hugged me tightly. She'd barely said a word all morning, and I was certain she was thinking about the worst possible outcomes. I wrapped my arms around her, inhaling her glorious scent. For weeks, I'd felt like all this was happening because of me. Maddy was racked with guilt, but she was in this by accident. Her parents and Abi being taken was my burden to bear. The only reason they'd been taken was because the guys I'd hired to watch over them hadn't been prepared. I should have warned them to be ready for something like this happening, then perhaps they'd have managed to keep them out of harm's way. All I could do to make up for it was to ensure I was the one who saved them.

"I'll be back soon," I whispered into Maddy's ear.

Her head bobbed up and down in a nod against my chest. "I know. Just make sure it's on two feet."

"I'll even be tap dancing if you want," I joked.

Maddy couldn't help but laugh. "In a tight little leotard or something?"

I nodded. "If my lady wishes."

Without another word, she kissed me. Her lips stayed on mine for a long time. No matter what I said or how much Maddy told me she believed me, the kiss had the distinct feeling of *goodbye*. When we finally pulled apart, Dad looked at me over her shoulder and tilted his head in the direction of the door. It was time to go.

Mom came over and gently pulled Maddy away from me. "Come on now, sweetie. Nico needs to go. Can you help me in the kitchen? I was thinking of baking some loaves of bread for tonight. Are you much of a baker?"

Maddy obliged and went along with Mom. She glanced over her shoulder as I stepped out the door, tears shining in her eyes. When I closed the door behind me, I took a couple of deep breaths before making my way down to the cul-de-sac where the fifteen-passenger van sat. Diego and Mateo had picked it up early this morning.

The side door slid open, and Sebastian leaned out. "Get in, loser! We're going to go save the day."

Once we got to the airport, we split into our teams. Sebastian hadn't budged on wanting to rescue Abi. He, Luis, and Mateo would head to Abi's safe house. Javi had surprised me by volunteering to go on one of the teams. I'd called him the night before to let him know what was going on, and he'd been hell-bent on going with us. He was with Gabriel and Rafael and would go after Maddy's dad in Oklahoma.

Felipe, Diego, and I would go after Maddy's mother in Chicago.

The nine of us huddled together and sorted out the tickets. Once everyone had what they needed, the three teams split up and walked to our respective gates. There was no big goodbye speech, no last hugs, no final declarations of brotherly love. It all seemed so tenuous that even attempting any of those things felt like it might tip the scales against us.

We'd all been on edge since we arrived at the airport. The walk to the plane did nothing to push away those feelings. Each and every one of us knew that failure wasn't an option. I'd done everything in my power to make sure this would go off smoothly. I'd even rented two vans identical to the one we'd used and had other members of the pack drive them. On the highway, we'd played three-card monte, swapping places, taking different exits from each other, coming back together, and then finally going in three different directions. If there'd been a tail, there was a much lower chance that we'd been followed. Hopefully, they thought we were either driving to Atlanta or Louisiana like the other two vans.

Felipe and Diego sat with me in the same row, but for the most part, we didn't talk on the two-and-a-half-hour flight. I tried to kill time by watching a movie but gave up after an hour. I couldn't keep track of what was happening. Instead, I pulled out the folder with all the information Maddy's birth mother had given us.

I'd already committed the blueprints and security codes to memory, but it was comforting to know I had my hands on the information. I was trying to memorize the security teams' lunch schedules, but that was more to keep my mind occupied. The only times we really needed to worry about were five o'clock in the afternoon and midnight. That was when the two shifts switched off. And at midnight, we'd make our move. God help us all.

Once we landed in Chicago, I sent Maddy a quick text, letting her know we'd arrived:

We made it. I love you. See you soon.

Maddy replied within seconds.

I love you too. Be careful!

Felipe, Diego, and I disembarked and headed straight for the rental car kiosk. The plan was for Diego to rent a car and go ahead of us. He'd scope out the area and see if everything looked like it was supposed to. The other teams would be following the same plan.

Felipe and I rented our own car and sent Diego on his way. We killed time by having lunch in an airport restaurant. As we were finishing our meal, Diego called me.

"Hey, big brother. I got good news."

"Let's hear it," I said.

"Everything is exactly like it should be. Looks good. No extra men, nothing out of the ordinary. I think if we can see the shift change happen as the schedule says at five, we're golden."

"Okay. We'll grab our car and meet you at the hotel. You still have the address?"

"Yeah. See you there."

On the ride over, I sent the other teams a text message letting them know we were a go. The others responded not long after. They'd found the same thing we had. The safe houses looked ripe for the picking. Things really seemed to be looking up.

We met up with Diego and all got into the same car before heading back for another recon drive-by of the house. The whole neighborhood was in various stages of construction. It looked like none of the homes were even occupied. We parked three blocks away, and I used the binoculars I'd brought to zoom in on the house. At five p.m. on the dot, a black SUV pulled up in front of the house. Six men piled out of the car as six others exited the building. They all wore the standard clothing of construction workers. They were hiding the fact that all these men were coming and going from a residential house by playing it off as construction. Cute. No one would call the cops if it seemed like all these guys were doing was working and trading out shifts, even if it was in the middle of the night.

Once the day-shift security left, the SUV pulled away from the curb. I glanced at the others. "Looks like we go at midnight."

"How ominous," Diego said. There was no humor in his voice.

"Let's head back to the hotel room. Try to take a nap. I've barely slept the last couple of days," I said as I turned the car in the direction of the hotel.

A few hours later, we were back in the car. To my surprise, I actually *had* been able to sleep for a couple of hours. Diego and Felipe both seemed well rested. Nevertheless, the trip to the house was stressful. The drive had the distinct feeling of a trip on the River Styx. Instead of Diego at the wheel, it was Charon the boatman, steering us toward death.

I shook that thought away, not wanting to fill my head with dark nonsense. I had enough to worry about without fantasies and nightmares taking over. My hands were clenched into fists on top of my knees. I was doing my best to keep them from shaking. I knew I was brave, but bravery wasn't a lack of fear, it was being able to push through the fear.

We pulled up a few hundred yards from the house, and Diego decided to park in the driveway of a house with a For Sale sign out front. I pulled out my phone and called Luis first.

"Luis, it's Nico. Are you guys in position?"

"Yeah," Luis whispered. "Good to go."

I checked my watch. "Seven minutes until midnight. As soon as the night shift pulls away, we make the move. We've got to keep it coordinated. Good?"

"On it, brother."

"Cool." I called Javi next. His team was ready and on the same page. All that was left was the countdown.

I was thankful all the locations were in the same time zone. Was that an oversight by the royals? Or was it blind luck? Either way, I was happy with it. Otherwise, there was no way this would have been a success, even with all the information Maddy's mother had given us.

"Car pulling up," Diego whispered.

Through the windshield, I saw the black SUV creeping up the road to the house. I sent one last text to the rest of the teams:

Good to go! Be careful.

I gave a curt nod, and Diego, Felipe, and I got out of the car, closing the doors as quietly as we could. The moon was masked by clouds, so the only light was the few street lights in the neighborhood. As Diego, Felipe, and I slunk through the shadows between houses, I kept an eye on the switching teams. There were some exchanged words, handshakes here and there, then the departing team piled into the car and pulled away.

Adrenaline surged through my body, making me feel both nauseous and excited at the same time. My pupils dilated, giving me even better night vision, and my breathing became quicker and shallower. This was the precipice, the last moment before we descended into chaos. I gritted my teeth and released a deep, rumbling growl before breaking into a run.

Diego and Felipe followed closely behind. The front door closed when we were less than fifty feet away. The men inside would already be dispersing to their watch posts. They'd have no idea what was coming for them. I leaped all six steps on the porch in one jump, landing softly in front of the security beside the door. From memory, I punched in the nine-digit code and held my breath. An instant later, the red ARMED icon changed to a green DISARMED icon.

I heaved a sigh of relief and glanced back at the guys, nodding once. Taking two steps back to get a running start, I burst forward, then took three heavy steps before lowering my shoulder and slamming my full weight and all my shifter strength into the door.

The cracking of the wood sounded like a gun going off. The explosion of wood, hinges, and glass burst through the night like the first cannon fire of war. War was exactly what this was. I crashed to the floor with the rest of the door. Felipe and Diego leaped through the opening, already shifting into their wolf forms. Before getting to my feet, I glanced around, taking stock of what we were up against, and my insides turned to liquid.

I saw four of the six men. Each one had already slung silenced submachine guns on their shoulders. They were startled but not as shocked as

I'd hoped. These were, unfortunately, well-trained men.

An older man with short blond hair fired a burst of rounds in Diego's direction, the silenced gun coughing out bullets. I watched in horror as the bullets punched holes in the wall, almost as though they were chasing my brother across the room. I shifted and sprang at the blond man. From the corner of his eye, he saw me coming and turned the rifle toward me. He was able to get off one shot, the bullet barely grazing my ribs, drawing a line of fire across my fur and skin. I buried my teeth into his throat, his larynx cracking between my powerful jaw. I turned away, leaving him to writhe and gag as he suffocated to death.

My instincts told me to move. I tucked my wolf body into a roll an instant before a burst of gunfire ripped through the drywall where I'd been standing a moment before. A grizzled-looking man with face tattoos stood there, teeth bared, screaming incomprehensible curses at us as he continued to fire at me. I sprinted around the room, drawing the attention away from my team. I ran into the kitchen, using the walls to guard me against gunfire. Once I circled through the dining room and back to the living room, Felipe had already tackled the tattooed man.

Felipe's jaw was clamped around the barrel of the gun. The man below was trying to push Felipe up and away. I saw it a moment before it happened—too fast for me to do anything to stop it. The man couldn't get his gun free. Instead, he pushed up to give his other arm access to his belt. A knife flashed up out of a sheath at his side. The arching blade moved like it was in slow motion, I howled out a warning to Felipe, but it was too late. The blade buried itself to the hilt into his body. He yowled in pain and tumbled away from the man.

With no idea how badly he was hurt, I snarled at the man and hit him full force, knocking the gun away from him. His knife was still inside Felipe, so the guard had no weapons left but his own hands. He screamed and fought back, pressing against my face and chest. One hand came too close to my jaw, and I clamped my teeth shut. The sound of three of his fingers snapping off was cathartic, and the echo of his screams was even better. This man might have just killed one of my best friends. His people wanted to bleed my mate dry. He deserved nothing better than this. I tore into his throat and left him bleeding on the floor, then spun in place to see if Diego was okay.

He had already shifted back to his human form and stood over the other two men. One looked dead, and the other was unconscious on his side. I shifted back and took a step toward him.

"You good?" I called.

"Yeah. Felipe?"

I turned and saw my friend slumped on the ground, a pool of blood slowly spreading under his body. My voice caught in my throat. "I... I don't—"

My words were cut off by another round of silenced gunfire. We were caught in some kind of crossfire. A man from upstairs was firing down at us, and someone else in the basement was shooting up the stairs toward us. My brother and I leaped toward the kitchen to safety.

The house wasn't complete, the walls were naked drywall, and the cabinets hadn't even been installed yet. There weren't a ton of places to hide. Panic started to swirl in my head and chest. I tried to steady myself, but the gunfire and screams of my enemies made that difficult.

"What do we do?" Diego shouted over the cacophony.

"Upstairs. We have to take him out first. He's got the high ground."

Diego looked around, and a patch of drywall exploded beside his head, bullets ripping into the plywood of the floor. "Any fucking ideas on how to do that, big brother?"

I took two deep breaths and nodded. "I'll run through the living room. The ceiling is vaulted, so there should be a banister or something he'll be shooting from. How high can you jump?"

"As a wolf? I don't know. Eight, maybe nine feet."

"When he's focused on me, you jump up and go for him."

"But—"

I was running before he could protest further. I had to move before the two men came together. Once that happened, we'd be done for. I sprinted across the kitchen in the same circuit I'd taken a few seconds earlier. I shifted, pushing myself to run faster. When I came out into the living room, I could almost feel the man's eyes and barrel lock on to me. I could hear the burst of gunfire erupting behind me. I ran and cut hard, sliding around a corner as a trail of holes opened in the floor beside my feet, inches from me. I heard the click of an empty chamber. The man was already dropping his clip and grabbing another.

A shadow emerged from the kitchen. Diego. I howled at the man, making sure his attention stayed on me as he reloaded. Diego galloped from the dining room and jumped. In an act of pure canine acrobatics, he leaped and placed his back paws on the lower newel post, then sprang upward nearly ten feet toward my assailant. The barrel of the gun, freshly loaded, turned toward me. I saw the inky black tube of the rifle staring at me like the eye of death. An instant before he pulled the trigger, Diego's jaw clamped on the man's trigger hand. His teeth sank deep, and the gun twisted as it fired. I felt the wind of three bullets as they whizzed by my head.

Diego used the full weight of his body to jerk the man's hand. His teeth were fully embedded in the man's flesh. It pulled the shooter off balance, and he tumbled over the edge of the banister. Diego let go once the man flipped over and fell straight down. I watched him turn his head and look at the floor before he landed on his face, the weight of his body crashing down above him. The sound of his neck snapping was like a wet stick breaking.

He lay in a heap of broken flesh on the floor. Before I could catch my breath, a voice shouted out behind us.

"Freeze, you fuckers!"

Diego and I shifted and turned to see the sixth guard standing at the top of the stairs. He had Maddy's mother's neck locked in one arm and a pistol pressed against her head with the other. She was sobbing and looked to be on the verge of going into shock. Her face was pale and gaunt.

"You move, and I blow this bitch's brains all over the wall. Got it?"

I raised my hands in supplication. My brain was spinning to find a way out of this. We were still two against one. There had to be a way.

The man spat on the ground in front of us. "The royals are gonna skin you fucking shifters alive. You understand that? No one stands against them. Pieces of shit." He pushed toward the door, and we had to back up. He looked like he'd pull the trigger any instant.

Forcing my voice to be calm, I said, "Listen, you can still get out of this. Leave the woman, and we'll let you go. No harm, no foul. Okay?"

The man gave a humorless chuckle. "Do you think I'm stupid? Why would I ever trust a shifter?" He sneered in disgust and turned the gun barrel toward me. "Maybe I'll go ahead and—"

His words were cut off by a scream. My whole body jerked, thinking I'd been shot. I looked down and saw Felipe's wolf jaw clamped around the man's Achilles heel. Blood spurted from the man's leg. Diego bolted forward and swatted the gun from the man's hand. I ran straight toward the guard, who was still screaming in pain. Maddy's mother finally slipped out of his grip, and I kicked him dead in the chest, his ribcage cracking from the blow. He flew backward through the door to the basement and tumbled down the stairs.

Diego took Maddy's mom into his arms, and she started to sob. She was having trouble standing, which made me think she'd been drugged. I knelt down to check on Felipe. He shifted back to human form, the knife still sticking out of his stomach.

Felipe grimaced in pain. "Fucker got me, Nico."

"Nah, bro, looks like you got him."

"We need to go, Nico," Diego said, hustling Maddy's mother toward the door. "They might have had time to call the guys who just left. No way we can take another six guys."

I scooped Felipe in my arms and stood, doing my best to keep the knife in his gut from moving. "Jesus Christ, man. You need to lose some weight. You're one heavy son of a bitch," I grunted as I walked toward the door.

"Well, I didn't ask you to sweep me off my feet like a princess. I hope you don't think you're getting lucky with this whole chivalry thing. You're cute and all, but I prefer the ladies." Felipe hissed in pain as we went down the steps.

The walk back to the car seemed to take forever. I kept waiting for headlights to come sweeping around the corner, for the reinforcements to come and finish us off. That would be the end of us. Felipe groaned in pain as I got him into the back seat.

"Diego, find the nearest shifter clinic. We need to get Felipe some help, and I don't trust any human doctors. They could have been paid off."

Diego started searching on his phone and looked over at me as I got into the driver's seat. "Couldn't the shifters have been paid off too? I mean, Javi's pack used to work for these people."

I nodded. "Yeah, but the chances are lower. Look at him. We've got to get him help. He's bleeding out."

"Okay, there's one about ten minutes from here. Says it's a twenty-four-seven clinic."

Diego gave me the address, and I punched the gas. We'd had a much harder time than I'd anticipated, which made me worry about the other teams. Were my friends or family dead somewhere? Had Abi or Maddy's father been killed? So many thoughts and so many terrible possibilities. I needed to call Maddy, but I had to get Felipe to help first. If that knife had punctured an organ, we might lose him. First get him to the doctor, then call Maddy. Hopefully, the others would get in contact with me soon.

Chapter 29 - Maddy

Nothing could get me to relax. The whole day had been one giant stressful slog. Part of me felt like I was in purgatory, like I'd died and was now stuck in this one day, reliving it over and over again, never getting closure.

Carlos and Julia had done all they could to keep my mind off the mission. Julia and I had spent the whole day baking, and she'd shown me how to make a bunch of different recipes—yeast bread, empanada dough, homemade donuts, and biscuits, among other things. The guys would be coming home to one hell of a feast. I did all I could to convince myself that they *would* be back.

There was only so much cooking you could do, though. After dinner, Carlos had spent a couple of hours telling me stories about Nico and his brothers when they'd been young. The stupid things he'd done, the broken bones and scraped knees. It had been a fun diversion, but even then, we were talking about Nico. My mind kept slipping away from the young Nico of the stories to the grown man who was halfway across the country trying to save everyone I held dear.

I knew they couldn't help it, but having his parents here with me made me think of my own mother and father, who'd been kidnapped. The stress was almost enough to make my skin crawl. Even my wolf was pacing nervously around inside my mind, waiting to hear the news.

I'd used all my remaining strength to try and push thoughts of Mom, Dad, and Abi out of my mind. If I dwelt on it too much, I'd become a mess—a non-functioning, debilitated, sobbing mess. Between what was going on with my wolf and trying not to have an utter breakdown thinking about my family, I was completely exhausted all the time. I wasn't sure how some people went years with those kinds of mental walls built up. A few weeks and I was about ready for a Valium prescription.

Midnight came and went. We were an hour ahead of Nico and his teams, which meant I had another hour to wait. Carlos and Julia sat with me in the living room. There was zero chance I'd ever get any sleep, so why even bother? None of us were paying any attention to the movie on the television, each of us lost in thought. At one a.m., the tension became almost palpable. Julia got up and began walking around the house, straightening up and cleaning.

Carlos had a small pocket watch that he kept snapping open and closed—a nervous tic. I looked at him and asked, "How long until we hear?"

He sighed. "No telling. The rescues should take less than fifteen minutes if all goes well. They'll need to extract, though. Get to safety. Who knows? An hour? Maybe two?" He gave a sad shake of his head. "Your guess is as good as mine."

The minutes dragged on and on. My eyes continued to flick toward the clock on the wall. Fifteen minutes. Then half an hour. Still no word. After forty-five minutes, I stood and joined my wolf, pacing in the real world instead of just my head.

At five minutes to two, my cell phone rang. I yelped, and both Julia and Carlos gasped. I nearly tripped over my feet as I ran to the coffee table to snatch up my phone.

"Hello? Nico?" My voice was high-pitched and panicked.

"It's me." He sounded exhausted, but I almost collapsed in relief at the sound of his voice. "I'm safe. I've got your mom. She's alive. I think they drugged her because she's a bit out of it."

I burst into tears. I couldn't help it. Hearing that Mom was okay was too much. All the hope, worry, and terror I'd kept bottled up inside were too much to keep in. I was sobbing like a child, and I couldn't stop.

"It's okay," Nico said, his voice a hushed coo. "Babe, it's all right. Calm down."

He did his best to settle me down. My sleeve was wet from wiping tears and snot off my face, but I finally managed to get myself under control. "How is everyone else?" I asked. "Daddy? Abi?"

"I don't know. No word from the others yet," Nico said.

That didn't help my anxiety. Could they have run into trouble? Had things gone poorly for the other teams?

"Do you think they're okay?"

Nico blew out a breath. "I'll be honest with you, I'm a little worried. We had a bit of an issue getting your mom out, Felipe got hurt pretty bad, and we still were on the road less than twenty minutes after we pulled up at the house. We're at a shifter clinic just outside Chicago right now, waiting on word. I'm not sure what's taking the others so long. I have to believe they were successful. They had—" His voice froze mid-sentence. "Hang on, Maddy. I'm getting a call. It's Sebastian. I'll let you know what I find out."

I almost cried out in anger and frustration. So much hung in the balance. All I wanted was to know. For the hundredth time, I wished I could have gone with them.

Julia touched my arm gently. "Nico? Diego?"

I nodded. "He's good, sounds like they both are. Felipe was hurt, but he didn't say anything about his brother. I think they're both fine."

"Praise God," Carlos muttered behind us.

My phone chimed that I had a text message. It was from Nico:

Abi is alive and safe. Sebastian has her.

I hugged my phone to my chest, fresh tears streaming down my cheeks. This time I did lower myself to my knees. Abi was okay. My best friend was alive and protected. Two of the three were okay. As happy and relieved as I was, I knew true peace wouldn't come until I knew whether or not my father was safe.

Carlos and Julia knelt on the ground beside me, wrapping me in their arms. I reminded myself again that they still had other sons out there in harm's way. They were as invested in this as I was. I reached up and put an arm around each of them, trying to offer them some semblance of comfort.

Twenty minutes later, I had composed myself enough to begin pacing again. Carlos and Julia both had worry in their eyes. It had been too long. Why wasn't there news from the third group? What could have happened? I texted Nico every three minutes, asking if he'd heard. Each response was the same. Nothing. I should have been overjoyed that Abi and my mother were safe, but I *needed* more. My daddy was still out there, along with Nico's family and friends.

Julia and Carlos were sitting on the couch, holding hands, and I was standing at the kitchen counter when I felt it—a sudden and intense sense of foreboding. The feeling was so intense that the hair on the back of my neck rose. Something bad was going to happen. I glanced at my phone, thinking it was going to be a phone call. Was Nico going to call and tell me my father hadn't survived? Or that one of his brothers had been killed trying to save my family?

Run!

I blinked. The thought had come from so deep inside my mind it was almost too hard to understand.

Run! Run! Run!

My wolf? She was screaming at me. I could feel her panic, almost hysteria. She wanted me to run. Something was coming here. Right now. I trusted her instincts and bolted, my feet slapping on the tile. I ran toward the stairs, remembering Nico's safe room. If I could get there and lock the door, I'd be safe from anything.

I slid to a stop at the base of the stairs, at the last instant, remembering Nico's parents. "Julia? Carlos? Follow—"

My words were cut off by a heavy crash at the door. I heard yelling voices and ran. I was too far away to help them. All I could do was run for my life. My feet moved so fast I was afraid I would trip and fall, ending my escape. I turned the corner and ran into the bedroom. At the far side of the room, I slid the false bookshelf out of the way and opened the heavy vault-like door.

I climbed in and turned to close the door. A man in black fatigues and a balaclava was running into the bedroom. He'd been right behind me! An icy finger of abject terror stabbed into my chest as he turned and saw me. His eyes widened in surprise, and I tugged the heavy door shut as he started running toward me. I slammed my hand on the big red button that read: **Secure**.

The locks latched, and I sucked in panicked breaths as the light above automatically turned on, along with the small video panel to the left. The man outside was banging on the door, but it was so thick that it sounded like he was miles away. I glanced at it, covering my mouth with my hand when I saw what was transpiring in the living room. Julia and Carlos had shifted to their wolf forms and were stalking around the room. One of the black-clad figures was on the ground bleeding, but Carlos was holding up his front forepaw like he'd been hurt. I didn't hear any blasting gunfire through the speakers, but I did hear the *thap-thap* of silenced weapons.

Glancing quickly at the other cameras, I saw there were three black SUVs outside the house. How had they gotten into the Lorenzo compound? I saw another video feed from the front gate of the community. A man lay unmoving on the ground. I clasped a hand to my mouth. Tears tracked down my cheeks. But they weren't tears of sadness—no, they were tears of terror. The royals were here, and they were going to take me.

There were two yelps of pain, and I glanced again at the living room camera. My blood ran cold as I saw Julia and Carlos collapse to the floor, their forms still and unmoving. Were they dead? Dear God, had Nico's parents died to protect me? I prayed that I was wrong.

On the video feed, a familiar form emerged from the front door—the slender, supermodel body and gorgeous face of Viola. Even though it was the middle of the night, she still wore massive designer sunglasses. As she stepped into the destroyed living room, she took the glasses off and glanced around at the destruction. My wolf growled in my head at the sight of her. I bared my own teeth in a silent snarl.

The man who must have chased me appeared on camera as he came down the stairs. He shared a few whispered words with Viola. I couldn't make out what they were saying. They were too quiet for the microphones to pick up. Viola surprised me by rearing back and slapping the man, who stumbled sideways before catching himself.

"Idiot," she spat at him.

Viola glanced around the room until she spotted the black bulb on the ceiling that contained the camera. She moved until she was directly below it and stared into the camera. I had the eerie feeling that she was staring directly into my eyes instead of a bundle of electronics.

"Hello, my dear Maddy. Can you speak through this pretty thing, or is this going to be a one-way conversation?"

I looked down and saw a button that read **Speaker**. I chewed at my lip for a moment before pushing the button and speaking. "Go away. I'm not coming out."

Viola's eyes widened in pleased surprise, and she clapped her hands softly like a child who'd gotten exactly what she wanted for Christmas. "Fantastic. It appears even these shifter dogs know what they're doing with technology. Now, Maddy, why don't you come on down, so we can talk about this like ladies?" Viola turned to her men and swept a hand. "Search the house. See if there are any others hiding."

I pressed the button again. "I'm not coming out. Just go!"

Viola knelt over the two wolf bodies at her feet and looked up at the camera again. "They aren't dead, my dear. Only tranquilized. Now…" She gave a little shrug. "If you do want them to die…" She snapped her fingers, and two of the men stepped forward and pulled out pistols. They aimed the guns at the sleeping bodies.

My breath was hissing in and out of my nose. I was on the verge of hyperventilating. Every muscle in my body vibrated with fear. What did I do?

But I knew there was only one thing I could do.

"All I have to do is say the word," Viola said. "But if you want them to stay alive, you'll come out." She shrugged. "My safe houses were breached. I would *really* love to know how you and all your little wolfy friends managed to accomplish that. Thankfully, I've been staying close, making sure I could keep an eye on you and the others. Lucky for me. Unlucky for you, it seems. Come now, sweetie, let's get this over with."

My finger hovered over the button to speak again, my hand trembling like a leaf. I should say no. I should tell her to go fuck herself. Except, that would sentence Nico's parents to death. There was no way I could do that. I'd never be able to live with myself. Even if I could, Nico would always know his mother and father had been killed because I was a coward. He'd say all the right things, tell me he understood, that it wasn't my fault, but deep down, he'd always resent me. Just like I'd resent myself. I couldn't let anyone die for me.

Viola was getting impatient. She waved at the two men. They pulled the slides of their guns back, chambering a bullet. I slammed my finger into the button. "Stop!" I shouted. "Stop. I'll come down. Please don't hurt them. I promise I'll come down."

On the video feed, Viola's bright red lips spread into a smile, revealing perfect pearly teeth. "What a good girl you are," she purred.

I gritted my teeth and unlocked the door. My wolf growled and raged at me, but I shoved her aside in my mind. She didn't want me to surrender, but there was nothing to be done. I couldn't allow them to die for me, and that was final, no matter what my wolf had to say.

The door had barely swung open when black-clad arms and hands started reaching in, dragging me out into the bedroom. They shoved me to the floor and pinned my hands behind my back, wrapping zip ties around my wrists.

"Ow," I hissed, kicking at them.

I struck one in the shin, and he barked out a curse before hitting me on the back of my head. Stars shot through my vision. I hadn't been hit that hard since the night I'd been attacked at the bar, and those men had nearly beaten me to death. Rough hands seized me under the armpits and lifted me up. The pressure of them carrying me forced my hands apart, causing the plastic of the ties to cut into my skin. I hissed in pain while they carried me, my feet hovering an inch off the ground as they moved.

Viola stood at the bottom of the stairs. The two men still held pistols at Julia and Carlos's heads. Fear jackhammered in my chest. These people were not the type to keep their promises. Would she have them killed even though I'd agreed? I tried to keep my eyes glued to her and not stray a glance toward Nico's parents. Maybe if I didn't look at them, she'd forget about them. Maybe she'd take her prize and go, leaving them safe.

Viola stepped toward me and ran a red, manicured nail gently down my cheek. "You are a beauty. Maybe, if you're very lucky, I'll leave enough blood in you so that you can come home and suck on that shifter cock some more. You'd like that, wouldn't you? Hmm?"

"Fuck you," I snarled.

"Oh my," Viola said, withdrawing her finger and smiling. "Such vigor. So much power. I'll be very intrigued to see how you feel once the full moon rises. A super moon, no less. It should be *very* enlightening." Viola glanced around at her men. "Time to go. The dogs won't stay asleep for long. I can smell them all over this place. Really, darling, I don't see how you can associate with mongrels. There's a reason my ancestors pulled Edemas and his family down from their little pedestal. Shifters, and especially werewolves, aren't meant to rule. They are meant to *be* ruled."

As the men dragged me out of the house, I glanced back and gave a small sigh of relief that Julia and Carlos had been left alive. I could see their chests rising and falling as the men dragged me out of the front door.

"Your ancestors were just jealous," I said. "They either weren't shifters, or their blood was so diluted they couldn't shift anymore, and they might as well have been human. That's what it was all about. Nothing but jealousy."

Without even looking at me, Viola swung her arm back and backhanded me. My head jerked to the side, and coppery, viscous blood pooled in my mouth. I spat it onto the ground just before they heaved me into the back of the van.

Before they got me there, I looked around to see if I could call for help. The problem was all the houses near Nico's were his family. His parents were unconscious, and his brothers were scattered across the country. The closest house where someone might be was over a hundred yards away. A hundred yards of space plus insulated walls. Shifters had enhanced hearing, yes, but not that advanced, and not when a shifter was deeply asleep. I winced in defeat as a hand shoved my head roughly into the back of the car.

I was pushed to the middle, and two men climbed in, flanking me. Sandwiched between two men, I had even less room to move. My hands were tied and pinned behind me. My wolf felt trapped, like an animal in a cage. She was making it hard to think as she writhed and whined inside my mind. I blinked and shook my head, trying to clear my thoughts. I had to stay focused, to think. My claws were extending and retracting involuntarily. I could hear the leather of the seat tearing as I tried to clench my fists.

Hearing the sound of tearing leather, Viola looked over her shoulder from the front seat. "Victor? Show our guest what we have for her." The man to my right pulled a hypodermic gun out and pressed it to my side. Viola went on. "If you don't keep your beast under control, I'll have my associate here put you to sleep like the two inside, understood? The tranquilizer works in seconds. Don't think you'll be able to manage any heroics before you go night-night. Okay, precious?"

I bit my tongue, holding back a retort. I closed my eyes as the car started pulling away from the house. All our planning. Everything we'd thought would work. It had all been for nothing. Nico and everyone else was too far away to help me. The royals had me. I was being taken to an unknown location. Tears slipped out of my closed eyelids. I was screwed.

Chapter 30 - Nico

I was glad to get good news from Sebastian. They had Abi, but it had been close. Mateo may have broken an ankle, and Luis probably had some broken ribs and a couple of shallow knife cuts. He'd apparently taken on two guards at once. If Sebastian hadn't been right there, he wouldn't have made it. That was good, though. Injured was better than dead by a long shot. Now, we just needed to hear from Javi.

It had been almost an hour since the initial break-in. They should have made contact already. What could have happened? Maybe they'd been unsuccessful, but… I shook my head, trying to push those thoughts away. I pictured my little brothers Rafael and Gabriel lying on a dusty floor riddled with bullet holes. *No*, I hissed at myself. I couldn't go down that road.

The problem was, sitting in the clinic waiting room gave my mind nowhere else to go. A thousand different thoughts circled through my brain. Had it been a trap? Maybe the third location was a ruse? An even worse thought, had Javi been lying all along? All he'd done was try to get close to us, let us lower our guards, and now he'd led my brothers into danger and killed them.

I clenched my fists and lowered my head. "Come on, Nico," I whispered to myself. "Stay in it. There's a good reason."

Diego sat beside me and punched my arm softly. "I know, man. I know. They're okay. I know it. Give them some time. Maybe there was a hiccup with the shift change or something. The guys could have been standing outside shooting the shit between shifts or something. Stuff happens."

I opened my mouth to answer, but the ringing of my phone silenced me. I answered it, bringing the phone up so fast it slammed painfully against my ear. "This is Nico."

"It's Javi. We got him." Javi's voice was strained, and I could pick up on the worry in his tone. It didn't sound at all like his normal cocky voice.

"Rafael? Gabriel? Are they good?"

"Yeah." Javi was huffing, and it sounded like he was running.

"What's wrong? I can tell by your voice that something's wrong."

"It was fucking weird, dude." He must have pulled the phone away because his voice became quieter, more distant. "Hey, hang on, guys, let's rest. I need to update Nico." He put the phone back to his ear. "Sorry. Anyway, we did as the plan said. We parked far enough away that they didn't notice. Then we waited until midnight. Everything went good as gold. These douches showed up in a black SUV, piled out, and traded places with the assholes inside. Those guys took the second SUV that was parked in the driveway. Then we moved in."

Everything sounded exactly like it should have. "Well, what happened after that? Why did it take so damned long for you to call me?"

"Getting there," Javi said. "We started moving toward the building, nice and slowly, but then the dudes in the house came piling back out."

"What?"

"Yeah, we were shocked as shit. We had to dive into the shadows. The guys poured back out of the house they just walked into. And they were hustling like they stole something.

"At this point, the boys and I freaked the fuck out. We were already thinking the worst. We weren't sure if the royals knew we were coming or what. But all the guys inside the building just packed the fuck up, and boom, they were out of there. Gone."

I narrowed my eyes as a headache formed in the center of my forehead. "Wait... you mean all the guards? They walked out? Without Maddy's dad? Why would they do that?"

"No clue. We thought about calling you guys, but we knew you all were knee-deep in shit yourselves. Best-case scenario, you were fighting your asses off. Worst case, the same thing had happened to you, and we didn't want to fuck with your head.

"We sat still for almost thirty minutes. We were sure they'd come back, but they never did. We snuck up even slower than we were going to. The door was hanging wide open, man. Didn't even need those security codes. We spent another thirty minutes checking the house. Right about this time, I started getting worried that they'd wired the building to blow or something. We still don't find jack shit. Finally, we head to the basement, and there's Big Poppa himself. Maddy's dad is just tied up on his stomach like a trussed turkey ready for the Thanksgiving oven.

"We untied his ass and got out. We didn't even bother going back to our car. That's why I'm out of breath. We've been cutting a path across the city. Making our way to the bus depot. Going to buy a ticket to the next town over, then hop a flight. I was worried they'd ambush us at the car or something. Probably just me being paranoid, but we didn't wanna take any chances."

"Okay, okay, that's… it's good that you got her dad. Give me a head's up when you're on the road."

"You got it."

I looked at Diego. "Did you hear all that?" I asked.

He looked as confused as I felt. "Why would they leave a hostage? That makes no sense."

My brain went into overdrive, trying to think of a reason for the bizarre behavior. A memory popped up, something that we'd seen in our initial recon of the locations. I grabbed Diego's arm. "Cameras. Did we say the locations had cameras?"

Diego nodded slowly. "Yeah. But we didn't find any direct lines out of the houses. The teams inside used them to monitor their areas. Even Luis said so."

"We fucked up," I said, feeling my heart start to slam in my chest. "Someone else was watching. Fuck!" I ran my hands through my hair, panic building like a wildfire.

Diego put a hand on my shoulder, trying to calm me down. "Nico, bro, chill. If they saw, why would they all run? Why wouldn't they have just sent backup? They could have had us dead to rights. Why just cut bait and leave the…" Diego trailed off.

I looked into his face and saw the dawning realization and horror forming there. The same thoughts had begun to worm their way into my own mind. I grabbed my cell phone and dialed Maddy's number. The phone rang and rang, then went to voicemail. I tried Dad's number next—nothing. Then Mom's—again nothing.

My eyes were already burning, on the verge of tears, when I logged into my security account and pulled up my home cameras on my phone. The first footage I brought up was the front gate of the Lorenzo community. Uncle Miguel was on guard duty. I watched as three black SUVs pulled up to the gates. A single figure dressed in black leaped from the car and raised a rifle at Miguel. My uncle tried to raise his own weapon, but the figure fired, cutting him down. Diego and I sucked in a collective breath. A fist of anxiety, shock, and remorse twisted inside my chest.

The cars moved away, headlights off, into the neighborhood. I knew exactly where they were going. They'd be there in seconds. I flipped through my video feed, cursing the program for not letting me move faster. I pulled up the living room. My parents were sitting on the couch, and Maddy was walking from the kitchen, a strange expression on her face.

My phone didn't allow access to the intercom. I was screaming in my head for them to run. Almost like she heard me, Maddy broke into a sprint toward the stairs. An instant later, the front door burst in. The next several minutes were chaotic. Maddy made it to the panic room. My parents fought the royals in my living room. I could hear Diego's ragged breathing over my shoulder as he watched the feed.

We watched Mom and Dad get shot and go down. It was like my heart vanished from my chest. They fell to the floor, unmoving.

"No, no, no, no…" Diego muttered. His voice was thick, and I knew he was either crying or on the verge of it.

The next few minutes were agonizing as Maddy was taken. I sped up the video and almost sobbed with relief when Mom and Dad started to stir. "They aren't dead," I hissed to Diego. "They're alive."

"Oh… oh, thank God," Diego muttered.

I had to sit down. My knees felt like jelly. So much emotion in such a short time—it was almost too much to bear. I sped the feed up until I was in the present time. Mom and Dad had shifted back to humans and were writhing on the ground, holding their heads. It looked like they had splitting headaches or something.

Mom rolled over and crawled toward the stairs. She was going to check on Maddy. They didn't know she'd been taken. I turned the video feed off and called Dad.

"Nico?" Dad's voice was groggy.

"Dad, it's me. Me and Diego. Are you all right?"

"My... damn... my head feels like it's splitting open."

"Tell Mom to stay downstairs."

"No, no, she's getting Maddy out of the safe room."

"She's gone, Dad. There's no need." My voice hitched, and I had to swallow before continuing. "They took her. The royals have her."

"Oh god... no." Dad was more distraught than I'd ever heard him. He called Mom back over and told her. "I'm sorry, son... I... I failed you. I'm so sorry." I could hear Mom crying quietly beside him.

"It's fine. We got outplayed. They knew we'd go for the hostages. They were waiting until we made our move. Once our forces were spread out, they went for her. You did all you could. I knew there would be retaliation, but I thought it would come after we rescued Maddy's family. None of us anticipated it would happen *while* we were saving them."

Diego patted me on the shoulder. I turned to look and saw the doctor coming through the door. "Dad, I need to go. We'll be home as soon as possible. You need to send someone to the gate. Uncle Miguel was shot. I'm... I don't know if he's okay."

"Sweet lord. Okay. Be careful, son. See you soon."

Hanging up, I stood to greet the doctor. "How is he?"

The doctor nodded and glanced at his chart. "Your friend is very lucky. The knife penetrated the abdominal cavity but missed the major arteries and organs. However, the spleen was perforated. We had to remove that, but he should be fine. Prognosis after splenectomy is better for shifters anyway. We aren't at risk of disease like humans are. We stitched up the fascia and closed the wound. We'll want to keep him for a couple of days."

"When can he fly home? We... uh... we're from Florida. We need to get back home."

The doctor nodded. "A human would need to wait at least a week. He's already healing pretty well. I'd say two days. As soon as he's discharged, he can head home."

Diego nodded and put a hand on my shoulder. "I'll stay with him. I'll make sure he gets home safe. You get home."

"Okay. Thanks, Doc."

I wanted to go and say goodbye to Felipe, but every second mattered. I had to get home and regroup. I jogged out the door and got into my rental car. On the way to the airport, I called the other teams and updated them on the situation. They took the news almost as poorly as I had. The other teams hadn't had to make detours to the hospital and were already boarding jets to get back home. My knuckles were white as I drove. I pushed my car as fast as it would go.

Checking the car back in and getting through security was like walking through mud. Nothing could have felt slower than this. Then I had to wait over an hour for the next flight. All the while, my wolf was raging inside me, desperate to lash out. I was right there with him. I would give anything to go on a run and slam my teeth into the neck of a deer—or even better, the throat of an enemy.

The actual flight wasn't much better. Thankfully, due to the late departure, the flight was nearly deserted. The last thing I wanted was to try and survive two and a half hours of small talk. My feet and hands fidgeted the whole flight. My body was wound tight with anxiety, anger, and worry. A thousand thoughts burned through my mind as we flew. Had the royals already bled Maddy out? No, that wouldn't happen yet. They'd wait until the full moon. We still had time. But they could have hurt her. If they so much as laid a finger on her, I'd rip their guts out. I fantasized about leaving Viola's bloody body broken and torn on the ground. Daydreams were the only catharsis I had at the moment.

By the time I burst through my front door a few hours later, I felt like a balloon on the verge of popping. Mom and Dad and my brothers ran to me. I took a moment to hug them all, thanking God that fate let them live, even if it chose to take Maddy. There was only so much loss I could take. At least with them, I'd have the support I needed to get her back.

"Where is everyone?" I asked Rafael.

"Maddy's parents and Abi are upstairs with Doc. We had him come over to check them all out. They were drugged with something. It's been hours since we got them, but they're still pretty loopy," Rafael said.

"What about you guys? How do you feel?" I asked, turning to Mom and Dad.

"We're fine. It's okay. We have more to worry about than us," Mom said, waving me off.

"Do they know she's been taken?" I said, gesturing upstairs toward Maddy's parents and Abi.

They all shook their heads. Dad put an arm around my shoulders. "We didn't tell them. Didn't want to worry them while they recovered. Doc agreed it was for the best."

My wolf was snarling in rage, and I clenched and unclenched my hands. It was like I was ready to burst. My mind raced to come up with a plan, a solution, anything to make this right. We weren't sure where the vial was, we didn't know where they'd taken Maddy, and there were only a few days until the super moon. I paced across the kitchen and slammed my fists onto the counter, then lowered my head. Desperation was fighting with hopelessness in my mind. Anger and fear warred in my chest.

I threw my head back and roared in rage. The sound exploded through the house. Everyone else froze where they were. The release of energy felt good, but I knew I had to stay calm. I was the alpha. If I lost it, then the whole pack would be in trouble, not just Maddy. I had too many responsibilities to let myself fall apart.

Sebastian walked up and put a firm hand on my back, and leaned in close. "We'll get her back, Nico. I know we will."

I couldn't even muster a nod for him. His confidence was a much-needed presence, but I couldn't match it. How could we get her back when we had zero idea where she was?

"I need to see them," I said, heading toward the stairs.

Before I climbed one step, a quiet voice spoke from the top of the stairs. "Nico?"

I glanced up and saw Abi standing there. "Abi? Shit, I thought you were still in bed." My gaze traveled over her body, inspecting the wounds—mostly bruises and small cuts. She also looked like she'd lost about ten pounds. She'd been petite to begin with, and the weight loss made her look almost emaciated.

I climbed the steps until I was by her side and put a supportive arm around her. "You need to rest. You look terrible."

Abi shrugged my arm away. "No. Where's Maddy? Where is she?"

My throat tightened, and my lungs seized up. I didn't want them to know, but there was no way to keep this secret. They were her family just as much as I was. "She, oh god, Maddy was taken. They have her. They came and got her while we were rescuing you guys."

Abi's hands shot out and clamped on my arms, one on each bicep. Even in her weakened and exhausted state, her fingers felt like steel bands, cutting off my circulation. "Where? We have to get her, Nico. Where did they take her?"

I looked into her fierce eyes and, for the first time, felt myself start to bend. My resolve weakened, and my will began to crack. I shook my head wordlessly. My mouth opened and closed, but no sound came out.

The door to the right opened, and Maddy's father stepped out. He looked equally as exhausted but had much worse wounds. His left eye was swollen shut, and his lip was split. There were bruises all along his jaw. Even in his weakened and injured state, he looked pissed, and why wouldn't he? I'd be furious if I'd been through what he had.

He took two heavy steps toward us. "Do you know where she is? Maddy, I mean?"

He'd heard us talking then. He knew she was missing. I shook my head. "No, Mr. Sutton. We don't."

He gave one angry shake of his head. "Call me Anthony. And I think I know where she is."

Abi and I both stared at him dumbly for half a second before I leaped at the news. I stepped up to him and put a steadying hand on his shoulder. "Mr... er... Anthony? You know where she is? How?"

I couldn't think of a single reason why this man would know more than we did, but I was happy to hear any news. Even a sliver of information was better than floating in the unknown. The longer we sat here doing nothing, the more impotent I'd begin to feel.

Anthony nodded and put a hand on the wall. He looked a little woozy. Once he'd recovered from his dizzy spell, he looked me dead in the eyes and said, "I heard some of the men talking. My guards. They were going to take us all to a place they kept calling 'The castle.'"

"Wait," I said. "Come downstairs. Everyone needs to hear this. The more minds working on this, the better."

Once we were downstairs, I sat Anthony and Abi down on the couch. The rest of us settled in around them. Anthony told us again what he'd heard. I looked around at them. "Anyone have any clue where this *castle* might be?'

Luis was the first to speak. "I might have an idea."

"Out with it!" I snapped.

"Okay, okay. There's a castle in Germany that the royals are known to frequent. It was part of Kenneth's research. They owned multiple residences. Villas, penthouses, and mansions, but the only castles they owned were the Edemas ruins and a castle in Germany. That's where the royals migrated to after the fall of Edemas's family. It's used as a sort of tourist destination at the moment. The front half is the museum and sightseeing venture. The remaining half and the rest of the estate is still used as a residence. That could be it."

"Okay, okay, maybe," I said. "Does that mean that's where the vault is? I don't want to plan a whole other rescue across the world just to get there and find they've moved her again."

Luis winced and shook his head. "Like I said, I'm pretty sure the vault was in the tombs near the Edemas estate. We never figured out if it was moveable, though. The treasure, due to its size, is probably still there, yes. The vial of blood? Who knows? Maybe the *vault* is a stone chest or something. So, yes, it could have been brought to the castle. We have no way to be sure." Luis looked at me with a sorrowful expression. "I'm sorry, that's all I know. It's the best I can come up with."

Everyone fell silent. Each eye in the room was looking down at the floor. We all looked like we'd been defeated. I forced my eyes to stay up and stared out the window at the bright blue morning sky outside. I refused to give up. Maddy was worth going to the end of the world. To the very gates of Hell if need be. I wouldn't stop. My lip curled back, and I growled low in my throat.

Chapter 31 - Maddy

The man beside me kept the hypodermic gun shoved painfully into my side for the entire drive. My ribs ached, and all I wanted was for him to take the fucking thing away. It was almost a relief when I saw the airstrip appear through the windshield.

This wasn't a commercial airport. It was a small strip about twenty miles away from Clearidge. I didn't even know this was here. A small jet airplane sat out on the tarmac. The steps had been lowered, and two men holding guns stood on either side of the stairs.

"Where are you taking me?"

Viola turned toward me and answered with nothing more than a smile, then turned back, and we continued the rest of the way in silence. The car pulled through a chain-link fence and parked right beside the plane. If I got on that plane, the odds of Nico finding me fell to almost zero, but there was nothing else I could do.

I dug down deep and mentally screamed at my wolf, begging her to help. Now was the time to shift. If there was ever a time that I needed her help, this was it. Instead of feeling her strength flood through my body, I felt the fear of a young girl. Being so near the royals actually made her fall even deeper into herself. All I could feel from her was terror and anxiety. The anger and rage she felt toward them were not enough to overcome the horror of being in their clutches. So, instead of my hands turning to claws and my jaw becoming a weapon, I was just a human. Weak, bound, and captured. I sighed, and even in my disappointment, I tried to let my wolf know that I didn't blame her.

The door opened, and the man beside me blessedly pulled the hypo-gun away from my ribs. He twisted a hand in my hair and yanked me out. Electric sizzles of fire shot through my scalp as he pulled. My feet shoved and scrabbled at the floor and the seat in front of me—anything to keep the pressure off my hair. I pushed myself out and fell onto the tarmac.

The same man leaned over to grab me again, and I snapped my teeth at his hand, just nipping his finger. He yanked his hand away, yelping in pain. "Asshole," I hissed at the man.

"Oh," Viola cooed. "She does have fight in her." She knelt and put her face right in front of mine. "I like when they fight." Viola stood and turned. "Bring her."

The men grabbed me under my arms and lifted me, carrying me toward the plane again. My toes banged on each stair as they hauled me up. Once inside, they tossed me into one of the big leather chairs, and one of them snapped out a knife and sliced off the zip ties on my wrists. I gasped in relief and rubbed at the red indents the plastic had left in my wrists.

It was a small plane. There were only eight seats—all plush, overstuffed leather. Instead of all the seats facing forward like a commercial plane, each of the two seats of four seats faced each other, with four facing the cockpit and four facing the tail.

Toward the back were a bathroom and a small attendant area, and up front were the two pilots. Even from here, I could see that the pilots had pistols in their shoulder holsters. Viola took the seat directly in front of me, crossing one immaculate leg over the other, and began typing into her phone. The other seats were filled with the guards. A male flight attendant appeared to lift and secure the stairs and door. He also had a gun on his hip. Did everyone have a gun? Did Viola? I didn't see how the skin-tight blazer and skirt could conceal a gun.

Within minutes, the jet taxied to the end of the runway, and the screaming noise of the engines roared. I was pressed back into my seat as the plane gained speed, and then the jet was in the air. My jaw clenched as I heard the landing gear pull up and stow away. There was a finality to that sound that I didn't like.

"Oh, Duncan?" Viola called to the attendant.

"Ma'am?" he said, giving her a deferential bow.

"Can I get a glass of Dom Perignon?"

"Of course, Ma'am. Um, anything for our guests?"

Viola glanced at me and raised an eyebrow. As much as I didn't want anything from this woman, I could feel my anxiety building with each passing moment. I needed something to take the edge off. "Whiskey, straight up."

Duncan nodded and disappeared. Viola frowned. "Whiskey? How very... butch."

I shrugged. "I like what I like."

Duncan arrived a few moments later with the drinks. The first sip of whiskey hit my throat, and it was the smoothest thing I'd ever drunk. I blinked and looked at the glass. I'd never had anything so good in my life. The bartender's curiosity overtook my anxiety and worry for a moment. I held the glass up and looked at Viola. "What the hell is this?"

She lowered her champagne flute and raised an eyebrow. "That? Oh, I think it's a Macallan. If I'm not mistaken, it's a 1926—probably a million-dollar-ish bottle. That glass"—she pointed a bright-red manicured nail at me—"is north of fifty thousand dollars."

I almost gagged, and my hand rattled. I grasped the glass with two hands to make sure I didn't drop it. I stared at the amber liquid and tried to imagine having enough money to pay fifty thousand dollars a shot. I looked at her again. "Why do you all even want the treasure if you already have so much money?"

Viola took another sip. "Darling, first things first. One, you can never *ever* have too much money. Second, I'm asking the questions. Let's begin, shall we?"

"Begin?" I asked dumbly.

Ignoring me, Viola leaned forward. "Did you exhibit any shifter symptoms during childhood?"

"What? No. No, I didn't."

"What about puberty? Did you reach sexual maturity earlier than any of your peers?"

"Huh? I… I don't—"

"Never mind. When engaging in sexual activity, have you ever experienced a desire to bite or claw your lover?"

"What the fuck are you—"

"Please, answer the questions."

I huffed out a breath. "No. I've never wanted to bite anyone while we were having sex."

Viola nodded. "Did you ever have any contact with your grandparents? Biological, that is," she added.

"No, never."

"Hmmm. Did your birth mother ever make contact with you while you were a child?"

Did I mention the fact that she was my pediatrician? Or all the letters she sent? Probably not. I shook my head. "No. What is all this about?"

Viola leaned back into her seat and finished her drink. She waved the glass, and Duncan appeared to retrieve it. "Just trying to connect some dots, dear. There are many things about the Hollander line we don't know. Much was lost in the Purging."

"You mean when you murdered dozens of innocent people and children? Is that what you call it? The Purging?"

Viola shrugged. "One of many names. It was long before I was born. Why should I care what happened to a few shifter babies three hundred years ago? Honestly. Do you weep over the children that died when Hannibal went to war with Rome? Do you wring your hands about all the women who were raped when the Christian army sacked Jerusalem? Or even more recently, do you have a vested interest in how the war prisoners were treated during the American Revolution?" She shook her head and pursed her lips. "I think not. What's past is past. Nothing to be gained by crying about what can't be changed."

I gaped at her. "Are you really that heartless?"

"Again, darling, we aren't talking about me. It seems there are many secrets about you. We did, of course, do a background check on you, but Kenneth did a good job of hiding things. Very unfortunate that he kept so many secrets to himself."

I felt a jolt of sadness at the mention of my uncle's name. The nightmarish image of him getting shot in the head flashed through my mind. "Don't say his name."

Viola raised her eyebrows. "What? Your blood uncle? You mean the man who sold you out to us for a chance to become a shifter? That's the name I shouldn't say?" Her lips curled into a cruel smile. "What can I say? He knew too much and wasn't sharing all he knew. If he ever truly believed we'd let him become one of you"—she curled her lip in disgust—"*things*, he was out of his mind. Now, tell me about the beast inside you. What is it like?"

I slammed the last of the whiskey back and tossed the glass to the floor. I'd hoped it would shatter, but the crystal was too thick. Instead, it thumped down and rolled against one of the guard's feet. "I'm not telling you shit," I spat.

"Maddy, we can do this the easy way or the hard way."

"I have nothing to say because I've never met my wolf, Viola."

For the first time ever, Viola looked taken aback. Her face went a bit ashen. "You... um... but you are a direct descendant of Edemas. Your wolf should be incredibly strong. You..." She looked away and paused like she was thinking. "You're saying you've not made contact with your wolf yet? Not shifted or spoken to her? You are an alpha, correct?" There was a strange desperation in her voice. I liked hearing it and decided to lean into that worry. Why should I be the only one who was scared?

I shrugged. "Maybe? Who knows?" I knew I was an alpha, but there was zero reason for me to give that information over to Viola.

She looked distraught and fidgeted in her chair. Viola chewed at her lip and stared blankly at the floor for several seconds. "If this doesn't work, I'm screwed," she murmured to herself under her breath.

I sat motionless as though I'd heard nothing. It was a relief to see the veneer of invulnerability crack a little. After a few seconds, Viola gathered herself, and the haughty exterior returned. "Doesn't matter," she said. "As long as the Edemas blood is concentrated enough, it should be successful. Regardless of whether you've shifted or not."

"The treasure is obviously a secondary objective. Why is this vial so important to you? What good is shifter blood to a human?"

Viola was still as a statue as she studied me. It was almost like she was dissecting me with her eyes, slicing away every layer of my skin, probing each of my organs, examining my soul. Then she said, "That's not really any of your concern, is it." A statement, not a question.

"I don't know if you remember or not," I said, "but you need my blood to open the vault."

Viola smiled back at me with a sickly sweet expression. "Yes, my lovely. Though I could just slit your pretty little throat and bleed you dry. That works too, no?"

I remembered my father's journal entry about the dream he'd had about Edemas and the witch. I knew Edemas would have thought of that. I grinned back. "I think you and I both know Edemas would never allow his blood to be taken by force. If you kill me and take the blood, it won't work. That's why none of this has worked all these years. You've murdered your way through the centuries. You stole and took the blood of men, women, and children, and nothing has opened the vault. I need to give my blood freely to open it. That," I pointed at her for emphasis, "is what you've finally figured out, isn't it? I know of the curse and about the witch Edemas hired. I know more than you think."

Viola stared at me, unblinking. The look on her face never changed. The smile was as perfect and white as always, but the eyes? The eyes told me all I needed to know. She wanted to tear my throat out. I had no doubt that if I weren't so valuable, she would. The perfectly coiffed and polished exterior hid an inky-black twisted monster. Then her smile vanished, and her shoulders relaxed. "Fine. I suppose you can hear the truth. Did your precious Kenneth tell you of the healing properties of werewolf blood?"

She bounced back and forth so quickly that I always seemed to be caught off guard. I blinked and shook my head. "The... what?"

She bobbed her eyebrows up and sighed. "Thought not. You see, ancient legends told of the power of werewolf blood. There were stories of injured werewolf kings in battle having their blood smeared on their warriors' wounds, and they would heal. It was even greater for humans. It is said that a single drop of werewolf blood, when ingested by a human, can heal any wound or sickness. My organization—er, family—want to break down this blood. Take the vial, study it, and synthesize the healing properties. Can you imagine what people would pay to be healed of any sickness? Tech billionaires? Presidents and prime ministers? What would they give to live?"

"But you already have so much money. This seems like overkill," I said.

Viola leaned forward and bared her teeth at me. "Again, silly girl. You. Can't. Have. Too. Much. Money." She smoothed the wrinkles out of her clothes and leaned back, regaining her composure. "But not only money. The power? We would hold the power of life and death in our hands. Plus, that blood can also create more werewolves—ones who would be under our control. What an army that would be! Any government on earth will give us whatever we want. We would become the true power behind the scenes. The real Illuminati, if you will. What person would try to bring down or stop the only people who can offer a chance to conquer death? We may not be a real royal family anymore, but we still have the ability to reign. I may not be a true queen, but I still sit on a throne."

I shook my head in disgust. "So, this is all about profit and power. Nothing more?"

Viola gave a short bark of a laugh. "What more is there?" She waved a hand at me. "Take a nap, child. We'll be in Germany soon."

With that, the conversation was over. I glanced out the window and watched the clouds drift by as we flew six hundred miles an hour through the sky, propelled forward toward my fate. I wondered if Nico had any clue where I was being taken. Would he even have the chance to get to me before it was too late?

Chapter 32 - Nico

"I'm sorry?" I stared at the woman incredulously.

The gate agent gave me an apologetic smile. "I'm sorry, Mr. Lorenzo. There's nothing I can do. You and"—she scanned down her screen—"your associate, Mr. Luis Ruiz, are on the no-fly list."

Dumbfounded, I stared at her. With no direct flights to Europe until the next day, we'd taken an immediate flight with a two-hour layover in Philly. From there, we planned to take a plane right to Germany. We'd only landed in Philadelphia less than forty minutes ago. I knew money could buy a lot of things, but this? That fast? I looked behind me at Luis, Marcus, Darren, and the Alabama shifter brothers. We'd brought them along as backup. They were free and clear, but I couldn't send them to fucking Europe alone to try and do this. They wouldn't even know where to begin.

I turned to her again, desperate for some way to get through this. "Miss? There has to be some mistake. My friends and I literally just landed from a flight from Florida. How could we get put on that list so fast? Is it possible that there's some glitch in the system or something?"

She shrugged, and the apologetic smile slipped, a more professional demeanor taking over. "I'm sorry, Mr. Lorenzo. There's nothing that can be done. You and your friend Mr. Ruiz can fill out a Traveler Redress form and submit it to the DHS. That's the only way to get off the list."

"How long will that take?"

She sighed and glanced over my shoulder at the ever-increasing line behind us. "You'll need to correspond with the DHS. No way for me to know, but minimum, three months. Maximum? They may not rescind it. Please, Mr. Lorenzo, there are others in line."

I turned and walked away from the desk, feeling more defeated than I had during this entire ordeal. Even watching them take Maddy hadn't been like this. I'd felt angry and pissed, this was… I couldn't even describe it. The super moon was only a couple of days away. I'd never get there in time. Luis clapped a hand on my back and pulled me away from prying eyes and ears. Marcus and Darren followed.

"What?" I asked.

"I think I have a way out of this. I know a guy in New York. It's only a three-hour drive." He shrugged. "Two if we haul ass."

I straightened and looked around. "What guy? How can he help? This is the fucking US government we have to circumvent, for Christ's sake."

"He owes me a favor. He's got his own jet. We can use that."

I shook my head. "A jet won't help. We still have to show our passports to get out of the country."

Luis lowered his voice and glanced around. "That's what I'm saying, man. He can get us falsified documents. Fake IDs, passports, everything."

I looked at him, taking a second to wonder how my best friend had made a contact like that in New York. Those questions would have to wait until later. I nodded eagerly. "Do it. Make the call. We'll go and get a car."

Luis had his phone out and to his ear in seconds. Marcus, Darren, and I moved over to one of the car rental kiosks. As we walked, my phone buzzed. Pulling it out, I saw it was my father calling. "Hey! Marcus?"

The shifter turned and raised an eyebrow. I pulled my credit card out. "Go and get us a car. I need to take this call."

Marcus nodded and took the card. I answered the phone, wondering what was wrong. "Hello?"

"Hey, boy. How are things?" Dad asked.

I sighed. "Not great. Sometime during our initial flight, the royals managed to get Luis *and* me on the no-fly list. We can't take our connecting flight. Luis thinks he knows a guy nearby who can help us out."

"Oh my god." He sounded more somber than I was used to hearing.

"Dad, are you okay? You don't sound like yourself."

There was a long pause before he answered. "I'm... Well, son, I'm ashamed of myself."

I blinked in surprise. "What? Why would you feel that way?" Even as I asked, I had a sneaking suspicion about why.

Dad let out a heavy sigh. "I was responsible for Maddy's safety. I'm a damned alpha. If anyone should have kept her safe, I should have. I feel like an old, weak piece of shit."

In my whole life, I'd never heard my father speak about himself like that. He'd always carried a quiet confidence. He had the demeanor of a true alpha and had led our pack for decades before retiring and turning leadership over to me. Hearing him say those things about himself hurt me more than I would have thought it would.

"Dad, you can't think that way. You and Mom did everything you could. You were overwhelmed by their numbers. There's nothing more you could have done."

"That's just it, Nico. I should have thought about all the possibilities. I should have had more people at the house with me, protecting her. Instead, I let the whole pack lie snug in their beds. My brother was shot, and he's in the hospital, maybe dying, and your mate was taken. All because I got complacent. This is on me and no one else."

Marcus turned and gave me a thumbs up. I nodded and gave a weak smile before speaking again. "Dad, I trust you with my life. I trust you with the lives of everyone I love. If it had been the other way around and Maddy and I had been there protecting Mom while you were out rescuing people, and the same thing happened, what would you say to me if I was acting like this?" Another long pause. I hoped it was because he was thinking it over. "Well?" I prompted.

"I see what you mean. I just… Son, I'll never forgive myself if something happens to your mate. That's what I'm saying. No matter what you say or what I tell myself, I'll feel like a failure and that it was my fault."

"Okay, then," I said. "I'll have to make sure we get her back safe and sound. That way, you won't have to worry."

Dad chuckled lightly. "You always were full of piss and vinegar."

"It's why you guys love me so much. Listen, I understand what you mean by keeping everyone safe. Call Javi. Have him bring his pack to our compound. That will be more than enough extra guards and fighters if it comes to that. I'm sure he will."

"All right, okay. I'll do that. Listen, Nico?"

"Yeah, Dad?"

"Be careful. I want Maddy back, but I want my boy back too. You understand?"

I sighed. "Dad, I'm going to do whatever is necessary for her to—"

"That's an order—from one alpha to another and from a father to a son. You get your ass back here. That's final."

"Yes, sir. Will do," I said with a grin. "Love you, Dad. Tell Mom I love her."

"I will, and we love you too."

I hung up just as Luis joined us. He beamed at me. "We're good."

"He can do what you said?" I asked. Marcus and Darren walked up with the keys and paperwork for the rental. Marcus handed my credit card back.

Luis nodded. "Passports and the plane. Thing is, his price is pretty steep. He did, however, cut fifty percent off because he owes me."

"I don't care," I said. "I'd happily go bankrupt if it means getting Maddy back. I'll pay whatever."

"All right, let's go," Luis said.

Marcus held up the keys. "Got us a Mustang!"

"Seriously?" I asked.

Marcus shrugged. "What? All we have are a couple of backpacks, and you said we needed to get there fast. I call front seat, though."

I rolled my eyes and shook my head. "Then I get to drive."

Chapter 33 - Maddy

I spent the rest of the flight napping and trying to ignore Viola. She continued asking probing questions about my wolf, my family, and anything else she was curious about. Duncan brought out food at one point when we were directly above the Atlantic. I was used to peanuts, and maybe a sandwich wrapped in plastic but Duncan placed a tray in front of me and lifted a steel dome. "For the lady, butter-poached cod, asparagus with balsamic glaze and garlic, along with pureed potato and celery root. Enjoy."

He disappeared to the small attendant station. I looked at the food. It looked like something that would be served in a five-star restaurant. I glanced back at the tiny station. How the hell had he cooked this? He returned with more dishes and served Viola, then he served the guards. I noticed the guards got the typical airline food I was used to. It looked like six-inch sub sandwiches wrapped in foil. Viola had some type of steak with vegetables.

As much as I didn't want to take anything from these people, my stomach ached with hunger. I hadn't eaten anything in almost twenty-four hours. Grudgingly, I grabbed my fork and dug in. The fact that the food was delicious annoyed me. I felt like I was betraying my conscience by enjoying the food, so I told myself I was using it for fuel. There was no way I'd have the strength to escape if I didn't eat.

"Seems you enjoy some things money can buy," Viola cooed as I finished and wiped my mouth with the linen napkin. The sound of her voice made my skin crawl.

"I enjoy not starving to death," I said, biting back a sneer.

Viola raised an eyebrow. "Whatever you say."

I turned away from her and looked out the window for the rest of the flight. Soon, the ocean gave way to beaches, then land. For the second time in a month, I was back in Europe. When I'd imagined globetrotting and traveling, I never really anticipated this.

Twenty minutes later, one of the pilots turned in his chair. "Miss Monroe?"

Viola turned her head lazily toward him. "Yes?"

"We'll be landing just outside Hamburg in five minutes. We're preparing for the final descent."

"Very well. Thank you, Todd." She interlaced her fingers and rested her chin on her knuckles as she looked at me. "Well, Maddy? I hope you enjoy Germany as much as I do. I'm sure this will be very educational."

I curled my lip in disgust and refused to answer. The landing was smooth, and within minutes we'd come to a stop on a small airstrip that looked like it was in the middle of the woods. One of the guards got up and stood in front of me. He produced another set of zip ties.

"Really?" I asked. "This again?"

"One can never be too careful, dear," Viola said while she stood and smoothed out her clothes.

The guard bound my hands, this time in front of me. Duncan opened the door and lowered the steps. All but one of the guards went out to stand on the tarmac, followed by Viola. One guard remained behind, holding the stupid hypodermic gun in the small of my back. He pushed me toward the doorway.

As I stepped out, Duncan nodded to me. "Enjoy your stay, Miss Sutton. Perhaps we'll see you again."

I looked at him incredulously. "Yeah. I'm sure I will. I'll make sure to fly Douchebag Airlines again real soon." I rolled my eyes and turned away.

I stomped down the stairs and walked toward the car waiting for us. Instead of a stretch limo, it was a massive stretch SUV. Something I'd never seen before. The guard behind me ushered me toward the back door and helped me get in. This time I was able to help myself and not get shoved in like a sack of potatoes. The interior was a U-shape of plush leather seats. Instead of an opening into the driver's area, there was a wall with a small LCD TV and a bar lined with liquor bottles secured with black satin ribbons so they wouldn't fall over during the drive. If I hadn't been scared for my life, I would have enjoyed the luxury I'd been experiencing the last few hours.

Viola got comfortable and pressed an intercom button. "We're all here. Proceed to the estate."

"Yes, my lady," the driver replied. A moment later, we pulled away.

Again, I spent the ride looking out the window, doing my best to act like everyone else in the car wasn't there. Despite my circumstances, I had to admit that the countryside we were driving through was beautiful. We passed through a few small villages that looked like they'd been cut directly out of a fairytale. We then went through a much more urban area, which must have been Hamburg. It seemed to be as big as a medium-sized city back in the States, but many of the buildings looked to be hundreds of years old. There was a sense of foreboding to it. Many of the buildings had dark gargoyles that hung out over the streets, all of which seemed to leer at me as we passed—as though they already knew what fate awaited me.

After Hamburg, we again ventured into the outward countryside. Eventually, we came to a fence that was over nine feet tall and ran for over a hundred yards with a steel gate in the center. The driver pulled up and must have punched in a code, for the gate slowly slid aside, and we entered the grounds of whatever estate the royals used as their base of operations.

Through the window, I watched as we took a winding driveway up a hill, and then the building was visible in the distance—a massive castle. Upon seeing it, my wolf spoke for the first time in almost a full day. *Home?* she growled. I frowned at the building. This couldn't be the castle my wolf grew up in. It was in the wrong country.

Finally giving Viola my attention, I asked, "What is this? My..." I caught myself before mentioning my wolf. "It seems familiar."

Viola smiled. "Ah, yes. I suppose it would if you've done your research. This is Edemas's castle."

My brow furrowed as I looked at her. "But his castle was destroyed in the... the Purging, or whatever you call it. It's nothing but ruins up in Norway."

Viola chuckled. "Oh yes, that's the original castle. When we migrated away from those lands, we built an exact replica." She shrugged and looked a little irritated. "Over the years, we lost much of our social standing, but not our money. My ancestors were savvy enough to make sure we never lost that. Part of this was opened as a tourist destination, similar to your Biltmore Estate in America. We make millions each year as greasy, fat foreigners pony up their money to walk through the few corridors we have cordoned off for them. Other than the location and a few… shall we say… special additions, this is exactly the same castle as the one Edemas ruled from in Norway."

I shook my head, trying to wrap my mind around the sheer amount of hubris these people had. We pulled around the building, leaving the big visitor parking lot and the front of the castle behind, along with its ticket gate, gift shop, and restaurant. To the side of the castle was a secondary gate that we passed through. The driveway took a turn, and we drove toward a large building set back from the castle. It looked like a small mansion. The driving path curled around behind this building until it dipped down into an underground garage. The car parked, and we disembarked. It seemed like all I was doing for the last day was getting into and out of vehicles.

The guards prodded me along behind Viola. We crossed the parking lot, our steps echoing through the cavernous concrete garage. Eventually, we headed into a long hallway lined with doors.

"In," Viola said when I hesitated to step into the hallway.

These were prison cells. Nothing else they could be. They walked me down to the furthest cell. Viola punched in a code, and the cell door popped open. It wasn't metal, but it was incredibly thick, likely reinforced, and heavily insulated.

A guard shoved me into the cell and spun me around. In one quick motion, he cut my bindings, turned, stepped out, slamming the door behind him. There was a *clack* as the locking mechanism slid into place, and just like that, I was alone.

The room was eerily quiet. It was as thickly insulated as I thought. There wasn't even a hum of air conditioning or water running through pipes. I was fully set away from the world here. A quick glance around showed me what I had. A small cot with a pad and one thin blanket and pillow. A single chair was bolted to the floor, and a strange toilet and sink combination and a security camera were in the corner. Other than that, the only other thing in the room was a TV monitor positioned so high on the wall I couldn't reach it even if I jumped.

As though someone knew I was looking at it, the TV suddenly clicked on. I was sure I'd see Viola's awful face smiling back at me, but instead, all I saw was a video feed of another cell that looked exactly like mine. A woman was pacing back and forth in that cell. From her body language, I could tell she was pissed. I stepped closer, craning my neck to see this person. Eventually, the other woman seemed to get bored of pacing and stopped where she was, jabbing her hands onto her hips. Then she glanced up at the camera, and my stomach sank.

My jaw dropped as I stared at the furious face on the monitor. It was a face I'd not seen in years, but one that was immediately recognizable: Doctor Stanford—the woman who, at one time, had been known as Gabriella Karson—my birth mother.

Chapter 34 - Nico

I drove the first hour, but my nerves were shot. After we got through New Brunswick, I had to give Luis the keys and let him drive. All I could think about was the time we were losing. The full moon was on the horizon. What if the royals had already taken what they wanted from Maddy? Thankfully, I didn't let myself dwell on it too much. Mostly, the guys talking kept me from falling too deep into my own thoughts.

"Seriously, man. I don't think it's gonna happen," Luis said.

Marcus chuckled and shook his head. "I'm telling you. 'Bama is gonna win the Natty again. I will say, yes, Florida will get to the SEC Championship, but my Tide are gonna roll you boys. Just like usual."

Luis groaned and rolled his eyes. "You guys. One day, you all won't be so cocky. You can't be good forever."

Darren burst out laughing. "True! But until that day? Roll tide, roll!"

"Oh god, I'm gonna puke. I should stick with soccer," Luis muttered.

"How far are we?" I asked, interrupting their football conversation.

Luis leaned forward, trying to see ahead of where we were. "Looks like we're coming up to the George Washington Bridge. From there, depending on traffic, less than forty minutes."

I spent the last part of the trip trying to keep my mind off what was going on. I ended up playing on my phone, but instead of getting my mind off it, I ended up checking the damned weather in Germany and searching for average flight times. I even looked up the website for the castle in Germany that the royals owned. I spent a solid minute just staring at the pictures of the stone walls, wondering if Maddy was inside them at this very minute.

Forty-five minutes later, the car lurched to a halt, and I finally looked up from my phone. To say I was confused was an understatement. The only time I'd ever been to New York had been on a layover when I was nineteen, and Dad had taken Diego and me on a trip up to Canada for a business meeting with some bear shifters he knew there. We'd had time to go see Times Square, eat lunch, and then head back to the airport. This was... not New York.

I glanced around and saw more trees than I did buildings. The buildings I did see weren't the stereotypical brownstones you saw on TV. Instead, they were the grassy lawns and rocky outcroppings tucked between sidewalks. This looked like a suburb of Chicago or something.

"Where the hell did you take us, Luis? This doesn't look like New York."

Luis looked over his shoulder. "Oh, it's New York. We're in the Bronx. This is Fieldston. And that"—he pointed out the windshield—"is my guy's place."

I opened the door and looked across the street. The huge building must have been at least five thousand square feet. The exterior was stone and stucco with moss and ivy growing up the north-facing walls. It basically looked like a castle. It made me a little wary. So far, all my dealings with castles had been in relation to the royals.

"Are you sure about this guy?" I asked as the others got out of the car.

Marcus glanced around and frowned. "Where are all the yellow cabs and stuff?"

"Jesus, guys. You really need to get out more. There's more to New York than high-rises and Madison Square Garden. Come on."

We followed Luis across the road, kicking yellow and brown leaves aside as we went. The late fall air was brisk, and I realized in my haste to get going that I was still dressed for Florida weather. We stepped up to the house, and Luis pressed the doorbell. I didn't hear anything ring inside, but a few seconds later, a response came from a small intercom beside the doorbell.

"Is that you, Luis?" came a drawling voice.

"It's me. Let us in, Donatello."

Marcus swatted his brother Darren in the arm and whispered, "Donatello? Like the Ninja Turtle?"

"Quit it," I hissed. "It's just a name. I've got a brother named Rafael. It doesn't matter.

Darren shook his head. "These people are *obsessed* with the Ninja Turtles, bro."

Before the Alabama brothers could embarrass Luis further, the door swung open to the slickest-looking dude I'd ever seen in my life—bright, almost-white blond hair combed back, small round glasses that sat at the bridge of his nose. His face looked like it had been carved out of marble by a Renaissance sculptor. He wore a fitted blazer over a dark gray turtleneck, skinny slacks, but bright white high-top sneakers. I did a double-take when I saw the Prada symbol on the side of the shoes. Everything about him exuded money and confidence. Who the hell was this guy?

The man—Donatello, I assumed—smiled. "Luis. My friend." He put a well-manicured hand out, and Luis shook it.

"Don. Glad you could help us on such short notice."

"Nothing makes me happier than helping a friend in need. Come in. All of you, come in."

Donatello stepped aside and swept an arm toward the foyer. We stepped in, and I was thankful there wasn't some cliché butler or maid running around. The home was large but not ostentatious. There were lots of dark mahogany and black walnut accents and antique furniture and artwork from what looked like the Victorian or Edwardian eras. Nothing about the house was modern. It was kept perfectly and elegantly how it must have looked in the roaring twenties. I could easily picture a Prohibition speakeasy party happening here with all the city's wealthiest families. As much as I hated to admit it, I was impressed.

"So, I understand you and your friends are in a bit of a bind?" Donatello said, giving Luis a wry grin. "Tell me what you need."

Luis nodded grudgingly. "Well, my three friends and I need fresh passports and identification, and we need your jet to go to Germany."

"Would you like a brand-new Ferrari and some ladies to enjoy for the flight as well?" Donatello asked, giving Luis another strange smile.

Luis put his hands on his hips and glared at Donatello. "You owe me. No jokes. Can you get what we need or not?"

Donatello's smile evaporated, but the good-natured glimmer in his eyes stayed. He put a finger to his chin and thought for a moment, then nodded. "I think this is doable. How soon do you need it?"

"Today," I said, interjecting into the conversation. "We've already lost a lot of time. We should be halfway to Germany by now."

Donatello raised an eyebrow at me, then glanced at Luis. "Is this your alpha? The one you were telling me about?"

"Yeah," Luis said. "He's right. We need this ASAP."

"Well," Donatello said. "I can get them, but due to the late nature, there's no way I can have them today. No one could on such short notice. For one thing, my jet is on lease and is on the way back from Los Angeles. It's due to land sometime this evening, and the pilot is required a full ten-hour break. But I can get it all to you, after my fee, of course. As we discussed, I'll give you half off due to our history. I'll also wave the cost of the jet fuel."

I hissed in irritation and shook my head. "There's no other way?" I could practically see time slipping through my fingers like sand.

Donatello gave a sad shake of his head. "Unfortunately not. I'll have to grease some wheels with some unsavory people as it is to get it done that fast. I'm your best option."

I did some math in my head. If we left the next day, we'd still get to Germany with time to spare before the full moon. As much as I hated it, this was our only option. We'd come too far to turn back or try another route. I nodded reluctantly. "Fine. Let's do it." I dug out my wallet and looked at Donatello, raising my eyebrow. "I don't suppose you take credit cards?"

Donatello chuckled wryly. "My good man, this is the twenty-first century. MasterCard or American Express?"

Over the next two hours, Donatello took us into a side room near what looked like a fully stocked bar that would have made Maddy envious and took our pictures—headshots for the new passports. He then provided us with a tray of cheeses, meats, and fruit for a meal. Most of the cheese looked like it cost more than my monthly truck payment. For the hundredth time since we'd gotten there, I wondered what Luis could have possibly done to have this guy be in his debt.

Some type of courier arrived not long after Donatello finished printing out the pictures. I watched Donatello hand the printouts and what looked like a massive wad of cash to the guy, and he was gone in seconds. I had to hope this friend of Luis's wasn't full of shit.

After eating, Luis called over to Donatello. "Hey, Don? You still have that pool table upstairs?"

"The Cappelletti? Indeed. Are you looking to pass some time?"

"If it's okay with you?"

Donatello nodded, and Luis, Marcus, and Darren headed toward the massive spiral staircase. Luis glanced over his shoulder. "You coming, Nico?"

I shook my head and eyed Donatello. "Nah. I'd like to get to know our benefactor here."

Donatello stepped over to his bar as the others went upstairs. He poured himself a scotch and glanced over at me. "A drink, Mr. Lorenzo?"

"Call me Nico. Got any vodka? I'd love to take the edge off a little."

Donatello bobbed his head appreciatively. "I have Chopin Family Reserve?"

I shrugged. "I literally don't know what that is. Is it like Grey Goose?"

"Oh, my friend. Let me change your life," he said and started making me a cocktail.

I sat in a leather chair that must have been a hundred years old in what Donatello called his smoking room. He handed me a martini glass with a thinly curled lemon peel hanging on the edge of the glass. "Lemon Drop. Simple but delicious. Lets the vodka really shine through."

I nodded in acceptance and took the drink. I sipped at it and was surprised at how good it was. I raised my eyebrows in appreciation and lifted my glass in a toast. Donatello smiled and sat across from me in a matching chair.

We drank in silence for several minutes. I looked out the massive bay windows to the tree-lined street outside and saw the lengthening shadows on the sidewalk. The sun would be down in less than an hour—one more night closer to the full moon.

Seeing the dark look that must have been on my face, Donatello said, "Luis told me a bit about this issue you have. Something about a kidnapping?" He smiled conspiratorially. "Very intriguing. Care to talk about it?"

Ignoring him, I changed the subject. "So, I don't see many personal items around here. Do you live in this massive place by yourself?"

He didn't look put off by my swerve to another topic. He took a drink and glanced around the room. "I enjoy my privacy. Let's say that, and leave it there."

"Fair enough," I said, taking another drink. "I do have to ask, how the heck did you make all your money? This place had to have cost an arm and a leg. Plus a private jet? Do you own a business or something?"

Donatello drained his glass and bobbed his free hand back and forth. "A little of this, a little of that. I try to keep my toes in multiple pools. Never get bored that way. Am I right?"

I chuckled. "I suppose. It makes sense."

This man was not someone I would typically deal with. He was a different breed than I was used to, mysterious to a fault, and seemed to enjoy keeping people in the dark. On the other hand, he appeared to be good-natured, didn't take things too seriously, and was willing to help a friend in need. He had the financial means to help us and acted like it was a pleasure to do so. I could like this guy. We might never be friends, but if all this worked out, I'd owe him more than whatever he owed Luis. Their score may be settled, but ours had only just begun to be tallied.

I finished my drink and held the empty glass up. "Can I call you Don?" He tilted his head in what I took to mean acceptance. "This was delicious. Maybe one more?"

A happy glimmer sparkled in his eye, and his grin spread. "I told you I'd change your life."

The rest of the evening was spent making simple small talk. The guys returned from upstairs an hour or so later, and given the desperate urgency of our mission, it was a strangely relaxing night. I'm sure it had something to do with the luxurious surroundings, but by eight o'clock, the guys and I were exhausted.

Donatello, seeing our fatigue, gestured up the stairs. "I've got five bedrooms other than mine. All made up. Go on up and take your pick. I'll stay up. I should have a call from my friend in the next hour or two about the IDs."

We thanked him again for his hospitality and made our way up to the guest rooms. I took the first door I found, a bedroom that was easily twice the size of mine at home. The four-poster bed looked like the most comfortable thing I'd ever seen. I collapsed onto it and fell into a deep sleep without even taking my clothes off.

Donatello woke us the next morning with a stack of passports, driver's licenses, and he'd even forged US visas for some reason. After a quick breakfast of pastries and espresso, he took us to a private airfield in Westchester County. The drive was forty minutes, and again, I felt as though we were walking through mud to get there. I was desperate to get in the air.

At the airport, Donatello wished us well, shaking each of our hands as we boarded the plane. I was the last one to say my goodbyes. He held my hand a moment longer than necessary and made sure I made eye contact with him.

I glanced at him curiously. "Yeah?"

He grinned at me. "Go, get your lady, my friend. Go get her and give those bastards hell."

I smiled back despite myself. "That is the plan."

"Goodbye, Nicolas Lorenzo. Perhaps we'll meet again."

I nodded and started up the steps, looking back over my shoulder once more before stepping inside. "Yeah. Maybe."

Within minutes, the plane was in the air, and we were making plans about what to do when we got to Germany. The entire day before had the distinct feel of a dream—surreal in some way. At one point, I chuckled to myself and nudged Luis. "So... I'm not crazy, right? All that happened yesterday, didn't it?"

He frowned at me. "What do you mean? With Don?"

"Yeah. It felt *weird*."

Luis grinned. "He has that effect on people."

It was nice to know I wasn't the only one who'd felt the bizarre nature of the experience. Maybe Don and I would meet again. It would be nice to have someone like that in my corner in the future. I owed him one hell of a debt, and I hoped to God I'd be able to pay it off. As we soared over the ocean, I kept glancing out the window, hoping to see land but knowing that was still hours away. *I'm coming, Maddy. I'll be there soon.*

Chapter 35 - Maddy

The moon tugged hard at me. It was like I had a thousand fishhooks in my skin being yanked toward the sky. Each day closer to the full moon made me feel more and more like I was going to lose my mind. My skin was tight and uncomfortable. I could almost trick myself into thinking I could feel my wolf right there beneath the skin, ready to explode out. My God, I wished she would. Then I'd finally have a way to fight back. At the moment, I would have killed for a massive, terrifying werewolf body to attack my captors. But other than anxiety, irritation, and pain, I got nothing else from her. So, I had to make do and keep my head clear.

There were no windows in my cell, but as I lay on my cot, I could still feel the pull. Although, that wasn't why I couldn't sleep. My eyes were open, and I stared at the dark ceiling, worry swirling inside me. For once, I wasn't worried about myself. Instead, I was worried about the woman I'd seen on that TV monitor. Gabriella. How had they gotten her? Why was she here? I didn't have any special bond to her, but she wasn't a complete stranger. I still had vague memories of her as my childhood doctor. Plus, she'd done a lot to help Nico and me. I couldn't just write her off. I wasn't that kind of person.

Everything that was happening was because of me. No matter how distant a relation, I didn't want someone to get pulled into my shit storm of a life and get hurt. Even with that thought, I had to wonder if I could risk my life for someone I didn't really know. Someone who'd been hiding and lying for decades. I'd probably have no way of knowing until the moment came.

After a few hours of fitful, uncomfortable sleep, there was a knock at my door. A small panel slid aside, revealing a man with a tray. He waited until I stepped forward to slide it through. I took the plastic tray warily.

"Good morning, Miss Sutton. Breakfast. Bread, sweet butter, two poached eggs, some sliced meats with cheeses and jam. What can I get you to drink?"

I stared at him dumbly before I found my voice. "Umm... I don't know... what is there?" I asked, acting as though I was at the most terrifying restaurant in the world.

"Water, fresh orange juice, and apple juice, or we could do a morning cocktail if you like? A Screwdriver? Mimosa? Bloody Mary?"

Oh, for fuck's sake. "Apple juice is fine. Thanks."

"As you will. I'll be right back."

My captor left me with my breakfast. They were strangely hospitable for people who had two women locked up against their will and were, more than likely, going to kill them or bring them close to death on the night of the full moon. I had no idea why, but my stomach betrayed me again. Since I was starving, I sat to devour the food.

By the time the guard returned with a tall glass of apple juice, I'd finished everything but the bread. I took the glass as I took large bites of the bread that I'd smeared with jam and butter. That whole day went the same way as the day before. I paced and napped and was bored out of my mind. At lunchtime, they brought me a tray of some kind of potato salad and a sandwich. Then, later on, another meal of sausages, sauerkraut, and potatoes. In the evening, Viola decided to show me my birth mother again. The TV came on for three minutes. I saw the woman who had birthed me sitting on her cot, eating a similar dinner to mine. After that, the TV went off, and my lights were shut off. Time for bed again, and while the pull of the moon was still obnoxiously present, I was too tired to toss and turn. I was able to fall into a blissfully dreamless sleep.

After my breakfast the next morning, a different guard came and opened my door to retrieve me. He stepped in without a word and took me by the arm, guiding me out to the hallway.

"Where are we going?"

The man said nothing. Instead, he continued down the passage, oblivious to any other questions I had. I gave up after a while and went along with it, knowing there was nothing more I could do.

He led me through a door at the end of the hallway and escorted me through twists and turns until we stopped in front of a door. He unlocked it and opened the door. He pushed me inside, and I froze in my tracks. Sitting at the table, with her face in her hands, was my birth mother. She didn't look at me, but I could see her shoulders stiffen. She knew I was here.

"Viola thought it would be nice for the two of you to have a moment to speak. She felt it would be a gracious show of kindness on our part since it'll be the one and final chance you will have.

Gabriella finally raised her head, and I saw the look of fear in her eyes as she stiffened even more. Without another word, he stepped out, closing and locking the door behind him. Silence filled the room, and I took the seat across from her. All I could do was sit there and wait for her to say something. After a few moments, her shoulders sagged, and a look of defeat came over her face.

"Why?" I asked. I hadn't even known what I was going to say until I opened my mouth. I wanted to know why. Why everything? Why all of it?

She shook her head sadly. "I already told you everything in the letters."

That pissed me off. Like what was in those letters could explain the motivation behind what she'd done all those years. "Why did you stick around? Playing my doctor and making me think you were someone else? That's what I mean. I don't understand how you could go years being my doctor and keep that secret." I hadn't truly understood how upset I was until I started talking. Once the words started coming, the emotions unfurled, spinning webs of anger and sadness in my chest.

Gabriella looked heartbroken. "I'd made plans to resign. Every time I'd see your name pop up on scheduled visits, I'd tell myself it was the last time. I knew I needed to get away from you." It seemed like she was in physical pain just thinking about it. "But each time I'd see you walk in…" She shook her head. "I couldn't let go. It was always just enough to get me through. Seeing you alive and well. Happy. Hearing…" She swallowed hard. "Hearing you laugh? I couldn't do it. I know it was selfish, but I can't apologize for wanting to be near you."

The raw emotion gave me pause. The way everything had gone down, the secret letters, the hidden envelopes, the lies, and faked death? All that had only been by necessity. Things that she'd had to do. My face softened.

Uncrossing my arms, I leaned across the table toward her. "Maybe... can we just talk a little? I don't know. Get to know each other a little?"

A hesitant smile spread across her lips that finally broke into a bright white smile. She nodded. "I'd like that. I'd like that a lot."

We talked for what felt like hours. I told her everything about my life through high school and college, choosing a major, moving, and buying the bar after graduation. I told her about Abi, my parents, Nico, and everyone who was in my life.

She told me about her life after leaving the pediatrician's practice. Her time on the run. She told me about her favorite books and movies. It seemed like she'd led a very solitary life. It was sad to hear that she had no close friends and had apparently never found anyone to share her life with after my father died.

I asked her about it, and she gave me a sad little shrug. "Once you've loved someone as deeply as I loved David... you find it hard to ever see that love in someone else. If for some reason you lost Nico, do you think you could ever love again?"

I thought about it for a moment and realized she was right. At best, I could try to find someone I was compatible with and force the feelings—trick myself into thinking it was the same, but that seemed both sad and dishonest. It wouldn't be fair to myself, and it definitely wouldn't be fair to the person I ended up with. I finally shook my head. "No, I guess not."

"See? It's difficult, but after a while, you learn to get used to being alone."

"What about Kenneth?" I said, remembering the way he'd talked about her. He'd betrayed me, yes, but I still felt that deep down, he was a better person than the one he'd shown.

My mother shook her head once. "I hadn't seen him in years. I didn't trust him anymore. I disappeared from him as well. As much as he helped me and worked to keep me safe and hidden..." she trailed off and shook her head absently. "He always looked at me like he wanted something more. There was always this hunger in his eyes. You're a woman, and you know what I'm talking about. That look some men get when they're thinking about the things they want to do to you in the dark?"

I nodded. Unfortunately, I did. There were always a few of those guys hanging around the bar, pushing women to give them their number, cajoling them for a dance, never taking no for an answer even though everybody and their brother could read the signs and feel the vibe. It was an unfortunate reality. It was sad that ten or fifteen percent of men could be like that and help ruin the reputation of the other ninety percent of their sex.

"Don't get me wrong," Gabriella went on. "I don't think he would have acted on that. Not in a million years, but it always made me nervous. He was also so obsessed with shifters. He told me once that he'd give anything to become one—to finally inherit this ancient birthright. I worried he might do something crazy to achieve those goals."

I told her about what happened at his cabin in Europe, including his death. The look on her face was a strange combination of sadness, acceptance, and irritation. She tapped her nails on the table and sighed unhappily. "I'm not surprised. It's exactly what I feared."

"He was in love with you. Even before David died."

"Again, not surprised. As I said, I always had a feeling. It's been over ten years since I had any dealings with him. I hope he's at least resting in peace now."

"Yeah," I mumbled, not knowing what else to say.

Gabriella looked me dead in the eyes, her voice suddenly hard and serious. "Maddy, I know why we're here."

"I figured you did. Not hard to put the pieces together."

"No matter what happens, Maddy. Do not do it. Don't give them what they want."

The door behind me burst open. I jumped in my seat and yelped in surprise. The guard stomped over and grabbed Gabriella by the arm, his free hand grabbing a handful of hair and yanking her from her seat. "I think that's about enough talking." He grunted as he pulled her toward the door.

She twisted and fought against him, finally looking back at me. "I didn't do all those things just for you to sacrifice yourself."

"Shut the fuck up," the guard hissed. He yanked harder on her hair, dragging her toward the door.

Frozen, I watched the struggle as he pulled her, inch by inch, toward the door. He had her halfway out when my mother called out one final message to me. "I'd die happy as long as you live, Maddy. I love you! Wake up. You have to wake up!"

The door slammed behind them, and I was left in silence. Her last words echoed in my mind. Several minutes later, a new guard came and escorted me back to my cell. I walked in a daze. Were they killing her? Was Viola murdering her while I sat on my cot? And what did she mean by her final message? Wake up? I was awake. I already knew what the royals wanted. I'd figured out the whole conspiracy and knew what the final plan was. What did she mean? I sat there for hours, thinking about all we'd talked about and trying not to imagine what was happening to her.

After not eating any of the food they brought for dinner, I lay down to sleep. The lights shut off a few seconds later. I dozed and was on the verge of falling asleep when my eyes snapped open. *Wake up!* My wolf.

Are you there? I asked her.

I could sense a change in the depths of my being, fueled by my mother's words. A deeper well of power seemed to open within me. My wolf's voice whispered from deep within my mind.

It's time.

Chapter 36 - Nico

As the jet descended to the runway below, I felt the pull of the moon. I glanced out the window as we touched down. The milky white orb floated above us. It was one day until the super moon, but already its power seemed to be leeching into my bones.

The plan was for Luis to join one of the daily tours tomorrow morning. We hoped he would be able to locate a possible hiding place of the vault or even Maddy's location. It was a pretty shitty gambit, but all we had to work with. At this point, we were desperate.

The jet stopped, and the pilot came out to open the door and lower the steps. As he did so, he nodded toward a large, heavy black case sitting directly behind the cockpit. "Donatello wanted you guys to have that. He thinks it will help in your mission."

Luis and I looked at each other with mirror expressions of confusion. There'd been nothing about a chest or extra equipment in our deal. We stepped over and undid several latches before lifting the top. We gaped at the contents. Several machine guns, magazines, and boxes of bullets sat in foam compartments. There was a secondary compartment with what looked like both grenades and plastic explosives with detonators.

"Holy shit! It's like Christmas for Rambo," Marcus said, fingering one of the guns.

Luis glanced at the pilot. "Seriously?"

The pilot shrugged. "I don't ask questions. I just do as I'm told. He did say if you get caught with those in Germany, you're in deep shit. So, be careful."

"Duly noted," Luis said.

We hauled the chest of weapons out of the jet and set it in an SUV that Donatello had arranged for us. My nerves were still too fired up for me to drive, so Luis took over. The Alabama shifters and I sat in the back, loading the guns and getting them ready. It was a good way to keep my mind off wondering what was happening with Maddy and what Luis was going to do the next day.

He'd go in with one of the tourist groups and find a way to peel off from the rest of the group. Then Luis would search as much as he could before finding a spot to hunker down and hide until closing. It was incredibly risky. He'd be, literally, in the lion's den.

Luis drove us to a hotel that was close enough to the castle that we could see it from our room on the sixth floor. Marcus and Darren went out to grab us dinner, leaving Luis and me to prepare for the next day.

Luis tucked a small block of the plastic explosive into a fanny pack. The detonator went into a small side pocket.

"What's the plan for that?" I asked, nodding at the bag.

"Well, if I can find where the vial of blood is kept, I can take care of the damned thing in a few seconds."

"Blow it up?" I asked.

"Hell yeah. Depending on where they've hidden it, it might do the job. Then their whole plan goes to shit. We'll see. I won't use it unless I'm certain of the location. I won't detonate until after it closes. I'm not trying to kill a bunch of innocent tourists."

I nodded and looked out the window again. The castle stood in the distance, looming like something out of a horror movie. Knowing Maddy was in there made my chest ache and my heart pain. So close I could almost touch her, yet here I was. Free while she was a captive. It pissed me the fuck off. I didn't know how I'd be able to sleep knowing she was so close.

"What are you thinking about?" Luis asked.

"Huh?"

"You look like you want to beat someone's ass."

I gestured toward the castle. "I do. The royals. I don't hit women, but if I get my hands on Viola, I'm going to kick the shit out of her. Or, better yet, let Maddy beat her brains in."

Luis chuckled. "I wish Felipe and Sebastian were here."

I got it. Being here without our friends felt strange. I'd had them stay behind because I needed people I trusted to help Dad watch over and protect Maddy's parents and Abi. There was no telling what the royals might do. If we were successful, their agents in Florida might retaliate. There was no one I trusted more than those two and Luis. Between them, my brothers, and Javi's crew, I was one hundred percent certain my pack was safe. It was what I needed to focus on this mission.

"I miss them," I said.

"Those Alabama guys are pretty cool, though," Luis said.

I nodded. "Yeah. They are," I said. It was the truth, but they still didn't hold a candle to our friends.

After dinner, we all went to bed, and I spent a few hours tossing and turning. My anxiety about the next day made getting any rest almost impossible. In the morning, it was clear I hadn't been the only one who'd struggled to sleep. Everyone looked tired and on edge.

We drove to the castle, and on the way, Luis donned a hat and sunglasses. It was a pretty garbage disguise, but they wouldn't think either of us would be in one of the tour groups. After all, they'd put us on the no-fly list and probably expected we were stuck in the States. The disguise was only an extra layer of protection. Marcus, Darren, and I were going to scout the outer edges of the estate. One of the lizard shifters would get even closer after shifting. While Luis was scoping out inside, we'd do the best we could on the outside.

After dropping Luis at the ticket booth and letting Marcus scurry out of the car in his lizard form, Darren and I drove to the outer gate, parked, and began to stroll along the outer perimeter. Fifteen minutes into our walk, Luis texted, letting me know he was inside. Five minutes later, he let me know he'd successfully broken away from the group.

"We're right on schedule," I said to Darren. He nodded and kept glancing through the ten-foot-tall wrought-iron fence that surrounded most of the estate.

Darren glanced toward me and pointed at the castle. "Got a lot of security."

Even from this distance, it was easy to see the men patrolling the grounds. Several were up on the parapets of the building itself, while others were out walking the woods and surrounding footpaths. We did our best to look like oblivious tourists enjoying a brisk stroll on the walking path.

My phone rang a minute or two later. It was Marcus.

"Hello? Marcus?"

"Yeah, it's me." He sounded out of breath and excited.

"What's up?"

"Okay, so there's more to this place than just the castle. I was going to do a quick circuit of the perimeter and then go inside like we planned. But there's this big-ass house behind the castle that you can't see from the visitor's parking. I decided to take a peek around there. It kinda looked like where they might be housing their guards or something."

"And?" I asked, wanting him to get to the point.

"Well, the place isn't some barracks. It's an actual house. I went through the whole place and went downstairs. That's where I found it. They've got fucking prison cells in there."

My heart started beating, threatening to break free of my chest, and an icy chill ran down my spine. "Are you saying you found Maddy?"

"I think so, man. I couldn't see into her room, but I found a surveillance room. They had the video feed of her room going. It was all I could do to see the screen without the guard guy seeing my slithery green ass in the corner. She looks like she's in a lot of pain, bent over and sweating. There was fur sprouting on her arms and face, but it vanished a second later. She looked at the camera once, and I could see her eyes. They were red like an alpha's. Whatever she was going through looked rough."

I cursed under my breath. In my haste to get here and save her, I hadn't given a second thought to her first shift. There was no way her wolf wouldn't come out during the super moon that night. I *had* to be by her side for her first shift. It was a promise I'd made to her, and by God, I was going to follow through on it.

"How do we get in there, Marcus?"

"There are no windows. It looks like there's an underground garage. There are a ton of guards. I'm not sure what the best option is. She's really well-guarded, and the place is like a fortress."

My phone chirped. Luis was calling. "Marcus, I gotta go. Luis is calling." I disconnected and answered Luis's call. "What do you have for me?"

He sounded irritated and pissed. "Well, I found the vault."

"Why do you sound like that's a bad thing?"

Luis sighed. "I went into the lower levels of the castle, and the thing has a damned maze of tunnels and passages. Everything looks to be hundreds of years old. Only a few of them even had electric lights running to them. I followed a few passages until I came across a couple of guards. They were taking one of the longest passages. I stayed in the shadows and alcoves while I followed them. They ended up at a chamber doorway. They were there to trade shifts with a couple of other guys. I heard them talking. The vial is definitely being held there."

"Again, you make this sound like a disaster. Wasn't this what we wanted? Can you plant the explosives so we can blow it tonight?"

"That's the problem. We were gonna blow it tonight if we found it. We didn't want to kill a bunch of innocent people."

"Yes, but that doesn't even matter now. It's so far away from the tourist area no one will get hurt. Hell, we could blow it this afternoon if we wanted."

"Same thought I had. One problem. I used my phone's GPS to see exactly where the vault was in relation to the castle. It's about four hundred yards from the actual castle. But it's directly below an old church. A church that has been converted into an orphanage."

I closed my eyes. "Seriously?"

"Yup. That place is over five hundred years old. If I use enough explosives to blow through the door and destroy the vial, the entire passageway will collapse, as will the foundation of the church. The whole place will collapse. We'll kill two or three dozen kids, and who the hell knows how many nuns."

"Son of a bitch," I said. "I guess getting rid of the vial won't be as easy as we hoped."

"What's the play?" Luis asked.

I mulled it over. We only had one option. Ambush. "Okay," I said. "Marcus found Maddy. She's in a house right behind the castle. If the vial is where you say it is, that means they're gonna bring Maddy over to the castle. We set a trap and surprise them as they move her. They'll use the tunnels. That's how I'd move her. No reason to trudge a hundred yards across the yard. They'll be in the tunnels, in the dark, on their home turf. Plus, their guard will be down because they'll be so worried about the vial. It's when she'll be the most vulnerable to a rescue. That's when we move. Maddy is the number one priority. We try for the vial if we get a chance or a good opening, but if we get out with Maddy and nothing else, that's what we take. I'm saving my mate tonight. I don't give a fuck about anything else."

Chapter 37 - Maddy

My body was tearing itself apart. That's what it felt like. All I could do was writhe on the cot and the floor. It hurt so much that I couldn't even scream. I lay there, beads of sweat dripping off my head, teeth clenched, hands fisted, vibrating like I was having a seizure. My wolf was right there with me. She was snarling and pissed. Her frustration melded with my own.

The moon was like a malevolent spirit hanging over us, trying to physically rip the shift into being. I could imagine alabaster white claws stretching down from the sky, digging into my chest and grabbing my wolf, trying to wrench her free.

The pain was so bad that I struggled to my knees, intent on getting to the toilet before my stomach expelled its contents. I didn't make it and turned slightly to vomit on the floor. A moment later, the door to my cell opened.

"What the hell is wrong with you?" the guard yelled. I could hear the irritation and disgust in his voice.

Rage unlike any I'd ever experienced surged within me. I snapped my head around and glared at the man. My vision went red, and I knew my eyes must have been the same shade. Alpha red. I growled, low in my throat, and he stumbled back. He managed to get the door closed and latched. I supposed it would have been too much to hope for him to have forgotten that little detail.

Once he was gone, a small respite came over me. I was still miserable, but at least I managed to get myself under control. I washed my face and rinsed my mouth out at the sink, then used an entire roll of toilet paper to clean up the mess I'd made. The last thing I wanted was to sit and stare at a pile of my own sick on the floor.

Sitting back on my cot, I hugged my arms to my chest and waited. For what, I had no idea. My shift, my death, my rescue—who knew? Before I could dwell on that too much, I heard the lock being disengaged again. The door swung open, and Viola stepped through, pulling Gabriella along behind her.

She shoved her toward me. "Maybe you can use the new little trick you showed us to control your brat. I need her ready for the ceremony at the height of the full moon. I don't want her to lose her mind before that. I trust you can do that," she said with a sneer before stepping out and slamming the door again.

Gabriella looked at me with sorrow. "Oh, Maddy. This is all my fault. You look just awful."

I sat, shivering, pale, my hair limp and greasy around my face, sweat dripping off my body. I nodded. "Yeah. You look great too."

Another wave of agony seized my guts, doubling me over in pain. One moment my birth mother was standing by the door, and the next, a wolf was nestling herself down around my body. Even in my pain and agony, my eyes widened in surprise. My mother had shifted. She was a shifter. What the fuck was going on? My thoughts and surprise vanished for a moment. The feel of her warmth, the softness of her fur, and the sound of her heartbeat lulled the pain away. Slowly, with the help of her comfort, the pain started to vanish. I didn't know if it was because she was my mother or if she was a shifter. Either way, I was grateful for the relief.

My true mother and father were the ones who raised me. They'd held me when I was sick and scared, had pretended to be Santa and the Tooth Fairy, and loved me unconditionally my whole life. They were my parents, but there was something about blood that was intense and unbreakable. Something the shifter side of me was unable to shrug off. Having my birth mother curled around me like that, bathed in the scent of her that was so much like my own, was more calming than any drug I could imagine. I barely knew her, but my wolf didn't seem to care.

Sensing my recovery, she shifted back to her human form but pulled me to her, cradling me in her arms. I let her hold me, my body still wanting the contact. *Needing* it. But I had to know what the hell was going on. I raised my head and looked at her. "You can shift? Kenneth never told us about that."

She sighed and shook her head. "He never knew. I kept that hidden. Everything you're going through is what I went through. I also became a shifter later in life. Not as late as you, though. It happened right after your father and I...well...he claimed me, the night you were conceived."

My eyes widened. "He turned you into a shifter?"

"No, no, not really. I was already distantly related to Edemas, your father and I were like, sixth cousins or even more distant, who knows. But your father's wolf was the reincarnation of Edemas. The strongest shifter to ever live. The werewolf king. Any other shifter and I would never have changed, but when he claimed me, and we became one, I felt my wolf's awakening the same night."

It was almost like what happened with Nico and me. She did understand what I was going through. "Did it take you a long time to shift?" I asked.

She shook her head. "No. Within a day or two, I'd learned how."

That little tidbit didn't make me feel so great, but it was good to know I wasn't the only person who'd endured the pain and irritation of turning into a shifter later in life. I'd gone nearly ten years longer than she had. Plus, my wolf had been suppressed with drugs. I was one in a million. Probably more like one in a billion.

"What's going to happen?" I asked.

She took in a shaking breath as she stroked my hair. "I don't know. I really don't. I'm sorry this is so rough for you. Like I said, it's my fault. If I hadn't given you those suppressants for all those years, this wouldn't have happened. You wouldn't be so miserable right now."

I ignored that. If she hadn't given my parents those drugs, the royals would have found me much sooner. I'd probably have been dead before high school. What I was going through right then sucked, yes, but it was better than being dead.

"What was it like when David shifted? Was he always a werewolf? Or did he shift into a normal wolf sometimes?" I asked.

"He could become either. Though the werewolf part of him was much stronger, and that was usually what took over. I only saw him as a normal wolf ten or twelve times. And on the full moon, he barely had any control. The werewolf came out whether he wanted it or not."

I nodded. "I'm afraid that's what's going to happen to me. I'm going to be some kind of awful beast."

"Do not call yourself that," she snapped. "Don't do it. Yes, the werewolf is frightening. I was scared of your father when he'd shift. The first time I saw it, I thought I'd have a heart attack, but you have to remember who your father's wolf was. That was Edemas reborn: full of rage, anger, betrayal, and vengeance. Your father couldn't control him. I told you about him coming home, dazed and covered in blood, with no memory of what he'd done. That was his wolf, not him. Yours is different. Your wolf isn't cruel or twisted by wrath."

Deep down, I knew she spoke the truth. I'd felt my wolf for months now. There wasn't a single scrap of cruelty in her. Simply because we shared blood with Edemas didn't mean we'd end up like him. That was something I could take solace in.

They let my mother stay with me, which was nice. It was a relief not to be in agony. While my body calmed down, I was able to prepare myself for what was to come.

"They'll be taking you next door to the castle soon. Sunset isn't far," Gabriella said. "That will be your one chance. You *need* to shift. You aren't cruel, no. But you need to use that strength to escape."

"I don't know if I'll be able to. Not on command anyway. I can feel it coming, but it may not happen until they've already gotten me into the castle." It was a fear I'd already thought about. That would be my luck. After all the struggle, I'd finally shift, but it would be too late to be of any help to me.

"Don't think like that. Tonight is the super moon. The pull of it will be stronger than any other full moon. I have faith, Maddy. It'll be there when you need it."

I looked at her, and a spike of worry wormed its way into my chest. "If I escape and don't open the vault, won't they do something to you in retaliation?"

She shook her head. "We can't worry about that. That vial of blood needs to be destroyed, yes. I don't believe for a moment the only reason they want it is to make more money. That's a good reason, but there are other things they can do along with that. Awful things. It needs to be destroyed, but I'm more concerned with you getting away. One problem at a time."

I gave a humorless bark of laughter. "Even if I do get away, what do I do? I don't know anyone in Germany. I have no money, no identification, and they'll be hunting me the moment I get away—if I even manage to escape."

Gabriella leaned in close. "Maddy, do you really think that mate of yours isn't already in Germany? If I had to guess, Nico is already riding to the rescue. Maybe you won't be as alone as you think."

I'd been so worried about dying and shifting that I hadn't allowed myself to think about Nico. My instincts told me that what my mother said was right. He wouldn't have left me to die. He would move heaven and earth to save me. A glimmer of hope erupted in my heart. He would come for me. He would.

They finally came and took Gabriella away. When they did, she looked at me and winked. Thankfully, my mother's calming presence remained, and I didn't revert to the agonized tantrum I'd been going through. I reached out to my wolf and found her more focused than ever before. Fully awake and ready. A surge of power billowed under the surface, like lava boiling beneath the stone of a mountain, ready to burst forward. I did my best to control it. My plan was exactly what my mother had said. Wait until they moved me. Once I was out in the open, I would finally shift and make my move. Run to the forest and not stop until I was miles and miles away. After that, I'd try to make contact with Nico.

The door opened a couple of hours later. Viola and four guards stepped into my cell. "I'm glad your little beast was put to sleep. I guess mothers *are* good for something," Viola said.

I didn't answer. Instead, I glared at her, hoping she could picture all the things I wanted to do to her. The guards came forward and helped me up. Surprisingly, they didn't tie my hands.

Viola must have seen my surprise and shrugged. "You and your wolf don't seem to be on the same page. If you haven't shifted by now, it's safe to say you won't, at least not until the moon reaches its apex. That's still an hour away. By that point?" She gave me an ironic smile. "Let's just say you'll be less trouble.

I gritted my teeth and followed her out. One guard stood behind me, a pistol pressed into my back. Another walked ahead of Viola, and the last two followed behind us all. The first crack in my plan happened when, instead of going right toward the garage and the outside world beyond, Viola and her retinue went left and through a door that led to a stairwell. We weren't going outside. I hid my surprise and worry as best as I could.

We went three floors down before coming to a landing and another door. Viola opened it to reveal what looked like an ancient stone passageway. We were moving to the castle underground. Not good. The panic and claustrophobia I suddenly felt made the urge to shift almost overwhelming. I couldn't do that here, though. I didn't have the passcode to get out of the upper levels, and I had no idea what kind of maze of tunnels there were down here. If I shifted now, I'd be stuck, and my one chance would be gone.

I followed while my mind raced a million miles an hour, trying to think of some new plan. Viola spoke over her shoulder. "When you get close to the vault, the spell surrounding it will activate. You'll see a wolf sculpture appear at the base. You will put your hand within the wolf's mouth, and the ritual will begin." She stopped walking and turned to stare into my eyes. "Please don't forget that your mother is back at the mansion. If you step out of line or try anything, I will give the order for her neck to be snapped."

I growled at her, deeper and louder than I'd ever growled before. The strength of it surprised me, and it must have surprised Viola as well because she took several quick steps back. Her eyes glanced down to my wrists, and I could see her wonder if it had been a good idea not to bind me. To her credit, Viola recovered her composure in an instant and gave me a sickly sweet smile before turning and proceeding down the passages.

A breeze filtered through the tunnels toward me, probably pushed toward us by opening and closing doorways ahead of us. I almost tripped over my feet when I smelled it. The faint breeze carried a scent toward us. It was familiar and filled me with renewed hope. Gabriella had been right. Nico and his friends had come for me. I could smell Luis. He was down here with me. His scent grew stronger the closer we got to the vault.

By the time we got to the final stone door, my wolf was almost beyond control. The door was opened, and we entered a new chamber. A huge stone boulder sat in the middle of the floor. I stepped toward it, and my knees went weak in its presence.

"My ancestors couldn't open it. Even the stone around the actual vault door is so strong it couldn't be broken. They chiseled out the stone as close as they could and transported the entire thing here hundreds of years ago. The stone weighs over ten tons. It was an incredible feat," Viola said, pride dripping from every word.

I could barely hear her. My eyes were locked on the stone. Ten feet tall, seven feet wide, and a one-foot square door was visible near eye level. I watched as a wolf's head appeared out of the stone beneath it. The stone itself morphed and changed like it was made of water. It sat with its jaw open, waiting for my hand. The power that radiated from the vault made my eyes water. The moon above pressed down on me, almost crushing me under its weight, even down here below ground. I trembled and went to one knee. Between the vault and the moon, it was too much. I could feel my wolf surging forward.

"What are you doing? It's too soon. Stand up," Viola hissed. "Put your hand in the wolf's mouth. Now!"

Then I felt him. Close and getting closer. Not Luis. Nico. He was coming. My mate was on his way. I relaxed, and at that moment... my shift began. Viola began to scream.

Chapter 38 - Nico

The power. My God—the power that I
felt. It was Maddy. I knew it was. As soon as I entered
the tunnels, I felt it. I'd come in through the church
above, as it had half the security of the royal estate. It
also had the added benefit of being close to the vault.
I shifted and sprinted down the hallway toward the
feeling of power, toward Maddy's scent, toward the
sounds of screaming.

As I got closer, three men ran past me,
heading for an exit. The look of abject terror in their
eyes gave me hope. Had I been in my human form, a
broad smile would have been plastered on my face.
The last corner revealed the doorway and the
chamber where they'd taken Maddy. I sprinted in but
slid to a stop, shocked by the sight that greeted me.

Instead of the werewolf that I'd
expected, she'd shifted into a regular wolf. She was
massive, larger than me, and in my wolf form, I was a
huge wolf. She was a head taller than I was and
absolutely gorgeous. Her fur was the same color as
her hair, dark and sleek, and such a deep shade of
red it looked like pools of blood. There was a powerful
aura around her, and it made me want to kneel down
and bite her all at the same time. When she turned
her gaze toward me as I entered, she truly did look
regal. This was what a royal wolf looked like.

"Shoot it," Viola bawled from the corner.
"Shoot the goddamned thing!"

I turned and saw the remaining guard,
eyes wide in terror, lifting his pistol toward Maddy. I
leaped through the air and clamped my jaw on his

wrist. The bones snapped, and the gun fell to the ground as the man screamed. He sprinted from the chamber, clutching his arm, still screaming.

"You bitch," Viola hissed. "If you're going to be a dog, then do as you're told. Be a good fucking puppy and do your damned duty. Don't forget, we still have your mother."

I froze. They had her mother? Icy fear shot through me. Had they attacked my compound and taken her again? Had they killed my pack? Maddy turned and leveled her gaze at me again. I could almost feel her thoughts. In her eyes, I found the truth. They had her birth mother. That's what they were holding over her head to get her to open the vault. Maddy stepped toward the stone monolith at the center of the room.

I shifted back to my human form and took a step toward Maddy. "Don't do this. Your mother wouldn't want that." I didn't really know her birth mother, but deep down, I knew it was true. She would happily sacrifice herself for Maddy's safety. I knew it made me selfish, but that was the option I was willing to take. Anything to make sure Maddy survived.

The eyes of the wolf's head on the vault began to glow red as Maddy neared it. A shimmering white orb of energy seemed to appear around. Maddy stepped across the threshold of the orb, getting closer to the vault. I ran to her, ready to yank her away from it. When I hit the barrier, it was like running into a stone wall. It was so hard that it knocked the breath out of me and sent me flying across the stone floor.

I looked on as Maddy shifted to her human form. It must have taken all she had to change back because she looked exhausted as she knelt on one knee. I scrambled to my feet and tried to push through the magical barrier again. I pounded my fists on it, but it was as unyielding as steel.

"Please, Maddy." My voice was thick with tears. "Don't do it. Please, baby. Please."

She turned her head toward me and gave a small reassuring smile and nod. "It's okay, Nico."

I shook my head and pounded at the invisible wall again. "No. No, Maddy!" Panic flooded my body. My vision went blurry as I watched her step even closer to the vault. "Please."

Maddy placed her forearm in the mouth of the stone wolf and looked at me again. In a whisper so quiet only another shifter would hear it, she said, "Before my heart stops, I need to bite you. I still haven't claimed my mate yet."

I stared at her, taking several seconds to understand what she was saying. Then it clicked into place. She was an alpha. Every alpha had to claim their mate to complete the bond. I'd claimed her, but she'd never claimed me. Once she did, our bodies and souls would become one. The magic of the claiming would breathe life back into her. It would save her if she were on the verge of death. Even through my tears, I smiled, in awe of how smart she was. She wasn't just going to her death without a plan.

An instant later, the jaw of the wolf snapped shut on Maddy's arm. She flinched, and blood immediately began to flow from her body into the vault. Veins of red began to appear through the stone. Her blood seeped into the rock, her power unlocking the door behind which sat the blood of Edemas.

Viola pressed herself against the barrier, a look of almost ecstasy on her face as she watched Maddy sink to her knees. "Yes," she muttered to herself.

"Bleed the bitch dry. Do it. My whole life, I've waited for this. We'll bring them all back."

I tore my eyes away from Maddy to glance at Viola. Bring who back? What was she talking about? Maddy groaned in pain, and Viola was forgotten. I looked toward her, and my wolf roared in anger. Her face was beyond pale. Her skin was so white it was like tissue paper, and the veins beneath were visible. She lifted her head and whispered to me again. "No matter what, don't... let... her get... the vial."

I couldn't give a shit about a dead man's blood. That was the least of my worries. All I wanted was to get to Maddy and save her before it was too late. As though she could see the thoughts forming in my head, she shook her head. "Don't let her," she repeated.

Maddy's head slumped forward—the only thing keeping her from falling to the floor was the wolf that slowly bled the life from her. Her heart was slowing down—I could hear it. Across the room, Viola was screeching in victory. Fury exploded inside my chest. I'd been so worried about Maddy that Viola had taken a backseat in my mind. But seeing her look so happy and pleased at Maddy's pain and suffering set me off.

I ran to her and wrapped my hand around her throat before she could react. She clawed at my hand, drawing bloody furrows across my skin. She kicked out at me, but the pain was minimal. Viola's face grew red, and I closed my fingers harder. Before I could choke the life out of her, there was an audible crack, and a pressure change caused my ears to pop. I dropped Viola and turned to see the barrier had fallen.

Viola gasped for air while I ran toward Maddy. The wolf's jaw had released her arm, and she was lying motionless. Ignoring what she'd told me about the vial, I patted her cheek, trying to wake her up.

Viola nearly tripped over herself as she ran toward the vault. She dug her fingers into the small doorway and tugged, but even unlocked, it was too heavy for her to slide aside.

"Help me," she screamed, looking at me, bruises already blossoming on her throat where I'd choked her.

Cradling Maddy in my arms, I looked at Viola and snarled. "If you're smart, you'll get the fuck out of here. Because once I save Maddy, I'm going to rip you limb from fucking limb."

She heard how serious I was, and fear crossed her features, though she did her best to mask it. She opened her mouth to say something, but a growl echoed from the door. I gave her a menacing grin. "Better run. My friends are here."

She looked around and saw Luis in wolf form standing by the door. Marcus and Darren stood behind him, holding the assault rifles Donatello had given us. Viola looked at the vault with longing before running to the other side of the chamber. There was a small passage in an alcove. She turned on her heel and jabbed a finger in my direction. "You're going to regret this. You all will."

Without another word, she disappeared down the hidden corridor. Forgetting her as soon as she was gone, I turned back to Maddy. I wanted to chase Viola down and rip her goddamned throat out, but Maddy was more important. I could still hear her heart. It was beating, but barely, like butterfly wings, faint and weak. I lifted her lips and rubbed at her gums, trying to coax her fangs out. "Come on, babe. You've gotta do it. One good bite. Come on. I know you can."

"What can I do?" Luis asked.

Ignoring him, I smacked Maddy's cheek harder, trying to get her eyes open. Nothing. The beating of her heart was growing weaker by the second. She was going. My breath was hissing in and out of my nose in panic. I could feel her slipping away. Tears started slipping down my cheeks. "No. Maddy? No. Baby, please. You can't leave me. You can't. Please? Wake up. Wake up!" I screamed the last two words, feeling my heart breaking.

Her eyes fluttered open, and I stopped breathing, afraid even one breath might tip her over the edge into oblivion. She locked eyes with me, then sank her fangs into me. The pain was sharp but sweet. It meant she was alive. Maddy was alive and had claimed me. The bond erupted almost at once, our hearts beating in sync, and the color of her cheeks grew pink as her body drew strength from mine. I wept happily as I watched the blood slip down my arm.

Chapter 39 - Maddy

The first thing I noticed was the low hum of sound. It was quiet and subtle but all around me. I wanted to open my eyes to see what was going on, but the bone-deep exhaustion was like a heavy blanket. I couldn't even move a finger, my waking mind barely able to pick out the sound. I sank back into a dreamless sleep less than a minute later.

When I woke again sometime later, the fatigue wasn't as awful. I managed to get my eyes open. At first, the light was too bright and sent shards of pain through my eyes right into my brain. I raised a shaky hand to shield my eyes. I was on an airplane. All around me, men were passed out asleep in chairs. Luis was there, along with two other guys who looked like the lizard guys—the ones Felipe got to help us.

Once I sat up, I had to hold my head and wait for the dizziness and nausea to fade before getting to my knees. Where was Nico? I wanted him. *Needed* him. As though he heard my thoughts, the bathroom door at the back of the plane opened, and he stepped out. He glanced up, and when he saw I was awake, his face broke into a happy smile. He was down on his knees with me a second later.

He kissed me gently on the lips. "How are you feeling?"

I rubbed at my head. "Like shit. But alive. So that's one thing." I looked him in the eye, a question on my lips, but I was too afraid to ask it. I swallowed and finally pushed through. "Did Viola get the vial? Does she have Edemas's blood now?"

Nico settled down on the floor beside me. "That's an interesting story."

I frowned at him. "What do you mean?"

"Well… this Edemas guy? He was a serious asshole. One hundred percent jackass."

I grinned dumbly, having no idea what he was talking about. "I think we'd already established that. What does it have to do with what happened with the vault?"

Nico shook his head ruefully. "The little door was solid stone. Even when your blood unlocked it, Viola wasn't strong enough to lift it, and all her men had run for the hills. She was pissed, which I couldn't give two shits about. She's lucky I had to save you. Otherwise, I'd have killed her. She ran. So once you were safe and stabilized, the guys and I slid the stone door aside. It really was heavy as shit and so small it was difficult for us to get a good hand on it."

I put a hand on his thigh. "Nico, for real, you're killing me here. What was in the damned vault?"

He looked at me with a funny, knowing smile for several beats before speaking. "Nothing."

I felt like I'd been slapped. "What? It was empty? The vial had already been taken? Is that what you mean?"

He shook his head. "Nope. Once the door was slid aside, the *vault* was basically a two-foot box carved into the stone. It appeared empty."

Catching the last sentence, I pushed him. "What do you mean by 'appeared'?"

"That was our lizard friends over there. We couldn't believe there was nothing inside, so Marcus shifted and climbed in to look around. He'd have a better view than we could. He found a little opening just big enough for a finger that we hadn't seen." Nico shrugged. "I had a hunch. So I wiped some of your blood off your arm where that thing bit you. Wiped it off with my own finger and shoved it into that hole. It worked. There was a click, and another stone panel on the top of the little mini chamber opened, and a scroll fell down."

I stared at him like he was speaking another language. "What the hell? A scroll? Like *The Dead Sea Scrolls*?"

He shrugged. "Basically. This Edemas guy wrote it. In fucking Latin. Randomly enough, Darren over there minored in it in college, and he was able to read it to us. To paraphrase, Edemas had visions of his betrayers searching for this vial. He'd hidden the scroll in the vault so that when the royals opened it, they'd see nothing and, hopefully, give up. He even sowed lies about where the treasure was. Apparently, it's not in the graveyard Luis saw the guys guarding either. The scroll gave us the actual location of the treasure and the vial."

I sighed and rubbed my head. All these goddamned games. What was the point of it all? This was ridiculous. I was happy the royals didn't have it, but I wished this wasn't so difficult. "What is the real point of this vial?" I asked. "Some say it can create werewolves. Others say it can heal any disease, so what is really going on here?" My frustration came through in my tone.

"It had instructions for how the vial is to be used. Or… I guess, how the power of the vial is to be accessed. Out of his entire bloodline, all the way back to his ancestors, Edemas was the strongest. His power was unrivaled. There's a ritual written there about how to bestow the power of Edemas to his descendants. With you being the only one, all that power is yours to inherit."

Even the idea of that filled me with anxiety. Did I want that? It was my birthright, but it was terrifying to think about. I didn't want to be some kind of werewolf demigod or something. Then again, if I were, I'd be strong enough to protect my loved ones. It hadn't been enough for Edemas, but it was a fighting chance.

"I think we should destroy it," Nico said. "That way, there's no chance the royals will ever get it. Edemas did a good job tricking them, but they'll know what happened soon enough. They'll keep looking for it."

He was right. I knew he was. Whatever power I could gain wasn't worth the chance that they could get their hands on it. "Yeah. We need to destroy it," I said. "It's the only way."

Nico nodded, and the smile on his face slowly slipped away. "I'm sorry we couldn't save Gabriella. We spent too much time finding the scroll. We had to get you out of there before they regrouped and came back. I'm... I'm really sorry."

I remembered the look of determination on my mother's face when they took her away the last time. A thought had wormed its way into my mind, and I shook my head. "She'll be okay. I think she's made peace with whatever happens. I want her to be safe, but we did all we could do. If anyone can give Viola and her organization a run for its money, it's her. Honestly, I think she let them catch her."

"What?" Nico couldn't have looked more confused if I'd told him I was from the moon.

"She's really good at hiding and running. After almost thirty years, do you think she'd slip up right before the super moon and get caught by accident?" I shook my head. "No. It was part of her plan. Maybe she used the chaos of my escape to break herself out. Or she stayed behind to give me a better chance of escape. I hope we find out, but I'm not sure we ever will."

A sudden wave of dizziness fell over me, and I almost toppled over. Nico caught me and helped me up into one of the chairs. "You need to be careful and take it easy. You lost a ton of blood. So much you should be dead."

His voice grew thick and heavy with emotion as he spoke, and there were tears forming in his eyes. I wrapped my arms around his neck and pulled him in tight, hugging him to me.

"I was so scared, Maddy," he whispered. "I thought I'd lost you. I'd never have forgiven myself if something happened to you. Don't you ever do anything like that again."

I kissed him. "I'm sorry. I promise not to almost die ever again."

He stared at me for a few seconds before snorting out a laugh. "Yes. Please don't almost die. Deal?"

"Deal. I love you."

Nico settled down in the seat beside me. "I love you so much. How is your wolf doing? Now that you've shifted, I mean."

That was a good question that was hard to answer. "Well, she feels much calmer and more at peace. I have to be honest. I was sure I was going to shift into a werewolf my first time. I'm sort of surprised I didn't."

"Well, if it makes you feel better, you were still damned terrifying."

I smiled, despite myself, and felt a flush of pride from deep inside my mind. My wolf liked hearing that. "Really?"

Nico nodded. "You were huge. Even for an alpha. A full head taller than my wolf. Your eyes were red like an alpha's too, but not a subtle red shine like most of us have. It was like your eyes were literally full of blood. So red, it was frightening. If I didn't know who you were, I'd have probably thought about running."

"Well, I'm glad you approved," I said, laughing and leaning into him.

A few hours later, we were back on the ground. Nico said he'd made a new friend who'd helped them get to Europe, and the plane belonged to him. He'd allowed us to land at an airfield near Clearidge. That was good because I was desperate to see my parents and Abi. It was pretty much the only thing I could think about for the last half of the flight. He'd let me know all three of them were staying at our house until we got back.

Nico barely had the car in park before I was out the door and running up to the house. I burst in and saw Mom and Dad sitting with Nico's parents on the couch. Abi was in the kitchen drinking a cup of coffee. Everyone froze when I came in, then the whole house erupted into movement. There was hugging, tears and sobs, and a thousand questions. It was the best five minutes of my life. I was happy to have them all back safe and sound. Nothing could have made me happier at that moment.

Once we'd calmed down and Nico came in, it was decided that all three of them would stay with us for a while. My parents were more than happy to do so. I think they'd been rattled by the kidnapping, but I think Abi had the worst of it. After our reunion, she withdrew and was quieter than I'd ever known her to be. It was strange, but she probably needed space.

Hopefully, after a few more days, she'd start to snap out of it. There was no reason to push her. She'd been through a lot—we all had. We each had to deal with what had happened in our own way.

That night, I slipped into bed beside Nico, and nothing had ever felt so comfortable in my life. I rested my head on his chest and listened to his breathing.

After a moment, Nico cleared his throat and nudged me. I glanced up at him. He looked worried. "You know we've got to brace for whatever is coming. You know this isn't the end of it."

I nodded. "Yeah, the royals are not going to be happy with what happened. Viola is their leader. She won't be happy we made a fool of her."

"She's going to want revenge. She's going to come for us."

I laid my head back on his chest. "I'd already figured that was coming. It'll be fine. It'll all work out as long as we have each other."

Chapter 40 - Nico

Maddy's parents were still living with us, even though we'd gotten back almost three weeks ago. I was actually happy about that. There was no way I could blame them for being scared to go home. I'd thought I would have to talk them into it, but they'd asked Maddy if it was okay the day after we got back. It was one less thing to worry about.

Abi was staying too, but something wasn't right. Maddy's parents were still sort of shell-shocked and wary, but Abi was worse. It was strange. She'd always been so bubbly and exuberant, but since getting rescued, she'd been withdrawn and quiet. Sebastian had been hanging out with us more often, hovering around Abi quite a bit, trying to help her. He'd get her whatever she needed, grab her food or stuff from the store, but even with him doing all that, she didn't really acknowledge him. She seemed like a ghost of herself. I mentioned it to Maddy one day after I got back from checking on things at the auto shop.

"Hey? Is Abi okay?"

We were standing in the bedroom, and Maddy glanced toward the door with a worried look. "I don't think so," she whispered. "She's not been acting like herself." She went over and closed our door before continuing. "I thought she'd get better after being home for a few days, but if anything, she seems to be getting worse."

I raised an eyebrow. "Do you think it could be some kind of PTSD or something?"

Maddy shrugged. "Maybe so. I don't know how to help her."

Neither did I. The only thing I knew to do was to increase security. Uncle Miguel had survived his shooting, thank God. But he'd probably never do guard duty again. I'd commissioned a company to come out and install motion-activated cameras all around the pack lands. We'd increased the amount of fencing, electrifying a lot of it and adding barbed wire. Several of the guys had volunteered to work as perimeter guards. It was the best I could do to keep things as safe as I could.

The entire pack had been on edge, and a little down since the royals broke in and took Maddy. The guys and I decided everyone needed something to lift their spirits. A massive cookout seemed like the best idea. The royals weren't gone, and we knew they'd be coming back, but for now, we needed to try to get back to normal life.

Felipe and Sebastian went out and bought almost thirty pounds of brisket to smoke. Mom and Maddy worked on a bunch of sides and salads, with my cousins Francisca and Eliza helping out. The entire pack was invited, and we had everything set up in my backyard that Friday night. It took almost a full day to prep and cook everything.

Once the party got going, it seemed like everyone was really enjoying themselves. Beer and wine flowed freely, food was plentiful, and laughter rang through the pack for the first time in weeks. I even saw Abi smiling a bit while talking to my family. It filled my heart with happiness. I was the alpha, and not only was it my job to protect and lead the pack, but I was also supposed to keep morale high.

I was standing over by the dessert table trying to decide if I wanted apple pie or chocolate cake when my cell phone rang. A quick glance showed it was Javi. I'd invited his pack to the festivities, but he'd declined. I wasn't sure what he might be calling about.

I answered the phone with a shrug. "Hello?"

"Nico?" He sounded panicked. "You need to turn on the news. Now. Right fucking now."

The frantic tone of his voice had goose flesh breaking out over my skin. "Javi? What's happened?" My voice was hollow and full of fear.

"Just turn on a fucking TV. You'll... shit... you'll see." Without another word, he hung up.

I ran inside as fast as I could. My family and friends must have seen how worried I was and slowly started to follow me in. I didn't pay them any attention, just grabbed the remote and turned on the TV in the living room as my pack started to trickle in, curious about what had me so worked up.

It took me a second to get to a news station, and when I did, my heart dropped into my stomach. A massive red banner was plastered across the bottom of the screen in big, bold letters: **SHIFTER CRISIS.**

"Nico?" Dad asked from beside me. "What is all this?"

"I don't know, hang on," I said, turning the volume up. There was some type of press conference going on in what looked like the White House Press Room.

A reporter stood and raised their hand, and the press secretary pointed at them to speak. "Yes, can you give any detail as to the crisis facing the country right now?"

The press secretary nodded. "Yes, as you may or may not have seen recently, we've had multiple reports of shifters going feral. We all know that this is a very, very rare situation with their race. Most of the time, it is handled within their packs or familial units, while other times, law enforcement becomes involved. This new situation is a bit worrisome. The reports show shifters are going feral spontaneously, as well as the fact that their animals or beasts have more than doubled in size. The Centers for Disease Control have been in close contact with the president as well as his chiefs of staff. We do believe that there is some type of unknown vector causing this. Whether it be an external cause like a virus or bacterium, or a type of biological warfare is unknown at this time."

I was clutching the remote control so hard in my hand the plastic was cracking. What the hell were they saying? This made no sense. I'd never heard of any such issues. Where were they getting this?

The press corps erupted in chaotic questions, and it seemed like thousands of flashbulbs were going off. The secretary managed to calm the reporters down and pointed at a woman in the front row who I'd seen for years on the nightly news. "Yes? Samantha?" the secretary said, gesturing to her.

She nodded and stood. "What is the administration's plan for dealing with this? From initial reports, there have already been nearly a dozen deaths by these infected shifters. How are you going to keep the public safe? Are there any cures in the pipeline?"

The press secretary looked uncomfortable for a moment, then glanced down at his notes before taking a heavy breath. I knew that whatever came out of his mouth next would not be good. Not for shifters anyway.

He nodded, finally looking up from his notes. "Yes, this situation is very dangerous. The population of the United States is almost thirty percent shifter. Those numbers, coupled with what is going on, have forced the president to... go to extreme lengths to protect not only the human population but the shifters as well. As of noon today, the president has instituted martial law, but only in regard to our shifter citizens. An immediate and mandatory quarantine is to be instituted for all shifters. Multiple facilities will be set up in each state for admission. The National Guard has been mobilized to help facilitate the quick and seamless check-in process in each state. FEMA has also been activated and will be assisting with the setup of these temporary hospitals and camps.

"As you can imagine, this is unprecedented, and the government must lean on our friends, and one of those friends is the Monroe Group. They were the first organization to discover this issue and bring it to our attention. The Monroe Group and many of its subsidiaries will be instrumental in helping make sure this is handled with the utmost care and expediency. With that being said, I would like to turn over questions to the executive president of the Monroe Group. Miss Viola Monroe." The secretary stood aside, and the camera panned over to a familiar face stepping up to the microphone as a new explosion of questions erupted.

"Son. Of. A. Bitch," Sebastian hissed.

Everyone in the pack had learned who this woman was, and multiple people growled at the TV as she smoothed her suit for the cameras. Maddy was pressed against me, her hands digging into me in fear.

Once the press had calmed again, Viola started speaking. "I'm sure there are many questions. I assure you that the *substantial* financial backing of the Monroe Group and thousands of our employees will be keeping a very close eye on what happens over the next several days and weeks. Mister Secretary was correct in that The Monroe Group scientists were the first to make the connection to this emergency. I myself was witness to one of the feral shifters. I can tell you that what you imagine isn't even close to how terrifying these sick individuals are. I barely escaped with my life. All I can say is that I fear for humanity. If this medical emergency can't be isolated and stamped out, then there is a huge possibility that all shifters may end up being affected and turning on humans.

"As heartbreaking as it may be, all shifters must understand that they need to move to the nearest detention center as soon as possible. If nothing else, they should do this to protect their human friends. The director of homeland security has informed us that any shifter who does not turn themselves into the nearest facility or refuses to be rounded up by government agencies will be considered enemies of the state and handled accordingly."

I was shaking. The mood in the room was one of panic. We all knew what was happening. They'd tricked the entire goddamned government into rounding us up and putting us in internment camps or arresting us. Or be shot and killed by the police or National Guard. How the fuck had Viola pulled this off? The tricky bitch was smarter and more powerful than I'd imagined.

Viola gave the crowd a sad shake of the head that could have won an Oscar. "The individuals more than likely do not know that they are infected. I have made the recommendation, and the administration has agreed, that all human citizens have the right to defend themselves. We want the nation to understand that if a feral shifter is seen attacking, you have the right to defend yourself or your loved ones in any way you see fit. With that being said, under the specialized martial law that has been instituted, any citizen who does defend themselves will be, for the duration of the crisis, fully exempt from any criminal wrongdoing."

Jesus Christ. I growled at the screen. Viola smiled back with perfect red lips and an icy cold gleam in her eyes. My blood was boiling. Rage, fear, anger, and terror all warred within me. With one swift action, she'd just put a bounty on every shifter in the country. Every asshole with a gun would be aiming for us. They could kill any shifter they wanted with no repercussions. All they had to say was we were attacking. We were wolves. We were supposed to be the hunters. Now?

We were the hunted.

Made in the USA
Monee, IL
20 April 2024

57254671R10364